THIS BOOK IS THE PROPERTY OF

OF THE
IMPERIAL
LAMPLIGHTERS

•

LIMNAEUS LINATOR
IN MINISTERIUM IMPERIA REX

BOOKS BY D. M. CORNISH

Foundling
Lamplighter
Factotum

PART TWO

Lamplighter

D.M. CORNISH

with illustrations by the author

FIREBIRD

AN IMPRINT OF PENGUIN GROUP (USA) INC.

*Title page illustration: Monster-blood tattoo puncted on the arms
of Lampsmen Assimus, Bellicos and Puttinger*

FIREBIRD
Published by the Penguin Group
Penguin Group (USA) Inc., 345 Hudson Street, New York, New York 10014, U.S.A.
Penguin Group (Canada), 90 Eglinton Avenue East, Suite 700, Toronto, Ontario, Canada M4P 2Y3
(a division of Pearson Penguin Canada Inc.)
Penguin Books Ltd, 80 Strand, London WC2R 0RL, England
Penguin Ireland, 25 St Stephen's Green, Dublin 2, Ireland (a division of Penguin Books Ltd.)
Penguin Group (Australia), 250 Camberwell Road, Camberwell, Victoria 3124, Australia
(a division of Pearson Australia Group Pty Ltd)
Penguin Books India Pvt Ltd, 11 Community Centre, Panchsheel Park, New Delhi - 110 017, India
Penguin Group (NZ), 67 Apollo Drive, Rosedale, North Shore 0632, New Zealand
(a division of Pearson New Zealand Ltd)
Penguin Books (South Africa) (Pty) Ltd., 24 Sturdee Avenue, Rosebank, Johannesburg 2196, South Africa

Registered Offices: Penguin Books Ltd, 80 Strand, London WC2R 0RL, England

Published in Australia by Omnibus Books, an imprint of Scholastic Australia Pty Ltd., 2008
First published in the United States of America by G. P. Putnam's Sons,
a division of Penguin Young Readers Group, 2008
Published by Firebird, an imprint of Penguin Group (USA) Inc., 2010

1 3 5 7 9 10 8 6 4 2

THE LIBRARY OF CONGRESS HAS CATALOGED THE G. P. PUTNAM'S SONS EDITION AS FOLLOWS:
Cornish, D. M. (David M.), date.
Lamplighter / D. M. Cornish. p. cm. (Monster blood tattoo ; bk. 2)
Summary: As Rossamünd starts his life as a lamplighter on the Wormway, he continues
his fight against monsters, making friends and enemies along the way, but questions
about his origins continue to plague him. Includes glossary.
ISBN 978-0-399-24639-5 (hc)
[1. Lamplighters—Fiction. 2. Monsters—Fiction. 3. Self-confidence—Fiction. 4. Identity—Fiction.
5. Tattooing—Fiction. 6. Foundlings—Fiction. 7. Fantasy.] I. Title.
PZ7.C816368 Lam 2008 [Fic—dc22] 2007033786

ISBN 978-0-14-241462-0

Printed in the United States of America
Designed by Katrina Damkoehler
Text set in Perpetua

For TJ,
my besterest friend

CONTENTS

	List of Plates	ix
	Acknowledgments	xi
1	Master Come-lately	1
2	Wings of the Dove	25
3	On Returning to Winstermill	43
4	An Interview with the Surgeon	58
5	Threnody Goes Forth	73
6	The Lantern-Watch	94
7	Morning to Mourning	108
8	Pots-and-Pans	132
9	Pageant-of-Arms	155
10	Numps	171
11	Hither and Thither	195
12	Punctings and Posters	218
13	An Unanswered Question	230
14	The Undercroft	247
15	The Way Least Went	263
16	The Lamplighter-Marshal	280
17	Hasty Departures	298
18	Wretchedness Revealed	316
19	Billeting Day	339
20	On Leaving Winstermill	355
21	The Brisking Cat	381
22	The Ignoble End of the Road	410
23	Wormstool	436
24	A Lamplighter's Life	460
25	Thickets and Thrumcops	488
26	A Show of Strength	510
27	A Light to Your Path	533
28	Before the Inquiry	551
29	A False Falseman	568
30	Quo Gratia	582
	Explicarium	603

Appendix 1(A)	702
Appendix 1(B)	703
Appendix 2	704
Appendix 3	705
Appendix 4	706
Appendix 5	710
Appendix 6	712
Appendix 7	714
Appendix 8	715
Map	716

LIST OF PLATES

Map of the Half-Continent	xii
The Lands of the Idlewild	xv
A Horn-ed Nicker	9
Lamplighter-Sergeant Grindrod	27
A Greater Derehund	53
Dolours	63
Threnody	77
Sebastipole	99
Herdebog Trought	117
The Snooks	139
Syntychë the Lady Vey	167
Numps	177
Doctor Crispus	211
Nullifus Drawk	223
Europe	235
Rossamünd	251
The Gudgeon	275
The Lamplighter-Marshal	287
Winstermill	303
The Master-of-Clerks	321
The Black-Eyed Wit	341
Critchitichiello	375
The Lentermen	387
Squarmis the Costerman	427
Wormstool	443
Mama Lieger	477
Sequecious	491
Wormstool Brodchin	525
Aubergene	537
Craumpalin	561
Laudibus Pile	573
Surgeon Grotius Swill	587

ACKNOWLEDGMENTS

TO GOD FOR KEEPING the door open, for showing me a life I never thought possible; my sweet new wife too for showing me a life I never thought possible, for patience and for reading all those drafts—this book is better because you help me; once again to Dyan for her dreams, her belief, for the passion, the struggle; Tim, for the cracking of the whip; Mr. Fickling, who trustingly watched on; Nille "the Swedish Translator," and to all those who toiled to turn Book One into other tongues; to all those publishers about this tiny globe of ours that have taken on MBT; Celia for making editing a joy and for rescuing me from my own heavy hand; Patricia for her quiet maturity and support and for knowing what to do; Helen, who keeps it all organized; also to my parents once more, my new ones too—Graeme and Kerry, and the Sweet Hamers, for reading this second stage in its early, ugly moments and loving it still; Sue Ellen for all that Latin; Graeme Rickerby—master of catchphrases and song—for slogg-porridge, Joey DeVivra and enjoying all the nuances of our difficult, wondrous language; James White, who wrote a book well before I ever did, made Sydney possible and showed the way—may you write again, sir; and Murray Whiteford, for card games and all the time spent at your house. Thanks too to the regular dwellers and commenters at www.monsterbloodtattoo. blogspot.com: Femina, Koallaku, Random Missfitt, MadBomber, Winter, Midwishin, Andre, Shayne de Comyn Esquire, Coz, Giant Fan, Dan S. Tong, Shyane, John, Kathryn, Daisy__Girl, Oriana, Jimmy Trinket, Steve, Sirk, Erin, Mark, John, Sookie, Arty Bel, Joaquin Rosada Martel, Markus, Inez, Troubardier, Ninjanna, sme0149, Samosin, Baraholka, Ravinn, Joyous Santina, Dozer911, Vahlaeity, Charlotte, Evil1I, Okyoureacab, Longinvs, Suspicious Hat, Bard, MooseGuy, Rosiegirl, Coinks, Dustin and to all those anonny mouses too. To Joshua Kipitza, for your cruorpunxis—keep creating, sir. To my time in Kansas, without which there would be no lamplighters.

This is the map of the southern and central portions of the Half-Continent. The area within the small rectangle is shown in detail on the following page.

THE LANDS OF THE
IDLEWILD

INCLUDING THE RANGE OF THE
IMPERIAL LAMPLIGHTERS
OF THE CONDUIT VERMIS

◉ MAJOR CITY

◎ MINOR CITY OR LARGE TOWN

▣ LONE STRONGHOLD

▭ RIVERGATE

⋯⋯ ROAD

///// SWAMPLAND

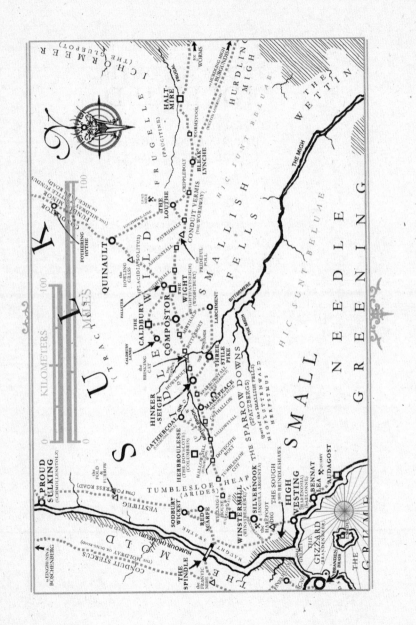

1

MASTER COME-LATELY

calendar(s) sometimes also called strigaturpis or just strig—a general term for any combative woman; the Gotts call them mynchen—after the do-gooding heldin-women of old. Calendars gather themselves into secretive societies called claves (its members known as clariards)—constituted almost entirely of women—organized about ideals of social justice and philanthropy, particularly providing teratological protection for the needy and the poor. They usually live in somewhat isolated strongholds—manorburghs and basterseighs—known as calanseries. Some claves hide people—typically women—in trouble, protecting them in secluded fortlets known as sequesturies. Other claves offer to teach young girls their graces and fitness of limb in places known as mulierbriums. Calendars, however, are probably best known for the odd and eccentric clothing they don to advertise themselves.

THE short run of road that went east from Winstermill to Wellnigh House had a reputation as the easiest watch on the Wormway—and for the most part it was. Known as the Pettiwiggin or the Harrowmath Pike, it was so close to Winstermill, the mighty fortress of the lamplighters, that those who used it were rarely troubled by nickers or bogles. Close and safe, the Pettiwiggin was ideal for teaching young prentice-lighters the repetitious tasks of a lamplighter.

For nigh on two months the "lantern-sticks," as they were

called by the scarred veterans who taught and chastised them, had been at their training. In another two, if each boy made it through, he would be promoted to lampsman. On that great day it would be his privilege to be billeted to one of the many cothouses—the small fortresses punctuating the long leagues of the Wormway—to begin his life as a lampsman proper.

At this middle point in their training the prentices were taken out on the road to begin the lighting and the dousing of the great-lamps that lit the Wormway. Until now they had marched and drilled, learned their letters and practiced at lighting on yard-lanterns safe within Winstermill. Rossamünd had found it all as boring as he once feared a lamplighter's life might be. Indeed, his first excursion out to light lamps had been uniformly laborious and uneventful, the overnight stay in Wellnigh House uncomfortable, and the return to the manse dousing the lanterns the next morning as dull as the night before. He keenly regretted that he might never become a vinegaroon as he had once hoped, and often thought to himself, *Oh, that's not how* they'd *do it in the navy; that's not what* they'd *do on a ram.*

For Rossamünd the first half of prenticing had been long, yet not quite as lonely as his old life at Madam Opera's Estimable Marine Society for Foundling Boys and Girls. Here at Winstermill he shared the trials of training with the other prentices, all boys of a similar age from poor and obscure origins like his. Together they fumbled through each movement of their fodicar drill; together they winced at each reluctant, shoulder-wrenching shot of pistol or fusil; together they balmed their feet after day-long marching. Yet the other lads were not nearly as keen on pamphlets or the matter they contained—tales of the heroic progenitors of the Empire and the monsters they slew. Most could barely read, despite the attempted remedies of "letters," the reading and writing class under Seltzerman 1st Class Humbert. None of them showed any interest in the vinegar seas or the Senior Service, nor desired a life of a vinegaroon. *Grass-combers,* Master Fransitart, his old dormitory master, would have called them—true lubberly, ground-hugging landsmen.

Rossamünd's failure to get to the manse in time for the start of prenticing meant he had missed that first crucial period when fragile bonds of friendship begin. He had been late only one week, but Lamplighter-Sergeant Grindrod had dubbed him "Master Come-lately," and the name had stuck.

One skill he had learned at Madam Opera's proved exceptionally useful. The hours spent keenly watching his old master and dispensurist Craumpalin had shown their fruit, for he was known for his facility with potives and restoratives. He had been made the custodian of the prentice-watch's chemistry, doling out repellents or healing draughts where necessary. This earned him a little respect, but it meant that out on the road, while the others carried a short-barreled musket known as a fusil, he was to content himself with his fodicar and a satchel of potives. However, he had seen the effect of both musket ball and repellent. As reassuring as it was to have a firelock in your hands that could cough and boom startlingly at an enemy, a well-aimed potive could deal with many more monsters at once and often more effectively.

The evening of this second prentice-watch, Rossamünd was called forward, joining the six others he had been listed with when he first began as a prentice-lighter. These were the boys of the 3rd Prentice-Watch, Q Hesiod Gæta. Though, by letter-fall order, Rossamünd's name should have appeared second-from-top in the appropriate triple-marked ledgers (*B* for Bookchild), he was nevertheless gathered with the six whose names were at the end of it, lads like Giddian Pillow and Crofton Wheede. For a second afternoon these six and Rossamünd stood in single file on the Forming Square as the other prentices looked on.

The platoon of prentices was sectioned into three quartos, one of which would go out on the road each evening to light the lamps, staying in Wellnigh House over the night and returning to Winstermill the next dawning, putting out the lights and getting back by midmorning. Each quarto was named after a doughty lamplighter-marshal of old: Q Protogenës, Q Io Harpsicarus and Q Hesiod Gæta, Rossamünd's own.

With a cry of "A light to your path!" Lamplighter-Sergeant Grindrod led the watch through the great bronze gates of Winstermill down the steep eastern drive known as the Approach and onto the Pettiwiggin. After them came the crusty Lampsmen 1st Class Assimus, Bellicos and Puttinger, veteran lighters glaring and complaining under their breath, barely tolerating the green incompetence of the prentices.

Much of the six-mile stretch of the highroad was raised on a dike of earth, lifting it almost a yard above the Harrowmath—the great flat plain on which Winstermill was built—giving a clear view over the high wild grasses. Ever the wayward lawn of the Harrowmath was mown by fatigue parties of peoneers and local farm laborers with their glinting scythes, ever it would grow back, thick and obscuring. At its eastern end, after five miles and eighteen lamps, the Pettiwiggin descended flush with the land and passed through a small woodland, the Briarywood. Tall sycamores and lithe wandlimbs grew on either side of the way, with shrubby evergreen myrtles and knotted briars flourishing thickly about their roots. Yesternight, when the prentice-watch had worked through it, Rossamünd had keenly felt the workings of mild threwd—that ghastly sensation of hidden watchfulness and threat that thrilled all around. This evening it had grown a little stronger as he went along, tiny prickles of terror upon his neck, and its subtleties felt like a warning.

There was a great-lamp to light at the beginning of the Briary, one at its end and another right in its midst. This middle light was found in a small clearing on the shoulder of the highroad.

After this only five lamps to go, Rossamünd consoled himself. Puffing at the stinging cold, he stared suspiciously at the darkling woods about him. The thorny twine of branch and limb crowded the broad verge, newly pruned by the day-watch fatigue party out gathering firewood. Anything might be creeping behind those withy-walls, lurking in the dark beneath the briar and winter-nude hawthorn, sneaking between thin pale trunks, hungry, waiting. Behind him the glow of the cold evening gloaming could be seen through a grandly arched gap in the tall trees where the Pettiwiggin entered the woods. The sky showed all about as pallid slits between the black of the lithesome trees. In the thin light Rossamünd adjusted the strap of his salumanticum—the satchel holding the potives—and checked once more that all within were in their place. He had been as eager as the other boys to start at lighting proper, but now here, out in this wild unwalled place, he was not so sure. He arched his back and looked up past the steep brim of his almost new, lustrous black thrice-high through the overhanging branches at the wan measureless blue of evening. Without realizing it, he gave a nervous sound, almost a sigh.

"Are we keeping you up, Master Come-lately?"

This was Lamplighter-Sergeant Grindrod. Even when he hissed angrily, the lamplighter-sergeant seemed to be shouting. He was always shouting, even when he was supposed to be talking with the habitual hush of the night-watch.

Rossamünd snapped back his attention. "No, Lamplighter-Sergeant, I just . . . !"

"Silence!"

Ducking his head to hide a frown, Rossamünd swallowed at an indignant lump and held his tongue. *Can't he feel the horrors growing?*

From the first lamp of the afternoon until now, the prentice-watch had stopped at every lamppost to wind out the light using the crank-hooks at the end of their blackened fodicars to ratchet the winch within each lamp. Bundled as best they could be against the bitter, biting night, they halted once again, stamping and huffing as Grindrod called Punthill Plod forward. The boy pumped the winch a little awkwardly and wound out the phosphorescent bloom on its chain, drawing it out into the glass bell of the seltzer-filled lamps, where it came alive with steadily increasing effulgence. The prentices not working the lamp looked on while Lamplighter-Sergeant Grindrod spelled out each rote-learned step.

The little thrills of threwd prickled all the more, and Rossamünd could no longer watch so dutifully. Something was coming, something foul and intending harm—he could feel it in his innards.

There it was: the clatter of horses' hooves, wild and loud. A carriage was approaching, and fast.

"Off the road, boys! Off the road!" the lampsmen called in unison, herding the prentice-lighters on to the verge with a push and a shove of their fodicars. Buffeted by the back or shoulders of several larger boys, Rossamünd was shoved with them, almost falling in the scramble.

"The wretched baskets! Who is fool enough to trot horses

at this gloamin' hour?" Lamplighter-Sergeant Grindrod snarled, mustachios bristling. "See if ye can eye the driver, lads—we might have a writ to write back at Winstermill!"

From out of the dark ahead six screaming horses bolted toward them, carrying a park-drag—a private coach—with such bucking, rattling violence it was sure to break to bits even as it shattered past the stunned lighters.

The prickle of threwd at Rossamünd's back became urgent.

"There's no coachman, Sergeant!" someone cried.

Rossamünd's internals gripped and a yelp of terror was strangled as it formed. A dark, monstrous thing was rising from the rear of the park-drag. Massive horns curled back from its crown; the slits of its eyes glowed wicked orange. Threwd exploded like pain up the back of Rossamünd's head as the carriage shot by, the stench of the horn-ed thing upon it rushing up his nostrils with the gust of their passing.

Some boys wailed.

"Frogs and toads!" Grindrod cursed. "The carriage is attacked!"

More horn-ed monsters could be seen, horrifyingly large, as the coach-and-six smashed on. They clung to the sides of the carriage, worrying and wrestling with the passengers within. The weight and fury of the beasts were so great the whole carriage tipped on to two wheels as it sped. A yellow-green flare of potive burst from a window, flinging one vile nicker from the vehicle in a high, hissing arc and leaving a fizzing trail of reeking fume that rained fur and flesh on the

A **HORN-ED NICKER**

prentices. Head aflame with false-fire, the monster crashed into the briars, a charred ruin. Even as this one flew, another beast leaped from the park-drag to the back of the lead mare. As large as the horse itself, the blighted creature bit into the mane and neck of the hapless, panicked nag. The horse shrieked its dying whinny and fell beneath the grinding hooves of its fellows. The whole vehicle careered and lurched as the team was brought down, sheer momentum tumbling the carriage from the Wormway. With a sickening clash of shattering wood and grinding bones, it skidded and smashed into a dense thicket of tall trunks on the farther side of the road.

For an agony of seconds there was a terrible stillness, the only sounds the mewling of a single mortally injured horse and Grindrod's muttered encouragements to the prentices.

Rossamünd struggled to accept what he had just seen, he and his fellow lantern-sticks agog at the barely lit suggestion of wreckage and mutilation barely fifty yards away among the trees.

"Ground crooks and present arms!" Lamplighter-Sergeant Grindrod gruffed, rousing the prentice-lighters from their stunned dumbness. "Form two ranks for firing by quarto, prentices in front, lampsmen at back! Master Come-lately, stand to our right with yer potives. Show yer flints bravely, lads!"

Driving their fodicars into the roadside to make a hedge of steel, the prentice-watch formed up in two lines behind these, facing the carriage wreck. With the coldly lambent light of the lamp at their backs, the six other boys crouched at the front, the four men stood behind.

Putting himself to the side of this formation, Rossamünd gripped two scripts in a trembling hand, a double dose ready for throwing. One was a cloth salpert of Frazzard's powder to stagger and blind; the other a fragile porcelain caste of loomblaze, a fiery doom. He desperately wished they had a leer with them to peer into the gathering dark and tell better where the monsters were.

Indistinctly lit at the edge of the great-lamp's nimbus glow, great horn-ed shadows stirred and began to stalk about the partly smashed cabin of the coach.

"At least five of the baskets, and as big and cruel as ye never should hope to meet," Lampsman Bellicos hissed in awe.

"Aye," Grindrod growled, his voice all a-hush now. "I bain't seen naught like 'em before. Have ye, Assimus?"

Lampsman Assimus grunted. "Where did they come from, I wonder?"

The lamplighter-sergeant's pale eyes glittered. "We'll have to work some pretty steps tonight if we're going to preserve the lads."

A murmur of dismay shuddered through the prentices.

Two or three of the huge, hunched shadows ripped and gnawed at the stricken horses. Others clawed at the broken carriage, trying to get to the tasty morsels within who, obviously still alive, could be heard crying out. Women's voices.

"That changes things! Other lives are in the balance now, and protecting 'em is our duty," Grindrod said firmly. "Ply your firelocks briskly, hit yer mark; a coward's mother never weeps his end. Master Lately! Time for ye to produce the worst yer salt-bag has to offer. Ye must defend us as we reload, boy! Prentices! Present and level on that blighted slip jack stumbling there!"

One of the horn-ed nickers had appeared on the road. Its silhouette was clear against the pallid glimpse of sky showing where the Pettiwiggin entered the wood.

"Ranks to fire together in volley!" With a rattle of unison action, prentice and lighter leveled their fusils on this creature even as it became aware of them. At the muted metallic dicker of many cocking flints, it fixed them with a gleaming, cunning gaze that seemed to say, *You're next . . .*

Potives already in hand, Rossamünd adjusted his salumanticum so that it would not tangle a good throw.

"Stay to the line!" Grindrod continued, low and grim. "Reload handsomely if ye want to live—it may come to hand strokes soon enough, but I *will* see ye to yer billets safe tonight!"

Rossamünd's throat gripped at his swallowing: to come to hand strokes—to fight hand to hand with a bogle—was to grapple with terror itself. Smaller, weaker-seeming bogles than these could make pie-mince of a large man. He knew what hand strokes would mean: gashing and iron-tasting terror. It was only barely learned duty that kept him to his place.

Grindrod raised his arm, the prelude to the order to fire, yet before he could complete the command a great churning disorientation tumbled over the prentice-watch.

Rossamünd reeled as the world was turned right ways wrong and outside in.

The prentice-watch fumbled their weapons and some cursed in fright.

"They've got a wit in there . . . ," managed Lampsman Bellicos through spasming, grinding teeth.

"And a bad one too . . . ," Puttinger wheezed.

Rossamünd had spent some time with a fulgar on the way to Winstermill all those weeks ago, and now here he was feeling the working of a wit. *So this is what it is to suffer their frission . . .* The sensation quickly passed, leaving a sick headachy funk.

The nicker on the road was gone.

There was a smarting flash from the ruined coach—some kind of illuminating potive that quickly became a glaring rose-colored flare lifted high by a small, slight figure. A woman was struggling from the wreck, dazzling the scene with a brilliant ruby light that stung the eyes. The monsters shied from that strange red glare, retreating into the darkness between tangled trunks.

"Ah! Bitterbright!" growled Lampsman Assimus, shielding his sight with an outstretched arm. "That's a smart bit of skoldin'."

"Aye," Grindrod growled, "but wantonly witting and

blinding us won't help us help them. Make ready and keep a squint so ye can see into that blasted night."

Amazed, struggling to see what was happening, Rossamünd squinted, his eyes watering in the quick, painful brilliance. Bitterbright was powerful chemistry that took great skill to keep burning, and amid the confusion he was desperate to see its maker.

Bold again, the monsters paced a careful circle about the woman, some of them showing as black shadows against the flare as they stalked between the calendars and the lamplighters, their feral stink wafting over the prentice-watch. The smallest nicker was at least seven foot, as far as Rossamünd could tell, the biggest maybe over nine. A-bristle with stiff fur, sharp and slender horns curving back wickedly over their long skulls, they swayed menacingly as they bobbed and lurched in complete and unnerving silence. Slowly the nickers arranged themselves with grim deliberation.

Lamplighter-Sergeant Grindrod kept his eye fixed on the monsters. "Level on that nearest brute. We'll see if we can't even odds a little."

No sooner had he said this than a slight figure sprang out from the carriage, a girl in strange costume, long hair flailing as she leaped. An angry, frightened call followed her, something like "Threnody, *no!*" The girl came on, dancing toward a monster, clutching at her temple. Once more Rossamünd felt that weird and deeply unpleasant giddiness of frission contract in the middle of his head then quickly flex in the pit of his stomach. His vision failed briefly this time and he reeled, as did all those of the prentice-watch. Bellicos retched; Rossamünd's fellow prentice Wrangle vomited and, finally overcome, three other boys collapsed.

Grindrod swore as he staggered. "Lackbrained wit! What's she playing at?"

"They're stinkin'calendars!" Rossamünd heard Assimus' angry whisper.

Rossamünd had read of such as these. They were a society of women—lahzars, skolds, pistoleers and the rest—set to doing good, protecting the weak and pursuing other noble causes.

The agony rapidly passed, as it had before, leaving its aching in Rossamünd's skull. Yet he kept enough of his senses to see that though his fellow lighters were reeling, the monsters were not suffering much at all. The striving of the long-haired calendar had done little to deter the nickers. She was not practiced enough at her witting—it was random, inept. And now the monsters pounced, the largest blocking Rossamünd's view of her in its ravenous intent.

Again they felt the wit's wild frission, driving every one of the prentice-watch still standing to his knees. One of the nickers fell too. With a weird shriek, two more oddly dressed figures pounced from the shattered wood and frame while a third, bearing the bitterbright, struggled after. By the swaying rose light the two dashed to the young wit's defense, prancing and whirling, dancing about her as they began a mortal struggle with the horn-ed nickers, their hands trailing long, lacerating wires. The monsters shied and cast about wildly, raging with disturbing strangled yips as the figures harried and slit first at one then another, keeping them at bay, pirouetting clear of every swipe.

One of the dancers misstepped, and that was her end as the horn-ed nicker gripped and ripped and clawed her—an end more terrible yet than Licurius' at the carving nails of the grinnlings. Bile bubbled up from his gullet as Rossamünd tried to conceive how a living person could so quickly be bent and rent to a meaningless mash. Not even the stoutest proofing could stop such elemental strength. Even as this woman was slain the other dancer became frantic and, with a grieving wail, danced madly about the killer of her sister, cutting at it over and over, slicing off one of its horns, severing a mangled arm, removing an ear. Another beast sprang from a thicket, snatched the flailing woman about her stomach and chewed its great fangs into her face. With a flash-and-bang that echoed through the spindly, spiny wood, someone still inside the cabin fired a pistola—a salinumbus by the flat, heavy slap of the discharge. Hit low with the shot, this ambuscading nicker tottered, dropping its maimed prey. Another thick pistol-crack and a glare of orange flickered about the head of the beast, followed quickly by boisterous crackling. Its head afire, the creature collapsed back with a strange, husky howling, tripping over its victims and falling to the earth. The glare of its burning added light to the furor.

As these things were happening, several nickers had closed with the long-haired wit, who cowered and sent out ineffectual flutterings of her witting powers. Even from where he stood, Rossamünd could feel threwd emanating from these monsters as the beasts sought to best their prey through anguish and mad terror alone.

His fellow prentices whimpered.

"Pernicious threwd!" cursed Assimus.

"Take your aim on that leftmost basket!" Grindrod cried.

The prentice-watch brought up their firelocks.

"Fire!"

With a sharp, rattling clatter the quarto fired, startling the horn-ed nickers, gun-smoke obscuring their view.

One of the monsters collapsed under many hits of musket ball and crumpled gasping to the verge. Sets of glimmering monster eyes—maybe four, maybe five—regarded the lighters malignantly.

"Reload! Reload!" Grindrod demanded, and the prentices hurried to comply.

The long-haired calendar sank to her knees.

The monsters looked to her again and closed for the slaying.

Yet the smallest calendar staggered in between. It was she who had set the bitterbright to burning and kept it bright for her sisters to see. She flung the glare at an encroaching nicker, the red glimmer dimming rapidly now that she no longer fed its chemistry. The beast recoiled as the potive struck and a smolder set in its fur, quickly turning to ruby flames that engulfed head and shoulders. Regardless, two others approached slavering noiselessly, tongues lolling and licking at the smell of blood and smoke.

By the light of the failing bitterbright Rossamünd could see that this brave woman wore the conical hat of a skold and white spoor lines down both sides of her face. A thick hackle of cream-colored fur wrapped about her neck and shoulders, and strange little wings protruded from her back. She looked fragile, vulnerable, doomed.

One set of glowing eyes, however, had stayed fixed on the prentices hurrying new rounds into their fusils. This nicker chose them as its next victims and pounced, taking five yards with each springing lope.

"By quarto!" Grindrod hollered.

The lantern-sticks struggled to get their weapons up in time as in five strides the beast was halfway toward them, foul breath steaming from its gnashing teeth.

Rossamünd lifted his arm ready to throw his chemistry.

"Level!"

The horn-ed terror arched itself as it ran at them, ready to pounce. Almost in unison the other nickers lashed at the calendars . . . and froze as if each was stricken. The monster rushing them toppled and skidded along the road in midstride.

"What the . . . !" Grindrod exclaimed.

"Saved," whimpered Crofton Wheede.

"She's a bane!" marveled Assimus. Both skold and wit, banes were rare and extraordinary.

Indeed, the calendar, though clearly struggling, was now touching her left temple, a gesture characteristic of a wit. The prentice-watch looked on in awe as, with a precise show of frightening potency, the woman caused the largest beast before her to writhe in paroxysms of agony while holding the other two frozen. So skilled was she that, unlike her long-haired compatriot, she sent no wild washings of frission to trouble the lampsmen and their charges. All Rossamünd could feel was a vague fluttering in his innards.

With a hoarse sound almost like a whinny, the monster bent on the lamplighters struggled to break free of the calendar's invisible grip. It stumbled sideways, tried to turn and lunge at the quarto of the prentice-watch, their weapons still leveled and ready.

"Fire!" Grindrod hollered, and the prentice-watch let go a clattering volley at the beast. It gave voice to a disturbing, sheeplike bleat and ceased its struggling.

Still the calendar bane held the other two beasts in a prison unseen while a pistoleer pulled herself from the ruin of the transport. She drew forth two long-barreled pistolas and fired both point-blank into the glimmering, helpless eyes of one of the pinioned creatures. With a violent jerk and gouts of black pouring from its head, the beast expired.

All that remained was the largest monster. A tortured thing it was now, twisting and thrashing upon the ground, a captive of its own agony. The woman never moved, never touched it, a hand always at her temple. Slowly the creature's movements slackened; slowly its writhings turned to twitchings and finally to nothing. Its terrifying orange eyes faded and at last were extinguished.

With an audible and weary exhalation, the calendar bane sagged to the ground.

Rossamünd let out a quiet relieved sigh of his own.

"Ye've done it, lads!" Grindrod exclaimed, proud and a little amazed. "Ye've just won through yer first theroscade."

It's not my first, Rossamünd thought but kept to himself.

"There'll be punctings for ye all after this tonight," the lamplighter-sergeant continued.

"It's been a prodigious long time since a prentice was marked," Bellicos chipped in.

The prentices grinned at each other weakly, happy simply to be alive.

I don't want to be puncted! Rossamünd fretted.

Grindrod turned to him. "Ye're carrying the salt-bag, Master Lately. Ye can come with me," he declared.

Leaving the lampsmen to organize the prentices into piquets, the lamplighter-sergeant stalked over to the wreck of the park-drag. The calendar bane and pistoleer were bent over one of their fallen while the long-haired wit sat slumped in the twigs and dirt by the bristled corpse of a dead nicker.

"The sniveling snot—almost ruined us all with her wanton wit's pranks," Grindrod cursed under his breath, then called as they approached, "Hoi, calendars! Bravely fought and well won, m'ladies! Lamplighter-Sergeant Grindrod and a prentice come to offer what aid we might."

Crouched by the body of her comrade whose face was a gory mess, the bane looked up at him. Her cheeks and brow glistened with a lustrous patina of sweat; her eyes were sunken and her skin was flushed. Rossamünd thought she looked more ill than injured. "We may have triumphed in the fight, but the loss of two sisters is never well," she returned in a soft voice, with a hint of a musical southern accent. "Lady Dolours you may call me, Lamplighter-Sergeant; bane and laude to the Lady Vey, esteemed august of the Right of the Pacific Dove. Your assistance is welcome. My sister languishes with these terrible bites to her face but will survive if attended to quickly. I would tend her myself, but I lack the right scripts. Do you carry staunches? Vigorants?" All this time she had not stood, and the effort of speaking left her breathless.

Keen to please, Rossamünd nodded eagerly. "Lamplighter-Sergeant, I have what she requires," he said emphatically as he fossicked about in the potive satchel. "Thrombis and a jar of bellpomash." The first would stop a wound's flowing and the second revive spirits when taken in food or drink.

"As it should be, prentice." Grindrod nodded curt approval. "Ye may give them what they need."

Rossamünd held the jars of potives as the pistoleer min-

21

istered to the gruesome injuries on her sister's face. He forced himself to keep watching, to not flinch and wince and look away from the gore: he was no use to anyone if he let others' wounds trouble him. With a fright he saw a flash on the edge of his sight, and was startled by a *Crack!* as Bellicos put his fusil to the head of a prostrate nicker and brought its twitching throes to an end.

"I must ask ye, lady maiden-fraught, what possessed ye to be traveling in the eve of a day with a six-horse team?" Grindrod folded his arms. "Ye ought to know it only encourages the bogles!"

The diminutive calendar called Dolours looked the lamplighter-sergeant up and down as if he were a blockheaded simpleton. "That I do," she returned wearily, "as does even the least schooled. The horses were proofed in shabraques, sir, and doused with the best nullodors we possess; and had we been allowed a night's succor by your less-than-cheerful brothers at Wellnigh, we would not have needed to venture forth so foolishly in the unkind hours." She held the sergeant-lighter's stare. "But we were refused lodging at that cot, directly and to our faces. No room for a six-horse team, or so they said."

"That can't be right." Grindrod scowled. "Of course six horses can stable in Wellnigh—wouldn't be much use if they couldn't! What other reason did they give?"

"No other reason at all, Lamplighter-Sergeant," the bane said coolly. "After this first exchange the charming Major-of-House himself simply refused entry and sent us on our

22

way. Little less than storming the twin keeps would have got us within."

"Bah!" Grindrod almost spat. "Another of the Master-of-Clerks' spat-licking toadies," he muttered. Aloud he said, "He's one of the new lot shifted up from the Considine. If what ye say be true, I'll be having words with the Lamplighter-Marshal—refusing folks bain't the way we conduct ourselves out here on the Emperor's Highroad. Succor to all and a light to their path," he concluded, with one of the many maxims with which the prentices had been indoctrinated from the very first day of prenticing.

"A light to your path," intoned the prentices automatically, as they had been taught.

"Indeed, Lamplighter-Sergeant," Dolours returned, "the Emperor's lampsmen seem not to be what they once were."

Grindrod bridled.

Rossamünd too felt a twinge of loyal offense. The lampsmen he had come to know worked hard to keep the roads lit and well tended.

"Attacks rise and numbers dwindle, madam," the lamplighter-sergeant countered, chin lifted in defensive pride, "yet the road has the same figure of lamps and still we have to compass it all. So I ask again: what be yer business on the road?"

The calendar stayed her ground. "As I understand it," she said slowly, "time is running short for your prentices to be sufficiently learned in their trade, true?"

"Aye, precious short. What of that?"

"It's a simple thing, you see," Dolours said, ever so quietly. She looked to the long-haired calendar—Threnody, they had called her—who glared at both the lamplighter-sergeant and Rossamünd. "This young lady desires to become a lamplighter."

2

WINGS OF A DOVE

fodicar(s) (noun) also lantern-crook, lamp- or lantern-switch, poke-pole or just poke; the instrument of the lamplighter, a long iron pole with a perpendicular crank-hook protruding from one end, used to activate the seltzer lamps that illuminate many of the Empire's important roads. The pike-head allows the fodicar to be employed as a weapon—a kind of halberd—to fend off man and monster alike.

FROM the little Rossamünd knew of these things, lamplighters rarely, if ever, employed women as lampsmen. As servants, as cothouse clerks, or even as soldiers maybe, but never a lighter.

Lamplighter-Sergeant Grindrod puffed his cheeks, his jaw jutting stubbornly. "Her?" Then he laughed—a loud, foolish noise in the mourning-quiet after the attack. "She near brought us all to ruin. She'll be lucky I don't clap her in the pillory for impeding the goodly duties of His Rightful Emperor's servants!"

Threnody stood, clench-fisted. "I am a peer, you lowborn toadlet, of rank so far above yours, you'll be lucky I don't claim quo gratia and have you clapped in irons yourself, you sot-headed dottard!"

Rossamünd tried to pull his neck into his stock as a turtle might.

His fellow lighters gathered near, awestruck.

The lamplighter-sergeant was agog. "Lowborn? Sot-headed? Quo gratia?" Grindrod's red face became an apoplectic purple. "I'm not the want-wit who frissioned my watch to a daze in the middle of a bogle attack! They wasted the surgeon's fees on ye, poppet!"

Threnody let out a tight, wordless yell, both her hands clutching her temple.

Rossamünd's head, his entire gall, revolted, and his sense of up and down collided. He staggered and fell, joining Grindrod, the lampsmen, the prentices and even the pistoleer writhing in the dirt.

"Enough!" cried Dolours, and the wayward frission ceased. The bane was the only one standing, her left hand to her temple, her right stretched over the now prone Threnody. She had witted the girl, striven one of her own. "Enough," she whispered again. Looking deeply unwell, she reached a conciliatory hand to Grindrod regardless, an offer of help.

"I can get to me feet meself, madam," he seethed, tottering dazedly as he proved his words.

As Rossamünd and his fellows unsteadily regained their feet, Dolours sighed. "That 'poppet,' Sergeant, is the daughter of our august and a marchioness-in-waiting in her own right: you'd do well to pay your due respect."

LAMPLIGHTER-SERGEANT
GRINDROD

Lampsmen Bellicos, Puttinger and Assimus muttered grimly.

The prentice-lighters looked to their sergeant.

"And a great liability she'd be to ye too, I am sure." Grindrod smiled. He nodded a bow, saying louder, "I apologize to ye." He wrestled with himself a moment, then with deliberate, frosty calm added, "I don't know where such a custard-headed notion sprang from, madam, but women bain't wanted in the lighters!"

"We know it well, Lamplighter-Sergeant!" The calendar bane stood unsteadily and Rossamünd saw her face turn a ghastly gray. Clearly she suffered from some feverish malady. She smiled sadly. "Perhaps you are right, but yet it is not an impossible thing for a woman to take her place in your quartos, I am sure?"

Grindrod's mustachios bristled and writhed as he considered her words. "Bain't really for me to say one way or t'other, bane," he said finally. "This shall have to be the decision of the Lamplighter-Marshal."

"Hence our journey to Winstermill, Lamplighter-Sergeant," Dolours countered.

"Well, our work tonight takes us in the contrary direction." Grindrod rocked back on his heels, his arms still folded across his broad chest. "However, I'll send back a transport with guard to gather the fallen and bring ye all back to Wellnigh. Now ye're six horses less they'll be having to give ye a billet, I reckon." With that, the lamplighter-sergeant pivoted on his brightly polished heel and stepped out on to the road, calling the prentices and lampsmen to him.

Sick with too much frission, Rossamünd came tumbling after, trying hard not to trip over the putrid bodies of the dead bogles. The lamplighter-sergeant made hasty arrangements: he and Bellicos and the other prentices would continue on to Wellnigh House, the sturdy little cottage-fortress to the east, continuing to light the remaining lanterns as they went. Rossamünd, however, as possessor of the salumanticum, was to be left behind to tend the calendars' wounds. With him would remain Lampsmen Assimus and Puttinger as a nominal guard and fatigue party to help with the fallen and to salvage the luggage.

With a cry of, "Prentice-watch in single file, by the left, march!" Lamplighter-Sergeant Grindrod, Lampsman 1st Class Bellicos and the wide-eyed, nervous prentices went on, leaving Rossamünd and the other two lampsmen with the vigilant, silent calendars.

Assimus and Puttinger ignored Rossamünd. Lampsmen rarely shared in chitter-chatter with prentices till they were full lampsmen themselves. Reluctantly they set to work finding belongings and goods amid the shatters and splinters, making a pile of the broken trunks and half-rent valises. Typical of the older men who worked on this easy stretch of road, they were crotchety half-pay pokers whose job was to babysit the lantern-sticks out on the road as they learned their trade. They paid no attention whatsoever to the lads unless duty demanded.

Feeling uncomfortable and unnecessary, Rossamünd hugged his arms against the searching chill.

Balding branches rubbed together with whispering creaks. Dry twigs rattled.

Exposed and neglected, Rossamünd looked to the calendars. Head bowed and shy, the young prentice fished about his salumanticum and brought out more bellpomash, offering it to Dolours with a nervous cough, "I thought you might need this, m'lady. I'm sorry, I have nothing more appropriate for a fever—no febrifuges or soothing steams . . ."

She remained silent for a breath, looking to Rossamünd's hands, then to his face. There was an unreal calmness in her gaze. Her spoors, those white lines that went vertically from her hairline across both eyes to her jaw, showed clearly in the night. They made her look serious, dangerous. Like Europe, she possessed a remote, almost casual deadliness.

Rossamünd began to regret his boldness.

"Thank you, young lampsman." The bane nodded graciously. "It was foolish of me to have left both ill and without the chemistry for even a simple vigorant. Dispense away."

Putting down his fodicar, Rossamünd set about his task, also giving out lordia—to restore their humours, which, as he had read in a book from Winstermill's small library, was essential after times of great stress and exertion. He had bought this from a hedgeman, a wandering script-grinder who had visited Winstermill not more than a month ago.

Each restorative was gratefully received.

Such a concentrated collection of teratologists Rossamünd had never seen before. While he dispensed, he sneaked beady, fascinated looks at their odd costumes. The calendars hid their well-proofed silken bossocks beneath mantles patterned in blue, orange and white. Dolours kept warm beneath a hackle of fur. She wore fleece-lined, buff-covered oversleeves called manchins tied to her shoulders with ribbons. Rossamünd could not help staring at her wings. Although they looked real—outstretched and ready to fly—he knew they were simply ornaments.

Each of the calendars' feet was shod with quiet-shoes: flat-heeled, soft-soled, coming to a pronounced, flattened point at the toe. The strange, ornate hats upon the calendars' heads—known as dandicombs—varied, however. The pistoleer—whose name, he quickly learned, was Charllette—wore a broad thrice-high; the maimed dancer had been wearing a tight, vertical bundle of black ribbon and many, many hair-tines—these were being removed even as Rossamünd watched. Threnody, evidently sulking, wore her own hair, with no hat or other flamboyant head covering. She, too, had a spoor: a thin arrow pointing up from her left brow—the mark of a wit. Rossamünd had read that wits were always bald; he wondered how it was that this one was not.

With sad, taciturn direction from Dolours, the lampsmen discovered the body of a sixth calendar in the mess of the carriage. The lampsmen placed it on the side of the road, near the lamp and away from the corpses of bogles. Beside it they laid the fallen dancer, covering both in their patterned mantles and returning to their vitriolic mutterings and the

31

search for luggage. If there was one thing Rossamünd had learned well, it was that lamplighters liked to gripe.

The three calendars stood by the bodies, their heads bowed.

The lampsmen stopped their labors and watched, staying very much apart from the women as they grieved. Thinking it polite, Rossamünd removed himself too, sitting on the side of the road. Sad in sympathy, he thought he could hear Threnody softly weeping as Dolours whispered almost inaudibly, "Fare thee well, kind Pannette. Rest thee easy, dear Idesloe. The dove fold you in her down-ed wings . . ." More was said, special funeral potives lit to ward off scavenging bogles and hushed laments sung while the lampsmen stared. The sad task over, the calendars retired to the edges of the lamplight.

Ritual done, the lampsmen recovered the last of the dunnage. "They expect her to join us!" Assimus piped up as he and Puttinger wrestled a trunk to the small collection of the calendars' belongings. "They expect us to let a girl join! Have you ever, ever heard of such a thing, Putt? I don't give a fig what the Marshal might do: I've never heard of such a thing in all my time!"

Threnody, obviously overhearing, fixed them with an attempt at a withering eye.

Rossamünd was caught by it, and though they were not his words, he blushed and shuffled awkward feet.

"You there," Threnody called, soft yet sour, "the little ledgermain. I am in need of evander, if you have this."

Rossamünd hesitated. Evander he did not have—only

gromwell, a cheap substitute courtesy of the miserliness of the clerks—though it did in a pinch. He said as much, and the young calendar snorted in mild disgust.

It will do, she said, and held out a hand to receive the restorative.

He stepped over and gave to her a drab brown flasket marked with a $\Gamma\rho$ to signify gromwell. Threnody took it, looked at it with a splenic expression, and then quaffed it in one brash gulp.

"That is all" was all she said as thanks, and with that said ignored him completely.

Rossamünd was not impressed. She could not have been more than a year or two his senior.

"I reckon she's taken a liking to ye, Master Come-lately," Assimus chuckled archly.

Rossamünd turned his attention to nothing in particular and fixed it there. This kind of jesting was, he had learned over the last two months, part of the lamplighter way.

"Not that you really want to get tangled with a calendar, boyo," Assimus continued quietly, unexpectedly willing to share his manifold experiences. "They're always getting in our road on the road, if ye get me, always interfering with their lofty machinations. Still," he said, patting the young prentice on the back, "since they've taken such a shine on ye, it seems it's fallen to thee to be their minder. Handsomely done, lad, a noble thing you've set to, sparing us the burden. Handsomely done!"

"But I thought it was the duty of all lamplighters to do the noble thing," Rossamünd returned seriously.

Assimus looked awkward in turn, then collected himself. "What do ye know of noble things, lantern-stick?" the lighter said churlishly. "What dangers have ye had to test yer thew? See what I've seen and then see if ye're so quick to judgment. Just keep to yer watching, and yer ignorant twitterings to yeself!"

Feeling chastened and foolish, Rossamünd did as he was told.

The cloudless night grew colder. The women whispered to each other in a foreign tongue, yet said little to their three guardians. The calendar pistoleer attended to the hurts of her half-chewed and mercifully unconscious sister while Threnody brooded and Dolours sat suffering her fever. Heavy pistolas hanging ready at her hips, Charllette picked slowly through the fallen nickers, frequently looking out into the darkling woods wanly lit by a rising moon. As she went from corpse to corpse, the pistoleer would crouch for a time, poking at the beast, then rise and move to the next, slyly stowing things in her stout satchel each time. Puzzled, Rossamünd watched her from the corner of his gaze, trying not to look open and curious. At one of the dead monsters he saw her stopper an odd-shaped vial, one he recognized—a bruicle it was called—used by physicians and surgeons to hold humours and by teratologists to hold . . . *monster blood!*

He was curious to see the manner by which it was done—his peregrinat, the waterproof almanac given him by Fransitart—was only vague on the subject. The epitome of failed nonchalance, the young prentice sauntered over to a beast and stared at it, looking for signs of Charllette's gruesome work. The horn-ed nicker's eyes were wide and staring, as vacantly black and blank and empty of energy as they had been wild, coal-fire orange when it lived. Rossamünd looked into them sadly. Such an impressive, stalwart creature, yet he could still sense its malign nature: definitely foe, never friend. And oh, the stink of it! Like a piggery, the jakes and an unmucked manger in one.

"These are ugly, festering articles." The hushed voice of Lampsman Assimus marveling to his right startled Rossamünd. "Look'ee here!" The lampsman poked at the heavy body with his fodicar. "This is one we hit—see the holes. Every bullet has its billet. I see those saucy coneys have taken their fill already, but we have claim on this 'un's ichor too. Draw some, Putt—we can get Drawk to punct us when we're off watch tomorrow."

Puttinger shook his head grimly as he drew forth a wicked-looking utensil.

A sprither, Rossamünd realized. It was a tube of steel bent into an S-shape with a needle point on one end and a short, flexible straw made of gut protruding from the other.

"They'll claim the kill, no doubting," Puttinger said in his thick Gott accent as he bent and stabbed the point of the sprither into a hole made by a musket ball. "But we had our hands in it!" He sucked on the straw briefly and squeezed it several times till the thick, dark brown blood—the ichor— of the bogle trickled out. Pinching the straw to stem the flow, he unstoppered a bruicle of his own and let the ichor drain into it. From what Rossamund understood, now that the ichor was contained outside the body, it was called cruor—spilled blood.

Rossamünd watched with rapt disgust. Then his own blood went cold. *They shan't mark me!* To be puncted with a cruorpunxis was foul to the young prentice ever since he had witnessed the end of the innocent Misbegotten Schrewd by Europe's hand. Not that he would *ever* express this aversion: an admission of such a thing would surely brand him a sedorner. With the lamplighters, as in the cities, monster-lovers were always hanged. More than once Rossamünd had seen a man hanged in Right Tree Angle, the square in what was once his part of Boschenberg. He had never relished the spectacle as many others appeared to do, with their jostling and jeering and hoots of derision. "Traitor! Traitor! Who's going to caress the nickers now?" Such were the cries as the poor convict's face went purple-black and his tongue swelled out.

Rossamünd shuddered at the vivid recollection.

"No blood-marking for thee, little lantern-stick," Puttinger said gravely, as if he were reading Rossamünd's thoughts. "Though thy chums did, thee did not have thy hand in this killing."

Rossamünd quickly returned to the present. "Aye, Lampsman." Oh yes, he was very glad to be excluded from the kill—even if these nickers were not so innocent.

Assimus stepped away and cautiously kicked at what was

left of a horse. He looked over to the calendars with a snort. "Horses indeed! Much smarter choice, oxen, for traveling in the night," he said to his fellow lighters, just loud enough for the calendars to hear. Only Threnody paid him any mind— an ineffectual glare. "Not nearly as toothsome and attracting to the nickers as a team of half-a-dozen glossy nags." He scratched his head. "Thing is, Putt, how is it so many of the hugger-muggers have found themselves this far west?"

Puttinger nodded gravely. "Our brothers is pushed too hard out east and are letting the schmuttlingers through. It is like the people is saying: the Marshal is struggling."

"The Lamplighter-Marshal will have it in hand, and no fear," said Assimus. "We just do as he directs and we'll win through. It's just like that dark time back in—when was it? Ye remember, Putt? When all those nasty spindly things came out from the Gluepot and with them schrewds in hordes and we went out to help . . . It was 'cause of the Marshal we got 'em then, and we still have 'im now and we'll get 'em now—easy as kiss me hand!"

"Yes." Puttinger did not sound convinced. He stowed the sprither and stepped away, looking suspiciously into the menacing shadows.

Rossamünd had read of nickers and bogles—"hugger-muggers" Assimus had called them—gathering in numbers in determined assault on some remote or ailing community. In days-now-gone maraudes of monsters would ravage everyman heartlands, even into the parishes and right up to the walls of a city. Such terrors were so rare now as to be mythical, yet it was still the greatest fear of the subjects of the Empire. Within every bosom dwelt the vague dread of cities overrun with murderous, civilization-ending bogles, of gashing pain and effusions of blood, of a world without humankind. Without vigilance, ancient history could too easily become present calamity. It was this dread that made Imperial citizens so determinedly vengeful whenever a sedorner was ferreted out from among them.

Yet here on the edge of the Idlewild, even Rossamünd had heard the growing rumors of monsters setting on people in the lands about with alarming regularity; read of it in the few periodical pamphlets he had managed to buy from the paper hawkers who drifted through the fortress. At first he had thought it just a part of rural life, but if weary veterans of the sinew of Lampsmen Assimus and Puttinger were troubled, then Rossamünd was moved to be doubly so. He was surely glad to be in the company of a bane, even a weary one.

In the carriage debris a part-crushed hamper had been rescued. By the light of the great-lamp, as the calendars and the lamplighters reluctantly gathered close for safety, Charllette rummaged among the cracked, dribbling pots and smashed, smeared parcels, sharing any unspoiled vittles she found. The pistoleer called Rossamünd's portion "a nice bit of coty gaute." He examined it skeptically: it looked like pie filled with odd-smelling chunks.

"It's quail pasty, lamp boy," Threnody said testily. "Just eat it."

Rossamünd did so and, even though it was congealed-cold, it tasted rather good.

In the encroaching dusk, green Maudlin rose over the eastern hills and showed how long the night had been. In due time the lamplighter-sergeant returned with a guard of four sturdy haubardiers of the Wellnigh House watch leading a dray pulled by a nervous ox. The animal was draped in a flanchardt, a covering blanket of proofed hessian. It was turned about and took the exhausted, injured or unconscious calendars, their two dead sisters, and their damaged effects back to Wellnigh House. It was agreed better to return to the cothouse rather than go on to Winstermill; better to get indoors as soon as possible while the night still lingered, and with it the threat of more monsters. The proper treatment of wounds would have to wait until the morrow.

"Amble ye by the dray, Master Come-lately," Grindrod commanded. "Keep yerself available to tend their hurts."

So Rossamünd walked, as did Assimus and Puttinger and the haubardiers, staying by the ox dray, ready if a script was needed. On the farther side of the woodland Rossamünd saw the crumpled bodies of the park-drag driver and his side-armsman. They had been mauled then tossed from the stampeding vehicle to land dead on the side of the highroad. Wrapped in canvas tarpaulins, they were laid on the dray alongside the remains of the two calendars.

The round hills of the Tumblesloe Heap loomed black against the starlit gray. The lanterns became more frequent: at last the cothouse was near. What swelling relief it was to finally spy the beacon flares and window-lights of the small twin keeps of Wellnigh House at the base of the hills. A pair of squat towers stood on either side of the Pettiwiggin, each fenced by a thick drystone wall. These were connected by a hanging gallery known as the Omphalon, a bridge with walls of solid wood and a steep-sloping roof that spanned the road. In this raised gallery were the lighters' quarters, and the sight of lanterns winking from its narrow windows set Rossamünd's thoughts to bed and sleep.

At last they entered the walled lane between the two keeps. Here they passed ornate warding censers, great brass domes that squatted in heavy three-legged stands on either side of the road. Within these domes, day and night, nicker repellents were burned, their poison fumes seeping through holes bored in the dull metal. On Rossamünd's very first night at Wellnigh House he had sucked a lungful of their foul fetor and for an instant thought his end had come, but the wind had mercifully blown another way and he recovered. From that day he learned to stay upwind of the censers or hold his breath and shut his eyes till he had passed.

What relief it was to pass through the thick oak gates in the broad wall of the northern fastness and stand safe within the cothouse's tiny foreyard. The unhappy deeds that had ruined the night were already common talk there, yet still the calendars received a barely civil reception. The long-faced Major-of-House was waiting for them in the yard and insisted on a brief conference with Grindrod while Rossamünd was made to remain in the cold. The lamplighter-sergeant looked mightily unimpressed with what he was hearing. Dolours approached them as they remonstrated under the light of a yard-lamp and the discussion came to an abrupt and obviously unsatisfactory end. The house-major raised a refusing hand, loudly declaring, "That is all, madam! I had my reasons. Take the matter up with our Marshal in Winstermill if you want further hearing." He dismissed Grindrod and called for Rossamünd with an authoritative wave.

The young prentice hurried over dutifully while, with stony face, Dolours turned wearily on her heel and returned to her sisters-in-arms.

"I'm told these blighted women have taken a liking to you, boy," the house-major said quickly, not stopping for the inconvenience of an answer, "so you can be their liaison. Meddlesome wenches—you may not find them so agreeable once you've spent time in their company. Take them now to the store on the farther side of the Omphalon. They may rest their troublesome heads there."

Rossamünd groaned inwardly. He led the women through the windowless watch room on the ground floor of the north tower, pointing the way down narrow passages of dark wood and through the cramped rooms of a structure built for efficient military function rather than genteel comfort. Up the tight stairway to the gallery he took them, and over, along the access way of the raised gallery and by the night sounds of the already sleeping prentices, to their room beyond in the southern keep. He became aware that a hushed, earnest talk between Threnody and the bane Dolours—begun in the front watch room—had now become a repressed yet passionate struggle. As he stood at the top of the southern stairs to point the way down, he heard Threnody exclaim through clenched teeth with petulant words too low and hissing to distinguish.

Arriving at their hastily arranged quarters, the calendars testily reviewed the inadequate lodging. Crates and goods had been rearranged and foldable cots squeezed between, all still dusty and crawling with earwigs.

Embarrassed, Rossamünd bid them fair night with a stiff bow.

Despite their weariness, Dolours and the pistoleer returned the compliment, the bane saying, "Grace and manners. We are obliged to you, young lighter. You have been a great service to us."

Threnody just frowned and, with a huff of spleen, lay on her ill-made cot.

His thoughts all for bed, Rossamünd went to his own lodgings, shuffling among the sleeping prentices, and threw himself down clothes, boots and all.

ON RETURNING
TO WINSTERMILL

cothouse(s) type of fortalice; the small, often houselike, fortresses built along highroads to provide billet and protection to lamplighters and their auxiliaries. Cothouses are usually built no more than ten to twelve miles apart, so that the lamplighters will not be left lighting lamps and exposed in the unfriendly night for too long. Their size goes from a simple high-house with slit windows well off the ground, through the standard structure of a main house with small attendant buildings all surrounded by a wall, to the fortified bastion-houses like Haltmire on the Conduit Vermis or Tungoom on the Conduit Felix.

Rossamünd woke, having slept very little, to the drum roll of "Stand While You Can," a merry martial tune rattled out every morning at five-o'-the-clock to rouse the lantern-watch.

Stand while you can, lads,
Stand while you can:
For the Glory of Ol' Barny,
Stand while you can.

He gave a gentle groan. The common-quarter night at

Wellnigh had been full of snores and night shouts and a paucity of proper rest. He should have been used to this: it was how he had spent all his sleeps at Madam Opera's. Two months' prenticing at Winstermill, however, with a cell of his own, had given him something he had never truly known, privacy. Cold and small though his cell might have been, with a cot lumpy like tepid slogg-porridge, he had come to prize its seclusion.

Rousing himself, Rossamünd rubbed grit-itchy eyes and sat, his head still swimming with nightmares of gnashing shadows and carriages attacked. Fouracres, the ambling Imperial postman he had met on his journey to Winstermill, had told him a lamplighter's life was dangerous, and now the prentice well understood why.

A life of adventure. A life of violence.

Bright-limns were turned and their cool light slowly revealed the long, low quarters. Waking and rising, the other prentice-lighters hubbubbed with restrained excitement, retelling last night's theroscade.

"What about that young calendar!" Hanging by his arms from one of the low, steeply angled rafters, Punthill Plod gave a saucy whoop that set the sleepier ones complaining. Mornings always were his better part of the day.

"Aye! She was a bit of a fine dig," Tremendus Twörp leered, "though she couldn't wit for a goose."

"Did ye hear old Grind-yer-bones last night?" Plod enthused. "We might get marked. Ye heard him: said prentices ain't been puncted in a precious long time!"

"I'm not getting one," Rossamünd declared, with more gladness than he meant to show.

"Why not, Rosey?" Plod stopped his rafter swinging.

"Lampsman Puttinger said I did not have a hand in killing anything."

"Oh" was all Plod said.

"Ye don't sound too troubled, Rosey. Don't ye want one?" Twörp added. "Perhaps there should 'ave been more so you could've got yerself a kill." He gave a sardonic grin.

"That was more than enough for me," Crofton Wheede put in, wide-eyed. "I thought we were done in and no mistaking! It was like how me poor mammy ended all over again . . ."

"Don't start on yer poor mammy, Wheede!" Eugus Smellgrove called testily, still lying abed.

"Aye," Giddian Pillow offered, "just be grateful they weren't one of them gudgeon-baskets I heard tell of—them ones running wild out Gathercoal way."

"They reckon a wit can't stop a rever-man," Wheede shuddered, clearly glad it had not been a brace of these vile creatures on the road last night.

Gudgeons! Rever-men? Rossamünd sat up. "Where did you hear about that?" he called.

"When we were in Silvernook the other day," Pillow answered. "Some fellow at the skittle-alley on the Hackstone Row says he'd come from Makepeace and that it was all abuzz about the quarry being haunted by some handmade beastie."

Rossamünd nodded, aghast. "But how did it get there? They have to be put somewhere, don't they? Rever-men don't just wander about on their own—do they? Someone has to make them. Someone has to place them."

"It probably got loose from a hob-rousing pit," Pillow offered with a grim and knowing look.

Hob-rousing was the illegal practice of setting monsters against gudgeons and betting on the winner. Rossamünd thought of Freckle and the rever-man once locked in the hold of the *Hogshead*. *Maybe that was where they were headed?* He was doubly glad now he had set Freckle free. "But that's wrong!" he exclaimed without thinking.

The others looked at him blankly.

"Well, I've heard it that the fluffs use the baskets for guards to protect all their jools and secrets," Plod said finally, rolling his eyes weirdly. He wiggled his fingers as if a great shower of coins were pouring through them, causing a chuckle among his fellows.

"I heard it said there's some poor fellow back at Winstermill who's all agog from what they reckon was a gudgeon fight," Smellgrove joined in, fully awake at last. "Was once a fine lighter but has never been right in his intellectuals since."

"Clap it shut, little frogs!" Assimus snorted, startling them all, stomping into the room to rouse them out to the sip-pots to wash. "Who talks on rever-men at this fresh hour of day? Git ye up and git ye at 'em! Out for yer scrubbing! Move yer carcasses!"

A line of tubs ran along a wall in a small yard adjacent to the foreyard of the northern keep. While the shivering boys scrubbed themselves in the freezing twilight, the topic of talk soon shifted to more friendly adventures. First it was the mischief done on the last Domesday visit to Silvernook and mischief planned for the next—for Domesday was the common, weekly vigil-day and their one occasion of rest. Much to the other boys' bemused disapproval, Rossamünd had never joined them on these half-drunken jaunts, preferring to spend his money on pamphlets and remain behind at the manse reading. In the time since he started at Winstermill he had ventured down to Silvernook only twice to get more pamphlets and to see if he might meet again with Fouracres, who had helped him so much on his way to prenticing. The restless postman had not had an opportunity to come to Winstermill. Silvernook and the dwellings of the Brindleshaws were his range, and he was so devoted to his "custom"—as he called the people he delivered to, he rarely had a common vigil himself. Their reunions had therefore been necessarily and unsatisfactorily brief, and Rossamünd was still hoping for a day where they might sit and talk in earnest.

The boys' chatter changed again to the most common topic—in what cothouse each prentice thought he would like to serve once prenticing was done and they had all become lampsmen 3rd class.

"I want to go to Makepeace Stile," Plod said eagerly. "They work close with them obstaculars to catch bandits and dark traders and such."

"What about Haltmire?" pondered Twörp, leering at Wheede. "Ye get to see plenty of nickers there."

"They don't send lampsmen 3rd class out there, Twörp!" Wheede rose to the goad. "It's too unfriendly for new lighters."

"Aye," said Smellgrove, "the way ye was whimpering last night I can see why."

Rossamünd did not particularly care: where he was sent was where he was sent. Surely it would all be the same: light the lamp, douse the lamp, light the lamp, douse the lamp, light the lamp, douse the lamp, always waiting for some monster to spring and deliver a horrible end . . .

Rossamünd contrived to wash only his face and not remove his shirt before being herded back to the gallery to dress in full. Today was the day when he was due to change his nullodor: the Exstinker he had promised both Fransitart and Craumpalin to wear, splashed on the cambric sash wound about his chest, under his clothes. But his precious Exstinker was back at Winstermill, wrapped up in an oilcloth at the bottom of his bed chest at the base of the lumpy cot.

Before putting on his quabard—the vest of rigid proofing all lighters wore over their coats—he stared at the embroidered figure upon it. Stitched in thread-of-gold was an owl displayed wings out, talons reaching, sewn over panels of rouge and leuc—red and white. Sagix Glauxes Rex—the Sagacious Imperial Owl—the sign of an Emperor's man. *For the Glory of Ol' Barny indeed!*

The prentice-watch messed on the usual farrats and small

beer (never as good as that served at the Harefoot Dig—always far too watery). Tomorrow's breakfast at the manse would be no better—dark pong bread swilled down with saloop, a drink of sassafras and sugar boiled in milk. The morning after that it would be farrats once more, then pong the next, then farrats, over and over.

Breakfast wolfed down, they paraded out in the yard of the northern keep before the sun had even peeped. Now they must douse all the lanterns back to Winstermill and be in time for limes, the morning interval between first morning instructions and second. This was where the prentices still at Winstermill were formed up to await the return of the lantern-watch, each given lime-laced pints of small beer to fend off ill-health. Ready for this returning and looking forward to limes, the boys stood shivering in the glow of bright seltzer lamps, the morning showing as a cold halo in a low and murky sky. This was the time of day figured safest, when night monsters had found their beds once more and daytime prowlers were still waking.

Surly and overtired, Assimus, Bellicos and Puttinger poked the boys into correct dressing with rough tugs and prods of their fodicars. Grindrod called them to attention and marched them out the gates. Back to Winstermill they went, to a little rest before resuming the solemn routines of their prenticing.

Back to Winstermill, that is, except for Rossamünd. He had been left behind as a courtesy from the lamplighter-sergeant to rouse the calendars and accompany them to the manse. Returning from the foreyard, he passed Mister Bolt, the night-clerk and uhrsprechman, sitting in the north keep guardroom behind a small dirty stool that served as his table, and asked him the time of day.

Groggy, smelling of claret and squinting with lack of sleep, Mister Bolt peered at Rossamünd. "*Quota hora est,* he asks!" the night-clerk said, taking out his heavy fob. "What time is it indeed?" He glared at its cryptic face beadily. "Why, lantern-stick, it's a little before the half hour of five-o'the-clock on this cruel chill's morning, and the bad half of a good hour till the drummer wakes the rest and I get to me fleabag" (by which he meant his bed).

By their own instruction the calendars were not to be troubled for another hour. At last Rossamünd had a moment of his own, without press or crowd or the impel of orders—a precious-rare commodity, he had learned, in a lamplighter's life. Secreting himself in a dim corner beneath the stairs that went up to the gallery, he hoped to remain inconspicuous, perhaps to read a little of his new pamphlet and avoid being discovered and set to some odious task.

He failed.

As the drums rataplanned again to wake the rest of the cothouse for another day, the house-major, on his way down to breakfast, spied Rossamünd. "You there! Lantern-stick! The one I spoke with last night," the officer barked. "Feed the dogs. Their meat is in the kitchen."

"Aye, sir," the young prentice said with sinking wind. It

was properly the duty of the house-watch to feed the dogs. The house-major must have known that though Rossamünd had been left behind, he was still part of the lantern-watch. He had rarely ever met a dog of any sort—they were not allowed in Madam Opera's—and any time he had, the meeting had not been comfortable. Shaken, the young prentice nevertheless obeyed without demur, asking directions of a kitchen hand.

"They're in the yard of the south keep," a rough-shaven kitchen hand explained, handing Rossamünd a rotund pot of dog vittles. "Mind the weight!"

Wrapping his arms about the pot's wide girth, Rossamünd did not find the burden a trouble and, arms full of reeking offcuts, made his way to the southern keep of Wellnigh. He wrestled the great pot past the house-watchmen, a half quarto of haubardiers pacing about the edges of the road who jostled him as he tried to get around them.

"Move your ashes, scrub!"

Tottering across the Pettiwiggin, he thumped with his elbow at the small sally port in the wall of the south keep yard. No one answered, and he kept thumping until one of the haubardiers came over and, with a sardonic grin, unlocked and opened the port to let him through. In the small, high-walled space beyond were the great kennels, built up against the keep's base, barred with stout iron founded in stone. This was the cage for the dogs, five Greater Derehunds—enormous creatures with spotted flanks and slobbering jowls—that waited hungrily. Such dogs were kept at many cothouses and at Winstermill too, there to howl and yammer with great commotion if a nicker was ever near.

The Derehunds began an awful growling as soon as they saw Rossamünd, all five hunched and threatening, a terrible gurgling rattle in their throats, pointed ears flat along their pied necks.

"Hallo there," Rossamünd tried, and waggled some stinking offal.

With a jerk one hound gave a savage bawling bark that sent the rest mad, leaping over each other, back and forth, crashing against the bars, baying like all wretchedness was loose.

Rossamünd leaped backward, scrambling and slipping on grimed cobbles.

Officers, lighters and haubardiers rushed from all points, some shouting, some soothing the dogs in vain, many demanding, "What did ye do?"

Some minor officer—a lieutenant—grabbed Rossamünd hard under the arm and pulled him away. "What are you practicing at?"

"Nothing, sir!" the young prentice quailed. "I . . . I just tried to feed them, as ordered."

"He's all right, sir," offered a lighter from the day-watch. "He was a part of that confustication last night."

"Ah, cunning beasts," said a haubardier in obvious admiration of the hounds, "they can still tell the stink of the monsters on ye from yester eve."

A GREATER DEREHUND

"Well, get him out of here," demanded the lieutenant. "Find him another task."

"You had best get back to them harum-scarum ladies, lad," the lighter said quietly. "Quick now, before the dogs get wilder."

Rossamünd gratefully left the pot and went back to the northern keep, up the stairs, over the gallery to the temporary lodgings of the calendars.

Threnody greeted his polite good morning with little more than a cold stare and silence. Dolours looked as poorly as she had on the night previous.

"May I offer you a draught mixed with bellpomash, m'lady?" Rossamünd inquired.

"You most certainly may," she returned gratefully.

Rossamünd went quickly to the kitchen and asked permission of the cook to prepare the restorative. The best he could do was to mix it with saloop and add some lordia too, but Dolours did not fuss. She drank it down and returned the bowl to him with a smile.

"My thanks to you. We will be ready presently."

He waited a goodly while by the door as the calendars prepared to leave.

Charllette the pistoleer was to stay behind and take a post-lentum back east by way of the Roughmarch, the threwdish gap through the Tumblesloe Heap. She would return to the Lady Vey and the stronghold of the calendars, bearing with her dispatches and the bodies of the two dead. Dolours, Threnody and the wounded dancer Pandomë, who lay unconscious on a bier with her face and head entirely bandaged, were to go west to Winstermill. Despite the bell-pomash brew, the bane still showed the strain of her malady and Rossamünd asked after her health once more.

"Why, I thank you, young lighter," Dolours replied. "Truly I would not have set out so ill had not the need been pressing. You understand the life of service, I am sure."

Rossamünd nodded wholeheartedly. "I shall recommend you to our physician when we return, m'lady. They say there's nothing he can't mend."

Dolours smiled and Threnody frowned.

When all was ready the small party set out in pouring rain—*fighting weather,* Europe would have called it. For a moment Rossamünd wondered where the terrible fulgar might be. Was she still in Sinster—that city famous for its transmogrifying surgeons, the makers of lahzars—to be mended after the near-fatal spasming of her artificial fulgar's organs? Would she soon return, as she had promised, to see how he was getting on? A quiet ache set in his gall: despite his abhorrence of her trade—at her indiscriminate killing—he was actually missing the teratologist. After all, she had rescued him from that scurrilous rogue Poundinch.

Instead of an ox dray, the calendars traveled easy in a small covered curricle drawn by two sturdy donkeys. These were led by a laconic leer Rossamünd had never properly met but knew from the milling of rumor and reputation to be Mister Clement. The fellow confirmed this with a sour introduction to the calendars, giving them all a dour look with his weird yellow and olive-drab eyes, as if the task was a great inconvenience. Before the leer put on his sthenicon Rossamünd marveled at his wrong-colored eyes, so different from Sebastipole's. For Clement was a laggard, like Licurius, better able to spy things hidden in shadows and darkness and nooks than a falseman, but less capable of spotting lies. His biologue in place, the leer took them out on the road. He talked little, instead bending all his energy to searching ahead and aside for the evidences of a monster.

After his experience at the strangling hands of Licurius, Rossamünd walked a little uneasily beside Clement. Exposed to the foul weather and equally silent, the young prentice was nevertheless grateful to have the leer's senses to forewarn them. That at least was a genuine comfort.

The calendars themselves also proved ill-disposed to speak, and the whole journey from cothouse to manse was accomplished in near silence.

They traveled back through the Briarywood, back through its hinting threwd, passing the scene of last night's violence. Despite a wet day, stains of spilled blood still showed black in the dirt of the road. Under a heavy guard of haubardiers, with the chortling morning chorus of birds making light of the grisly work, a toiling fatigue party from Wellnigh House's day-watch struggled to build and light a pyre of the fallen nickers and dead horses. The bodies of slain monsters needed to be disposed of promptly, for it was held that, left to rot, a nicker's corpse always attracted more of the living kind.

Walking through the Harrowmath, Rossamund started and stared at every rustle in the high grass. The rain increased and his thrice-high filled with water, which spilled inconveniently whenever he moved his head.

With each lamp they passed he felt a steady urgency to wind out the bloom, even though it was day. He had been in lessons (Readings on Our Mandate and Matter with Mister Humbert) in which the prentices were belabored with the notion that the Conduit Vermis was the spine about which many towns and villages grew; that the road allowed these towns to be knit as more than just remote settlements; that it was for the lamplighters to toil and keep the Wormway clear; that if they did not, then the whole of civilization might fail and fall to rapid ruin. To light the lamps meant that the kingdoms of humankind could sleep well that night. Every lamp they passed was a memorial to him of this heavy responsibility. He sighed, letting his fodicar drag in the soupy slick that filmed the hard-packed clay of the revered road.

"Lift your lantern-crook, boy!" came the rough command of the leer, and the young prentice obeyed with an unthinking start. Shrugging his shoulders against the wet, Rossamünd pushed on. Between the silence of the calendars, the taciturn concentration of Clement, and the broad, brooding Harrowmath, he lamented how different life might be as a vinegaroon or——he wondered for a moment——even as Europe's factotum.

AN INTERVIEW WITH
THE SURGEON

post-lentum(s) among the carriages more commonly used to traverse the highroads and byroads of the Half-Continent, post-lentums deliver mail and taxi people (for a fare) from one post to another. They are manned by a lenterman or driver, an escort (usually armed and armored) known as a side-armsman or cock robin (if wearing a red weskit of Imperial Service) or prussian (if wearing a deep blue weskit of private employment) and one or two backsteppers—either splasher boys or post runners or amblers—sitting upon the seats at the back of the roof. When traveling dangerous stretches, another backstepper may join—a quarter-topman possessing a firelock and a keen gaze—for extra protection. This crew is collectively referred to as lentermen. Po'lent is the common term for these vehicles, an abbreviated derivation of po(st) lent(um).

WINSTERMILL grew step-by-step before them. An ancient stronghold, massive and lonely upon the flat moors of the Harrowmath, it was familiar and welcome to Rossamünd already. He still marveled at the squat, gray cartography of its lichen-blotched roofs and their chimney spires, at the mightily thick outer walls and the foundations upon which the fortress was lifted high above the plain. When he had first observed it those two months gone he had thought it like some great, overgrown manor house, but now he knew the fortress to be much more. Once a small outpost of the Tutins of old, the fortress of Winstermill had accreted over the centuries: towers added, floors added, the whole mound of Winstre-slewe built up and encircled with a thick wall. Once it had stood at a junction of trade routes; now it had grown over and submerged these roads in its footings. The western run of the Wormway and the north–south course of the Gain-way made tunnels in Winstermill's foundations and joined beneath the very fortress. As far as Rossamünd knew, these tunnels were called the Bowels—if they had any other name he had not heard it. In the evening, great grilles were low-ered over their gaping mouths to prevent monsters and va-grants from setting up a home there, and mighty steams of repellents were regularly flushed through in the small hours of the morning to force out any unwelcome lurkers. These duties were reserved for the house-watch, and Rossamünd was glad of that. Not in all recorded history of the current Empire had a monster ever won its way into the manse.

The broad Imperial Spandarion that usually flapped proud and defiant above the battlements hung limp now in the day's damp. The morning was already long, limes missed and second morning instructions well under way. Rossa-münd had never felt so tired. Passing through the mighty gates, their arrival counted by the tally-clerk and his cur-sors, they were greeted by one of the house-guard calling down to them from the wall.

"Hoi there, me fellows! There's Lady Dry-stick ready to

lash us with her dim-wits. Wit us too, like ye did our mates!" News of Threnody's actions had already traveled ahead.

"Don't goad at her, chum," came another. "She's as likely to fish us as soon as fart, from what I hear!"

"Fish" was a vulgar term for frission. Rossamünd shot a look to Threnody, sitting stiff on the seat behind. The young calendar's chin jutted high in supercilious display, yet she betrayed her anger with the clenching and unclenching of her fine jaw.

The donkeys' hooves and carriage wheels made a harsh grinding in the white quartz gravel that formed a broad drive from the gate to the manse's main entrance. The drive skirted three acres of paved ground known as the Grand Mead, which fronted the manse itself. It was large enough to contain kennels, several strong-houses, room for the parading and evolutions of the whole fortress and yet still allow for the frequent coming and going of carriages and other conveyances. There was even space for a well-tended green by the wall of the manse proper with benches and a grove of pines for the officers to sit beneath. Here a convention of territorial rooks would caw and cackle every evening before returning to their roost in the manse's ridge-caps, eyeing everything angrily and keeping pigeons away. At the end of the drive stood the Scaffold, a single gaunt tree that Rossamünd had observed the night he first arrived.

As he walked by the curricle, Rossamünd watched a company of haubardiers working through drills under the shadow of the eastern wall, standing and moving in well-practiced order. He could not see the other lantern-sticks; they would be at readings now, suffering dire boredom in the Lectury with Mister Humbert. A post-lentum came through the gates, overtook them and rattled on to the covered stables to the right of the main building. The postilion blew his long horn to herald their arrival. *The post is here! The post is here!* its call declared.

Rossamünd felt an instinctive thrill, the sweet anticipation of a letter from a loved one—from Verline perhaps (it had been a whole month since her first missive), or Fransitart . . . or maybe even one from Europe.

It was obvious the arrival of the calendars was expected, for a welcome of officials turned out in their finest threads emerged from the manse. As Clement took the curricle through to halt before the front doors, the women were greeted first by Podious Whympre, the Master-of-Clerks. An officious man who smiled too much, he was dressed in sumptuous Imperial scarlet. He had only that year become acting second-in-command of Winstermill, and with the promotion his influence had grown. Joining him, and accompanied by all their particular secretaries, were other senior martial-bureaucrats: the Quartermaster, the niggardly Compter-of-Stores, the rotund General-Master-of-Labors and his Surveyor-of-the-Works, and a scowling General-Master-of-Palliateers. Even the rarely seen Captain-of-Thaumateers was in attendance. A small file of clerks—the chief of which was Witherscrawl—followed, along with a guard of troubardier pediteers in their bright lour-covered, proof-steel loricas and soft square pagrinine hats. Rather than their usual poleaxes, the pediteers bore high umbrellas to provide a roof against the steady drizzle.

Yet one among them refused to dress the dandy. A skulking fellow in a midnight-dark soutaine, he hovered at the Master-of-Clerks' back and stared viperlike with ill-colored eyes of red orb and pale blue iris. This was Laudibus Pile, leer and faithful falseman to Podious Whympre. He could often be seen whispering at the Master-of-Clerks' ear, a telltale saying what was truth and what was lie. To Rossamünd he was a false-seeming falseman, and he was glad he had little to do with this fellow or his master.

The one person missing was the Lamplighter-Marshal.

"Lady *Threnody*, you honor us at last." The Master-of-Clerks bowed, a perfect study of civility. "And Lady Dolours. We are met again. It has been almost a year since you helped us against those brutish ashmongers in the Owlgrave."

Dolours gave the man a tired, knowing look.

"And what relief it was," the Master-of-Clerks continued without pause, spreading his arms to include the various lampsmen in attendance, "to receive report that our tireless lighters did rescue you this yesternight gone. How happy it is you have both arrived sound and intact."

The bane had been looking most poorly but now she presented a hale front. "Clerk-Master Podious Whympre," she said with a subtle frown at the falseman Laudibus a-whisper-whisper behind the man, "a delight." She paused. "For the good deeds done last night I am grateful. Your

DOLOURS

Marshal is not present, I see. Matters more pressing keep him from us?"

Even Rossamünd knew that the absence of the Lamplighter-Marshal was a great affront. Of all the officers of Winstermill, the Lamplighter-Marshal was not only the most senior, but also had the reputation as the most punctual and gentlemanly.

"Ah, ever-astute Lady Bane, you do your clave proud. The Lamplighter-Marshal, I am certain, would give sincere apology for his nonattendance were we able to find him." Though the Master-of-Clerks' face was apologetic, his eyes were bright.

Dolours stepped past and went to push through the gaggle of officers and clerks. "It is well, for proper meetings must sadly wait; our sister Pandomë is deadly hurt. I hear your physic Crispus is of fair repute. Would you consent to his immediately attending to her wounds?"

The Master-of-Clerks was obliged to step quickly, moving from the precious cover of his troubardier-held umbrella and leaving his falseman behind. "Indeed, madam, Doctor Crispus is a man of many parts," he said, his smile broadening almost to a sneer as a troubardier hurried to cover him with a high parasol. "Alas, however, he is gone away to Red Scarfe to tend a disturbing outbreak of the fugous cankers. Ah, but all is not a loss! Grotius Swill, our surgeon and the physician's locum, remains with us. He will serve, I'm sure."

The calendars looked less than pleased.

"Whatever you might provide," Dolours said wearily.

Even as the bureaucrats dispersed, the Lamplighter-Marshal, the Earl of the Baton Imperial of Fayelillian himself, hastened from the doors of the manse. He was a grand-looking old man with long white mustachios, although unfashionable; he wore no wig, rather his own hair kept short as a true lighter's. His mottle-and-harness were simple—quabard over platoon-coat—worn easy and naturally. In a way he looked just like an ordinary lampsman, the most physically capable, shrewd and dangerous ordinary lampsman you might ever meet. Yet there was a barely perceptible atmosphere of weariness about him, a sense of harassment and overwork. He acknowledged the calendars warmly enough, saying through a rueful smile, "My most sincere apologies to ye, dear, dear Lady Dolours; what a bumbling scrub I must seem. It is unforgivable that I was not here in the first to meet ye." Mustachios a-bristle, the Marshal flashed a look of veiled wrath at Podious Whympre. "I would have been more timely, but found myself needlessly summoned to the farthest end of the manse. I have only now been told of yer arrival."

Nodding an obsequious bow, the Master-of-Clerks tut-tutted. "Those new clerks are quite useless. Unacceptable, sir, unacceptable. They shall be most particularly reprimanded."

There was a small silence.

The Lamplighter-Marshal offered his hand to Dolours. "It's clear ye're unwell, m'dear. Let's withdraw to

65

the quiet of my duty room. I hope its comforts will make amends. How is yer bonny august, the Lady Vey? She sends communication?"

The two turned their backs on the Master-of-Clerks and, without a further word to him, went inside. With a pointed show of proper manners, Podious Whympre bowed to their retreating backs.

As the bureaucrats dispersed, two porters were summoned to carry Pandomë to the manse's infirmary. Rossamünd had never—thank the Signal Stars!—been required to attend an appointment with the surgeon. Brought by especial request of the Master-of-Clerks, Grotius Swill, according to the common-mess rumor, held staunchly to the surgeon's creed of amputating first and investigating later; of fossicking about far too much in people's innards rather than administering the tried and proved chemical cures of dispensurist or physician. *How did the rhyme go?*

Honorius Ludius Grotius Swill
Saws off your limbs, but eschews the pill;
For a cough he removes fingers, a sneeze he'll take toes,
And fevers will cost you your ears and your nose.

Rossamünd shuddered—he would never allow someone to dig about inside him, and could not understand why lahzars and the like would pay to submit themselves to such abominable treatment.

With Threnody walking alongside her injured sister, he led the way through the empty vestibule down the Forward Hall and left through the right angles and long passages that led to the infirmary. They moved through the domain of the bureaucracy of Winstermill, a place that had a reputation as a strange and uncomfortable place for those not of the clerical set, even for experienced lighters. They passed white wooden doors from which would sporadically emerge a secretary, clerk or servant. These would pass in turn with a muttered apology or impatient sneer, to disappear in another white port along the way. Going deeper into the manse, the smoky perfume of the dark, venerable wood of furniture, beam and wainscot soaked the atmosphere. It grew strongest as they entered a large passage known as the Broad Hall. Several doors went at intervals down either side, the spandarions of the local city-states mounted between. The first door on the left was painted a pale lime green.

Through this was the infirmary.

Rossamünd stepped up and gave a reluctant tap. An epimelain answered almost instantly, her broad brown skirts and oversized apron filling the entire doorway. The woman's expression exquisitely stated, *Yes? What do you want? I have no time for this!* without the use of a single word.

Hat in hand, Rossamünd bowed. "This wounded lady needs a physic's mending, miss."

The epimelain looked over him to the stricken calendar, to the porters, then to Threnody and back to Rossamünd.

She gave a soft, high "humph," turned and sashayed away. This was enough permission for the porters, who immediately went in, shoving Rossamünd aside. Threnody followed them without a thank-you. Within was a long hall, well-made beds down either side, pillows arranged identically against the wall with prim regimental exactitude, bed ends forming a squeezy aisle along which the epimelain's skirts brushed and rustled noisily as she hurried between. A few beds were occupied, various ailing souls coughing or sighing in their discomfort, and another woman dressed similarly attended the bedside of one of the ill.

Behind a lectury desk was the person they sought: Honorius Ludius Grotius Swill, the carver of lamplighters, their surgeon. He was short and thin and sported a meticulous mustache and a fixed frown. Dressed immaculately, he sat with a flam-toothed saw in one hand and a hone gripped in the other, sharpening the blade to and fro, careless of the patients about him.

"Your pardon, surgeon."

With a small start, Surgeon Swill stood and faced the woman. He looked at the group a little confusedly. "Come, come," he said, finally fixing his attention on Rossamünd, "let me look you over."

"Ahh . . . not me, sir." Rossamünd gestured nervously to the stretcher-borne Pandomë. *"Her."*

Surgeon Swill looked to the calendar. "Very good. Leave her here."

The porters laid the bier on the closest empty bed and retreated promptly without so much as a good-bye, leaving Rossamünd and Threnody with Swill.

Threnody stepped up, chin high. "I'll have you know, sir, that I have been under the steady knife of the finest transmogrifer in or outside the Empire. Before I submit her to your ill-learned investigations, quacksalver, I would have you understand this: my mother is the Lady Vey, and should you mishandle my sister, your days of lawful practice shall end."

Rossamünd looked at the floor. This was surely not the way to go on if she was seeking to become a prentice-lighter.

The surgeon looked at her coldly. "Moving about the odd organ is enough for *some* to claim great talent, but there are subtler things one can do with a knife. My ill learning will be learning enough to set your sister to rights." He took up a weird-looking monocle, its protruding end a completely opaque black smoothness, and squinted it into his left eye. It was an even stranger instrument than Rossamünd had seen Doctor Verhooverhoven wearing at the Harefoot Dig when treating Europe so ill from spasming. It was some kind of obscure biologue, he was sure, designed to make a surgeon's or physician's work more effective.

Threnody stood close and watched suspiciously as Swill bent over the bed and scrutinized the injured, unconscious Pandomë, peering pedantically through the monocle at every cut, gouge and contusion. The epimelain hovered, waiting to serve any command. Swill worked in silence but for a periodic "mm-hm" and the scratching of stylus on paper as he made notes of what he discovered.

Fascinated, Rossamünd shuffled forward to get a clearer sight of what the surgeon saw.

Swill straightened and pinned him with a wintry eye. "Stand back, prentice! It is not necessary for *you* to see so closely. Indeed, all of you—please give me space to work."

Threnody bridled. "Tell me, surgeon, can you mend her?" she asked sternly. "Or should we wait for Doctor Crispus?"

Swill straightened and, after a pause where he clearly calculated his answer, said sourly, "I might serve under him, young madam, yet I can tell you I have observed and performed things *Doctor* Crispus would not credit as possible. What the good doctor has spent a lifetime acquiring, I learned in months. So, to you, dear, I say 'yes' to your first inquiry, and 'no' to your second. This has become intolerable! If you want the best for your sister-in-arms, then I must be allowed to labor in quietude. Do me the service of leaving!"

Spreading his thin arms, Swill went to usher them out of the surgery. To Rossamünd's dismay, Threnody was clearly reluctant to depart and made to stand her ground. Swill balked at her stubborn immobility, and only after a foolish, pointless standoff did she allow herself to be guided out to the less gruesome side of the door. It closed with a deliberate thump.

"Do you know much of this Grotius Swill fellow, lamp boy?" Threnody demanded.

"He seems competent enough, miss. I think he is supposed to be under Doctor Crispus' charge," Rossamünd offered helpfully, ignoring the girl's imperious tone. "I must confess I've never been ill enough to need either his or the doctor's work."

Threnody looked less than satisfied. "He did not seem to be under anyone's charge to me. He'd better do right: I made no idle threat in there."

Rossamünd was not in the smallest way impressed. "I ought to return you to your Lady Dolours," he said simply.

At the Lamplighter-Marshal's duty room the smiling registry clerk Inkwill greeted them.

"You'd best go in, m'lady."

Threnody entered into the mystery of the duty room, leaving Rossamünd without a word of thanks or farewell.

"You might want to idle here, Prentice Bookchild," suggested Inkwill kindly. "I think that young lass will be needing more guidance shortly." This was an unwelcome hint, or so Rossamünd thought, that he and his fellows might have to put up with this pompous peerlet for a good sight longer.

As he waited an unwelcome pressure built in his bladder, but Rossamünd dared not leave. Instead he paced the Forward Hall uncomfortably back and forth, pressure growing, until the door opened with a bang. Sergeant Grindrod emerged from the duty room looking grave. He nodded brusquely, said nothing and moved on. Soon after, Threnody stalked out, followed by Dolours and the Lamplighter-Marshal himself. "What say you, young fellow? We're going to have a lady in our midst!"

The Lamplighter-Marshal had clearly come to his decision. Threnody was to be the first girl prentice at Winstermill.

THRENODY GOES FORTH

fusil also known as a fusee or carabine or harquebus; a lighter musket with a shortened barrel that makes for simpler loading, is less cumbersome to swing about in thickets and woodland, and saves considerable weight. Its shorter length also makes it handy as a club when the fight comes to hand strokes. This makes the fusil a preferred weapon of ambuscadiers and other skirmishing foot soldiers, and also comes a-handy for the drilling of smaller folk in the handling and employment of arms.

T HE morning did not improve after its irregular beginning. Rossamünd took Threnody to the Room of Records, where she gave all her particulars and was paid the Emperor's Billion; the master proofener, where she received her two quabards—one full dress and one for continual day wear; the library, for her books on matter and drills and regulations; the armory, for her fusil and fodicar; and every other necessary place. Throughout, she showed nothing but arrogance and high-handed rudeness. She near drove the normally good-natured Inkwill to distraction with each painfully extracted detail for the register. She wrangled with the proofener's yeomen over the constitution of regulation dress. She insulted the librarian over a matter book, insisting it was arrant drivel, that the books *she* had learned from back at Herbroulesse were far superior. She quibbled with the wool-slippered master armorer over the one-sequin pledge required to secure her firelock and fodicar. And throughout she ignored Rossamünd in the manner of someone used to the attendance of servants.

He had led her from place to place without complaint and with an ever-sinking feeling and the sharp jabbing of an overfull bladder. Joyful relief had come only when he finally showed Threnody to her own newly appointed cell where her luggage waited for her. While she changed to a lighter's harness, Rossamünd made a quick dash for the jakes and returned in time for her to emerge with a wrinkled nose.

"Ugh! The stench of too many boys, too close together," she said.

Rossamünd stayed mum. He had spent his life with too many boys, and it had made him insensible to any such odor. "Come along," he said instead, and guided her up to the dim, high-ceilinged mess hall in the rear quarters of the manse, where a roll of drums declared middens was about to be served. There the other prentices arrived as a mass and, as they lined up, stared in open wonder at this newly presented lantern-stick before them.

Threnody went forth now in a rich, elegant variation of the gear of a lamplighter: silken platoon-coat, quabard, long-shanks, galliskins and a black tricorn sitting prettily upon her midnight tresses—all of the finest tailoring, as sumptuous as that of any of the Master-of-Clerks' flunkies. The other prentices, by comparison, looked like drab weeds.

Threnody ignored them all as she had ignored Rossamünd. In their turn the boys kept unashamedly at their gawping, some turning puzzled looks on her fortunate companion.

Rossamünd felt anything but fortunate as he received their middens meals, served by two short, fat cooks from the pots hanging in the gigantic fireplace at the farther end of the room. Steaming with faintly appetizing smells, the larger pot was, as always, full of skilly, a savory gruel of leftover meat; the smaller with vummert, a mash of sprouts and peas.

Threnody scowled at the food, at the cooks, at the boys and at the hall as she sat at one of a pair of long tables that filled the mess.

"Are . . . are you all right, miss?" Rossamünd asked cautiously, painfully aware that she had just occupied the usual seat of a less-than-friendly lad known as Noorderbreech.

"Yes." Threnody's voice cracked a little. "No . . . What care is it of yours—"

"Look here, miss, I . . . ," complained Noorderbreech, leaving his place in the line of unserved boys. "Look here, normally I sit there."

Threnody did not move, did not even give a hint she had even heard.

"And—and that would be my apple," Noorderbreech insisted.

A look came into Threnody's eye that Rossamünd recognized—a haughty, dangerous look. She glanced at the fruit mentioned, which sat on the table before her. It appeared to be the same as all the other apples placed evenly along the benches for the prentices to take away with them when the main meal was done. Threnody picked it up with a study of feminine grace. "*This* apple, do you mean?" she said, and bit into it deliberately, daring Noorderbreech to retaliate.

The lad puffed himself up as threateningly as he might.

Uncowed, Threnody crunched away as happily as if she were on a vigil-day hamper. Every boy—and the kitchen hands too—held their breath.

"Give me my apple, girly," Noorderbreech growled, "and go take yer place at the far end. This is where we sit."

"This apple?" She took another bite. "You mean *this* apple, don't you? . . . *Have it then!*" The apple flew the full length of the bench in a well-aimed arc. It landed with a *crack* and a *hiss* right in the midst of the hottest coals of the fire.

Everyone became very, very still. Some even stopped chewing.

Rossamünd wanted to shrink in on himself.

"I'll sit where I like and eat what I please, you loose-jawed bumpkin," she hissed with such vehemence spittle flew.

Wide-eyed, Noorderbreech stumbled back, mouth agape as if he were trying hard to prove Threnody's insult true, finding for himself a vacant place at the far end of the other bench.

THRENODY

The prentices sitting near Threnody shifted away, afraid or glaring. No one other than Rossamünd dared put himself too near. Angry mutters began to stir. Rossamünd did not know what to say and fixed his attention on his food, avoiding every other eye in the room. Yet the filling of stomachs finally took priority even over so shocking an event as just witnessed. The hubbub of general chatter and the patter of forks and spoons on plates swelled once more.

Threnody made to eat as if naught was wrong. "Who can eat this glue?" she snarled eventually, pushing the slopping pannikin of skilly away in disgust. "Must everything be against me today?"

"Against you, miss?" Rossamünd dared after a few pensive chews.

"I save us from the ambush of those ungotten baskets," she suddenly fumed, floodgates inexplicably let free, "and all *Lady* Dolours can dwell upon is the possibility of bad things that never even happened! We were thrown about inside the drag, tumbled roughly in its wreck, and Dolours so unwell she was scarce capable of fighting. What else was I supposed to do?"

Remembering the startling and dangerously incompetent effect of her wild witting, Rossamünd could not quite see how Threnody had done any more than make a bad situation worse. The way he remembered the play of things, it had ultimately been Dolours who had saved them all, the lamplighters included. Indeed, given that the prentices had dispatched two of the horn-ed nickers themselves, Ros-samünd figured a little more gratitude might have been shown. Still, he held his tongue: he would not gainsay a woman in her distress, especially not one as fiery as this. She had done her bit, and had not flinched from the fight—and none should fault her on that. This girl had passion. All she needed was practice.

"I reckon you did as boldly as you knew to, miss," Ros-samünd said matter-of-factly.

She gave a little start, as if this was the last encourage-ment she expected.

"You saw me take on those wretched bugaboos, then?" she said.

Felt, more like. "Aye, miss."

"I'll not shrink from the fact that I did not defeat them alone. Oh no," she declared with a flourishing wave of her hand, "my sisters and I did it together, mastered and de-stroyed the nickers."

Rossamünd thought on the valiant fight the calendars had made as a troupe. "It was a genuine, heroical spectacle, miss," he said. "I've never seen such a thing as happened last night."

"So it was, I know. Yet they *made* me apologize!" Thren-ody seethed. "They made *me* apologize to that . . . that pompous muck hill."

By "apologize" Rossamünd could only assume she had been made to repent of her clumsy, ill-advised witting; and by "pompous muck hill" she meant Grindrod, the lamplighter-sergeant. He thought she might consider herself fortunate not to have been made to apologize to the lampsmen and prentices as well—it was their lives she had endangered.

"Yet it was *we* who were refused at Wellnigh!" She balled her fists.

"Hardly seems fair, miss."

"Hardly, indeed! Pannette dead! Idesloe dead!" the girl continued. "And *Dolours* insists *we* make amends like *your* lot were the worst done by! To think I actually wanted to join in with you clod-headed blunderers!"

"Don't count me in too quick with the clodheads or the blunderers, miss," he replied.

"Well, since you are but half the size of all the other boys I suppose it would be hard to do so."

Rossamünd blinked at the sting of her insult. He knew he was undersized: his embarrassingly truncated fodicar was continual evidence. Dumbstruck and mortified that those near might have heard her, he realized she was no longer even paying him any mind. Instead she was looking up over his right shoulder. Rossamünd became aware of the looming of somebody there. He looked up to find Arimis Arabis at his back.

The oldest, most worldly-wise of the prentices, Arimis Arabis was top of the manning lists—both by letter fall and ability. The frankest shot with a fusil, he also considered himself handsome. Though Rossamünd could not see it, a gaggle of dolly-mops in Silvernook confirmed Arabis' self-approval every Domesday, following him about on his jaunts about town and giggling at everything he uttered.

"Hullo to thee, Rossamünd," he drawled, all charm and swagger. He leaned on Rossamünd's shoulder and smiled knowingly at Threnody. He must have been down in the cell row cleaning up for eating and missed her petulant antics with the apple. "I see it's true. We have a fair Damsel of Callistia among us. Would you care to introduce her?"

"No, he would not," Threnody answered frostily. "Go away!"

Arabis' grin vanished. "Just making friendly," he retorted. He took his hand off Rossamünd's shoulder immediately and straightened. "But you seem to know as much about being friendly as you do about witting." He clapped Rossamünd on the back as he left. "Fair travels with that one, matey," he sneered, and made his way to the other table and immediately began to talk to the prentices there. Laughter rose, and these boys glanced over at Threnody in disapproval.

Rossamünd glumly sucked at his food.

Threnody raised her chin a little higher—a telltale sign, he was beginning to notice, of impatience or anger or embarrassment.

"Did I hear your name a-right, lamp boy?" She was staring at him again. It seemed she needed someone to stare at right now. There was a vindictive gleam growing in her eye. "It can't really be so, can it? Rossamünd?"

"Many folk find some fun in my name, though I don't," he replied evenly. "It is what it is and I am who I am."

Threnody had enough grace to drop her gaze.

For a while they ate in silence. Rossamünd fretted vaguely and wished that, just for today, middens was not quite so long. Threnody poked at her food and screwed up her nose at the small beer.

"Too small by half," the girl muttered at the beverage.

"It certainly is that, miss. Much better down at the Harefoot Dig," Rossamünd returned, happy to punctuate the awkwardness.

"Anything anywhere is better than here." Her face was tight and unhappy.

Rossamünd could not be quiet in the face of such misery. "I don't understand. If all this makes you so wretched, why join us?" he asked.

"You're an impertinent little lamp boy, aren't you?" She sniffed loftily. "Since you inquire, I joined because I wanted to, why else?"

"Why not stay as a calendar?" Rossamünd could not reckon such a thing. Calendars were mystical, romantic figures who resisted the powerful and helped the destitute. They confronted monsters whenever these threatened and offered help wherever folk floundered. The way of a calendar was a goodly adventurous life if ever one existed: making life better, not just mindlessly destroying monsters for pay like Europe or the other pugnators.

"If you knew my mother . . . ," she replied thickly, almost to herself. "If you, too, were pinned in the never-relaxing clutch of Marchessa Syntychë, the Lady Vey, August of the Right of the Pacific Dove, then you would understand. No choices. No schemes of your own."

"But you *did* have a choice." He could not help himself. "You chose to come to Winstermill and be a lighter."

Taken aback, the girl pursed her lips. "That was a rare lapse of my mother's. For once she let her grip slip. Mother and I are always at odds. I go left, she goes right. I say black, she says white. If I want something one way, she will always have it the other. If I was ever truly listened to—if what I wanted counted, if she had ever faltered for a moment and remembered that underneath that waspy bosom she has a heart and think me her daughter . . ." Threnody seethed— her haughty mien subsumed by anger. "And not just a tool to preserve her precious clave, then I might never have become a blighted lahzar!"

Skilly forgotten, Rossamünd listened, motionless.

"I wanted to serve the Dove as a spendonette, blazing away at monsters with my pistols, not . . ." Threnody pressed her knuckles against her brow, wincing. "Not spend the rest of my life swallowing down cures to quell revolting organs that do little more than ache!"

He knew enough about wits to know what she meant. Cathar's Treacle, twice a day, else headaches, spasms or worse would beset her.

"But once transmogrification was forced on me—well, I chose the path of the lightning-throwing astrapecrith just like the Branden Rose—"

Rossamünd's attention pricked at the mention of Europe by her more famous title, but he did not interrupt the talk bubbling out of the girl prentice like froth from an over-shaken beer bung.

"—But oh no! Dear Mother was not having that! I was ordered to become a wit because the clave needed wits, and a good calendar *always* obeys her august. I would never have managed so long but for Dolours."

Middens was nearing its end. Other prentices were rising and depositing their pannikins, mess-kids and tankards on a broad palette for cleaning.

"Finally I made it all so terrible at home that Mother could bear me no longer. She's agreed to this," she said, looking about to show the mess hall and all the prentices, "only because it has made *her* life simpler, not through any care for me. And here I can become a pistoleer. Not quite the good calendar spendonette I wished for, but . . ." She shrugged, all angst submerged with baffling alacrity. "Well, you have my life's tale before you, so return in kind: why have you taken up with the lampsmen?"

Though it was time to leave, Rossamünd paused in thought. "Because I had no choice either; because it was this or be cooped in the foundlingery forever. I'm a book child, and we get what we're given and say thank you, like it or no."

"How little we have in common then." Threnody tipped her plate, skilly and all, into the pail just meant for the slops.

The attack on the calendars' carriage so close to Winstermill had caused no small stir among the lighters. It was universally agreed that the six fusil-bearing lads should all be marked with a cruorpunxis for their part. It would be a small drawing of a drip of blood, as was commonly awarded when a prentice had a hand in the slaying of a monster but the actual killer was not clear. In the bosom of many a hardened campaigner there rose too a genuine, almost paternal concern for the batch of young lantern-sticks. Such was this concern, it prompted the Lamplighter-Marshal to cancel the prentice-watch and move drills and tutelage normally conducted in the fields below Winstermill back within the fortress walls. Consequently, that afternoon, targets—the handling, firing, cleaning and right use of a fusil—was to be held in a long foyer of dark, aromatic wood called the Toxothanon in the westernmost end of the Low Gutter below the beautiful Hall of Pageants.

"*Right, lads! Stand by twos at your lane!*" Benedict, the Under-Sergeant-of-Prentices, stood behind the gaggle of lantern-sticks. "After two months of this I am expecting good aim and handy reloading." To those of Rossamünd's watch he said, "As for you lads who prevailed last night, I am expecting to be dazzled."

Standing in her own firing lane beside Rossamünd,

Threnody took to the fusil with elegant aplomb, handling her firelock with an accomplishment equal to all but the frankest shot among the prentices. Much to Arabis' wry dismay, almost as many of Threnody's shots as his own found the center bull in the targets fixed to the great bales of straw at the farther end of the lanes. Benedict twice acknowledged her wicked aim and went as far as to say, "You might make yourself useful yet, young lady." Her self-satisfaction was so clear, Threnody almost glowed.

Unfortunately Rossamünd, who was an indifferent shot at best, had the worst day at targets yet, missing many of his shots entirely, one ball lodging itself in a low crossing roof beam. His woeful aim did not, of course, escape the keen observation of the under-sergeant.

"Master Bookchild! For shame, not one solitary ball true, sir. Sergeant Grindrod would say your fusil work is a clattering, gaffing embarrassment and a wanton waste of powder. One night's pots-and-pans for you. Let's hope some good hours scrubbing will teach your arms to hold a franker aim."

With sinking soul Rossamünd kept to the work: make ready, present, level, fire—over and over, till they were lined up for Evening Forming and the quiet tolling of mains brought a merciful end to the training day.

Entering the manse via the Sally—the side door and only correct entry for the prentices into the manse—and stowing their fusils in the armory cupboard, the lads made their way back up to the mess hall and food. While they ate their boiled pork, boiled cabbage and soggy boiled rice, Mister Fleugh, an under-clerk to the Postmaster, hustled into the mess hall crying, *"Post is arrived!"* An excited hubble-bubble warmed the room as the under-clerk extracted crushed packages and bent letters from a mostly empty satchel.

"Clothard . . . Onion Mole . . . Bookchild . . ."

Rossamünd found a letter slapped before him, its water-stained and slightly smeared address still clearly stating:

Master Rossamünd Bookchild
Apprenticed Lamplighter
Winstermill Barracks
The Harrowmath
Sulk End

. . . written in Verline's unmistakable hand. Trembling with delight, he prized open the rough seal. Dated twenty-third of Brumis, it must have taken a week to make its way down the Humour through High Vesting and back up to Winstermill. It read:

My dear courageous Rossamünd,
Thank you, for your dear letter of the 13th of Pulchrys. What gladness we had at the news of your safe arrival—and

my, what adventures you had! That Europa Branden Rose woman sounds very frightening, but what a thrill to meet someone so famous! You always wanted adventure, and had I been you I think I might have had my fill of it after such a journey. Little wonder you were at Winstermill fortress a week late. Still, far better late than absent.

My hope for you is that you are safe, that you are taking to your tasks with ease and that you have found like-minded souls there to share in further adventures, of which I am sure you are having many more.

Dear Master Fransitart is still determined to come to you. Time has done nothing to still his unease, and if, as you say, you know not of what troubles him, then I must confess to be at a loss. Craumpalin is no help. He and dear Fransitart worry like old women about you. In fact they seem to be having second thoughts about your life with the lamplighters, though since you say you are settling to the routine there they may be less troubled. I shall write more on this when I can.

What is joy, though, is that Master Craumpalin's restoratives have begun their marvels on your dear Master Fransitart and he suffers much less from the strains and aches of his seafaring ways. Your old dispenser sent beyond the Marrow to his contacts (he called them) for the scripts, and they have answered wonderfully. I do not fret for dear Fransitart's fortunes so much should he travel now.

Master Craumpalin is very happy with your report of how well his bothersalts performed. He bids me insist that you keep applying his nullodor, that you wear it at all times no matter where you are at. This was the first time I ever heard of such arrangements. I can only assume you know of what he speaks. He was in serious earnest when he declared this, so I offer to you to take him at his word and do as he bids.

Time for writing letters has come to its end, as anything worthy must.

Take great care of yourself. Return when you are at your liberty to do so. Forever your

P.S. Dear little Petite Fig (I am sure you remember her—how stoutly you defended her from the older boys). Well, the dear little one said that last night she saw Gosling moving about the street out front, spying on us from the lane across the way. Madam declared it impossible, but sent Master Fransitart and Barthomæus with him to see. Of course they found nothing, and we are all perplexed. Even the littlest fret, for he has already become a frightful legend though gone only a month. I did hear that the lad had tried to reunite with his family, but that they did not want him back. (Who could spurn their own child so? It defies fathoming, as Master Fransitart would say.) So perhaps he has taken up loitering about here for want of anywhere else to go? I can only hope naught will come of it. The thought of his presence oppresses almost as much as when he lived with us. Fransitart will think of something.

Write back to me soon.

I wager he is hanging about the foundlingery. It's the kind of weak prank he would do. I am glad to be rid of him! Rossamünd shook his head, banished any further thoughts of his old foundlingery foe and reread the welcome missive.

Threnody looked at him and then at the paper.

"You have received an amiable letter, I see," she said.

"Aye, miss," he replied, "all the way from my old home."

He was well aware that she had received no friendly communication from home: jealousy was writ clear on her face. With a slight cough, Rossamünd put the letter away and began to eat.

While pudding (figgy dowdy filled with raisins and all poured over with a runny, barely sweet sauce) was being served, a summons came for Threnody from the Lady Dolours. Still suffering her fever, the bane had remained as a guest of the Lamplighter-Marshal, watching over the recovering Pandomë and convalescing herself. The messenger—a little lighter's boy, too young to start his prenticing—delivered his message with many a faltering "beg yer pardon" and clearing of the throat.

"I must go to take my alembants," Threnody declared to Rossamünd and, under the guidance of the small messenger, departed without another word. As she left, every other set of eyes but Rossamünd's followed her and their gaze was not kind. She was going to take her plaudamentum, and whatever other draughts wits needed to keep their organs in check. *Now that surely is an imposition!* An image of Europe blossomed in Rossamünd's memory, of her ailing by a dying fire, teeth blackened by the thick treacle she had drunk, dead grinnlings lying near. How glad he was not to be dependent on such foul chemistry.

At the very end of mains was a brief period called castigations. This was the time when the record of that day's minor infringements was reiterated and impositions meted out.

Following centuries-old custom, Grindrod stood at the large double doors of the mess hall and boomed, "Lamplighter-Sergeant-of-Prentices stands at the port!" An ancient civility: the prentices' mess hall was the refuge of the prentices alone, accessed by those of higher rank only after the senior-most prentice had granted permission. The boys ceased whatever they were doing and sat up straight. Arabis stood. In a clear confident voice he called, "Cross the threshold and bear up to the hearth; this hall bids thee welcome!"

Courtesies complete, Grindrod entered in a fine display of regular military step. With him came Witherscrawl, walking with civilian slouch and bearing a great black ledger—the Defaulters List, in which each day's misdemeanors were marked. With a look of dark satisfaction, Witherscrawl stood before the great fire, opened the Defaulters List and stared shrewishly at the boys. "On this Maria Diem, being the sixth of Pulvis, HIR 1601 . . . ," he began, and proceeded to call off all those caught for minor breaches and the appropriate disciplines.

Rossamünd waited for his own name to be called. He knew what was coming.

"*Bookchild*, Rossamünd, prentice-lighter—accused of wasting black powder and of mishandling his firelock, the penalty being one imposition of scullery duties to be performed three nights hence on the ninth of this month, during the appropriate period."

Pots-and-pans!

The imposition was a guilty weight in Rossamünd's innards. He had washed many a dish in his time at the foundlingery, but not as a punishment. Rossamünd stared straight ahead, not lowering his eyes or his chin.

The next day, Threnody spoke very little to anyone but Rossamünd, even then only briefly, as a mere acquaintance and not someone to whom she had bared her soul. The experiences of Noorderbreech and Arabis had quickly schooled the other prentices to leave her alone, and most of the lads began to mutter against her, darkly declaring that girls should not be allowed to be lighters. Even so, there were still some secret doe-eyed looks sent her way, and many sniggering asides when she left the mess hall morning and night to make her treacles. Chin in air, the calendar ignored them all, rather setting her attention firmly on learning her new trade. She proved quickly that she already possessed most of the skills required, and those few she did not know she was apt to learn. Despite having never marched in her life, it took no more than her first afternoon of evolutions to step-regular with as much facility as the rest. It had taken the other prentices more than a week and much cursing and bawling from Grindrod and Benedict to do the same. Rather than being impressed, the boys resented her quick learning and smug self-awareness. Though there had been no open discussion, it became a general accord that none of them wanted her in his prentice-watch.

Moreover, Threnody's advent posed a disruption to the symmetry of the manse's fine lists, and any one of the three quartos might be lumbered with her. With the suspension of the nightly prentice-watch, the question as to which Threnody would join remained unanswered.

6

THE LANTERN-WATCH

skold-shot leaden balls fired from either musket or pistol, and treated with various concoctions of powerful venificants known as gringollsis, particularly devised for the destruction of monsters. These potives are corrosive, damaging the barrels of the firelocks from which they are fired and eating gradually, yet steadily, away at the metal of the ball itself. Left long enough, a skold-shot ball will dissolve completely away. Very effective against most nickers and bogles, some of the best gringollsis actually poison a monster to the degree that it becomes vulnerable to more mundane weapons.

As winter deepened, the weather had steadily soured. Great squalling showers would blow up from the Grume, or heavy thunderheads roll in over the Sparrow Downs. On the second morning since the carriage attack and Threnody's arrival, the prentices stepped-regular for Morning Forming out on Evolution Square. The night's driving rain had blown away to the northeast, leaving murky puddles and a low solemn sky, and Grindrod stepped over a small mire as he stood before them.

"The Lamplighter-Marshal and I have revised our conclusions," he called to the two ranks, obediently still. "Knowing yer way on the highroad is too important to yer survival as full-fledged lighters. I told him that ye should never fear to tread the highroad just because of a single theroscade. Such is the lighter's life, gentlemen," he declared. "No good will come of keeping ye from it. Therefore, from tonight, the prentice-watch shall resume."

The murmur that inevitably buzzed among the prentices over breakfast was mostly of excitement, though there was a groan or three of anxious concern. Some of the boys were quietly happy to be kept off the road with monsters threatening. Rossamünd's six watch-mates showed off the bandages about their arms that covered the small droplet-shaped cruorpunxis they had received the night before. Their marking had been done in evenstalls without much ceremony by Nullifus Drawk, one of the manse's skolds and its only puctographist. Now even Wheede was boldly pronouncing to the more timorous, "Ye don't have to worry, chums, if a hob comes a-calling—we'll see him off for ye!"

For the remainder of the day, under the earnest eye of Benedict, the prentices practiced the handling of a fodicar as tool and as weapon: trail arms, port arms, order arms, shoulder arms, present arms, reverse arms, quarter arms, over and over. Once a fodicar had made no more sense in Rossamünd's hands than had a harundo stock at Madam Opera's. Effectual instruction and plenty of time to practice had seen him improve a little, though today this did not prevent him from fumbling badly once and nearly letting his lantern-crook fall to the ground.

At four o'clock that afternoon, at the end of yet more

fodicar drill, the prentices formed up on the square for Lale—the time when that night's lantern-watch got ready to go out to lighting. Their backs to the Low Gutter, they waited anxiously as maids brought out saloop and fruit for sustenance. Waiting for his food, Rossamünd noticed Dolours standing under a tree over on the Officers' Green, wrapped thickly in furs and observing them all closely. He looked to Threnody to see if she saw her clave-fellow too but the girl was making a distinct show of not noticing the bane. Peering from Dolours to Threnody and back, Arabis and his cronies muttered dark things to each other about the unsuitability of women for the lighting service.

As a post-lentum arrived with its usual hullabaloo, Rossamünd fidgeted and drank his saloop in nervous gulps. Lantern-watch was resuming on the very night his quarter was rostered to serve. Grindrod stood before them. One by one each lad was called forward and, after a pause, Threnody too. She was to be bundled in with him, the other latecomer, to the dismay of his own quarto and the open relief of the other two, lifting their quarto's number to eight. Rossamünd gave her a quick look as they lined up before the others, but she kept her eyes front, ignoring him.

While Benedict continued drills with the fourteen left behind, Grindrod marched Q Hesiod Gæta to the gates, forming them up in the designated place on the southern edge of the Grand Mead. Lampsmen Assimus, Bellicos and Puttinger were waiting there to take them out for the night's lighting.

Bellicos thrust a box into Rossamünd's hands, saying simply, "Hold this!"

Taking it, Rossamünd immediately felt a deep unquiet. Looking within he found it contained many musket balls that shimmered a telltale blue-black rather than the usual dull lead-gray. *Skold-shot!* These were bullets treated with pestilent and mordant scripts—poisons and distinct acids made to do monsters far greater harm than an ordinary ball ever could.

"Before going out tonight," the lampsman said sourly, "each of ye is to load yer fusil with one of these." With great respect, he took a pair of privers and, from the box Rossamünd still gripped reluctantly, plucked out a single ball. He held it up for the prentices to see. "Salt lead we call it, or skold-shot if you prefer. I want ye to take one from the box Master Lately here holds just as I have with these here privers, and load it into yer firelocks. Let's us give any nasty hobnicker a good cause to pause."

The prentices obeyed, all but Rossamünd; he carried no fusil, for he had the salumanticum. He stood and obediently offered the box for the other lads. Each took a turn and a ball. Even the lampsmen and Grindrod took rounds, filling their own bullet bags from it. When the loading was done, Rossamünd was grateful to pass the foul-smelling box back to Bellicos.

Grindrod seized Threnody with his steely stare. "I am here to tell ye plain hard: if there's a peep of witting out of ye—even a wee fishing flutter—you'll be out of the lighters with no coming back!"

The girl lighter frowned truculently in return, but the lamplighter-sergeant appeared not to notice. He paced before the quarto when they had returned their firelocks to their shoulders. "It has been decided that a leer should be sent with us to improve the security of ye precious lambs. Not that *we* needed fancy-eyed gogglers to watch out for us when we were lantern-sticks."

Assimus, Bellicos and Puttinger snickered.

Rossamünd struggled to imagine the lamplighter-sergeant as a fumbling, square-gating lantern-stick.

"Ah!" Grindrod looked toward the manse. "Here struts the fellow now."

Leaving off a conversation with Dolours, a tall dark fellow stepped toward them. He bore a finely made long-rifle, wore a tall thrice-high upon his head and a dark coachman's cloak that hid all other attire and accoutrements, including his boots.

Mister Sebastipole! Here at last was the lamplighter's agent who had hired Rossamünd back at Madam Opera's. He looked straight at Rossamünd—with those disquieting red and blue eyes that signified his status as a falseman—as he stopped before the prentices, but if Sebastipole recognized him it did not show.

"Well, Lamplighter's Agent Sebastipole"—there was a coolness in the manner of Grindrod's address—"are ye ready to coddle we lowly lighters?"

SEBASTIPOLE

"If you and your lampsmen are ready to depart, Grindrod," Sebastipole replied evenly, "I am ready to coddle." The leer turned and bowed to the boys. "Good evening, prentices."

"Good evening, sir," they all responded, as was their duty.

"Let us light the way." Sebastipole led the prentice-watch down the stonework of the Approach. With a sharp toss of his head the leer drank something from a small black bottle. Whether this was some special concoction to enhance senses or prevent the sthenicon's organs from growing up his nose, Rossamünd could not know. Drawing in several solid sniffs, the leer took out his sthenicon from its wooden case under his cloak. Rossamünd was certain he saw a hint of disgust as the leer strapped the ordinary-looking box to his face.

Rossamünd breathed in the frigid airs. The whole Harrowmath stretched about him, a slightly undulating moor of rippling, swaying reeds, weeds and grass. It stretched far south to the low hazy fells of the Sparrow Downs, and reached long into the north where paler greens gave over to the great straw-gray expanse of Sulk End. This unbroken pastoral flatness continued all the way around to the west where, on clearer days, great, distant windmills could be seen, sails lazily turning. Rossamünd had observed these very mills from the Vestiweg after his escape from the *Hogshead*. To the east, the stark, diminishing line of the Wormway ran out from under Rossamünd's feet. On it went with the merest curve, right through the dark of the Briarywood and out the other side, on to the ancient, bald hills of the Tumblesloe Heap. There it disappeared into the mystery of the shadowy cleft of the Roughmarch. Though he had never ventured so far, Rossamünd knew that over the Tumblesloes the Idlewild began. Normally he might admire the vista, but this evening it held only threat.

With a heavy sigh, he dutifully followed his comrades.

Down the Approach they went, down on to the Petti-wiggin, dark with the chill gloom of Winstermill's late afternoon shadow. The line of twenty-four lanterns they had to wind began here, at the bottom of the stonework ramp. Lantern East Winst 1 West Well 24 was the very first lamp on the Wormway, and as such was treated to special honors, writhen with a confusion of curls and finials of skillfully wrought iron. It even bore two gretchen-globes at either side of the main lamp-bell. They were small examples of the phosphorescent pearls formed inside the bellies of kraulschwimmen, spat out for brave divers to collect from murky seabeds. It was an ostentatious show of Imperial wealth that such precious items should be used to light this remote place. It was an equal show of the lamplighters' vigilance that the local banditry had never tried to steal them. Assimus and Bellicos wound out the bloom, for no prentice was ever allowed to touch this most prized of lights.

Watching with his fellows, Rossamünd wondered at the strangely lumpy spheres of the gretchen-globes with their soft, innate radiance, disbelieving that such beauty could come from the foul innards of some monstrous sea-beast. He looked to Threnody to see if she too was amazed by these pearlescent lights, but she stood stock-still, arms folded against the cold and all the world too. On the other side of her, Punthill Plod was nonchalantly inching closer, his rapt and imperfectly hidden admiration showing he did not share his messmates' ill opinion of her. He was trying so very hard not to look hopelessly, gormlessly smitten, and doing such a poor job of it, even Rossamünd could see his intent.

"Things of rare purity, are they not?" came a strange, almost squashed voice behind them.

Rossamünd looked to find Sebastipole there, his face hidden behind its sthenicon, its flat wooden front looking blankly at the gretchen-globes. The young prentice wondered how the lights might appear through the bizarre device.

"Aye," he agreed, unsure if the leer remembered him. He spoke low to avoid Grindrod's attention.

As Assimus and Bellicos did their work, the lamplighter-sergeant was loudly describing the winding to the prentices, a quick revision he performed at the beginning of every watch.

"I have it on good authority," Sebastipole continued quietly, "that there are whole navies who use even more marvelous liaphobes than these as sea lights on the backs of their rams."

"Aft-lanterns, sir." Rossamünd could not help giving the correct term. It was as reflexive as a blink.

"Aft-lanterns?"

"Aye, Mister Sebastipole, aft-lanterns are fixed to the frame through the taffrail at the stern of a vessel."

Threnody snorted dismissively. "Know-it-all," she muttered. "You sound like an edition of Lot's Books."

"You remember me, I see." The leer looked pointedly at Rossamünd, passing over Threnody's aside. "Glad to see you made it to us after all. Bravo. I should know better than to misname the parts of a ram in the company of a marine-society lad." Even through the strange sonics of the sthenicon, the leer's humble pleasure at Rossamünd's recognition was obvious.

"Altogether too much lip-flapping happening," Grindrod barked, addressing Rossamünd and Threnody and conveniently ignoring that Sebastipole outranked him. "Are ye wanting more impositions, lippy-lucies?"

"No, Lamplighter-Sergeant!"

"Then attend to the winding, lantern-sticks, or ye'll attend a week's worth of the foulest duties my cunning can devise! Have ye got me?"

"Aye, Lamplighter-Sergeant!"

Grindrod gave Sebastipole a quick and frosty look.

The leer made no comment.

The lantern now glowing, the prentice-watch moved on, each watchman—man and boy—keeping a full fodicar's length behind the next: the correct drill-book formation. The official wisdom had it that such spacing gave each lighter room to swing his lantern-crook, and the nicker a harder time attacking more than one lighter at once. This practice went against the natural urge to bunch together for protection, and Grindrod was continually correcting their gaps as the boys instinctively drew close to each other. "Step back there, Wheede! Ye want to march behind the fellow, not take him home to yer mammy! If ye were any closer, Plod, I'd have to separate ye and Pillow with a chisel!"

It was proving to be a drizzled, windy night. The Harrowmath sounded alive with the hiss and rush of southerly gusts through its grasses, accompanied by the tuneful buzzing of a rabble of frogs sending their sweet night music into the gloaming. And with this, along the gap of road between each lamp, the gritty, crunching unison footfalls of the regular-stepping prentice-watch added its own even rhythm.

Rossamünd felt safer with Sebastipole at the work tonight. The leer swayed his sthenicon left and right, left and right, as they moved away from the manse—a thorough, never ceasing reconnaissance.

At Lantern East Winst 8 West Well 17, Rossamünd was required to wind out the bloom, his shortened fodicar just barely reaching the ratchet. Twice he tried getting the crankhook into the ratchet housing way above him in the crown of the lamp. Twice he failed, the hook end uselessly hitting the outer bracket of the housing and failing to slot home. Rossamünd had been issued this shorter lantern-crook in the belief that he could not handle one of full size, yet it had proved inadequate for the task. Winding out the bloom was one of the hardest skills to learn and a tool that barely reached the ratchet did not make it any easier.

The other prentices shuffled in the cold and groaned their impatience.

"Thank ye for the wait, Rosey!"

"Master Come-any-later-and-we'll-be-here-till-Chill-ends!"

Even the lampsmen shuffled their feet as they watched and grumbled testily.

"What ails ye, Master Lately?" fumed Sergeant Grindrod. "If ye cannot get the crook in the hole, then what business have ye being a lighter? Ye boys'll be the end o' me afore I can make ye fit for lighting!"

Rossamünd could not help but agree. As he was about to fumble a third time, Threnody stepped up. Her expression dared Grindrod to argue. She took the fodicar in a firm hand and guided it true. The hook end connected into the ratchet with that pleasant, snug, metal-on-metal sensation that told it was properly engaged.

"Ah . . . Thank you, miss," Rossamünd breathed. Shame-faced, he lifted the lantern-crook up for three ticks of the gears and let it fall under its own weight; lift and let fall— *up two three, down two three* it went, to work the gears that wound out the bloom.

The other prentices were stunned to muteness by Threnody's actions.

Threnody said nothing and stepped away, keeping apart from the other lighters.

"Well, by front door or back, one still gets into the house." Grindrod was clearly amused. "Wind it out faster, lantern-stick, there's only a set count of hours in a night!"

With much puffing and aching arms, Rossamünd did his duty, the lamp rewarding his effort with a gradually increasing gleam, and the prentice-watch moved on. Behind them the brooding safety of Winstermill, with its thousand lamps and window-lights, diminished with every vialimn lit.

At East Winst 15 West Well 10, Rossamünd fared better with the winding, and at her own lights Threnody displayed her natural facility, working the ratchet with ease.

The glow of Lantern East Winst 17 West Well 8 on the approach to the Briarywood was discovered, once it was wound out, to have become a purulent yellow-green. The seltzer water had been gradually deteriorating.

Time to change the seltzer, just like a bright-limn.

A clothbound record was produced from Bellicos' satchel and the lantern's state recorded for Wellnigh House's seltzermen to attend to the next day. The wind gathered pace as this was done, buffeting out from icy storehouses down in the southeast, making ears noisy with its passing and quieting frog song. On the walk again, Rossamünd twisted and craned his neck to relieve his hearing from the gusting airs, desperate to catch suspicious, dangerous sounds. Sebastipole kept at his ceaseless vigilance.

Too soon they reached the Briary, its tops creaking in the wind but at its roots deathly still. The pyre of nicker corpses was a soggy charred mass that, even after three days, hissed and steamed with incomplete combustion. Wet woody smells sat heavy in the atmosphere. It was as if the threwd had worsened, not diminished; that the killing of the horn-ed monsters in the wood had only stirred that place, not quelled it. Even the hardheaded, stonehearted Grindrod felt the horrors tonight. The lampsmen hurried the prentices through, insisting upon winding the great-lanterns here themselves to save time and their nerves. At each winding Rossamünd truly expected Sebastipole to cry out that a nicker was nigh upon them—yet he did not.

With Phoebë lifting her nightly shrinking face over the darkling hills, the prentice-watch found themselves gratefully passing the great fuming censers of Wellnigh House and entering the safety of the cothouse confines.

"How was it?" one of the house-watch asked.

"The threwd grows" was Bellicos' curt reply.

"Aye," the house-watchman returned, "don't it always, these days?"

7

MORNING TO MOURNING

burges small flags for signaling, made in sets of distinct patterns for the representation of letters, numbers, cardinal points, titles of rank or social elevation, even whole words. The color of a burge is first and foremost for distinction, though the meaning of the colors can be inferred if a small multistripe, multicolored flag—known as the parti-jack—is flown with them. Burges are used for both civil and military purposes on land and the vinegar seas.

As it had been on their previous prentice-watches, Rossamünd's quarto was rudely awoken before the sun had properly started its own day. In the hurry of breakfast Rossamünd thanked Threnody for her help with his lantern-crook.

"I could not help myself," she said a little stiffly. "It is the way of a calendar: strive against the oppressor, relieve those oppressed, work for those who cannot afford a teratologist's labors, feed them that cannot afford the food, give roof to the roofless, a bed to the bedless." She spoke her creed with the monotone of rote learning.

The prentices were blessed with a friendly greeting from

Sebastipole as they formed up to leave, a profound contrast to the surliness of Assimus, Bellicos and Puttinger. The leer at the lead, out went the lantern-watch, out into the early gray when the air seems especially clear and still and cheeks hurt with the cold and everyone speaks in a hush; out to quell the lights for the glory of Ol' Barny once more. Dawning glimmers expanded to an astounding rosy brilliance as they returned—as they must—through the Briary's brooding shadows.

Red dawning, traveler's warning . . .

Even the hard veteran lampsmen kept quiet and looked often to the leer. Rossamünd was sure he heard suspicious rustlings and rattlings in the winter-barren woods, thick with faintly luminous fogs, but Sebastipole did not give an alarm.

Out on the raised dike-road of the Harrowmath and free of the claustrophobic thicket, the prentice-watch walked a little easier. From some hidden roost in the wild pastures the occasional lonely trilling of a wagtail echoed about the quiet. At lamppost East Winst 5 West Well 20—only four more lamps till they could consider themselves safe within the fire arcs of the manse's great-guns—Grindrod allowed them to take their ease. For a moment they sat on the roadside to sip at skins of water, chew on hardened slogg-porridge and listen to the tinkle of a runnel that flowed under the highroad. Called the Dribble, it apparently came from boggy ground to the north, went through a pipe beneath them in the dike's foundations and down to a small marsh known as Old Man's Itch in the south. Rossamünd loved its bubbling melody and was grateful they had stopped by it.

Only Sebastipole did not stand easy, but took a quick drink through a tube stuck into his sthenicon and resumed his silent survey. Something in the gloom of the Briarywood through which they had passed only a little more than an hour before seemed to fix his attention. Noticing the leer's pointed stare, Rossamünd tried to discover what lay there. *Surely not a monster?* All he could see was the thick mist condensing up from the grasses and settling over the highroad. However, he did spy a hard-covered transport emerging from the rising fume. It was a boot truck pulled by a fully shabraqued mule hurrying as fast along the Pettiwiggin as the fractious creature could manage.

"First traffic of the day," called Bellicos. "Clear the way!" This was redundant, for all of the prentice-watch were sitting easy on steep verges.

"He cracks on apace!" spat Assimus.

Though it was still a fair way off, the broad blue and white stripes that covered its windowless sides could be easily spotted. It was a butcher's wagon; something that belonged in a town or city.

"He is out of his normal pond," Puttinger mused.

"What business has a butcher got in the early morn on haunted roads?" Bellicos wondered aloud.

"I reckon I've seen him and his before," Assimus posited. "Comes and leaves from the manse twice or thrice a year, more frequent yet ever since the old Comptroller-Master-General left."

The approaching vehicle did not distract Sebastipole. He pushed at one of the three small, slotted levers on the side of his sthenicon and kept staring beyond it, farther down the road. After a long, far-looking scrutiny, he pushed at the biologue box again from the other side. "We must hurry ourselves, Lamplighter-Sergeant," the leer said carefully, precisely. "There is good reason for that truck's speed: it has picked up a follower."

"At what cardinal, leer?" Grindrod gruffed.

"Directly east."

The lamplighter-sergeant took out his perspective glass, a privilege of his rank, and took in the view indicated. "Shadows within shadows," he growled obstinately after a thorough scrutiny. "I see naught to trouble us."

"Yet there is *trouble* there," Sebastipole persisted patiently. "It remains in the fogs but will emerge soon enough. You must move now, man! There is an umbergog eagerly on that butcher's slot!"

An umbergog! Rossamünd was gripped with fascination and dread. Umbergogs were reputed to be among the largest of the land-walking nickers, some bigger even than ettins and far more cantankerous and misanthropic. The only ettin he had met had not seemed mean at all, rather sad and confused. He could see something there, emerging at the edge of clarity, clearly enormous and coming their way.

"Though our follower is still nigh on two miles distant," Sebastipole said, never moving his gaze from the distant menace, "it is moving extraordinarily fast. I suggest you pick up the rate—quickstep or double-quick, Mister Grindrod, and leave off the learning and the dousing till a friendlier day."

Grindrod bridled, but nevertheless he said, "Aye, leer, good advice—"

"Not again!" quailed Crofton Wheede, too frightened to care that he had interrupted the lamplighter-sergeant.

"What's the chance of two theroscades within a week?" whimpered Giddian Pillow.

"Steady, lads, steady," Grindrod cautioned. "Ye faced 'em four nights gone and ye'll do it again today if needs be. Now to yer marching—we'll beat this hasty hugger-mugger home yet! The basket is still a goodly way that way," he said, pointing open-palmed, soldier fashion, to his left. "And we have but three parts of a mile to succor and security at the opposite point. Keep yer dressing and eyes forward if ye want to avoid trouble: a threat near or far should never be allowed to ruin good and steady order! By the left! At the double-quick, *march*!"

So they marched fast, Threnody keeping pace with the best of them. Frequently Sebastipole halted to assess the threat, the lampsmen watching him almost as often, waiting hawklike for his reaction. Each time he simply spurred the prentice-watch on.

"How is it," Rossamünd heard Puttinger wheeze in his thick Gott accent, "that the basket does not go for the pile of charbroiled corpses in the Briary?"

"The stinker finds something more to its likin' in the butcher's buggy, I reckon," Bellicos offered.

The butcher's truck rushed past with a noisy clatter even as the prentices themselves fled. The driver and the side-armsman were muffled up to the nose against the chill, their eyes unfriendly, frightened and staring ahead. The donkey was gasping, near blown, but still they pushed it as if all the blightlings and baskets of the Ichormeer pursued them. In its flight it left a faint unfriendly trail of moldering meat smells and the faintest whiff of something foul and horrifyingly familiar—*Swine's lard!*

A nauseous chill rushed through Rossamünd's innards. He wrestled off the horrors, his memory lurching back to rever-men slavering in a vessel's dark hold. *But here?* He cleared his head with a shake.

"I reckon I recognize 'im," Crofton Wheede gasped. "He's the knackerer from the woods above Hinkersiegh where my sires are from. What's 'e doing all the way here?"

Almost immediately a horizontal gout of smoke erupted from the manse followed by the small thunder of cannon, which sent clouds of startled birds bursting into the gelid morning with a great clamor from every hide and roost on the Harrowmath. The fortress was firing one of its long-guns, seeking the prentice-watch's startled attention. Burges were run up beneath Ol' Barny, small flags lit bright in this clear morning and signaling the same warning Sebastipole had just issued.

Bellicos pointed to the signal and cried out, *"There's a nicker on the Harrowmath!"*

Behind, Rossamünd heard Sebastipole say, as if to himself, "As I said . . ."

"So yer prescient observation shows true, leer. Well done to ye." The lamplighter-sergeant did not actually sound pleased or impressed.

The prentices kept bravely at their marching, but began to look about wildly, losing what was left of their even gait, quickly ceasing to step-regular altogether. Rossamünd stepped directly into Tremendus Twörp's broad back, receiving a blow to his chin and nose from the lad's flabby shoulder blade. Threnody managed to gracefully avoid the collision.

"Reform yer file, ye clod-footed blunderers!" Grindrod barked angrily. He looked back. "Where is the beast?" He looked again through his glass and must have found something, for he said, "What an ugly article . . ." With a grunt, Grindrod passed the perspective glass to Bellicos.

With eight hundred yards still between them and Winstermill's sturdy gates, some hulking thing was emerging from the fog. It had gained on them alarmingly. Even at a distance Rossamünd could see its giant size: a lumbering brute with a great spread of spikes about its head. And how fast its massive legs did carry it! Even as they watched it seemed to draw closer.

"I reckon it's the Herdebog Trought!" wheezed Bellicos with the callous calm of a hardened campaigner. "Even from here I can recognize the basket. I remember it from its rampagings in '87."

"Can't be!" muttered Assimus. "It's meant to have been chased by the Columbines all the way up into the northern marches of the Gluepot and destroyed there."

"It's coming!" Wheede shrieked.

The other prentices whimpered.

"I don't want to die by the jaws of a nicker . . . ," burbled Twörp.

"Cease yer panicking!" Lamplighter-Sergeant Grindrod bellowed. "I've been in far tighter contests than this."

"Grindrod!" Sebastipole barked, surprisingly clear from his boxed face. "With Puttinger, take the prentices back to the manse as quickly as you think they can stand. Assimus and Bellicos and I shall be rear guard. Go now, Lamplighter-Sergeant—there's not a moment to lose!"

The lamplighter-sergeant repeated the orders as if they were his own. The prentices hurried away; the double pace doubled again, leaving Sebastipole and the two lampsmen to do what they might to put the beast off. At East Winst 3 West Well 22 the prentices paused, panting like overworked dogs. Rossamünd looked back, and his eyes went saucerlike.

The umbergog was bearing down at prodigious speed now, pulling itself along with the assistance of its long powerful arms. Less than two lantern-spans were between it and the rear guard. Half as tall again as the ettin Rossamünd had met in the Brindleshaws, this nicker was like some enormous malformed deer, its great antlers spreading out above its head like a regiment of pikes. Its hide, knotted and matted in thick curling beards about its chin, throat and down its chest, was like clots of dirty pale brown felt. The black fur about its small, weeping, rage-red eyes radiated down its cheek like points on a wind rose. It gave vent to a bellow like the lowing of a mighty, maniac bull, its hot breath expelled into the cold as billows of yellow steam.

"At the doubled-double now. Lead on, Mister Puttinger." Grindrod hung back. "I'll keep an eye out rearward."

The prentices hustled forward, barely held panic spurring them. The thump of a long-gun pounded ahead of them, and the metal it threw flew close enough for Rossamünd to hear its unnerving, shuddering whine. The gunners of the fortress clearly thought the beast close enough to try their aim. The shot struck the earth to the north of the road, tearing a gap in the weeds and sending up a small spray of root-clogged soil well to the right of the charging monster.

Assimus, Bellicos and Sebastipole each discharged their locks though they were well out of range, then retreated at a run.

"Mister Puttinger, take the boys on," Grindrod ordered. "I will stay to aid the rear guard."

"Yes, Lamplighter-Sergeant!" the old lampsman cried obediently.

Threnody made to hold back too as Grindrod dropped behind; she was fearless and clearly itching to do her part.

"Keep up, girly!" Puttinger hollered with quick fury, and grudgingly she picked up her pace again.

116

HERDEBOG TROUGHT

The prentices were running now in line, a maneuver for which they had had little training. Soon their formation was only a ragged farce of a file. Yet what they lacked in skill they compensated for in speed. Straggling, struggling to breathe, they were near enough to the fortress now to hear the terrible, distant baying of the manse's dogs lusting to be let at the mighty beast. With this came the distant clattering of alarm posts tumbled out on drums, and the *dong-dong-dong* of the warning bell hung high in the Specular, the bell tower of the southern gatehouse. Yet as close as they were, Rossamünd doubted they could reach the manse in time. The battlements buzzed and milled with agitation as little, far-off people called encouragement from the walls.

"Leg it, lads! Leg it!"

Soldiers began firing from the ramparts, their muskets cracking hot but doing little more than fouling the air with their fumes. A few spent balls thwipped through the tangled grasses on either side of the road, posing more danger to the boys than the beast, and the ragged shooting soon stopped.

Ahead of them the butcher's truck kept at its cracking pace, the winded donkey whipped to push beyond all endurance. It neared the Approach and the succor of Winstermill, and Rossamünd bitterly wished he was upon it; yet instead of going up the steep ramp, the truck clattered on to disappear into the Bowels beneath the fortress.

At the head of the prentices' line, Crofton Wheede stumbled as the road changed from tamped clay to pavers of dressed stone. He tripped out of file, dragging Giddian

Pillow with him. The other prentices avoided the tumble, but Rossamünd proved less nimble. Wheede's toppling fodicar caught him about the shin and pulled him down. He saw a glimpse of gray sky and whirling horizon and hit the ground with a lazy puff of fine road-dust, his hat spinning off into the Harrowmath grass. A deft roll and Rossamünd was up on his feet again looking east, then west, then east again. Threnody slowed, this time to help him, fright now clear on her face, but the other prentices ran on, screaming panicked encouragements over their shoulders. Wheede and Pillow scrabbled to their feet and were off like hares from a covert, pelting after the others without a rearward look, deserting fodicars, fusils, knapsacks, even a mess-kid in their renewed flight. Red-faced and gasping, Puttinger half turned but, seeing the lads back on their feet, continued his own retreat.

With quick glances left and right, Rossamünd could see that he was not going to get away. None of them were: not Sebastipole nor Grindrod nor the lampsmen dashing after them, not even Puttinger and the fleeing prentices. Only the butcher's truck was safe—the very one that had brought this terror. Surely there was something he could do other than run uselessly? Surely he could attempt something to help his fellows escape?

From his salt-bag he took out one of two leakvanes he carried. The small box contained two scripts separated by a heavy film of treated velvet. When mixed these burst into a repellent of the foulest kind. He had never used a leakvane, nor seen one till he joined the lighters, and under less testing circumstances might have hesitated to try it. Yet, with carelessness born of necessity, Rossamünd pulled the red velvet tab that kept the two volatiles apart and hurled the box as far as he could—a surprising way for so small a lad. The leakvane landed with a skipping bounce on the Pettiwiggin, falling between him and the retreating lampsmen. Rossamünd had no idea how long it would take for the chemistry to erupt from it and only hoped it would not go off till after the men had passed over.

The guns of Winstermill spoke again, five deep, rippling coughs, booming so close in succession they were almost one sound. The distinct and frightening howl of twenty-four-pounder cannon shot came high and to the right. Three shots went well wide. One glanced off the umbergog's right arm to ricochet crazily into the Harrowmath hay. The last was a direct hit. It struck squarely in the monster's ribs with a thick, dull slap, forcing a coughing belch from the Trought. The creature's flesh rippled violently under the blow, but the shot did not penetrate and dropped uselessly to the road. The umbergog staggered and bellowed at the buzzing walls of Winstermill. A thin cheer of many smaller voices answered it faintly from the battlements.

Before the beast the four men of the rear guard fled, and as they ran the leakvane burst prematurely ahead of them with a hissing pop. Too soon it sent out a foul, warding steam, a smoking hedge that hung between Rossamünd and the senior lighters. They waved their arms angrily and the prentice could hear Grindrod's indignation carry on the wind.

"What are ye doing, ye twice-stunted ape!" he roared. "Are ye trying to trap and kill us?"

The leer leaped through the repellent and, following his lead, Bellicos darted about the side of the boiling smoke. So encouraged, Assimus and the lamplighter-sergeant hastily followed.

The fortress guns boomed a third time. The tearing shriek of their shots quickly followed.

With surprising and terrifying dexterity the beast ducked their fire and sprang forward, leaping nearly one hundred yards, as Rossamünd could tell it, in that single bound.

"Run!" Sebastipole commanded. "Perhaps your chemistry will purchase us a little space!"

Puttinger and the prentices were near Winstermill's precipitate ramp; perhaps they would be safe after all? Rossamünd could only wish he were among them.

The umbergog was closing. Only a single lantern-span and the clouds of leakvane repellent stood between. The young prentice was sure he could feel its powerful footfalls through the paving of the Pettiwiggin, yet when he dared a rearward look the creature had slowed. The smoke of the leakvane had been spread about by contrary breezes, and the reek boiled broadly over the road, going down either side of the dike and into the thick weeds. The Trought was obviously confounded and pulled short stupidly, turning its dripping nose up at the fume. So close and so tall was the creature that it eclipsed the rising sun.

The leer, the prentice and the three lighters ran. They had not gone far when Rossamünd realized with horror that somehow Threnody was still behind them, making a stand before the hefty beast. Even now she took careful aim at the giant with her fusil while it sniffed bemusedly at the leakvane's brume. Realizing what Threnody was doing, Sebastipole pulled up and turned, unshouldering, cocking and sighting his long-rifle in a single, easy action.

Hiss-CRACK! went Threnody's fusil, its gun-smoke acrid, the sound of Sebastipole's own fire quickly following.

One of the shots was true. It struck the umbergog just as the brute was daring to push through the broiling barrier of repellent. The monster gave a mighty yelp far out of proportion with the smallness of the hit and staggered back, cracking the paving with its footfall and sending up a spray of gravel and dust.

Such was the sting of skold-shot.

With gloved hands, the leer instantly took another skold-shot ball from a cartridge box hung over his shoulder and, quick and cool, reloaded his long-barreled firelock.

Ahead of them Threnody did the same.

"I would appreciate it if you would come away now, m'dear," Sebastipole called to her, but she did not acknowledge.

The nicker, its abdomen now splattered with new-flowing gore, bounded at them, head up, mouth gaping, its ponderously oversized antlers pointing wide along its back. Rossamünd could feel the pounding of its mighty strides shaking the road beneath his feet.

Undaunted, both Threnody and Sebastipole coolly fired again.

Hissss-C-CRACK! No more than a hundred yards from them, a gout of ichor came from the top of the umbergog's head, and a piece of shattered antler spun off. A prodigious shot, whoever it was. The beast cried its agony again as it was sent headlong, sprawling upon its knees across the road and sliding down into the Harrowmath.

Sebastipole, seeing Rossamünd, called, "If you have another of those leakvane boxes, I suggest you employ it now—we could do with the help, I think."

Rossamünd quickly produced the second leakvane from his salumanticum. He pulled its red velvet tab, gave it a brisk shake and tossed the little box a short way up the road.

"Now, let us be off!" Sebastipole cried.

The Herdebog Trought was getting to its feet again, pulling itself up by those powerful arms, coughing and snuffling and shaking its great, bloodied head.

As they ran, Sebastipole put himself between the monster and the two prentices.

Rossamünd fossicked about in his salt-bag for a dose of Frazzard's powder. He did not know how it might work on a nicker so big, but some potive in hand, however inadequate, felt far better than none. He looked back over his shoulder.

Half standing, the Herdebog Trought peered at Rossamünd, Threnody and the valiant leer as if seeing them for the first time, then at the fleeing lamplighters, almost to the Approach now, almost home. It seemed puzzled, sniffing once more at the air, stooping to smell the ground and casting about confusedly. Rossamünd did not get the same sense of pure malignancy from this creature as he did from the horn-ed nickers. The umbergog felt driven more by anger than malice.

The second leakvane burst at last with a *whoof!* of toxic smoke. Giving a wild bovine shout, the startled monster leaped up and over them, passing close overhead. With a great shudder of the ground and cracking of flagstones it landed on the opposite side of their small group. By some cause of Providence, the Herdebog Trought had let them be. It lumbered away down the Pettiwiggin, covering a prodigious distance even as Rossamünd watched, its attention fixed on the tunnel-mouth into which the butcher's van had fled.

Grindrod and the two lampsmen were close to the fortress now. They had caught up to the prentices, who were struggling to make the last few dozen yards. The nicker was gaining on them all. The musketry resumed on the walls. Puffs of dirt flicked up as balls missed or deflected from the monster's shaggy hide.

Rossamünd could just see Bellicos turn and stand his ground. He cried something over his shoulder and flourished a pistol. There was a tiny puff of thick white from his hand and a pathetic pop of pistol shot.

The nicker hesitated. It must have been hit.

But one shot from such a sidearm, skold-shot or otherwise, could never stop such a gargant—not even Sebastipole or Threnody's fine aim had managed that—and the beast recovered in an instant.

Sebastipole loaded and fired his long-rifle as quick as he might in support of the lampsman, scoring a glancing hit on the monster's rump, a fine shot that did naught to stop it.

Wailing *"No!"* Rossamünd watched helpless as the Trought galloped forward and caught up Bellicos in its gangling violence, crumpling and crushing the fellow as it ran on, flinging what remained to the eight winds. A cry of indignant dismay came from the watchers on the wall. Bravely the fellow had stood and bravely he had fallen, gaining a precious little space for his comrades.

With Grindrod, the two remaining lighters and the prentices still on the road, the umbergog was upon them. Yet just as it had disregarded Sebastipole, Threnody and Rossamünd, the nicker ignored the prentice-watch too as they scattered either side of the conduit into the concealing weeds below. The beast stayed fixed on the Bowels and, ignoring all the firelocks firing, lumbered right up to the great gap in the foundations. The Trought was too big to fit within, and reached into the tunnel with its great arms, bellowing into the cavity in rage. There was a clamorous ring of metal as the ponderous grille was let to drop on the umbergog's questing limb. Roaring, clearly wounded in head and body, the beast wrenched free of the pinning portcullis.

The yowling of the dogs became louder as the heavy bronze portals of Winstermill were swung open to release a company of troubardiers, the manse's entire complement. They were led by Josclin, the lighters' only scourge. His entire head was wrapped with protective bandages of potive-treated fascins. The soldiers with him stepped high and stoutly, going out to defend their brothers, long spittendes—barbed, cross-pieced pikes—ready in their hands, their boots clattering boldly on the dressed stone of the Approach.

Another was with them, wrapped in a cloak of orange, blue and white. It was the Lady Dolours, without her wings, her bald head wrapped in a soft cap. Standing on the edge of the ramp and looking down on the Trought, she raised a hand to her forehead. Rossamünd suddenly feared for the Trought's life: regardless of poor Bellicos, he was sure the beast did not deserve such an end. Fully expecting the poor Trought to expire instantly, he was amazed when the hugeous thing stumbled away from the fortress, slipping down the side of the highroad dike.

Why does she not kill it?

Rossamünd could see Plod and Wheede huddled on the same side of the road, frozen in confusion, wailing their fright. Close by, the Trought, equally distressed, collapsed to its haunches in the grass of the Harrowmath, steam rising from its heaving back into the morning cold.

The troubardiers pressed forward with a derisive yell. Spittendes lowered in bristling threat, they formed on the road with dangerous alacrity. The scourge stepped before them, standing on the verge, twirling a sling filled with some deadly potive. Ten yards from the panting beast he gave a shout and flung his chemistry. The nicker raised an arm to ward off the hissing projectile, and the potive struck it with a dirty splash. The Trought recoiled screaming as part of its forearm was dissolving to the bone. Even its ponderous mass was not enough to save it from the ancient script.

The troubardiers charged down the side of the dike with a battle-yell, joined by the yammering dogs led by their handlers from the gate, and by the jeers of the lighters on the wall. Threnody shouted with them, thrilling to the hope of victory soon won, thrilling to the hope of revenge. Rossamünd just watched, not knowing who to feel most sad for: man or beast.

At last the monster half turned and staggered to its feet for several heavy steps, then made off into the long grass of the Harrowmath. With pestilential steam streaming from the bubbling stump of its left arm it fled north, faster than the heavy pediteers could follow. The dogs were let go at last, great black tykehounds dashing out from the fortress and down the Approach, past the ranks of the troubardiers, to chase the wounded creature down and hold it at bay. Cheers grew louder, great hoots of victory from the men on the walls, many shouting the lead dogs' names.

"Fly, Drüker!"

"At 'em, Griffstutzig!"

"Get the masher, boys!"

The troubardiers halted at the base of the dike and gave voice to another derisive cry as the Herdebog Trought quit the scene.

In the awful silence that followed, Rossamünd retrieved his hat from the southern slope of the highroad. Torn between his grief for Bellicos and for the Trought, he joined Threnody and Sebastipole as they returned hastily to the manse. For much of the way no one said anything, the prentice hugging himself as his awareness of the cold returned.

"Will they kill it, sir?" he asked in a small voice.

"Most certainly," Sebastipole returned. "The brute has killed one of our own and must be slain in turn."

Kill or be killed, went Rossamünd's thoughts. "Oh," he said aloud. "That was some frank shooting, sir," he ventured after a lengthy silence. He said this with sad yet genuine admiration, trying hard to ignore the red stains of Bellicos' pointless ruin on the road. "And you too, miss," he said to Threnody.

Flushed, staring out toward the far-off, fleeing umbergog, Threnody had said nothing since her valiant stand. She now gave a zealous, self-satisfied smile. "I just wish it had been doglocks in my hands and not a fusil," she said warmly.

In his turn the leer bowed his head in thanks for Rossamünd's compliment. "Improved aim is one of the genuine boons of this vile biologue," Sebastipole said mildly as he removed his sthenicon with a sucking intake of breath. For several beats the leer seemed as if he had been struck a heavy blow, slowing his pace, dazed and blinking rapidly. "But you, young woman, have clearly got a fine eye," he finally continued, still giving his head small, violent shakes. The sthenicon was returned to its ordinary-looking box, and a kerchief produced into which Sebastipole blew his nose over and over. "And I thank you both for standing stoutly with me through it." He acknowledged them both with an admiring nod and Threnody smiled again, clearly thinking she could now take her place among the men.

Rossamünd did not feel so confident. "I am so sorry for the leakvane bursting too quick, sir. It was—"

"Not another thought, young sir!" Sebastipole insisted. "It was well intended and did its trick in the end. Tarbinaires like those leakvanes of yours are contrary contraptions even in the wisest hands."

Dolours came down to them as they walked up the Approach, full of concern for her mistress's daughter. She went to wrap an arm about Threnody, but the girl bristled and with an angry sound refused the bane's comfort. Dolours looked to the heavens for a moment and followed.

Within the manse's fortified bosom, they found Grindrod and the prentice-watch gathered safe at last, formed up on Evolution Square as if they had just returned from a typical lantern-dousing. Every boy looked exhausted, harrowed; most bore tear stains on their cheeks. Crofton Wheede still wept even as he tried to hide it.

The lamplighter-sergeant was doing his best to console the traumatized boys. "Well, ye lads have surely had a violent passage through yer prenticing . . ." It was with almost obvious relief that he turned his attention to Rossamünd. "As for ye, Master Come-lately, ye're a fool of fools, boy! I'll have yer gizzards for gaiter straps for putting yer vile puffings in our way! I thought it was the end of me! Of all the sponge-headed bedizened . . . Were you trying to kill us all?"

"That will be enough, sergeant-lighter," Sebastipole warned, becoming very grave. "You know very well the placing of the leakvane was intended only to deter the nicker and give us a screen to retreat behind."

"I'll remind ye, Sebastipole," Grindrod said, leaning into the leer's face, "that the prentices are *my* charge—"

"And I'll remind *you*, Grindrod, that both *you and they* are mine," returned the lamplighter's agent, stepping to a grateful Rossamünd's side.

Grindrod stared at Sebastipole and then changed his tack. "Fine bit of marksmanship, leer," he said. "Almost as good as the girl."

Sebastipole simply blew his nose and turned his attention to Rossamünd. He gave the prentice an owlish look. "It has been a pleasure to serve with you, young master Rossamünd." He smiled politely. "I go to join the inevitable coursing party. We will trap it and so bring its end. Thank you again for your assistance, sir." He looked over at Threnody, who stood silent on the edge of the group, unsure how to join in. "And you, young woman. I would happily have either of you at my side on any future outing."

Rossamünd was even more confounded. This was high praise, but it left him terribly troubled. What part had he played in what was to be the Trought's ineluctable end? The killing of the horn-ed nickers had seemed right, necessary, but the Trought's destruction brought only baffled dismay. Indeed, Rossamünd felt most angry at the butchers, for baiting the beast. *Was it really swine's lard I smelled?*

Threnody did not answer either, but stood with arms folded and chin raised.

Mister Sebastipole was quickly away, clearly intent on joining the group that was forming by the gate, eager to hunt the nicker that had just slain one of their own. The clamor of the tykehounds could still be heard coming distantly from the Harrowmath.

Grindrod bent right down into Rossamünd's face. "Ye, sir, will *never* make it to lampsman if ye get in the way of yer fellow lighters and near cause their deaths."

Rossamünd fumed silently. He had done all he could to protect and defend his fellows. Mister Sebastipole had said he had done rightly; he would not back down. Nevertheless, he was wise enough to not speak. He knew what little good it would do him.

"Ye can forget yer Domesday vigil tomorrow, lanternstick!" the lamplighter-sergeant hissed. "Pots-and-pans for ye all day. Think yerself well off, for I would cheerfully make it worse!"

8

POTS-AND-PANS

evolutions training in the correct movements in marching and the right handling of weapons and other equipment. Evolutions are taken very seriously in military organs, especially in armies, where pediteers are drilled over and over and over in all the marches and skills required until they become a habit. Failure to perform evolutions successfully is punished, sometimes severely, and this is usually enough to scare people into excellence.

THE coursing party that finally left by the middle of that very same day was constituted of the scourge Josclin and another skold Rossamünd had never met before, Clement, Sebastipole, a quarto of lurksmen, a platoon of ambuscadiers and musketeers, the tractors of the dogs, and two mules with their muleteers to bear comestibles. No one thought the coursers would be gone long, and everyone expected them to return victorious.

Dolours had not joined in the course, which Rossamünd thought strange given her venturing out to help fight the Trought. "Not well enough to travel," he overheard the bane say in a brief word with Threnody.

Bellicos' death was a heavy blow to everyone at Winstermill. He might have been a world-weary veteran pensioned off, so to speak, along the safest stretch of the way, but he was one of their own. Reports of lighters from other parts of the highroad coming to their end were common enough, but this was the first lighter from the manse to be killed in a long while. Ol' Barny was flown at half-mast, and the lighters, pediteers, servants and even the clerks wore long faces and did their duty perfunctorily.

At limes, and more so at middens, the other prentices—those who had been safely in Winstermill washing and breakfasting and marching while their fellows were fleeing the umbergog—nagged those of Q Hesiod Gæta to recount every particular of their flight. Their own deaths so nearly realized that morning, those of Rossamünd's quarto were unwilling to endlessly repeat their small parts in the rampaging of the Trought. Deeply shocked, they had no heart for the usual showing away and idle brags, but sat together in the mess hall in a melancholy huddle. Threnody would not sit with them, but stayed very near, cleaning her fusil ostentatiously. Unsatisfied, their fellows diverted themselves, wondering what the coursing party might do to the creature, wandering off to ignorant conjectures about whether Clement or Sebastipole or Laudibus Pile was the best leer.

"Did you see how the basket tried to get into the Bowels?" Crofton Wheede wondered quietly, his haunted gaze looking at nothing. "I thought he was after us, but he was set fast on that meat cart."

"Maybe they were baiting it," Smellgrove offered in a whisper.

"They looked too a-frighted for that," countered Pillow.

"Exactly," said Threnody from outside the circle. "Besides, who'd be simple-headed enough to bait an umbergog?"

"Me dead dad," Wrangle muttered, flashing a look of suppressed fury at the girl.

"Maybe they were delivering parts for the dark trades." Rossamünd spoke up, thinking of the hint of swine's lard he had detected.

That struck the others dumb.

"Carry for the dark trades right under our noses?" Smellgrove snorted.

Rossamünd shrugged. "I've seen some bad fellows try to get a rever-man through the Spindle. It's not impossible."

His fellow prentices looked at him oddly and lapsed into ruminative silence.

Soon the mood of the Hesiod Gæta prentices affected the whole platoon, and a heavy glumness settled on them all.

For Rossamünd, the sorrow of the lampsman's passing and the Trought's imminent destruction was far bleaker than he had reckoned upon. In a few months he had seen so much death—violent and stark and shocking quick—nothing like the glorious end that his pamphlets described for its heroes. The life of adventure *was* a life of violence. He had been seeking this, but now found he did not want it; men died, monsters died, and only grief and self-doubt remained. Barely eating his skilly and ignoring all about him, the young prentice felt a light touch on his shoulder. It was Threnody, looking at him with guarded and unexpected sympathy, perhaps to show that she understood. Rossamünd was not sure anyone could. Who else was able to comprehend sadness for the slaughter of a monster?

Grindrod was determined not to let the boys wallow in the aftermath. They were set to marching, stepping-regular across the Grand Mead and back, across and back, left, right, left . . . for what remained of that grief-struck day. "Good practicing for tomorrow morning's pageant-of-arms," as the lamplighter-sergeant put it. However, Grindrod was himself more irascible than usual, and bawled out even the slightest error. "Keep to yer dressing, ye splashing salamanders! I didn't stand out here hollering at ye for more than two months to witness this clod-footed display! Step-regular like I have showed ye! Swift and even!"

The Lamplighter-Marshal visited the prentices at mains. He told them that he had halted the prentice-watch once more, and spoke quietly to each member of Q Hesiod Gæta. "It is a hard thing to lose a brother-in-arms, Prentice Bookchild," the Marshal said gently, pale eyes genuine in their commiseration. "Grieve freely, and remember well why it is we stand here against the wicked foe."

But what if the foe is one only because we make him so? Rossamünd quashed the troubling thought.

"Lamplighter-Marshal, sir?" piped Smellgrove. "What happened to that butcher's wagon?"

The Marshal smiled. "Ah, those fellows hid scared in the

Bowels till middens then went down the Gainway, very anxious to be gone——not like ye stout gents standing afore the front of stiffest dangers!" He looked at all the prentices with fatherly esteem. "Bravely done, my boys, bravely done!"

Every face, whether it had suffered trauma that day or not, beamed at him.

A double tot of grog was given out as a treat that night, an especial consideration to the boys who had suffered that morning. They all drank openly in memorial to Bellicos, and the eight quietly in thankfulness for their own survival.

"A confusion on the nickers!" Arabis boisterously cried the habitual toast.

It was repeated lustily by all but Rossamünd, who barely murmured, "A confusion on the nickers," and then mouthed, *and an end to my own.*

Mains came to its end and evenstalls began. While the other prentices, Threnody with them, went to their confines to polish and prepare for tomorrow's full parade, Rossamünd was required to present himself at the kitchen for his scullery punishment. He was given no dispensation for the terrible attack of the Trought. Exhausted, he stowed his hat, frock coat and weskit safely in his cell, put on a smock issued to all prentices for laboring duties, then hurried out.

Only four sharp turns from the prentices' mess hall were the enormous kitchens with their sweating, white daubed walls and high ceilings of intersecting smoke- and fat-blackened beams. Cookhouse, buttery, small-mill, scullery and slaughter yard were together run by the culinaire, a woman infamously known as the Snooks. She was stout and lumpy and not much taller than Rossamünd, dressed in gray, with a puckered perspiring face, its age hidden beneath a trowel's worth of boudoir cream. Worse, her lips and jowls were pinked with rouge, making her look like an ancient kind of good-day gala-girl, such as those Rossamünd had passed in less seemly parts of Boschenberg.

A near-mythic fear of her made pots-and-pans an excellent punishment for defaulting prentices. From her throne at the end of a long-scarred bench the Snooks glowered at Rossamünd through thick double spectacles as he entered the steam, stink and sweat.

"Hark 'ee, another weedy lantern-stick sent by old Grind-yer-bones to do me dishes!" she cried at him above the clangor of chopping knives and stirring ladles. "Ye lads come to me so often I don't have any labors for me scullery maids to work," she added with a chuckle, a strangled wheezing gurgle.

Rossamünd swallowed a gasp at the sharp, distinctly unpleasant odor of the kitchens. He had expected they would always smell sweet, of baking crusts and roasting sides: where Mother Snooks sat reeked more of fat and some acrid cleaning paste. "I've come for pots-and-pans."

"Yes, yes, I know that!" the Snooks snapped. "It's the only reason ye bantlings come to me." She squinted at him through fogging glasses, her lips pursing and puckering over and over. She took out a small, well-thumbed tally book and flipped many pages. "Let us spy on who we've got ourselves

137

here," she muttered, running a stubby finger as if down a list. "Ninth of Pulvis . . . ninth of . . . Ah! Here ye be! Ye pasty li'l sugarloaf," she stated in small triumph, then looked hard and close at the page. "Oh." She gave Rossamünd a quizzing look. "Ye're not the new girl, are ye?" .

"Ah . . . No, ma'am." Then it occurred to him what she meant. A little glimmer of self-respect expired within. "I . . . I just have a—a girl's name."

The Snooks gave a strange, high snort and her gurgling forgery of a laugh. "Well, perhaps we should find ye a pretty pinafore to wear!" This made her laugh even harder.

Rossamünd stood stiffly and waited for her to stop.

She wagged her head and dabbed at an oily tear. "The burdens some of us have to bear, eh?" she sighed. She marked the tally book with the greasy stub-end of a pencil and put the book away somewhere in her apron. Pointing into the confusion of the cries and the cooking she instructed him, "Off ye go—scullery's through there and down yon stairs. Philostrata is always ready for the help."

Rossamünd rolled up the sleeves of his smock and made his way through the bustling kitchen. He passed the small-mill, where the pistor ground and pounded the flour in a great granite mortar ready for hasty pudding, the little treat allowed the prentices on Domesdays. His stomach gurgled. Some might have said it was bland stuff, hasty pudding, but as an interruption to the repetitive menu, it was a small ladling of bliss. Rossamünd stepped aside as the furner stoked the ten-door oven that dominated the center of the great

THE **SNOOKS**

room, bumping into one of the baxters as she prodded and checked her baking breads.

"Oi there, pip-squeak," the baxter warned. "Best mind yourself, afore you wind up in one of me loaves!"

At last in the farther corner he found an oblong hole in the floor through which steam was continuously venting in churning swirls. The scullery cellar. Paved steps went down and Rossamünd descended till he was standing by a line of scrubbers, great wooden vats brimful of frothy, near-scalding water. The rosy-faced scullery maids, arms up to elbows in suds, greeted him with singsong cheer. The head scullery maid, Philostrata, handed him a soap-greasy cloth. "Sooner to start is sooner to end." She pointed with a nod to a tub crowded about with unsteady piles of grimed crockery and smeared turnery.

Vinegar flies floated about the stack delicately.

Pots-and-pans!

The water was tremendously hot, but when Rossamünd flinched, the nearest scullery maid chided him gently. "Don't be a mewling great babbie, now." She smiled. "You'll get used to the scald. Young lantern-sticks need to grow into hardy lighters."

Rossamünd washed pots, pans, plates, griddles, saucers, fine Gomroon porcelain, dainty Heil glassware, sturdy mugs, cutlery and turnery. Sweat dripped from his brow and soaked his shirt as he scrubbed away the grease and washed off the spittles and scraps. The water turned into a foul, tepid soup that was promptly replaced with steaming new water poured from large coppers and made sudsy with great scoops of scarlet-powder. Scullery hands bustled about taking washed plates, drying them, hustling them off to be stored.

As the scullery maids worked they gossiped and griped. ". . . Did you see what *she upstairs* had delivered today?" one woman huffed with a ceilingward glance and a dripping poke of her thumb in the vague direction of the Snooks. "We only used to get the finest, but now *she* rules the roost. Acacia says *she* carts in this awful cheap wheat dust from Doggenbrass! *She* ought to know better!"

"Tut!" another maid exclaimed. "The finest fields in the Sundergird just north of us, and *she's* importing poor stuffs from across the Grume! All because of that pinch-a-goose, Odious Podious."

"Larks! Been here but three years and it's like he rules the place!"

"Or like he wants to," came the first scullery maid's shrewd answer.

"Mm-hmm," her colleagues-in-suds agreed.

Rossamünd washed for an hour, his puckered hands becoming insensible to the steaming water, and was relieved when Philostrata told him that his job was done and he could leave. Feeling a weight lifted, he hurried up the scullery steps eager for the seclusion of his cell.

His joy was premature.

Finding the happy prentice without a task and ready to leave, the Snooks put a heavy arm about Rossamünd and guided him over to an enormous fireplace filled with chains and lumpish levers. The pendulous fat of her limb flowed about either side of his neck. Rossamünd strained his head away from the noxious mixing of her posy-perfume and the funk of her armpits. Before him was a great cauldron, removed from its hooks over the hearth.

"Now I want ye to hop into there," the Snooks said, pointing to the enormous pot, "and scrub away till it all gleams."

The young prentice regarded the cauldron with sinking, wide-eyed disgust. With a helping hoist up and over from a soup cook, he was made to climb inside, and to his horror the pot was still warm from its cooking. He was expected to scratch at the crust of ages within with little more than a bent butter knife and an old brush. Squashed on his knees, Rossamünd labored in dread of being forgotten and having some boiling, putrid fish-head stew poured atop him. Hacking at the crust with the handle of the brush, he had managed to make a fair pile of burnt smithereens at the bottom of the great pot when he felt it being lifted and saw the stone mantel of the fireplace loom over the rim to eclipse the smoke-stained white ceiling. They were going to boil him!

"*Ahoy! Ahoy there! I'm in here!*" he hollered. "*I'm in here!*"

The cauldron was tipped on its side and Rossamünd rolled on to the slate-paved floor. Small unidentifiable pieces of char stuck to his face, hands and clothes.

"I'm sure ye're very tasty, me lad," the soup cook grinned, "though I reckon yer boots might make for some prodigious chewing."

Shaking just a little, Rossamünd grinned with him. Brushing off the char, he presented himself back at the Snooks' chair. The kitchen was beginning to empty now, staff retiring for the night as their duties finished, and Rossamünd was hopeful he would be among them.

Regarding him through light-reflecting lenses, the Snooks pursed and unpursed her lips. "What to do with ye now, eh?" she muttered. "What to do with ye now . . . I tell ye what, boyo," the old potato sack of a woman offered at last, "I need ye to do a little favor for yer old Mother Snooks. What do ye say?"

"W-What would I have to do, ma'am?"

"Why, just carry a trifling thing up some stairs for me, that is all."

"I . . . er . . . ," Rossamünd started.

"Or shall I tell dear Grind-yer-bones just how contrary ye are? I'd be happy to give ye a more regular place in me kitchen." The Snooks gave him an appraising look.

Rossamünd made a strangled noise.

"I'll take that to be a 'yes,' shall I?" The culinaire grinned wickedly. "Good lantern-stick."

With that she took him back through the cookhouse and out into a small quadrangle that he never knew existed. It was sunk right down like a well amid the lofty walls of Winstermill and was lit dimly by the light showing from the kitchen door and slit windows. Stars showed through the high oblong hole above, blue Gethsemenë—the brightest—winking at him silently. In the twilight Rossamünd could tell the place was both manger and slaughterhouse, the stink of pig's sweat, lanolin, dung and blood mixing with the smoke of a fitfully glowing brazier. By it a man stood, warming his hands, clearly oblivious to the stink. He wore a striped apron and a belt holding wicked-looking carvers—a slaughterman.

The Snooks went to him. "Well, hello there, Slarks," she said in her friendliest voice. "Give my parcel to the lad."

"Right you are, Mother Snooks." Slarks hesitated, looked dubiously at Rossamünd from crown to boot-toe and then went to fetch this "parcel." With a grunt he hefted a sack and handed it straight to the young prentice. "Watch out, lad—it might be a mite weighty for you!"

Rossamünd grappled with it clumsily, expecting to be toppled by a ponderous weight. It smelled strongly of pigs and made vile squished noises, but it was not heavy.

The slaughterman regarded Rossamünd. "You're a wiry little stick, ain't you?" He indicated the sack with a wink. "We won't be havin' the soup this week, eh?"

Rossamünd had no notion what he meant.

"Follow me, me darling dumb-muscle, follow me!" The Snooks led the way back through the kitchen, past the mill to the pantry stalls. Into the leftmost of these the culinaire ambled, going to the very back. Behind a stack of wheat and barley bags was a red door, ironbound and locked. With a large key, the Snooks released the door, picked a bright-limn from the wall and took Rossamünd beyond into a small cold room. Here were kept all the sweet dainties and rare nourishments set aside for the officers—and especially the

Master-of-Clerks. Labels—handwritten, hand-pasted—identified the contents of many sacks, bags, boxes, tins and other containers: pickled peaches, plums, apricots, small black fish and so much more Rossamünd could not catch a glimpse of in the swinging light as he was rushed through the store. For a breath they paused before a meat safe and several enormous earthen pots of unknown content.

What now? Rossamünd wondered.

Partly concealed behind the pots was another door barely big enough for the old woman to fit through. A second key opened this port, and she encouraged Rossamünd through with a firm hand.

At first Rossamünd thought he had been shown into some kind of cupboard, but as the Snooks pushed in with her bright-limn he discovered that it was actually a landing. Before him he discerned a tightly winding wooden stair going up and going down. It was a furtigrade—a secret stair—cunningly built in a cavity between the walls, barely lit with ill-kept bright-limns fixed to the banister posts.

"This nasty squeeze'll take ye right up to where ye need to go." The Snooks patted a rail. "For too long I've been jamming me girth between them banisters, and now I hurt right deep in here," she said, patting her right hip tenderly. "I'd rather not climb anymore."

The meager width of the furtigrade was such that Rossamünd marveled that the Snooks had been able to make the ascent at all.

"So that's why ye're here and that's where ye're to go

145

with yer bundle. Just take the stairs all the way till ye come to a door and can't go no more. Bang hard low down and go through. To ye left ye'll find the surgeon's door, dark purple and banded in iron. Knock three times, then a pause, then three more, then another pause, then two."

Very unsure, Rossamünd shifted his load. "The surgeon, ma'am?" he asked bemusedly. "Do you mean Swill?"

"Aye!" she snapped. "And ye tell him when he asks—and I know he'll ask," the corpulent culinare insisted as sweat-melted boudoir cream congealed on her brow in the cool of the landing, "that Mother Snooks is a-getting too age-ed to be running errands through back ways and is fed up of nasty, dusty, too-steep, too-narrow stairs. That she has seen fit to send me—that's ye, boyo—in her stead."

Rossamünd hesitated.

"Up ye go, boyo!" She gave a ghastly grin.

That was enough for the prentice; he climbed. Each stair was just that inch higher than was comfortable to climb, requiring him to lift his feet awkwardly, every step creaking a protest as it bore his weight.

One—two—three—four—five—six—seven—eight—nine—ten, he counted under his breath, *switch back!*

The whole structure seemed to tremble slightly with every step. Between the rough stone wall and rickety rail there was barely room for the prentice to swing his elbows. *The Snooks must have been squished like pudding in a dish to come up here.*

Gritting his teeth determinedly, Rossamünd climbed in the stuffy, dusty, closetlike dark, marveling at this secret stair and wondering how many folk in Winstermill knew of its existence. Eyes wide to make the best of the weak light, he hoisted the sack over his back. Something soft and blunt bumped and prodded again and again into his kidney.

One—two—three—four—five—six—seven—eight—nine—ten . . . Switch back!

Over and over, higher and higher, and it was colder and darker as he went.

On a landing by a dirty green bright-limn, Rossamünd put the sack down. As he caught his wind he indulged a little curiosity.

He toed the bag. It rocked and squelched softly.

He gingerly undid the cord that bound the top, already loose and in need of retying—or so he told himself. The sack sagged open but that was all.

He lifted it up to the light and peeked within . . . and sat back with a stifled yelp.

An eye had stared back at him.

Rossamünd recoiled, but the eye did not blink or twitch or twinkle with life. A little shaken, the prentice returned to his investigations. He pulled at the sack's mouth, carefully, cautiously, and there was the eye again—a dark, sightless eye and an anemic forehead a-bristle with short, white hairs . . . and a blunt, broad-nostriled snout. The smell of swine was strong now.

Looking closer he found it was indeed a pig—or the head of one, at least—sitting atop a gelatinous knot of gizzards. He grimaced. *What could a surgeon possibly want with a pig's head?*

147

He closed the sack and tied the cord about with the best version of the previous knot he could manage. He had read that physicians and surgeons like to practice stitching wounds on pig bits. *Or maybe he just wants to cut it up and see what's inside?* Rossamünd carried the sack for several flights more, uneasy with his package now he was aware of its gruesome contents, holding it away from his body as best he could.

At last the flights stopped at a square portal.

With a low, whistling puff of relief, Rossamünd caught a breath.

There was no handle on the door before him, no grip or lock, just two solid panels of wood, big enough, he figured, for the Snooks to squeeze through. He thumped it hard and low and with a *thunk*, a *click* and a *whir* that made Rossamünd flinch and shy in fright, the portal opened. The gap revealed the other side was better lit. The prentice gladly snatched up his package and crouched through and saw that the panels which had slid clear of the portal were really the back of a heavy bureau. On the farther side of the square opening he was amazed to find himself in a tight whitewashed corridor. There was a purple door at its farther end, just as the Snooks had described. What business did Swill have with such a secluded venue? Through the smudgy mullions of a small window set almost three feet into the wall Rossamünd could see the frigid night, clear and starlit above the gray mass of Winstermill's roofs, and beyond this the dark line of the low hills of the Brindleshaws.

He rapped at the door just as he had been told: three

knocks, three knocks, two. He could not hear any sound beyond, and was beginning to hope he could just leave the sack there and go back down to the kitchen. *Douse-lanterns must be soon?* Surely his imposition would be done by now?

The port slowly opened.

Rossamünd came to attention.

Holding a bright-limn high, the owner of a flat round face regarded him shrewdly. "Aye?" Her thin lips contorted. This certainly was not Grotius Swill. It was the epimelain from the infirmary.

He declared more boldly than he felt, "Mother Snooks sent me up," and held up the sack. "I have a delivery for Mister Swill."

"Surgeon Swill to you, young man!"

"Surgeon Swill," Rossamünd mouthed obediently.

The woman looked suspiciously down the long, narrow passage. "Stay," she insisted, and with a crisp rustle turned and swung the purple door closed. Yet it did not shut, and Rossamünd was left with a sliver of a view into the room beyond. Her bright-limn made ghastly shadows as the epimelain shuffled across the room. He heard the creak and latching of some other door, then stillness. Trying not to make a sound, the young prentice peered through the gap between door and jamb. In the barely lit apartment was a long, low table with shallow gutters carved down each side that bent to a stoppered drain at its end. On the floor next to this sat a wooden pail of sawdust. Between this table and thin, shuttered windows in the right-hand wall stood a life-size armature of a human body made of wood and porcelain complete with removable parts, which Rossamünd at first thought with a start was a sickly person retired into the corner. When he realized what it was, he stared for a moment in horror. Worse yet, what he could see of the back wall was neatly arranged with several tall screens showing oddly proportioned people in various states of flaying, dismemberment or decay. In such grisly surroundings, Rossamünd wondered how a person could possibly remain in his right mind.

He pushed at the door just a little, his compulsion to see more overcoming his terror of being caught.

Near the door on a stand was a tray a-clutter with tools designed to prize flesh apart, or clamp flesh together; things to gouge and maim—all of them laid tidily inside velvet-lined boxes. Next to these were clumps of frayed cloth he recognized as pledgets and yards of tow, which must have been for tying off free-flowing wounds. Clustered above were many lamps shuttered with mirror-backed hoods that would reflect and intensify their light when lit.

He took half a step inside the door. Between the windows was a gaunt bookshelf carefully stacked with papery piles weighted with jars and pots of desiccated bits and parts: wizened embryos of unguessable genus, distorted eyeballs, withered organs, all decaying slowly, slowly, one tiny bubble at a time in preserving alcohols. Stacked with them was a small library of books. Rossamünd struggled to make out their titles with such little light: *Phantasma-*

goria one read perhaps; the thickest of all maybe showing *Ex Monsteria*. He had learned enough from Craumpalin to realize that these were rare books on forbidden subjects not normally required for a surgeon to read—and Rossamünd longed to look into them.

Swill's voice, angry and loud, came from some other room deeper within. Rossamünd pulled away from the fascinating slivered view and as he did, glimpsed a terrible sight: the flayed skin of a person, glistening as if fresh, pinned out on a frame that stood right by the door. He stoppered a cry of fright and took a clumsy rearward step.

Better light flooded the apartment and determined steps tramped toward the young prentice from behind the purple door. It flung wide and Grotius Swill stood there wearing a brown leather apron besmeared with darker brown stains, his own bright-limn up by his face. He looked furious.

"I . . . I have this for you, sir," Rossamünd quailed, lifting the foul sack. "From Mother Snooks."

Swill took it, looking over his shoulder—gaze catching for but an instant on the flayed skin—and back to Rossamünd. "Where is the Snooks? Why has she sent *you?*"

"She is down in the kitchens, I reckon, sir. She says her hip hurts too much to climb the stairs tonight." He delivered the message exactly as the culinare had told him.

Swill's lips pursed tight as he listened. His eyes became cold slits.

"I see," he said after a long pause. "And you are her porter, are you?"

"I . . . I've j-just done what I've b-been told, sir," the prentice stammered.

"Have you just? By which way did you come, child?" The surgeon's voice was pinched and menacing. "Who saw you come here?"

Rossamünd tried to hide his fright. "I—ah—I came by—by the f-furtigrade, sir," he said in a small voice, pointing back to the barely distinguishable shadow of the bureau. "I—I don't reckon anyone could have seen me, sir, not at all."

"I see." Swill scratched at his throat. "Wait there," he said quickly, and the door closed, properly this time. Presently it reopened.

"When you see the Snooks again, give her this." Swill presented Rossamünd with a sealed fold of paper. "It's my reply." He smiled inscrutably. "She will understand."

Something thumped loudly in the darkened surgery behind. There was a short, stifled yelp and a muffled, maniac gibbering.

"Go on now, quick-quick, get along! Patients need my ministrations." The surgeon gripped Rossamünd's upper arm and hustled him back toward the hidden doorway. "Be certain to give that painted crone my reply," he insisted as the prentice clambered quickly back through the hole in the wall, knocking his head.

The prentice needed no further encouragement but rushed down the furtigrade, gasping, taking two or three steps with each stride, daring even to leap whole flights in his panic, the furtigrade shuddering dangerously. Pig's heads. Flayed skins. Clandestine stairs. *What is all this?*

With douse-lanterns imminent, the kitchens were near empty, only the night staff remaining to stir the pots and bake breads for the morrow's hungry. The Snooks was still at her domestic throne, waiting for him. "Did ye get the surgeon his bag?" she hissed.

"Aye."

"Did ye deliver me message?"

"Aye."

"Well?" The Snooks thrust her grinning, oily face at the prentice. "How did he like our new arrangement?"

"H-He just said 'I see' . . ."

"Is that all?" She grabbed Rossamünd by his sweat-stained smock front. "Just 'I see'?"

The prentice pulled away from her. "And he told me to give you this," he said. The Snooks took the sealed fold of paper slowly and, reading it, went gray, her boudoir cream showing in ugly mealy blotches over her now ashen complexion.

Rossamünd shuffled his feet and the Snooks gave him a sharp look.

"Ye may go," she barked.

The prentice hesitated.

"Ye're clear, ye're free! Go! *Begone!* I'm sick of the sight of ye!" the culinare cried, waving the paper in his face. Rossamünd dashed from the kitchen.

"Douse lanterns!" came the call as Rossamünd entered his

own cell. He quickly shut the door and turned the bright-limn, undressing for bed in the settling gloom. Smock-less, shirtless and shivering, Rossamünd sneaked out to the passage between the cells and scrubbed at the sweat and the cook-room stink as best he might with the frigid water of the common washbasin. The cold and a silly fear of something creeping at him from behind made him leave off washing, and he dashed back to his cold cot to shiver the night away, his bed chest dragged out to barricade the cell's door.

9

PAGEANT-OF-ARMS

august ruler of a single calendar clave; typically a woman of some social stature, perhaps a peer, or noble, with a social conscience. To have any chance of affecting their surrounds, calendars need money and political clout, and those with high standing socially possess with these attributes natively. A clave that does not have ranking gentry or nobility at its head and core, or at least as a sponsor, will most certainly be marginalized. Augusts are seconded by their laudes, who are their mouthpieces and their long reach. With a well-organized and talented clave with her, an august can be a daunting and influential figure in Imperial politics and society.

ROSSAMÜND was woken by a heavy pounding on his cell door and a rough voice crying, "A lamp! A lamp to light your path! Up, you lounging lumps! Up and at 'em—it's a fine day."

It took a few nauseated moments for the prentice to realize he was not in fact being boiled alive in an enormous bottomless cauldron, but lay pinned in tangled blankets on a lumpy horsehair mattress in a freezing cell in the basements of the Imperial outpost of Winstermill. As the rousing groans of the other prentices coughed across the gap between cells, Rossamünd dragged the small chest away from the cell door. *What was it I saw in Swill's apartment?* he fretted. *Do people know about his room up there? Those were mighty strange books . . . and what about that flayed and pinned-out skin? Do I need to tell anybody about it? But who to tell?* At that moment a larger problem loomed, driving these unsettling things from his thoughts: the Domesday pageant-of-arms.

The ritual of Domesday for those under Imperial Service at Winstermill was a military formality of unquestionable antiquity. Every Domesday morning, the whole fortress turned out on the Grand Mead, all bearing arms before the main building in a pageant of flags, polish and rich, bright harness. Two-and-a-half hours of marching and speeches, it was a show of strength of which Rossamünd had quickly grown weary. He had once dearly wanted to see such spectacles: an array of soldiery gathered as if ready for battle. Watching was one thing but participating quite another. To march in a parade was a ponderous and worrying chore where evolutions must be well performed or impositions were imposed.

Sitting shivering on the edge of his cot, he looked forlornly at his unprepared harness. Metal must be polished with pipe clay and galliskins whitened, boots and belt blacked and brightened. Denied the opportunity last night, Rossamünd had to do his best to prepare now, which meant skipping breakfast. With sinking wind he could hear the other prentices stepping singly or in twos up the stairs of the cell row on their way to eat.

Threnody appeared at his open cell door, already washed and fed, immaculate in her perfectly presented mottle. "Well, a good morning to you, lamp boy," she said, with a supercilious grin. "Not ready, I see." She sniffed the night-stale air of the cell and pinched her nose. "Has someone been using you to wipe out the inside of a lard vat?" she exclaimed in an affectedly nasal voice.

Rossamünd blushed deep rose.

"You'd better get your pace on or you'll never be ready," Threnody continued unhelpfully. "I have heard how these things go: you'll be censured, brought before a court-martial, and stretched out on a Catherine wheel if you go out looking less than perfect." She shook her head.

Rossamünd knew she was just being painful, though certainly more pots-and-pans could be expected for a slovenly showing out.

Threnody huffed and put her hands on her hips as he was struggling to fold his cot corners. "Leave off, lamp boy!" she insisted. "I'll do that! You just set to your clobber."

The girl worked a modest wonder, folding the corners on the bed neater, pulling the sheet and blanket tighter and smoothing the pillow better than Rossamünd knew was possible. All extraneous items went into the bed chest, all inspected items arranged in regulation order on the small stool in the corner. Rossamünd's cell had never looked so deftly ordered.

"Turn out for inspection!" came Under-Sergeant Benedict's warning cry. There was a boisterous clatter as all the prentices scurried to their cells from the mess hall or wherever they had been.

Threnody quit the room without another word or even a glance back.

Fumbling buckles and buttonholes, Rossamünd finished dressing in a flurry, still wrestling with his quabard and his baldric as he took his place at the doorpost. Teeth rubbed with a corner of a bedsheet, hair combed with his fingers, he stood at attention by his door with only moments to spare.

Grindrod ducked his head to enter Rossamünd's cell, and looked about, betraying the slightest surprise at its excellent state. He bounced a carlin off the blanket pulled and tucked drum-taut across Rossamünd's cot. "All is in order, Prentice Bookchild," he said after he had peered into every cavity of the tiny quarter. "As it should be. Move out to the Rear Walk and make ready for the pageant."

Assembling with the rest along the tree-lined pathway of the Cypress Walk on the southern side of the manse, Rossamünd mouthed an earnest "thank you" to Threnody. To this she responded with the slightest suggestion of a curtsy, then snapped on a serious face as Grindrod stalked past to check the prentices' dressing. With a cry the sergeant-lighter took his twenty-two charges out to form upon the Grand Mead, to take their place at the rear of the pageant. Before them a crowd of much of Winstermill's inhabitants were also gathering in fine martial order, rugged against the cold.

Marching and standing with the companies of pediteers,

peoneers, artillerists and thaumateers there were very few lampsmen—not even a platoon, seltzermen included. Most able-bodied lighters had been sent east, needed out on the road proper to replace the steady—and increasing—losses from the various cothouses. Yet that small, aged group stood in their place bearing their fodicars proudly, resplendent in the rouge and or and leuc—red and gold and white—of the Haacobin Empire, and glossy black thrice-highs. Only Assimus and Puttinger looked a little worse for wear, their evolutions poorly handled.

Formed on the soldiers' left was a veritable army of bureaucratical staff: clerks, under-clerks, registers, bookers, secretaries, amanuenses, file boys. Each pageant made Rossamünd more aware of the diminishing ranks of lighters and the swelling number of clerks.

Rooks cawed from the pines by the Officers' Green, spry sparrows and noisy miner birds hopped and flitted about the battlements, watching on shrewdly. The thin flags borne by color-parties at the front of each collection whipped and cracked in sympathy with the winds that rushed spasmodically across the Mead, joining the great ponderous snapping of the enormous Imperial Spandarion billowing above the gatehouse.

At his very first pageant, Rossamünd had trembled at the sheer number of folk gathered, at the steady pounding din of feet marching on the quartz gravel and at the stentorian hooting arrogance of flügelhorn, fife and snare. Yet now he was inured to the martial spectacle. It surprised him how quickly he could reconcile such astounding wonders and think them a workaday commonplace.

All the soldiers and their commanding officers were now gathered on the Grand Mead, decked in their finest.

"Stand fast!" came the cry from Sergeant-Master Tacpharnias.

With a rattling shuffle, the lighters, soldiers and staff came to attention as the seniormost officers strutted peacock-proud up on to a temporary podium—erected every Domesday for just this purpose—and stood before the assiduously ordered soldiery. It was the task of the highest ranked to take turns addressing the parade, and first always was the Lamplighter-Marshal. Although he was a peer of some high degree, in his soldierly simplicity the Marshal was unlike many of those standing with him. They were stiff and starched, their rich, finicky, bragging uniforms boasting of more in themselves than they really possessed.

His volume modulating with the breezes, his words punctuated by the calling of the birds, the Lamplighter-Marshal spoke loudly and confidently about the details of the routines of Winstermill, on subjects almost everyone had heard before. He reminded them of duties botched and the need for vigilance, for care, for the particular regard of one another. The pageant listened dutifully, for most loved their dear Marshal and knew these things needed to be said. However, their attention became genuine when the marshal-lighter turned to the disconcerting excesses of bogle and nicker.

"These theroscades have now become an ever-increasing problem," he said gravely. "Almost each day reports come to me and I am applied to for aid. Yesterday I learned that the whole 2nd Lantern-Watch of Ashenstall was slain without quarter, not six nights gone, and also lamps pushed over on the Patrishalt stretch. Today already I have been informed of the taking of a family in the broad of day by the walls of Makepeace." There was a chorused murmur of angry dismay among the lighters and pediteers, while the clerks remained quiet. "Aye, and no doubt ye are all informed of the assault witnessed five nights ago by our own barely breeched prentices." The murmur grew to a growl, a rumble of solidarity and resentment. "And yesterday morning were yourselves witness—as was I—to the end of one of our doughty veterans on the claws of a blighted beast!"

The growl turned voluble.

"How dare the baskets try such things!"

"We'll have our own back at 'em, just you wait!"

"My brothers!" The Marshal's steady voice stilled them. "From loftiest officer to lowliest lighters' boy, we must stand together—and we will. We have fought the long fight for eons beyond the telling of books. Humankind stands and will stand the longer if we *stand* together. Even now a faithful band seeks the very beast who slew our brother, as we, undaunted, continue to keep the way clear and safe. Lighters! We are the bulwark between our fellow men and the raging monstrous malice: we are the brave band who shall always light the way! *Of discipline and limb!*" he cried with a burst of steaming breath, jaw jutting proudly and a deadly gleam a-flashing in his eye.

"*Of discipline and limb!*" cried the many hundred throats before him, Rossamünd's own among them.

Smiling with paternal grimness, the Lamplighter-Marshal took his place at the head of the line of most senior officers as the Sergeant-Major-of-Pediteers stepped forward with a rousing monologue of his own. After him came the bureaucrats, their ornamental wigs drooping curls almost halfway down their backs: the Quartermaster, the Compter-of-Stores, the rotund works-general, each complaining about some unheeded quibble of clerical detail or neglected civil nicety. Last of all was the Master-of-Clerks. With saccharine gentility and that never-shifting ingratiating smile, he droned about some new bit of paperwork required, some new process to record the change of watches. At times he would say things that Rossamünd did not understand but had the vast plethora of clerks chuckling knowingly. As the bee's buzz went, the clerk-master was the darling of the bureaucrats of Winstermill. They looked up to him—so Rossamünd had learned—not just as their most senior officer, but as a genius of perpetual administrative reinvention. His only joys were the minutiae of governance and refining of systems that already worked. Tending to the clerical quibbles of fortress and highroad Rossamünd had heard Assimus and Bellicos (when he had lived) griping to each other—Podious Whympre was getting a better grasp upon the running of the manse than the overworked Lamplighter-Marshal.

Near the Master-of-Clerks—as always—was Laudibus Pile, lurking at the back of the podium, looking out over the pageant with narrowed, quizzing eye. For a beat Rossamünd was sure the falseman had fixed him with his lie-seeing eyes. The prentice was held in this distant interrogation till Pile seemed to see what he sought and, satisfied, looked for another to play this game upon.

Piebald gray clouds stretched over them from horizon to horizon like a roof on the day. Beneath these drifted smaller, knobbled cumulus blown up by southern winds, increasing the impression of a vaporous ceiling. Cold clouds these were, but not rainy ones. With the winds came the faintest scent of the Grume, the great bay to the south. Breathing deeply of this sweet-yet-acrid hint, Rossamünd could have sworn he heard carried with it the faintest wailing of whimbrels—the elegant, scavenging gulls of the southern coasts. The great, hopeless longing to serve at sea sat like cold gruel in his bosom.

Snap! went the flags in the winds.

With a cry from the gate-watch that cut through the Master-of-Clerks' chidings, the bronze gates were swung open and a glossy red and brown coach rushed through with all the self-importance of a post-lentum. It was a dyphr, a small carriage pulled by two horses, its sides raised and roof lowered.

"Eyes front, you slugs!" barked Grindrod, as several boys turned their heads to see.

The vehicle dashed past the parade, peppering those standing nearest the drive with fine gravel flicked from its wheels, and pulled up sharply before the great steps of the manse.

Most of those on the podium made to continue, a bloody-minded show of their disregard for the impetuous arrival. Yet, as the Surveyor-of-the-Works finished his housekeeping plaints and before the Master-of-Clerks could return to reiterate, the Lamplighter-Marshal stepped forward and, to general relief, ended proceedings prematurely. Finally, with a blare of horns and a rattle of toms, the pageant-of-arms was done.

Grindrod dismissed the prentices with a simple order of *"Port arms!"*—perhaps keen himself to be on with the vigil-day rest. "Master Lately, be sure to report to the kitchens," he reminded Rossamünd with no evident satisfaction. With that the lamplighter-sergeant walked abruptly off to join other sergeants milling at the edge of the Grand Mead to watch the small carriage.

Released from the painfully motionless dumb show of the pageant, the delighted prentices hurried off to get ready for the jaunt to Silvernook, all interest in the dyphr forgotten in their eagerness to be away.

Rossamünd stayed. He was intensely curious to know of the passengers and in no hurry to start a long day of pots-and-pans.

Threnody too observed the carriage, her expression strangely intense. She gave a soft groan. "Yes, Mother, I have been a good girl . . ."

Rossamünd looked askance at her.

She appeared not to have noticed he was there. He gave a subtle cough.

Threnody nearly betrayed her surprise, but with a haughty toss of raven tresses recovered. She cocked an eyebrow emphatically at the lentum and said bombastically, "Who is it that has so quickly come in yonder conveyance, you want to ask? Why, it's my mother, come to chastise her wayward daughter no doubt, and sermon me on the honor of our clave."

"Your mother?"

"Indeed. She cannot leave me be for a moment! I am not a week gone and she is come to crush me back into her shape."

The Lamplighter-Marshal now approached the carriage with Inkwill and a quarto of troubardiers. He was followed by the Master-of-Clerks and that man's attendant crowd. Dolours too had appeared, walking over from the Officers' Green, her favorite spot it seemed, from where she must have been watching the entire pageant unheeded. Two calendars had already emerged from the dyphr clad in the mottle of the Right of the Pacific Dove, and they acknowledged the bane's approach with subtle hand-signs. Rossamünd recognized one as Charllette the pistoleer, though the other he did not know. Standing proud upon the manse steps, the marshal-lighter greeted the passenger within the carriage with elegant manners, giving a gallant bow as he handed her out.

"Well betide you, O Lady Vey. A hale welcome to you, August of the Columbines, and to your attendants, from we simple lighters." His declaration was gracious without being fawning.

The last passenger, a woman with hard eyes, hooked nose and a sardonic curl to the corners of her mouth, emerged and responded with equal decorum. "Well betide you, sir," the Lady Vey enunciated beautifully. She was tall, with black hair the hue of her daughter's, yet hers was as straight as Threnody's was curly. Like everyone that morning, she was dressed against the chill in a thick mantle of precious, fur-lined silk with a sumptuous fitch of bristling white dove feathers about her neck and shoulders. Lady Vey stepped away from the dyphr with all the poise and arrogance of a peer. She glared at the lowering sky and pulled her mantle close with a twirling, theatrical flicking of its hems.

So that was the Lady Vey, the great august of a calendar clave. So that was Threnody's mother.

"Ah! There is my laude, the Lady Dolours," the woman declared with a tight smile.

"Always her *first*, isn't it, Mother?" Threnody muttered. "Never a kind thought or concern for me . . ."

Dolours bowed low, with apparent deep and genuine respect.

"She has been abed with fever, gracious August," the

SYNTYCHË THE LADY VEY

Lamplighter-Marshal declared. "But our locum has seen to her as best he can."

"And Pandomë, my handmaiden?" The august looked at the faces about her. "I hear she is badly hurt."

"Your handmaiden mends well in the infirmary . . . and your daughter too has been installed safely in her new role. We are glad to have her among us."

"Yes, very good." The Lady Vey looked over her shoulder and gazed around slowly. She saw her daughter immediately, as if she knew where she was all along. Something profound and complex transmitted between mother and daughter, something beyond Rossamünd's comprehension. For all her tough talk and showing away, Threnody seemed to flinch, and hung her head in uncharacteristic defeat. The Lady Vey swept up the manse steps, unheeding of the bureaucrats and the attendants all deferring a pace to give her room as she slid past.

Threnody rolled her eyes, bravado quickly returning. "Off to my executioners," she said with ill-feigned indifference.

Rossamünd frowned and blinked. "Pardon?"

"My mother is *never* happy with me," she sighed. "And I go to find out just how unhappy she is . . ."

"Oh."

Hardening her face and hiding her dismay, Threnody obeyed some invisible command and left to join the new arrivals.

Left alone as the day-trippers left for Silvernook, Rossamünd went his reluctant way to the kitchens.

Mother Snooks did not want to see him. Looking haggard, she dismissed the young prentice from her sight almost as soon as he entered. "Be on ye way! Whatever wicked crimes ye have to serve yer wretched day atonin' for, it won't be done here. Go!"

Knowing full well that Grindrod had just departed on a south-bound lentum, Rossamünd was puzzled as to what to do next. It was tempting to exploit this as a twist of fortune and take an easy day after all. However, if he did not serve one imposition now, he would only have to serve two later. Knocking at the sergeants' mess door, he asked Under-Sergeant Benedict instead.

"Well, Master Bookchild," the under-sergeant said, stroking his chin, "we must find you another task, else our kindly lamplighter-sergeant might set you more. If the Snooks won't have you, then perhaps Old Numps will."

"Who?" Rossamünd asked.

"He's a glimner working down in the Low Gutter. You'll find him in the lantern store, Door 143, cleaning lantern-panes. You can clean them with him—a nice simple task for a vigil-day imposition."

Rossamünd felt anxious. He had heard of the mad glimner in the Low Gutter. It was the same fellow Smellgrove had been telling of at Wellnigh.

"Be on your way, lad," Benedict instructed, "and work with Numps till middens. I'll report to Grindrod that your duty—we'll call it panel detail—was served. Don't look so dismayed."

169

Rossamünd tried to blank his face of worry.

Benedict smiled and scratched the back of his cropped head. "The glimner might have the blue ghasts from a tangle with gudgeons, but from what I hear the fellow is harmless." Rossamünd did not share the under-sergeant's confidence.

10

NUMPS

seltzermen tradesmen responsible for the maintenance of all types of limulights. Their main role is to make and change the seltzer water used in the same. Among lamplighters, seltzermen have the duty of going out in the day to any lamp reported by the lantern-watch (in ledgers set aside for the purpose) as needing attention and performing the necessary repair. This can be anything from adding new seltzer, to adding new bloom, to replacing a broken pane or replacing the whole lamp-bell.

EXCEPT for targets in the Toxothanon, Rossamünd had never gone down into the Low Gutter. He had often wanted to explore its workings, but he now descended the double flights of the Medial Stair with flat despondency. A Domesday vigil wasted.

Despite a gathering storm roiling to the south, Rossamünd did not hurry. He took time to stroll through the Low Gutter, fascinated by this hurry-scurry place. There were many here who rarely participated in a vigil-day rest. Great fogs of steam seeped from doorway seals and boiled from the chimneys of the Tub Mill, which stood on the other side of a wide cul-de-sac at the east end of the Toxothanon.

It was a-bustle with fullers entering and leaving, burdened with bundles of laundry in varying states of cleanliness. The prentice stood aside for a train of porters hefting loads of clean clothing back to the manse, wondering if any of his own clobber was among them.

Crossing a wide cul-de-sac, the All-About, and passing by the Mule Row, a neat three-story block of servant housing, Rossamünd could hear the hammering of a smith or a cooper, and with this the sawing of a carpenter. In the narrow lane beyond, muleteers trotted their mules in and out of the ass manger, mucking their stalls, scrubbing the animals, feeding them. Beyond the manger rose the near-monumental mass of the magazine, where much of the manse's black powder was stored. This structure was said to have ten-foot-thick walls of concrete but a roof of flimsy wood, there only to keep out rain. If there was ever an explosion, it would be contained by the walls and erupt through this frangible top far less harmfully into the air.

Dodging a mule and its steaming deposit, Rossamünd made his way across the street to where two besomers sat beneath an awning determinedly binding straw with wire, making ready for brooms.

"Well-a-day to you, young lampsman. What can we do for you?" one of the men called as the prentice approached.

"Hello, sirs," said Rossamünd, and touched his forehead in respect. Almost everyone in Winstermill was of superior rank to a prentice-lighter. "I seek the lantern store and Mister Numps."

A queer look passed between the two besomers.

"Do you, then? Well, just keep on your way past us, past the well, and the magazine, through the work-stalls and behind the pitch stand—that large hutch yonder there. You're looking for the big depository that's built right against the east-end wall. You want to go through Door 143."

Bidding thanks, Rossamünd followed the friendly directions and found himself before a low wooden warehouse built beneath the shadow of the Gutter's eastern battlements. On the rightmost door he found a metal plate that read:

Even as the prentice approached the door the rain suddenly arrived, falling quick and hard. Unprotected by any eave or porch, Rossamünd ignored all polite custom, opened "143" without a knock and ducked inside.

The depot beyond was truly the lantern store, he discovered, as his sight adjusted to the scant light. On either side of him were shelves, ceiling-high and sagging with all the equipment needed to mend and maintain the vialimns or great-lamps. Rows of lamp-bells without their glass stood on their collets in a line or hung on hooks from the roof beams. Whole wrought lantern-posts were laid flat in frames, ready to replace any ruined by time or the action of monsters. There were rolls of chain for mending the winds and with them spools of wire. At the end of this crowded avenue of metal and wood hung a massive rack of tools used for repair work. Chisels and heavy saws, sledgehammers, crowbars, mallets, rivet molds, powerful cutters and clamps and other devices were arranged upon it, all for the singular problems a seltzerman might face.

Despite the rain hammering on the lead-shingle roof, Rossamünd could make out a small, infrequent tinkling in the gloom, like two people touching glasses at a compliment. He could not fathom why some happy pair might be taking a tipple in the dim lantern store. Curious, he followed the sporadic noise deeper into the store. A low, lonely singing, true in tone, deep yet sweet, came through the dust and tools.

> *Will the Coster sat in posture,*
> *Upon his bed of hay.*
> *Will the Coster spake, "I've lost her!"*
> *Head sadly hung to sway.*
> *Such sad posture for Will Coster:*
> *"She ne'er should gone away."*
> *But Will Coster, he has lost her,*
> *And grieves it ev'ry day.*

Beguiled, Rossamünd stepped out from among the shadows and equipment and into light. An old-fashioned great-lamp lit the space, with seltzer so new it glowed the color of summer-bleached straw. Cluttered about it was a motley collection of damaged and ruined bright-limns, great-lamps, flares, oil lanterns, even a corroded old censer like those that burned at the gate of Wellnigh House. Right in the middle of it all was the singer. He was alone, sitting on a wicker chair and bent over an engrossing task. He hunched strangely in his seat, his face a dark profile against the seltzer light, his legs pulled up oddly in front. His buff-colored hair was in an advanced state of thinning, and what little he possessed grew lank and thin to his jawline. He was winter-wan, and glimpses of his pallid skull gleamed in the clean light.

There was another "chink," and the prentice saw the fellow put a small pane of glittering glass upon a stack and then, with the same hand, replace this with another dull piece. This he placed in his lap and, still with the same hand, tipped grit paste from a clay jar on to a cloth laid out on a broad barrel. He did something remarkable then. He put down the jar and, with a deft movement of his leg, picked up the cloth between nimble toes and began to polish. He used his foot—bootless and stockingless even on this inclement day—as easily as another might use a hand.

"H-Hello," Rossamünd said softly.

The fellow hesitated only briefly then kept polishing, round and round with his toe-gripped cloth. "I felt you there a-shuffling," he said quietly, almost a whisper, so desperately fragile that Rossamünd stepped closer to hear it better. "Have you come to help me or to hurt me?"

"I—ah . . . to help, I hope." The prentice smiled nervously to show that he was not a threat.

"You smell like a helper" was the baffling reply.

Thrown by this, Rossamünd stuttered, "Um . . . A-are you M-Mister Numps?"

The fellow looked up and blinked languidly once, showing a shadowy preview of a lopsided face. Rossamünd tried not to gasp or start in alarm, yet he still took an involuntary backward step. The fellow's face, from the right-hand brow and down, was a-ruin with scars. His cheek was collapsed, the right-side corner of his mouth torn wider than it should have been. The cicatrice flesh went farther, down the man's neck, mostly hidden by his collar and stock.

"No one has called me 'mister' for three years," Numps said with a sad inward look, speaking with that gentle voice from the left side of his mouth. "But I was a 'mister' before. Mister Numption Orphias, Seltzerman 1st Class . . . hmm, that's who I was before. Just Numps now."

"Ah . . . well, hello, Mister Numps. I've been set duties with you."

The glimner frowned thoughtfully. "All right then," he said mildly, and went back to fastidiously polishing the pane in his lap, pressing hard at some stubborn grime. Rossamünd could see that these stacks of glass panes were for the frames of the lamps and lanterns, big and small.

"What can I do, sir?" Rossamünd looked about uncertainly.

"Well, you can tell me what *your* name is, sir," Numps re-

NUMPS

turned, fumbling and dropping his cleaning rag, then picking it up again with a bare foot.

Rossamünd forgot himself a moment, transfixed by this simple, uncommon action.

"My name is Rossamünd, Rossamünd Bookchild, prentice-lighter."

"Hello to you, Rossamünd Bookchild, prentice-lighter, lantern-stick." Numps smiled shyly then frowned. "Oh, wait. That's not polite. Shouldn't say 'lantern-stick' to a prentice, should you? Just Rossamünd then, Mister Rossamünd," he finished, grinning bashfully. "Aye?"

"Aye!" Rossamünd returned the grin. This surely was no madman, just a simple, gentle fellow. He reached out his hand for shaking.

Numps sprang from his seat, the pane falling to splinter on the boards. His broken face was aghast, wide eyes dashing up and down from Rossamünd's friendly limb to the prentice's horrified expression.

It was only then that Rossamünd realized the fellow's right arm was missing and not just the arm but the entire shoulder too. Not knowing what else to do, Rossamünd dropped his hand. "I'm so sorry . . . ," he mumbled.

"Oh dear, oh dear," Numps whimpered and begun to shuffle those vulnerable bare feet about in the shards smashed over the floor. "Oh dear, Numps is dead."

"No! Stop!" Rossamünd cried. "You'll cut yourself."

Yet this just seemed to distress Numps more, and he continued to shuffle and murmur, "Oh dear, oh dear . . ." A pan and brush were handy, propped against the shining great-lamp. Rossamünd snatched these up and flicked the broken glass from the floor and into the pan as quickly as he could. Yet he was not fast enough to stop the glimner from cutting himself badly, and the man began to splish about in puddlets of his own blood.

"Mister Numps! Please sit, sir." Rossamünd tried to nudge the fellow away from harm. He held him off with his elbow and swept up the remaining shards from beneath Numps' feet, brushing up blood with them. "You *must* sit down, sir, please! Or step away!" Not seeing any other course, Rossamünd stood and gripped the man by one shoulder and what remained of the other and shoved him back with surprising ease against the wicker chair.

Numps sat heavily without resistance, saying over and over, "Oh dear, oh dear, so much red. Oh dear, oh dear, ol' Numps is dead . . ."

"We must get your feet seen to by Crispus—no, wait, he is gone away . . ." Rossamünd managed to wrestle Numps' feet into a better position to see their injuries. His right foot was slashed with small cuts, especially between the toes, and the blood flowed easy and terribly free. His left foot had suffered only minor scratches. "I'll take you to Mister Swill—"

"*No!*" Numps screeched. "Not the butcher and his butcher's thoughts!" He wrenched his feet from Rossamünd's grasp. The prentice was knocked against the barrel, bumping his head painfully. The glimner's own chair tipped and fell, sending Numps sprawling head over end with a flail of limbs. He lay on the boards, his wounds still bleeding free.

"But you need to have your foot mended," the prentice pleaded.

"No! No no no . . . ," Numps insisted in return and began to sing. "Too much red, Numps is dead . . ."

Rossamünd sat for an exasperated pause, rubbing the smarting egg already swelling at the back of his head. He could not see how he could force Numps to do anything the man did not want. *I'll fix him myself, then. I'll use my salumanticum!*

He grabbed at the nearest, cleanest looking rags and pressed them to Numps' bare foot, insisting the man hold them there. "I will be back with potives. Just press firm till then!" he said rapidly and, forgetting his hat, dashed up the avenue of metal and out Door 143. The rain, prodding him like fingers upon his crown, hurt his bruised scalp. The inclement weather had driven all others indoors. The windows of the Low Gutter glowed red, orange, yellow, green, while the noise of working still rang out above the fall of water.

Rossamünd was quickly soaked as he dashed up the nearest stair to the Grand Mead, his hasty feet *splicker-splack splicker-splack* in the quickly growing puddles, his thoughts tripping with him, *I didn't mean to scare him, I didn't mean to scare him* . . .

Across Evolution Green he ran, all the way down the Cypress Walk, turned right through the Sally at the side of the manse and dripped water all along the polished floor and down the steps to his cell. His salumanticum always sat beside his bed chest. He took it up and made hasty inventory of its contents. What he needed most was missing: the black powder called thrombis that made wounds clot rapidly. It was all used on Pandomë's wounds. Indeed, he had attempted to restock his salt-bag soon after the attack on the calendars, but was still waiting for the correct permission papers from Grindrod.

"Off to the dispensury, then," he muttered to himself, and ran out of his cell and up the steps again. "Surely they'll give some to me for an emergency!"

The dispensury was accessed from the infirmary. Entering, Rossamünd recognized Pandomë in a nearby bunk, despite the bandages that hid most of her face. She was still senseless. With a shudder, the prentice thought of Numps' ruined features.

From the other end of the long room Surgeon Swill glanced at Rossamünd dismissively at first, then beadily, discomfortingly, causing the prentice to hesitate. Yet the surgeon said nothing and returned his attention to an attending epimelain.

Through the dispensury door was a small white anteroom with a barred window at the farther end. He stepped up to this dispensury window.

It was not attended.

A velvet rope hung by, and the prentice gave this two hearty tugs, which set a hidden bell to violent ringing. Standing on tiptoes, Rossamünd peered through the bars. From the aisles of boxes, bottles, drawers and shadows emerged a sharp-nosed, flabby-jowled fellow with a high collar and a crotchety, querulous mien. This was the almonder, Obbolute Fibullar, script-grinder and assistant to Volitus—Winstermill's dispensurist. He was a difficult fellow, about as opposite in temperament to Craumpalin as Rossamünd reckoned possible. The prentice cleared his throat and, as confidently as he could, made his request.

"What d'you need thrombis for, lantern-stick, coming in here to drip and dribble all over my floors and on to my counter?" Obbolute leaned toward the bars and glared down at him. "Are you bleeding?"

"No, sir. I am run out of thrombis," Rossamünd returned, startling himself with his own, unexpectedly "what-else-do-you-reckon" manner. He held up his salumanticum as evidence.

The dispensury door swung, but Rossamünd, intent on getting the needed potive, ignored this.

"You can wave that salt-bag about and gum away rudely all you like, young fellow." The obstructive almonder sat back. "I'll need a chit of authority from your commanding officer."

"But . . ."

"Aye, aye, always 'but,'" Obbolute mocked. "No chit, no parts! That's the way it runs here. Time to learn it, don't you think?" He looked up beyond Rossamünd, dismissing the prentice with that single gesture. "Ah, welcome back among us once more, sir. How went the course? Did you get the basket?"

Rossamünd looked up quickly and straight into the mildly amused red and blue eyes of Sebastipole. The prentice had no notion that the coursing party had returned.

"Well, my boy," he said, ignoring the almonder, "glad to see you again. I have just come back from the hunt. A grim event when all was done."

"Hello, Mister Sebastipole," Rossamünd replied. There was no time for chatter. Mister Numps' foot must be attended to. His thoughts spun quickly. Terrible glimpses of Numps dead in a puddle of red ran through his head. "Please, sir. I need thrombis urgently."

Sebastipole looked at him strangely. He turned to Obbolute, producing a fold of paper. "I will be needing puleblande, a six-months' dose, and the same of gromwell too, for all it's worth. And . . . pass me your stylus, man."

"Of course you will, sir." The dispensurist half turned, ready to fetch these potives, all polite eagerness to this reader-of-truth. He pulled the pencil from behind his ear and pushed it through the bars.

"And," the leer continued, looking down to Rossamünd again as he scratched words on to the fold, "a salumanticum's worth of thrombis too, or any other siccustrumn you might have."

Rossamünd could have cheered for joy and thrown his arms about the leer.

Obbolute's eyes narrowed as Sebastipole handed paper and pencil through the barred gap. A glimpse of temper trembled across the assistant's brow. He clearly wanted to contradict this request, yet how could he? A chit had been provided and, more so, the leer was his superior.

"I, ah—well, I," he spluttered, his thoughts clearly at war, "what were you needing that last item for, sir?" He looked narrowly at Rossamünd.

"Because this lighter needs it and you will not give it him," Sebastipole returned, his sangfroid as much as his rank impossible to argue with. "Perhaps you will give it to me?"

A hoarse grumble from his throat and a pointed pause was about all the contrariness Obbolute dared as he filled the order. The leer took the potives with a solemn thank-you that the almonder did not acknowledge. As they left the infirmary, Sebastipole gave Rossamünd the thrombis.

"So tell me, young Rossamünd," he said, "how have you recovered from our excitement upon the road?"

At any other time the prentice would have been all for question-and-answers and exploring his confusions, but this was not that occasion.

"I am well, sir . . . ," he answered, looking over his shoulder down the passage to his path back to Numps.

The leer squinted at him sagely. "Indeed? So tell me, what gives you such cause for haste?"

"Someone has cut himself terribly, Mister Sebastipole, and I need to get to him right quick to stop the bleeding!"

"Why did you not bring this 'him' to the infirmary?" Sebastipole pressed.

"Because he most definitely refused to come, sir . . . refuses to be seen to by Swill—um, Surgeon Swill, I meant." Rossamünd could not obey forms of right conduct any longer. "I really must go now, sir—please give me leave."

"Yes, yes! In fact I shall do one better." Sebastipole put a gloved hand on Rossamünd's shoulder. "Lead on and I will help how I can. Perhaps persuade this fellow to get to the infirmary where he belongs."

Rossamünd dashed back out the Sally, into the rain and down to the Low Gutter, Sebastipole just one step behind.

"Where do you take us?" the leer called over the rush of falling waters. "Who is it that is hurt so urgently?"

Through gasps and rain, Rossamünd called over his shoulder. "To the lantern store"—*puff*—"Door 143"—*wheeze*—"It's Mister Numps—he's cut his foot with glass . . ." He almost staggered in a muddy puddle.

Sebastipole caught the prentice under his arm, saving him from the fall, and dragged him on. The leer quickened his stride, flying down the alley by the Pitch Stand, Rossamünd trying as best he could to keep pace.

Throwing back Door 143 and springing inside, they found Numps sleepy yet still holding the rags to his foot.

"Oh, Numption," Sebastipole hissed.

Rossamünd was amazed at the genuine distress held in that expiration.

"Ready your thrombis, prentice—quick and steady. Now I understand your dilemma."

Hands a-tremble, Rossamünd opened the box and brought out a small sack of the "bonny dust"—as Craumpalin used to call it.

"We must act apace!" The leer righted the toppled wicker chair and wrestled Numps' leg upon it. "How did this happen?"

"I just went to shake his hand." Rossamünd's confession babbled out. "Just to make his friendship, and he jumped and started and the glass fell from his hand and smashed about his feet."

Numps looked up with slow eyes. "Oh, Mister 'Pole, oh dear, you're swimming in my red again . . . Oh dear, Numps is dead . . ."

"Yes indeed, Numps, I find you all bloody like before. Easy, now. We'll fix you right, just like then." Once more Rossamünd was struck by the gentle anxiety in Sebastipole's voice. He never expected a leer might show such tenderness.

"There is glass still in the cuts," the leer continued. "Do you have forceps? Or spivers?"

Rossamünd shook his head, but had a thought. "I spied pliers on the rack there though, sir," he said, even as he went to fetch them. "Here, sir."

"They will do." Sebastipole snatched them. "With haste, Rossamünd, grip his leg under your arm and hold it firm and sure. This will not be easy—I am no man of physics."

186

The prentice obeyed with alacrity.

Numps writhed and wailed as the leer poked and probed and tugged at the wounds. *"Help me, sparrow-man! They tear me apart! Limb from limb!"* The glimner cried, *"Sparrow-man!"* while Sebastipole shouted, "Don't mind his calls, my boy, just hold him steady!" Rossamünd never let go of Numps' ankle nor allowed his squirming to disrupt Mister Sebastipole's delicate work.

"Bravo, my boy," Sebastipole muttered as he pulled out a wicked-looking shard, "you have yourself a strong grip there."

The make-do surgery was mercifully brief. With light-headed relief the prentice tapped hearty mounds of the thrombis on to a particularly nasty laceration under the knuckle of the big toe. It was from here that most of the blood had come. He watched as the dark powder quickly mixed with the gore, coagulating to a sticky, adhering mass wherever it did. When he was satisfied the thrombis had done its work, Rossamünd bound Numps' foot as tightly as he could with all the swathes kept in his salumanticum. He sprinkled more thrombis between each bind till the box of it was all but empty and only Numps' toe tips showed.

Dazed from pain and distress, Numps remained supine among the old lamps.

"When Crispus returns, I'll ask him to come here and do what he can," said Sebastipole. "Till then you'll just have to hop about, Mister Numps. Fetch that handle cup." He spoke suddenly to Rossamünd, and pointed to a ladle lying by a

187

puncheon of water near at hand. "He will need fluid. One who has let free much blood always does."

Rossamünd filled the cup and carefully brought it over.

Sebastipole let Numps drink with noisy thirsty gulps, cradling the glimner's head as he did.

Crouching by, Rossamünd watched, feeling it all his fault. "I'm so . . . so . . . sorry for . . . ," he tried.

"Don't fret, prentice-lighter," Sebastipole said. "Our Numps has never been right in the intellectuals since surviving a theroscade. He has hurt himself before. It was providential I met you when I did, wouldn't you say? Had I not needed pule-blande so urgently I would have already been in a meeting with the Lamplighter-Marshal."

"Will Mister Numps mend, sir?"

"Doctor Crispus cites it the worst case of malingering horrors he has ever encountered," Sebastipole continued, putting a friendly hand on the glimner's shoulder. "We do what we can, do we not, Mister Numps, but it just isn't the same, is it?"

Clearly dazed, Numps still managed to answer. "No, Mister 'Pole, never the same, poor Numps, and poor glass too." He started to look around the floor about him.

"You know Mister Numps well, Mister Sebastipole?" Rossamünd asked, feeling a sudden surge of affection for the leer, so different from the other leers the prentice had encountered.

"We are acquainted, yes," Sebastipole said.

Rossamünd hoped he might say more and waited, but

the leer showed no inclination to speak further. He stood, helping Numps to sit against the glowing great-lamp. The glimner was shivering, and the lamp offered no heat.

Retrieving his thrice-high from where it dropped, Sebastipole said, "Sit easy now, Numps. Don't you tread on those clever feet of yours—we don't want them to bleed again."

To this Numps nodded slowly. "Poor Numps' clever feet. You put me back together again, Mister 'Pole."

"Indeed, we did what we could." The leer looked pointedly at Rossamünd. "This young master and I shall find you a blanket."

Rossamünd followed as he went to the farther end of the lantern store.

Sebastipole turned over a bright-limn sitting on a shelf and its soft glow soon revealed a pile of sacks neatly folded in a flimsy crate. He gathered several and deposited them in Rossamünd's arms, declaring lightly and loudly, "These will answer nicely!" He fixed the prentice with his disconcerting eyes. "It was I who found him," the leer said low and serious, "alone and horribly mangled after the other two seltzermen had been devoured or carried away."

Rossamünd's ears rang as his attention became very focused. "Devoured, sir? Carried away?" he said, equally softly.

"Yes, carried away." Sebastipole paused, closing his eyes. "It was in the first year that our Master-of-Clerks arrived. I remember it so because one of his first acts was to insist on a thorough inspection of all the great-lamps along the

189

road. Numps and others had been attending to a vialimn out east beyond the Heap, past the Roughmarch and Tumblesloe Cot. As you know, seltzermen go out in threes—two to work, one to watch with a salinumbus at the half cock—and return before the lantern-watch starts. But this day they did not arrive by the correct time, a remarkable thing, for as you know a lamplighter's life *is* punctuality." Wry and knowing, Sebastipole looked to Rossamünd, the blue of his eye showing strangely bright in the seltzer light.

The prentice was too intent on poor Numps' story to notice this small joke.

"Though not normally enough to stop the work of a lantern-watch," Sebastipole continued with a cough, "what they found sent them quickly back to Tumblesloe, half the lanterns still unlit. By East Sloe 10 West Dove 13 the seltzermen's tools lay scattered, their cart shattered, its mule torn and mostly eaten, and too close for comfort, they could hear a horrible inhuman calling from the hills."

Rossamünd let his breath out slowly. "Were you with the lamp-watch, Mister Sebastipole?"

"No, Rossamünd, I arrived the next day. Myself and Mister Clement and Scourge Josclin and a dragging party of pediteers, lighters and dogs. We did not have to go far to find poor Numps, though. He was sitting up against the same lamppost where the previous night only signs of attack had been present. His arm was gone, torn from his body at the shoulder. His face and jaw were badly gouged, yet somehow he managed to live, even to crawl back to the

190

road. The cold must have kept him alive, freezing the flow of his terrible wounds. Before or since I've never known a man to survive such mortal harm."

"Frogs and toads!" Rossamünd whispered in awe.

"Indeed." Sebastipole stood. "But it gets more remarkable still. For not only had a man so mortally mangled and co-matose somehow pulled himself along for who knows how long, he had also bound his own wounds and stuffed the socket of his shoulder too, using grasses and leaves with an expertise not even a two-armed man might achieve. How he did this is a puzzle that still beggars solving . . . We bundled him back to Winstermill. He woke on the way, yammering from the horrors and saying such things as you heard him cry today, especially about that little sparrow-man. From what I know of it, Crispus fought to revive the man while Swill thought it more a mercy to let him languish and die."

"What a merciless sod-botherer," Rossamünd growled. "Little wonder Mister Numps refused to go to the infirmary with only the surgeon about."

"Indeed." Sebastipole stroked his chin. "Fortunately for Numps, Doctor Crispus is the senior man and a brilliant physician. Though I wonder if it would not have been the greater mercy to let poor Numption pass."

Rossamünd shuddered, glad never to have faced such an impossible choice. "What of the other seltzermen?" he could not help but ask. "Did you ever find them?"

"We searched as much as we dared." The leer rubbed at his neck like a man exhausted. "Josclin followed me as I followed the smell of the slot and sight of the drag far up into Hallow Sill. It was not like any monster's trail I had pursued before: foreign and much fouler. It was a trace I had only smelled once before, but knew only too well. It was gudgeons. For a week we searched but found only torn clothing and discarded equipage. The calendars of Herbroulesse joined us for a time, speaking of a mighty combat heard in the woods beyond their walls, and of driving off some terrible fear two nights before; but still there was no trace of the other men. I am sure they had been eaten, for the drag I spied through my sthenicon showed little hint of human traffic, and the slot smelled only of death and that evil revenant stink. We traced it back in hope of finding where the revers had come from. Yet the trail ended nowhere, out in the wilds of the southern marches of the Tumblesloes. We returned to Winstermill with nothing more than tatters and conjecture, though Lady Dolours searched on. A tenacious woman, she followed the foul, foreign trail far into marshy lands along the northern marches of the Idlewild, but she too returned with nothing."

Rossamünd's attention pricked at the sound of Dolours' name. "The calendars helped you?" he asked.

"Indeed. I have worked with them from time to time, and they with me—especially the Lady Dolours—snaring corsers and commerce men, foiling the dark trades where we can, beating off the bogles and the nickers. It's inevitable; in a ditchland everyone must cooperate or perish in their isolation. The Idlewild prevails because of *their* work as well as ours." Sebastipole peered at Rossamünd.

"How did a gudgeon find a way out here?" asked Rossamünd. "Did it come from a hob-rousing pit?"

A cold and dangerous look set in Sebastipole's weird eyes. "Not very likely. Such criminal and vile practices do not last long about here, my boy."

"But I thought a dead monster was good whichever way it's done?" Rossamünd spouted the usual dogma.

The leer regarded Rossamünd closely for a moment. "Some folk might say it's so," he said carefully, "but I don't care for the justifications they offer on rousing a bogle against a gudgeon. Coursing monsters as we have done is a needful thing, but making sport of them, especially with something as abominable as a revenant, is useless and cruel. More so, it ties up the monies of men who can ill afford it and is ruinous to the lives of the wagerers who lose." He stopped, took a breath. "We came down very hard on the lurchers after Numps' theroscade."

"Why the lurchers?"

"Because these are the beginning of the whole rotten chain of the dark trades. You can only get live bogles from the lurchers or human remains from the corsers. If you stop them, then you stop the therlanes, who then can't supply the commerce men, who have nothing to give to the ashmongers, leaving them without stock to sell to the massacars or the rouse-masters. Try as we might, there have yet been other gudgeons marauding, though never again an assault on a lighter. Enough now! Let us tend again to the needs of Numps. I can hear him shuffling about. We have muttered overlong on his past and now should labor for his present, after which I must leave you to your duties as I attend to mine."

Rossamünd returned with the leer, back to the clutter of lamps and lanterns. There Numps, against instruction, had moved to sit again in his wicker chair and, patiently humming, was polishing another lantern-window.

11

HITHER AND THITHER

course (verb) to hunt, particularly to hunt monsters; (noun) the hunt itself, usually referred to as a coursing party, or in such phrases as "to go on a course." A course is, obviously, a dangerous affair. One undertaken lightly will always result in the doom of some, if not all, of those involved. A prospective courser is always advised to take at least one skold and one leer—or, if they are unavailable, a quarto of lurksmen, even a navigator or wayfarer, and a hefty weight of potives and skold-shot. Not to be confused with "corse," meaning a dead body, a corpse.

THOUGH Rossamünd was wanting to ask Sebastipole of the coursing of the Trought, the leer soon left him and Numps, saying that he was well overdue for an interview with the Lamplighter-Marshal.

Numps, wide-eyed, watched the leer leave and then bent to his labors once more, humming as he cleaned. Rossamünd did not know how to talk to Numps. He was afraid to frighten the nervous glimner again and so he moved slowly, looking for work to do. He found a rag, sat on an empty chest on the other side of the bright great-lamp and silently began to polish lantern-windows.

Wrapped in the canvas sacks for warmth, Numps did not

complain. He did not even acknowledge Rossamünd. Instead he took every pane the prentice cleaned and polished each one again just as fastidiously as if it had never been worked, adding it to the stack of other lustrous panes. Frustrating as this was, Rossamünd did not grumble but kept at the task. Every so often he would lean down and check Numps' feet, to make certain no blood showed through the bandages, or chide the glimner carefully if, from habit, he should try to use his foot to grip or hold. They kept at this for an hour or more till he accidentally grasped at the same dirty pane the glimner grasped from the top of the diminishing stack.

"Oh" was all Numps said, letting the pane go and humbly placing his hand in his lap.

"Sorry, Mister Numps . . . and I'm sorry about before. For scaring you and making you drop the glass and cut your feet."

Numps must have rarely received an apology, for with each contrite word that Rossamünd uttered, the glimner interjected with a blink and an odd, hesitant "Oh."

"That's just silly poor Numps forgetting his-self. All a-flipperty-gibberty since Mister 'Pole found me swimming in red." He hung his head. "I've never been as I was." He sat like this for several minutes, Rossamünd not daring to move or interrupt. "Time to make seltzer!" Numps suddenly straightened, ready to get to his feet.

"*No!* Mister Numps!" Rossamünd lurched to his feet, forgetting his caution in his concern for the man's wounded sole. For an instant he feared he might have spooked the man again, but Numps just looked at him, puzzled, holding himself between sitting and standing. "You must have a care to stay off your bad foot. Hop on your good foot like Mister Sebastipole said, till Doctor Crispus has declared you whole."

Offering himself as a small crutch, the prentice helped Numps out of his seat and guided the limping glimner over to where he pointed: a collection of barrels and chests gathered in a corner between the wooden wall of the store and one of the tool-cluttered shelves.

"They say I'm struck with horrors," the glimner said, pressing down heavily on Rossamünd with each hop, "and I know I'm not the old Numps, just poor Numps now; but I still remember how to mix the seltzer—they still come to me to make it 'cause no one makes it as well. I might be rummaged all about up here," he said, patting himself on the side of his head, "them pale runny monsters saw to that, but that don't mean I have forgotten."

Numps prized off the lid of one barrel, releasing a distinct tang into the stuffy lantern store, and Rossamünd immediately recognized the sealike odor of sweet brine— the beginning of seltzer water. Humming tunefully, the glimner began to take all manner of chemicals from chests and boxes close to hand. With precise care he dripped, scooped, tapped and tipped each part into the barrel of brine. At each addition he stirred with slow, fine movements; first one turn of the clock then the other for set counts that he spoke under his breath. "Once clockingwise, fours contrawise . . ."

Rossamünd knew the basic constitution of seltzer water: spirit-of-cadmia, bluesalts, chordic vinegar and wine-dilute penthil-salts. He had been shown this by Seltzterman Humbert, and at first Numps followed the recipe properly but then he put in only half the chordic vinegar, left out the penthil altogether and began to add other things—unusual-looking things. Of what Rossamünd saw, he recognized a dash of ethulate and pinches of soursugar, plus a fine sandy powder that smelled like the vinegar sea and sludge that looked ever so much like the muckings of a gastrine.

"What are these for, Mister Numps?" the prentice inquired of the extra parts. "I have seen seltzer made—Seltzerman 1st Class Humbert has shown us, but he never added these."

"Oh . . . ah . . . Mister Humble-burt is good at the simple seltzer, but this is our own seltzer. Better seltzer for Numps' friends. Numps and his clever old friend, we figured this, figured it out before poor Numps' poor clever old friend went swimming in his red too. No one else knows how to do it right and his clever old friend is gone now but Numps still remembers; makes the bloom bloom it does, good for Numps' friends."

"What friends, Mister Numps?" Rossamünd was finding it hard to follow the thread of wandering talk. "Do you look after all the bloom?"

The glimner became silent at this, and would say no more on the subject of bloom or seltzer or friends new or old. Rather he kept pointedly at his mixing until he had made three kegs full of seltzer—smelling far more rich and full than seltzer usually did.

As the day waned someone came a-calling. At first they simply heard her. "Numps! Numps!" was the demand. "Hullo there, my darling muddle-head! Help me git this glass through yer door!"

"Oh, oh, oh," fretted Numps, up to his bicep in seltzer. "The barrow woman is here. The barrow woman."

"I'll go. You stay here."

Rossamünd answered the shout in the glimner's stead, stepping down the avenue of shelves to discover a woman wrestling a heavy load through Door 143. She wore a buff-leather apron over her maid's clothes and was towing a barrow stacked high with panes and lantern-windows. When this laboring lady saw a well-presented prentice-lighter she pulled up short and smiled. "Oh, hello, my lovely."

"Hello," Rossamünd replied. "May I take that?" He had gripped the barrow by the handles before she could reply.

"What a precious little mite you are!" she exclaimed. "Doing my job for me? And grateful I am too." She leaned toward him and whispered conspiratorially, "That seltzer-man is a bit too gone in the intellectuals for my liking. I don't much enjoy having to come down here. Folks avoid him, you know."

"No need then for you to see him today, mother labor," Rossamünd replied peevishly.

The woman gave Rossamünd a sharp, appraising look. "Ye must have done summat right bad to be sent here, lad." She peered closely, seeking the fatal flaw. "Ye've got to take him in hand, pet, if ye're going to get anything done with him," she said. "He's naught but a limpling-head," she finished loudly, for Numps to hear.

Rossamünd felt a surge of anger. He almost forgot his manners as she bid good day, scowling after the woman as she left.

With her departure Rossamünd and Numps set to stacking then polishing these new deliveries and kept at this for what remained of the day. Neither spoke, and there came no other noise but the chink of picking up and putting down till mains was rung and Rossamünd realized he had missed middens, entirely forgotten. With a bow he went to hurry off. "Good evening to you, Mister Numps," he said as he left. "I hope your foot heals right quick. Don't walk on it nor use it for any work, please. Wait for Doctor Crispus to see you."

Numps blinked at him, nodded—with a small, cryptic smile lighting his face—and said, "Will you come back tomorrow and check poor Numps' poor foot?"

"I will, Mister Numps."

Rossamünd returned to the manse, wishing he had met this fascinating fellow well before today.

The other prentice-lighters were not due back from Silvernook till after mains—part of the vigil-day privilege. Rossamünd took himself to the mess hall to eat alone. There he found Threnody back from interviews with her mother and by the fire, sitting on a tandem chair reading a book—a novel no less, that most frivolous of frivolous things. Two small pots, one of delicious muttony-greasy and one with gray pease, bubbled over the fire for any who had stayed. On the table there was also some hard-tack and apples still untouched from middens, and piping Domesday pudding. As he was serving mutton into a shallow square pannikin, Threnody walked wearily over and did the same. She sat before Rossamünd, full of mystery and reticence.

Rossamünd broached the hush. "I thought you'd eat with your mother."

"So did *she*." Threnody smiled sourly, then added, "I told her I was a lighter now and was duty bound to mess with my fellows-in-arms."

"She came a fair way to see you. Did she not insist?"

Bent over her food, the girl looked at him sharply through her brows. "She ranted and railed, as always."

"What did she say?" Rossamünd knew he had asked too much as soon as he said the words.

Threnody stared at him owlishly. "Insufficient to detain me . . . clearly."

Muteness descended and stretched out into a heavy awkwardness. The cooking fire crackled in the hearth. Merry fife music, distant, rhythmic stomping and timely claps drifted through the mess-hall door. This was the ruckus of soused lampsmen and pediteers cozy in their own mess-room making happy on their vigil-day rest.

Rossamünd sighed. Threnody *was* hard work. "And Pandomë—is she healing?"

Threnody bowed her head.

Have I said too much again? Rossamünd wondered.

"She . . . recovers," the girl replied eventually. "She will return with Mother though both physic and surgeon agree that she is unlikely to fight again." For a breath she looked truly, openly sad. "Do *you* think I'm to blame, Rossamünd Bookchild?"

Rossamünd hesitated. "Blame?"

"For Pandomë's hurts!" Threnody stared hard at him. "For—for Idesloe's death . . ."

He was unsure of how to soothe her sorrow.

"I returned from Sinster's sanguinariums little more than eight months ago," she continued, her whispered words spilling, wide eyes imploring. "I have only been *allowed* to begin using my new 'skills' in the last month. Yet, I am a wit: what else could I do? I had no pistols. We were attacked. I did my part, defended my clave, did duty to *them firstmost*! The others were all too battered by the crash. I had to act! If I had been made a fulgar I would have done better, and better yet as a pistoleer—you saw how frank my shots were against that umbergog thing. It was not some self-centered display of valor. Was it? Did I set us all to risk like Mother insists I must have?"

This was more than Rossamünd wanted to answer.

"Practice makes it, miss," he tried, feeling very inadequate. "It's as my dormitory master used to say: learn it as rote and it'll work freely like hearth-softened butter, if you get my meaning."

Impatience flickered across Threnody's face. "I'm not sure that I *do*." Her earnest openness vanished like the snap of a closing lid.

"Well—I was—" Rossamünd started and did not know where to go—*trying not to be rude,* he concluded to himself.

Threnody arched an eyebrow.

"Will you be returning to your mother this evening?" Rossamünd quickly changed tack.

"No, she has said all she wanted to say—and more besides," Threnody answered sourly. "We are done. Fortunately she will leave again tomorrow and take Dolours and dear Pandomë back to Herbroulesse."

With a thump the prentices, soused and swaggering from their vigil-day excursion, bundled into the mess hall.

The strange, strained conversation ceased.

"Hoy there, you sobersides! You should have seen it!" Punthill Plod effused.

"Seen what?" Threnody returned icily.

"Aye, Rosey, you missed a real bust-up," bragged Arabis, completely ignoring Threnody. "A carriage was attacked by some nickers—horses dead, lentermen dead, passengers dead."

"Just like we saw on lantern-watch," Plod continued.

"I heard them say in town that it was done by some nasty grinning blightlings," Crofton Wheede added.

Rossamünd's milt went cold. *Grinnlings?*

"That company of lesquins we saw camped just a mile farther down was not much use to them poor folks, was it?" said a prentice named Foistin Gall.

Rossamünd's ears pricked up at the mention of lesquins, those gaudily dressed sell-swords—the best, most arrogant fighters, who gathered into legions and sold themselves to fight in the petty wars of the states.

"What are *they* doing there?" Threnody frowned.

"People are saying because we can't stop the baskets on the Wormway that the Gainway is under threat!" said Onion Mole in awe.

"Not as under threat as that sweet li'l dolly-mop at the Drained Mouse, not from the looks you were giving her, Moley," guffawed Twörp stupidly, and several boys brayed in drunken delight.

Threnody gave them all a single dirty look and left.

Mind spinning with memories of Licurius collapsing under a press of grinning bogles, Rossamünd was not long in following.

The routine of the next day began as it always did, with the ritual wake-up cry, hurried dressing and stomping out to line up for morning forming on the Cypress Walk by the side of the manse. There Grindrod confirmed the attack on the carriage between the fortress and Silvernook, everyone slaughtered. He quickly moved on to properly inform the prentices that the coursing party had returned the previous day while the boys were living it large in Silvernook. The coursers' homecoming had been somber. They were less five dogs, including the leader Drüker, and Griffstutzig was badly hurt. An ambuscadier was dead, the badly wounded Josclin borne back on a litter. These were bitter blows indeed after Bellicos' death. Even mortally hurt, the harried umbergog had proved a terrible adversary, trapped in a hollow on the western flanks of the Tumblesloe Heap far to the north. It was slain at last by the chemistry of Josclin and a final, fatal shot from Sebastipole's deadly long-rifle. The severed head of the vanquished monster had been dragged all the way back by the mules.

The prentices did not know how to react to this: was it good news? Was it bad?

Grindrod also advertised that that very night in the Hall of Pageants there would be the puncting—the marking with the monster's blood—of those who had had a hand in slaying the Herdebog Trought. Collected from the dead umbergog at the time of its slaying, the cruor was in the care of Nullifus Drawk. He was apparently eager and ready to mark the monster's killers. Rossamünd did not want to go. He had lost his fascination for cruorpunxis. Their gaining was surrounded by too much sorrow and confusion. He well understood why his old dormitory master was ashamed of the tattoo he wore.

After breakfast the prentices were set to more marching. Rain set in, a gray shimmering swathe, and dripping-drenched they formed up along the side of the gravel drive to mark the Lady Vey's otherwise unfeted departure. *"Present arms!"* came the order. Next to Rossamünd, Threnody obeyed, staring fixedly ahead, chin high, a sardonic half smile barely hidden. For her part, as the dyphr clattered by, the august ignored her daughter and the twin-file of prentices with her, her neck held stiff and chin raised.

As mother, as daughter, Rossamünd observed.

For 2nd morning instructions the prentices went to the lectury for lantern workings with Seltzerman 1st Class Humbert. Rossamünd liked the subject: he actually understood and admired the mechanism of a seltzer lamp and the constitution of seltzer water itself. This study was a relief from marching and evolutions and targets. In fact, and despite himself, he welcomed the safety of routine. The last week had been as event-filled as ever he wanted. Too much adventure left him craving easy predictability. With a contented lift in his regular-step Rossamünd entered the lectury carrying stylus, books and lark-lamp—a small replica of a great-lamp given to all the prentices. Rossamünd was intrigued by the curious way its covers folded open upon many hinges, fascinated with the down-scaled workings revealed within, which were just like those that operated the real lights of the road. He paid close attention to all that was taught, but most of the other prentices could not have given two geese about the what or how or why of a great-lamp's internal parts. Humbert noticed neither. He simply droned on.

Rossamünd had quickly learned that lampsmen naturally, though unfairly, regarded seltzermen as failed lighters who only ever ventured out into the wilds with the sun, and then only when need demanded. They were appreciated, certainly—repairing the great-lamps was necessary work—but not respected. Consequently, it was with mixed gratitude that Rossamünd received Mister Humbert's uncharacteristic praise when, in the face of his fellow prentices' ignorance, he speedily identified a limp, pale yellow frond the seltzerman held up as "glimbloom drying out and past saving, Mister Humbert."

"Correct!" the seltzerman returned. "How long can the glimbloom survive out of seltzer before it reaches this irrevocably parched state?"

"No more than a day, Mister Humbert."

"Well, Master Bookchild, you know what you're about with them parts." The seltzerman 1st class brightened. "It takes just this kind of nous to keep these plants working. We'll make a seltzerman out of you yet."

"Aye," Rossamünd heard muttered behind him, "or maybe you'd make a good weed-keeper, Rosey?" There was the sound of soft laughter.

Rossamünd did not look around.

However, Threnody did. "Better to be good for something than a good-for-nothing bustle-chaser," she hissed, unable to tell between good-natured jape or insult.

"Young lady!" Mister Humbert called long-sufferingly. "You might be the only lass at prenticing, but don't think

207

you'll have special concession from me. Please turn around and refrain from disturbing the others."

Skipping the sit-down meal at middens, Rossamünd grabbed some slices of pong and hurried to Door 143 in the Low Gutter and his promised visit with Numps. The Gutter was busier on a normal day, and Rossamünd had to negotiate the bustle of laborers and servants and soldiers. He entered the lantern store quietly and heard speaking: not one of the soft monologues of Numps, but the voice of a learned man.

Rossamünd became very still and listened.

". . . Poor old Numps wouldn't tolerate Mister Swill, eh?" the voice declared. It sounded like Doctor Crispus. He must have returned from his curative tour. "I must say I can barely compass the man myself: entirely too wily, all secrets and heavy-lidded looks and smelling of some highly questionable chemistry . . ."

Although he was aware that it would be proper to make his presence known to the speaker, a guilty fascination held Rossamünd and he remained tense and quiet.

". . . Coming with his uncertain credentials, when all the while a proper young physic might have been satisfactorily summoned from the fine physacteries of Brandenbrass or Quimperpund. A product of the clerical innovations of that Podious Whympre. Everything in triplicate and quadruplicate and quintuplicate now! One thousand times the paperwork for the most trifling things, and all requiring our Earl-Marshal's mark. How the poor fellow bears with the smother of chits and ledgers is beyond me: my own pile near wastes half my day!"

As Rossamünd moved to the end of the aisle he found it was indeed Doctor Crispus, sitting on a stool and ministering to the dressings on the glimner's foot with intense concentration. He had examined Rossamünd on the prentice's very first day as a lamplighter, and had had naught to do with him since. Numps was sitting meekly on a barrel waiting for the physician to finish. He looked up at Rossamünd before the lad had made a sound and smiled in greeting. The physician himself had still not noticed Rossamünd.

"Ah, Doctor Crispus?" the prentice tried, shuffling his feet to add emphasis.

With a start, the physician stood and quickly turned, catching at his satchel as it slid from his lap.

"I have come to help Mister Numps again," Rossamünd added.

"Cuts and sutures, lad!" Crispus exclaimed with a flustered cough. "You gave me a smart surprise!" A towering, slender man—Doctor Crispus must have been the tallest fellow in the whole fortress and probably of all Sulk End and the Idlewild too—he was sartorially splendid in dark gray pinstriped silk, wearing his own snow-white hair slicked and jutting from the back of his head like a plume. He wore small spectacles the color of ale-bottles, and a sharp, intelli-

gent glimmer in his eye boded ill for any puzzle-headed notions. "Ah, hmm . . ." The man composed himself. "Master
Bookchild, is it not?"

"Aye, Doctor," the prentice answered with a respectful
bow. "At your service, sir," he added.

"And so you have been, Master Bookchild," the physician
said, clicking his heels and giving a cursory nod, "of service
to me, and more so to this poor fellow here, as I understand
it." He gave a single, paternal pat on Numps' shoulder.

Numps hung his head and smiled a sheepish smile.

Rossamünd did not know what to say, so he simply said,
"Aye, Doctor."

"See, Mister Doctor Crispus, see: Mister Rossamünd has
come back again and Numps has a new new old friend. They
let him in, did you know? They never let my friends like him
in before, did they? Maybe one day they'll let the sparrow-
man in too?"

Crispus smiled ingratiatingly. "Yes, Numps, yes. I see."

Baffled but deeply gratified by this reception, Rossamünd
asked, "How is your foot today, Mister Numps?" The bandages seemed still tightly bound and in their right place.

"Oh, poor Numps' poor foot," Numps sighed. "It hurts,
it itches. But Mister Doctor Crispus told me well stern this
morn that I was to *leave it be* . . . so I leave it be." He wiggled
his toes.

"And so you must." Distractedly the physician pulled a
fob from his pocket. "Ah! Middens is already this ten minutes gone," he declared. "I must eat like any man jack."

DOCTOR CRISPUS

"Doctor Crispus?" Rossamünd dared.

"Yes, Master Bookchild, quickly now: middens is not the meal to be missed. Breakfast maybe, mains surely—but never middens." Crispus took off his glasses and dabbed at them with the hem of his sleek frock coat.

"Was Mister Numps right not to want to go to Swill?" Rossamünd inquired.

The physician nearly blushed. "Oh . . . Heard my complaints, did you?" He paused thoughtfully for several breaths. "Please disregard an unguarded moment. Those were just professional frustrations requiring a little letting. It's a small understanding between Numps and I—whenever we meet: I run away at the mouth, he listens. That being so," Doctor Crispus carefully continued, "I would rather you came to me with your ills, or the dispensurist or even Obbolute if I'm incommunicado; or just go sick until I return, than put yourself into the hands of that hacksaw." With a cough Crispus looked Rossamünd square in the eye. "I would thank you not to say any more of that which you have overheard."

Rossamünd ducked his head, going shy from the confidence this eminent adult was putting in him. "Not a word, Doctor." He nodded gravely.

"How-be-it, eating is overdue." Doctor Crispus pointed at Numps' legs. "I have applied new bandages but that is all: your use of the siccustrumn was exactly right. The lacerations are deep but the potive has been well applied and is doing the healing work far better than any I could now.

You have been given charge over a salumanticum for good reason, prentice-lighter."

Rossamünd bowed again, unable to hide his grin of delight.

"Enough now, food awaits." Doctor Crispus gathered up his satchel and stray instruments. "After that it's back to that stout fellow, Josclin—may his skies seldom cloud."

"Is he mending, Doctor?" Rossamünd ventured.

"If you are a wagering man, Master Bookchild," Crispus said as he began his exit, "I would put my haquins and carlins on Mister Josclin's full recovery! Good diem to you and good diem to you, Mister Numps. I shall return in a few days to ensure your clever foot—as you call it—is still mending. I have seen you return from the very doors of death, my man. Your foot will not unduly trouble you."

With that the physician hustled out of the lantern store.

Numps immediately began cleaning panes. "Mister Doctor Crispus and Mister 'Pole doesn't know all what happened." The glimner did not look up, but spoke into his own lap.

There was a long pause.

"Doesn't know what?" the prentice pressed as gently as he could.

"He didn't tell it like things happened . . ." The glimner went on. "I didn't go a-crawling back to the lamppost . . ."

Realizing what Numps was talking about, Rossamünd leaned a little closer.

"I remember . . . Even now when I sleep I remember.

213

Poor Numps was dead in his puddle of red, no crawling about for him. It was the little sparrow-man that helped me."

Rossamünd's attention prickled. "The little sparrow-man, Mister Numps?" he asked very very quietly. This was the type of talk that could get you branded "sedorner."

"Yes, yes." Numps smiled, looking up at last. "They might have got my arm to gnaw on, but they didn't get all of poor Numps. It was the little sparrow-man that fought the pale, runny men—"

"I heard you were hurt by rever-men!"

"Oh aye, aye! Pale, runny men ripping us all to stuff and bits and that little sparrow-man came and tore *them* limb from limb and saved me—my first new old friend. He plugged all the pains with weeds and stopped the red from its flow-flow-flowing . . . Fed me dirty roots. That made me feel safe."

"That little sparrow-man?" Rossamünd repeated.

"Aye, this big"—still gripping a pane, Numps adumbrated a creature of short stature with his hand—"and with a large head like a sparrow's, a-blink-blink-blink."

A hunch tickled at the back of Rossamünd's mind. *Could it be the same creature?* "I think I have seen him myself," he said.

Numps became all attention, and he too bent forward in his seat.

"Not a long time ago I spied him," Rossamünd continued, "on the side of the Gainway going down to High Vesting, a nuglung with a sparrow's head all dark about the eyes and white on his chest, blinking at me from a bush."

A little taken aback, Numps blinked quickly. "Yes yes, Cinnamon—he helped me! I reckon he's got more names than I've got space in my limpling head to count, he's been about for so, so long . . . Long-living monsters with long lists of names."

Cinnamon, Rossamünd marveled. "How do you know this, Mister Numps?" he whispered.

"Hmm, well, because he told me," Numps answered simply. "Cinnamon is poor Numps' friend too, see, 'cause it was him that beat the runny men."

Rossamünd felt something between awe and a habitual, thoughtless horror. "You are friends with a *nuglung?*" he breathed, reflexively looking over his shoulder for unwelcome listeners.

Numps grinned. "Ah-huh. Cinnamon said he was come from the sparrow-king who lives down in the south hills. He keeps an eye out for old Numps, sends his little helpers to watch."

"The sparrow-king?" Rossamünd scratched his face in bewilderment. His thoughts reeled at the thought of a monster-lord living near.

"Yes yes," Numps enthused. "The Duke of Sparrows, the sparrow-duke; he has lots of names too.

The Sparrowling
Is an urchin-king
Who rules from courts of trees.
He guards us here

From the Ichormeer
And keeps folks in their ease."

"Have you seen the Duke of Sparrows, Mister Numps?"
Numps shook his head. "But I would like to, though."
"So would I," Rossamünd admitted.
"But you can see him anytime, Mister Rossamünd!" The glimner pulled a perplexed face. "All the old friends would be your friends, wouldn't they?"
The young prentice hesitated. "All the *old* friends? What do you mean, Mister Numps?"
"Yes, yes! My poor limpling head—the nuggle-lungs and glammergorns and the other old friends."
"I—I have one old friend such as this," Rossamünd dared. "His name is Freckle. He is a glamgorn who helped me when we were trapped in a boat with a rever-man. We set Freckle free."
Numps listened to this short telling with growing intensity. At its conclusion he grinned rapturously and did a little sit-down dance, chiming,

"Yes yes, you set him free,
trapped in gaol is no place to be.

. . . you are a good friend indeed for Numps to have who sets his fellows loose from traps. Good for Freckle too."
"I don't like to tell anyone about him," Rossamünd warned. "You should not say either, Mister Numps, about

216

Freckle or Cinnamon. Most people don't like those who are kind to nickers."

Numps' enthusiasm vanished. "I remember that folks hate the nuggle-lungs." He nodded glumly. "And the hobble-possums and all the gnashers, friend or bad. I remember that them that talk with them nor think them friends are hated too. Don't be a-worrying and a-fretting, I won't say naught 'bout Cinnamon nor Freckle, and I'll not say naught 'bout you neither."

They set to polishing panes again, Numps redoing Rossamünd's as he had done the day before. This time the prentice did not mind. He was already being wooed by the timber-and-seltzer-perfumed ease of the lantern store, the rumble of rain on its shingle roof adding a merry, monotonous melody. It was with profound reluctance that he returned to his usual tasks at middens' end.

12

PUNCTINGS AND POSTERS

graille(s) tools of a punctographist. A marker needs four particular utensils to make a cruorpunxis upon the skin: the guillion—also called an acuse or zechnennadel—the needle dipped in cruor and then pricked into the skin; the orbis—in full, orbis malleus, a disc-headed mallet with which the guillion is tapped to puncture the skin and leave a mark; the sprither—the device used to extract the blood from a monster in the first place; the bruicle—the container in which cruor is kept till needed and into which the guillion is dipped every twenty taps or so to refresh the blood. Other tools necessary to a punctographist are a notebook and stylus to take a likeness of the fallen monster's face (either by description or by the presence of a corpse—or the head at least). From this the design of the mark is then figured, usually in consultation with the "markee."

T HAT night after mains the prentices gleefully attended the evenstalls puncting, happy to have something to celebrate. Waiting for the officers and other senior ranks to enter before them, the lantern-sticks formed up along the low fence that hedged the Dead Patch, where the corpses of the first common lighters and pediteers had been buried into the very foundations, feetfirst to conserve room. There they waited dutifully as the higher ranked—dazzling in the polish of their uniforms—entered the hall. The Dead Patch always made Rossamünd fretful; he

associated graveyards with the dark trades and, after his experience in the hold of the *Hogshead,* with rever-men too. It
was just as well the Dead Patch was properly lit, for this
helped a little with the prickling terrors that crept under his
scalp and down his neck. He shivered at thoughts of boat-
holds and foul things snatching from the dark.

"Be still!" Threnody complained alongside him.

"Be still yourself," Rossamünd spat back, under breath,
with a rapid glance in Grindrod's direction. Despite himself, Rossamünd was growing weary of Threnody's fractious
manners. On his other side he felt Wrangle shift minutely
and dart a worried, warning look at them both.

Threnody stared hard at him from the corner of her eye.
"What's your trouble, lamp boy? Missing your old nurs-
ery maid?"

"Shh!" Onion Mole hissed over his shoulder.

"Shh yourself, dolt," she hissed in turn.

There was never any talking when the prentices were in
line, but if Rossamünd did not say something she might go
on and on at him. "Clamp it, Threnody, or we'll all get pots-
and-pans! For you prenticing might be just to get away from
your mother, but for me it's my life."

Threnody went pale and did not say another word.

Rossamünd was grateful when he and his fellows were
finally ordered inside, making their solemn way over the
ledger-stones of long past heroes that paved the path to the
Hall of Pageants.

Within was a small oblong amphitheater. On three sides

tiered stalls of seats rose about a rectangular floor. Displayed grandly at the farther end of the amphitheater were the mighty antlers of the Herdebog Trought, each one lustrous black and as long as two tall men lying end-on-end. The monstrous trophy had been stood upright in a makeshift frame, the violent curves of both antlers spreading out over the stalls from one side of the hall to the other. Removed from the Trought's corpse with sectitheres, the horns had required a whole platoon of peoneers to bring them into the hall. Rossamünd had faced the Trought upon the road and seen its great size firsthand, but the dimensions of its antlers astounded him. The rancid musk of the monster was in them, tainting the air thickly, and he could see the damage from Threnody's or Sebastipole's shooting: an obvious pale gouge in the glossy black velvet. The strong smell brought up unwelcome confusions. He wondered sadly how long the creature had walked the world before the ambitions of men had interrupted its ancient existence.

Before the antlers were two chairs and a small desk arrayed with odd-looking tools.

The Hall of Pageants was filled to standing room, everyone decked in their best and cleanest. The greater ranks sat in the lowest, most padded and plush pews. At the very back on the highest, farthest, least comfortable benches, the prentices took their place. Troubardiers stood along the wall partly silhouetted against the long, thin windows that showed the last blood-orange glow of sunset against a turbid cloud bank rolling north in a close, blue sky.

"Stand fast!" came the cry, and the room stood to attention, hats off indoors and respectfully in hand. The Lamplighter-Marshal and the Master-of-Clerks and all those of eminence filed from some hidden ingress and took their easy seats in the frontmost rows. They sat and the rest of the room followed. The baritone buzz of quiet eagerness resumed till two men stepped on to the floor and strode conspicuously to the chairs.

Quiet reigned again.

Bemused, Rossamünd knew the first man to be Nullifus Drawk, skold and punctographist. The other was Sebastipole.

Both men bowed to the Lamplighter-Marshal and the senior officers.

Rossamünd could not imagine the leer and lamplighter's agent as the stripe of person who would actually want a monster-blood tattoo. It shocked him to see Sebastipole standing before his comrades calmly rolling up his shirt's white sleeve, waiting to be marked. Rossamünd thought he glimpsed at least one other cruorpunxis showing from under the rolled cloth.

As Sebastipole sat, Nullifus Drawk addressed the room, crying, "Officers, lighters, foot soldiers, clerks! It has been decided that Josclin and Sebastipole do share the distinction of slaying the mighty Herdebog Trought, that the falseman's aim did play its part as much as the scourge's potives. Yet as our brother Josclin is lying broken but well mending in the infirmary, it will be, as you can see, our goodly agent Sebastipole who will gain his prize tonight."

Nullifus Drawk took up a guillion needle and a small disc-headed orbis. Dipping the point of the guillion into a beaker of the Trought's cruor, he referred to a small notebook that lay open on the table and found his place on Sebastipole's bare arm. There he began to gently yet rapidly strike the broad, blunt end of the needle, *tap tap tap*. The hall was profoundly silent as each observer savored the marking of yet another victory over the monstrous foe.

Fixated yet appalled, Rossamünd was convinced that Sebastipole was not enjoying this spectacle. He was certain that, as when he put on his sthenicon, the leer found the puncting distasteful. Yet truly, disappointingly, Rossamünd knew it could not be so. "Like chasing after Phoebë," Verline would have said—wishing after impossible things: a leer's *job* was to seek, to find and, inevitably, to join in the killing of monsters. Could he be what Rossamünd considered a good man and still do this? Could a man be wrong for doing what he thought was right?

Threnody showed sympathy neither for the monster nor the men. By his other side his six watch-mates gingered their bandages beneath their coats, impatient for the punxis to be healed and tattoos ready to show away.

Tap tap tap. Drawk hammered lightly with his guillion, dipping frequently into the cruor dabbing at the stippled place on Sebastipole's arm with thick pledgets. The leer sat stiff and still, never flinching. For a week or two the mark would be invisible other than a suppurating scab, which would finally slough off and reveal the craftily formed image.

NULLIFUS DRAWK

And so they all watched till the honor was done, then gave a rousing cheer.

Stepping regular at the rear of the file, Rossamünd was grateful to leave the closeness of the Hall of Pageants, which was almost toxic with the exhalations of a crowd and the heavy musk of monster. Breathing deeply of the clean frosty night, he resolved never to see another puncting as long as his days had span.

Dismissed, Rossamünd hurried with the other prentices past the Dead Patch, some of them distracted by a collection of lighters, pediteers and laborers gathering around a tree by the lamp at the top of the Postern Stair.

Threnody pulled at his arm, their earlier conflict clearly forgotten. "Come," she said as she dragged him toward the inquisitive group.

Rossamünd resisted. "It'll be douse-lamps any minute. We have to go to our cells."

"By the dove's wings! Something interesting in this regulation-strangled den of boredom and you want to go night-nights?" She yanked at his sleeve and pulled him over to the tree. This trunk was a common place for public messages to be fixed, and against the tatters of older bills, rotten and moldy and mostly illegible, a large new bill had been posted. Taking the risk of being late, Rossamünd squeezed between the lampsmen and pediteers and their muttered complaints and stood with Threnody before the proclamation. It read:

NOTICE TO THE PEOPLE

Generous Prizes offered to ALL

TERATOLOGISTS

of Fine Repute & Sturdy Thew
to Aid in the REPELLING *of an*

ONSLAUGHT *of*

NICKERS

along the rightful lanes of
HIS MOST SERENE HIGHNESS' HIGHROAD
THE CONDUIT VERMIS

Applications to be made to the Marshal of Lamplighters
at the Imperial Fortress WINSTERMILL MANSE
or with the Most Excellent Peers & Civil Masters of the
habitations of the IDLEWILD

Satisfaction Guaranteed or WRITS *of the* COURSE *will be w'held*

Printed by Three-Gutter P.º Old Box L¹, Silesti-bole

"Elsegood brought this' un up from the Nook," said Assimus to his colleague and the world in general. "Bills just like this here one are all about the Sulk End and the Idlewild, he says, even down in Winstermill and maybe over the Gizzard in Brandenbrass and Fayelillian and even down in Doggenbrass."

"Aye," coughed an old corporal-of-musketeers, "inviting all manner of violent, adventurous foringers to the manse— to *our* home." The man looked the type to consider anyone not from Winstermill a "foringer."

"There's another one of these just been handed about the officers' mess," growled a haubardier. "*We* can handle the baskets. Don't need no outside hesistance, thanks all the same. The Marshal'll keep it all in hand."

"So ye say, Turbidius," countered the corporal, "but ye have to give that it's been a cram-full of theroscades un-checked these last couple o' years, particularly this year, and most particularly this winter. The Marshal ain't kept that all in hand—it be his name on the bill, bain't it? He's the one admitting to needing help."

Assimus ground his teeth. "And if *ye* was buried under a mountain of paper and chits such as our Lamplighter-Marshal be these few years, then I beg to suggest ye might be needing some help too!"

Rossamünd was, more than anything, boggled at the idea of the manse full of teratologists in all their weird gaudery. As people moved on to their business, a notion dawned on him. *Maybe Europe will be coming?* Reading the bill closely, he did not doubt that her "thew" would be sturdy enough, though he wondered if her "repute" might be fine enough. She would have been finished in Sinster by now, surely. The thought of her returning into his life made Rossamünd feel strange. He was apprehensive yet oddly hopeful.

"I don't know why the Emperor don't send us some more lighters from them kinder highroads like what's down in the Patricine—like the Conduit Axium or the Bridle," continued the corporal.

"Aye, or reinforce us with a battalion o' musketeers or such," some other voice put in. "He's got more'n enough to spare with all his armies up in the Seat and down in the Alternats."

"Aye, well, the Emperor's too busy using them same musketeers to fight with our hereward neighbors and has none to spare us in our troubles."

Rossamünd had some notion of the wars being fought to the west of the Empire with the princes of Sebastian and the landgraves of Stanislaus and Wencleslaus. This was an age-old struggle with the sedorner-kings that lived just beyond the grasp of the Haacobin Dynasty, accused of traffic with the monsters and worthy of annihilation. Centuries had gone and still these realms had refused to be subdued.

"Ye'd think our most Serene Highness might reckon it more important to fight the nickers nigh on his doorstep," that other voice put in.

"Aye, and ye'd think it wouldn't be much use conquerin' some other folks for loving the nickers when your own home is overrun with 'em!" the corporal concluded. "Don't he know how tough we've got it?"

With a corporate grumble of agreement people retired for the night.

"Listen to them mew about how hard it has been! What do they know?" Threnody growled as the crowd thinned. "My sisters have been stretched to exhaustion for years defending the people. These grot-headed lightermen don't know to recognize an ally when they've got one!"

Close by a sparrow flitted through the dark from one withered conifer to the next, disappearing into the foliage to twitter from its covert. With a last sharp tweet, it burst out and dashed away, followed by its mate, going southeast up across the roofs of the Low Gutter to disappear over the wall.

"Those things are uncommonly active of a nighttime," Threnody remarked. "Maybe they're watchers for the Duke of Sparrows . . ."

Rossamünd started. *How does she know of the Duke of Sparrows?* He turned to stare where the bird had flown to hide his surprise. Were they truly being watched? "How can you know that?" he asked.

"I have heard Dolours say an urchin-lord dwells in the Sparrow Downs," the girl said smugly, clearly pleased to get a reaction out of him. "The Duke of Sparrows, who she says watches over things and keeps other bogles at bay."

"What would the Duke of Sparrows have to watch in here?" Rossamünd marveled aloud, his sense of the lay of things shifting profoundly.

"Who can know?" Threnody replied dismissively. "We

can't even be certain such a creature exists. Oh, never-you-mind, lamp boy. Dolours is often quietly telling me things like that: enough to make some people cry *Sedorner!*" She finished with an untoward shout.

Rossamünd looked about in fright.

"But I'm not one of those mindless folk," Threnody concluded, "whatever Mother might insist."

"Is that why Dolours did not kill the Trought?" Rossamünd said in the smallest whisper.

With a start, Threnody stared at him. "What do you mean, lamp boy?" she demanded.

"I—I would have reckoned she could slay it with one thought, but she just seemed to drive it away—"

"How would *you* know what the Lady Dolours can and can't do?" Threnody stood tall and arrogant.

"Well—I—"

"Bookchild! Vey!" demanded Benedict from the step of the Sally. "Inside at the double! Get to confinations afore the lamplighter-sergeant sees you!"

I hope the Duke of Sparrows does *exist,* thought Rossamünd as he obeyed the under-sergeant. The notion of a benevolent monster-lord out there seeking to help humans and not harm them was almost too good to be possible.

13

AN UNANSWERED QUESTION

caladines also aleteins, solitarines or just solitaires; calendars who travel long and far from their clave spreading the work of good-doing and protection for the undermonied. The most fanatical of their sisters, caladines are typically the most colorfully mottled and strangely clothed of the calendars, wearing elaborate dandicombs of horns or hevenhulls (inordinately high thrice-highs) or henins and so on. They too will mark themselves with outlandish spoors often imitating the patterns of the more unusual creatures that their wide-faring ways may have brought onto their path.

B Y the new week all manner of teratologists began to fetch up at Winstermill, braving the unfriendly traveling weather for the prospect of reward—an Imperial declaration *always* held the promise of sous at the end. There were skolds and scourges, fulgars and wits, pistoleers and gangs of filibusters and other pugnators. Some appeared alone, others brought their factotums, and a few swaggerers were served by a whole staff of cogs—clerks and secretaries and other fiddlers of details. There came too the learned folk: habilists and natural philosophers, with their pensive expressions and chests of books. Even peltrymen—trappers and fur traders—answered the call. Bloodless and severe, they arrived from all the wooded nooks, lured from their own perilous labors by the lucrative promises. Every one of these opportunists and sell-swords would come there by foot, by post-lentum, by hired caboose, by private carriage, and stay for a moment and no more than a night, just long enough to gain a precious Writ of the Course. This Imperial document was a guarantee of payment that gave the bearer the right to claim head-money for the slaughter of bogles.

With all these came the usual motley crowd of hucilluctors, fabulists, cantebanks and clowns, pollcarries, brocanders selling their secondhand proofing, even wandering punctographists. Peregrinating, posturing upstarts were coming and going and milling about the manse, some foolishly camping near the foot of the fortress on the drier parts of the Harrowmath. More a nuisance than a novelty, they soon found themselves firmly encouraged to shuffle on to other places.

Yet it was among the teratologists, of course, that Rossamünd discovered the most unusual folk of all. Once in a while there arrived a person dressed in the likeness of an animal or bird, or monster even; and wherever these animal-costumed folk went and whatever they did, they went and did in dance. He recognized something of their prancings in the two calendars who had fought in the Briarywood. At limes, between fodicar drill and evolutions, a pair of these slowly spinning, skipping teratologists danced through the gates on foot, costumed as cruel blackbirds.

"What are they, Threnody?" Rossamünd stared at these, fascinated.

She looked at him as if he were the dumbest boy on watch. "Sagaars, of course!" she answered contemptuously.

Rossamünd stayed dumb.

Threnody narrowed her eyes and wagged her head. "With all those pamphlets you read one would think you'd be sharper, lamp boy," she continued with a huff. "Sagaars live to be dancing all the day long—some even try it in their sleep—and while they dance they kill the nickers with venomous theromoirs. Several serve my mother and the Right."

"Like Pannette and Pandomë?"

Threnody hesitated, closing her eyes. "Yes," she whispered, "like Pannette and Pandomë."

As these pugnators pranced proud and upset much of the manse's rhythm, the little varying schedule of prentice life remained. So it went, day come and day go, till Rossamünd was sure the whole of the east must be squeezed full with the monster-wrecking bravoes. As opportunity allowed, he would carefully and keenly review the arrivals, hoping—daring not to admit he hoped—to spy a flash of a deep scarlet frock coat with flaring hems. He could not rightly say why he was so keen to see Europe: he had known her only for the short side of a week, and she was the epitome of deeds he found very hard to reconcile. Regardless, he missed her. Yet with such frequency of arrivings and leavings, such a plenitude of lahzars, Europe, the Branden Rose, was never among them.

By the middle of the week something finally did break the prentices' routine. The morning was clear and achingly cold; the cerulean sky flat, brilliant, puffed all over with clean white fists of cloud rushed northwest by a whipping wind that was bringing fouler weather with it. The prentices were out and swinging their fodicars about in a tidy and orderly manner, postilion horn-calls an irregular, intermittent music. Teratologists and their attendant gaggles had been steadily coming and going all day. Some would take a turn on the borders of the Grand Mead as they waited for connecting posts or the resolving of kinks of paperwork.

It was limes, and the prentices were formed up and formally sucking on their bitter lemon rinds and sipping tinctured small beer while Grindrod watched to make sure they swallowed it all. This would normally be the time that a quarto would be returning from lighting, had the prentice-watches not been suspended. Rossamünd was considering paying a call on Numps at middens when Benedict marched on to the ground.

The under-sergeant muttered for a moment with Grindrod, then summoned Rossamünd out of file, to the surprise of all the lantern-sticks. Benedict wore an odd expression—somewhere between bemusement and admiration—as he took the young prentice aside. "You have an eminent visitor, prentice-lighter, and have been granted the time to spend with them," he said officiously, adding in a friendly undertone, "and might I say you keep some odd and powerful company, lad."

"Who——" Yet before Rossamünd could finish asking he smelled a welcome, well-known perfume drift past. Heart pounding, he spun about. There, in all her healthy bloom, was Europe, the Branden Rose, the Duchess-in-waiting of Naimes, the one who had saved him from a foul end, the one he himself had rescued.

"Well hello, little man," she said in her silken voice, smiling, amused, maybe even happy to see him. "Still fumbling your way through, I see."

"Hello, Miss Europe." He could barely manage a hoarse wheeze. It was such a strange sensation to see her familiar face in these now familiar precincts. Her hair was pinned up but without the usual crow's-claw hair-tine; her deep scarlet frock coat was of another style, made from some kind of short-cropped hide——like the head of a new-barbered lighter——its glossy reds shifting and mottled. Over this she wore a short black pollern-coat with broad collars and sleeves of creamy-hued fur that was faintly spangled at its cuffs with darker spots. Her black boots were trimmed with fur, which made a fuzzy hem at the top of each boot and protruded between the buckles up the sides. This was Europe rugged against the cold.

Rossamünd did not know what to do with himself: some of him wanted to throw his arms about her in sheer delight.

EUROPE

The significant part—that part which governs in the end what we really do rather than what we wish we might—was afraid. So he just stood and stared. "You've come," he managed.

The fulgar raised an amused eyebrow. "So it would appear. I have come to knave myself to these kind lamplighters and the citizens of the Placidia Solitus, in so desperate straits they send their pleading bills all the way south to Sinster." Her face was straight but her voice amused. "What's a kind-winded girl to do when such plaintive notes are sung?" She was in finer fettle than of their last parting, rosy-cheeked with a shrewd twinkle in her eye. The surgeons of Sinster must have done their infamous work well. "Tell me, little man . . ." Europe leaned forward a little. "Why did you not write me? Did you not miss me?"

"I thought you would be too busy to read any letter of mine, Miss Europe," Rossamünd answered.

"Why, I do believe he blushes!" Europe laughed. "That young lady certainly watches us keenly," she said, shifting subjects. "She knows you?"

Rossamünd looked and saw Threnody standing alone on Evolution Green, the other prentices gone now, dismissed for readings. Her arms folded and her face shadowed under the brim of her thrice-high, she was clearly paying Europe and Rossamünd pointed attention.

"Aye, Miss Europe, that's Threnody. She's a prentice like me." Rossamünd attempted a small wave.

Threnody flushed, turned on her heel and marched away without a rearward look.

236

"A girl as a lighter—how intriguing. I think she might have set her heart on you, little man."

Rossamünd blushed deeper shades. "Hardly, miss! She's never happy with anything I say and spends most of her time either ignoring me or huffing and puffing and rolling her eyes. Besides which, she's older—"

Europe gave a loud peal of honest mirth. "My, my!"

At the start of the Cypress Walk, Threnody turned to the happy, incongruous sound, and Rossamünd was sure she glowered.

Touching the corners of her eyes, the fulgar asked with a smile still in her voice, "And how did she find her way here to vex you so?"

"She was a calendar before, but she has come here to get away from her mother."

Europe gave a wry smile. "I know how she feels," the fulgar murmured. "Mothers are best fled . . . Now come along, little man, I have been granted the rest of the day with you by your kindly Marshal. Let us get out of this cold." She handed him a small, beautifully wrapped parcel. "It is just as well I brought this trifle for you. Your neck is bluer than a wren's."

Within the gaudy, fashionably spotted package was a magenta-red scarf made with fine twine.

"It's tinctured sabine," the fulgar explained airily. "You can only get it from this one little fellow on the high-walks in Flint. It looks good on you—matches prettily with the harness."

Rossamünd was happily dumbfounded. Europe wanted to spend the day with him *and* she had given him a present. When they had last parted company she had not said a word in final farewell, nor even waved good-bye. Yet here she was seeking his company. He felt rather odd following the fulgar with a present under his arm. Heads turned as she led him down along the drive and through the coach yard: lentermen, postilions and yardsmen gazed, distracted, habitually disapproving of her trade but heartily admiring her face and grace.

"I have sent the landaulet back to Brandenbrass." She chatted easily, oblivious to the stir she was causing. "It was too much trouble to find both horse *and* driver at once. It will be a relief not to have to fuss about stabling and repairs and thrown shoes. Let another worry about that . . ."

She led him up a steep flight of stairs to the guest billets. Like a small wayhouse, it lacked a common room but had private rooms in its stead, and secluded dinner rooms as well as a lounge for guests to receive guests of their own. This last was Europe's destination, a small, warm apartment with comfortable chairs along each wall, thin windows looking out to the business of coach yard and Mead below. A well-fueled fire crackled in the friendliest of ways in the corner.

Summoning refreshments, the Branden Rose took off her pollern and sat on a long tandem chair, stretching out like a man, her back slouching, long legs crossed over at the ankles.

"So how *is* the life of a lamplighter turning for you?" she inquired complacently. "Still as adventurous as that pawky postman made it out to be?"

Perching himself on the edge of the settee adjacent to the reclining fulgar, Rossamünd put his hat beside him as his eyes roamed the room. "It has been mostly come and go and march and stop, Miss Europe, and very little time for reading or thinking. But in the last couple of weeks there have been two theroscades. I have also met a glimner called Mister Numps and delivered a pig's head to our surgeon for the Snooks."

Europe fixed him with her sharp hazel gaze. "Tell me of these monsters attacking."

Refreshments arrived in the hands of a bobbing porter and Europe ordered food for the two of them. As they waited Rossamünd recounted the two theroscades, starting with the horn-ed nickers assaulting the carriage and the deeds of the calendars. "That is when Threnody joined us."

"The girl lampsman who was so fascinated earlier?" Europe asked, oh so casually. "She is a *wit*?"

"Aye, and she's the daughter of the calendars' august."

"My. How very impressive. The Lady Vey's progeny is a wit, a calendar *and* a lamplighter?"

Rossamünd ignored the sarcasm. "You know of her mother?"

"We have had occasion to meet, yes." The fulgar raised her hand as if to say that was all she would tell.

Heeding this, Rossamünd pressed on with an account of the flight from the Herdebog Trought and Bellicos' death, still so large in his memory. His telling was briefer, more subdued.

Europe sat a little straighter. "It is a . . . difficult thing to lose one you know to the wickedness of some unworthy nickery basket," she said softly. "Do you wish you had become my factotum after all?"

"I've wished a lot of things since being here, Miss Europe," Rossamünd demurred, "but I am signed to serve as a lamplighter now and have been given the Emperor's Billion and all."

"So you choose to be stuck on one stretch of road for the rest of your days? What a waste."

The two of them looked at each other for a long moment until Rossamünd dropped his gaze. "I don't want a life of violence," he said.

"You're living one now!" the fulgar retorted. "I tell you, child, this life is nothing but violence—even if you do not seek it, others will bring it to you." She leaned forward and fixed him with a terrible eye. "Do not make the mistake, Rossamünd, of living easy behind the feats of others and all the while thinking yourself better for not joining the slaughter."

Cheeks burning from her rebuke, Rossamünd shrank back, confronted with how little he knew of this pugnacious woman.

"How can we not be violent when violence breeds in the very mud and makes monsters of us all?" Europe persisted. "Stay here and you will be fighting just as you have been, always fighting: if not with nickers then with men. What did you think a life of adventure was?" She smiled condescendingly. "It *is* a life of violence. Come with me, and at least your foe will be clear."

"Not *all* monsters are our enemies," Rossamünd insisted doggedly.

Europe regarded him with an unfathomable expression. "Truly?" she said eventually. "You might want to shift yourself to Cloudeslee if you insist on spouting talk like that. Sedorners get short shrift in the Emperor's countries."

"But what about that poor Misbegotten Schrewd? He was just simple, not wicked, yet you killed him all the same. And you wanted to slay Freckle when he had helped me. I could never join you in that!"

Europe sat back, her gaze dangerously glassy, a threat in her tone. "Next you'll be telling me those triply undone blightlings were right for killing my dear Licurius."

"No!" he said quickly, eyes wide with horror. "I would never say that!"

There was a strained silence.

Europe sipped at a glass of deep red toscanelle and looked away. "You are a small and ignorant urbanite; once you have lived and watched and been forced to such things as I have you will not be so simple-headed."

Rossamünd could not collect his thoughts sufficiently to answer. He was right but so was she, though he wished she was not. Mercifully they were interrupted by the arrival of meals.

For a time they ate and did not speak.

"Little man," Europe finally offered between bites, "tell me of this pig's head and that Snooks fellow, the surgeon."

"Oh, the Snooks is not the surgeon, that's Grotius Swill—"

Europe stopped eating. "Did you just say Swill? Honorius Ludius Grotius Swill?"

"Aye." The young prentice stopped his chewing too.

"Hmm. I have heard of the man," the fulgar said gravely. "He has an evil reputation in Later Sinster. What has he done to you?"

"Naught! I only took up the guts and head of a pig to him," Rossamünd explained, and told of the attic surgery and the books and the flayed skin. "What is his reputation?"

"I heard that the fellow was caught dabbling in the darker habilisms and had traffic with folks all but the most scurrilous butchers avoid. Rumor is a poor transmitter of truth, but it was said that the Soratchë were becoming increasingly curious about his exertions."

Rossamünd frowned at this revelation. "The who, miss?"

"The Soratchë: they are a loose confederacy of those do-good calendar-kind keen on foiling massacars."

"Is Swill a massacar, then?" Rossamünd gasped. "We should tell the Lamplighter-Marshal!"

Europe raised a calming hand. "There was much conjecture in Later Sinster, but nothing proved. I am sure your kindly old Earl has things well in view. In such a tight place as this fortress, genuinely nefarious deeds would be hard to hide."

Aye, but what if the fortress is not as tight as it should be? Rossamünd wondered. Even he could tell the manse was creeping to disarray in the failing grip of the overworked marshal-lighter, a punctilious clerk-master and men so stretched that there were none left to plug the breaches. Rossamünd shifted his thoughts. "Miss Europe?"

"Yes, little man?" the fulgar replied absently, taking out and chewing on a little rock salt.

"What was it like going to Sinster?" he asked. "What did you do there?"

Europe cocked her head and looked to him, a wry, energetic twinkle in her eye. "The journey was brief," she said. "I left High Vesting the same day as you; took a fast packet down to Flint—where the doughty crew discouraged a curious sea-nicker with their fine gunnery and well-aimed lambasts. Then a barge up the Ichabod and I was under the transmogrifer's catlin not more than two weeks after I first met you."

"You saw a sea-nicker, miss?" Rossamünd's imagination ran with the image of a ram firing its broadside at some enormous, marauding, eel-like thing with spines and needle teeth. He had never seen a sea-nicker or a kraulschwimmen, nor any such creature—not for real—just poorly executed etchings in his pamphlets.

"I actually saw very little of it but for a great amount of splashing and some distant screaming," the fulgar answered. "I was directed to the seating deck soon after it appeared. It was a close-run thing for a time, but the fast packet was truly that and we outran the beast in the end. A good thing, for I do not think I would have been much help had the thing won its way aboard us. Even if I had been at my best, the puddles and splashes on deck would have taken my arcs to places they were not intended."

"Did the surgeon mend you?" Rossamünd pressed.

"Yes, he did." Europe straightened, rubbing her arm as if it ached. "I feel greatly improved. He told me to keep to my treacle and it will be less likely for my organs to vaoriate in future as they did that night in the Brindleshaws." Bitterness returned briefly to her countenance.

"Vaoriate, miss?"

The horn of a post-lentum sounded, dulled by wall and window.

"Spasm," she said distractedly.

There was a hasty knock at the door. It opened and a porter put his head inside. "The post's ready, m'lady. Do ye need yer bags lumbered out?"

Europe nodded and handed him a chit so he might retrieve her luggage from a stowage closet below.

"Listen, Rossamünd, I am leaving on the last post today. I would sooner have you with me than not—your flair for a good treacle is hard to forgo. Yet as you say, you have taken the Emperor's Billion and a solemn oath on the day of joining. Imperial Service is not something that can be put on then off again like some ill-tailored jackcoat. If you proved faithless in this, then what trust could a girl put in you?" she said slowly, with deliberate calm. She stared at the floor, lips pressed thin. "However, I wonder if you young prentices should not first be schooled in the rotten core of the Empire you serve before being offered a shiny Emperor's Billion."

"A rotten core, Miss Europe?"

"Ask your Marshal, little man—he is more recently schooled in Imperial machinations than I. Such things I escaped a long time ago." She paced out of the room without a rearward glance.

Down in the foreparts of the coach yard, the Branden Rose mounted the lentum ready to depart for the Idlewild and the mysteries of the east. Standing on the highest step, she stared darkly for a time at the spandarion rumpling in the fitful wind that moved above the battlements, and at the house-watch that moved along them.

Below, waiting, Rossamünd watched her silently.

"I go to do my usual labors—find a nicker, kill a nicker," said Europe finally by way of farewell. "I may be wintering at the Brisking Cat on the highroad at the Sourspan Bridge. If you wish to write me, send to there and I shall get it either way."

"I will," the prentice answered. There was a pause. He wanted to say that he sometimes regretted not taking up her repeated offer of work, yet could not think how. Moreover, after his refusals such sentiments seemed a little late and a little foolish. Either way, he could never willingly accept a living made through a perpetual, thoughtless slaughter of bogles.

Europe peered at him knowingly.

"Do not be troubled, little man," she said finally. "The last word is yet to be said on your service: just because you begin along one way does not mean it will be your end. Go back inside, Rossamünd. I will wait for thee, if thou wouldst come with me. Go back to your lampsmen chums," she said as she entered the carriage. "And stay well clear of that Swill fellow." The lentum door was shut with an impatient bang by the splasher boy.

"Good-bye, Miss Europe," Rossamünd called to her.

With a brash hoot of its horn the post-lentum was whipped on and took the Branden Rose—still without a factotum—out of Winstermill. As suddenly as she had arrived, so she left.

Watching her depart, Rossamünd was caught in a collision of many emotions, but above them all he felt as if he had been left behind.

14

THE UNDERCROFT

The Skillions the southeastern corner of the Low Gutter in the fortress of Winstermill. It gains its somewhat derogatory name from the many small, wood-built single-story sheds, warehouses and work-stalls found there. These are a recent addition to this part of the Gutter, it previously being the site of a stately old building designated for multiple uses, including the growing of bloom and the making and storing of lanterns. This reputedly burned down in mysterious circumstances two generations ago, outside of any current occupant's memory.

THOUGH the menagerie of teratologists had begun to move into the Idlewild, disturbing reports continued to arrive at Winstermill. One told of the cothouse of Dovecote Bolt east of the Tumblesloe Heap that had lost three lamp-watchmen to an unseen ünterman. Another told of a small band of nickers having the audacity to attack Cripplebolt near the farthest end of the Wormway, destroying lamps in the process. For three days—the report said—they maintained a kind of siege before relief arrived from the fortress of Haltmire.

The weather grew foul, either storming or foggy. Roads became nigh impassable. With the continued monstrous threat to the Wormway, the regular merchants from the south became reluctant to deliver. Only paying triple or quadruple the fair price for the essentials seemed to make them willing to come up from Silvernook and High Vesting. Informed by the Master-of-Clerks that the coffers could ill afford such prices, the Lamplighter-Marshal was forced to introduce restrictions to the diet and habits of the manse. Starting with the prentices, the fortress had been on short commons for the whole week. Rumors abounded of the clerks getting better fare than the lighters, of certain well-to-do officers using private resources to purchase delicacies for themselves but not share them about.

Worse yet, the lighters discovered during a wet and dismal pageant-of-arms that their customary vigil-trip was canceled. The prentices were in foul spirits by the time they were dismissed to loiter about the manse with little to occupy themselves. "Who does the Marshal think he is, making us miss our stingos!" some of them grumbled. Small arguments broke out between boys harboring worthless grudges. Other prentices bickered over their high-stakes card games of lesquin and punt-royale, and cell row and mess hall became unbearable. Rossamünd sat on an easy chair in the corner of the mess hall, regretting he had not gone with Europe. He had been reading and rereading the same line in an already well-read pamphlet while beside him a semantic spat between Smellgrove and a stocky prentice by the name of Hapfauf revolved endlessly. To Rossamünd's surprise Threnody sought him out and suggested they take a walk outside despite the inclement weather. He took only a little convincing to go. He rugged his neck with the scarf that Europe had given him and followed, Arabis giving him a sly wink as he exited.

Out into the biting squall they bravely ventured, clutching their regular-issue oiled pallmains tightly about, heads bowed against the sleet, ducking involuntarily at the mighty cracks of thunder that snapped above the Harrowmath. Having never owned a hat till he had left the foundlingery, Rossamünd found them an absolute boon for keeping rain off the face. He could endure the foulest weather if his dial was not being splashed and pelted with water.

"Who *was* that woman yesterday?" Threnody had found a small garden lean-to by the vegetable patch and they were at least now out of the rain. "Was it truly the Branden Rose? It certainly looked like it was. How do *you* know her?"

"Aye, it was. She and I met on my way here." It seemed a too-simple explanation. He wriggled uneasily, trying to get comfortable atop a rather smelly sack that was digging into his buttocks and dampening the seat of his longshanks.

"But how did someone like *you* meet someone like *her?*"

"Well," he said slowly, aware of how foolish he might sound, "the truth is that she found me hiding in a boxthorn on the side of the Vestiweg."

"What in the Sundergird were you doing there? Hardly anyone travels that way—at least not anyone in their right minds. It's just a supply road for the Spindle."

He told Threnody the story of his journey, beginning with

the day Sebastipole had come to select him. As he told it he was struck by the extraordinary nature of that adventure—had he really done all those things and survived those dangers?

She leaned in close as he told his story, never interrupting, and when he had finished, she stretched and let out a sigh. "Who'd have thought it, lamp boy? A stick like you fighting pirate captains and, what did you call them? Grinnlings? And all the while that amazing woman is feeding you whortleberries and letting you make her treacle?" Threnody's face was alight with a deep, previously hidden enthusiasm. "I always have to make my *own* treacle. Mother has drummed into me that you should always make your own—that way you know what is in it and that it will work. But, oh! Tell me, what does a whortleberry taste like?"

Rossamünd opened his mouth to answer but the girl plowed on.

"I tell you, if I hadn't seen the Branden Rose talking to you I wouldn't believe a jot of your impossible story." She hesitated. "Is this all really the truth?"

"Of *course* it's the truth. She wants me to become her factotum!"

"*You!*"Threnody barked an incredulous laugh.

He scowled, wanting to say several things at once but saying nothing at all.

For a few moments they sat in silence together.

Threnody took out a vial of sticky red liquid. About to take a draught from it, she noticed Rossamünd's scrutiny and said testily, "What do you goggle at, lamp boy? It's just

ROSSAMÜND

Friscan's wead. Have you never seen a girl drink her alembants before?"

Rossamünd gave a wordless splutter and quickly looked out to the sodden view.

"I should have been a fulgar." Threnody spoke softly after she had secreted the vial. "They only need two treacles; did you know that? I have cartloads of potives to take. Wits need so many different treacles and alembants at so many different times it's a wonder we do anything else at all. If anyone needs a factotum, it's a wit." She glowered at the wintry garden patch, and Rossamünd wondered what he was meant to say in reply. He had only rarely seen her take a sip of her many draughts: a far greater variety of red and blue and black liquors, taken far more frequently than Europe's.

"It does seem somewhat unfair . . . ," he offered into her angry silence.

"*And* she gets to keep her hair."

"Well, you have kept your hair," Rossamünd remarked cautiously.

Threnody looked at him acidly, as if he had made a foul and tactless jest, then out at the saturated roofs of the Low Gutter. Her expression was unfathomable. "Well, yes." She fiddled absently with a raven curl. "I have . . ."

Rossamünd was beginning to regret coming out with her. He decided to try a different tack. "I've met a man called Mister Numps—"

Threnody cut him off before he could finish his sentence.

"Of course, Mother does not think the Branden Rose is much good at all. In fact, she very much dislikes her."

It was best to remain silent.

"But really, she and my mother have a lot in common."

Rossamünd waited. He could not fathom what these two women might share.

"They were at the sequestury in Fontrevault together when they were my age. The Branden Rose was set to be a calendar, you know, except that she was expelled. I grew up hearing all about her: about the scores of men that pursued her; about how she loves herself most of all. Mother says she is an embarrassment to her state, her mother and her entire lineage, that if Mother had such a proud heritage she would never carry on so." Threnody paused. "The Branden Rose was the reason I so wanted to be a fulgar," she murmured, looking sadly at her elegantly shod feet.

Between these revelations of Europe's mysterious past and Threnody's twists of mood, Rossamünd could think of nothing to say. He looked dumbly out the open front of the lean-to to the dripping garden. A damp sparrow, all puffed and ruffled, was sitting atop a bare stake sunk deep in the moldy loam. It regarded him with definite, unsettling wisdom, as if it knew only too well the trials of being a boy making sense of a girl.

"So this Mister Numps is a glimner living in the Low Gutter," Rossamünd tried again. "I'm going there this afternoon. You could come if you want." He immediately regretted the invitation.

Fortunately Threnody did not take him up on it, but stood and strode quickly to the doorway, tossing her hair over her shoulder. "Have you even been listening to me at all?" she demanded. "You would have to be the rudest, most ignorant boy I know!" And with that she left him.

Rossamünd blinked hard, frowned, took a deep breath. Verline had been much easier and a thousand times more pleasant to be with than these bizarre, belligerent women. Rossamünd might live till he was a thousand and still come no closer to understanding them. The sparrow chirped cheekily and left with a whir of wings. The young prentice could have sworn it winked at him before it vanished.

Middens was a desultory affair. No one seemed to know why or when, but the Snooks had mysteriously departed Winstermill, and the new culinare—hired particularly by the Master-of-Clerks—did not possess the talent to make strict rations appetizing. The food was plain, the smells were unsavory and the company was decidedly unhappy. While Threnody and Rossamünd had been outside, Smellgrove and Hapfauf's disagreement had ended in blows, and with other boys taking sides, half the prentices had earned themselves pots-and-pans. Now one side of the hall was not speaking to the other side.

Threnody ignored Rossamünd utterly.

As soon as he could, Rossamünd took up his saluman-ticum and made his way down to the Low Gutter to see Numps. After watching the man make his special seltzer he was hoping he might learn a chemical trick or two from the glimner today. He was cold and damp when he arrived but, once safe within the lantern store, he shook off his pallmain and left it and his thrice-high on a hook by the door to drip themselves dry. He was thankful to have his new scarf. One of the detractions of seltzer light was that it gave no heat, and consequently the store was often too cold.

"Hello, Mister Rossamünd," the glimner chuckled. "Chill's biting my feet today." He lifted his legs to show spatterdashes buckled about his shins, his bare soles poking a little from the bottom. Numps waggled his toes on his healing foot. "Numps' frosty feet are bitten with the cold, but Mister Doctor Crispus says I can use them again."

Rossamünd grinned. "Afternoon, Mister Numps. Another day for furbishing the lantern-lights?"

"Ahhh." Numps touched his handsome nose and chuckled again. He cupped his hand about his mouth and whispered loudly to no one particular, "I've got one on Mister Rossamünd. He doesn't know it's not to be light-cleaning today, does he?"

For a moment Rossamünd thought the glimner was actually talking to some third person. "What will we do today if we don't clean?" he asked.

The glimner just gave that merry little chortle in answer and stood. Wrapping himself in old oiled canvas and secreting a bright-limn and a small, plump satchel beneath it, Numps made to exit.

"Come along, Mister Rossamünd," he said softly and

stepped outside, rain swirling in from without. Putting his own dripping pallmain and hat back on, Rossamünd followed, thoughts alight with puzzled wonder.

Producing the bright-limn to guide them, Numps took a left turn by the lantern store down through a riddle of narrow alleys, another left, then a right and along an ill-cobbled lane with a trickling drain that sneaked between the fortress wall and the black planking of a great storehouse. Beneath the high eaves of the store, it was more like a tunnel, and so cramped they were forced to walk sideways. Hammering rain found its way through splits and cracks to dribble from above. Rats and other nervous skitterers stared from time-gathered detritus or scurried before them, disappearing down unexpected gaps and grilles in the stonework on either side. While they went, Numps gave sweet voice to brief nonsense songs about fish and frogs at a tea party, men wooing milkmaids with whortleberry jam and some old general with a wooden leg and no army.

Creeping carefully, taking heed not to trip on the litter of planks, broken lamps, musket stocks, various tins and pots half-filled with stagnant water or worse, wire spools, wire knots, broken bottles and even a pile of unidentifiable bones, Rossamünd stayed behind the glimner. *Where is this place?* he marveled, stepping over the remains of an older foundation, some agglomeration of brick and stone and cement. They were clearly in a forgotten precinct of Winstermill.

The tunnel-like lane ended abruptly, depositing them in a small, remote square where two other cramped lanes and their drains joined and gurgled down a large, sunken grate. As clear of debris as the lane was full, the square was surrounded on three sides by stone foundations and wooden walls and on the fourth by the works of Winstermill's battlements. Weakly illuminated through a drizzling opening between roof and wall, it felt as removed from the bustle of the fortress as any haunted, lonely spot out in the wilds. Wind and rain wailed on high, lightning crashed, but down here it was still; the bubbling waters and Numps' lilt the only tunes.

Pausing, Numps put a finger to his mouth, indicating quiet. They could have talked at volume for all anyone would have heard. Bemused, Rossamünd nevertheless nodded, and clamped his lips together for emphasis. Giving him the lantern, Numps crouched by the sunken grate and reached down between its squared bars, grabbing at something on their underside. There was a slight clank and the grate sprang up slightly, splitting in two like a gate. It was an entrance. Stone stairs led down an arched tunnel into damp warmth and darkness. The water of the drains did not pour directly into the hole revealed, but was caught in a gutter about the rim and channeled into a pipe at one corner. The dark below smelled faintly familiar; the sweet salt of seltzer blended with that almost-but-not-quite neutral odor of high humidity.

Without hesitation, Numps went down, encouraging Rossamünd to follow, pointing downward. Rossamünd squeezed past and Numps closed the grate again and came after. "Down, down, down we go," the glimner enthused, giving Rossamund a gentle nudge.

As they went the din of wild weather above was dulled almost to silence. The prentice could hear drops dripping steadily below, and occasional soft mechanical squeaks as well echoing up the stone stairway. This stair went deeper than Rossamünd expected, down into what must have been part of the structures of old Winstreslewe, the ancient bastion founded in Dido's time upon whose ruined piles Winstermill had been raised.

The stair ended in a low undercroft of indeterminate size, its slate floor crowded with square columns and arches of brick. Packed between each pillar were large, squat, square vats of blackened wood. Some vats shone clean light to the low ceiling, others a verdant grassy green and yet others showed little light at all. Together they lit the vast subfoundational space with soft effulgence like an early, misty morning. The warmth here was peculiar: the close air tepid and clinging. A tinkling music sounded in the dimness, made by the sporadic drizzle that formed in the humidity and dripped from the rough ceiling into the vats.

"What is this place?" Rossamünd breathed, swinging the bright-limn about to shine on Numps' face.

The glimner grinned in lopsided delight. "This is where the bloom is made," he whispered. "Oh, where it used to be made long, long before old Numps became poor Numps. This old Numps and his old friend found these baths and we put some little bit of bloom from a broken lamp in and we kept it alive till it grew to fill one bath and then the other bath and then the other and then more baths still! I have kept them alive, all these times." Numps' smile became sentimental, even paternal. "They're my special friends—like you and Mister Sebastipole and Cinnamon. Look, go on—look inside." By the kindest pressure on Rossamünd's upper arm, the glimner encouraged the prentice to peer inside a vat. "But be careful not to let the light shine in too long, and stay quiet, 'cause they like it still and dark and peaceful."

The black wooden vats had a girth of roughly twice the width of Rossamünd's cot and, straining on his toes, the prentice could see that within was water or something akin to it, perhaps a little greener. In this water was row on row of trailing plant-like growths, long horizontal strands of a kind of submerged grass waving in its rippling bath.

Bloom! Rossamünd realized. *Native, unsprung, unprismed bloom!*

To most they would have been simply a plant; just some kind of dull, underwater weed; boring old bloom: but to the prentice it was wonderful to see it growing freely, long and wild, bushy and eagerly verdant. Puncheons of the stuff were sitting in most domiciles the land over, stumpy, pruned sprigs ready to put into a bright-limn when the old had died. Here it was closer to how it might be in its native dwelling, the littoral waters of southern mares.

Rossamünd stared for a long time, enjoying the deep echo of the drops, the faint trickling of the rippling water set in motion by some unseen agent, watching the elongated tendrils swaying, swaying, swaying in the green. It was a place of near-complete peace—a model of subterranean calm.

"This is wonderful . . . ," he breathed.

Numps beamed even as he took the bright-limn from Rossamünd's hand.

"Too much light," he explained, and sat down on a nest of hessian and hemp. "I come here and the bloom trickle-trickle-trickles to me and gives me sleep and kind noises."

They sat for a time, both silent in this hidden undercroft of bloom baths.

"How does the rippling in the tubs happen?" Rossamünd asked at last.

Numps stood, leaned into the vat, shone the light within and said, "By the flippers flapping, of course."

Rossamünd looked again and saw flat paddles waving slowly in the depths like the swimming feet of an idling duck. Numps took him farther into the undercroft, threading past many more baths than Rossamünd had first reckoned. In the midst of it all Numps halted and pointed with open palm and a self-satisfied expression to a large brassbound wooden contraption. It was a pull-box, a small kind of gastrine about the size of a limber. From its flywheel a series of wheels and belts drove all the modulating paddles that set the tub water to gentle motion, squeaking occasionally in their lazy to and fro. Rossamünd could see the convoluted connection of the belts all about the roof of the undercroft, one reaching down to the paddles of each vat.

"I feed it and muck it—and the bloom too, and keep it

all running myself. No one else will." Numps closed his eyes like a fellow foundling reciting verse in one of Master Pinsum's lessons at the foundlingery. "Sometimes I put a little of one of my friends into a great-lantern that's to go back out to the road, and these live and live and live much longer than the poor things they grow otherwise."

In anyone else, this claim would be discounted as pure boast, but not with Numps; not with such obvious proofs of his skill before them.

Rossamünd was powerfully impressed. "What do you feed the pull-box?"

"The cuttings and prunings and dead bits from the bloom," Numps returned matter-of-factly, though a self-satisfied grin ticked at the unscarred corner of his mouth.

"What do you do with the pull-muck?"

Grin growing, clearly proud of himself, the glimner answered, "Feed it to the bloom. They reckon it's the tastiest stuff they ever have tasted. They feed the pull, the pull feeds them—on and on and on and on."

"Why aren't these used in all the lamps all the time?"

"Oh, they have their own blooms up there," Numps replied, "in tubs not so old and leaky nor hard to get to. I always have to plug the cracks and gaps in this soggy wood." He patted the side of a bath tenderly. "Besides, the master-clerker and all his clerker-chums wouldn't like a thing like this. It's him who says where the bloom comes from nowadays."

Rossamünd stood and watched the entire mechanism in

silent admiration, just listening to the deep soothe of the trickling, rippling waters. "You'd have to be the best seltzer-man ever there was, Mister Numps!" he whispered.

"Ahh, not poor limpling-headed Numps," the glimner said bashfully, then grinned.

They sat then, side by side in the soporific warmth, the glimner and the prentice, Numps humming, Rossamünd wishing heartily that he could come here again. Safe and warm and brimming with peace, it was simply the best place in the whole Half-Continent. In the soft darkness of the old forgotten bloom baths, Rossamünd slept.

15

THE WAY LEAST WENT

moss-light also known as a limnulin or limulight; this is a small, pocketable device, a simple biologue consisting of a lidded box holding a clump of naturally phosphorescent mosslike lichens (either funkelmoos or micareen), set on a thick bed of nutrient to keep it alive. This nutrient bed can be reinvigorated with drops of liquid similar to seltzer. The light provided by a limnulin is not bright, but can give you enough to see your way right on a dark night, and is diffuse enough not to attract immediate attention.

WITH a panicked, convulsing suck of breath, Rossamünd awoke. He sat up in disoriented fright, looking every way with hasty, sightless alarm as the swilling of water trickled all about. Then easy realization brought peace: he was still in the undercroft, with the bloom baths.

Numps stirred more peaceably, saying sleepily, "Oh, oh, wake up, sleepyheads, no time for dozing."

"What's the o'clock?" Rossamünd asked loudly, still a little mizzled.

Numps scratched his head. "Uh, sorry, Mister Rossamünd, I'm a glimner, not a night-clerk."

Rossamünd got to his feet. "It feels late," he said, and ran up the steps to observe the sky through the grate. With profound consternation he discovered that the clear black dome of night hung above. He could not quite believe it. His heart skipping several beats, he opened the grate and clambered up to the square to get a better view. Maudlin green was riding high in the dark. It was desperately, impossibly late. Douse-lanterns had come and was long gone and all prentices should be in their cells asleep. No one was permitted to roam the grounds at night, especially not some lowly lantern-stick. A quick trot to the jakes across the hall was all a prentice was allowed during the night-watches. To be at large now was the worst breach, punishable by an afternoon in the pillory by the Feuterer's Cottage.

Rossamünd leaped back down the steps, three at a time, utterly flustered, dreading the worst punishments. "I'm late. I'm locked out. Frogs and toads, Mister Numps! How am I to get back into my cell?"

Numps was still sitting as the prentice had left him.

"I have to go right now, Mister Numps." Rossamünd's voice quavered with anxiety. "It's past douse-lanterns . . . Oh, I'm in *so* much trouble . . ."

"Oh—oh—um, oh dear—there's better ways home again." Numps nodded. "Numps' hiding-hole goes more places than just here." With that he stood and jogged off through the baths.

Rossamünd followed.

Through the convoluted clearances between the battery

of baths they hastened. In the farthest corner of the under-croft was a hole in the wall, round like a drain. Upon a hook at the apex of the drain's arch hung a bright-limn with the healthiest looking bloom Rossamünd had ever seen glowing bright in its near-clear seltzer. Beyond the throw of clean light the cavity of the drain was exquisitely black and blank and mysterious. Numps took the bright-limn off its stay and, with a solemn nod to Rossamünd and a soft "shh," entered the round gap.

Close behind, the prentice saw that they were in a tunnel, most probably an ancient sewer pipe. On left and right down the length of the tunnel they passed the small dark mouths of lesser pipes beady with reflecting retinas and echoing with light patters and rodent squeaks. The gray-mousers that haunted the manse could grow happily fat down here.

In this moldy, claustrophobic place Rossamünd's sense of distance began to distort, and with it time. To him it felt that they had walked far enough to be somewhere out on the Harrowmath. Several times the tunnel kinked and branched till Rossamünd was disoriented and very glad that the glim-ner knew the way. Numps finally took a right turn and they began to descend. The new way was of greater diameter than the previous drain and took them down so sharply that Rossamünd was made to lean backward with the effort of climbing, scrabbling at the slimy bricks to prevent a slip.

Lifting the bright-limn high, Numps paused when the tunnel became level again. "We are right under the manse-house," the glimner said, looking up and ducking his head.

Looking to the immuring bricks just above, Rossamünd shrank a little at the thought of the great press of masonry, the tons of stone and hundreds of sleeping lighters and staff all on top of him. It was so deep not even the vermin ventured here.

Shouldn't we be going up? Rossamünd fretted.

Numps continued forward, and there, by an intersecting pipe, was a small door of corroding iron a few feet above the floor, reached by three large steps. He grinned at Rossamünd, his geniality made ghastly by the play of seltzer light on his scars. Rossamünd smiled back, alive to the immense trust the glimner was showing him, the secrets the man was revealing.

"Through here now, and up, up, up," Numps said softly. He produced a key pulled from somewhere on his person, unlocked the rusty door and shone the seltzer light through. Beyond was the landing of a tight stairway of near-failing timbers, rising into shadows of architectural gloom.

Another furtigrade!

Unlike the one reached through the kitchens, this was not lit at all.

How often does he come here? Rossamünd's whole sense of Winstermill shifted with the thought of the glimner wandering about beneath them as they labored, ate, even slept.

Numps stood by the door, waiting.

"Mister Numps?"

"I don't like to go up to the manse." The glimner's face was drawn and gray, his eyes animated with deep troubles.

"I won't go any farther—oh dear no; I don't like it in the manse . . . never have."

"Can I find my own way from here?" Rossamünd asked.

The glimner clucked his tongue. "Mister Rossamünd can indeed go himself."

"What more is ahead?" the prentice asked.

Numps looked to the furtigrade distractedly. "Oh—oh, more tunnels, more stairs: just go up—up—up—up—do not stop at any doors until the very top and turn the bolt and slide the door, down the passage and through the hole and you shall come out on to the lectury floor."

A start of panic knotted in Rossamünd's innards. "Are you sure?" he pressed.

Numps nodded emphatically. The glimner had led him a long and twisted way but now he must go ahead alone—to a place that might not lead anywhere. *I could be lost or found out late!—between the stone and the sty, as Fransitart would say. I found my way to Winstermill and I can do this too.*

Stepping onto the tiny landing, Rossamünd looked up. He could see only a few flights above, beyond which darkness brooded. He listened: he could hear nothing but his own workings beating, *lub-dub lub-dub*.

"You must go gently-gently," said the glimner. "Some others are up here too, all a-wandering. I hear them sometimes down here but they don't hear me. Oh no." He took something from his satchel and pressed it into Rossamünd's hands. "Here, Mister Rossamünd, take this; it's too dark up there." It was a small pewter box, like those in which pedi-teers carried their playing cards, but this had a thick leather strap attached and felt almost empty. The prentice did not know what to say.

"It's a moss-light," Numps explained. "Push——push at the top."

Rossamünd did as instructed. The top panel proved to be a lid that, when slid up, exposed a diffuse blue-green glow within. With a closer look he found the box was hollow with a glass top, and stuffed with a bizarre kind of plant, its tiny leaves radiant with that odd, natural effulgence like bloom.

"So you will find the way." Numps blessed Rossamünd with his crooked smile once more.

"Oh, thank you, Mister Numps." Rossamünd felt a small relief: at least he would see his way—even if he was not certain *where* that way would lead him.

"Go, go." Numps bobbed his head bashfully. "Up up to the top, slide the door, through the hole and off to bed just like me. Bye, bye . . ." Mumbling, he shuffled back along the reverse of his path.

By the eerie nimbus-light of Numps' gift, Rossamünd began to climb the furtigrade. It was steep, of course, and so very cramped he was obliged to climb slowly. Heeding the warning that the glimner had given of others above, he worked hard to make his footfalls light and prevent the flimsy stair from creaking. Three flights and still the furti-grade went on. At the fourth the looming shadows resolved themselves into a doorway, but the stair went on. *No stop-*

ping at any doors, Mister Numps said. Rossamünd continued to climb. His ascent was soon foiled, however. Not more than another two flights higher he discovered to his great dismay that a part of the stair had collapsed, making a wreck of gray splinters that made the furtigrade impassable. He could go no farther. *What now?* His mind's cogs raced. *I'll try the door I saw below.*

Rossamünd crept down to this door, the glow of the moss-light muffled against his chest, and listened: nothing but drips and the rush of his heart. He dared a little more light and peered gingerly beyond the doorway. The floor of the space was a mirror of the ceiling, a broad shallow drain that formed a vaulted junction with three other tunnels. Forward or back he was lost, he figured, but back meant certain discovery and the pillory while forward at least held a chance of undetected return. *So forward it is . . .*

He had heard somewhere—probably from Master Fransitart—that when caught in a maze you should always go left and eventually you would win free. Taking a deep breath he went left. If this did not work he would simply return and choose again.

Rossamünd followed the leftward tunnel and it took him farther and farther from the junction, finally terminating in eight steps that led up to a brick wall. *A dead end!* But there, hammered into the mildewed bricks with corroded pegs of iron, was a crude ladder. Hanging the moss-light by its strap about his neck, the prentice scuttered up and pulled himself through into a deep tight valley in the masonry that smelled of century-settled dust and stillness. Brittle twig-weeds sprouted from any suggestion of a crack between floor and wall. How they managed to live at all down in this subterranean night he did not know.

Leftward was blocked by a wall, and so Rossamünd went right. In the meager moss-light, he thought he could discern what looked like the blank sockets of windows high in the walls above. Soon this architectural chasm ended bluntly in a redbrick barrier fronted by yet another furtigrade going up and going down. Up was closer to Winstermill, he reasoned, so he began to wearily climb again.

The night was never going to end!

I should never have come this way. I should have knocked on the Sally door . . . or even the front door.

Becoming used to this creeping dark, he took the ascent a little more confidently, but the stair sooned reached its end. At its summit he was confronted with a wall into which was sunk an oblong trap-hole, about his height and nearly an arm's-length deep. It was blocked by a stained panel of dark rusted iron fixed with a corroded handle and barely held shut by a sliding bar of wood and iron. Rossamünd tried it in hope, and the flaking metal resisted at first but then slid back with a loud crack. *Maybe this is the door Numps was thinking of . . .* He tugged, and the door did not shift. He shoved with hearty frustration, and in a small burst of rusting dust from its age-blackened hinges the portal bulged inward—just a little. Through this crack was a glimpse into blackness, and from it exhaled the foul odor of decay, so much like that far worse hint he had once detected in the hold of the *Hogshead.* In the bowels of the cromster it had been heavily masked with swine's lard, but here it was full and oppressively potent, smothering him in its dread stink.

A rever-man! he intuited, stepping away from the door. *Down here? But how?* He could not believe it.

There was a sound, some nondescript evidence of motion; a step, a shuffle—Rossamünd could not tell, but he knew something moved behind that stubborn-hinged door.

I must try another way! He reached for the handle of the panel to shut it.

Some misshapen thing lurched at the space from the black within. Pallid hands, blotched and scabbed, gripped door and post and wrenched powerfully. Metal groaned, wood buckled and the door-gap widened. A pale head thrust through, craning and twisting right, then left, its spasmodic breath coming in a quivering wheeze. Its toothy, lipless mouth seeped saliva, at which it sucked almost as often as it breathed. The abominable creature twisted about and fixed its callous attention on him, pinning him with its morbid fascination. With a white flash of dread he realized this was a gudgeon. Here truly was a *rever-man*—uncaged, unfettered, dreadfully free.

Rossamünd bit back a scream. His innards churned. His thoughts wailed. *A rever-man! A rever-man here in Winstermill!*

For a breath Rossamünd's mind was overthrown as he tottered back, struggling to fathom what he saw. Yet with the cold, radiating dread that cried *Run! Run!* in a tiny, terrified voice within came a wholly unexpected rage. Faced now with a rever-man, a blasphemously made-thing, uncaged and visible, Rossamünd's terror did not overcome him. His hand went instinctively to his salumanticum and found the Frazzard's powder.

The gudgeon shifted its grasp. Tiny little piggy eyes regarded him coldly—soulless, dead—as slowly, inexorably the panel-door was forced open. Large, furry, inhuman ears swiveled and twitched at either side of its long and bulging skull. Swathes of filthy bandages and even a rope were wrapped about its trunk, keeping its heaving chest and stitch-grafted abdomen together. What struck Rossamünd most was the utter absence of any threwd about the thing. *A threwdless monster: how could you ever tell it was coming?* Indeed, it was devoid of even a flicker of real vitality: a man-made thing, a dead thing. Yet its full and putrid reek, unmasked by swine's lard, was potent. The gudgeon opened its slavering mouth and a long tongue like a lizard's lolled obscenely, flicking in the dusty air. Even as Rossamünd stumbled backward onto the furtigrade and down the way he had come, the abomination stared with hungry curiosity as the crack between door and wall grew ineluctably wider.

"Hmm," it seethed, licking at the gap between it and the prentice, "yooouuu mmmake mmeee huuunnngreee . . ."

With one powerful spring, the made-monster flung itself through the gap, viper-quick, at Rossamünd, slamming into the balustrade as it made pursuit.

Tripping, nearly falling, Rossamünd blundered down the

stair. The gudgeon staggered and turned with a dry, rattling hiss. On the lower landing Rossamünd twisted and flung the potive at it as it pounced at him from on high. His aim was as true at a natural throw as it was off with a firelock. The Frazzard's powder burst against the creature's neck and shoulder with a flash of bluish sparks and a series of tight detonations that sounded like the popping of corks.

"Aaiieeee!" The creature hit the wooden steps with a crash and tumbled into Rossamünd as it fell. A thousand stars erupting across his senses, the prentice was crushed over and over between wooden step and rever-man. Together they toppled a whole other flight, then another, striking the banister rail on the lower landing hard, causing it to crack dangerously.

The gudgeon was on him in an instant, pressing him down, its whelming stench all about him, teeth snapping *clack! clack!* seeking to nip at exposed flesh: fingers, knees, cheeks. In white, blind terror Rossamünd heaved the abominable creature off and shoved it—almost threw it though it was twice his size—across the tiny landing. Free of its imprisoning bulk, he sprang up the stairs he had just descended so painfully, pointlessly crying, *"Help! Help!"*

"Ahhh! Yoouuu liiittle beeeast!" he heard it hiss behind him. The rever-man was fumbling about on hands and knees, its piggy little eyes burned out by the Frazzardian chemistry. The distinct peppery-salty smell of the spent potive spiced the close fug of the furtigrade. "I caaan stiiill heeeaaaarrrr yoouuu . . ."

The gudgeon shuffled toward Rossamünd and he turned to face it, scuttering up each step upon his bottom.

It made a strange cackling. "I could eeeat *yoouurrr* kiiind aaall the looong looong daayyy!" It sprang catlike at what it believed to be Rossamünd's position, and struck the banister three steps below the prentice with enough force to smash the rails to flinders, which toppled down into the darkness. Nothing could stop the gudgeon. It bounced off the ruined wood, its arm a spasming dead weight, the left shoulder dislocated and deformed by the blow—the vile creature so utterly ravening it was destroying itself to get to him. It pounced again.

Rossamünd kicked out with all the might his horror could muster—and missed. The unhallowed thing gripped his flailing leg and bit at his shin, a bite meant to tear away muscle. Its crooked teeth met proofed galliskins, cruelly pinching flesh against bone but failing to penetrate. Once again Rossamünd had been saved by the wonders of gauld. With a yelp, he lashed with his free leg, striking the putrid thing upon its face. The gudgeon must not have been well knit, for its jaw gave way with sickening ease under his boot-heel; teeth sprayed and clattered about the stair. The cobbled-together thing gurgled and shrieked and sought to grasp Rossamünd in a death grip. Kicking again, the prentice got his footing and bounded up the stairs.

Below, the gudgeon was hissing and sucking through its mangled mouth, struggling once again up the furtigrade

THE GUDGEON

seeking nothing but gory murder, utterly heedless of its broken parts.

Rossamünd extracted another salpert of Frazzard's powder. *Oh, for something more deadly!* Yet he did not dare use the loomblaze for fear it would cause the dry, dusty furtigrade to take fire, and start an unstoppable conflagration right within the foundations of the manse. He threw the potive hard on the step before the gudgeon, seeking to make a brief barrier, to give the abomination second thoughts. The potive popped and crackled as it erupted and sprayed the gudgeon again. With its cries of rage oddly flat and muffled in the squeeze of the dusty furtigrade, Rossamünd dashed up the stairs, pain jarring up his bitten shin.

The foul thing was staggering up after him—he could see it through the frame and rails—eyes fizzing, weeping gore, utterly ruined by two doses of Frazzard's powder, jaw a crooked mass, mouth dribbling unstoppably. There was something almost pathetic about this abominable creature with its terrible injuries, yet it did not heed its damage. With long, clumsy reaches of its arms, the gudgeon slapped its hands on a higher step, felt the way and pulled itself up, gaining pace. There was no escaping the thing. Rossamünd could only try to flee up the furtigrade and out into the unknown cavities of the vault above.

"Help!" he cried, a small pathetic sound in this claustrophobic fastness.

The gudgeon slunk around the landing below, starting up

the very stair he was upon. It jabbered at him incomprehensibly, trying to form vile taunts with its broken, dribbling maw.

"Help!" Rossamünd bellowed again. He knew it was hopeless, but sanguine hope kept him crying.

He set his feet on the creaking boards of the tiny landing by the wrenched door, giving himself a little space to fight from, and seized a caste of loomblaze from his salumanticum. He had to risk it or perish. Rossamünd watched the ill-gotten thing climb, and waited. Waited till it was close enough.

"Whhyyy-bbll-ssooo-blbb-ssstiiilll-blbl, littbblle-bbl-mooorsel-bbl," the horror drooled and, despite blindness, gathered itself to pounce.

With a tenorlike wail, Rossamünd leaped down the stairs and grappled the foul creature once more, hitting the banister rail as they collided, wrenching it with an ominous crack. The gudgeon tried to pound at him, but Rossamünd was in close, too close for its swings to be effective. It thumped at his shoulders, pushing him down beneath its wrath. He gagged and spat bile. Yet as it smothered him, the prentice gripped the gudgeon about its festering neck and shoved the caste of loomblaze down into the foul, broken mouth, right into its crop. The gudgeon tried to chew off his hand, its broken jaw doing little more than a gory flapping. It wrapped its tongue about Rossamünd's wrist and with groping, gripping hands sought to gouge at the prentice's face. Straining and twisting his head, Rossamünd wrenched himself loose and away, bringing his arm back sharply to chop at the creature's throat, where the frangible vial had lodged. At the second blow the gudgeon gave a convulsing, gargling shriek: a half-human, piglike squeal. Yellow-green gouts of light flared from its mouth and nostrils as the loomblaze erupted within its neck. It writhed and arched its back, still screaming as Rossamünd kicked it away and fumbled for safety on higher steps. He watched in horror as the burning rever-man toppled against the already weakened rail. It gave way and the beast plummeted through the thin gap about which the furtigrade wound, shattering the rail below; falling, colliding and falling again a score of times more than Rossamünd could follow, before abruptly halting, a small bright fire in the darkest depths below.

Laboring for breath, shin a torture, his mind's eye revisiting the horror over and over in a giddy spin, Rossamünd pulled himself away from the edge of the gap. He shook himself, stood, and on wobbling legs went as fast as he could down the furtigrade, terrified that some other revenant-beast might be waiting for him above. Far down the dangerously shuddering stair, deeper still, he could see the dying flicker of the loomblaze burning. The frame of the furtigrade began to crack and sag, the age-rotten wood not able to support such rough use. Back at the walled valley he leaped from the tottering stair and ran, legs still shaky, back the way he had come, finding the original four-way vault. Going left again he pushed on, listening always for sounds of pursuit, another caste of loomblaze ever ready in his grasp. So intent was he on knowing if he was followed he took little notice of the perpendicular twists and the turns, choosing left when he could, going either up or down with an instinct born of desperation. If he hit a dead end he would simply turn about and take the next left, eyes wide as wide could be, ears pricked for any wheezing shuffling of a gudgeon in pursuit.

Driven by the nauseating urgency to be free of this crowding, dusty labyrinth, Rossamünd pushed on through more and more cramped passages and buried, forgotten rooms. Stumbling dizzily several times, he had no notion of how long or how far he had come, but at some point the way became straighter and the architecture familiar. At the top of a solid flight of stone steps he stopped in front of a door with a very ordinary-looking handle in it, just like those on the doors of the manse. Excited, he tugged. The door resisted at first, but after a determined pull it opened with a clatter. The relief was powerful, hysterical. Rossamünd sprang out, all sense of decorum abandoned. *"Raise the alarm!"* he hollered. *"A rever-man! A rever-man!"*

And there, on the other side, he found himself staring directly at the shocked face of the Master-of-Clerks.

THE LAMPLIGHTER-MARSHAL

telltale(s) falseman retained by one of office or status to inform their employers of the veracity of others' statements or actions, to signal if fellow interlocuters are lying or dissembling or masking the truth in any other way. If they could afford to, most people of any prominence would employ telltales, but there simply are not enough falsemen to fill so many vacancies. This means that a leer can earn a truly handsome living as a telltale. Then there are those honorable few who do it simply because it is their job and responsibility. Despite this rarity, many of the prominent work hard to nullify the advantage a telltale will give, either by employing their own falseman, or having a palliatrix (a highly trained liar—even rarer than a falseman) attend in their stead.

R OSSAMÜND did not much like the Master-of-Clerks, but right then the officious fellow was an astoundingly welcome sight.

"Blight your eyes, boy!" the clerk-master almost shrieked, pale and breathing hard from the fright. "You were nigh on the end of me! Where have you come from? How did you get here? Where did you get that running gash upon your crown?"

"A rever-man below us, sir! A rever-man in the tunnels underneath!"

"A 'rever-man'? What do you mean?" the clerk-master snapped, recovering his composure and sitting again on his seat at the long table that dominated the room. The man was without his gorgeous wig, looking slightly ridiculous, his head bound with cloth and showing tufts of cropped wiry hair.

Rossamünd could not believe the man did not know what a rever-man was. "A revenant, sir! A gudgeon!"

"Nonsense, child! Utter fiddle-faddle!" The Master-of-Clerks flicked his hand in angry dismissal.

Laudibus Pile appeared as if from nowhere. "What is the trouble, sir?" he purred with his oily voice, his disturbing eyes narrow and calculating as he saw Rossamünd standing where he should never have been.

Looking about in a daze, Rossamünd began to realize he was actually in the Master-of-Clerks' private file. He had been here just once before. "Mister Pile!" he effused, unaware that he had just cut across his superior. "I fought a rever-man down in the tunnels of old Winstreslewe!"

"The boy has a wound to the head. He is delirious! He forgets himself! Send for Surgeon Swill," Podious Whympre seemed to demand of the air itself.

Rossamünd felt at his head. His hat was gone, lost somewhere in the horrid under-dark. His hand came away bloody. "I am not delirious." He frowned at the red. "I fought a gudgeon!" He could not understand the resistance, the lack of action.

"I do not know what you are jabbering about, child, but I would recommend you lower your volume and mend your manner," the Master-of-Clerks ordered with a dangerous look. "You are in thick enough without adding insubordination to your troubles!"

Feeling equal parts perplexity and fright, Rossamünd obeyed.

All the while Pile had been shrewdly examining the young prentice. He now bent to murmur into the Master-of-Clerks' ear.

Exposed, the prentice held the leer's gaze regardless. He had no lies to hide.

"I see," said Whympre at the leer's secret words. "Well, young prentice, show us this—this *rever-man*." He spoke the word as if it were a vulgar thing. "Take us to where you think you found such an unlikely creature."

Rossamünd turned to go back down. He did not want to return to the benighted maze beneath but was eager to prove what he had been through. It was then he realized he did not know how to return to the scene of violence, so keen had he been on getting out. Some of his lefts had become rights in the end, and there was no telling precisely which and when. He hesitated.

Surgeon Swill arrived in the enormous room and all notions of going below were subordinated as, with an intently professional expression, he examined Rossamünd's hurts. "This is a nasty blow," he declared after a silent observation of the young prentice's head. "The boy must surely be in a daze. How did you get the wound? Knock your cranium on a doorpost or the like, yes?"

"No, sir, the basket did this to me!" he said, watching nervously as the surgeon reached into a sinister-looking case.

"He persists with this daft notion of a monster in the cellars," the Master-of-Clerks said with strange, affected sympathy. "Poor, foolish child."

"Indeed. Clearly dazed," Swill insisted, producing a bandage. "Such an injury can make one believe he sees all kinds of phantasms. Bed rest and a callic draught are the best for you, young lantern-stick. Let this be a lesson to you not to be dashing about after douse-lanterns!"

Callic draughts were for drowsing the mentally infirm—Rossamünd knew his potives too well. He did not want an addled, forgetful sleep. He wanted to tell the horrible news that the unthinkable had happened: that a monster had been found inside Winstermill. As he submitted to the bandage being wrapped about his crown, Rossamünd was keenly aware of the unsympathetic gazes upon him. "I have to tell the Lamplighter-Marshal!" he insisted.

"And so you shall," said Whympre, "and illuminate him *and* me both as to your illegal surveyings and nocturnal invasions. I warn you though, child, your chatter about buried bogles will not wash with him either. The only event for which we have proof unavoidable is your trespass in my rooms."

"Mister Sebastipole will confirm I tell the truth, sir," Rossamünd said obstinately with an angry glance at Pile.

The falseman gave Rossamünd a cold, almost venomous look.

The Master-of-Clerks and the falseman and the surgeon exchanged the merest hint of a pointed glance.

Whympre declared firmly, "Well then, it's off to the Marshal we go, prentice. He will not be pleased, for he is always busy with his papers. Batterstyx!" he called to the air. "Batterstyx! My perruque!" An aged private man appeared from some other door bearing the clerk-master's lustrous black wig. Once it was fitted to the great man's satisfaction, the Master-of-Clerks strode forth. "Come along!"

Rossamünd was marched through the perpendicular geometry of the manse. Accompanied by the three men, he was taken from the far back corner to somewhere near the front, where the Lamplighter-Marshal's duty room was found. Pile knocked for them and they waited.

Presently this port sprang open and Inkwill emerged, looking overworked. "Master-of-Clerks," the registry clerk said, managing a wry smile. "What troublesome punctilio troubles you now, sir?"

Whympre sniffed as if to indicate Inkwill was beneath his notice. "We have a disturbing breach of security to relay to the Marshal. Go tell this to him."

Why not just tell him of the rever-man? Rossamünd thought angrily. He knew there were forms to follow, but in a circumstance such as this, surely they could be put aside?

"Aye, sir." The registry clerk nodded, his eyes going a little wide at the bandage about Rossamünd's head.

The door closed, there was a wait; it opened again and

Inkwill reappeared to gesture the four through. The anteclave was empty of its usual crowd of the Marshal's secretaries and assisting clerks, yet many piles of paper remained. Even to Rossamünd—for whom these countless documents had no relevance—such a mass of paper gave the room a feeling of nagging, insurmountable and never-ending labor. Inkwill guided him through the thin lane between desks.

"Stay here, prentice," the Master-of-Clerks ordered.

Rossamünd obeyed, his head starting to throb uncomfortably, while Whympre, Swill and Pile went on into the Lamplighter-Marshal's duty room. Very quickly Inkwill was back, dashing through the anteclave without a word.

More waiting, and the throb in Rossamünd's pate grew into an ache.

Inkwill returned now with Sebastipole in tow, the leer giving Rossamünd one look and saying, "That is a fine bump you have got yourself, my boy. Follow me, if you will," before going directly in to the Marshal.

In the shadow of Sebastipole, the young prentice inched his way into the very soul of Winstermill's existence, hands habitually gripped before him at a now absent thrice-high. To Rossamünd's left, the Master-of-Clerks had stationed himself on a richly cushioned tandem chair. Swill was on his right, poised stiffly on the edge of a hall chair, alert, waiting. On the clerk-master's left stood Laudibus Pile, leaning against a false architrave, head down. But right before him, behind a desk piled with documents, sat the Lamplighter-

Marshal, the eighth Earl of the Baton Imperial of Fayelillian. He appeared drawn, and sharply aware of the entire substance of his manifold burdens, and was staring keenly at Rossamünd. "Good evening, Prentice-Lighter Bookchild," he said, his warm voice crackling slightly with weariness. The Marshal's quick gaze, penetrating and wily, seemed to sum up Rossamünd, standing as stiff as an Old Gate Pensioner, in one acute look. He cleared his throat and gestured to the hall chair. "Please, take your ease." Despite dark sags of sleeplessness, the man's amiable, fatherly appearance remained. Indeed, with his sweeping white mustachios, a noble lift to his chin and a white-blond forelock curling almost boyishly upon his brow, the effect this close was magnified.

Sebastipole stood at the corner of the massive table while Inkwill showed Rossamünd to his seat, positioned squarely before the great man.

"I am told by the clerk-master," the Marshal continued, "that ye believe yerself to have fought with a homunculid in the ancient tunnels below us. Is this so, prentice?"

"Aye, sir." Rossamünd swallowed hard. He was about to let the whole tale burble out, when, with a cold stab in his innards, he realized he might betray Numps by telling of the undercroft. With a flicker of a look to the two leers, Rossamünd faltered and went silent.

With this, Laudibus Pile raised his face and, with a dark glance at Sebastipole, fixed Rossamünd with his own see-all stare. It was profoundly daunting to have a twin of

THE
LAMPLIGHTER-MARSHAL

falsemen's eyes—red orb, blue iris—staring cannily from left and right. Rossamünd shifted on the hard seat in his discomfort.

"Are ye well, son? I hope that wound does not overly trouble ye," the Lamplighter-Marshal said, nodding to the thick bandage about the prentice's head.

"A little, sir."

"I did my best to mend him, Lamplighter-Marshal," Swill put in. "It is a nasty cut underneath all that cloth and I am sure, however it was sustained, it is enough to knock the sense out of the boy."

"So ye said before, surgeon," the Marshal said gravely. "Tell me, Rossamünd, do ye feel knocked about in yer intellectuals?"

"Somewhat, sir, but I was fully aware before and I am fully aware now."

The Marshal smiled genially. "Good man." He shuffled some papers before him. "The good clerk-master has told me his take on yer tale, prentice, and is skeptical. I would like to hear yer own recollection and we shall go on from that. Proceed, young fellow."

Rossamünd cleared his throat, took a rattling, timorous breath, cleared his throat a second time and finally began. "I had missed douse-lanterns, sir, and found a way under the manse and it took me through all kinds of furtigrades and passages . . ." And so he told of the terrific events, passing very quickly over the how of his presence, avoiding any

288

mention of the bloom baths or Numps, concentrating most on the battle with the prefabricated horror.

All present listened in unmoved silence until his short recounting was finished. Upon its completion the Lamplighter-Marshal nodded gravely and smoothed his mustachios with forefinger and thumb. "I am not a commander who likes to set one fellow's telling against another's, yet ye seem a rather slight lad to be the conqueror of so fearsome a thing as a rever-man. More than this is how such a beastie ever won into places no monster has ever made it to before. How-be-it, my boy, ye were the only one present and my telltale finds no fault with yer summation."

Rossamünd had not been aware of any communication between the Marshal and the lamplighter's agent, yet somehow Sebastipole had made what he observed clear to the Lamplighter-Marshal. The leer gave a barely perceptible nod to the prentice. "Indeed, sir, what he has told us has contained no lie."

He believes me after all! Rossamünd could have done a little caper for joy, but kept still and somber.

Laudibus Pile darted a calculating, ill-willed squint at Sebastipole.

"As it is, this is a most difficult situation, prentice." The Lamplighter-Marshal became very stern. "Ye have placed me in a bind, for on the one hand ye must be applauded—surely awarded—for yer courage and sheer pluck at prevailing in such a mismatched contest as ever a fellow was set to."

Rossamünd's heart leaped with hope.

. "Yet," the Lamplighter-Marshal went on firmly, "the circumstances surrounding yer feat of arms are drastically irregular, would ye not agree, lad? To be out beyond douse-lanterns though not of the lantern-watch or the night-watch is a grave breach. Entering restricted parts of the manse, another grave breach. Perhaps we should simply all be glad for the blighted thing's destruction. But a rule for all is a rule for one, and a rule for one is a rule for all, do ye agree, Prentice Bookchild?"

The prentice swallowed hard. "Aye, sir." Though he had never heard entering the underregions of Winstermill for-mally proscribed, this revelation did not surprise him—most things were out-of-bounds for a prentice.

The Master-of-Clerks stirred. "If I may interject here, most honored Marshal, with the observation that my own telltale does not find all particulars of the prentice's retell-ing wholly satisfying."

With a single, stiff nod, Laudibus Pile confirmed his mas-ter's claim.

"When falsemen disagree, eh?" The Lamplighter-Marshal became even sterner, hard, almost angry—with whom, Rossamünd could not tell, and he swallowed again at the anxiousness parching his throat.

"In fact, sir," the Master-of-Clerks pressed, "I might go so far as to state that one does not need to be a falseman to detect the irregularities in this . . . this one's story. Perhaps your telltale does not see it so clearly? I am rather in the line that this little one is just grasping for glories to cover his defaulting." He bent his attention on Rossamünd. "You have waxed eloquent upon your fight with the wretched creature, child, and the proof that you came to blows with *something* is clear; but I still do not follow how it is that *you* came to be in the passeyards at all or why it is that your journey took you to my very sanctum? You avoided the question before, but you shall not do so now."

"The passeyards, sir?" Rossamünd asked.

"Yes." The Master-of-Clerks flurried his fingers impatiently. "The interleves, the cuniculus, the slypes—the passages twixt walls and beneath halls, boy!"

"Oh."

The Lamplighter-Marshal raised his right hand, a signal for silence, stopping the Master-of-Clerks cold. "Yer point is made, clerk-master. Prentice Bookchild, ye have a reputation for lateness, do ye not? As I understand it, ye have gained the moniker 'Master Come-lately,' aye?"

"Aye, sir."

"But, as I have it, ye do not have a reputation for lying, son, do ye?"

"No, sir."

"So tell us true: how is it ye found such well-hidden tunnels as those ye occupied tonight?"

Ashamed, Rossamünd dropped his head then darted a look to the Marshal, whose mild attentive expression showed no hint of his thoughts or opinion. "I was with the glimner, Mister Numps, down in the Low Gutter, and I forgot the time so——so I went by the drains so I could get into the manse after douse-lanterns." He was determined not to implicate Numps in any manner, but with a falseman at both sides, it was an impossible ploy. Yet Rossamünd was desperate enough to attempt to dissemble. "I found them . . . through . . . through somewhere under the . . . the Low Gutter, sir——"

Laudibus Pile's glittering gaze narrowed. "Liar!" the falseman hissed caustically.

"Ye will address an Emperor's servant with respect, sir," the marshal-lighter pronounced sharply, "be he above or below ye in station!"

"He does not lie, Pile!" Sebastipole added grimly.

"He dissimulates!" Laudibus snapped, with a black look to the Marshal then his counterpart.

"Indeed he might," Sebastipole countered smoothly, "but he does not lie."

"Enough, gentlemen!" The Marshal cut through, and there was silence. He returned his attention to Rossamünd. "Now, my man, whitewashing tends only to make one look guilty. Say it straight: we only want to find how this gudgeon-basket got into our so-long inviolate home, and so stop it happening again. Where did ye gain entry into the under parts?"

"Through the old bloom baths." Rossamünd dropped his head, feeling the most wretched blackguard that ever weaseled another. "Under the Skillions, where they once tended the bloom." He did not mind trouble for himself near half as much as implicating Numps.

The Marshal just nodded.

"What old bloom baths?" asked the Master-of-Clerks sharply, forgetting his place perhaps, interrupting the Marshal's inquiries. "How, by the blight, did you find such a place on your own? A place, I might add," he continued with the barest hint of a displeased look to the Marshal, "that *I* have only heard of tonight! You cannot expect us to believe you discovered such a place in solus!"

"In solus, sir?"

"By yourself," he returned tartly. "Who showed you where they are?"

"I—" Rossamünd did not know how to answer.

"Speak it all!" Laudibus Pile spat.

"*Silence!*" barked the Lamplighter-Marshal. "Another gust from ye, sir, and ye *will* be exiting these rooms!"

An undaunted, cunning light flickered in the depths of Pile's eyes, yet he yielded and seemed to retreat deeply within himself.

After an uncomfortable, ringing pause, the Master-of-Clerks fixed the prentice with his near-hungry stare. "You must tell us, prentice," he said softly, "how then do you know of such a place?"

"It is common enough knowledge that there are ancient, seldom visited waterworks and cavities underneath our own pile, sir," came Sebastipole's unexpected interjection.

"I think, Master-of-Clerks," was the Lamplighter-Marshal's firm and timely addition, "that ye may leave this line of questioning now. The boy has been brought up short enough with the night's ordeal *ipse adversus*—standing alone! What is more, it brings no clarity to the more troubling details."

The Master-of-Clerks became a picture of pious obedience. "Certainly, sir," he returned respectfully, smoothing the gorgeous hems of his frock coat. "I am just troubled that the existence of those old bloom baths is what has allowed the creature—if such exists—to find its way in. If that be so, then we will most certainly have to do away with the whole place," the Master-of-Clerks declared officiously, "to be thorough."

From across the Marshal's desk Rossamünd could see the tension in Sebastipole, the lamplighter's agent's jaw tightening, loosening, tightening, loosening with rhythmic distraction.

"But the rever-man was shut up in some old room a long way from the bloom baths," the young prentice dared.

"So you say, child." The Master-of-Clerks smiled serenely at Rossamünd, a sweet face to cover sharp words. "Yet if a mere prentice can find his way so deep in forgotten places, then why not some mindless monster, and these unvetted baths may well be the cause."

The Lamplighter-Marshal raised his hand, stopping Podious Whympre short. "There is no need and nothing gained from despoiling those old baths," he said firmly. "They have been here for longer than we, and are buried deeply enough, and no harm will come from the quiet potterings of faithful, incapacitated lighters."

"You already know of it, sir?" the Master-of-Clerks replied with a studied expression. "This—this continued unregistered, unrecorded activity? Why was I not informed . . . sir?"

"I do know of it, Clerk-Master Whympre," the Marshal replied, "and I iterate again it is not the case of most concern. I could well ask ye how it is that there is a way down from yer own chambers into these buried levels."

The Master-of-Clerks blanched. "It is a private store, sir. I had no idea it connected to regions more clandestine," he explained quickly.

Other questions continued. Rossamünd felt unable to answer any of them to full satisfaction: did he have any inkling of where the gudgeon had come from?

No, sir, he did not. It had, by all evidence, been locked in the room rather than having arrived from somewhere. In the end he simply had to conclude that he truly had no idea of the how or the why or the where of the gudgeon's advent.

Did he recognize where he found the gudgeon?

No, sir, he did not.

Would he be able to find the place again—or give instructions to another to do the same?

Rossamünd hesitated; he could only do his best, sir. He described his left-hand logic to solving the maze and as much of the actual lay of the passages and the rest as he could recall.

And all the while the Master-of-Clerks was looking at him with his peculiar, predatory gaze. Pile seemed to sulk, and said nothing.

"I will look into this, sir," Sebastipole declared. "Josclin is still not well enough; Clement and I shall take Drawk and some other trusty men and seek out this buried room." With that the lamplighter's agent left.

"If you could excuse me, Lamplighter-Marshal." Swill stood and bowed. "I must attend to pressing duties," he said with a quick look to Sebastipole's back.

"Certainly, surgeon," the Marshal replied. "Ye are free to go—and ye may depart too, clerk-master. Yer prompt action is commendable."

"And what of this young trespasser?" The Master-of-Clerks peered down his nose at Rossamünd. "I hope you will be taking him in hand. Whatever other deeds might or might not surround him, you cannot deny that he has contravened two most inviolate rules, and it is grossly unsatisfactory that he has violated my own offices."

"What I do with Prentice Bookchild is between him and me," the Marshal returned firmly. "Good night, Podious!"

With a polite and contrite bow the Master-of-Clerks left, his telltale and the surgeon following.

Grindrod was admitted in their stead, hastily dressed and looking slightly frowzy.

"Ah, Lamplighter-Sergeant!" the Marshal cried. "Ye seem to have been missing one of yer charges, but here I am returning him to ye."

"Aye, sir." Grindrod stood straight and, appearing a little embarrassed, gave Rossamünd a quick yet thunderous glare. "Thank ye, sir."

"Not at all," the Marshal answered. "Ye make fine lamps-men, Sergeant-lighter. This young prentice has been doing the duties of a lamplighter even as his fellows sleep. Return him to his cot and set a strong guard over his cell row. Fell doings have been afoot. We shall discuss his deeds after."

The lamplighter-sergeant looked stunned. "Aye, sir." Thunder turned to puzzled satisfaction.

"Our thanks to ye, Prentice Bookchild," the Lamplighter-Marshal said to Rossamünd. "Yer part here is done; ye played the man frank and true. Ye may turn in to yer cot at last. Be sure to report to Doctor Crispus tomorrow morning. Good night, prentice."

With that the interview was ended.

Rossamünd left under the charge of Grindrod, feeling a traitor. While he was sent to sleep, he was aware of a grow-ing bustle about as the soldiery of the manse were woken up to defend it from any other rever-men that might emerge from below.

"I don't know whether to castigate or commend ye, young Lately!" the lamplighter-sergeant grumped as he led the prentice along the passages. "Just get yer blundering bones to yer cot and I'll figure a fitting end for yer tomorrow."

For another night Rossamünd readied himself in the cold dark and slept with his bed chest pulled across the door to his cell.

17

HASTY DEPARTURES

sis edisserum Tutin term, loosely meaning "please explain", this is an order from a superior (usually the Emperor) to appear before him and a panel of peers forthwith to offer reasons, excuses, evidence, testimony and whatever else might be required to elucidate upon whatever demands clarity. A sis edisserum is usually seen as a portent of Imperial ire, a sign that the person or people so summoned are in it deep and must work hard to restore Clementine's confidence. A sis edisserum is a "black mark" against your name, and very troublesome to remove.

ROSSAMÜND awoke with the worst ache of head and body that he had ever known and his bladder fit to burst. He hurt like the aftermath of the most severe concussion he had ever received in harundo practice. For a time he could not remember much of yesterday, though a lurking apprehension warned him the memory would be unwelcome. With the sight of his salumanticum discarded on the floor and the bed chest blocking the door recollection struck. A gudgeon . . . a gudgeon in the forgotten cellars of the manse, right in the marrow of the headquarters of the lamplighters! A monster loose in Winstermill!

He dragged back the chest and opened the door to find Threnody there, leaning on the wall as if she had been waiting.

"You missed the most extraordinary pudding at mains last night," she said dryly. Evidently she had elected to speak to him again.

"Aye . . ." Rossamünd knew by "extraordinary" she did not mean "good." Threnody had always hated the food served to the prentices, and the new culinaire was achieving new acmes of inedibility.

"You might be a poor conversationalist," she continued as they went to morning forming, completely heedless of the thick bandage about his head, "but at least you're interesting. Between Arabis having the others ignore me, and Plod mooning and staring all through the awful meal, it was a very long evening." She peered at him. "Where's your hat?" But by then Grindrod was shouting attention and all talk ceased.

In files out on the Cypress Walk it was obvious the manse was in a state of agitation, with the house-watch marching regular patrols about the Mead and the feuterers letting the dogs out on leads to sniff at every crevice and cranny. Under a louring sky the atmosphere of the fortress was tense and watchful.

"Do *not* be distracted by all this hustle ye see today, lads," Grindrod advised tersely. "There was an unwelcome guest in our cellars last night, but the rotted clenchpoop is done in now." He looked meaningfully at Rossamünd. "Just attend to yer duties with yer regular vigor."

At breakfast the other prentices stared openly at Rossamünd's bandaged head.

"How's it, Lately?" asked Smellgrove as Rossamünd sat down with his fellows of Q Hesiod Gæta. "Is the bee's buzz true?"

"What buzz?"

"That you came to hand strokes with a gudgeon last night," said Wheede, pointing to Rossamünd's bound noggin.

"Ah, aye, it nearly ruined itself trying to destroy me."

"Pullets and cockerels!" said several boys on either side.

Insisting others shift to make room, Threnody sat next to him. "Have any of you others fought one before?" she asked knowingly.

Universal shakes of the head.

"Because I can tell you," she boasted, "that a full-formed lamplighter would struggle to win against one, let alone a half-done lamp boy."

"I have heard it that wits can't do much to them either." This was Arabis, listening at the far end of the bench.

Threnody lifted her chin and pretended she had not heard him.

"Tell us, Rosey," asked Pillow, "how did you do the thing in?"

"I burned the basket's head out with loomblaze!" Rossamünd said, with more passion than he intended. "It went smashing down through the stair into the pits deep underneath."

There was an approving mutter of amazement. The looks

of awe turned Rossamünd's way were simultaneously intoxicating and hard to bear. He ducked his head to hide his confused delight, but one incredulous snort from Threnody and his small, uncommon joy was obliterated in an instant.

After breakfast Grindrod did not say any more about Rossamünd's yesternight excursions. However, he did seem to address Rossamünd with a touch more dignity as he sent him to Doctor Crispus for further examination. "Ye may take yer time, Prentice Bookchild: well-earned wounds need proper treating."

"Cuts and sutures, my boy, you certainly have a bump and a gash upon your scalp to show for some kind of scuffle," the physician declared as he cleaned the nasty contusion on Rossamünd's hairline and rebandaged it.

"Swill tried to recommend callic for me last night," Rossamünd said pointedly.

Crispus wagged his head in disapproval. "Fumbling butchering novice," he said, clucking his tongue. "Even a first-year tyro would know callic is not for concussions. By your current alertness I can assume he did not succeed in his fuddle-brained prescription?"

"No he did not, Doctor. I know enough of the chemistry to have not taken any even if he had."

"My apologies, Rossamünd. He certainly is not who I would have here," Crispus complained. "But the young quackeen is only nominally under my authority; rather he answers to the Master-of-Clerks himself. Very unsatisfactory, and a clear nuisance when he comes a-quacking in my trim infirmary." He clucked his tongue again. "A mere articled man strutting about as if he is a senior surgeon."

"He certainly reads some strange books for a surgeon," said Rossamünd.

"Does he, indeed?" Crispus blinked owlishly.

"Aye, sir." Rossamünd squinted at the ceiling in recollection. "Dark books, from what my old Master Craumpalin told me."

"Where did you see these, child?" the physician pressed.

"In Swill's apartment, way up in the manse's attics. Mother Snooks sent me up the kitchen furtigrade, delivering a pig's head to him."

"The kitchen furtigrade?" Crispus looked utterly amazed. "I did not know one existed, though Winstermill is old enough to have a thousand such obscure places. You certainly have had a tour of the slypes, haven't you?"

"And the attic apartment?"

"Oh, that place is just his personal library, a place of private reflection. 'Do not disturb' and all that. I've never begrudged him this: a professional man must have his sanctuary for study—I have one of my own. In our profession there are some strange tomes—some better had we never read them, of course. And as for the pig's head—well, a surgeon must practice his sutures, I suppose."

Rossamünd was unconvinced.

Sebastipole entered the infirmary and, after asking of Rossamünd's health, went on to request a personal word.

WINSTERMILL

The dressing of the wound complete, Crispus left them and attended to other patients.

"Did you find anything in the tunnels, Mister Sebastipole?" Rossamünd asked eagerly but in a low voice.

"There was no gudgeon corpse," the leer answered.

Rossamünd's soul sank.

"And all that was left of the stair was splinters and wood-dust," Sebastipole went on.

Rossamünd's dismay deepened. His desperate struggle must have wrenched the ancient furtigrade too much.

"I have heard of gudgeons so cunningly made they dissolve into a puddle after they expire," Sebastipole expounded further. "Do not worry, Rossamünd, you are believed," he added, seeing the young prentice's dismay. "But I must tell you it was touch and go to even find your path; we found our way more by your instructions than your trail. Were you using a nullodor last night at all?"

Rossamünd felt a caustic flush of guilt, as if he had been caught out. "You can smell a nullodor?" He had no reason to feel this, yet he did.

"Actually, no: they do their job just as they should—all smells gone where applied. It is rather that absence of scent that is the telltale signifer. Think of it like reading a letter where a clumsy author has cut out his errors with a blade and as you read there are great holes in the sentences. You know something was there but you'd be hard-pressed to say what it was." Sebastipole sniffed, then blew his nose. "Such a ruse will work against a brute beast but not against the pragmatical senses of a well-learned leer." He looked at Rossamünd searchingly.

"Oh," the young prentice said in a small voice, "and there were no smells down there?"

"Exactly so." The leer's expression was impenetrable. "The whole area was a great blank, with only the merest suggestion of many obliterated smells. If you pressed me I might say that more than one nullodor was employed, but it is too hard to prove so now."

"Oh . . . I am sorry, Mister Sebastipole," Rossamünd murmured. "My . . . my old masters have me wearing a little each day . . . to keep me safe, they said, from sniffing noses." He could not see the sense in hiding it now.

"Indeed?" The leer looked astutely at him, held him with a silent, penetrating regard. "I detected a nullodor on you the night we went out lighting together."

Rossamünd ducked his head and blushed. "My old masters are very protective of me."

"And you are very obedient to *them*, it would appear."

Rossamünd nodded sheepishly.

Sebastipole smiled. "Yet, Rossamünd, I *did* manage to detect the merest smell of your foe. It was exactly like the foreign, foul slot of Numption's attackers."

"What does that mean, sir?"

"I have not encountered enough gudgeons to know beyond doubt, but the similarity seems suspicious to me. It may well mean the creature that beset Numption and that which you slew last night—though separated by three years or more——have come from the same benighted test, made by the same black habilist. If that is so, the wretch has grown arrogant enough to try his constructions on us again!" The anger in Sebastipole's eyes was made more terrible by their unnatural hue. "More galling still, we did not find how the homunculid found its way in. Others could come."

Rossamünd's imagination fired with the abhorrent scene of the fortress overrun with rever-men.

"Hmm." The leer became ruminative. "I can say that it certainly did not come from the region of Numption's bloom baths."

"I did not want to tell about them," Rossamünd confessed forlornly.

"I know you did not, Rossamünd." The leer spoke up quickly. "You are an honest fellow and your honesty last night made proceedings easier. Fret not for dear Mister Numps: he is protected, and his 'friends' with him. I asked him to let us in and only took those with me who would treat him kindly."

Rossamünd felt a little relief at this.

Sebastipole put an encouraging hand on the young prentice's shoulder. "No more nighttime wanderings for you, my boy. Play the man, Rossamünd, be not afraid but be on your guard and carry your salumanticum with you always: strange and suspicious things turn in the manse now." With this warning the leer left him, and Rossamünd went out of the infirmary and rejoined the slightly awed prentices stepping regular out on Evolution Green.

At middens Rossamünd rushed down to the lantern store, the guilty conviction that he had failed Numps a heavy weight right in the pit of his gizzards. Yet what else could he have done? *Oh! If only I hadn't slept past douse-lanterns!*

His compunction was not eased either when Numps looked at him only very briefly with big, timid eyes and said nothing for a long time. "I heard it that you were set upon by a pale, runny man yesternight, Mister Rossamünd," the glimner eventually muttered softly, not looking up from his working. "Just like old Numps was."

"Aye, Mister Numps, I was," Rossamünd answered.

"Oh dear, oh dear—I'm sorry, Mister Rossamünd, I'm sorry! You wanted my help and I showed you into trouble—poor, limpling-headed Numps!"

This made Rossamünd feel more miserable than ever. "I—I could have turned back, I suppose. Besides, I beat the rever-man and got out."

Numps stopped polishing the lamp-pane gripped by the nimble toes of his left foot.

"It is me who must say his sorries, Mister Numps, for telling them about the bloom baths," Rossamünd blurted out. "I did not want to say . . . but I had to be honest—I . . . I . . ." Rossamünd's words felt very thin and meaningless.

For a while Numps sat, staring at his lap. Finally he

looked up. "Fair is fair. One 'sorry' each. You had to fight the runny man because of Numps' limpling head and then some people want to talk and talk about it and ask things, the same things over and over till you're all done with it. I remember it, just the same on the day of all my red."

"Aye, I suppose." Rossamünd was not soothed by all this sorrying.

The hollow sensation of friendship part-fractured persisted, and the two cleaned panes in reflective silence.

"Mister Sebastipole reckons my gudgeon and the one you fought might come from the same maker," Rossamünd finally tried. "He said they could not find where my rever-man got in, though. Do you have any notion, Mister Numps?"

Numps shook his head. "No one can get from out there into here." He smiled. "Even I know that. Only the sparrows of the Sparrowling make it here . . . oh, and you. But I reckon they let you in 'cause you look right, but it is still clever to cover the smell." He tapped his handsome nose and his smile grew cryptic.

With the chime from a bell, Rossamünd realized with a sault of fright in his chest that middens was ended. Having learned his lesson for lateness only too well, he scrambled his tangibles together, and with a quick bow and a short "good afternoon," took hasty leave of the startled glimner.

Though the discovery of a gudgeon within was disconcerting news, Rossamünd's victory over it was powerfully encouraging, and the lighters particularly held him a mite-sized example of true lampsman valor. Among the greater share of the clerks, however, the rumor prevailed that he had made the whole tale up to cover his disobedience. From what Rossamünd had heard, the Master-of-Clerks was furious that no disciplinary action was to be taken for either Rossamünd's lateness or his unauthorized presence in Whympre's chambers.

"I think that bump on yer brain-box serves ye a better reminder to do yer duty than any reprimand I can give ye," the Lamplighter-Marshal had declared during a brief interview the next morning.

Coursing for rever-men beneath the manse continued, Sebastipole finding alternative routes into the foundations other than Numps' undercroft. The progress was slow and incomplete, the searchers hampered by the strange terrain and, as rumor would have it, by the Master-of-Clerks' insistence that underneath was the sole property of the Emperor and not somewhere for lighters to be roaming about carelessly or without proper permissions or reports in triplicate.

Meanwhile the prentices went on with their routines, and the awe of the other lads toward Rossamünd waned. Out on Evolution Green each day, Rossamünd noticed Laudibus Pile sometimes lurking, watching them at their marching and training where he had never lurked nor watched before. It was not constant, but enough to be annoying.

"See, it's *him* again," he pointed out to Threnody as the prentices were between drills.

"Perhaps he finds our movements appealing," she offered lightly. "Though what interminable stepping-regular and fodicar movements have to do with lighting lamps I do not know. I'm glad there is only a month left of it."

Scowling at the leer, Rossamünd was glad too that the last month of prenticing was approaching. He would be able to serve on the road at last and do his part.

On the last day of Pulvis, with only one month and four pageants-of-arms left till Billeting Day, Rossamünd was with Numps again at middens. Door 143 gave a rattling bang, and Sebastipole quickly appeared from the avenue of shelves and parts. He was disturbingly, uncharacteristically agitated, the blue of his eyes too pale, their red like new-spilled blood.

Rossamünd stood, frowning with dismay. "Mister Sebastipole?"

"Young Master Rossamünd. Good, I am spared the time to find you too." The leer's brow glistened with perspiration.

Rossamünd had never seen Sebastipole so agitated—not even when he was facing the Trought. "Are . . . are you distressed, sir?"

"Hello, Mister 'Pole." Numps was clearly delighted to see the leer. "Come to see my friends again?"

"Not today, Numption," the leer answered, returning the glimner's smile with one of his own, brotherly and warm despite his mysterious urgency. "I am glad you have Rossamünd for a friend now too, for today I will be leaving."

The prentice's innards gave a lurch. *Sebastipole leaving?* Rossamünd did not care for such a notion: the manse felt safer with the leer somewhere at hand.

Attention now fixed on a particularly grimy lantern-window, Numps nodded. "All right, Mister 'Pole, Numps will see you again soon, then."

"You're going, Mister Sebastipole?" Rossamünd asked.

"Indeed," the leer returned, "I will most probably be gone for a goodly while."

The glimner finally looked up from his rubbing. "More days than Numps has fingers or toes?"

"Yes, Numption, more even than that." Sebastipole gave him a sad, affectionate look. "I do not know for how long I will be absent."

Numps' joy collapsed. "But why?"

The leer crouched down and looked up at the glimner.

"The short of it is, my old friend, the Lamplighter-Marshal has been served a sis edisserum. Do you know what this is?"

Though Sebastipole was talking to Numps, Rossamünd nodded. This Imperial summons had played infrequent but significant parts in the more exciting stories in his old pamphlets.

Numps just blinked slowly, his look of distress mixing with increasing confusion.

"It means that the Marshal must appear before the Emperor's representatives posthaste," Sebastipole explained, "and as his falseman—his telltale—I am to go with him."

"But why does the Marshal have to go?" Numps persisted.

The leer hesitated. "Because . . . because the Emperor's ministers have ordered him to meet with them all the way down in the Considine."

The Considine? Rossamünd was amazed: he had hoped to see the subcapital as a vinegaroon visiting as part of a ram's crew, to tread slowly into harbor and admire its grand buildings and massive walls. "Why have they done that?" he piped, with questions of his own. "What has the Lamplighter-Marshal done?"

Sebastipole looked at him squarely. "He has *done* nothing," the leer said with contained anger. "But somehow they have already heard of the gudgeon in our bowels and he is required to explain both this and what they consider our failure to check the great many theroscades and depredations along the highroad."

"It's not the Lamplighter-Marshal's fault that bogles and nickers attack!" Rossamünd could not believe the folly of such a notion. "Nor that the rever-man was found in here! How can he explain something he couldn't know? It was those butchers who brought the poor Trought down on us, not the Marshal!"

"I suspect there is more behind this sis edisserum than a

simple 'please explain.' Someone plots the Marshal's embarrassment, perhaps, or his removal."

"Who would want such a terrible thing?" Rossamünd asked indignantly.

"Maybe those who covet his popularity with the lamplighters and the people of the Idlewild, and his position as a peer," answered the leer. "Those who will happily destroy any good just so they can have it their way, without any thought to wisdom or right."

How could anyone be black-hearted enough to wish ill on such a great man? Rossamünd reflected bitterly.

"But why do you have to go?" Numps interjected, frowning with intense, puzzled concentration.

"I go because the Marshal needs me." Sebastipole became kinder. "I must see through all the lies and traps of cunning men for him. While I am gone you must be careful, do you follow me, Numption?" The leer bent his neck sideways to look Numps in the eye. "If you are scared, hide with your hidden friends. Yes?"

The glimner nodded, his head dropping dejectedly. "Yes Mister 'Pole, if I'm scared I will hide, yes."

Standing, Sebastipole turned to Rossamünd. "Watch out for my friend, Rossamünd. Only you and Crispus show him any abiding kindness, and the doctor is a man daily beleaguered with too many tasks." Sebastipole gripped Rossamünd firmly by his shoulder, startling him. "Will you do this?" the leer asked, uncommon anxiety clear in his queer-colored gaze.

"Aye, Mister Sebastipole," Rossamünd said seriously. "Aye, I most certainly will."

"Bravo! Good man! Now I must go. We have been given little time to satisfy the summons."

"You come back again, Mister 'Pole," Numps insisted.

"You know I have to go away at times. But I always return, do I not?" He fixed Numps with a firm look. "Do I not?"

Sniffing, Numps eventually, grudgingly, nodded.

"And I will write to you as I have before," the leer pressed, "and Doctor Crispus will still be here . . . and so will Rossamünd."

At that Numps looked at the prentice and gave a pathetic smile.

Nodding, Rossamünd grinned awkwardly in return.

Sebastipole sat with Numps for a little longer, then said, "And now, friend Numption, I must *must* go and *you* must trust me and Rossamünd as your friend." Sebastipole stood.

"Yes, Mister 'Pole," Numps relented. "You *are* my for-always friend, and Rossamünd is my new old friend. I will see you back here soon again, yes?"

"Yes, you shall—as soon as is possible. May well betide both of you," he said with feeling. "We shall meet again—I will make certain of it! Until then I will write if able, though there will be much work to do, great labors perhaps, but I will still attempt a letter. Good-bye!" With that, he turned quickly with a flick of his coachman's cloak and exited the lantern store.

Numps began to sing and mutter.

Rossamünd could feel—almost see—the glimner withdraw into himself, no longer heeding the prentice sitting by him. Rossamünd quietly returned to the manse and left the glimner to his introspections.

18

WRETCHEDNESS REVEALED

Considine, the ~ one of the alternats or subcapitals situated at strategic places within the Haacobin Empire. Alternats were founded to allow the Empire to keep greater control over its subject states, most of which lie beyond inveterately threwdish land, well past easy reach. Large armies and navies are kept at each alternat, ready to venture forth and chastise any overweening state or peer or defend the lands against the monsters. In the Soutlands, the Considine is the larger, older and therefore senior of two alternats, the other being the Serenine, farther south.

THE prentices were not even properly awake when the Lamplighter-Marshal, Sebastipole, the Marshal's adjutant, accompanying secretaries and a small quarto of lifeguards left in three lentums that next morning. Preparing for parade with a heavy heart, Rossamünd marched out with his subdued fellows to find the entire pageant-of-arms in similar mood. The sudden departure of their beloved Marshal to duties in the Idlewild was not so uncommon, yet word had got about that it was a sis edisserum that had taken him away—and this was shocking. Rossamünd could almost sense resentment bubbling under this veneer of fine martial order as they gathered on the Grand Mead.

The weather shared the oppressive mood. There had been frost that morning after a clear, cold night. But as the sun climbed to its meridian, powerful winds blew from south of southeast, their gusts only partly foiled by Winstermill's ponderous walls. Clouds so thick they were almost black arrived on its threatening breath, and the tang of rain and lightning was heavy on the air.

Standing preeminent before the entire population of the manse, Podious Whympre, Master-of-Clerks and next in line of command after the Lamplighter-Marshal, looked out upon all those now under his sway, peacock-proud, and peacock-preened. Laudibus Pile, Witherscrawl and his genuflection of sycophants stood close behind.

Wooden screens had been pegged to the ground with guy ropes and stakes to spare Whympre and his tail any ruffling buffets of wind. His audience simply endured and, during the course of the pageant, many hats found wing in the gusts and crashed into the northern wall or sought the broad meadows of the Harrowmath.

"Our beloved Lamplighter-Marshal has been recalled to the Considine," Whympre began with clerkly sobriety. "The Emperor is concerned for the proper administration of his beloved highroad and seeks an accounting from our own faithful Marshal. A Most Honorable Imperial Secretary"—murmurs through all ranks—"arrived from High Vesting bearing the directive of the subcapital late yesterday evening with a sis edisserum marked by the Emperor's own Chief-of-Staff." He took a breath, waiting for the troubled rumbling of the assembly to still. "Therefore, our dear, dear Marshal was compelled to leave at first change of watch this morning and may well be gone for an extended time."

Though the lighters and auxiliaries already knew the Lamplighter-Marshal had departed, there was nevertheless a small roar of dismay at this final confirmation. It was unheard of—powerfully discomfiting to all—and only with the severest reprimands was a pretense of order maintained.

"With his absence," the Master-of-Clerks continued, "need must fall to me to take the daily toil of our glorious manse in hand. I shall endeavor to lead in his stead, in a manner truly befitting an outpost of the most Serene and Mighty Emperor. In that capacity I shall be forced to assume the rank of Marshal-Subrogat . . ." He continued like this for a numbingly long stretch. His loyal aides did the same, extolling the Master-of-Clerks, inflating his virtues, sounding as if they were trying to convince those gathered of the clerk-master's fitness to lead. Within all this gabbling came the first significant announcement: the Master-of-Clerks was to allow vigil-day visits to Silvernook—beginning on that very day. Even as he said this, near a dozen lentums began to roll out from the yard, ready to take those interested in a day on the town. In their delight the wind of many lifted and they began to think their new executive officer a capital fellow after all. A happy mumbling stirred through the prentices, though Rossamünd did not share their easily won enthusiasm.

"Button it shut, flabberers, or ye'll all be staying in yer

cells for the day!" Grindrod growled huskily, and stillness was purposefully restored. For the entire pageant till now the lamplighter-sergeant had been glaring up at the clerk-master, mustachios bristling in disgust. "What does he know of lighting?" Rossamünd heard him mutter to Benedict.

The Master-of-Clerks mollified them all still further by adding that they could expect roasted mutton with thick gravy for mains and treacle crowdy for puddings, with rich bully-dicey to be served at middens for those left behind. Had it been allowed, all the other prentices and many lampsmen and pediteers and the clerks would have shouted for glee.

"The hearts of the crowd are found in their bellies," Threnody muttered after they were marched back to the Cypress Walk and dismissed by their unusually subdued officers.

"Perhaps the change of command might be a turn for the good," a prentice pondered a little too loudly.

"Cleave yer tongue to yer teeth, Gall!" Grindrod bawled, sending the loose-lipped prentice white with fright. "Ye're as shatterbrained as yer nuncle the lictor! Pots-and-pans for ye tonight and the rest of the long week! The marshal-lighter is as fine a man and officer as anyone could ever hope to share a generation with! And if a single one of ye goes down to Silvernook today, ye'll have my mark as a baseborn runion fink not worthy of a lighter's fodicar!"

All the lantern-sticks were astounded at his outburst. None said another peep about the Marshal's departure— good or bad—for fear of another flaring of temper. Not one prentice took the day in Silvernook either, and if any were disappointed by this, he dared not show it.

Brooding, Rossamünd sat on his cot in his cell. Threnody, having invited herself in, was perched on his bed chest, her back against the wall.

"Is it just me," said Threnody, "or have the Lamplighter-Marshal's troubles turned out rather nicely for our new Marshal-Subrogat?"

"I suppose they have," Rossamünd agreed guardedly. "It cannot be helped that the clerk-master is next in rank." *Mister Sebastipole does have a notion that* someone *might be seeking the Marshal's ruin.* "How long would it take a message to get from here to the Considine and back?" he asked.

"You would need a fortnight," Threnody said huffily. "Why?"

Rossamünd scratched at his bandage. "What has my head turning is Mister Sebastipole saying yesterday that someone in the subcapital must have already heard about the reverman and was calling for an explanation. Barely a week has passed—"

"You already knew the Marshal was leaving on a sis edisserum and you did not say?"

"It was not my information to tell!" Rossamünd returned indignantly.

"Oh truly? *Very* convenient." Threnody rolled her eyes. "Will you always be this dim?"

"I cannot say," Rossamünd countered, an angry rush in his belly. "Will you always be this rude!" His mouth spoke

THE MASTER-OF-CLERKS

before his kinder thoughts could marshal themselves to intervene.

Threnody gaped.

"Oi, Rosey!" called Arabis down the steps of the cell row. "I saw your old middens-chum blubbering on the Mead."

Rossamünd leaped off his cot and put his head out of the cell door. "You saw what?"

"Aye, what's-his-name—the Numps or somewhat like it." The older prentice shrugged. "The daffy cove looked mighty put out by something."

Numps! Blubbering on the Mead?

Leaving Threnody flabbergasted in his cell, Rossamünd was up the steps, down the passage and out on to the Cypress Walk in a twinkling. Before he was clear of the Walk, he could hear a distant, agonized wailing coming from the Grand Mead, and very quickly he recognized it as coming from the throat of Numps. There were rapid steps behind: Threnody was following.

Clear of the manse, he saw—at the farther end of the Grand Mead on the edge of the gravel drive—Numps, hampered between two hefty troubardiers of the Master-of-Clerks' own foot-guards. The glimner was writhing and pulling against their restraint. Rossamünd had never seen him so wild and so awfully animated.

Then he saw why.

Upon the gaunt beams of the Scaffold, the great dead tree that stood at the northern end of the manse, great tendrils of still verdant bloom were hanging upon the gaunt branches to dry and slowly die. As Rossamünd well knew, glimbloom will not live long out of water, becoming parched and yellow, its tiny leaves finally rotting to slime. Between the ladders and the many, many barrows holding the bloom stood the Master-of-Clerks directing an industrious band of peoneers with remonstrative gusto. Beside him a man Rossamünd recognized as the portly works-general stood, shamefaced, determinedly avoiding the sight of the grief-racked glimner while Witherscrawl wrote Phoebë-knows-what in a portable ledger.

The old dead tree was already draped with such a vast amount of bloom that it looked to have wondrously re-turned to life; and the stuff was so vigorous-green and thick it could have come from only one place: Numps' secluded undercroft.

A shout of anguish escaped Rossamünd before he even knew to stop it. He ran the length of the gravel drive, heed-less of any shouts or reprimands, groaning, " . . . This is all my fault, this is all my fault . . ."

Doctor Crispus ran into the narrow scope of Rossamünd's panicked vision, striding fast on his long, stiltlike legs, cry-ing something to the troubardiers that Rossamünd could not understand in his rush. With a great waving of hands and arms, the physician remonstrated with the foot-guards—who did not relax their detention of Numps—before turn-ing away sharply to confront the Master-of-Clerks.

As Rossamünd got closer he could see that one of the men had a pincer grip on Numps' arm while the other corralled him with the shaft of his poleax. Though the two foot-guards were much heavier men than the glimner, they were hard-pressed to keep him in hand. The prentice pulled up smartly before the struggling three, skidding on the quartz pebbles of the drive, cut to his heart at the expression of utter desolation wrenching Numps' already distorted, tear-washed face. Bent with agony, the glimner howled, "My friend! My friend! They're killing my friend!" pushing and pulling at the grip of the foot-guards.

"Let him go! What are you doing?" Rossamünd hollered.

"Clap up your squealing, little sprat!" one of the soldiers spat. "Get back to your quarters!" For added effect the man shied at Rossamünd with a steel-shod boot, roughly shoving him away.

Rossamünd yelped as the force of the push sat him on the gravel. All he wanted to do was set Numps free. A burst of Frazzard's powder in the foot-guards' vile puds would have served perfectly, but the prentice was without his salumanticum.

Amid the horrible yawling, he heard a shout of anger behind him.

"Poke at him like that again, you bamboozle-winded dung sop, and you'll spend the rest of Chill confusing your head for your tail!" It was Threnody, arriving to intervene. She planted herself before the lofty foot-guard, hand raised to temple in a wit's telltale attitude.

The man looked down at her, his expression thunderous. "Shove it up your wheeze-end, little harridan!"

His fellow foot-guard glanced at Threnody hesitantly; however, Rossamünd was sure he could see nervous perspiration twinkling on the fellow's brow.

"All this fuss and trouble is hardly worthy of you, my people," the Master-of-Clerks declaimed, interrupting the contest of wills as he strode imperiously toward them. "The bloom must be left to die. They are well likely to be responsible for that wicked gudgeon finding its way in and causing our generous, unfortunate Marshal such embarrassment!"

Rossamünd knew this was a bald, pettifogging lie: monsters did not care two figs for bloom. "That's not tr—"

The Master-of-Clerks raised his hand. "*Silence!* Stop your rabble-rousing and get back to your duties! I will not tolerate such affronts. What a foolish weight of grief wasted over a few dripping weeds. Foot-guards, stuff a rag in its nose and return this one to its place of labor—"

"Your sturdy roughs have done their worst, man!" Doctor Crispus said with cold deliberation, glowering at one of the fellows as if he should know better. "As the manse's physician, I declare this poor fellow has taken a great strain of soul today and now needs a gentler hand. By the rights granted me through the Accord of Menschen over the health of pensioned military persons, I demand he be released to my care and relieved of any more manhandling."

"We are not at war, sir!" Whympre contradicted.

"I think you shall find that the Accord differs with you, sir." Crispus was not to be so easily beaten. "As would the brave lighters out there on the road."

The Master-of-Clerks considered, eyes narrowing, lips pursing. "This is most decidedly irregular, Doctor. I would advise you to go back to your infirmary and keep your opinions within its four walls."

"The clerking of our Emperor's manse is for you to determine, sir—the healing of its limbs is mine." Crispus stood tall, looking down on the clerk-master with the peremptory authority of the learned. "Inside the infirmary's four walls and out!"

Tear-diluted spittle was running freely from Numps' nose and mouth as he began to sag in the cruel grip of his restrainers.

With a cold glare the Master-of-Clerks eventually nodded. "I can see the wretch is ridiculously distressed. Please! Take him and set him to ease if he needs it. He will see the wisdom of today as time brings clarity. Guard-Sergeant! You may let that Numplings fellow go."

The troubardiers obeyed and Numps collapsed. Rossamünd was at his side in an instant.

"Lady Threnody." The Master-of-Clerks gave a slight, barely respectful bow to the girl lighter. "If I see you attempt to strive again I shall call your mother here and have her take you away." While the peoneers worked callously on, he strode into the manse, Witherscrawl, the works-general and foot-guards scuttering after.

"Look at them leave to heel, like the curs they are!" Threnody hissed.

Numps lay curled about himself, making strange gulping noises, whispering "Oh, my friend . . . oh, my friend" to himself between sobbing gasps, his eyes red and swollen, his cheeks gray and drawn. Oblivious to the sharp pebbles of the drive, Rossamünd knelt and embraced the glimner as best he could, an awkward, inadequate reach across the man's convulsing back.

Doctor Crispus was unwilling to provoke Numps further by taking him into the manse. Calling for two porters and a stretcher, he had the glimner taken to the lantern store. Rossamünd and Threnody accompanied them as, whimpering and unresponsive, Numps was set gingerly on his pallet in a small, nestlike domestic nook of the store.

"I shall return presently with a soothing draught for the poor fellow," Crispus instructed Rossamünd. "There is no circumstance under which this would have happened if the Marshal was still present," he concluded heatedly.

"My, how kitten does play with father cat away," Threnody concurred. "The clerk-master behaves a little differently without someone to check him."

"Indeed, my dear. The worm has turned, I think." With a bow, the physician left.

Speechless with shame and regret, Rossamünd could think of no comfort as Numps lay curled about himself, rocking on his cot by the clean, cold light of the well-kept great-lamp. When he did finally find voice, all he could say for a time was, "Sorry . . . I'm so sorry."

But all he got in reply from Numps was, over and over, "My friend . . . you're killed again . . ."

"If I had known the Master-of-Clerks would treat your baths so, there is nothing that would have made me tell of them!" Rossamünd said bitterly, tears threatening.

"There's no way you could have guessed ahead to that fellow's wretchedness, Rossamünd," Threnody murmured, touching him on the arm and actually managing to bring some comfort. "I'm sure Dolours would say something much the same were she here," the girl added as a qualification for her soothing.

When Crispus returned, it was a bitter fortune that the glimner, so insensible with shock, went quickly to sleep under the influence of the physician's soother. Crispus, Threnody and Rossamünd sat for a while by Numps' side, watching over him.

"What is going to happen to him, Doctor?" whispered Rossamünd.

"He will recover, my boy." The physician smiled kindly. "I have seen him through worse and will see him through again."

Rossamünd was in doubt. "He should have gone with Mister Sebastipole."

"I do not think the Considine is a good place for him either," Crispus replied. "In fact, you would have a hard time getting him out of Winstermill. It was remarkable that he even ventured up on to the Mead today."

Rossamünd sat in silent thought. "Doctor Crispus, what will happen to Winstermill—to us all—without the Marshal here?"

The physician sighed, deep and sad. "I have not one notion, my boy, though if today's travesty is an indicator of our new leader's method, then it just might be an unhappy end for us all."

"Here I was beginning to enjoy the life." Threnody's muttered words were heavy with irony. "I was telling Rossamünd before, good Doctor, that events have fallen very *well* for our dastardly clerk-master."

"Why, child, I suppose they have." Crispus stroked his chin. "Yet I can hardly conceive of him orchestrating all the manifold trials that have beset us and the brave Marshal most of all."

"I have been a pupil of Mother's long enough to know only a prod here and a coaxing there is enough to bring another down," Threnody waxed sagaciously. "Their troubles do the rest for you."

The physician looked at her for a moment. "Is that so, child? I wonder at the rather bleak nature of the lessons your good mother holds."

Rossamünd marveled at this glimpse of the bizarre life the girl must have led before she joined the lighters.

Inevitably Crispus' duties called him away, and middens' call coaxed Threnody back to the manse.

Rossamünd was left to continue the observance alone. Sitting there in the quiet of the store, he began to arrange a plan in his grieving thoughts: a scheme to offer some small consolation to the harrowed man. It was quite simple, and required only a clear occasion to be done. He would go to the Scaffold and rescue what bloom he could. The best time was mains, when the manse was a little stupid with the filling of its myriad stomachs, and the vigilance of its watch directed more outward to the Harrowmath. Prentices were allowed a relative freedom of movement during meals, and he was going to make full use of the privilege. Rossamünd would take a smock and a barrow—of which there was a conspicuously ample supply all about this part of the Gutter—and, like a gardener, steal on to the Mead and take back the bloom. The plan fixed so firmly in his mind as the only way he might make any kind of amends, he determined to go through with it that very evening.

He stood to put the plan into motion. The smock would be from his own trunk. Of all its intended uses, he reflected, impersonating a groundsman was probably not among them. The wooden barrow—found in the lantern store itself—he hid in a gap between the Principal Stair and front boarded wall of the store, wedging it behind a rain barrel, and with it a rusty fodicar to aid him in hooking the bloom down.

Preparations done, the prentice looked in on the insensible glimner one last time and returned to the manse.

The evening was as blustery a one as Rossamünd could recall. Clouds blossomed and expanded, unraveling from horizon to horizon over the whole Harrowmath: low, mountainous-dark, and turned an oddly luminescent, muddy hue by the westering sun they hid. Southerly, loam-perfumed winds blustered over the shorter walls of the Low Gutter; wild, freezing vortices spun across the Mead and down the Cypress Walk, prodding Rossamünd with every gust, bringing to his cold aching ears the angry hiss of the tempest-tossed grasses on the plain.

Gripping the thin linen smock and its meager extra warmth about him, the prentice skipped down the postern stair and scurried along the poorly lit lanes of the Gutter. His healing crown aching under the bandages, he wished he still had his hat to protect his head from the blustery buffeting. This was a bad night to be in the open, but it was a good night for clandestine or nefarious deeds. He reckoned upon less chance of discovery or questions by this route, and his reckoning proved right. Not one other soul crossed his way but a gray grimalkin, one of the tribe of mousing-cats allowed free roam of the whole fortress. Wise enough to leave the vermin to themselves on such an ugly eve, it blinked knowingly at him from its shelter beneath a stack of unused hogsheads, puncheons and barrels.

Past the bill-posting trees, across the All-About, by the Magazine and between the warehouses and work-stalls he went, arriving at the lantern store in a state of thrumming anxiety. He hastily pulled the barrow from behind its rain-barrel nook. Rossamünd pushed it up the long cartage-ramp—the Axial—to the edge of the Grand Mead, the axle creaking quietly and the wheel making a pleasant, continuous crunch on the gravel. The Mead proved as empty of people as it had been that very first evening the coach had deposited him at Winstermill. Back then he had thought the manse huge and vacant, but now he knew the Mead's current state of inoccupation made a lie of the fortress's hectic daytime activity. Honey-hued window-lights flickered invitingly—glimmering like watching eyes in the gatehouses, the Cursory, the Feuterers' Cottage and the Yardsman's Row. Snatches of ribald songs reached him modulated on the wind's frenetic breath, but the great, walled valley before him was deserted.

Rossamünd paused. He knew that it was possible hidden eyes were looking from cavities in the structures where the most faithful house-watchmen kept a diligent eye. There was very little he could do about these unseen observers but hope his thin ruse of a groundsman on a late errand would fool them.

Rossamünd took a steadying breath.

Lit behind by one of the few lamps on the grounds, the Scaffold was unmistakable: a stark shadow of limbs so unnaturally perpendicular that Rossamünd could well see how it earned its name. The dying bloom still thickly furbished every branch as high as the peoneers' ladders had reached, warping and writhing violently in stormy gusts. Touched with a ghastly yellow hue, the plants were clearly drying, their vigor failing. Steeling himself, Rossamünd pushed the barrow steadily along the left-hand edge of the drive, walking with a show of purpose directly to the dead tree, hurrying only when he crossed the brightly lit ground before the manse's front doors. Under the tree, the hanging bloom was far too high for him to get with his diminutive reach. Even the corroding fodicar was little help, the single hook requiring impossible precision to snag the wildly wind-dancing tendrils. Over and over Rossamünd swung and poked at these elusive targets till he was near to sobbing with the futility of the task. Too often when he did achieve a hooking, the failing plant would tear and shower him with its wilting leaflets.

Frogs and toads! Confinations will be starting soon.

It had been his great Plan with a capital *P* to fill the barrow with great armfuls of the stuff, but now he was hard-pressed to gather a handful. He threw the fodicar down in disgust and it bounced butt-end first off the iron-hard roots of the Scaffold, flipped over several times and skidded clatteringly to a stop against the wall of the manse.

With a clinch of dread at such a din, Rossamünd froze— he had never meant to hurl the fodicar so hard or so far—and instantly realized he need not have toiled so fruitlessly. For there, all about the fodicar's final rest were intact fragments of bloom, ripped from the tree by the gale, scattered now like summer-fallen blossoms on the Scaffold's leeward side. The prentice's entire soul leaped for the joy of it, but quickly squeezed to fright again as the noise of watchmen stirring in one of the many structures on the Mead's edge reached him. With terror's thrill, Rossamünd dashed the barrow over to the fodicar. Voices were becoming more distinct, sounding nearer, coming from the coach yard around the corner. He grabbed at all the bloom he could reach, dumping it rapidly in the barrow. The crunch of a footfall on gravel was all too clear. The prentice snatched up the fallen lantern-crook, took grip of the barrow's handles and hurried off across the Mead, dark excitement broiling in his innards. At any moment he expected to be hailed. He forced himself not to run. With every step nearer the Axial, he dared to hope he might escape unseen, and hope and dread seesawed desperately till—at last!—he was trundling down the ramp descending to the Low Gutter. Only when he was back by the gap between the Principal Stair and the lantern store did Rossamünd finally begin again to breathe.

Not waiting to discover if he had been seen or followed, the prentice fumbled off his smock, tipped all the bloom from the barrow on to it, put the barrow back behind the rain barrel, and the fodicar with it. Rolling up the smock and hefting this bundle over his shoulder, he scampered back through the comparative calm of the Low Gutter, up the Postern Stair and into his own cell just as mains was ending.

Never had he prized the privacy of his cell as much as then. In the quiet of the tiny room, with the door shut, Rossamünd spread the smock out, and heart a-thump with hope, sorted through all the scraps of bloom. He was quickly and bitterly dismayed to find much of the stuff terribly yellowed. Yet among all the dying bloom-shreds he found six still-healthy tendrils, limp but not beyond restoring. He could have whooped for joy.

His messmates began moving and stomping about outside, shifting about the cell row as they readied for bed. Rossamünd got into his own nightclothes and, with a quick check out the cell door, made three rapid forays. Some of the other prentices gave him odd looks but none stopped him. Bare feet slapping on the cold slate, he carried water from the cistern, via his biggin, to pour into the chamber pot. Thus the aquatic environment the bloom required was in some way restored. Rossamünd took his time tenderly arranging the survivors so that each was properly submerged.

His nerves were so tightly strung, a soft bang at the door spooked him mightily.

"It's douse-lanterns, Bookchild," came a hard, warning voice.

Intent on tending his haul, Rossamünd had missed the day's-end cry. All clatter and flurry, the prentice tried to hurry the last two precious sprigs into the chamber pot.

The cell door opened and in thrust the lamplighter-sergeant's head. "Did ye not hear the——" he began, then saw the bloom. Grindrod's eyes went wide, but sharp anger was quickly replaced with understanding. "Where did ye get those, prentice?"

"I—ah—from the—the—" Rossamünd floundered: it was theft either way—a flogging offense, twelve of the best under the lictor's hand.

"From the Scaffold?"

"Aye, Lamplighter-Sergeant."

"Good man, Master Lately. As ye were." The merest hint of an untypical smile showed on Grindrod's face. "Douse yer lantern, the day's deeds are done, lad . . . and keep *those* well out of sight. What our new Marshal doesn't fathom won't turn into trouble."

Confused, relieved, Rossamünd pushed the chamber pot under his cot, tumbled all the dead bloom together with his smock, stuffed it into the bed chest and turned his bright-limn. In the fading light he readied for sleep. His heart still pattered fast and he lay awake for a long time, astounded at his own audacity and wondering why Grindrod had just abetted him in his crime.

Immediately after the sunup call *"A lamp! A lamp to light your path!"* rang through the cell row, Rossamünd was out of his cot and pulling the chamber pot with its leafy guests out from under his bunk. He had continued to use the pot for its intended purpose during the night, having learned from Numps that one's night waters were good for the bloom. Seltzerman 1st Class Humbert had reluctantly said the same when, amid much snickering and guffawing from his fellows, Rossamünd had sought to confirm the fact during readings. Nevertheless, one of the bloom sprigs had not survived the night, and he was down to five.

While the others lads washed, Rossamünd hid the pot between his bed chest and the wall under his valise and salumanticum to foil the questing chambermaids on their morning rounds.

Food gobbled (farrats, raisins and small beer) and barely more than an awkward "good morning" exchanged with Threnody, Rossamünd was rushing back to his cell, an idea illuminating in his mind like a thermistor's bolt. He fished out the chamber pot from its hide, took out his lark-lamp, prized off the lugs and opened the top of the bell. Into the glass-bound cavity he managed to fit all five fronds, stuffing the sixth in with all the dead bloom wrapped in his smock and hiding it again in the bed chest. He filled the lark-lamp with water from the cistern and by breakfast-end had the bell-top secured back in place and the lamp safely back in his bed chest.

All through the rest of the day, he was in anxious expectation of discovery. At morning parade he waited for the Master-of-Clerks to arrive and announce the wicked theft of bloom-rubbish from beneath the Scaffold. Through morning evolutions Rossamünd kept looking guiltily over at the gaunt tree, convinced a mercer would run up and announce that "some unknown miscreant had meddled with the rightfully exposed collucia plants!"

None of this happened.

By middens, Rossamünd was eager to restore the rescued glimbloom to Numps.

The glimner was still in bed, sitting up, sipping at some fine-smelling broth—probably a kindness of Doctor Crispus—and looking utterly spent from all his grieving. Gratified the man was cared for, nevertheless Rossamünd felt his heart ache to see Numps so woebegone.

"Mister Numps," Rossamünd ventured, "I—I tried to save your bloom yesternight, but . . . but this was all I could get. The rest was too high off the ground." He proffered the bloom-packed lark-lamp and the glimner's eyes went so round Rossamünd feared they might pop right from their sockets. For a terrible beat or three of his anxious heart, the prentice thought he had woefully miscalculated, and simply added to the glimner's distress.

"You rescued poor Numps' poor friends," the man managed brokenly. He took the small lamp in shaking hands and gradually his hauntedness gave way to profound delight as joy blossomed into ecstasy. "Oh, my friends!" Numps cried, in both shouts and tears. "Oh, my friends!" The unscarred side of his face became wet with weeping, yet the riven side stayed dry, his ruined eye tearless.

19

BILLETING DAY

fetchman also fetcher, bag-and-bones man, ashcarter or thew-thief ("strength-stealer"). Someone who carries the bodies of the fallen from the field of battle, taking them to the manouvra—or field hospital. Despite their necessary and extremely helpful labors, fetchmen are often resented by pediteers as somehow responsible for the deaths of the wounded comrades they take who often die later of their injuries. Indeed, they are regarded as harbingers of death, sapping their own side of strength, and as such are kept out of sight till they are needed.

DESPITE the dramatic events, many of the lantern-sticks were largely unperturbed by the Marshal's departure. Grindrod and Benedict did their utmost to preserve the routine. The next day the prentices had just completed the usual afternoon reading on Our Mandate and Matter with Seltzerman Humbert when Benedict hustled into the lectury declaring in amazement, "They're holding Billeting Day early!"

Almost the moment these words were out, the grandiose figure of the Master-of-Clerks, the Marshal-Subrogat himself, appeared at the lectury door, gracing them all with his presence. He held his chin at a dignified tilt. As always, the man was served by his ubiquitous retinue: Laudibus Pile; Witherscrawl, and now Fleugh the under-clerk; the master-surveyor with diagrams of the manse permanently gripped under his arm; and two troubardier foot-guards. With them also came a lanky, frightening-looking fellow dressed all in lustrous black: heavy boots, black galliskins over tight leggings, black satin longshanks. His trunk was swathed in a sash of sturdy proofed silk, neck thickly wrapped in a long woolen scarf yet—most oddly—his chest and shoulders and arms were bare, despite the aching chill, showing too-pale against all the black. His head was bald, and a thin dark arrow pointed up his face from chin to absent hairline, its tines splaying out over each brow. He was a wit. More disconcerting still was that his eyes were completely black—no white orbs, just glistening dark. This was some strange trick of chemistry Rossamünd had not heard of. The combination of this blank, pitch-dark stare with Pile's snide, parti-hued gaze stilled the whole room as they moved within.

With a thump of determined footfalls Grindrod appeared behind them all, muttering to himself, his face screwed up in silent invective. "Sit" was all he said.

The prentices obeyed with meek alacrity. When all shuffling and snuffling ceased, the Master-of-Clerks paced before them, hands behind his back, puckering his lips and squinting at the platoon as if shrewdly appraising them all.

"Brave prentices," he declaimed, "you have worked at your practicing with admirable zeal and laudable facility. Fully confident in your fitness, I am convinced you are ready

THE BLACK-EYED WIT

for full, glorious service as Emperor's lighters, and have decided it timely for you to be granted your billets and to be sent promptly to them."

That had most of the prentices scratching their heads, pained frowns of lugubrious thought creasing several brows. *Does that mean it's Billeting Day or what?*

How would he know what the state of our fitness for service is? was the spin of Rossamünd's own thinking. *He has naught to do with us!*

With a harsh, self-conscious throat-clearing, Grindrod stood forward, clearly struggling to contain his temper. "Sounds an admirable conclusion, sir, but the lantern-sticks bain't ready for the work. Ye let a half-trained lad out on the road by himself and ye might as well toss 'im straight to the fetchman!"

"Pshaw! I'll not have your womanish obstructions, Lamplighter-Sergeant-of-Prentices." The Master-of-Clerks enunciated Grindrod's full title in the manner of a put-down. "They are required out on that road to make up for the appalling losses incurred under my predecessor."

The Lamplighter-Sergeant went purple with indignant rage, but the Master-of-Clerks carried on, not allowing the man an opportunity to press any further dissent.

"Staffing at the cothouses must be restocked. We have twenty-one—no, twenty-two"—he corrected himself with an enigmatic look to Threnody, sitting straightbacked at the front of the room—"hale souls trained in the lampsman's labors, and as ready as anyone can be, surely, to wind a simple glowing weed in and out its chamber. It is a terrible waste of a resource and one I have decided can be better employed filling these gaps on the road than lolling about here being taught the same thing over and over. It is not difficult work, Sergeant. If they have not come to grips with the task by now, I fail to see how another month will make it so."

"Another month is all the difference, sir!" Grindrod glowered. "They're bare-breeched bantlings who set to whimperin' at the slightest speak of bogles! Ye should be hiring those blighted sell-swords bivouacked outside the Nook, or get them lardy magnates in the Placidine itself to spare a platoon or two of their blighted domesticars! Either way, sir, trained, professional men-at-arms used to the rigors of war. Ye might not know, sir, hidin' behind yer ledgers and quill pots, that it's war out upon the road, sir, and it's we lowly lighters who are in the van!"

The Master-of-Clerks bridled for a moment and then, with admirable equanimity, said soothingly, "I'm sure you're a fellow who knows his business well enough when teaching a poor lad his first clues, but it now falls to me to choose their best uses. That is to be the end of it, Lamplighter-Sergeant—I do not want to be put in the position of having to take you in firmer hand. Indexer Witherscrawl," he said, dismissing Grindrod with a turn of his gorgeously bewigged head, "read the tally if you please."

The sour indexer stepped forward, glared at the prentices—at every single one—and especially at Threnody. "Harkee, ye little scrubs! Here is the Roll of Billets, of who will go to where and when they will leave. Listen well—I shall tell this only the once!"

What! The prentices could not quite believe this: they were to be denied the full honors of a beautiful and especial ceremony. There were supposed to be martial musics; the whole manse was meant to turn out in respect at the boys' success in prenticing and their coming into full rank as lampsmen. A susurrus of deep displeasure stirred about the boys.

Grindrod did nothing to quell them, simply folding his arms. In fact, he showed open pride in the prentices' muttering rebellion.

"I said, quiet!" Witherscrawl shouted, and a foot-guard rapped the floor with the shaft end of his poleax, its cracking report startling the whole room to dumbness.

With a foul sneer, the indexer raised a tall, thin ledger close to his face and from it began to read out names in letter-fall order: Arabis to go to Cothallow, Childebert to Sparrowstall, Egadis to Tumblesloe Cot just beyond the Roughmarch, and so on.

Attention focused.

"Mole to Ashenstall . . ."

Onion Mole went white with dismay. The other prentices winced, Rossamünd with them. A long way east, Ashenstall was one of the harder billets on the road, isolated and with few vigil-day rests.

Apprehension grew. They could not assume only the kinder billets would be given.

"Wheede to Mirthalt . . . ," droned the indexer, "Wrangle to . . . Bitterbolt . . ."

With a chill, Rossamünd knew his name was next, languishing at the end of the lists along with Threnody's . . .

"Bookchild to Wormstool . . ."

. . . and this chill became a frigid blank.

Some of the other prentices gasped.

Wormstool!

This was the last—the very last—cothouse on the Wormway, well east of Ashenstall, with only the grim Imperial bastion of Haltmire between it and the Ichormeer. Built at the "ignoble end of the road," Wormstool was no place for newly promoted prentice-lampsmen. Situated too near the sodden fringe of the dread swamp, it was held as one of the toughest billets of all. Only those who volunteered ever went there, yet here he was, a mere prentice, being *sent*. The Ichormeer had once been just a frightful fable to him. Now Rossamünd was going to live and work as a neighbor to its very borders, where all the bogles and the vilest hugger-muggers that ever dragged themselves from putrid mud haunted and harried. Absorbed in his shocked thoughts at this revelation, he did not hear where Threnody had been sent.

Witherscrawl finished his recitation.

The Master-of-Clerks presented himself again. "I will be wanting you all to your billets as soon as can be done. With time to travel in consideration, those farther out will leave sooner. Therefore those prentices stationed farthest away will be leaving on the first post of tomorrow morn.

Well done to you all, my fine fellows—you are now all full lampsmen!"

Confused and silent, the prentices were dismissed and that was that: Billeting Day—such as it had been—was over, an insulting sham.

The Master-of-Clerks left without any further acknowledgment, taking his "tail" with him. Grindrod followed, and an angry, muttered conference could be heard out in the hallway, terminating suddenly with the Master-of-Clerks' high clear voice saying, "Cease your querulous bickerings, Sergeant-lighter! It will be as I have decided it. They have been sent where needed. If you are so concerned for the children, then get back to them and make certain they are ready for their great adventure. Good day!"

At first Rossamünd's fellows were bemused. As the day progressed most were reconciled with their early promotions and many proved pleased with their billets, however untimely and however tawdrily they had been portioned. At lale—held indoors owing to inclement weather—they buzzed and boasted excitedly to each other about the various merits of their new posts, those billeted at the same cothouse gathering together in excited twos or threes. Every lad congratulated the others for their good fortune and the 7q extra they would all receive each month now that they were lampsmen 3rd class. For Onion Mole and even more so for Rossamünd there was baffled commiseration: he was the only prentice to be billeted at the ignoble end of the road.

"Why are they sending you so far, Rosey boy?" asked Arabis, still smiling about his prime posting at Cothallow, one of the smartest cothouses on the road.

Hands raised, Rossamünd shrugged.

"I reckon you'll be going tomorrow morning, then?" Pillow wondered aloud.

"It's a handy thing ye've had practice with yer potives." Smellgrove patted him on the back.

"Aye." Wheede grinned. "The baskets will have to watch they don't get a pud full of bothersalts."

Rossamünd ducked his head, grateful for their fumbling encouragements.

Threnody had guzzled her saloop and was rising to leave.

"Where are you going?" he asked her quickly.

"Out from here," she answered flatly.

"Where are you billeted?"

"Didn't you hear?" she asked tartly. "I'm going to Dovecote Bolt. That Odious Podious thinks he is such a funny fellow—told me my mother would appreciate me being so close."

"We'll be billet-mates!" cried Plod happily.

"Oh, hazzah," Threnody replied with a wry twist of her mouth, and departed.

For the rest of the day, as Benedict strove, in Grindrod's absence, to keep the animated prentices in line, Rossamünd's mind was a hasty turning of half thoughts and unhappy conclusions. He was leaving—packed off posthaste to the worst billet in the land. Most likely he was leaving for good, to die at the hands of some ravenous nicker fresh plucked from the ooze. He had to tell Numps—just as Mister Sebastipole had done—that he might not see the glimner for a long time. Once again, mains became the prentice's chance to venture out. When the meal came around he took only a hard loaf of pong to chew "on the foot" and hastened to the lantern store.

As he went to leave the mess hall, he passed Threnody, back from making her treacle in the kitchens. She snatched at his arm. "I must talk with you," she hissed.

Rossamünd wrenched free. "Not now, Threnody. I must visit Numps to tell him I'm going," he insisted in return.

She glowered at him. "What do you have to do that is more important than me? I have things to tell you—a surprise."

"Truly, Threnody, it must wait," he declared, pulling his arm free of her and dashing off, leaving her stunned and scowling.

In the early night he ran down to the Low Gutter. The sweet smell of rain-washed air—the promise of showers—was blowing up from the southeast. Passing through Door 143 just as water began to fall, Rossamünd emerged from the shelves as his ready, if somewhat forced, smile of friendliness became a puzzled grimace. Numps was not in his usual seat by the glow of the postless great-lamp and the never diminishing pile of panes. Nor was he down the next aisle of shelves getting mineral fluids or other such things for cleaning stubborn crust.

"Mister Numps?" he called.

The rain a-hammered on the roof.

Ringing ears.

Nothing.

"Mister Numps?" He turned slowly by the glimner's empty seat, hoping the fellow might just shuffle out from behind a barrel or stack of lantern-windows. Horrid thoughts of some frightful crisis began to intrude into Rossamünd's imagination, yet there was no evidence of trouble. Rossamünd searched down every aisle and behind any pile he could see: no Numps. *Destroying his bloom is one thing, but surely he is too unimportant to be hurt or carried off?* Rossamünd's mind cogged. *No one could be bothered, even if they* did *remember him.* He thought of the undercroft and the old bloom baths. *Surely not there? It's been boarded up and blocked* . . . This was the only alternative he knew.

Careful not to attract attention with any untoward huff or hustle, the prentice slipped through the mazelike interstices between the work buildings, trying to find the path Numps had taken him that one wet day. Twice he thought he had got himself irrevocably lost, yet, though seen only once, the particular features of the twisting route were quickly familiar again and Rossamünd was soon dashing down the tunnel-like alley. He skidded into the discarded square and its gurgling drains, startling a sparrow that had been bobbing by the sunken grate. The entrance to the undercroft had indeed been sealed with boards, but these had been pulled away and collected in a tidy stack by the grate. Next to this stack sat an equally orderly collection of the bolts used to pin the boards in place, partly piled on top of a soiled official ordinance bill stringently demanding everyone to go away in painfully formal terms. Kneeling in the wet, the prentice leaned over the grate and tried to reach under as he had observed Numps do, to feel about for some kind of catch or spring or other lever.

"Mister Numps!" he called, hoarse and wary, down the hole while he searched. "Mister Numps!" Nothing even vaguely catch or latchlike presented itself to his questing fingers.

"Oh hallo, Mister Rossamünd." The soft voice of the glimner echoed strangely from below, giving Rossamünd a fright. "I reckoned you were a guardsman fellow come to take my bloom again."

"Mister Numps!" With rushing relief, Rossamünd thought he could just spot the pale oval of Numps' upturned face in the dark of the subterranean stair. "Are you safe? Are you hurt again?"

"Oh dear . . . I don't want to be found by the Master-Clerker . . . ," the glimner quavered. "I didn't want to be found without Mister 'Pole here."

Rossamünd smiled sadly. How he wished he could provide

the glimner a greater sense of safety. Instead he had things to tell that he knew would be hard for the poor man.

"I have to go too, Mister Numps," he began. "They're sending me away . . ."

"Oh . . . oh dear . . ." Numps sighed, sounding bewildered. He must have climbed higher in his distress, for his pallid face became closer. "Numps' friends all going . . . "

"The Master-of-Clerks called Billeting Day today," Rossamünd confirmed, "and I am leaving to my cothouse—and there's nothing I can do about it."

"Tell Mister 'Pole—he won't let you be sent away. Even poor old limpling-head Numps knows it's too soon for prentices to go a-working. Write Mister 'Pole, he won't let you go—I have his address, see . . ." Numps rummaged about in pockets.

"I will . . . I will write him a letter," said Rossamünd. "Maybe he can help us, even from the Considine. Things are so bad with his and the Marshal's leaving. You should stay hiding if you can, Mister Numps—the fortress is downside up. Will you be able to eat and all?"

"Ah, Mister Rossamünd." Numps tapped his brow. "There are many things Numps knows that people don't think he knows. There is food a-plenty if you go to the right places." The glimner was oddly calm. "Besides, Cinnamon's friends are watching over Numps-a-hiding so you can reckon me as safe."

Rossamünd thought of the sparrow he had startled, pecking at the grate, and smiled. He did not know what help these little agents of the Duke of Sparrows might be—if that was indeed what they were. What did that kind of attention mean? He wanted to believe that goodly urchin-lords existed, that Numps was well looked out for, but the old common suspicions persisted.

A distant rataplan of the drums meant that mains was at an end and confinations about to begin.

"I must go, Mister Numps. We will both write to Mister Sebastipole, yes?"

"Yes."

"And you'll stay safe and secret, yes?"

"Yes."

Rossamünd wanted to hug the glimner, but shyness and the grate prevented him. Instead he just stared into Numps' melancholy eyes, and the man stared back.

"Good-bye!" The prentice reluctantly turned to leave.

"Good-bye, Mister Rossamünd," he heard the glimner call behind him. "Numps won't forget his new old friend—don't you forget him . . ."

"Never, Mister Numps!"

Heavy with fear for the glimner's fate, Rossamünd ran back to the manse. For the rest of confinations he packed, stowed all he had ever possessed and prepared himself for leaving at first light. In the last few moments before douse-lanterns he lay on his cot and with his stylus hastily scratched out a letter on a blank page torn from the back of the peregrinat.

To Mister Sebastipole
Lamplighter's Agent & Falseman to the Lamplighter-
Marshal of Winstermill
Epistra Scuthae
The Considine
The Patricine
2nd Heimio HIR 1601

Dear Mister Sebastipole,
I have no certainty this will make its way to you, but I
try anyway.
I write to you, Mister Sebastipole, on the last night of my
prenticing in Winstermill, for since you left with the Marshal,
the Master-of-Clerks has taken all in hand and declared Billeting
Day early. Tomorrow I travel to the cothouse of Wormstool.
But it is not this that troubles me. It is rather Mister Numps
that I am worried for. The Master-of-Clerks (he calls himself the
Marshal-Subrogat now) destroyed Mister Numps' bloom (the
stuff he was growing down in the deserted undercroft) the very
day you departed, and Mister Numps (as I am sure you can well
imagine) was sorely troubled. I managed to save a little part of
it, but the baths are shattered and most of the bloom is dead.
I fear for Mister Numps, that he isn't safe with only the good
Doctor Crispus to watch out for him. Would there be any way
you can help him, or even get him away from the manse?

He thought of adding:

The last I saw of him he still hid where his bloom was
once grown.

. . . but realized the letter might be intercepted and read
by unfriendly eyes and so he left it out. Instead he quickly
completed the letter.

I hope you and the Lamplighter-Marshal fare well, and that all unjust things are righted soon.

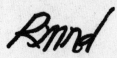

Rossamünd Bookchild,
Lampsman 3rd Class
HIHF Winstermill
Conduit Vermis
Sulk End

20

ON LEAVING WINSTERMILL

Idlewild, the ~ officially known as the Placidia Solitus, a gathering of client-cities (colonies) along the Imperial Highroad of the Conduit Vermis. Each town, village or fortress is sponsored by a different state of the Empire—Brandenbrass, Hergoatenbosch, Quimperpund, Maubergonne, Termagaunt, even Catalain. Established in the late 15th century HIR, it is the latest great project of what is grandly termed cicuration—taming by farming; purgation—taming by force; and hossesation—taming by landscaping, originally proposed by Clementine itself. The Inner Idlewild or Placidine, from Tumblesloe Cot to the Wight, was declared "regio scutis"—a fenceland—over a decade ago. This heralded a brilliant success of the great labor of pushing back the monsters and the threwd. The marches from the Wight to Haltmire—otherwise known as the Paucitine (also the Frugelle)—are still considered ditchland.

I
N the clear, bright and oppressively cold morning Rosamünd watched Winstermill recede as the postlentum took him away. Threnody sat opposite him in the cabin, snuggled in a nest of furs. The first he knew of her joining him was her appearance on the Grand Mead that morning, baggage and all, as he waited for the lentum. Originally billeted at Dovecote Bolt, the girl was not supposed to be here in the carriage, the first to take freshly promoted prentices out to their new home. Somehow late

the day before, she had succeeded in having her posting changed and was now with him on the road to Wormstool. Perhaps this was what she had been so intent on telling him the evening before. "It's too dangerous just for one" was all she had said in explanation as they had waited on the cold Mead earlier that morning. "I'll keep watch on your flanks, and you'll keep watch on mine."

Rossamünd wondered briefly how the besotted Plod would feel about her change of destination. She was surely the most gorgeously accoutred lamplighter along the whole of the Wormway in her scarlet and gold harness and mass of midnight ringlets. Under one arm she clutched a day-bag, while a linen package and a mysterious round box sat on the seat beside. One hand was kept warm in a fuzzy white snuftkin, the other clutched a duodecimo novel, which she was reading with pointed concentration. Despite her infuriating twists of manners and mood, Rossamünd was at first glad she had come along. But beyond the initial word she had been ignoring him, for reasons he could not quite comprehend, spoiling the sweetness of her original gallant gesture.

Has she come with me just to have someone to still pick on?

Rossamünd had reading matter of his own. Before the lentum-and-four had departed, he had ventured to the Packet File to deliver his letter for Sebastipole and had been given another missive in return. He still clutched it in his hand, forgotten in the haste of his embarkation. With him in the cabin he had also brought his restocked salumanticum, his old traveling satchel with its knife-in-sheath attached holding his peregrinat, and a parcel of wayfood. On the seat next to him was his precious valise crammed with smalls and other necessaries for five days' travel. Anything over that and he would just have to make do. The rest of what he owned—most of it issued by the lamplighters when he first joined—had been stowed in an ox trunk and fixed to the roof of the lentum along with Threnody's sizable collection of luggage, their fodicars and fusils.

In his pocket his buff-leather wallet was bulging full with traveling papers, reissued after the ruin his old ones had become on his way to Winstermill. There was also a work docket already bearing its first remarks: the period of his service as a prentice and the tasks undertaken, by which was a "CS" for "Completed to Satisfaction"; under "Conduct" was the comment "Late for prenticing period" and two small "i's" for his impositions—pots-and-pans with the now-vanished Mother Snooks. It was all signed off by the Master-of-Clerks himself, now the Marshal-Subrogat.

With these papers was a fair wad of folding notes and coin—his three months' wages as a prentice and a large portion of the money Europe had given to him in High Vesting. As for a hat, there had been no time to replace it, and so here he was venturing out with little more than the bandage about his head.

The east wind whistled low on the Harrowmath, the usual odor of the long grass rank with the rot of sodden veg-

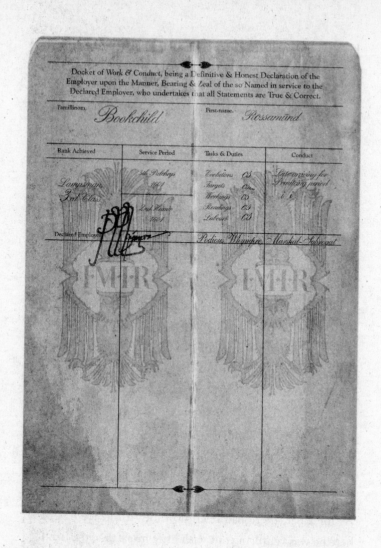

Docket of Work & Conduct, being a Definitive & Honest Declaration of the
Employer upon the Manner, Bearing & Zeal of the so Named in service to the
Declared Employer, who undertakes that all Statements are True & Correct.

Familinom. *Bookchild*		First-name. *Rossamünd*	
Rank Achieved	**Service Period**	**Tasks & Duties**	**Conduct**
Lamplighter 3rd Class	*5th Pitchboy 1601* *2nd Hesion 1601*	*Evolutions CS* *Targets CS* *Workings CS* *Readings CS* *Labours CS*	*Late arriving for Pointing period* *t.c.*
Declared Employer		*Podious Whympre*	*Marshal-Subrogat*

etation. Mixing with the flat nonodor of his newly applied
Exstinker, it became an unpleasant half stink in Rossamünd's
nostrils. He rubbed his nose with the back of his hand and

sighed his melancholy. An untimely departure, an uncertain way ahead, and Numps left in the rough care of the lighters, yet Rossamünd was glad to be out of Winstermill and on the road once more. He even entertained the hope he might see Europe on the way through.

He looked down at the letter and opened it, his hands slightly trembling.

It was dated the nineteenth of Pulvis, Solemnday— almost a week ago.

Rossamünd,

I have to tell ye of the profound and sorrowful news that on the night of the 5th of this month, the marine society was burnt down and that Madam Opera did perish in the fire along with, to my ever-living grief and shame, many children and Master Pinsum too, with valuables and papers burnt or maybe stolen.

Verline and we other masters all survived. Perhaps we should not have lived with so many young kilt. But survive we have and are seeking now to find berths for all the poor younkers made wastrel once more.

That wretched utterworst Gosling set the spark, or so it appears. Barthomæus and I chased at rumors of him a' watching the building many times afore the fire, but obviously turned up naught. The splints say he has fled the city. He always was a yellow-gutted dastard and I should have ended him long ago but for the restraint of conscience—and Verline, bless her.

With all that has got to be done for the tots it appears that Craumpalin and I shall be arriving to ye later than expected, but can't be knowing when. Expect us maybe in two months.

With great respect and sorrow etc.

Frans, Mstr, Ex-Gnr.

I am sorry about being so long in scratching this down and sending it on to ye, but our labors have not let me do so sooner. Thanks to ye for yer own letter dated 13th of Pulchrys, it survived the fire and we esteem it like treasure. Hold yer course, my boy, hold yer course—I know it is hard. Remember I said once that paths need never stay fixed.

Also Craumpalin sends greeting: he says that he is most proud and very happy with the usefulness of his bothersalts and tells ye (as do I) to keep wearing his Exstinker, if ye do not already.

Miss Verline is safe with her sister and her new niece and would send ye her best—as ye well know—if she knew of this letter.

Well-fare-ye!

Rossamünd could not believe what was written. He read again. ". . . the night of the 5th of this month . . ." That was the very night the horn-ed nickers had attacked Threnody and her sisters in their carriage. Yet it was not until his third time through, slowly and painfully, that the full impact of his old dormitory master's terrible news struck home. He turned his face away from Threnody, hiding in the collar of his pallmain, and wept as he had not wept in the longest

360

time, letting all the bleakness sob out. He wept for the dear dead children, for Master Pinsum, and even for Madam Opera, who may not have been the kindest, but was by no means the worst; for the grief caused to his beloved carers; for fury at Gosling's malice. The fury passed but the grief remained, and Rossamünd lost himself in sad, wordless reveries, only vaguely heedful of the progress of the carriage as it followed the Pettiwiggin along the Harrowmath.

They were passing through the Briarywood when he roused at last with thoughts of Fransitart's arrival—and dear Craumpalin coming too. *I must write to let them know I will not be at Winstermill.*

"What's wrong with you, lamp boy?" Threnody said, her voice raised only a little over the dull rumble of the lentum. "Why do you cry?" She looked at Fransitart's letter. "Who is the correspondence from?"

Rossamünd became suddenly very aware of the girl: aware of her proximity; of his unwanted tears. He wiped at them quickly, sniffing impatiently. "My old dormitory master back in Boschenberg . . . ," he answered reluctantly. "He . . . he sends sad news."

"Sad news?" Threnody folded the duodecimo in her lap.

"My old home was burned down by an old foe," Rossamünd managed. "Madam Opera died in the fire. She was the owner . . . and a . . . a mother, I suppose—in a strange way. She named me—marked it in the book . . . "

"You're a better soul than me, Rossamünd."

"How?"

"You weep over the death of some wastrel proprietress, yet I can only wish my very own mother might perish in a fire."

With a frown, Rossamünd returned to the window and broodily observed the passing scene. He knew she was just trying to be kind. It did not help that she was not very good at it.

The post-lentum clopped between the twin keeps of Wellnigh House without hesitation, under the Omphalon, and on through to the Roughmarch. With a feeling very much like going through the Axles of Boschenberg, Rossamünd realized with equal parts dread and expectancy that he had never been farther east than this point, that he was hurtling into what were, for him, unknown lands.

A great-lamp at every bend, the Roughmarch Road twisted serpentlike through a valley clotted with thorny plants of many kinds—sloe, briar, boxthorn and blackberry, its spiny runners thickly stickling the verge. As with the wild grasses of the Harrowmath, fatigue parties were regularly sent out from Wellnigh House and Tumblesloe Cot to pull and prune these plants, to resist the threwd and deny monsters a hide from which to ambush. Yet either side of the way was only partially hacked and cleared, and Rossamünd could still feel the haunting watchfulness here, strong but strangely restrained. He stared at the high bald hills, dark and silent, and pulled up the door sash to keep the threat outside, glad he did not have to work the lamps on this stretch.

If Threnody noticed the threwd, she did not show it. Indeed, she started to hum as she read her book and paid Rossamünd and the rest of the world little heed.

They drove down out of the hills where a creek bubbled alongside the Wormway, spilling over lichen-covered rocks, beneath twisted roots of writhen, leafless trees and south under the road to make a bog at the foot of a short cliff. In as much time as it took to walk to Wellnigh House from Winstermill, they were passing the walls of Tumblesloe Cot, not pausing there either. The cothouse was built away from the highroad, right up against the cliffs that marched upon the eastern flanks of the hills. Nothing could be seen of it but the stonework curtain wall and the tops of a handful of high chimneys. They were in foreign lands now—the great divide between the Idlewild and the rest of the Empire had been crossed.

"Welcome to the Placidine," said Threnody. "Dovecote Bolt is next, at the junction with another road; if you left the highroad and took this other pathway north it would lead you to my old home, Herbroulesse."

Rossamünd looked at his peregrinat maps and saw the path she was talking of and her home too, both important enough to be mentioned. He did not want to be, but he was actually impressed. While it had stood, Madam Opera's marine society had never featured on any map he knew. "What will your mother think of what you're doing," he asked, "going off to dangerous cothouses?"

"She would lecture at me and I would disagree and we

would start screaming and I would be sent away somewhere with Dolours till Mother could bear to see me again."

"But what about the Emperor's Billion?" Rossamünd pressed.

"What about it?" Threnody snapped. "My mother has a larger mandate than that! Our clave's Imperial Prerogative takes precedence over simple tokens."

"Imperial Prerogative?"

She gave him the by-now-familiar *are-you-really-that-stupid?* look and said after a sigh, "It allows us to do and be without the states troubling us. It is granted by the Emperor himself, and not *every* clave has one." She finished with a proud sniff.

Before them the Conduit Vermis descended into a broad, shallow valley of scruffy pastures hemmed to the north by a spur of bald hills and to the south by the rolling, pastured fells of the Sparrow Downs. It was an unremarkable land. Rossamünd stared at the distant downs, wondering if an urchin-lord truly was there watching and sending out its little sparrow-agents from its leafy courts.

As the day grew longer, traffic began to pass going the other way. There were other post-lentums with returning dispatches; barouques and landaulets, perhaps taking the well-to-do to High Vesting or Brandenbrass; dyphrs dashing on errands; crofters commuting in curricles between land and town. They also began to overtake slow-moving higglers with their trays of fripperies, stooklings with their enormous bundles of sticks, laborers with their barrows, vendors with their donkey carts; and always, whether in their direction or against, the ox drays and mule crates of the merchants.

Another lamppost flicked past.

It was going to be a long stretch to Wormstool.

"Ah," Threnody exclaimed, of a sudden, stirring Rossamünd from his sorrows, "I am sharp-set—it must be time for middens."

The prentice craned a look out the window at the gunmetal sky. The sun hid behind the even cover of clouds. He could not tell what hour it was—surely well past midday, yet his stomach told the time more truly with a noisy poppling gurgle.

Threnody gave out a peculiar laughing bark. "Your gizzards think so too, it appears!" She extracted a ditty bag from among her cushions and wraps, and shared her pong with dried-and-salted pork and a handful of millet, all washed down with a brown bottle of small beer.

Sick of the little varying diet of the Emperor's Service, Rossamünd took some food and ate perfunctorily. Dull grief would not let him eat. However, once started, he found his appetite returned and he supped heartily enough.

At the meal's end, Threnody took out a vial of sticky red Friscan's wead.

Rossamünd stared fixedly out of the window as she drank, not wanting to invite some petulant overreaction.

With shadows growing long as the bulk of Tumblesloe

Heap brought an early sunset, and their rumps sore from too much sitting, they passed the lantern-watch of Dovecote Bolt wending west, fodicars on shoulder, winding out the lonely lamps. The lampsmen hailed the lenterman, but paid no heed to the passengers.

Gloaming finally gave up to darkness as they followed the glittering chain of new-lit lamps and arrived at the cothouse itself. Dovecote Bolt was a high-house: whitewashed walls upon exposed stone foundations, with a fortified stairway to the only door at the very top of the structure, a high wall extending behind it and a crowd of glowing lanterns at its front. It was built close by a sludgy ford over the beginnings of a little stream known as the Mirthlbrook. Just before the ford the post-lentum turned, went through a heavy gate and halted in the modest coach yard at the rear of the cothouse.

The splasher boy opened the door, unfolded the step and said with a parched croak, "First stop. And an overnight stay till tomorrow's post."

As luggage was retrieved, lampsmen appeared from within bearing bright-limns to light their way and dour expressions to greet them. The seven-strong garrison of this modest cothouse seemed very tight, veterans with a long record of service together. However, they had little cheer for new-promoted lampsmen, looking especially hard at Threnody as she mounted the stair and entered the guardroom. It occupied the entirety of that floor, and with benches and trestles, doubled as a common room for meals. The two young lamplighters were directed to the cramped office of Dovecote Bolt's house-major, found in an attic-space loft of the steep roof.

Introducing himself as Major-of-House Wombwell, he spoke to them in a stiff yet welcoming manner.

"Good evening to you, young . . . er—prentices!" he said, eyeing Threnody with a confounded expression. His eyes became wider as he saw the small spoor upon her face. "Why have you come to us from our glorious manse? Well-nigh is the usual range of your watch, is it not?"

"Ah," said Rossamünd, "we are on the way to our billet, sir."

"To your billet?" The house-major bridled. "Preposterous! Billeting Day is not for another month."

"It has been called early by our dear new Marshal-Subrogat," Threnody explained with affected amusement.

"Marshal-Subrogat?" the man quizzed her.

"Aye, sir," Rossamünd answered, getting a word in before Threnody for fear of some rash statement from her. "The Master-of-Clerks has filled the place of the Lamplighter-Marshal."

"So it is true, then: the Lamplighter-Marshal is called away and that old fox Podious is top of the heap. They even let lasses serve as lighters now, I see—troublesome times are here . . ."

The house-major asked them some further questions

on minor details of Winstermill's running and then they were dismissed. Threnody, much to the bemusement of the lighters, was granted access to the kitchens to make her plaudamentum.

"Blighted Cathar's baskets as lighters—by my knotted bowels, who'd reckon it?" Rossamünd could hear the house-major mutter as they left him.

"Would you need help with your treacle, Threnody?" Rossamünd offered as they were shown down to their cots by the cot-warden: a surly, scabby-faced lighter— one of the permanent house-watch, too old now to walk the highroad.

The girl paused, contriving to look bemused, amazed and annoyed all at once. "No thank you, I will boil my own," she huffed, and left him to find the kitchen.

When she returned, they were served mains by the same surly cot-warden now acting as kitchen hand. Incongru-ously the meal of boiled beef, onions and rice from the tiny kitchen tasted better than anything made by Winstermill's vast cookery.

Left well alone on their cots by the lampsmen, Threnody read as Rossamünd contended with a bout of the blackest sorrow.

When the lamp-watch arrived from Sallowstall, their thumping and calling reverberating through the boards above, Threnody made trouble by asking for a privacy screen. Churlishly, the old cot-warden and two of the lighters answered her demand, setting a dusty old screen for her with much ungracious puffing and banging and stomping. Finished, the cot-warden left them, muttering grumpily, "Anything else yer highness wants doing . . ." Behind the screen, by golden lantern-light, Threnody did those mysterious things girls did before going abed. When she was done, she pushed the screen away and got into her rough cot. She was in a voluminous white nightdress, her hair gathered and hidden beneath a sacklike, ribbon-tied crinickle. Rossamünd had never seen her in this way. She had been careful never to show herself after douse-lanterns back at Winstermill. The nightclothes and hat made her look curiously vulnerable. He prepared for sleep more publicly, his wounded head throbbing as it had not done for some days.

Sleep was hard-won that night. Rossamünd wrestled with his troubles as he lay in the cold listening to Threnody's easy breathing.

Fed a hasty breakfast the next morning, they were allowed barely enough time for brewing Threnody's treacle. A slap of reins and a shout, and the lentum went on, the weird song of unseen birds echoing across the foggy valley their only farewell. Feeling empty and exhausted, Rossamünd bid the Bolt a silent good-bye. Threnody slid over to Rossamünd's side of the carriage and, pulling back the drape, stared at the low northward hills where Herbroulesse was hidden, still dark despite the morning glow. "Till anon, Mother," she murmured, and kept her vigil till they were well past the cothouse and the lesser road too.

The day's journey took them past dousing lampsmen returning to Sallowstall and on to that place itself, the quality of the road improving from hard-packed clay and soil to flagstones. With a blare of the horn, the post-lentum stopped at Sallowstall, a well-tended cot-rent with broad grounds and thick walls.

The mail was passed over and horses changed. Over the ford, scattering half-tame ducks, and out of the thicket of trees, the lentum resumed the journey.

As the afternoon wore on, the pastures on either side of the Wormway became neater, their boundaries clearer, their furrows straighter, less weedy. Much of the land was a dark, fertile brown. This was a very different land from the grayer soils of the crofts Rossamünd had known about Boschenberg. Nearing Cothallow they saw peoneers levering at the road with iron-crows while a grim-looking guard of haubardiers stood watch.

"Thrice-blighted baskets have taken to tearing up the highroad," Rossamünd heard someone call to their driver as the post-lentum cautiously passed along. Flagstones had been torn up and thrown aside, and a great-lamp bent over like a wind-broken sapling, its glass smashed, the precious bloom torn into shreds and yellowing.

Nestled in a wooded valley, Cothallow was long and low, its thick granite façade perforated with solid arches from the midst of which slit windows stared, closely barred and ready to be employed as loopholes. Their stay was not much more than a shouted "Hallo!," an exchange of mail and a hurried change of horses. The lenterman was clearly keen, with the advance of day, to be at the next destination.

A sparrow alighted suddenly on the lowered door sash and, ruffling its wings, inspected first Threnody then Rossamünd with keen deliberation. Threnody peered at the impertinent little bird over the top of her duodecimo. It trilled at Rossamünd once and loudly, and then shot off with a hum of speedy wings as the post-lentum jerked forward to resume its travels.

"I've never known such birds to be so persistent," Threnody exclaimed. "He looks just the same as that one watching while we talked in the greens-garden by the manse."

Rossamünd leaned forward. "Perhaps the Duke of Sparrows is watching *us?*" he whispered.

"I can't think why he would watch after us particularly," the girl answered with a frown.

"Maybe he's making sure you don't go witting the wrong bogle," Rossamünd muttered with a weak grin, feeling anything but funny.

"Is there such a thing?" Threnody said seriously, looking at him sharply.

Rossamünd very much wanted to say "yes" but held his tongue.

The crowns of the hills about were thick with trees, but their flanks were broad with deep green pastures, thin breaks of lithely myrtles. Here cattle lowed and chewed and drank from the runnels that wore creases down the hillsides. Crows cawed to each other across the valley.

Their day's-end destination was the community of Makepeace, built amid sparse, elegant, evergreen myrtles, right on the banks of the Mirthlbrook. It was the first significant settlement upon the Conduit Vermis, a village sequestered behind a massive, foreboding wall. Rossamünd could see the top bristling with sharp iron studs and shards of broken crockery, which seemed to make a lie of the Makepeace's friendly name. Crowds of chimneys stretched well above the beetling fortifications, each one drizzling steamy smoke into the still, damp air, showing a promise of a warm hearth and even warmer food. Rossamünd imagined every home filled with humble families—father, mother, son, daughter— living quietly useful lives.

Upon either side of the gate were two doughty bastion-towers, both showing the muzzle of a great-gun through enlarged loopholes. Situated immediately by the northern tower, the cothouse of Makepeace Stile merged its foundations with those of the wall. A high fastness much like Dovecote Bolt yet greatly enlarged—maybe five or six stories—the Stile was near as tall as the chimney stacks of Makepeace and must have dominated the view of the west from within the village.

The post-lentum eased into a siding between the cothouse and the highroad, its arrival coincident with the departure of the lamp-watch.

Alighting from the carriage, Rossamünd heard a cry sound from down the gloomy road. *"The hedgeman comes! Be a-ready to make your orders, the hedgeman comes!"* It was uttered by a portly figure pulling his test-barrow and strolling toward the town from the same direction the lentum had just come, as if there was no threat from monsters.

A hedgeman! Rossamünd's attention pricked. These were wandering folk, part skold, dispensurist and ossatomist who cured chills and set bones (for a fee) where other habilists would not venture. He had not noticed them passing the fellow earlier, though they must have.

"The hedgeman is here! Come a-make your orders, the hedgeman is here!" came the cry again, and this time Rossamünd recognized the crier.

Mister Critchitichiello! Mister Critchitichiello, who made his living hawking his skills to all and any along the Wormway. When he had first arrived at Winstermill, Rossamünd found it much easier to ask the kindly hedgeman to make Craumpalin's Exstinker than go to Messrs. Volitus or Obbolute, the manse's own script-grinders. Now, with the current batch near its end, and more required to last him at his new billeting, Rossamünd hurried over to the man through traffic and the rain.

In the manse the hedgeman was a popular fellow. Rossamünd had to wait his turn while the small crowd of brother-lighters ordered eagerly. Mostly they came for love-pomades made to secure the affections of Jane Public and the other dolly-mops—the maids and professional girls living in the towns about—or find a cure for the various aches and grumbles your average lampsman seemed always to possess. Out here, however, two days east of Winstermill, Rossamünd was the only customer.

"Well 'ello there, young a-fellow." Critchitichiello greeted Rossamünd in his strange Sevillian accent, grinning at him from beneath the wide brim of his round hat. "I a-remember you from the fortress. Yes? Back then you wore a hat and not a bandage."

The prentice nodded cheerily.

"Hallo, Mister Critchitichiello. Triple the quantity of my Exstinker, please. I have the list for it if you need to remember its parts."

Critchitichiello smiled. "No—no, I remember. Old Critchitichiello never forgets such clever mixings." He tapped his pock-scarred brow knowingly. "I'll have it ready for you in a puff, Rossamündo. You see! I even remember your name though we meet but once."

Rossamünd followed the hedgeman as he set his test-barrow down under the eave of a small stall built against the eastern wall. A remarkable little black-iron chimney poked out and up from the back, puffing clean little puffs of smoke. Critchitichiello unlatched and unfolded his barrow, the lid swinging up to provide a roof from the rain.

Master Craumpalin would want to see this! Rossamünd thought sadly of the charcoal ruin that Master Craumpalin's own marvelous test had become. He gripped the list of parts

CRITCHITICHIELLO

made by the dispensurist's own hand as if it were a precious jewel. He had read the recipe many times and knew it well: mabrigond, wine-of-Sellry, nihillis, dust-of-carum, benthamyn. As he observed the testing—as making a script is called—Rossamünd habitually ran through the steps in his mind. *Start with five parts—no! Fifteen parts wine-of-Sellry in a porcelain beaker over gentle heat.*

A familiar savory smell wafted, like fine vegetable soup, as the liquid began to simmer.

Add one—ah, three parts nihillis and . . .

Pumping at an ingenious little foot bellows connected to the test-barrow, the hedgeman looked up from his work, and with a frown of friendly concern said, "You know, Rossamündo, I have a-made many nullodors along these many roads, but with this a-one here I cannot figure how it might a-do its job." Critchitichiello shrugged, thick-gloved hands raised palms-to-the-sky.

Rossamünd blinked. The hedgeman was such a kindly fellow he did not want to gainsay him. Yet he knew Master Craumpalin would never give him something that was crank. To question his old dispensurist's scripts was unthinkable.

"It has done what I suppose it was meant to do," he offered guardedly. "I have no complaint." *Add the benthamyn.*

"And good that is!" Critchitichiello kept smiling. "Yet I tell you. Up till a-now its parts are all just as they ought—a simple base for a nullodor, but put a-this in"—and in went the tiny benthamyn pellets, six parts, just in time—"and suddenly it's like a-no nullodor I've ever heard made. It might foil some noses, but not a nicker's sniffing."

Rossamünd nodded patiently. He had no answer for the hedgeman. Instead he watched in silence as the mabrigond and dust-of-carum were added in right and timely proportion.

"Don't a-mind me, Rossamündo, my fine a-fellow," the hedgeman said perceptively. "Just a curious old noddy am I . . . I'm-a sure this no-stinker answers for what you are a-wanting it for."

Rossamünd certainly hoped it was so.

Critchitichiello poured the deep blue liquid into a fine new bottle and Rossamünd reached for his wallet.

Taking payment, the hedgeman looked beyond him with twinkling eye. "That sweet lass has been a-watching you for a little while," he said mildly. "Is she your sweetheart?"

Sweetheart? Rossamünd looked around and saw Threnody standing beneath a lantern already lit against the dim afternoon. She was leaning against it and looking his way very, very intently. "Oh, that—er . . . She isn't my sweetheart, Mister Critchitichiello," he said emphatically.

"Ah. Too a-bad for thee. Though . . . ," Critchitichiello said with a flourish of a bow, a conspiratorial whisper and a glance at Threnody, ". . . if you's a-needing an amorpoti—a lover's brew—just remember your a-friend, Critchitichiello."

With a blush and a garbled farewell Rossamünd quit the awkward scene.

Threnody pulled a cryptic face as he approached. "What have you had that ledgermain making?"

"Mister Critchitichiello is no ledgermain," Rossamünd came back, still tetchy. "He's the genuine article, a true dispenser."

"Ledgermains. Imperial fumomath. However you like it, lamp boy," she insisted. "That does not answer my question, does it? What did the man make you?"

"It's a . . . a nullodor. For my salumanticum."

Threnody stroked at her lips. "A nullodor! A waste of good parts. What do you need a nullodor for?"

What has everyone got against them? First Critchitichiello, now Threnody. Rossamünd did not care to quibble. Craumpalin had given it to him and told him to wear it, and that was good enough.

In silence they entered Makepeace Stile together.

As douse-lanterns approached and while Threnody polished her teeth with expensive dentifrices, Rossamünd decided it was time to write his own letter back to Fransitart.

Dormitory Master Fransitart
by the care of Lady Praeline
Versierdholte
Halt-by-Wall
Boschenberg City
Hergoatenbosch
4th of Heimio, HIR 1601

Dearest Master Fransitart,

I have got your letter and read its most terrible and sad news. I wept for you all, especially the little ones and Master P and the poor Madam, but am so glad to know that you and Miss Verline and Master Craumpalin (his poor dispensury!) still live. Though you might feel that you should not have survived the fire, it is too sweet a consolation for me that you survived to share your regret. And though you have all taught me to return evil with good, I cannot help but wish foul ends for that dastard Gosling. I can hear you scolding me in my head even as I write this. What is to become of you all now?

The other reason I write to you is to tell you that I have been sent early to my first billet, a place called Wormstool, far east along His Most Serene Highness' Highroad, the Conduit Vermis—almost the last place before the blighted Ichormeer. Can you believe it that I shall be so close to such a terrible place? Though it is a long way out from Winstermill, I shall probably be already established there by the time you get this. When you do travel, please come to me there—I am sorry it is so far away.

I am delighted that Master Craumpalin might be with you when you see me, though I most solemnly wish it was under better reasons.

Please give my most loving regards to all I care for. Tell Miss Verline I am safe. Tell Master Craumpalin I still wear his Exstinker. A hedgeman made me some more today, and he was baffled as to how it worked. He seemed good at his trade but perhaps not as good as our own dispensurist.

It is wonderful to hear that your health has improved with Master Craumpalin's help—may you stay in fine fettle always, from your old charge, and with love,

Rossamünd Bookchild,
Lampsman 3rd Class
Makepeace Stile
Makepeace
The Idlewild

I do not wish to alarm you, but some nights ago I fought with a rever-man in the cellars of Winstermill Manse. This is the second I have ever met and they are broken and disgusting things that only need to be destroyed. I worry for a friend I left behind. His name is Mister Numps, a retired seltzerman. Please look in on him if you pass through the manse.

Tell Miss Verline that I love her and her new niece very much.

Of Discipline and Limb!

THE BRISKING CAT

knavery offices where a person can go to hire a teratologist or three or as many as are needed. Such establishments gain their name from the term "knave," that is, any person who sells services to any paying client, as opposed to a spurn, who serves a retaining lord or master. When entering a region for the first time, a teratologist may register at the local knavery to make it known that he or she is about and going on the roll offering services. In doing this monster-hunters are agreeing not to shop their skills through other neighboring knaveries or their own advertisement, thus denying the knavery its commission. The knaving-clerk will take a request from a customer and offer a selection of monster-hunters to solve the dilemma. Once the teratologist has been selected, he or she is approached with an Offer of Work, which may be accepted or rejected. Work is more steady for teratologists who use the knaving system, though they usually make less money for service rendered.

T HE next day, thick with rain, was an early start again. Leaving his letter with the Post-Master at Makepeace Stile, Rossamünd followed Threnody as she dashed to the post-lentum waiting in the foreyard of the cothouse. Back and shoulders becoming rapidly sopped, the young lighter did his best to shield his bandaged crown with his satchel.

Traveling certificates and nativity patents approved by the officious gatemen, they passed through Makepeace to continue. Rossamünd saw little of the town through the obscuring downpour, only narrow buildings with glowing, narrow windows, water spouting from the edge of every horizontal surface on to even narrower streets. A soot-grubby child no more than ten scurried from eave to eave past the slow-going lentum—a char-boy, perhaps from Gathercoal, come to serve an errand in this cleaner town. Wondering what hard labors were this small lad's lot, Rossamünd caught his eye and they traded mournful glances.

Out the other side of Makepeace the road broadened and they discovered the lamps ahead had been left to shine on in the storm-dark morning. This was most certainly not good traveling weather, and the lenterman kept the pace slow for fear of skidding off the road.

The scene continued cozily pastoral: fortified farmsteads glimpsed at the end of private, tree-lined drives nestled among thickets of domesticated trees and were surrounded with fastidiously tended fields and drystone walls.

Every six lamps or so were low concrete-and-stone strongworks, squat boxes with loopholes and steps that went into the earth down to three-quarter-buried iron-bound doors. Rossamünd had never seen the like, and no one at Winstermill had ever talked of such things.

The sun was one quarter along its meridian when they met a convoy of large covered drays trundling the opposite way in a long line, every one under the guard of a skold or scourge. Drawn by great trains of flanchardt-covered oxen, each bore hundredweights of finest-grade charcoal from

Gathercoal, likely intended for Winstermill, High Vesting and the settlements of the southwest. It took the long end of fifteen minutes to pass the last dray.

They ate middens with stores granted from Makepeace Stile's pantry (a rind of hard, smelly Nine-cheese from Tuscanin; apples; strips of dried, river-caught fish) and Threnody went back to reading. Taking pointed notice of the book, Rossamünd read the small white letters printed on its burgundy cover—*The High and Illustrious Ladies of the Magna Scuthës.*

"What is that book about?" he asked absently.

The girl made as if to continue reading but, after a pause, she marked her place, closed her book, laid it primly on her lap, cleared her throat and looked up. "It is about the adventures of city women and their flash swells."

"Flash swells?"

She looked owlishly at him for a moment. "The rich young men who live such fun and easy lives in the cities."

"Oh, you mean dandidawdlers." Rossamünd thought of the frilly, fussy fellows he had observed making a nuisance on the streets of Boschenberg. "Is it interesting?"

"I think so, yes, though Mother doesn't like books such as these."

"Why not?"

"*She* says they're full of vile gossip and innuendo and *she* says they grossly exaggerate the successes of the protagonists without making enough of the consequences of their foolishness."

"You sound like you've had this said to you often." Rossamünd gave a mild grin.

"I could recite to you all of Mother's words better than the *In Columba Alat*," she returned wryly.

"The In Columna what-tat?"

"*In Columba Alat*," Threnody explained, with uncharacteristic patience. " 'The Wings of the Dove'—it's our cantus, the rule we—I mean the Right—lives by."

"How does it go?"

"I don't know." Threnody grinned. "I've forgotten it."

"But I thought you just said you knew it well," Rossamünd returned a little dumbly.

Threnody sighed long-sufferingly. "I do." She picked up the duodecimo and opened it again. "I was just making a jest," she said, and went back to reading.

"Oh." Rossamünd frowned. "Sorry."

Soon after, the horses were watered at the cothouse of Sparrowstall. Blackened spikes ran in rows along every ridge-cap and gable, set there to prevent weary birds or overadventurous nickers from taking roost.

A little over two hours further and they arrived at Hinkerseigh, much larger than Makepeace, with thicker walls and higher, more numerous bastions all filled with well-tended great-guns. It was a growing town—nearly a city, its people squeezed for room; some of the less well-heeled had been forced to build beyond the safety of the town's stony curtain. The Mirthlstream flowed right into the place under the wall to drive many waterwheels of industry within as it passed through. As it was a client-city belonging to the Imperial state of Maubergonne, Hinkerseigh's taciturn gatemen were dressed in harness of orot and gules—orange and deep red. They scrutinized Rossamünd and Threnody's documents cursorily and waved the lentum through.

The carriage crawled down the narrow main street, moving little faster in the midst of the cram of traffic than a town-and-country gent out on a lazy Domesday ramble. At a coach-host, the Draint Fyfer, the lentermen stopped to change teams. The broad, covered yard was thronged with public coaches and private carriages; horns hooting, sergeant-yardsmen bawling, under-yardsmen obeying, porters and box-boys and mercers scurrying. Exiting the lentum first, Threnody dashed off into the rain with little more than an "I'll be back!" and was gone before Rossamünd could call after or follow. With a shrug he took a midday meal and waited alone.

The warm commons of the coach-host was as impossibly crowded as the yard without, a-press with merchants' wives and farmstead ladies, nannies and their bantling charges screeching for attention; slightly damp higglers and shysters en route to more spendthrifty places; and off-duty pediteers; all waiting for a break in the weather. It was only twenty minutes or so before Rossamünd was called for by the hollering splasher boy to board the po'lent, yet it took Threnody more than an hour to return. She appeared suddenly by the carriage door, grinning broadly and quickly handing an oblong oilskin-covered something to the splasher boy.

"We'll still be in a tight bit o' hurry to make it to the next cot in time!" the driver said, louring down at her from his high seat as she climbed aboard. "So I recommend ye hang on ter something." He proved good to his promise, for no sooner had Threnody settled into her nest of furs than the lentum surged to motion.

"What were you doing?" Rossamünd shouted above the noise of transit. "We've been waiting for a while . . ."

Threnody looked at him unrepentantly. "I always like to try a little shopping when I can."

Rain began falling so hard its rattling drum on the carriage roof made conversation impossible. Threnody raised the sash on her side to keep its splashings out, yet Rossamünd left his down to see what passed and tolerated the wet. As Hinkerseigh disappeared in the fog of the deluge, the highroad narrowed. The lenterman whipped up the new horse-team's rate and kept the poor beasts at a dangerous, transom-shattering speed for several miles, slowing only occasionally to rest them. The post-lentum dashed right past Howlbolt, not even slowing for courtesy, noisily scattering a coven of ravens that had settled before the cothouse.

The valley became deeper, the Mirthlbrook drawing close by the Wormway again, broader now, its banks choked with willow, swamp oak and hawthorn, its waters rushing over and through sharp rocks and keeping pace with the lentum. The stream's opposite bank was steep, almost clifflike, tangled with dark young woods.

"That's the Owlgrave," Threnody shouted above the roar

THE LENTERMEN

of the rain and road. "It's said that monsters like to go there to die when they are mortal-hurt or sick of the world."

Rossamünd stared at the choked rise imagining he could see some languishing nicker up among the rocks and trees. He had always thought monsters lived on and on till someone slew them, and the idea of them pining away was odd, disturbing. *So that is where they end,* he pondered, *but where do they begin?* His reading had informed him of many theories. Some scholars said monsters grew on trees, others that they grew "buds" on themselves, which dropped to the ground and grew into other monsters. The worst way was congress between everyman and ünterman, which was said to spawn some wicked half-human abomination, the ultimate excess of outramour. Implicit in the accusation of sedorner was the suspicion of such a union. Most habilists said such a thing was impossible, but common folks still believed it, and that was enough.

Out the other side of the lentum Rossamünd saw the flicker of a lighted lamp, then another. Regardless of pelting rain and threatening lands, the lantern-watch of Bitterbolt, the next cothouse, had faithfully wound out the lamps.

The Wormway went down and over a large stone-arch bridge with lit lanterns upon either abutment that passed over the broad stream of the Bittermere. Before this bridge was a foreboding collection of buildings, each four or five stories of dressed stone, baked bricks, mortar and lead shingles. It was a mighty rectangular accretion, its roofs thorny with high chimneys. There was no encircling wall; the lowest floors were absent of any openings—not even a single door, and the few second-story windows were heavily barred. Even the undersides of the sills of higher windows and the gutters were garlanded with thorny wire. The footings of the entire pile were assiduously smeared with a slippery-looking black substance, a repellent no doubt. This was a place that never intended a monster to ever gain a foothold. The winds and the rain had blown themselves out. In the stillness, the comfort of sweet wood-smoke and the savory promise of that evening's prandial preparations wafted down to them from the place.

"The wayhouse of the Brisking Cat, good folks," the side-armsman called helpfully from his perch.

Upon the other side of the highroad was a low brick building with no sidelights or transoms or even a case-ment. Its strong doors were half buried into the chalky ground and a siding-lane with sturdy walls upon either side branched off and went down to them. At the top of the lane stood a filigree lantern-post. Fixed to this was a badly stained signboard upon which was painted a lion, its claws reaching.

The lentum descended the lane and went through iron-wood gates opened for it at the end. Through the gates and within the low building was a great stablery for horse and carriage, much of it tunneling back into the hillock itself. The reek of hay and hoof-trodden pats made the air foul.

Grinning ear to ear, the splasher boy opened the door for them with a touch to the brim of his tall stovepipe hat. "We've done all right to get you here afore the daisy hay was done," he said excitedly.

"Excuse me?" Threnody scowled. "The what was done?"

The splasher boy looked at her as if she were Jack Simple. "The daisy hay . . ." He grinned at Rossamünd as if he knew, but Rossamünd had not heard the term either. "It's the right time of day for travel! Only lighters and fools go out after sundown—oh . . ." The splasher boy went bright red as he realized who he was talking to and quickly found other things to do.

"I see," said Threnody.

As Rossamünd and Threnody alighted, another person was arriving on foot, let in by the small sally port fixed in the heavy ironwood gate. The last gasp of a gust blew through the door, bringing with it a sweetly salty and familiar scent.

"Did you get your hob-gnasher, Madam Rose?" one of the gaters asked.

"That I did, Master File," the newly arrived wayfarer declared briskly, and lifted a large leather satchel bulging with something lumpy and vaguely head-shaped. "And a might of trouble it gave me too."

It was Europe!

The Branden Rose was wearing her usual deep red fighting garb, and was muffled against the cold with the spangled-fur pollern. Three heavy-harnessed gaters attending bowed in quiet deference.

Threnody made to follow a porter and continue on through to the wayhouse, but stopped when she realized Rossamünd was just lingering and staring.

Eventually Europe turned, with narrowed eyes that went wide—just for a moment—then knowing. She swaggered over, an eyebrow cocked. "Well hello again, little man," the fulgar said softly as she approached. "Have they finally let you out of Winstermill?"

"Hello, Miss Europe," Rossamünd greeted cheerfully. "We're on our way to our new billet." Smiling at her, he saw that the fulgar's eyes were badly bloodshot, an almost complete and ghastly red.

"Where is that?" Europe smiled tightly in return.

"Wormstool—what's happened to your eyes, miss? They're all red like a falseman's."

The woman's brow furrowed. "It comes from a long day arcing. And what have you done to your head, little man? All bandage and no hat!"

"I lost it in a fight."

The fulgar raised an amused eyebrow. "In a *fight,* was it? I cannot leave you for a moment. Well, at least you did not lose my gift," she said, looking at his fine scarf. She turned a cool gaze to Threnody. "I see you have brought the august's daughter with you."

"I . . ." was yet forming in Rossamünd's mouth when Threnody interjected.

"You're the Branden Rose, aren't you?" she asked, with a look of profound, barely contained excitement. Rossamünd had never seen her look quite so enthusiastic—it was odd.

"My name precedes me, I see," said Europe, a subtle smirk fluttering at the corner of lip and eye.

"And you really do know *him?*" Threnody glanced at Rossamünd.

"Aye——" he began.

"Indeed!" Europe replied civilly. "We are old wayfaring chums, are we not, little man? We have been on many an adventure already."

"I am Lady Threnody of Herbroulesse," the girl lighter began, barely waiting for an answer, "daughter of the Lady Vey, August of the Right of the Pacific Dove," finishing with affected gravity as she tried not to betray her eagerness.

A hint of disdain fluttered across Europe's face. "I heard rumor that the Marchioness Vey had issue by some clandestine means, and here breathes the proof. Might I say you are dressed peculiarly for a calendar?"

Threnody looked down at her gorgeous, if slightly travel-ruffled clothes. "Oh, I'm not a calendar anymore. I'm a full lamplighter now."

Europe's smile was patient, polite. "Good for you, my dear. So I now know something of you and you already know something of me and we are all met. How lovely." Europe did not look as if she thought it lovely at all, but rather boring. "Come! Time for easy chairs and warm meals."

They were let through a heavy door by a broad-set gater with thick mustachios wearing a black-felt liripipium, its long peak almost trailing in the straw-rubbish. As Europe and her two guests approached, he opened the way and took them along an arched, brick-lined tunnel that must have been burrowed right under the Wormway. At the other side their guide hammered upon another door, crying, *"Ad asper-tum! The Branden Rose and two companions,"* to those beyond. They were admitted through a block-room and climbed slate steps to a broad wood-paneled vestibule of the way-house proper.

Footmen in plush asked for their names, took baggage and stowed weapons in an armory-stand to be retrieved on call. This was a very fine establishment indeed. Europe handed over the satchel. "Put it in the cold room for me: I will be requiring it tomorrow to claim my prize."

A horse-faced woman clad in a style of dress that Ros-samünd had never seen before, made of heavy velvet with

broad hanging sleeves and a pretty white palisade cap, rustled over to greet them. She paid studied respect to Europe
and politely introduced herself to the two young lamplighters as the enrica d'ama. " 'Allo, young travelers," she said in
a sweet voice and a delicate southern accent, "I am Madam
Oubliette, the proud owner of this fine 'ouse. If you are
seeking any service you must call on me or my man Parleferte." She indicated a gaunt, harassed-looking steward.
"Any time of sunup or moon-down. Now please, 'ave your
ease in the Saloon."

A footman announced them over the moderate hubbub
of other conversation. "Her Grace, the Branden Rose, Europa of Fontrevault, Duchess-in-waiting of Naimes; the Lady
Threnody of Herbroulesse and a guest!" was the ringing cry,
to which few of their fellow patrons paid any attention.

"Yes, yes," Europe huffed. "Get on and show us our
place, man!"

"How do you feel, *guest,* on being just a *guest?*" Threnody gibed Rossamünd quietly. "Shall I call you *guest* from
now onward?"

Rossamünd did not acknowledge her.

Before him was a great hexagonal space with balconies,
boxes and claustral-booths rising on every side for three
whole floors—the privatrium, each reached by a confusion
of stairs and walks. The radiating beams of the lofty ceiling were carved with forms of intertwined cats in various
attitudes of hunt or play. Every beam met in the middle
and from this zenith hung a collection of great-lamps gath-

ered together like some bizarre chandelier. Beneath this, in the middle of the space surrounded by the privatrium, was a raised oval stage hemmed in by a semicircular tapery-counter at one end where drinks were being pulled or poured. About the tapery were tables and chairs and people sitting at them in a variety of attitudes: animated, upright, slouched, slumped, even leaning dangerously. Rossamünd was so amazed by it all he stumbled on his own feet more than once before the three were settled in a second-story claustra—a somewhat private stall of leather high-backed benches around a square table.

"The Brisking Cat," Europe declared grandly as they sat. "Wayhouse, knavery and my current abode."

The Saloon was wall to wall with pugnators and their hangers-on, coming, going and ordering about the staff with high-handed carelessness. Rossamünd watched the galli-maufry of teratologists in wide-eyed wonder. Indiscriminate monster-killers written about in public print or gossiped about in civic rumor, a fabulous collection like the pages of a pamphlet come to life. Seeing his fascination, Europe began to name some of them.

"There are the Boanergës—the 'Sons of Thunder,' " she explained, watching three grim-looking fellows huddled together in grim conversation, periodically glancing suspi-ciously over their shoulders. "A competent band, each one a fellow astrapecrith, though none too bright."

"And that is the Knave of Diamonds," said Threnody, keen to show her worldliness. Rossamünd looked and saw a large man pass below. He wore a "crown" of tall spiked reeds upon his head; upon his body a heavy-gaulded smock or lambrequin of dirty white with its single, large red diamond on the front; and upon his fierce face a large deep blue diamond spoor.

A solitary calendar from a different clave than Threnody's walked across the Saloon floor and took a booth across the other side. She was wearing a bossock of prüs and sable checks and her face was striped like that of a grazing animal from far beyond the Marrow. She wore a dandicomb of long, elegant horns that her claustra was fortunately high enough to contain.

Threnody watched her closely. "She need not have come," the girl huffed with the strains of territorial jealousy. "The Right has these troubles in hand."

"Who is she?" Rossamünd said so softly he barely spoke at all.

"She's a caladine," Europe answered.

"Entering our diet without a by-your-leave," the girl lighter added icily. "I doubt she has presented herself to Mother. Saphine is her name. She is from the Maids of Malady."

"Truly?" said Europe. "Your surgeon had perhaps best watch himself."

"Miss Europe?"

"I have the understanding that these Maids of Malady have allied themselves with the Soratchë. Maybe they lend their help to the Soratchë, and Saphine is coming to investigate that Swill fellow. Wheels inside wheels, and all that."

Rossamünd hoped this was true. He stared at the caladine until she felt the scrutiny and turned to look at him.
Flushing, the young lighter looked away quickly and found a
teratologist *he* knew by sight. He had seen etchings of her in
the more sensational pamphlets. Epitomë Bile was her name,
a woman written of as a myth: lupine and pitiless and astoundingly daring. Yet here she was, a woman as real as his
own hand, all in glossy black soe, white-faced with staring,
black-rimmed eyes and oddly cropped black hair.

Europe showed clear distaste. "Cruel and heartless," she
warned. "Stay well clear of her."

Aye, Rossamünd wondered, *but has she ever sparked a child
in the head?*

Epitomë Bile looked up, caught Europe's cold eye and
returned it, giving a slow, taunting curtsy. A wicked smile flitted across the strange woman's mien. The two teratological
women kept each other fixed with stares of mutual loathing,
until Epitomë Bile walked out of the common room, sly,
malevolent amusement never leaving her face.

Rossamünd felt a shiver of dismay. He hoped never to
cross her path more closely.

Europe clucked her tongue quietly and looked elsewhere.
"There you have the Three Brave Brothers," she said, pointing
with her chin to a group of men below them (just returned
perhaps from the course), turning her guests' attention to
other things. "They actually number four, are not related
to each other . . . and are not particularly brave, either." Rossamünd, who had read of these Brave Brothers, was stunned

to see walking before him their infamous scourge, Sourdoor, in his swathes of black lour—proofed velvet.

"And so my kind gather, looking for violence." Europe sighed. "Collecting together like crows about a corpse."

All the great folk, and the lesser known too, strutted the common room and the privatrium, eyeing one another, ego against ego, and generally getting in the way of the way-house's even routine.

"The Maid Constant." The fulgar indicated a wit with an arrow-spoor pointing up from each brow and brilliant-hued blue hair. "She too must needs wear a wig, as you do, my dear, but her hair was green last week and blue for this."

Threnody went beetroot blush and sat up. "No wig for me, madam," she said quickly, glowering nervously at Europe.

"Not yet, anyway," Rossamünd put in, trying to be helpful. She glared at him.

"By-the-by," said Europe, unconcerned.

The fulgar rattled off many more names, of so many teratologists that Rossamünd could not keep track, and he simply listened to the smooth sound of her voice. His wonder became a little numbed, and he sat a little easier in the comfortable booth. The young lampsman felt the strains of the road ease out into the soft seating, and he became quickly acquainted with just how tired he was. Food was ordered—from the Best Cuts, of course, Rossamünd trying "Starlings in Viand-Royal Sauce"—and an awkwardness persisted while they waited for it to arrive, wetting their thirst with the sourest rich-red wine Rossamünd had ever been served. With the wine came a tankard of steaming Cathar's Treacle for Europe.

"It's testtelated in bulk in the kitchens, by a tandem of skolds of faultless reputation," she explained, "at a hefty charge, of course. You may want some yourself, my dear." She nodded gravely at Threnody.

"No thank you, Duchess," Threnody returned, still sitting stiff-backed, hands clasped on the table before her. "I have always been taught that one does best to make one's own plaudamentum."

The fulgar became suddenly expressionless.

"Indeed," she said, after a long, discomfiting moment, "one would prefer to have it made perpetually by the same trusted hands at a day's two ends, but what one wants and what one gets are rarely the same. The one I once had confidence in is . . . no longer available—and another unwilling." She peered at Rossamünd.

Threnody looked sharply at the Branden Rose, then narrowly, almost enviously, at Rossamünd.

He tapped purposefully at the tabletop, not meeting either gaze. He had vowed to serve the lamplighters and the Emperor, yet as the troubles of the lamplighters increased, so did the appeal of being the Branden Rose's factotum. *If only she was more careful about which bogles to kill.*

Providentially, mains arrived and all talk ceased for a time as, in the rust glow of red-, orange- and yellow-glassed lanterns, they ate in hungry silence.

Music swelled from the oval stage below them: sweet

chamber-sounds of fiddle, violoncello and sourdine, and adding mellifluously to it a soaring female voice. Rossamünd felt he had heard this singing somewhere before and, looking down to the stage, saw a quartet of scratch-bobbed, liveried musicians and, in a halo of light, Hero, the chanteuse of Clunes. Dressed in a smoke-green chiffon dress with broad, gathered skirts, black rumples at the elbows, her hair piled and rolled and festooned with flowers of similar color to the chiffon, she was the very same songstress he had watched in raptures at the Harefoot Dig. Yet here she was now, projecting sonorous verse all about the great room, arms reaching out imploringly. Rossamünd forgot his food and listened, heedless of time's passing, arm on balustrade, cheek resting on arm, his eyes just a little doelike.

Threnody affected to be unimpressed. "It is adequate, I suppose," she said in the applause between songs, "if you like those Lentine styles."

Rossamünd decided he liked the Lentine style very well and could not understand Threnody's remark.

Her own meal finished, Europe lounged on the comfortable bench and picked at a sludgy, creamy-colored delicacy known simply as cheesecake, soaked in syrup of peachblossoms. With it came sillabub—a curdled concoction of milk and vinegar. She let Rossamünd try a little, and he came away from the taste smacking his lips in disgust. She did not, however, offer any to Threnody, who had become more and more sullen and sour-faced as the night deepened and did not show any care.

Washing out the vile aftertaste with the bitter small wine, Rossamünd asked solemnly, "Miss Europe, what do you know of Wormstool?"

"It is remote and dangerous and no place for new-weaned lamplighting lads and lasses." Europe scowled. "What can your masters be thinking, sending you out there?"

"Oh, I was not sent," Threnody said piously. "I *asked* to go. Those with greater capacities have to wait on those who do not. It's how *I* have been taught and . . ." She looked at her fellow traveler. "Rossamünd will need the help—as you yourself probably well know."

"Oh?" Europe turned a piercing gaze on the girl. "And who will look out for you, my dear?"

"Rossamünd," the girl returned simply. "We lighters stick together, just like calendars."

The fulgar laughed unexpectedly. "Aren't you an adorable little upstart?" she purred.

Chin lifting then dropping, Threnody clearly did not know whether to be offended or pleased. She looked out into the Saloon at nothing in particular.

"Now tell me, young Rossamünd," Europe demanded, "what were you fighting that cost you yet another hat?"

"It was a rever-man, miss," the young lighter said simply.

Europe went wide-eyed. There was a pause, incredulity hovering at its fringes. "Truly?" she said eventually. "How did you manage to get tangled up with one of *those?* More to the point, how did you survive it?"

"I found it deep in the cellars of Winstermill the very next night after you left."

"Ah! You're playing a leg-pull on me, little man." The fulgar started to smile knowingly. "Your old home is far too tough to crack for some rotten-headed thing like a reverman. That old Marshal of yours must be sadly slipping if he let one of those wretches in."

Rossamünd's gall twisted at this. "I don't think he is slipping, Miss Europe, but still, sure as I sit here, it was a gudgeon I wrastled right down in the bottom of the fortress." He went on to tell the whole tale, elaborating especially on the moment when he jammed the loomblaze into the rever-man's gnashing maw. That moment was powerfully satisfying to recall. "It was somewhere in that fight I lost my hat," he concluded.

"Aren't you the one for getting yourself into fixes not of your own making?" Europe's knowing gaze had not slipped for the length of his tale. "You are still the strangest, bravest little man. Throwing a gudgeon about and blasting it to char is beyond even some of my ilk. You're not as helpless as you seem." She looked at Threnody.

"Maybe." Rossamünd tried not to look too pleased. "It was gangling and poorly made, with too-long arms and hairy, piggy ears, just like those"—he pointed to a sizzling porker's head that was being carried past at that very moment by a struggling maid—"and no great feat to best."

"The Lamplighter-Marshal said it was a mighty deed," Threnody stated proudly in a strange change of tack.

"I should think he would," the fulgar said, taking a sip of wine. "You did him a great service, Rossamünd."

"Yet it still did not stop the man receiving a sis edisserum from the Considine," the young lampsman said sadly.

"Truly?" Europe murmured. "You don't hear of that happening every diem. Your Marshal *must* certainly have gone awry then."

Rossamünd did not hear her. His thoughts had pounced on his own words, *hairy, piggy ears.* The gudgeon had large, furry, leaf-shaped ears, *pig's* ears, like those on the meal just gone by; pig's ears very much like those on the swine's head he had carried up to Swill . . .

And Europe had told of the dark hints that surrounded the surgeon; and it held that if Swill knew of the kitchen furtigrade when Doctor Crispus did not, he might be well aware of other secret ways, even down to the moldering cellars. Why, truly, would he need his deliveries of body parts if not to make a rever-man? . . . And there was the flayed skin.

Swill is a black habilist! A massacar!

The horrid, impossible idea rolled about his mind's view, an image of the surgeon clandestinely making gudgeons in his attic apartment: wobbling, raving creatures cobbled together from kitchen offcuts and dug-up corpse bits, then held and hidden in the fortress's depths. The young lighter could little fathom how such a capital evil as monster-making—or "fabercadavery," as the peregrinat called it—could go on undiscovered within Winstermill's precincts. How was it possible that amid such a crowd of zealous invidists monsters were actually made?

With low and stuttering urgency, Rossamünd explained his deductions as best he could. He talked mostly to Europe, who listened without interruption, her arms folded and her brow deeply creased with a scowl.

"The rever-man had pig's ears," he repeated excitedly. "I carried a pig's head up to Swill from the kitchens. That's why he reads from those banned books—they are full of all manner of ash-dabblings."

"Well, one hardly needs to be an auto-savant to have spotted Swill as a nefarious cad!" Threnody argued.

A great roar of applause erupted about all levels of the Saloon: Hero had come to the end of her recital and was now bowing deeply to her adoring audience with great, cheek-busting smiles. Threnody looked down at it all and curled her lip. "Yes, well, I suppose she was passable," she sneered as she clapped politely.

Rossamünd barely heard her or the cheers. *Swill is a massacar!* Sebastipole said he had not found how the rever-man could have got in: the fortress really *was* impregnable. It would not have to be if the abomination was already being kept inside Winstermill—indeed if it had been made there in the deep parts. Was it mere coincidence that Rossamünd had found his way out only through the Master-of-Clerks' rooms? Swill was most certainly his man, brought in espe-cially. It all fitted too horribly.

"My, what a hive of troubles you have kicked," the ful-gar said. "The Soratchë were right to suspect him, it seems, though one thinks they might have pressed their suspicions a little further."

Threnody made a face as if to say she did not think much of the Soratchë.

"But why do such a terrible thing?" Rossamünd could not fathom it.

"Why else, little man, but for the oldest reason of all?" The fulgar paused. "Money, of course. There is much to be made from the making and trafficking of rever-men and other made-monsters—as you have seen firsthandedly, with that filthy fellow Poundinginches or whatever his name might have been."

Rossamünd nodded. What precious relief it had been when Europe had rescued him from that vile rivermas-ter and sent him to the harbor-bottom with one arc to his beefy chest.

"All manner of people manage to require the service of the dark trades," the fulgar continued. "I have already caught the whispers of at least two rousing-pits within reach of here, and they are genuinely lucrative for those at the right end of the wagers. These must be supplied, and it seems Swill is the man to do so."

The young lighter shivered at the implication of her words.

"If you know of such horrid places, why do you not do something about them?" Threnody interjected. "Or tell someone who will?"

Europe's expression became owlish. "Because, my dear, if I have heard rumors, then others certainly will have too. The excisemen and obstaculars and your once-sisters are better fitted to the chore."

"But rousing-pits have monsters in them," Threnody continued querulously. "Surely that should move you!"

Europe fixed her with that dangerously glassy stare.

"Child, I am *not* some mindless invidist. I rid the world of teratologica for money's hand, not sport."

Threnody locked eyes with her.

Rossamünd ducked his head at the fizzing tension between these two lahzarines. He wanted to intervene, yet did not dare tangle with the friction between them, as inscrutable as the movements of the planets. In the end the standoff proved unbearable and he spoke. "What of the Master-of-Clerks?" he tried. "Swill is *his* man. Doctor Crispus said it so."

"Every mad habilist needs a patron." Europe sounded almost flippant, though her grim expression told otherwise.

"Why did you not speak of this before, lamp boy?" Threnody growled.

"Because I did not think of it till now, Threnody," Rossamünd sighed.

"I must write of all this to Mother!"

"For the little she might do," said Europe, "with the clerk-master sitting in control behind those unapproachable walls and little proof to go on but one small bookchild lamps-man's conjectures."

"*She* is a great woman," Threnody bridled, "and will do more than some to rid the Empire of a traitor."

"But what if I'm wrong?"

"If you are wrong then rumors are exploded, suspicions disabused and everyone goes on to other troubles," Europe said bluntly. "Yet for now we have the suggestion of seri-ous, dastardly things, little man," she said. "Gudgeons loose in Winstermill, marshal-peers summoned to the subcapital and prentices sent too far east: something is truly, deeply amiss in your reach of the world. Keep your eyes wide, Ros-samünd. You are in a dangerous tangle if all this turns out true. It may be that your assignment to Wormstool is not a simple lapse in wisdom." She reached over to put a hand on his shoulder. "You should have become my factotum after all," she said wryly.

Rossamünd could not help but agree. He could not now think of anywhere safer than by Europe's side. He noticed Threnody was looking at him with an envious scowl.

Europe summoned a footman and made provision for their bunking. There was no room elsewhere in the wayhouse. "You can join me in my quarters if you wish, Rossamünd. There is a bed for one other there," the fulgar explained. "Or you may join your friend in the dog-dens."

The "dog-dens" were the billet-boxes, tight cupboards—barely comfortable but inexpensive accommodation that all wayhouses possessed. Rossamünd felt such a strange and unwelcome tearing of loyalties he did not know how to act. In the end he chose to stay with Threnody, figuring that she had joined him voluntarily and stuck by him, and so he should do the same and sleep in the squash of the billet-boxes. The girl lighter was clearly gratified by his decision, looking as if she had just won some great moral victory.

With an enigmatic sniff, Europe paid the reckoning and bid them good sleeping. "I must retire. A girl needs her sleep to keep her beauty." At that she left, reemerging surprisingly on the farther side of the Saloon to speak quietly with the horn-wearing caladine.

Seeing this, Threnody demanded, "Why does she talk to *her?*"

"Probably to let her know of our suspicions about Swill." Rossamünd's hopes lifted. Distracted by Threnody, he did not see Europe leave, but when he looked again she had disappeared to some other part of the wayhouse to do whatever occult things that fulgars did in the night hours.

With her departure Threnody leaned across the claustra. "Well, *she* is a disappointment—" she said, "dull and ordinary and not at all heroic. And I thought I wanted to be like her."

Utterly baffled and not wanting a fight, Rossamünd ignored her and stared out at the emptying Saloon.

"You don't really want to be her factotum, do you?" Threnody persisted, a hint of that envious look returning. "Being with her is like sucking on a lime dusted in bothersalts."

No, Threnody, that's what it's like being with you! The bitter thought rose unbidden, but Rossamünd said, "I've made oaths to serve the Emperor, Threnody. I've accepted his Billion. I'm not free to be anyone's factotum—Miss Europe's, yours or even Atopian Dido's, were she still alive!"

Apparently satisfied, Threnody too took her leave and went off to find a place to make her plaudamentum.

Rossamünd was left to be shown to his billet-box alone.

22

THE IGNOBLE END OF
THE ROAD

rimple a curious-looking hairy-leather purse made from the entire skin of a small rodent, shaved, with a drawstring at the neck hole, and the skin of one limb sewn back on itself as a loop to fix on to a belt. Actually looking like some bloated rat, a rimple is all the fashion as a coin-bag among the wayfaring classes.

THE new day and Europe, teeth still blackened from her morning dose of plaudamentum, met the two frowsty young lighters as they were arranging themselves in the stabulary to leave with the first post.

"How was your night in the dog-dens?" she asked a little tartly.

"Like sleeping inside a sideboard drawer." Rossamünd yawned. "I do not fathom how older folk can manage a single blink."

Europe simply nodded. That was the sum of her sympathy. "I will be answering a plea for aid from some sorely put and well-heeled people from Bleak Lynche," she explained to the sleep-deprived pair. "They need help with a gudgeon, wouldn't you know. It would appear we are going on a concomitant path, little man." Europe looked at Rossamünd pointedly. "So you shall wait for me as I complete my dealings with the knavery-underwriter and we shall travel together."

Rossamünd agreed readily.

Threnody did not even acknowledge that the fulgar had spoken, speaking only when Europe had left them. "So we are to do everything *she* says, are we?"

"Hmm" was all Rossamünd replied as he stretched, arms in the air, to rid himself of the kinks and knots gained through his insalubrious night's sleep. Their arrival at Wormstool was not expected; the delay of an hour or two would change nothing.

They waited in the knavery. There, as Threnody penned a letter to her mother, Rossamünd wrote two of his own, one to Sebastipole and the other to Doctor Crispus. He told them in guarded terms of his suspicions regarding Swill and the rever-man beneath Winstermill. It was worth running the risk of prying eyes if someone who might be able to do something were to know.

During the delay Threnody decided to liberally apply some flowery-sweet perfume, splashing enough to challenge the salty-sweetness of bosmath, Europe's signature scent. Where she had procured the essence from Rossamünd did not know, but the funk of it filled the knavery waiting room.

The morning was well advanced by the time Europe's negotiations with the knavery-underwriter were completed.

411

With the proof of the head she carried in the sack, her prize was paid and her forearm etched by the punctographist on hand, with another small cruciform of monster blood. One less monster to trouble the lives of man. Consequently the three left with the third post of the day.

"It's a post-and-six," Threnody declared optimistically. "We should make good time."

Leaving the missives with the knavery-clerks, to whom they paid 4g a letter to have them properly sealed, they ventured out under a flat gray sky to the cheerful, unseasonal warbling of a magpie. The carriage was badly sprung and very noisy, rendering conversation below a constant shout impossible. For Rossamünd this was a small mercy, filling the frosty, aromatic silence between fulgar and wit with welcome clamor.

Across the Sourspan and over the Bittermere the lentum-and-six jerked and shuddered uncomfortably. No longer following a watercourse, the Wormway traversed hill and dale, the apex of most rises giving Rossamünd a grand view of the land about. The green upon the downs was grayer, the trees sprouting from them sparse and gnarled, growing in the shadows of enormous granite boulders lichen-blotched and anciently weathered. Indeed, the entire quality of the land declined markedly only a few leagues east of the Bittermere. There was a rumor of loneliness here, Rossamünd growing more certain of it the farther the lentum carried them—an absence of people, yet an absence of monsters too. In the struggle to possess it, the land had become useless to both.

They passed Bitterbolt and watered horses at the sturdy sprawling fortalice of Mirthalt. There the lighters wore dogged expressions and barely reacted to the premature advent of the young lighters.

They arrived at Compostor in the mist of day's end. Bigger than Hinkerseigh, it was built on a broad hill, its curtain walls descending into foggy vales on all sides. There was a genuine air of money in this small city of long, broad avenues of stately sycamores and multistoried manors, of wide parks as green and tame as the land without was gray and wild.

"Tonight we shall stay somewhere out of the way," Europe pronounced as they were granted entry to the city by the heavy-harnessed watch. She directed the lentermen to a hostelry called the Wayward Chair. From the outside it was a modest establishment, but the room proved of a high standard at odds with the humble façade. Regardless, Threnody oozed dissatisfaction. Throughout the leg from the Brisking Cat to here, she had sat gingerly, leaning forward to spare herself the bumping of the carriage seat. Now she looked terribly wayworn and irritated, lagging behind as they were shown to their rooms by a pucker-faced bower maid.

They were successfully installed in the apartment: luggage deposited, beds turned, the fire stoked, food brought and Europe's treacle brewing in the kitchens. Without a word, Threnody exited the room, her makings in hand, slamming the door as she left.

"I don't know what ails her." Rossamünd felt he needed to apologize.

"It is just night-pains, little man."

"Night-pains?"

"Indeed." Europe sat in a glossy leather recliner before the hearth. "All lahzars must endure them and wits more so than fulgars. It is the cost of having these unusual organs inside—the price of power, if you like. A little bit of justice, I do not doubt some might think."

After about as much time as it took to brew plaudamentum the girl returned, still in foul spirits. She stomped right past the two, glaring at them both, and disappeared into the adjoining room where a bower maid was turning down the beds. There was a shout and the maid hurried out, looking even more puckered and near tears.

"That will be all, my dear," Europe said, handing the quickly brightening maid a whole sou. "You may go."

Listening to the thump and bluster of the girl in the bedroom, Rossamünd asked, "Miss Europe? How can we stop Swill and the Master-of-Clerks?"

"I have warned that Saphine lass you may remember from the Cat, and you have written your letters." Europe peered at him, her hazel eyes intent, thoughtful. "Beyond that there is not much else, and even what we have is insubstantial. I think you will find it very hard to lay a solid accusation against Swill or his clerk-master. If they have been able to carry on as black habilists right under the lighters' feet, then you may be certain, Rossamünd, they will have all traces of their dabblings well in hand and can easily obliterate any trails that might lead to them."

"But I fought with their rever-man!" Rossamünd persisted. "I saw the flayed skin! There—there was even that butcher's truck that smelled of swine's lard, just like Poundinch used to hide in his cargo, that's why the Trought attacked!"

"At this instant it would be what you say against what they would say," Europe countered calmly.

"But we have Sebastipole! No one doubts a falseman!"

The fulgar took a deep breath. "And I am sure they would have a falseman of their own. Use one falseman to cancel the other out—typical Imperial politics."

"Who can stop them, then?" Rossamünd despaired, an image of Laudibus Pile's sneering face looming in his imagination.

"Well, it certainly won't be *you,* little man, will it—sent out here at their very behest?"

"No." Rossamünd hung his head.

"And with Whympre the current lord of Winstermill," Europe continued, pressing the point, "I cannot see how they will be stopped in a hurry."

"You could, Miss Europe."

Europe laughed a strange, sardonic laugh. "Oh, little

man!" she sighed. "Rescuing empires from their own corruption is not my game. You'll just have to trust that all wicked things bring themselves to an end in the end."

"But who says what is wicked?" Rossamünd blurted.

"Enough now," the fulgar said with sudden impatience. "You wax too philosophical for weary travelers."

The young lighter ducked his head in apology.

"Do not speak of these things to another, do you understand me?" Europe said sharply. "They will not believe you, and word of any loose talk or unguarded accusation might find its way to the wrong ears."

"Aye, Miss Europe." The young lighter retreated to his comfortable bed. He slept eventually. His last sight through the door ajar was the motionless fulgar lost in her unfathomable recollections before the dying embers in the hearth.

The new-morning world was sunk in fog. The lenterman was cautious and they left Compostor at a measured crawl. Threnody's wind had improved little since yesternight and she dozed and stared out the opposite window and said naught.

There was little to see from the window but fathomless gray until the lentum slowly crested a hill and drew clear of the obscuring shroud. Rossamünd was graced with a view that until now he never knew possible: all about was a puffy lake of cloud, glowing a russet golden-white in the climbing light, lapping at the contours of spur and gully as an ocean touches the sandy shore. Other hilltops poked through and made dark islands in this stark fog sea. On one pinnacle about a mile distant, Rossamünd thought for a moment he spied movement. He looked closer and saw a large, long-limbed something gamboling in the clear, cold dawn looking for all the world to be hooting at the glaring day-orb. It must have been very tall indeed to be visible from so far, but as he went to call his fellow travelers' attention to it, the carriage descended into the murk and the unsettling sight was obliterated.

"Such things are common here," Europe said in answer to his hurried, hollered description. "This remains true ditch-land, whatever maps might say. Here monsters have free rein and are stopped only by walls and vigilance—and me," she finished, a twinkle in her eye.

The brume persisted for much of the first half of the day, lifting only slightly to hang above as a somber, driz-zling blanket. In the haze loomed the Wight, raised where two trunk-roads met with the highway. The fortress-city had grown rich on tolls extracted from grain trains coming down from Sulk and luxury trading caravans going north. Negoti-ating its streets, Rossamünd saw that the military very much intruded on the public: watchtowers in municipal squares, barracks fronting a common park with its soldiers monopo-lizing the green for their evolutions. Nevertheless, women in tentlike dresses promenaded with parasols and met with men in finest silks. Together these would take their spiced and scented infusions in public places of high fashion and then be carried home in gilt, leather-covered mule-litters.

Insisting on a change of carriage as well as team, Europe took them to a tiny corner shop known as a small-market or kettle. It was a cluttered affair, full of such a disparity of goods that it took Rossamünd some time to even orient himself before being able to decide on purchases. With much of his money—almost a full year's worth—still encumbering his wallet, Rossamünd first bought a fine black thrice-high with satin-trimmed edges. It squatted rebelliously on his bandage, refusing to sit right, and became so annoying he removed the dressing so that the hat might fit as it should.

"I don't know the nature of the wound you had," declared Threnody, peering at his scalp, "but there is no evidence of it now."

Rossamünd also purchased a quarter of a rind of his old favorite—fortified sack cheese; a small jar of preserved apricots; dried fruits; half a cured pork sausage; and boschenbread. This last was just like from home: golden-dark and doughy, with a scrumptious hint of ginger. Verline had made boschenbread every Bookday, enough for every foundling. He carried two pounds of the stuff away in a big brown bag and shared it liberally with a quietly amused Europe, with Threnody—who declared she did not like it and left her piece barely nibbled—and even the bemused lentermen.

A new lentum took them out of Wightfastseigh. The replacement carriage was a public coach rather than the post, better sprung, with windows covered in iron grille work, and carrying an extra backstepper, a quartertopman who held a salinumbus and rode alongside the splasher boy. It was a vehicle intended for travel in threatened places. It was also quieter on the road.

On this side of the fortress-city they began to pass wayfaring metal-mending tinkers, script-selling pollcarries and brocanders shopping their secondhand proofing; those who dared the dangerous way in hope that isolation might make people willing to buy their inferior goods. The life expectancy of such as these would not have been long and only desperation could surely drive someone to such work; Rossamünd had a sudden glimpse of his privileges, when measured against the lot of these ragged gyrovagues.

As Ashenstall drew near, its window-lights and lanterns glowing merrily against the dour evenfall, the post-lentum eased its pace, its driver clearly intending on making that cothouse their night-stop.

"I have no desire to spend a night in the insalubrious squish of one of your cot-rents," Europe declared testily. She pulled down the grille and rattled her purse ostentatiously at the lenterman, shouting, "Drive on! Take us to the Prideful Poll. It will be well worth the anxiety if you persevere!"

There was a hasty discussion between the carriage-men and a quick conclusion.

The lentum pressed on, going faster now.

Rossamünd could hear the horses' frequent whickering, even over the clangor of the carriage's hasty progress. They well knew the unfriendliness of the dark and—shabraqued or not—the tasty treat they presented to night-prowling nickers.

419

The sun was an hour set and the waning moon well up on its course when Europe pointed through the grille of the window at a square, keeplike structure with a rounded roof built into the cutting on the northern side of the highroad right opposite a great-lamp. Its own gate lanterns made a well-lit spot upon the road before the thick encircling wall. Suspended between them was a circular sign with the silhouette of a proud-looking head and large white letters beneath that read *Prideful Poll*.

Another wayhouse.

They drew into the slender coach yard and a warm welcome as strong gates closed out the nighttime fears.

The next morning, though their rimples were decidedly fatter after Europe's financial incentives, the public-coach lentermen were unwilling to take her and her two young passengers down on to the Frugelle. The nighttime dash to the Prideful Poll was one thing, but a trot along that threatened place was "quite another tan of leather!" as the side-armsman put it. "No amount of counters will get us to shift down on to that there dour place."

Not at all inclined to argue, Europe dismissed them, declaring, "No matter, we shall take the next post east."

Post-lentermen were more game than public coachers.

As they waited, the woman and the girl sipped the Prideful Poll's best claret, while Rossamünd stared from an east-facing window at the bleak view. Below was a gray arid plain strewn with countless tufts of dark vegetation. His Imperial Highness' Highroad, the Conduit Vermis, ran out like an anchor cable down on the flat, going steadily east, curving slightly south as it did. This stretch before him showed on the maps as the Pendant Wig. More than a league away Rossamünd could see a tiny structure by the road—a cothouse: Patrishalt. The thrum of loneliness was a constant pang here—subtle threwd exquisitely balanced between threat and welcome. He could feel it through the glass, fluttering within him uncomfortably.

They did not wait long. The day's first post pulled into the cramped coach yard with a trumpet blast, bearing no passengers and keen to take some on board. Out in the yard the monotonous wind wailed its melancholy up from the eastern lowlands, bringing a faint stink of rot on its breath. With a quick inspection that all their luggage was intact, Rossamünd entered the coach and they were away. Speed was a traveler's best defense out here.

The Wormway wound down the flanks of the hills, following a shallow cleft eroded by a seasonal brook. The post-lentum gathered momentum as it descended the face of the hills. It crossed the Lornstone, an old brick bridge that spanned a gully thick with sighing swamp oaks and stunted pines. On seven great arches the Wormway crossed the bridge and continued along on a stone dike that reached out for a mile into the Frugelle. The great flat was a continuous low thatch of thorny, stramineous stubble. Trees collected in dell or hollow, writhen, dwarfish things, their gray trunks rough and fissured. The unsettled threwd nagged persistently, not foe but certainly not friend.

The travelers' breath steamed inside the lentum cabin. Threnody shivered, glared at the glimpse of frosty sky showing through the grille of the lentum windows and wrapped her furs closer about.

Europe proved unperturbed by it all, rugged in a long, thickly furred huque, hair down in a long plait; she watched everything through her pink quartz-lensed spectacles with regal equanimity. Nothing reached her, and for this Rossamünd was deeply grateful. For no matter how the lugubrious threwd pressed in or the chill gripped, the young lighter felt that all things might be compassed with the Branden Rose at the lead.

"My, this is a dreary land," she said, looking around at her two companions. "Yes?"

Rossamünd nodded.

From her den of furs Threnody raised an eyebrow and barely shrugged.

"And dreary company too . . ." Europe arched her spoored brow.

Along his side of the road Rossamünd discovered the low, half-buried strongworks he had first spied between Makepeace and Hinkerseigh. This time they were positioned at every third lamp, looking very much like sunken fortifications. *But to what purpose?* Rossamünd wondered.

Built on the connection with the northeast running

Louth-Hurry Road, Patrishalt was much like every other cothouse they had passed. With nothing to recommend it as a rest-stop, the lentum delivered a small amount of mail and carried on.

The country varied little, and by the time they achieved Cripplebolt two hours later, all three passengers were dozing. When the lentum was back on its way east with a fresh, new-shabraqued team, Rossamünd tucked into the provender bought at Wightfastseigh. Threnody grimaced from over her duodecimo with open disgust as he chewed on the pork sausage in one bite and took a spoon of preserved apricots, plopping about in their earthen jar, in another.

Hiss-CRACK! A musket shot just above shattered the delight of his light repast. It was followed by a short series of thumps joining the din of travel, a pause and then *Hiss-CRACK!*

"What is happening?" cried Rossamünd, ducking at the smack of the second discharge. A puff of gun-smoke burst above, on his side of the lentum, to be whipped away by wind of the vehicle's passage.

"I think you'll find they are warning off a passing nicker," Europe said calmly.

Threnody clambered over to the same side and joined him in a search of the passing land without, frustrated that her view was blocked by the window-grille. "I cannot see what they shoot at," she complained, leaning over Rossamünd. "They'd better hit it, the cheeky bugaboo!" she hissed.

"For the nicker's sake let's hope they do." Europe peered

briefly through the window-grille. "It would be a kinder death to have a musket ball in your meat than come to hand strokes with me."

There were no further shots and no beast assailed them. The lentum made good time on this flat straight road, and in the paleness of the eastern quarter of the evening sky they spied the rectangular towers of a settlement a-sparkle with lights easily seen from the straightness of the plain. The township of Bleak Lynche.

As the lentum drew closer, Rossamünd could see that every structure was three or four or five stories tall, raised close together and with no gate nor surrounding wall to protect them. *How is that possible!* It was only as they entered the town and crept between these towers that he realized none of the buildings had ground-level doors opening out to the dangerous world. The higher stories were accessed from the ground only via retractable iron ladders, and an arrangement of covered walks—the lynches—stretched the short gaps between structures, their weight carried on sturdy arches.

The hard-packed dirt of the Wormway went right through the middle of the town, leading them to a small wayhouse called the Fend & Fodicar, its sign a fodicar and a spittende crossed. Upon the other hand was a large oblong fort of four levels and, like every other building here, a flattened gable roof of red tiles. This was Bleakhall, the lamplighters' bastion and the only structure to be surrounded by a wall, which protected a coach yard and steep stairs to a third-story door. With the yell of its horn the post-lentum was let through gates as thick and tall as the bronze portals of Winstermill and rattled slowly into the tight area within, brightly lit by slow-burning flares lifted up on lampposts. A quarto of heavy-harnessed haubardiers met the carriage and humbly did the tasks of yardsmen: helping the lentermen take the horse-team in hand, organizing the setting down of the luggage. The postilion opened the doors of the lentum and lowered the folding-step, handing the women out of the cabin. The haubardiers were puzzled by a calendar in lighter's vestments and they were downright astounded by the dangerous graces of the fulgarine peeress. Europe played the part with practiced ease, feigning ignorance at their awe with a studied grandness. Threnody met them with her typical superciliously lifted chin. Rossamünd just helped to carry the bags.

The three were shown up the steps through a door of solid black iron, the postilion following after with a mailbag. Beyond was an antechamber slit with murder holes in roof and wall. A cheerful "halloo" from their haubardier guide, and a second black door at the farther end was winched open. Europe, Rossamünd and Threnody were admitted to a watch room furnished sparely with a clerical desk, a large clock and other doors to left and right.

They were met by a young man in a powdered scratch-bob, standing behind the desk. He was wearing the unmistakable white oversleeves of an altern-lighter and the same surprised expression as all the other officers of previous cothouses at the sight of newly made, newly arrived lighters. Stuttering a little at Europe's steady scrutiny, he greeted them all stiffly. As he sorted through the few items in the mailbag, he informed them that their Major-of-House and Lamplighter-Captain were away at Haltmire for an urgent conference with the Warden-General. "How-be-it, young lampsmen. You have come to reinforce us?"

"No, sir, we're meant for Wormstool," Rossamünd explained.

"Wormstool, is it?" The altern looked a little put out. "Well, they need it more, I suppose, though we are all sorely put. You can journey there with the lantern-watch tomorrow morn. I'll have the costerman take your dunnage across later in the day."

"I'll set owt termorrer," the costerman drawled with a thick Sulk End accent, entering at the altern-lighter's summons. Squarmis was the man's name. He was a withered, greasy fellow in many heavy layers of cheap proofing and a short-tailed liripipium. There was something indefinably odd about the man, something vague and unsettling. For a dread instant, Rossamünd swore he caught a hint of swine's lard on the fellow. When he thought no one was paying him any mind he sniffed more deeply, but only got a nose full of the man's natural unwashed odors and the waft of strong drink.

Squarmis looked at them shrewdly. "A jink for yer goods in the cart will cost ye one an' six."

Even Rossamünd could tell one sequin, six guise was

426

SQUARMIS THE COSTERMAN

thievery for such a short ride. It was more than the young lighter was paid for a month of prenticing.

"You must be jesting," said Threnody, incredulous. "How can you practice such domestic brigandry?"

"We all have owr burthens, miss," Squarmis said with an unctuous smile and fingers greedily gripping for the fare. "Does ye wants yer parcels delivered safe across this nasty world or does ye not?" The avaricious fellow was so brazen he was not daunted even by the presence of Europe.

"This is your best service, Lieutenant?" the fulgar queried the young altern-lighter, talking as if the costerman were not there.

Blushing slightly, he bowed a little. "My apologies, ma'am, th-this scoundrel is all there is to offer. He has been g-given sole commission to work here by the Master-of-Clerks' office, so we have little choice."

"Very well."

Before the costerman slunk away the altern passed him a red-leather wrapped dispatch, an official document normally sent only by the Marshal—in this case the Marshal-Subrogat, Podious Whympre. "This has arrived for you," the young officer said.

What does Podious want with him so far out here?

Squarmis took the dispatch between smudgy fingers. "Thems will be my orders from *yer* surpeereeors." He leered knowingly and wandered back through the side door from which he had come.

Blushing, the altern-lighter apologized once again then

asked of Rossamünd and Threnody, "How would you like to meet your new comrades?"

"I think a time of rest for us all at your wayhouse would do better," Europe cut in quickly. "Camaraderie can come later."

"Ah—right you are, madam." With an open palm, he gestured them to follow. He took them through a door and down a passage over the high lynche that connected cothouse to wayhouse. Though it was covered with its own tiled roof, the sides were open to the winds, and an eerie inhuman ululation carried faintly from the flatlands. Somewhere inside the bastion the muffled yammering of the cothouse dogs and the answering shouts of their tractors could be heard. The altern seemed hardly to notice as he guided them.

The Fend & Fodicar's enrica d'ama, Goodwife Inchabald, greeted them all familiarly. "Oh 'ello, my darlings! Come for a taste of me hasty pie, 'ave you?"

"Her fare is as poor as her welcome is warm," Threnody murmured into her plate when their meals were served.

"Miss Europe, what of this rever-man you have to dispatch?" Rossamünd asked.

The fulgar took a sip of beer and betrayed only the slightest distaste. "There are people who dare to actually live out there on the flat," she said, "and out there is where I am to go. Some puzzled eeker-folk with more sequins than sense, it seems, have a rever-man in residence in their cellar. My intermediary is a fellow here by the name of

Dimbleby: I am to find him tomorrow. More than that I do not know."

"What is it doing out here?"

"The rever-man? Who can say?" Europe sighed wearily. "It might have escaped from a strong room in the mines up north."

"Maybe it is one of Swill's," Threnody added.

"It could have come from a rousing-pit," Rossamünd put in. "There is probably one out here too."

"It might have." The fulgar was starting to sound a little exasperated. "Out in this rustic remoteness anything might be."

"Will you be taking help?" Joining her on the hunt for a gudgeon was factotum work Rossamünd would be happy to do.

Europe let out a puff of air and reviewed the room and its few hard-bitten patrons. "In the morning I will attempt to find myself a lurksman among these frowsty folk. If it weren't for your oaths of service I would take you too."

"Why are you *so* insistent on Rossamünd as your factotum?" Threnody demanded.

The fulgar looked at Threnody as if seeing her for the very first time. "Child, do not mistake my tolerance of you for acceptance."

Threnody's mouth opened then shut, but no sound came out. She looked to Rossamünd, dropped her eyes and looked mortified for a merest twinkling. With admirable spirit, she recovered, and, chin jutting proudly, ate the rest of her tasteless meal.

There was a long, unpleasant silence.

Europe ate little more, and soon left the two young lighters, to inquire of a bed for the night and board for an indeterminate duration. Threnody took out a duodecimo and read as if Rossamünd was not there. To pass time, he sorted through his salumanticum, resettling vials and jars, salperts and castes, all in their padded boxes or cushion pockets, making the most necessary scripts easy to extract.

Europe returned, her arrangements made. "I'm glad to see you're in a habilistic turn of mind," she said. "How would you take to trying your hand once more at making my treacle, little man?—to keep your practice up?"

"I might as well make you some too, Threnody, if I'm already at it."

"No!" she said frostily. "Stop asking me."

Stung, Rossamünd took up Europe's lacquered treacle-box—remembering only too well how uneasy it had made him feel—and allowed himself to be led to the small kitchen. There, while Europe left to arrange her luggage and Goodwife Inchabald hovered nervously to make sure he did not spoil her clean stoves, Rossamünd brewed. He discovered the steps of making were vivid in his mind and Sugar of Nnun still filled him with sickly dreads. The disturbing half smell of the finished treacle filled the close space.

"Well done, little man," Europe said quietly, reappearing as if drawn by the reek. With a toss of her head and those unladylike gulps she drained the bowl. "Well, good night, Rossamünd," she continued—Rossamünd trying not to stare at her stained mouth—"Tomorrow I knave myself in earnest, and you will be on your way to your lonely billet. I shall be about if you have need of me. Remember well my warning at Compostor." Her voice dropped to a whisper. "Keep what you know to yourself. It will profit no one just babbled about—and don't go getting yourself maimed or slaughtered." She looked at him until the young lighter felt like a squirming worm on a hook.

"Good-bye, Miss Europe," Rossamünd whispered. He felt like he was ever saying this to her.

Without another word the fulgar gathered her treacle-box and departed, leaving the young lighter to make his way back across the lynche to Bleakhall, passing Threnody without acknowledgment.

Halfway across the bridge she caught up with him. "What, no Brambly Rose? How ever will you get on without her?" she said sardonically. "How you can stomach her hoit-a-toit I do not know." Threnody sniffed sourly. "I can see well now why Mother does not like her."

"I would have thought your mother's dislike of her would have recommended Europe to you," he countered.

She fixed him with a withering eye. "Well, I go to make my own treacle, as any *good* lahzar should. You should come and see how it is really done."

Rossamünd declined.

"I shall leave you to your moon dreams of the Lady Europe, then!"

Baffled and tired, Rossamünd did not offer a response.

Across in Bleakhall the kindly altern showed him to a long, open hall with benches for meals at one end and a double row of cots at the other, all beneath a lofty ceiling a-crowd with exposed beams. The distinct, dank smell of seldom-washed men mixed with wood-smoke and lock-oil: the telltale odor of a cothouse and something a little more acrid and unpleasant. After three days in the funk of a lentum cab shared with two perfumed women, Rossamünd had lost his dullness to the smell of too many men together. He tried not to breathe deeply.

It was the full of night now, and the lantern-watch from Wormstool had already arrived, their lighting done. They were sitting with their Bleakhall brothers about the common table drinking bottles down to the mud, swapping bawdy jokes and playing at checkers. They seemed hard and rough, like the *Hogshead* bargemen, but altogether much neater and thoroughly clean. For all their coarse language and rough manners, they seemed careful with how they looked, cursing at each other if ever a splash or splatter threatened to soil their harness. Each wore a baldric of Imperial red: they were citizens of the Empire, claiming no particular stately heritage.

Rossamünd felt very dull and frowzy. He noticed Threnody, who had soon returned—teeth slightly stained with plaudamentum—self-consciously pull and play at her hems and fringes whenever she thought the lampsmen were not looking.

She barely acknowledged him, however.

The "Stoolers," those lighters—Rossamünd quickly learned—from Wormstool, and the "Bleakers" were fascinated by the two young arrivals, but especially by Threnody. She made much of being superior to their attentions, yet from Rossamünd's vantage she relished every rough jest or idle tease.

"How come they're sending them out to ye?" a Bleakhall lighter asked. "We need replacements just as much . . ."

"More's the point: what's the Marshal doin' billetin' such pink li'l morsels out to us?" one extraordinarily hairy Stooler—one Under-Sergeant Poesides—added.

"Aye!" Rossamünd heard one lighter whisper theatrically to a brother-in-arms. "What do they takes us for, wet nurses?"

"Doesn't he know we eat 'em alive out here?" Poesides added, raising sinister chuckles from his amused colleagues.

Rossamünd grinned sheepishly.

Threnody sniffed superciliously as she said sourly, "You might find us a little hard to chew!" inciting a general "ooooh" and loud laughter.

"I can see thy arrow-spoor, Miss Muddle!" A rather thickset sergeant sporting raven-hued mustachios and a bulbous nose grinned and pointed to Threnody's brow. Isambard Mulch was his name. "Going to fish our heads from inside our tummies after we've eaten ye, are ye?"

Some small lighter, old enough to surely have earned retirement, aped exaggerated actions of eating then keeled over, clutching dramatically at his head and stomach. The laughter became a roar, Rossamünd joining them. Even Threnody broke a smile.

"Ahhh there, lads," Sergeant Mulch cried, pointing to the girl's reluctant grin, "she's human-hearted after all!"

Her smile vanished and the guffaws roared louder still.

Perhaps service at the ignoble end of the road might not be so wretched after all.

23

WORMSTOOL

gourmand's cork also known as a throttle or a gorge; the projecting "knuckle" of cartilage in a person's throat, in which is situated the vocal cords; what we would call the Adam's apple. It is called the gourmand's cork (a gourmand being one who is a gluttonous or greedy eater) because of the tight sensation you can get there when feeling nauseated, which vulgar folk hold is the voice box trying to prevent or "cork" any further eating.

ROSSAMÜND was turned out into the small yard at the foot of Bleakhall the next morning to discover thick fog smothering the land, deadening sound, diminishing light, dampening spirits. There was no wind, not even a gentle breeze; just the clammy touch of tiny, infrequent eddies. In the unsettling quiet the half quarto of lampsmen who were to be his billet-mates, perhaps forever more, said very little above common greetings and introductions. One old fellow, who presented himself as Furius Lightbody, Lampsman 1st Class, checked the two new lamplighters' harness and their equipage. He paused when he spotted Rossamünd's salumanticum.

"Good lad," he said. Lightbody tugged on its strap to

test the repair, then patted a satchel of his own, showing a hand missing the third and fourth fingers. "Wise. We've all got one."

Rossamünd nodded. "Why are there five of you?" he asked in a hush.

"Them city-scholars say it takes three fit fellows to best a single hob-possum" was the gruff return. "That's all well and good for them and their books, but out here we reckon five of us stands a better chance. In truth there should be more . . ."

Lampsman Lightbody attached a bright-limn to the head of each of their fodicars, fixing the bottom of the small lamps—known as crook-lights—to the shaft to prevent them from swinging about noisily.

"Why do we not take a leer with us?" Rossamünd wondered aloud, looking worriedly at the thick airs.

" 'Cause we don't got one to take," came the simple answer. "The Hall's fellow is with his own lamp-watch, and Crescens Hugh—he being our own one-and-only lurksman—is off-watch. Even he needs his sleep."

Another lighter named Aubergene stood before them. He was a much younger fellow with black hair, angular features similar to Sebastipole's and a protruding gourmand's cork that bobbed disconcertingly as he addressed them with suppressed, whispered enthusiasm. "Don't you fuss too much about this soup, young fellows, it's just Old Lacey," he explained kindly. "It's the fleermare. Comes in off the Swash and leaves everything dripping, but without it there'd be no water for us or the plants—it rains dead seldom about here. Take these . . . it's phlegein," he said to Threnody's blank look at the small tubes the man held out to them, "or falsedawn if you like. In case you lose us. Just pull the hem." He indicated a small silk protrusion on the bottle. "Strike the raised end on the ground and hold it high, well away from your face."

Threnody went to refuse, tapping the fine-drawn arrow on her brow, as if it were an answer to everything.

Aubergene looked at the spoor with a slight hesitation. He puffed his cheeks out and in and said, "That'll help you find us, lass, but not us you. Take it and let us get on."

Sergeant Mulch led off, and as Rossamünd then Threnody followed the five bobbing lights out the heavy gates of Bleakhall, Rossamünd looked back at the barely visible mass of the Fend & Fodicar. He tried to guess which window Europe slept behind.

Leaving Bleak Lynche, it was impossible to reckon distances between lanterns. In the opaque fumes the beclouded nimbus-light of a great-lamp could be seen only when the watch drew very near. The assiduous lampsmen worked, stoutly feeling their way one great-lamp to the next, each lighter nothing more than the suggestion of a shadow and a bobbing globular glow, communicating only rarely in terse whispers. Rossamünd had never been anywhere so completely blank: anything could leap out and snatch them away. Ears were a-ring with anxious straining, eyes bugging to keep sight of the will-o'-the-wisp gleam of the leading crook-lights. His throat was in a constant constriction of dread; he did not know how the lamplighters of the Frugelle ever managed to do their work without blubbering into an overwrought mass. No amount of practice on the Pettiwiggin could have prepared him for this. It was a relief to learn that neither he nor Threnody was expected to wind any of the lamps on this blind morning. Nevertheless, he waited impatiently for each lamp to be wound, *one—two three—up, down-two-three, one—two—three—up, down-two-three,* cringing at the ringing clatter of the cogs and chains. Though the mechanical sounds were muffled by the turgid airs, Rossamünd found them a clashing of cymbals in the tomblike silence, sure to attract some nasty lurker.

The all-too-sluggish encroachment of the new day's growing light served only to illuminate the fog itself, making it pale and almost phosphorescent; a yawning whiteness where the only tangible thing was the hard-packed road grinding under his boot-soles. This luminous nothingness obliterated any sight of the crook-lights, and forced the lantern-watch to march closer than the regulation spacing.

Suddenly the column stopped.

Rossamünd could sense the lampsmen becoming very still.

The fellow immediately before him—Rossamünd thought it was Aubergene—crouched and indicated the young lighter do the same. Rossamünd obeyed and repeated the motion for the benefit of Threnody behind.

I am the very soul of stillness. He repeated Fouracres' old formula. *I am the very soul of stillness . . .*

Motionless and listening, he understood almost instantly. Something was snuffling in the veiling murk off to the left, its shuffling movement faint yet obvious in the dry crackle of the stunted Frugelle grasses. Staring out into that awful blank, Rossamünd had a prodigious sense of the malign intent of this sniffling, searching something. He carefully, haltingly, squeezed a hand into his salt-bag, thankful for resorting its contents. He felt for the especially wrapped john-tallow—one of the un-used gifts bestowed by Master Craumpalin when Rossamünd was still a foundling starting out. He withdrew it with fastidi-ous care lest the oiled paper make a give-away rustling of its own. Working it free of the bag, he put the parcel on to the road and gingerly grasped two corners of the complex folds of the wrapping, careful not to touch the actual wax. All this he did by feel alone, his eyes busy looking into the impenetrable fog, darting left and right at each new noise.

Before him he could hear Aubergene ever-so-gently cocking some kind of firelock.

The snuffler was getting closer.

On the other side, Threnody was a hardly discernible shadow—was that her arm he saw reach for her temple?

With a sudden flick of wrist and fingers, Rossamünd pulled the wrapper apart, letting out the sweaty, unwashed smell, and, quick as fulgar's lightning, flung the john-tallow, packaging and all, out into the cloudy soup. He could almost feel the attention of the malignant stalker catch the smell and follow the invisible arc of the flying repugnant. Sure enough, the sounds of scuffling moved away.

Oh, glory on Craumpalin's chemistry! Rossamünd's heart sang.

Aubergene did not appear to notice the young lighter's action and the lighters stayed as they were for longer yet—Rossamünd's senses frayed, his haunches aching—till as a man, they decided it was safe enough to push on. Not one mention was made of his deed; none had noticed. The young lighter had no way of knowing if it *was* the john-tallow that drew the sniffing thing away, and therefore he kept any boasts to himself.

Unexpectedly, only two lamps later, the vertical bulk of Wormstool materialized—they were arrived at last. The cothouse—if it could be called a "house"—was a tall octagonal tower topped with a flattened roof of red tiles a-bristle with chimneys. Entry was gained by the ubiquitous narrow flight of stone-and-mortar steps that bent about three faces of the tower as it climbed to a second-story door.

Rossamünd held his breath and squinted against the noxious fumes drizzling from the smoldering censer at the foot of the steps.

At the top, the thick cast-iron door opened on to a watch room. Entering, Rossamünd found an eight-sided hall, the walls slitted with loopholes, where watchmen periodically wandered from one to the next and mutely observed the land beyond. Not even the entry of the lantern-watch distracted them from their lookout.

In the very middle of the hall was a squat lectern, and behind this sat an uhrsprechman. Wet-eyed, limp-haired, the man looked all too ready for sleep, shuffling and settling papers clumsily at the close of his night-vigil. He watched the arrivals hawkishly, screwing up his face as he tilted his head back and peered over his glasses.

" 'Allo, Whelpmoon," the stocky, hairy under-sergeant named Poesides said to the fellow as they passed. "Ye look a mite piqued, me old mate. Just be glad you've not had to be out *there* this mornin': pea soup so thick that a laggard couldn't scry through it—and a stalking lurker thrown into the bargain."

Whelpmoon nodded briefly, said nothing, and kept at his staring.

Looking beyond him, Rossamünd saw a great kennel occupying three whole walls which kept a pack of dogs: spangled whelp-hounds—giant, sleek-looking creatures that eyed Rossamünd suspiciously and let forth warning growls from their heavy-barred cage.

"Them daggies never takes to strangers," Lampsman Lightbody chuckled.

From this room the lampsmen gained access to higher floors by a wooden stair at the left of the entrance. From it dangled a sophisticated tangle of cords and blocks, much as could be found on a vessel. Rossamünd asked what these were for.

"Ah," answered Lampsman Lightbody eagerly, "these stairs are the genius of the major and Splinteazle our seltzerman—naval men, both of them, with cunning naval minds." He nodded approvingly.

WORMSTOOL

Rossamünd's ears pricked at this mention of the Senior Service.

"It's dead-on impressive," Aubergene added. "You see there—that cord, how it leads up through that collet in the ceiling? If ever a nicker or some other flinching hob makes it in here and we need to retreat, we can pull levers up on the next floor connected to that cord and cause this whole construction to topple, leaving the foe stuck down here while we ply fire from on high."

It was indeed "impressive"—as an idea at least. No sooner had Rossamünd ascended a few steps than the whole flight wobbled alarmingly, beams groaning, the rope tackle shaking. The lighters did not seem to notice, and climbed happily up to the floor above, while Threnody and he followed one careful step at a time, knuckles whitening on the worn-smooth banister.

Gratefully achieving the top, Rossamünd heard Aubergene declaring, "Our reinforcements all the way from Winstermill, sir—ain't it nice to know we're not forgotten?"

Rather than dwelling safely on the very top floor of the tower, as many officer-types might, Wormstool's Major-of-House held office in the very next level; working with his day-clerk on one side and cot-warden on the other, all seated behind the same wide desk of thick, hard wood. It looked solid enough to serve as barricade and fire-position should need arise. Rossamünd could well imagine musketeers firing from behind it with their firelocks, shooting at some intruder who had managed to win its way up the rickety stairway.

The house-major was even better turned out than his subordinates—creaseless platoon-coat of brilliant Imperial scarlet and a black quabard so lustrous, with its thread-of-gold owl, it almost gleamed. The man was most certainly of a naval bent, for there were several scantlings of main-rams and cruisers pinned to the angled walls about him and a great covering of black-and-white checkered canvas on the floor, such as Rossamünd would expect to find in the day-cabin of a ram. The house-major stood with a fluent, perfectly military motion.

"Miss Threnody of Herbroulesse and Rossamünd Book-child, Lamplighters 3rd Class, come from Winstermill Manse, sir," Rossamünd said firmly as he stepped before the immaculate officer.

The house-major fixed them with mildly skeptical amusement. "Well, aren't you a pair of trubb-tailed, lub-berly blunderers?" he exclaimed in a trim and educated accent that gave no hint to his origins. "We've not received a brace of lantern-sticks in a prodigious long time, and nei-ther have we received word to be expecting any! The dead of winter means infrequent mail and is an off time to be sending anyone so far—how long have you been prenticing for? I thought lantern-sticks weren't deemed fully cooked till chill's end."

Rossamünd and Threnody looked to each other.

Threnody spoke up. "We were told that Billeting Day was done early because the road was in need of new lighters."

"Is that rightly so?" Taking his seat, the house-major stared at her and, more particularly, her spoor. "It is not common to have one of your species make lighter, especially not one that is a tempestine too—are you not a little too new from the crib to be cathared?"

Threnody bristled but controlled her tongue. "Perhaps."

The house-major held her with his steady gaze. "As it stands, we are thankful the Ladies of Columbris have the numbers to spare us one here."

Bemused, Threnody gave half a curtsy.

"As to what you have been told regarding us," the officer continued, "aye, new lighters we do need: a large quarto of doughty, veteran lampsmen to cover our losses, not a brace of new-burped lumps such as yourselves. Is that not so, Sergeant-Master?" he barked to the big, silver-haired cot-warden.

"Aye, sir." The cot-warden smirked. "Though a company of the same would be better."

"I've heard it said that the marshal-lighter is ailing," continued the house-major. "Can he have decreased in his powers so much as to send you here?"

"Oh, it wasn't the Lamplighter-Marshal, sir"—Rossamünd wrestled with the desire to cry out in the Marshal's defense— "it was the Master-of-Clerks who sent us."

In one breath the officer's eyes widened, in another they narrowed. "Did he . . . ," he said slowly. "Since when has *that* lickspittle been sending lighters or directing policy?"

"Since the Lamplighter-Marshal was shipped off to the Considine with a sis edisserum in his hand and 'that lickspittle'—who now calls himself the Marshal-Subrogat—took the run of the manse," Threnody stated tartly.

"Is that so, Lamplighter?" The house-major looked arch. "And I'd rather you addressed me as 'sir' or 'house-major.'"

"Sir," she added after only the briefest hesitation.

The day-clerk, who had been fossicking about in the newly arrived post-bag, passed a telltale red-leather dispatch over to the house-major.

"So the poor old war-dog has been called to account, has he?" the house-major continued. "The bee's buzz has been that he was losing grip of the whole 'Way. In a fight he's your man, but give him pens and paper and he's all a-sea . . . Well, it's of little use, by either hand," he concluded, picking up the dispatch and opening it almost absently. "Most folk tend to declare this place *hic sunt beluae*—here be monsters—and forget us altogether." He began to read.

Rossamünd shuffled his feet carelessly in the pregnant pause. How could they think the great man "poor" or "old"? However, like it or no, he was not about to set his commanding officer straight on the actual score of things.

"And here our glorious new Marshal-Subrogat confirms your report," the house-major suddenly said, holding up the dispatch, "though I still challenge his wisdom for sending you lantern-sticks out early. This is where only the best and hardiest get billeted. I'd say it's been an awfully long consult-a-ledger period of time since shining-new lampsmen 3rd class were ever billeted to us fresh out of the manse." He rattled the letter. "But here you both are, out to proudly join the hardiest and most soldierly of all the lighters on the 'Way." He fixed both newcomers with appraising scrutiny. "And that means we reckon they must have sent you to us because *you're* the hardiest and most soldierly of all the lighters too."

Swallowing pointedly, Rossamünd hoped he would be. "Aye, sir!" he said.

"Yes . . . sir," said Threnody.

"Now I know you and your situation"—the house-major stood again—"I am Major-of-House Thyssius Grystle," he said, bowing slightly to Threnody. "Also allow me to name Cot-Warden Hermogenës, or 'Sergeant-Master' to you." The cot-warden was slightly advanced in years with gorgeous silver hair held back in a whipstock and an impressive scar across his forehead. "And Linus Semple, our day-clerk"—a typically short and slender fellow in clerical black, a deep green fronstectum jutting over his brow.

Both men stood and bowed to Threnody with civil niceness.

"Our watches are septenary, changing every Newwich, and none of this slovenly two-watch business either! There are three lantern-watches here, done in lots of two so there's enough men on the road—and even then it's a stretch. So! Wet as your backs might be, two more is still two more. Even though you arrived with the dimmers I'll have you stay with the sluggards till you learn our idiosyncrasies—"

"Excuse me," Rossamünd piped, "the 'sluggards,' sir?"

448

"Aye, young lighter, the sluggards—the day-watch, as opposed to the dimmers, who are the lantern-watch. *You* watch while *they* sleep! What have they been teaching you back thereward—playing at skittles?"

"Ah, no, sir—sorry, sir." Rossamünd could almost feel Threnody rolling her eyes beside him.

House-Major Grystle's expression relaxed. "You may take your ease now, Lampsmen 3rd Class, then get to light duties after middens. The cart from Mill to Stool is a long time traveling and I see no benefit from putting tired lighters needlessly to work. Sergeant-Master Hermogenës shall direct you to your final billet. I imagine that oily grub goose Squarmis is bringing your ox trunks and other dunnage?" he concluded with a knowing look.

"Aye, sir," said Rossamünd.

"Carry on. Share your first breakfast with us and get your wind back today, for tomorrow—whatever old Grind-yer-bones might have had you doing—your life for the Emperor truly begins. Leave your Work Dockets with me, Lampsmen. Show 'em to their billets, Mister Harlock."

The silver-haired Sergeant-Master took them higher into the tower, up another steep stair, this one of sturdy, immobile stone instead, gradually winding around the entire structure as it rose. From this proximity Rossamünd could well see the handsome scar—a cicatrice any warrior would wish to have on display, a visible proof of valor—and more particularly, the man's unusually pale gray eyes, nearly silver—like his hair. "You might—like just now—hear some call me Harlock," he said with a faintly Sedian accent, while they climbed, "on account of my hair. That's a privilege you earn. For you two peepersqueeks it'll just be Sergeant-Master, am I clear?"

"Aye, Sergeant-Master!"

The common-mess where mains was served was found upon this next floor, two levels higher than the front door, the region designated "the kitchens" sharing the octagonal space. The ceiling high above was choke-full with beams and struts and supports of dark, polished wood; as gorgeously complex an array as Rossamünd had seen before only at Bleakhall. In here, they were told, everyone ate together, whether lampsman 3rd class or Major-of-House. Other cot-fellows were already beginning to gather, and a muscular, rotund man worked the pots and ovens on the far "kitchen" side. The third floor above the entrance, holding heavy tools and small machines, was for specific labors: tinkering, weapon-smithing, harness-mending, lantern repairs and the like. There was also a coop of chickens—for eggs—with a cock whose dawning crow Rossamünd soon learned was far more effective for rousing out the day-watch than any amount of drumming. There were stores kept here high up from the reach of rats and it was obvious now why the ceiling of the common-mess—being also the floor of this level—was so oversupplied with supporting woodwork.

On the top floor they were shown the bunk-rooms, set high and safe from the ground. This level was divided into equal quarters by wooden "bulkheads"——movable walls of about eight feet in height that stopped well short of the beams of the roof above. In the quarter farthest from the stair was where Rossamünd and Threnody would be sleeping; sharing the quarter, so the sergeant-master said, with the other younger lighters—both in their early twenties: Aubergene Wellesley, whom of course they had met, and another fellow, Fadus Theudas, currently on house-watch. Rossamünd looked at the room that was to be his "home." It was not as bare as the cells of Winstermill but gone was his privacy, his sleeping quarters to be shared again. Here the lampsmen were allowed to decorate their own spot, tack etchings and pamphlet-cuttings onto bed heads; have more than the standard issue of pillows or coverlets; and their own collection of other bed-furniture —stools, chests, side tables and the like. He realized too that though there were eight cots in here, only two were currently occupied.

"How many lighters are here at Wormstool, Sergeant-Master?" he asked.

"Less than there ought to be, Lampsman Bookchild," the cot-warden replied. "Put what dunnage ye have on yer billets and come down to the mess with yer kids or yer pannikins."

"I shall need privacy screens about my cot, then, if you please . . . Sergeant-Master," Threnody said.

"I shall see what we can arrange for ye, lass," he said, and left the two young lighters to settle.

"No more time to ourselves," Rossamünd observed

glumly. "At least we are allowed to put pictures up." He could think of several engravings from his pamphlets he might cut out and display, favorites by eminent pens like Pill or Berthezene.

"Hmm." Threnody looked about with mild distaste. "It will suffice, I suppose."

Rossamünd wondered if she was beginning to regret her willfully chosen profession and her hasty decision to throw in her lot with him.

Beds selected and bags dropped they returned down to the common-mess. Major-of-House Grystle called for general attention and semiformally introduced them both to their new messmates. The general reaction from the Wormstoolers was at first one of bemused disappointment. They were of the same opinion as the house-major, and it was manifest on their faces: *Why billet lantern-stick novices with us? Send real lighters with long experience and a steady arm in a fight.*

Nevertheless, the men proved friendly, and cheerfully ate a fine breakfast of spiced, lard-fried swampland mushrooms known as thrumcops and a strange kind of bacon Rossamünd was told was made from rabbit-meat. It was all a remarkable enlargement on "Imperial-issue provender," and Rossamünd only regretted he could not stand the smell or taste of these thrumcop mushrooms. Instead he filled his eager belly with coney-rinds and griddle-fried toast.

"This is so much better than breakfast at the manse!"

he declared, which drew the universal approval of his new comrades.

"Aye, aye!" Lightbody nodded emphatically, looking very pleased with himself. "No short commons for we Stoolers, lad. The world about proves bountiful for a keen eye, sharp nose and frank aim."

"Ye can thank our round-bellied poisoner fer the fine flavors too," said Sergeant Mulch. "Sequecious is his name, a true culinaire from up Sebastian way." He pointed to the enormously fat man in a red and beige striped apron, grinning and frying behind a large, flat hot plate that divided the "kitchen" from the mess. "He's meant to be some kind of prisoner from them wars Clementine and Sebastian are always in. He was sent here a year ago as a slave of the Emperor, I suppose, but he wants to change his nativity and become a paper nationalist of the Empire, strange fellow—"

"Cain't speak more than 'alf a sentence of Brandenard neither," interjected Posides. "And we're meant to watch over 'im and make sure 'e don't scarper off. Though where 'e's going to go out 'ere I don't know!"

"At least he's fat," argued Lightbody. "Never trust a gut-starver who bain't fat—I've been told, 'cause a thin one don't respect food enough to treat it right."

"What we actually lack is greens," Aubergene chattily added between chews.

"Just so," said a trim-looking man, the cothouse's dispensurist, one Mister Tynche, giving Rossamünd a welcoming smile, "and all we lack at times are some consistent, decent antiscorbutics. If it was not for the sovereign lime from Hurdling Migh and the nutrified wine sent ready mixed from Quinault and the Sulk, it'd be all black gums and lethargy here."

"Which is why that wriggler Squarmis can ask so much for his goods and time," Aubergene enlarged. "Sir!" he suddenly called across the trestle to the house-major. "Sir! Did ye hear of the nasty lurker we almost met this dousing?"

"Aye, 'Gene, I surely did," House-Major Grystle replied. "It was a good thing it wandered away like it did, else I might be less five—no, seven!—brave lighters. *You can spare the horses, but don't spare the lighters!*" he cried, and all the mess joined him, chuckling heartily, someone else calling huskily, *"A confusion on the nickers!"*

As one the Stoolers raised their mugs of three-water grog, took a swig and slammed their tankards back on the trestle, making a hearty wooden clatter. Rossamünd went through the motions and hoped no one noticed his lack of enthusiasm.

Threnody said little for the whole meal, sitting straight and taut, her eyes never leaving her food, and anyone who attempted to speak with her soon gave up in the face of her monosyllabic reluctance.

"What do we call you, girly?" one friendly young fellow of the day-watch tried. "Lamp-lass 3rd Class?" He chuckled in a cheerful way, as did those about him.

Threnody looked at the man sidelong, her fork hovering

before her mouth. "Probably anything but *girly* might be a good start," she said quietly.

"Watch out, Theudas!" Sergeant Mulch guffawed. "She's got the tongue of a whip, has our new lady lighter!" which everyone thought a great joke.

The young fellow called Theudas, red-faced, went back to his eating, while Threnody looked rather pleased with herself.

After the morning meal, dishes were collected and washed by the men of the day-watch themselves. Rossamünd tried thanking Sequecious the Sebastian cook for a brilliant meal, to which the man, in a thick accent simply repeated, "Tank yee! Tank yee!" with that unceasing grin.

Dishes done, Rossamünd and Threnody were directed back to their bunks, joining the lantern-watch for their prescribed rest. Threnody's screens were brought and erected with much better grace than at Tumblesloe Cot. They were put about the farthest bed from the others and, once up, the girl-lighter disappeared behind them, not to be seen again till much later.

Rossamünd organized himself, sorting satchels and bags. He pulled out a bag of boschenbread and offered a piece to Aubergene, who was sitting on his own cot, already in a long nightshirt.

"Why, thankee, Ros—ah—Rossamünd, isn't it?" he said to Rossamünd's offer.

"Aye," the young lighter replied, "Rossamünd—Rossamünd Bookchild of Boschenberg."

"Ahh, hence the bread and your baldric, aye?" Aubergene

made a little salute with his tasty morsel, pointing at Rossamünd's black and brown baldric, now hanging from an iron bedpost. "So why did they billet you here, truthfully? Everyone is here because of something . . ."

Because the Master-of-Clerks is a conniving, wicked blackguard! went across Rossamünd's thoughts, but he said, "I'm not sure, it's just where they sent us." Taking Europe's warning, he was not about to leap into some long-winded, barely believable story of events real and suspected. "What about you?" he quickly added.

"Me? Oh, I've got a dead-frank aim, and—uh—I calfed after the wrong girl" was all he said, leaving Rossamünd with more questions. Yet before he could ask them Aubergene himself quickly added, with a slightly gormless smile, "Well, welcome to the Stool."

Rossamünd grinned in return.

The cots proved just as uncomfortable as Winstermill's—some things in military service always stayed the same, it seemed. Windows were shuttered, blocking the diffuse, surprisingly bright light coming through the fog without. He peeked through a shutter. The fume was slowly dissolving, clearing the eastern view. The young lighter stared at the hazy horizon and could not quite believe that maybe only a day's lentum-ride farther began one of the most feared places in all the Half-Continent, maybe even the world. "Have you seen the Ichormeer, Aubergene?"

"Aye," the lampsman replied soberly. "It's all foul bottomless bogs and stinking pools the color of your heart's blood; half-dead thickets of red-leafed thornbushes and floating islands of red weed. Every path you take is treacherous and the rot of it all stays in the back of your throat long after you've escaped the place. I don't know how they managed to build the Wormway across it, must have cost a whole trunk of lives." Aubergene shook his head. "What the more, it's where the nickers are said to be born or somesuch—however that happens. You don't want to be going there, Rossamünd. I surely never want to return."

Rossamünd listened with rapt attention. Despite—or perhaps because of—the lampsman's lurid description, he was more keen to see the infamous place. Lying down to sleep, he found his imagination ran for the longest time with thoughts of a corrupted, bloodred swampland where loathsome things slithered and groveled in the noisome muds.

They were woken after middens by the arrival of costerman Squarmis, surprisingly delivering their heavy luggage intact and unmolested. Ox trunks properly stowed at the feet of their cots, Threnody's extra packages crammed underneath, the two new lighters were set to task. It was with profound and sinking horror that Rossamünd discovered the very first duty set aside for them: feed and muck the dogs.

Oh no!

"Ye've done this before, aye?" said Lamplighter-Sergeant

Mulch. "And if ye haven't, well ... I suggest ye learn quickly. It's an easy job and a good way to start, so hop to it now." There was a familiarly gruff manner in this lamplighter-sergeant, very much like the one they had left behind at Winstermill and perhaps all the sergeants the Half-Continent over.

"Dogs don't like me so much, Lamplighter-Sergeant," Rossamünd tried forlornly.

"They'll get used to ye," the man insisted, "especially if ye hold them out a little bit o' food."

"We will do splendidly, Sergeant," Threnody said flatly, and taking Rossamünd under his arm, pulled him with her down to the kennels.

But they did not do splendidly.

As at Wellnigh House, so it was here. No matter how tasty a morsel Rossamünd held out to them, the dogs went wild. Threnody's solution of sending him down to close off and muck out the other end of the cage failed miserably; the dogs bayed and yammered and made such a ruckus at him that all of Wormstool came running with cries of *"Nicker on the doorstep!"*

They soon realized what was what. There was no nicker anywhere, not even after a full quarto of the Stoolers searched the perimeters of the cothouse with Crescens Hugh the lurksman at their lead.

"I dun't know, mates, it's all cry and no nickers," Hugh declared when the searchers returned and the front door was secured once more. Everyone professed themselves mystified and the incident was dismissed.

Lamplighter-Sergeant Mulch just shook his head when all was done and declared, "The dogs truly don't like ye, do they, lad?"

24

A LAMPLIGHTER'S LIFE

combinades hand arms that are a clever combination of melee weapon and firelock. The firing mechanism on most combinades is an improved wheel lock, being more sturdy than a flintlock, and able to take the jars that come when the weapon is used to strike a foe. Added to this, the lock mechanism, trigger and hammer are usually protected by gathered bands of metal, a basket much like those protecting the hilts of many foreign swords. When edges and bullets are treated with gringollsis, combinades become very effective therimoirs (monster-killing tools).

ON the second day Rossamünd's life as a lamplighter started in full. Now he was properly arrived in this wild place, he was careful to replenish his bandage with the recent-made Exstinker, dawdling with his preparations until the other lighters had gone to breakfast. Obeying instructions, he ventured out fully harnessed, a necessary precaution this close to the monsters' realm. He quickly discovered the day-watch consisted of little more than rounds of chores, beginning—navylike—with the scrubbing of all the floors, soap-stoning and swabbing and flogging every story of the tower as if they were the decks of a ram.

Nothing more was said about the incident with the

dogs, though the young lighter was not required to muck and feed them anymore. Instead he and Threnody helped in the kitchens or in the Works—as the third floor from the entrance was named, carrying and fetching for Onesimus Grumely, the house-tinker and sometime proofener, or tending the fortlet's bright-limns and lanterns with Mister Splinteazle, Seltzerman 2nd Class. Yet Rossamünd soon discovered his favorite task was to join sentries, watching through the loopholes in the walls or from the observation benches upon the roof. Dubbed the Fighting Top, it was a place he quickly decided was the best in the whole cothouse. From there, high and safe, he could marvel at the whole flatland of the Frugelle with little interruption and still be considered working.

Threnody did not share his enthusiasm for the view. "This is an ugly place," she declaimed darkly as they watched with Theudas after middens. "All I can see is a hundred nooks for bugaboos to flourish."

Even as she spoke there came a single flash of lightning far away north, leaping from the flat cover of cloud straight to the earth. A second distant bolt had Theudas ducking.

"What, by my aching bowels, was that?" the lampsman exclaimed.

The peal of thunder took a long time to reach them, and by then it was only a sullen grumble.

"Maybe Europe has found her rever-man!" Rossamünd stared in the direction of the strike, heart thumping with fright.

"Maybe," replied Threnody, her tone saying, *Who cares!*

Threnody's sour misgivings and the regularity of lamp-lighting life soon dulled the novelty of a new location. A day's beginning was marked by the usual rattle of drums and its end by the cry *"A lamp! A lamp to light your path!"* declaring the arrival of the Haltmire lighters—stern, stiff fellows that the Stoolers called "Limpers." Then, as at Winstermill, was a little time for each day-watchman to do as he pleased before douse-lanterns. However, Rossamünd found the sameness of each day—as at Winstermill—a real and surprising comfort; for all their overfamiliarity, the routines were powerfully settling.

Different from the manse, however, were Domesdays. Out here they were not free of labor; indeed the lantern-watch had no rest at all. It was a day of reduced work, but House-Major Grystle was of the opinion that idle hands make waste, and the vigil was a make-and-mend day where clothes were patched and proofing was mended.

Yet in between light Domesday duties and any spare moment of an evening, the Stoolers enjoyed what Rossamünd soon considered his favorite pastime: sitting in the mess to play at checkers and the card games of lesquin and pirouette. They conducted themselves with far better grace and mirth than the prentices and, though the stakes were high, there was no bickering on the shuffle or squabbling over who could bet what or when. At pirouette—where the winning hand had the losing hand do a silly dance—they went easy on Rossamünd, letting him learn; but Threnody they needed to give no such grace. She quickly showed herself a match for all, even Mister Harlock, the sergeant-master, who proved shrewdly adept at outwitting most of his billet-mates. Young Theudas, however, was far too sharp and beat all with great *whoops!* of victory as he mercilessly had everyone—even Rossamünd—hopping one dance or another as they lost the round.

"Kindly Ladies Watch the Happy Aurangs again!" he declared triumphantly, throwing down both queens, both duchesses and both aurangs.

Half the success of the game was knowing precisely what made for a winning hand; there was a long list of combinations, just like the Hundred Rules of Harundo, and Rossamünd was slow to remember them all. Once again his own hand was pathetically meager, the worst of the round and now—for the fifth time that night—he was made to gambol about, curling his arms in and out calling, "I'm a monkey! I'm a monkey!" his face attaining the hue of the red side of his quabard.

"Go easy on the new babbies," Lamplighter-Sergeant Mulch chuckled while the other Stoolers guffawed at Rossamünd's antics. Threnody looked on with an expression of almost feline satisfaction. Mysteriously, Theudas never seemed to trump her, and she had not yet been made to dance a single turn.

Mulch's well-intentioned interjection only made Theudas more gleefully determined to win, and Rossamünd was made to turn a jig many more times before he won his first hand. Of all his billet-mates, Aubergene or Lightbody were perhaps the most unfortunate at cards.

"Ye'd have to be the most losingest two I ever clapped eyes on!" Under-Sergeant Poesides would laugh almost every night as he watched either unfortunate lighter lope about foolishly as the winning cards directed. He and all the others—whether Stooler, Bleaker or Limper—would refuse to play them at the more serious hands of lesquin. Here the spoils of victory were grog rations and favors; the lowest-valued favor was to stand in for kitchen duties or firelock cleaning, the value quickly escalating to the ultimate prize: having another take your place to muck the jakes. Out here sewer-workings were not nearly as sophisticated as at Winstermill, and the water closets needed frequent flushing with buckets of old dishwater and cleaning with broad, blunt shovels on long handles—an odious job, the most unpleasant task for the day-watch.

The house-major would play no game of chance against his men—especially not lesquin—declaring solemnly that "an officer should never take from those under his command nor be seen to be overborne by them either."

Near the end of their first week new stores arrived on the back of a long dray that had lumbered the dangerous Wettin Lowroad up from Hurdling Migh. Rossamünd knew only vaguely of this city: an isolated settlement—so his peregrinat told him—semi-independent in its remoteness and filled with a stern yet hospitable people. The driver of the dray and his grim-looking side-armsman were both pale-looking fellows. They had apparently made the northward journey often, but the threatening rumor of bogle and nicker had forced them to hire a scourge for protection.

This hireling was called the Scarlet Tarquin. He—she—it—sat stiffly now at the front of the truck swathed entirely in red fascins, bandaged crown to toe in protective cloth with only two round lenses protruding at the eyes. Laden with salumanticums, stoups, powder-costers and all the appurtenances of skolding, the scourge simply watched but did not offer help. Passing the red-wrapped teratologist as he and Threnody tumbled down the steps to help unload, the young lighter was affronted by a faint, yet powerfully unpleasant whiff of potent chemistry. He stayed well clear of this scarlet scourge as he worked.

On the dray were piled crates of musket balls, wayfoods and script parts; butts of rum, wine and black powder; sacks of flour, cornmeal and dried pease; even three bolts of undyed drill for making-and-mending day. While two lighters stood at guard on the road, every item was hauled up by a limber-run sheer on the fourth floor, its winch arm swung out from broad double doors—the store-port high in Wormstool's wall. Climbing onto the dray, Rossamünd helped Theudas and Poesides shift and tie each load to the sheer cord.

Standing below by the flat truck, the tired and humorless driver was arguing vociferously with Semple the day-clerk about the excessive charge for service this time.

"Thy wants thy goods timely and whole, do thee not?" the driver was saying. "Safe passage for cargo dern't come cheap nowadays." He glared at the Scarlet Tarquin for emphasis.

Rossamünd did not hear the reply, for Poesides moved away with sudden violence, giving a great shout: *"Watch it, lad! The knot's come loose! Load's goin' to fall!"* The under-sergeant tried to grab at him but did not get a grip as he stumbled away.

"Clear out below!" came a sharp cry from the store-port above.

Rossamünd looked up and there hurtling down to crush him was a butt, set free by a poorly tied knot—a knot he had wound himself. The young lighter hesitated in his fright, stupidly heedless of his own danger and more concerned with the possible harm to the stores.

"Rossamünd!" Threnody yelped.

Yet he stood transfixed as the heavy barrel dropped on him; instead of leaping aside he caught the entire weight in his arms with little more than a slight *huff!*—just as you might catch an inflated ball. The weight of the load drove him to the truck-top, pinning him on his back. He held the butt on his chest for several astounded beats before lifting it and setting it carefully back on the tray, keenly aware of the equally astounded faces all turned to him, even peering in amazement from the fourth floor.

"Did ye see that?" he heard drift down from above. "Fifty pound of musket shot and he catched it without a trouble!"

"How'd you do that?" Theudas exclaimed. "That was a full butt of balls! It would have smashed even Sequecious flat!"

Threnody rushed to the side of the dray-truck and looked up at him. "Rossamünd! Are you whole?"

"I—I believe so . . ." was all the young lighter could get out. He tugged at the white solitaire about his throat, seeking better breath.

"That's enough heavy loading for ye, lad," Poesides declared. "Ye can't depend on freakish catches all the time in this job. Take a spell inside. Have Mister Tynche or Splinteazle take a look at ye if ye reckon it necessary. I'll leave ye in the hands of the lass."

Rossamünd obeyed, Threnody helping him up each stairway.

"You should have been pounded to pea-mash by that bullet-barrel," she insisted.

"My chest does hurt, if that's more satisfying," Rossamünd answered wryly.

"Oh, ha-ha." Threnody did not look amused. "You should hardly make a jest of such a horrid thing. I thought you were done in! Poesides has it right: most certainly a freakish catch."

Talk of his feat buzzed about the cothouse in an instant, and other Stoolers popped their heads out from nooks to send funny looks his way.

Safely deposited on his bunk, Rossamünd took off his proofed-silk sash and his quabard to relieve the bruised tenderness in his ribs.

"What is that about your chest?" Threnody asked, crouching by him and looking at the loose collar of his shirt.

Rossamünd's innards almost burst open with fright. *Oh no, my Exstinker bandage!* "It's—it's—it's . . . it's for putting on nullodor," he tried.

"What, the one that Critchety-crotchety ledgermain fellow made you?" the girl lighter questioned.

Frowning, Rossamünd nodded.

"You don't *use* it, do you?" Threnody snorted.

His frown deepening, he nodded once more.

"When? Even out unloading carts?"

"Aye!" Rossamünd hissed in exasperation. "All the time! It was a command of my old masters' back at the foundlingery."

"Aren't you the obedient little munkler, then?" Threnody looked narrowly at him. She turned and left him to recover alone.

Later in the day, when goods were safely stowed and the dray left, returning to Bleakhall and then home, presumably to Hurdling Migh, Rossamünd was called to House-Major Grystle's desk.

"What is this that I have ear of: you snatching falling loads as if they were light parcels?" the house-major queried.

"I couldn't well have let it fall to crash, sir." Rossamünd was a little baffled by the fuss made of his fortunate grab.

Grystle gave a baffled blink of his own. "No, I suppose you couldn't have at that." He dusted a fleck off his pristine sleeve. "A powerful fine catch either way, Lampsman. I did not know they raised you so strong in Boschenberg—the lords at the Mill would be well advised to prentice more of your countrymen."

"Aye, sir."

"Maybe we should make you our fellow to challenge those stuffy Limpers to a wrench-of-arms?" The house-major gave a kindly smile.

Rossamünd did not really know what his superior was talking about. "Maybe, sir" was all he could think to say.

After a clumsy pause that grew into an uncomfortable silence, Rossamünd was dismissed.

Quizzical eyes were on him all that night at mains, the story growing some in its retelling. Aubergene asked him how he was feeling after catching half the load of the dray.

"It was really just one butt, nothing more," Rossamünd explained.

"Aye, but I heard it was a very full one."

Rossamünd shrugged.

Fortunately the incident quickly receded into the routine. Not more than two days later he was able to enter a room without there being that strange, deliberate silence. It was not completely forgotten, however, for it earned Rossamünd a new name: "The Great Harold" they began to call him, or "Master Haroldus," after the hero of the Battle of the Gates. Not even in the face of the awe of the prentices when he killed the gudgeon had Rossamünd ever felt so complimented. He had been given a new name—a proper military nickname—and the quiet, hidden joy of it had him smiling himself to sleep for the rest of the week.

"I thought Harold was a skold," was all Threnody said in quibble one breakfast.

"Aye, he was," Aubergene answered her, from across the bench, "but he was a dead-mighty one."

Thankfully, she did not say any more to spoil Rossamünd's delight, nor did she venture another word about the barrel or his Exstinker bandage.

Proving to have suffered no permanent discomfort from his catching feat, Rossamünd was soon employed in his very first excursion away from the cothouse. On the opening day of the second week he was sent with Poesides, Aubergene and Lightbody to carry stores to a poor old eeker-woman—an exile who had fled across the Ichormeer from somewhere east. Rossamünd was astounded that lighters would seek to aid one of the under class, a reject of her own society and unwanted in the Empire as well.

"Ah! Master Haroldus has come to lend us his mighty hands!" Poesides said in kindly jest as they readied to leave.

The other lighters smiled warmly in response as Rossamünd ducked his head to hide his delight.

The necessary stores—foodstuffs, clothing, repellents, a small quantity of black powder and balls—were lifted onto their backs and they departed, Whelpmoon observing them blearily as they filed out the heavy front door and down the narrow steps. Cold was the morning, its soft breath stinging cheeks, the eastern horizon orange-pink with the sun's rising.

"Where are we going to?" Rossamünd asked Aubergene quietly as they crossed the road and stood on its northern verge.

The lighter adjusted his grip on the long-rifle he bore. "There's a small seigh out north near the banks of the Frugal where an old dame lives. Mama Lieger is her name. The bee's buzz is that she likes to talk to the bogles and that's why she lives far out here—fled from Wörms to escape accusing tongues."

"Aye, and now we're the sorry sods who 'ave to do 'er deliveries," interjected Lightbody. "I've 'eard it she was some wild strig-woman when she was younger, coming from one of them irritable troupes of wild folk from the Geikélund out back of Wörms."

"Didn't the folks where she's from try to hang her?" Rossamünd had a vision of a terrible destructress with flashing blades and flying hair having monsters around for supper.

"I reckon she must have got away afore they could." Aubergene smiled.

Rossamünd shifted the uncomfortable load and stared a little suspiciously at the uneasy threwd that brooded out beyond the road-edge. "Why doesn't she have Squarmis the costerman do the delivering?"

" 'Cause that filthy salt-horse won't take things to the likes of her," answered Poesides, "and she could ne'er afford him to if ever he did. No, lad, it is our honor to take these supplies to her. She bain't the only eeker to get our help: it's the lighters' way out here, to succor all kinds in need without fault-findin'." He gave an acerbic sideways look at Lightbody.

"But isn't she a sedorner?" Rossamünd pressed, feeling a glimmer of hope. "I thought lighters would have said *all* sedorners were bad folk and done them in somehow."

"A lamp's worth is proved by its color, lad." The under-sergeant gave him a curious look. "Mama Lieger has done good for us, so we do for her benefit as she has done for ours . . . and maybe—if she does hold conversationals with the local hobs—she might put in a good word for us with them. But just have yer intellectuals about ye, else she'll have ye believing that some monsters are not so bad after all."

"Aye . . . " Aubergene muttered, "though some might agree with her on that one."

Almost stumbling down the side of the highroad, Rossamünd looked in surprise at the lampsman, a dawning of respect rising in his bosom.

"Stopper that talk, Lampsman!" Poesides barked. "Her saying such things is one bend of a crook, but ye spratting on so is a whole other. I don't want to have to leave ye with the old gel when we get to her house."

Aubergene ducked his head. "Aye, Under-Sergeant," he murmured.

Poesides fixed Rossamünd with a commanding eye. "We're all about quiet when walking off the road, so silence them questions for now."

The youngest lighter obeyed and said naught as the under-sergeant traveled an unmarked path through the thick lanes and thickets of thistle and cold-stunted olive and tea trees. In single file the three followed after, walking as carefully they could without going too slow. The shaley soil clinked softly as their boots broke the damp, fog-dampened surface, to reveal the earth beneath still dry and dusty. This was indeed a parched place, yet life still flourished, making the most of what little moisture it gleaned from the damp southern airs.

Always searching left and right, all four kept eyes and ears sharp for signs of monsters. Tiny birds chased on either side of them, flitting rapidly through the thick twine of thorny, twiggy branches, rarely showing themselves but for a flash of bright sky blue or fiery, black-speckled red. Rossamünd wanted to stop, to be still for a time and breathe in the woody smells and quietly observe the nervous flutterers, but on they marched, pausing only for a brief breather and a suck of small beer.

Two miles out from the Wormway the difficult country opened out a little and began to gently decline, a broad view of the Frugal vale before them, gray, thorny, patched with dark spinneys of squat, parched trees. Aubergene and Lightbody moved to walk on either side of Poesides. Keen to prove himself a worthy, savvy lighter Rossamünd did the same, stepping straight into a spider's web strung between two man-high thistles and still glistening with dew in the advancing morning.

"Ack!" he spluttered and scrabbled at the stickiness on his face, terrified some little crawler might be about to sink fangs into his nose or crawl and nest in his hair.

"Hold your crook in front of your face," Aubergene offered in a hush, clasping his long-rifle vertically in front of him in example. "Catches the webs and keeps your dial safe of them."

There was not a glimpse or hint of a single monster the whole way, yet the land still heeded them and knew they walked where men seldom did or should. Choughs scooted away with a flash of their white tail feathers at the lighters' advance through the cold land, looping low through the stunted swamp oaks, letting out their clear calls: a single note bright yet mournful, ringing across the flats. As the day-orb reached the height of its meridian Rossamünd spied a high-house—a seigh—very much as its those eeker-houses he saw from the Gainway down to High Vesting. This one looked older, though—very much as if it belonged here, grown somehow rather than built by human action; a sagging pile hidden behind a patch of crooked, fragrant swamp oaks. Its too-tall chimneys looked near ready to topple; its roof was entirely submerged in yellow lichens; weedy straw grew from every crevice in the lower footings. In this place the threwd was different somehow, so gentle and insinuating that Rossamünd hardly perceived it; the watchfulness was not so hostile—indeed, it was almost welcoming. Rossamünd might have liked to stay here. He looked pensively up at the high-house.

There was no stair to the gray-weathered door nearly twenty feet above.

Poesides took Rossamünd's fodicar from him. "We really must get ye a right lengthened crook," he muttered. Hefting it up, the under-sergeant deftly hooked a cloth-covered chain hanging well above their heads from the wall by the door. He gave it a series of deliberate tugs and waited.

Aubergene and Lightbody kept watch at their backs.

There was only a brief wait before the lofty door opened with a clunk and a small head peeped without.

"Ah-hah, das güt aufheitermen!" Rossamünd seemed to hear, a soft woman's voice speaking incomprehensibly in what he could only presume—from his prenticing with Lampsman Puttinger—was Gott. "Guten Tag, happy fellows!" the voice called a little louder in Brandenard.

"Mother Lieger!" Poesides gave a hoarse cry, trying to be heard without making noise. "We have yer stores."

"Güt, güt," and the head disappeared. What had appeared like a small, moldering eave over the door shuddered and, with a click, began to drop smoothly to the ground, lowered on thick cord.

It was an elevator. They were rare in Boschenberg and, no matter how simple this device was, out in the wilds was the last place Rossamünd expected to find one.

Each lighter was raised up on this small, worn platform. Poesides went first, and as the smallest Rossamünd was sent up next, finding the elevator more stable than it first appeared. He had no notion how Mama Lieger might operate this device if ever she left the house, but this pondering did not occupy his mind long. At the top he found a tiny front room—the obverse—with loopholes in the back wall and another solid door too, which was currently open. The woman was not there, though domestic bustle was coming from some rearward room. Rossamünd waited as the under-sergeant worked the mechanism that raised the platform. All present, Poesides led them through the second door to carefully deposit their burdens in a small closet at the end of a short, white hall.

"Ahh," came that soft female voice, getting louder as the speaker appeared from a side door. "I must be thanking you once again for keeping a poor old einsiedlerin's pantry full."

Bearing a tray of opaque white glasses, Mama Lieger turned out to be a neat, rather dumpy old lady, silvery tresses arranged in a precise bun, neither too tight nor too relaxed. Her homely clothes of shawl, stomacher-dress and apron were sensibly simple as was the interior of her humble dwelling. Run-down as it was, the parlor into which the men were invited was clean and tidy, any drafty holes plugged with unused flour-bags neatly rolled and wedged into the gaps. Yet for all this orderly homeliness there remained in her puddingy features evidence of the sharp, hawklike face she would have once possessed and a disquieting keen and untamed twinkle in her penetrating gaze—something deeply aware and utterly irrepressible. Serving them the piping, sharply spiced saloop the old eeker-woman looked

MAMA LIEGER

Rossamünd over hat-brim to boot-toe. "Who is this new one, then?" she smiled, her expression most definitely hawkish. "Do they make lighters in half sizes now, yes? To take up less room in your festung—your fortress—yes?"

Poesides and the lampsmen gave a hearty chuckle.

"I—" Rossamünd fumbled for a proper response.

As she passed a drink to him, the young lighter noticed the hint of a dark brown swirl sinuating out from under the eeker-woman's long sleeve, its style and color looking so very like a monster-blood tattoo. Rossamünd nearly missed his grip on the cup of saloop.

Mama Lieger noticed him noticing her marks and peered at him closely. "What a one you have brought me, Poesides." The neat old lady's wild, black eyes gleamed disconcertingly. "It is so very clear this one has seen his tale of ungerhaur; have you not, my little enkle, yes? Poor young fellow, I see the touch on him—I see he bears the burden of seeing like Mama Lieger sees, of thinking like she thinks, yes?"

Is she calling me a sedorner too? Rossamünd looked nervously from her to his billet-mates: he did not relish being ostracized so early in his posting.

"Aye, aye, Mama." The under-sergeant came to his rescue. "Ye'd have everyone lost in the outramour if ye could," he said tightly.

"That I would and the better for the world if you all were. Not to matter, you stay out here for a long time and the land will quietly speak to you—mutter mutter—the schrecken—

the threwd—changing your mind: is that not right, my little enkle?" She peered at Rossamünd once more.

"I—ah—" *How can she talk such dangerous words so freely?* He wondered at the mild expressions of his fellow lampsmen, sipping tentatively at their piquant saloop and trying not to show how unpleasant they found it. *Why doesn't Poesides damn her as a vile traitor and have her hanged from the nearest tree?* These fellows weren't mindless invidists—monster-haters—not at all. Rossamünd did not know what to think of them.

Apparently heedless, Mama Lieger sat in a soft high-backed chair and engaged the older fellows in simple chatter for a time, yet her shrewd attention constantly flickered over to Rossamünd.

Uncomfortable, Rossamünd looked at the mantel above the cheerily crackling fire. There he spied a strange-looking doll, a grinning little mannish-shaped thing with a big head and small body made entirely of bark and tufts of old grass. Even as he looked at it the smile seemed to expand more cheekily and, for a sinking beat, Rossamünd was sure he saw an eye open—a deep yellow eye that reminded him ever so much of Freckle.

The eye gave him a wink.

Rossamünd jerked in fright, spilling a little of his saloop.

All other eyes turned on him.

"Ye got the horrors, Lampsman?" Poesides asked in his

most authoritative voice, a hint of disapproval in his eyes, as if Rossamünd's behavior was a shame to the lighters.

"I—" was all Rossamünd could say for a moment. He gripped his startled thoughts and chose better words. "I have not, Under-Sergeant, I—I was startled by that ugly little doll," he finished weakly.

"An ugly doll." Poesides looked less than pleased.

Mama Lieger stood spryly. "He is never ugly!" she insisted, rising to stand by the wizened little thing. "My little holly-hop man. He is just sleeping his little sleeping-head." She patted the rugged thing with a motherly "coo," and turned a knowing look on Rossamünd.

He could not believe she was being so bold, nor that his fellows did not seem overly perturbed. Rossamünd looked fixedly into his glass of too-spicy, barely-drunk saloop and did not look up again till they were shuffling out of the room to leave. It was a relief to be going, despite the friendly threwd. The four made a hasty journey in the needling cold, Rossamünd as eager as the others to be home, back to the familiarity of the cothouse, their path easier for the lightening of their backs. He was glad too for the enforced silence to stopper his questioning mouth and for the distraction of the threwd growing less friendly again to occupy his troubled thoughts. With Wormstool clearly in sight, a dark, stumpy stone finger protruding high upon the flatland, Aubergene dared a quiet question.

"What were you getting all spooked at with that unlighterly display in front of the Mama, Rossamünd?"

Rossamünd flushed with shame. "That—that holly-hop

480

doll moved, Aubergene," he hissed. "It winked and grinned at me!" he added at the other lighter's incredulous look.

"You're a dead-strange one, Lampsman Bookchild." Aubergene gave a grin of his own. "Maybe Mama Lieger is right and you can see like she sees?" He scratched his cheek with an open palm. "I've sure seen the dead-strangest occurrences since being out here; changes the way you think, it does. Perhaps you can put in a good word to the monsters for us too, 'ey?"

Rossamünd's guts griped. Was the man being serious? Yet Aubergene's grin was wry and teasing and Rossamünd grinned foolishly in return.

"Hush it the brace of ye!" Poesides growled. "Ye knows better . . ."

Of one thing Rossamünd was becoming more certain: he was quickly growing to like these proud, hardworking, simple-living lighters. He could begin to imagine a lamplighter's life out here with them.

During their third week and an endless round of chores, Europe stopped by Wormstool, accompanied by a lampsman from Bleakhall as her hired lurksman. She had managed to persuade his superiors to release him to aid in her vital task of keeping the Paucitine safe—that was how she told it at least. Thoroughly impressed to be meeting the Branden Rose, the Stoolers joked with their Bleaker chum, declaring him the most fortunate naught-good box-sniffer in all the Idlewild.

"Aye, and I'm earnin' more a day than ye all do in a month," he bragged.

Europe ignored them as she spoke briefly with Rossamünd.

"Did you catch the rever-man?" was almost the first thing he said to her. "Was that your lightning we saw last week?"

"It might well have been. The basket was well knit and required a little more—push, shall we say. I never found out where it came from, though. Tell me," she said, changing the subject, "are you happily established in this tottering fortlet?"

"Aye, happily enough," Rossamünd answered. He wondered how he might fare trying to persuade Europe to hunt only rever-men. *Probably not well,* he concluded, and asked conversationally, "Have you been to the Ichormeer yet?"

"No." Europe frowned quizzically. "There is no call to go picking fights one does not need."

Threnody had come down to the mess but caught one glimpse of the fulgar, and with a polite grimace and a forced "How-do-you-do" went straight back up to wherever she had come from.

"How is our new-carved miss finding the full-fledged lighting life?" Europe asked amusedly.

Rossamünd watched Threnody's petulant retreat. "I think she might be sorry for leaving Herbroulesse."

Europe clucked her tongue. "The appeal of an adventurous life seldom lasts in the bosom of a peer's pampered daughter."

Rossamünd was not sure if the fulgar was talking about Threnody or herself.

"Tell me, Rossamünd, have you received any replies to your letters?"

It took a beat or two for the young lighter to realize she was talking of his controversial missives to Sebastipole and the good doctor. All the worry for Winstermill and Numps returned in a flood. "No," he answered simply. What else to say?

Europe's eyes narrowed. "Hmm."

"What can it mean?" Rossamünd was suddenly afraid that he had done the wrong thing in sending them.

"Nothing," Europe offered, her voice distant. "Everything. It probably simply indicates that your correspondents are too busy with their own affairs and, more so, that there is little they can do and little to be said as a result."

"Oh." His soul sank then lifted angrily. "There are times in the small hours I want to board a po'lent and hurry back to face Swill myself. I beat his rever-man and I can beat *him* too!"

"I am sure you can, little man," Europe chuckled, "should you get that close . . . Keep at your work here, Rossamünd. Let the rope run out—they will eventually choke on deeds of their own invention. Such are the bitter turnings of Imperial politics: you have to endure much ill before you prevail. Pugnating the nicker is a much simpler life . . . and you live longer too," she finished with a smirk.

After an exchange of respectful greetings with House-

Major Grystle, Europe was soon on her way again, hired lamplighter lurksman in tow.

"I go to Haltmire now, to solve problems for the Warden-General," she declared in farewell, adding quietly to Rossamünd, "It should prove to be an intriguing venture—I hear some distant grief has quite soured the Warden's intellectuals. So wish me well."

"Do well," Rossamünd answered anxiously.

Her departure left a hint of bosmath and something for the lighters to talk about on the boring watches long after.

As for Threnody, the lamplighters of Wormstool themselves had scant clue how to live with a female in their number. Regardless they proved proud of her all the same. "Our little wit-girl" they called her, and would "ma'am" her wherever she went in the cothouse. They would grow shy when she descended to the well in the cellars to do her toilet, and some even doted a little, going to some lengths to make sure she had ample supply of parts for her plaudamentum and other treacles. At every change of watch, when the Haltmire lighters would arrive, the Stoolers would boast that they were better than their Limper chums, "'cause we have a wit!" That there were no others amazed Rossamünd. He had assumed lahzars would be standard issue on this leg of the Wormway, yet there were only two skolds at Haltmire and nothing better than a dispensurist at the four cothouses.

Clearly enjoying it, Threnody quickly grew comfortable

with the attention. She took to wearing a pair of fine-looking doglocks in equally fine holsters at her hips, bearing them everywhere and playing the part of pistoleer at last.

"Where did you get *those*?" Rossamünd inquired one middens.

"Beautiful pieces, aren't they?" The girl beamed.

He had to agree: they were indeed attractive, made of black wood and silver, every metal part engraved with the most delicate floral filigree, elegant weapons despite their heavy bore.

"Do you remember the prolonged stop we made at Hinkerseigh?"

"Aye." He recalled most of all that she made them wait.

"These were why I was gone. I purchased them from Messrs. Lard & Wratch of Chortle Lane, finest gunsmiths in the Placidine." Her beam widened. "I have longed for them for so long, looking in on them any time we made an excursion to that town."

"How much did they cost?" he whispered. "How did you afford them?"

Threnody's smile vanished. "Don't you know that you *never ever* ask a woman how much *anything* costs!" she declaimed.

Rossamünd was sure that any regrets she might have had for coming to Wormstool were cured.

A common practice of a dousing lantern-watch was to leave the first two great-lamps on their route still undoused. These morning-lights were left glowing to provide a little light to the surrounds of the cothouse while the sun still tarried on the lip of the world. Part of this practice involved members of the day- or house-watch then going out and dousing them when the day-shine was brighter.

On Gallowsnight Eve, with every vertical protrusion in Wormstool hung with toy nooses of string and slight rope and neckerchiefs to herald this ghoulish festivity, Rossamünd and Threnody were sent to douse the morning-lights. They did this under the eagerly watching eye of Theudas— eagerly watching, that is, of Threnody. He was only slightly less recently joined to Wormstool than they and could not be happier for it, now that this dark-haired peerlet had arrived. At the base of East Worm 1 West Halt 52 Threnody and Theudas swapped a little chatter while they let Rossamünd struggle to douse the lamp.

"So how is old Grind-yer-bones?" Theudas inquired. "Still grinding away on all the poor prentices?"

"I can tell you," answered Threnody, "that he was none too happy about us being sent out so soon. Went into apoplexies arguing with the Master-of-Clerks."

"Ahh, dear old Grind-yer-bones, he's an awkward basket." Theudas shook his head. "The kind ye want on yer side in a fight. We always reckoned he ate spent musket balls for his breakfast as the only things that might satisfy his stomach of a morning."

Clang! Rossamünd took another swing at the ratchet and

missed. The other two seemed more than content to simply watch as he flailed.

"Here, let me help you, Rossamünd," Threnody piped, going over to him. "He has never been much good at crook work," she said motheringly over her shoulder. "I've had to help him with the winding before."

"Is that the truth, Master Haroldus?" asked Theudas with an incredulous laugh.

"Just the once," Rossamünd muttered angrily.

"Little wonder then ol' Grind-yer-bones was so reluctant to ever let you out," marveled Theudas. "Whoever heard of a lighter who couldn't light?"

Threnody gave a short braying laugh but saw Rossamünd's face and became serious. "He can throw a good potive though," she offered.

"All I need is a proper length crook!" Rossamünd growled as he tried again. With a belated *clink* he got the crank-hook home in the ratchet slot and with angry jerks began to wind in the bloom.

25

THICKETS AND THRUMCOPS

thrumcop also called a bog-button and related to a larger, tasty and oddly threwdish fungus known as austerpill, thrumcops are a funguslike mushroom with a deep brown pileus spotted with swollen off-white circular patches. The essence of thrumcops can be used in rudimentary repellents, giving rise to the idea that eating them on their own will cause this essence to seep through your pores and make you less appetizing to a monster.

THE restless airs of the Frugelle were rarely still, winds ever blowing from the lower cardinals. If they came from the west they smelled of parched rock and hinted too of fennel and loam; if from the south they brought with them a tang of the ocean deeps; but from the east the winds' cold breathing carried the sick stink of rot and fire-damp—the portentous, threwdish reek of the Ichormeer. It was on one of these putrid easterly days, with the sky lowering and threatening gales, that Rossamünd and Threnody were set the task of joining Sequecious the Sebastian cook to find more thrumcops to store for more breakfasts. House-Major Grystle showed great concern for their safety, handing over a portable timepiece to Rossamünd.

"Take this hack-watch, Lampsman," the man added, "and be gone no more than three quarters of one hour. Just a brief search and back here again. Someone will be watching from the roof, and if you are in distress, send up a flare."

"Aye, sir." Rossamünd cradled the remarkable device for an awed moment then hid it as safely as he could on his person. He was given charge too of a tubelike flammagon—a flintlock flare-thrower, which he hung from his shoulder along with his salumanticum.

Still in his kitchen apron and wearing a broad-brimmed catillium to cover his bald pate from the pale glare of the clouds, Sequecious the cook carried with him a large cauldron. This pot was of such girth that another man might have struggled to carry it in both arms, yet the fellow dangled it in the crook of one powerful, flabby arm. In the other, Sequecious bore a boltarde with pistol-length wheel locks extending from the pole on either side of the axlike blades. The blade edges were patterned with a distinctive spatter of congealed black; the telltale spackle of a weapon smeared with aspis, one of the more effective venificants or distinct monster poisons.

Like so many of the firelocks and hand arms of the Wormstool lighters, it was not prescribed issue. These fellows may have behaved in an exemplary manner and kept their harness to a higher-than-drill-book standard, yet their personal weapons were as diverse as the personalities who wielded them. Perhaps Rossamünd's favorite was an ax-carabin belonging to Aubergene, with its wooden butt thinned to a handle—the stock and barrel not much longer than that of a pistol—and the muzzle fixed with a thin, sliver-crescent ax-head counterbalanced by a war-hammer fluke. It was an elegant piece, and Lampsman Aubergene was clearly proud of it.

With many grins and some wordless gestures Sequecious got the two young lighters to follow him; Threnody regarding every request with scorn but obedient nevertheless.

Standing on the edge of the highroad facing north, the cook pointed to a thick stand of regal swamp oaks away to the northeast, about two hundred yards into the flatland. "Thrumcops are being best found in there, tank yee," he said with a happy nod. The tallest and largest of the few copses and thickets that dotted the otherwise unrelieved flatness of this land, it was as close as the Frugelle came to a forest. Despite all the warnings and suspicions of threwd, Rossamünd was eager to explore the somber wood.

In a spray of dust and stones, they slid down the short, steep side of the road, the cook almost upending himself in his career. He laughed the near-miss away and led them off into the weird world of the Paucitine flats. Semidried stands of mustard weed and thistles thrice Rossamünd's height made lanes through the small, tough grasses. These lanes would run for seven or eight yards before another lane would cross it and block the way, making a weedy maze that was hard to contradict. Sequecious waddled confidently along a stubbly, stony route that would have had Rossamünd disoriented but for the glimpses he caught of Wormstool.

SEQUECIOUS

The fortalice was a conspicuous landmark in this vast, remote cosmos. The Imperial Spandarion flicked and cracked on high from the rooftop, as the lampsmen's washing strung out beneath whipped in unison.

There must have been water about, despite the arid soil and thirsty plants, for as they walked the young lighter could hear frogs croaking, creaking and ponging at every hand; it might have been a friendly chorus, but the uneasy threwd, amplified by the fetid eastern breeze, turned the amphibious music sinister. Sometimes they would stop, leaving an eerie hush that set Rossamünd anxiously searching for a lurker.

Untroubled, Sequecious pushed effortlessly through a thicket and the young lighters followed in the wake the great man's girth made, unhindered by stem or twig. They were in the stand of swamp oaks at last, a dim grove that soughed uneasily in the wind.

Clearly pooped by the effort of the short walk, the cook puffed, "Yee find out yonder, boyo," pointing to the farthest end of the modest wood. "An' yee, girly, go between." He indicated the middle ground to an unhappy-looking Threnody. "I am being right hereabouts. Look in between th' roots an' under tha leaves an' be putting thrumcops in these an' I bring them back to pot when full, tank yee," he concluded, giving the two an old post-bag each.

Barely comprehending the cook's odd talk but following his intention, Rossamünd went to his designated end of the trees, his footfalls gritty on the dry, spongy mat of needles that kept the thicket floor clear of weeds and other choking grasses. Threnody walked a little ahead of him. He could hear her muttering, "I've been in the hands of the best sectifactors in the land and they have me out here looking for toadstools." Without another word she turned aside at an arbitrary place and began looking about the ground with little conviction, toeing here and there among roots.

Rossamünd moved deeper into the grove.

Wings whirring, a sparrow alighted suddenly on an overarching branch. With a sharp turn in his innards, Rossamünd had the odd, almost threwdish sense that this was the same bird that had flown up to the doorsill of the carriage when the post-lentum was waiting at Cothallow. He stopped, hands on hips, and stared at the remarkable, persistent bird, which swiveled its head, observing him cannily in return.

"Hallo," Rossamünd said softly, "has the Sparrowling sent you?"

The sparrow chirruped loudly.

Was that a reply?

The tiny bird chirped again and shot away, Rossamünd losing sight of it in the thick foliage. Cautiously he followed its path until he came to a small dell whose entire opposite flank was overrun by a large boxthorn crowding the roots of several tall swamp oaks. A loud chattering sparrow-song sang from within.

Rossamünd froze, looking left, looking right, but nothing untoward appeared. He glanced behind and could just make out the massive white bulk of Sequecious clambering about the farther end of the woods. Threnody was not visible, though Rossamünd thought he could hear her foraging a short way off. Keeping an eye out, he crouched on his haunches and began to carefully poke and rake among the needles and dry soil along the lip of the dell, prospecting for the round fungus with distinct white spots. Somewhere in the treetops, doves softly cooed ... *cuh-coo-hoo-oo, cuh-coo-hoo-oo* ... in the hissing quiet. Becoming engrossed in the search, Rossamünd worked his way from tree to tree, half filling his bag in quick time. It was only very gradually that he became alert to creeping movements nearby, a sound different from the constant susurrus of the needle-leaves, a sly stepping on needly ground. He first thought it was Threnody, but the subtle sounds were from the entirely opposite direction. Without putting down the sack, the young lighter eased his free hand into his salumanticum.

A dark shape sneaked into view, creeping around the side of the boxthorn, a small figure, mottled and unexpectedly familiar ... Was it? Surely not! *It couldn't be* ... Yet it *was!* Shuffling on the opposite side of the small dell was Freckle. There before him was the glamgorn who had comforted him in the hold of the *Hogshead,* one hundred and fifty miles and over two months away. For a shocked breath they simply looked at each other.

"Freckle?" Rossamünd hissed, remembering himself and looking quickly about, too startled to fuss with greetings. "You can't be here! There's half a platoon of lighters in that cothouse back there." He pointed over his shoulder at the shadowy tower. "Many of them, watching us!"

"No, no, no, little once-weepy Rossamünd, it is *you* that cannot stay, and stay you can't," the little fellow said musically, hopping from one foot to the other, deep yellow eyes catching the meager, dappled light brilliantly. These eyes were limpid and anxious-wide, and Freckle's cheeky, once-happy face was now drawn with worry and fatigue. "Not here. Not with these people who don't know yet what they ought never to know. I have come and you must get away with me."

"What do . . . ? But how . . . ?" Rossamünd wanted to dash over and hug Freckle, but this would be the action of an outramorine—the worst kind of sedorner. Indeed, Freckle himself proved keen to keep a little space between them.

"I kept a good long look and I saw you and I followed you and I waited," the little barky-skinned bogle said quick and low, "and sometimes Cinnamon would do the following and the waiting for this one while I went on other ways."

Cinnamon has been watching too? Rossamünd could not quite fathom what he was hearing.

"I have watched you learning all the dividing, conquering ways with your friends who would not be friends if they knew. Come along now, now come along," Freckle said, waving with his hand. "You saved me so I save you. The Sparrowling will have you and keep you, just as he ought. You belong nowhere, but it is safer for you to be with him. He—"

"Rossamünd?" came a soft, too-familiar voice. "Wh—what are you doing with that—that thing?"

Threnody! "Ah—I—" He looked back. There she was, picking through the underbrush, looking deeply anxious.

She was staring with stark intensity at Freckle, and even as she came, the girl put her hand to her forehead.

"Threnody, NO!" Rossamünd cried and was instantly overwhelmed with her ill-practiced scathing, which drove him to his hands and knees. "Threnody . . . no . . ." Gritting teeth, Rossamünd forced himself to clarity, growling under his breath as he struggled to sit and reach into his salumanticum for something to——*to stop Threnody from hurting Freckle!*——but it did not matter, for the clever little glamgorn was already clean away. Threnody sprang after it, sending again, running wildly past the boxthorn and into the net of low branches through which Freckle had first come. Her hat was sent flying as she crashed through the growth, falling at Rossamünd's feet. He heard her flailing about fruitlessly, feeling the frequent edges of her scantly managed witting.

Rossamünd had seen Freckle avoid a fulgar, and now the glamgorn had eluded a wit—albeit an unskilled one.

Forcing herself back through the thickly interleaved branches Threnody returned, the clinging stems tangling with her hair. With a prolonged and angry grunt she pushed clear, yet something remained behind: her lustrous black curls. They were now a knotted mass weighing down several snaring twigs. For an awful breath Rossamünd thought the wicked undergrowth had wrenched her hair from her very scalp. With another shock he realized it was actually a *wig*. She had lost her hair from witting after all.

The girl stood in the clearing, blinking and pale, caught in a confusion of shame and fear and doggedness, her now bald head part hidden beneath white bindings.

"Haven't you ever seen a wit without her hair before?" she said darkly as she snatched her wig back from the twiggy snare, bringing most of it with her.

Utterly astounded and perplexed, Rossamünd said nothing.

Sequecious came rolling over, rubicund face dribbling sweat.

"What is being yee problems?" he huffed, then puffed, "No yelling or crying, tank yee! Come! Come! We must be to going back at castle," which was his term for Wormstool. "Yee noises make for th' ungerhaur to come!"

For the short walk back to the cothouse Threnody remained tight-lipped, fidgeting with her wig, unable to set it right without a looking glass. "If mother had let me be a pistoleer . . . ," Rossamünd heard her mutter, "and not made me into a stupid hair-losing neuroticrith!"

They achieved the safety of the cothouse unharmed. Hands on head, Threnody fled to her cot. Down in the cellar, Rossamünd washed himself, expecting some angry observer to hurry down and haul him before the house-major as a monster-loving outramorine. Required in the common-mess, he went as quietly as he might. Despite his fears there was not one comment; no one grabbed him and cried *Sedorner!* as he shuffled past the observers on the entry floor. Shamefaced and with his head down, he returned the hack-watch to the house-major. Grystle said naught, while Semple the day-clerk simply gave Rossamünd a firm, gentlemanly nod—a greeting and nothing more. *No one saw me with Freckle! They do not know!* Rossamünd could not decide which was the stronger emotion: his guilt or his relief.

In the common-mess he and Threnody came back together and were set to cleaning the thrumcops: sitting at the trestle, lopping the stubby stalks just above the ring, rubbing dirt from the spotty caps.

Vanity restored, Threnody refused to look at Rossamünd.

"Th' good in these here," Sequecious chuckled, holding up a thrumcop, "is these are being making us uneatable to the ungerhaur. Gets in tha sweats and so we tastes too bad. Very very good, tank yee."

Rossamünd nodded, scarcely following the cook's monologue, wrinkling his nose at the off-smelling fungus. *I don't blame them.*

Sequecious rolled out of earshot.

"What were you doing with that blighted bugaboo today?" Threnody whispered in a passion. "You had your salt-bag— you could have fought it. Instead I find you *talking* to it?"

"I—I was . . ." Rossamünd had been caught and there was nothing to do but admit it.

"Tell me, what in the Sundergird were you doing with it?" Threnody pressed. "Swapping potive recipes? Bogles are for slaying or driving away, not chitter-chatter! I did not get it, and now the little blightling will be off to murder someone's chickens—or worse!"

"Not every bogle is a ravening gnasher, Threnody, deserving nothing but a hasty death—and certainly not Freckle! He helped me—"

"That's the talk of a sedorner, Rossamünd! Watch your words," Threnody seethed under her breath, looking to Sequecious obliviously chopping at something in the kitchen proper. "I cannot believe you actually know the wretched thing's name."

"I'm not a sedorner just because I can see that not all monsters are bad," Rossamünd countered quietly but hotly. "Else you could accuse me a murderer just for saying that not all folks are good!"

"Ugh, lamp boy!" The girl rolled her eyes. "You sound more like Dolours every time we talk! You should have been an eeker, not a lamplighter. You're most fortunate the cook did not spy what was what, or someone else on sentries for that matter. If you meet the thing again, *get rid of it!*"

"I will not!"

Threnody looked at him with slit-eyed scorn. "To be hung on a Catherine wheel is a bad way to end," she warned.

"How is it a good end to murder a friend?"

"You just don't understand, do you, lamp boy? Well at least you can trust me to keep this between you, me and the rising moon."

Rossamünd did not answer. He was happy he did not

understand and if understanding meant slaughtering every bogle in sight, he never wanted to either.

They worked on in angry silence.

Between the guilt over the accidental tryst with Freckle and the regret for his falling-out with Threnody, Rossamünd kept to himself that night. Instead of joining his fellows in the gap between the Limpers' arrival and douse-lanterns for games of checkers and lesquin and tots of grog, he sat on his cot and wrote a letter to Fransitart. Dating it the fifth of Herse, he described his safe arrival, gave his new address and sent his deepest affections to all who had them. It was a brief message. He did not mention the incident with the friendly glamgorn, though it sat heavily in his thoughts: such things should never be committed to paper. Rossamünd had never mentioned Freckle in any of his previous communications home. Asking the house-major if he might use his wafer, Rossamünd sealed the missive in a second blot of paper.

The next morning he went to Aubergene, intending to ask him to pass his letter on to the Post-Master of Bleakhall at the end of the next night's lighting-leg. The lampsmen had just returned from dousing, and were down in the cellars washing. Aubergene stood by a well bucket with hat on yet shirt off, showing bare back and shoulders crawling with scars and cruorpunxis: gruesome faces that glared and sneered from shoulder, back or chest, mute witness of a lamplighter's violent life.

Rossamünd almost slipped the last few steps in shock.

Of course he had seen cruorpunxis before, but not so many on one person. This fellow seemed too young to possess such evidence of experience and slaughter. What great and terrible things had Aubergene done to earn such markings? How many of those snarling faces had actually deserved to end so ignobly as pictures to adorn a man's trunk?

Shaking, the young lighter turned and hurried back up and away. *I thought Aubergene was only against the worst monsters—how many of the worst ones can there be?* He would ask someone some other time for the letter to be delivered.

Later that week an unexpected thing occurred. A letter came for Rossamünd.

> Rossamünd Bookchild
> Lampsman 3rd Class
> Wormstool Cothouse
> The Pendant Wig
> The Idlewild
> 16th Heimio HIR 1601

> Rossamünd,
> I thank you for your communications of the 2nd of Heimio and the 6th of the same. I shall start with congratulations on your promotion. Its gaining might be early but it is still well deserved; you shall make a fine lighter.
> The matter of Numption and his bloom baths was so disturbing I nearly took the fast advice-boat in harbor back to the manse. Whatever I can do from here I will and shall.
> As you have no doubt deduced from the address line, the Marshal and I remain in the subcapital. The whole process of

interviews and reviews goes interminably slow. One day we might get a brief meeting to simply make a time for another *brief* meeting that *might* occur another week later. After all the rush and bluster of the first summons, the bureaucrats here are in no great hurry to give us a hearing.

All of this is made more troublesome by the unsettling buzz that the Marshal might actually be relieved of his post, and the longer we are delayed our proper review, the more likely this wretched injustice becomes. There is certainly something most insalubrious and cunning in the coincidence of events. What you have written to me in your second communiqué is unfortunately of no small surprise, but with so many good folk all so unfortuitously removed from the manse there is currently little that can be immediately done. What is more we need harder proofs than we currently have.

I wish I could write you happier things, but now is not that season. Nevertheless it is wise to remember that the most important battle to win is the last.

Of Discipline and Limb,

Scholijde

Lamplighter's Agent
Falseman to the Earl of the Baton Imperial of Fayelillian,
Lamplighter-Marshal of Winstermill
Epistra Scuthae
The Considine
The Patricine

Do not write to me upon these matters any further— some seals have been tampered; information is going where it should not.

Once he had read it, Rossamünd simply looked at the missive numbly. He wished too that Sebastipole could have written happier things. Eventually numbness turned into an anxious, angry gripping up under his ribs as he realized just how helpless he was to aid the Lamplighter-Marshal or Sebastipole or even Numps. So much good in Rossamünd's small sphere was being brought to dust by the skillful machinations of a self-serving few. He showed the letter to Threnody, who snorted cynically when she was done reading it.

"The Marshal and the Agent flummoxed too: what are we to do now?" she said, apparently more interested in cleaning and admiring her pristine pistolas. "The honorable suffer and the crafty prevail."

Rossamünd thought to show it to the house-major, yet what would it matter to him really, besides which he was sure Sebastipole would rather his private messages were not shown about. So Rossamünd continued to heed Europe's warning and keep his thoughts to himself. Yet no matter how many nights he lay half sleeping, fretting over a solution, it never came. All he could see before him were limitless days of duty at Wormstool—small, remote, irrelevant.

Surely something good will come from all this wretchedness?

One crisp, clear and early evening where the air itself felt as if it could snap with the chill, Rossamünd was at sentry on the roof with Under-Sergeant Poesides and Lampsman 2nd Class Theudas.

The Fighting Top was a spectacular perch when no fog was about to hide the scene, a whole-compass view of the Frugelle, flat as flat could possibly be in any direction he cared to look. There were no hills, few very shallow valleys—mere depressions in the earth, and endless withered shrubs and drought-blasted trees. Indeed, from up on the roof, the only notable feature—apart from a tiny wood of swamp oaks to the northeast—was the Wormway itself. The Pendant Wig went west on the left hand, and kinked to east-northeast on the right: the final length of road before all habitation ceased completely and only wide, empty wilds were left. On the horizon, drawn as a deep reddish-purple line, was the western border of the fabled Ichormeer, the Gluepot, the Blood-Marsh, a brooding mark on the edge of vision. He could almost feel threwd radiate from it, reaching even here, like the heat of a bonfire.

Yet tonight, sitting quietly, Rossamünd observed the lantern-watch at the lighting instead, already four lamps down the way. How he loved the beauty of the gradual increase in the light of a newly wound great-lamp, the colors shifting from grassy-green through straw-yellow and, if the water was new, to wine-vinegar clear.

As he watched, a fifth lantern began to glow green.

High off the ground, on watch with brave men, he felt his troubles markedly diminished here. A long and distant caw of a crow drifted in on the cold, fennel-perfumed breeze while restless wrens twittered and dashed about in the thistles. Rossamünd relished the lightening of his soul.

Threnody and he were talking once more, though they were yet to fully heal, and the passing of only a little time left him feeling less troubled about Freckle. He gave an almost contented sigh.

Poesides, who had been staring out to the south with a perspective glass, suddenly scuttled across the narrow walk between the tiles and the wall, crouched behind a rain-butt and waved the two others to do the same. "Stay out o' sight," he hissed excitedly. "There's some li'l bogle-thingy creeping down by the runnet there, not much more than one part of a mile yonder. If it don't spot us we might get a chance to take a few shots at the pot and spare ourselves a nasty end when we're out lighting."

Grinning grimly, Theudas peeked over the battlement. "I see it! The movement by them dwarfish willow-myrtles, aye?"

"Aye!" On his haunches, Poesides edged forward, easing up his firelock, creeping its muzzle on to the rim of the fortification.

Straining his neck, Rossamünd could not see what they saw among the low twine of dry long-grass and tangled thickets of parched trees all across broad moorlands. Then he did: something small and furtive not more than two hundred yards away, making quick scutters from root clump to root clump along the shallow bed of a barely running creek, one of the many that curled east then north past the cothouse, to eventually drain into the sluggish river Frugal. In one horrid breath Rossamünd realized he was looking at Freckle. The midget glamgorn obviously thought it was being rather cunning, coming at the fortlet from behind, and seemed unaware that it was observed.

Does he still want to take me away?

"Come on, Master Haroldus, get yer firelock up," Poesides chided. "Ye cain't hit naught with it slack at yer side."

"But what would Mama Lieger say?" Rossamünd cried.

The under-sergeant hesitated for a mere beat. He gave the young lighter a look as if to say "Who has a care for what Mama Lieger might say!" and lifted the butt of his own long-rifle, leveled it and, nice-and-easy, squeezed the trigger.

Hiss-CRACK!

The shot cracked out across the flats. Water hens burst from some covet away to the right and quit the scene in fright; teals hurried away, their wings whistling loudly; little wrens scattered to all points, their angry chirrups and the hurry of their flight filling the air.

Miss—miss—miss . . . Rossamünd panicked, on the verge of a scream.

Poesides cursed under his breath as he realized he had missed his mark.

Rossamünd could have burst with relief.

"Cunning little skink," the under-sergeant growled. "I reckon he ducked that!"

"Let me have a pull," said Theudas. "Where is it?"

"Leftmost of the three thickets, down by that huge thistle-bush," answered Poesides, sitting back down on the angle of the roof, rapidly reloading his long-rifle.

"Ah, I see it . . . ," the younger man muttered, "I think."

Making a show of presenting his fusil, a cold sweat of guilty horror clinging in the small of his back, Rossamünd had gratefully lost sight of the glamgorn again. For the first time he was glad for his lack of skill with a fusil. The chance of him actually scoring a hit was remote at best at this range. "Shouldn't we just send someone out to grab it or fright it off?" he asked in a hoarse croak, wanting to buy the little fellow some time to escape.

"What!" Poesides exclaimed huskily. "And chance some bigger basket springing at us from some nell? I have seen little blighters cooperatin' with some great gnasher, lure ye along thinking ye're in for an easy marking to add to yer skin and *boo!* Out of no place: something thrice as big, and ye're the mug being chased right back the way ye came." He primed the pan. "Our li'l mite out there is probably in cahoots with that nasty skulker we almost met out in the fog the other morn," the under-sergeant added as he rammed the wadding home.

"No! I heard that handsome Branden Rose dig got that one," Theudas corrected.

"Well, either way, ye can't let a bogle go free—it just ain't moral."

Rossamünd just wished Freckle would get away and save himself. He winced as Theudas took aim.

Hissss-FSSST!

A misfire!

Theudas had taken a shot, yet all he got was a flash in the

pan, no burst from the breech, nor ball hurtling from the muzzle. "Not again!" he cried. "I don't care what Shuddercrank says, there *is* something a-foul with the touchhole!" Amid a flurry of uncouth words Theudas wrestled with his weapon to find the fault.

"It's fossicking about in the thicket over yonder . . . Do you think it suspects it's been found out?" Poesides chuckled, and humming "Stand While You Can" to himself, paused between the third and fourth stanza to let go another shot. "Ah, blight it! It's surely a crafty li'l bugaboo!"

The musket fire brought the other lampsmen, poking their heads through the trap in the roof or out of the unshuttered windows a floor below, to catch sight of the spectacle. Aubergene arrived on the Fighting Top bearing his own longrifle, but he and the onlookers were to be disappointed.

The glamgorn was gone.

Rossamünd sat blank-faced, frazzled nerves tingling in strange and anxious relief.

"Well, either we hit it, or it found some way to scurry off," the under-sergeant said, chewing his bottom lip, " 'cause there ain't been a movement down in the creek for a little while now." Poesides searched through his perspective glass till it was too dark to see, and prevailed on Crescens Hugh the lurksman to aid him. Yet, to Rossamünd's secret delight, not a trace of the diminutive creature could be discovered.

He lay his head to sleep that night with the barred, misty light of the waxing moon shining on his face through a high window, feeling keenly the huge difference between him and his fellow lighters. After their visit with Mama Lieger, Rossamünd had nurtured the notion that these men were of a more subtle cast. Yet after that afternoon's shooting, they had confirmed themselves to him as unthinking monster-haters. What they called moral, he called mindlessness; what he would call right knowing, they would call treachery most foul. He lay and watched the moon a long time, understanding full well Phoebë's cold isolation.

26

A SHOW OF STRENGTH

Scale of Might, the ~ originally an anecdotal reckoning of the number of everymen it takes to best an ünterman, it has since been extensively codified by Imperial Statisticians, but simply put it is deemed possible for three ordinary men armed in the ordinary manner to see off one garden-variety bogle, and about five to handle your more common nicker. Add potives or teratologists to the group and this number fluctuates significantly—depending on the quality of potive or skill and type of monster-slayer.

THOUGH they had served at Wormstool for well over a month, House-Major Grystle still did not send Rossamünd or Threnody out on lantern-watch, but left them on permanent day-watch. This arrangement allowed two other better experienced lampsmen to go out lantern-lighting who might otherwise be held back. At full strength, the lamp-watch of Wormstool and her sister cots along the Pendant Wig had once been nine or even ten strong for every outing. This number was reckoned sufficient to see off most threats, and if not, there were always the half-buried fortifications Rossamünd had been so curious about along the roadside.

Called basements or stone-harbors, these cramped fort-lets were just big enough to fit a quarto of lighters and their accoutrements, preserved foods and a firkin or two of stale water. Every other lampsman had a key to their stout doors and the lantern-watch could seek refuge in them for well over a week: more than long enough, it was thought, for the monsters to lose interest and move on, or for a rescue to liberate the trapped.

To give them time to better accommodate to a lamps-man's life the house-major decided to put Threnody and Rossamünd under the charge of Splinteazle, Seltzerman 2nd Class. They would accompany him on many tasks, replacing bloom, refitting lantern-lights, cleaning panes—a task that always made Rossamünd glum as he brooded on the plight of poor Numps. Whenever they went out a run down flat cart went with them, its sagging planks laden with the nec-essary stocks of tools and parts. This cart was kept in a solid stone outbuilding attached to the back of the cothouse and was drawn by a he-donkey with incredibly large ears, which earned the poor creature the name Cuniculus—or "Rabbit." This stolid beast was kept in the cellar and brought carefully down the cothouse steps whenever he was needed. Rossa-münd greatly enjoyed the work, but Threnody did not and would stand by restlessly while they labored.

One cold, misty morning Splinteazle and his two aides set out to restock the basement found at the bottom of the lamp at East Bleak 36 West Stool 10. Haggard and blotched from a life spent at sea, his skull wrapped in a tight black kerchief—vinegaroon fashion—under his cocked thrice-high—Splinteazle whistled to the rising sun. Today he was in particularly good spirits, for today was Dirgetide, the last day of winter, which, apart from a great slap-up meal for mains, meant a season of fewer theroscades.

The delicate mist softened the arid land with its opalescent sheen, filling dells and hollows and runnel-beds with cloudy film. Gray birds with black hoods dipped and rose from perch to perch among the stunted swamp oaks, calling on the wing, giving their maudlin, churring songs to the hazy morning.

"Ahh," muttered Splinteazle, staring at them, "the sthtorm-birdsth are out: it'll be rain today, and our butts'th filled again with fresh water." Missing his two front teeth, the seltzerman had a naval burr that was marred with a lisp.

For all the condensation, it was still a thirsty walk. Wearing his new hat and pallmain and wrapped in Europe's warm scarf, Rossamünd had come laden with fodicar, his knife in its scabbard attached to his baldric, salumanticum and his own satchel holding a day's ration. He took a drink from a water skin.

"Here'sth a mite o' wisthdom for ye," Splinteazle said, stooping to the roadside. "I've stheen yee both take a sthecond and even a third gulp of ye water. At that rate ye'll have drunk it out and be wanting. A better way isth to avastht yer drinking and pick a pebble like I've got here and plop it into yer mouth to sthuck." He did as he explained, putting a small, pale stone between his thin lips. "Keepsth yer mouth watering and thirstht at bay."

Obeying, Rossamünd was amazed to find the advice was sound. On the verge as they walked, he noticed scattered many smooth pebbles, and wondered if they were made this way in the mouths of so many vanished generations of thirsty lighters working interminably up and down the road. With faint repulsion, he thought of how many maws the very rock he sucked on might have previously inhabited, and mastered the urge to spit it out.

They crossed the path of Squarmis plodding east on some cryptic errand. The costerman paid the young lighters no mind but engaged in insults with the seltzerman as they passed.

"Slubberdymouth!" Squarmis drawled in abusive greeting.

"Fartgullet!" Splinteazle returned without hesitation.

Only Rabbit was pleased to see the costerman, or rather the fellow's mean old she-ass, who nipped at Rossamünd walking by. Braying and bellowing, the seltzerman's donkey tried to turn and follow the retreating object of its passion. Splinteazle fought to keep the brute beast's head pointed in the correct direction and stop Rabbit running off after his sweetheart.

"Lamplassth!" the seltzerman grunted as he wrestled his donkey. "Help me hold the Rabbit. Nothing will turn him now, daft basthket! Bookchild! Go down to that sthwamp oak yonder and get me a branch. It'sth the only thing to move him."

Rossamünd spotted the appropriate tree not more than a dozen yards north off the highroad. With a dash he descended the side of the road and ran a lane through the thistles to the small swamp oak. He grasped a branch and tore it off with ease and saw yellow eyes watching from a gorse patch not more than five yards away. Pebble or not, Rossamünd's mouth went dry.

"Freckle?" he called softly. The little fellow had survived. What is more, he was still watching out for him.

"Hurry there, lad!" came Splinteazle's urgent call.

The eyes disappeared with a rustle, and feeling both disappointment and elation, the young lighter hustled back to the road.

The seltzerman had spoken true: Rabbit adored the taste of swamp-oak needles more than even the she-mule. With Rossamünd going ahead using the branch as a lure, the creature was induced to walk on.

"Poor old Rabbit," Splinteazle chuckled tenderly, once the donkey was walking freely again. "He'sth hopelessthly sthmitten on Assthanina—that'sth that filthy Sthquarmis fellow'sth lady mule, don't ye know—Rabbit goesth braying after her every time we're in town. Poor deluded fool of a donkey don't realizthe that Assthanina is not in the amorousth way."

For Rossamünd's part he wanted to keep looking out to the north into the scrub and try to spy Freckle. Yet he feared giving the persistent glamgorn away and forced his eyes to stay to his front.

When they arrived at the basement, the seltzerman took out a large cast-brass key and descended to unlock the heavy, narrow entrance to the stone-harbor. The lock and hinges whinged rustily and proved of little use. The inside of the basement was stuffy, cavelike and typically cramped. Though he could stand tall, Rossamünd saw that Splinteazle was forced to move about in a ducking hunch. The young lighter examined the view from the tight slit of a loophole. The mist was coming in thicker, and he could not see more than a small arc of the road and flatland to the north.

They slowly unloaded the flat cart, which creaked in a kind of inanimate gratitude for the relief of the burden on its aged timbers and axles.

"Ye're sthtrong and quick for a wee lighter, lad, and that'sth the truth. Young Master Haroldus'th indeed!" To Threnody's sluggish unwillingness the seltzerman warned, "Take up the sthlack, young hearty, and clap on sthome sth-peed; that'sth no way to stherve yer Emperor!"

"I might wear your colors, sir," she hissed, snatching some small box, "but I do *not* serve your besotted, bedizzled Emperor."

"Besthotted, eh? Bedizzthled?" he said as she turned. "Isth that what they taught thee in thy sthequethtury? What do-esth ye think taking the Emperor'sth Billion meansth?"

The stores were kept under a trapdoor in a rough-cut pit in the back corner of the outwork. For each new puncheon or cask or crate they carried in, an old one had to be removed and taken up and put on the cart. Even with Threnody re-luctant to do the task, restocking was completed quickly and the three were soon strolling home. Along the return, a shrill cry, brief and birdlike, pierced the gauzy stillness four times, tangible alarm in its echoes.

The three workers became very still.

Rossamünd stared about, trying to see everywhere at once.

"It'sth a water hen," Splinteazle stated in ominous whisper. "They only cry when the worstht of blight'sth basthket-sth are about. Sthomething wicked-foul musth surely be out there. We mustht hurry!"

Not much farther on, they found that East Bleak 41 West Stool 5 had been smashed: bent over like nothing more than a broken grass-blade, the lamp's still dizzing seltzer already soaking into the hard surface of the road.

The smell of monsters—the telltale stink of pungent musk and almost animal filth found them, floating on the quickening breeze.

"Hi," Splinteazle exclaimed in the barest of whispers, "catch a nosthe full o' that reek! They're sthurely sthome of the wortht bugerboosth ye're ever likely to hide from."

The next lamp they discovered missing altogether, ripped footing and all from the verge.

"Desthtroying me lovely lampsth!" cried Splinteazle. "Killin' me bloom!"

Rossamünd became aware of a threwdishly unpleasant, impelling sensation buzzing behind his eyes. It grew with each step, spreading to the base of his head, to the core of his innards; an external, ambient yet powerful compulsion to act, to do something or else suffer displeasure. *From who?*

Is Mama Lieger doing this? What am I supposed to do? Rossamünd had no notion, but the dread of this sensation waxed terribly. Oddly, Threnody and Splinteazle did not appear to heed it.

And the closer they drew to Wormstool the stronger the bestial smell became.

Though the cothouse was a mile away and part hidden by the mists, Rossamünd could make out swamp harriers gliding the clearer air above in hungry expectation. The mad baying of the dogs came faintly. Even from this distance they could make out something large, perhaps an ettin pounding against the cothouse. Rossamünd instinctively checked his salumanticum. There was nothing in it that would affect something so enormous.

"The cothousth is attacked!" Splinteazle wailed and set off down the road at a run, pulling the contrary Rabbit with him, the young lamplighters following his lead. A lantern-span closer, they saw more than just an ettin attacking their home. On the road before the tower and in the scrub about its foundations a crowd of monsters prowled, an entire menagerie of them, numbering a score or more of myriad kinds and sizes. They seemed to work in concert, hooting and hissing and yowling up at the besieged lighters within, drawing and dodging shots fired from loophole and roof. This was a theroscade of a kind that Rossamünd had only read. The three rushed on in thoughtless, unspoken agreement, marching into this overwhelming danger regardless.

The powerful ettin, much heftier than the Misbegotten Schrewd, flourished a lantern in its massive hands and with it smashed at the door of Wormstool. An old cart looking very much like Squarmis' old bone-shaker was lashed to its head with rope and harness leather, providing some protection from musket fire above, the thills thrust out over its back like horns and the wheels looking like weird ears. Pops of smoke were puffing from the slits of every floor of the tower, and from the crenellations of the Fighting Top as well. Much of the fire was concentrated on the ettin, the beast swatting at the balls as a man might at flies. Many of the shots must have been true and deadly, for Rossamünd and his companions were not much farther up the road when the giant nicker tottered, righted itself and threw the lamp at the walls. The post hit the cothouse with a clarion ring, ricocheted and spun off madly to crash on to the road. Stumbling, the ettin staggered away north into the flatlands, clutching at its bloodied head and shoulders. With a dull crunch of splintering wood, the ettin ripped the cart away and hurled this heedlessly too as it fled.

"Look at that belugig run! Come now, fellowsth!" Splinteazle cried to Rossamünd and Threnody. "We mustht join the fight!"

Once more Rossamünd felt the malignantly compelling threwd; felt it throb and saw the remaining monsters at the cothouse's feet respond obediently. Smaller nickers and larger bogles began to scamper up the stairs: things with hunched bodies and long legs, bounding a dozen steps in one leap; gaunt, stilt-legged bugaboos that took each step with the mincing grace of a dancer; bloated bogle-beasties that lumbered after.

"The door is breached!" wailed the seltzerman, abandoning Rabbit to run to the aid of the assaulted tower.

Mind a whirl of useless garble, Rossamünd followed and Threnody with him, checking the priming of her two doglock pistols. The young lighter could scarce believe that he was willingly throwing himself into the fray. He reached into his salumanticum for a caste of loomblaze.

The tower of Wormstool was close now, no more than a hundred yards away, the clamor of the desperate struggle within audible even down on the road. Not more than a hundred yards from the cothouse near the base of the first lantern, Rossamünd cried, "HI! HI! OVER HERE!" carried away by his desire to help. A pack of monsters still at the foot of the steps and circling about Wormstool's foundations turned to Rossamünd's shout. With hoots and howls, they swarmed at the three, loping and leaping down the road with appalling speed.

Splinteazle was ahead of the two younger lighters, brandishing his fodicar in one hand and a salinumbus in the other. The monsters closed and he fired, sending one flailing, spurting to the road-dust. At the shot Rossamünd threw his vial of loomblaze high and wide, wanting to avoid the seltzerman, and it erupted over the heads of two stragglers, their shrieks clear in the general din. Threnody fired too, pistolas thrust forward in classic pistoleer pose, but the power of the doglocks must have thrown off her aim, and they had little effect on the beasts. The seltzerman swung his lantern-crook with all his might, hitting the foremost bogle hard but doing little harm. Was Splinteazle *that* old and infirm? He struck it again with all his force, and Rossamünd watched with a numb kind of horror as once more the blow hardly troubled the gnasher. Cackling and barely hurt, the beast tackled Splinteazle to the ground and, finding all the weak parts of his proofing, rapidly clawed the hollering seltzerman to shreds before Rossamünd knew to act. With a shriek of her own, Threnody flung her fine pistols down and scathed powerfully, stunning Rossamünd but driving the bogles back amazed. Yet it was too late for the old seltzerman.

Numbness turned to terror and Rossamünd hesitated. The will-filled threwd resisted him, undermined his resolve. If the seltzerman could perish so easily, what hope had he?

Undismayed, the gaggle of nickers pounced again, some outflanking them as the rest rushed headlong. The monsters were on them, the stink of the beasts surrounding the two young lighters. Threnody sent forth her frission, which this time left Rossamünd untouched but gave the pack of gnashers a smart jolt. They howled at her in rage. But she could not keep such a barrier up for long, and too soon something sleek and full of claws leaped at her. Shouting wordlessly, Rossamünd leaped to meet the beast. Dancing aside from its swiping talons, he brought the butt-end of his fodicar down with as much strength as he could muster. To his utter astonishment the monster's back buckled and bent the wrong way under the blow and it fell, naked surprise on its bestial face. But he did not have time to wonder over its end, for Threnody's fishing faltered and the other nickers sprang, sneering hungrily and more intent on the girl-wit. In the frightening, gnashing whirl of a fight where he was one of the players and life and death stood on his own deeds, Rossamünd did not fuss about where his feet were, what his hands were doing. He just hit. One with a great lump of warts and lard that pronked on two legs like a rabbit's tried to leap about and get behind them. Threnody scathed again, a little weaker. Rossamünd stabbed at Rabbit-legs as it jumped. The pike-end of the fodicar went straight through its belly, the astounded beast expiring in midspring, collapsing on the road and skidding away. The Hundred Rules that had baffled Rossamünd so continually at Madam Opera's were suddenly making sense. The young lighter swung his lantern-crook again with ease, giving another bloated monster second thoughts as he caught its lunge with crank-hook and pike-end then shoved the bogle clear away. It glared at him with an odd expression.

At his back Threnody's sometimes clumsy, sometimes competent striving continued. For all her inexperience, she was actually gaining him space and protecting them both from being overwhelmed.

The monsters pulled away, dismayed at the ferocity of such tasty little morsels, rethinking their foe. Rossamünd and Threnody stood back to back and watched in turn. Of the eight or so bogles that had sought their lives, perhaps half had perished: one shot by Splinteazle, two struck down by Rossamünd, one or possibly two hurt by the loomblaze and another drooling and broken and sitting harmlessly by the highroad, a victim of Threnody's successful witting.

"Do you feel it?" she gasped.

"Feel what?"

"The threwd!" Threnody opened her eyes. "Working entirely on the destruction of this place. It snatches at me every time I wit!"

Rossamünd nodded. "Aye, I feel it."

Indeed, the malign feeling waxed strongly even as they spoke, and the monsters prowled closer.

BOOOOM! An almighty crash reverberated about the Frugelle, startling flocks of complaining birds to wing. Down the road smoke began to issue from Wormstool, belching from a fourth-story loophole. A tongue of flame licked out and up the outside wall. A lighter stumbled out of the high door of the cothouse and started down the steps. A large nicker with great, snapping jaws emerged and pounced on the retreating lampsman, crushing him down onto the stairway, jumping on him over and over till his screams ceased and red flowed.

Threnody stared in dumb shock.

Taking shrewd advantage of the distraction, the four remaining monsters rushed the two young lighters. Shrieking fiendishly, they charged in, then skittered away again when Threnody rallied and finally strove. They were testing her.

She began to growl in frustration as time and again they fooled her into scathing pointlessly, wearing her down. Rossamünd threw another charge of loomblaze at the largest bogle, the one with peglike teeth in its spadelike jaw, but missed. The fiery chemistry burst bright but uselessly in a thicket of bushes beyond the road, and the dry branches eagerly took to flame.

Observing the commotion, the slayer of the lighter on the steps descended and pranced up the conduit, joining its fellows on the road. The largest of them, this new beast strutted on its thin legs and slavered through its long snout at the two young lighters. It regarded them beadily then called across to them in a weird, slobbering voice, "What are you, pink lipsss?"

"I hate it when they talk!" Threnody seethed.

"What are you, pink lipsss!" it slobbered again. "Why do you ssside with themmm?"

"I think it's talking to you, lamp boy," Threnody muttered. "Maybe it's been chatting with your Freckle friend."

Rossamünd swallowed hard but did not answer. *Pink lips?* This was the meaning of Rossamünd's name—rose-mouth, pink lips. How did it know his name? Perhaps it had indeed been talking to Freckle? He looked to the tatters of Splinteazle's corpse beyond the monsters. His resolve hardened. He held out his fodicar, presenting arms as at a parade, inviting a challenge.

With a vicious snarl the slobbering nicker lunged at them, the other monsters rushing with it, whooping and yammering. Threnody witted, laboring to keep her frission under control. For a moment she checked the charge, Rossamünd standing with fodicar and loomblaze ready, by her side. The monsters writhed and backed away. Suddenly the girl gasped, and without warning her frission faltered. The beasts were at them again, the slobberer foremost, and Rossamünd sprang too. He hurled the potive with wicked aim, missing the slobberer and hitting a stocky bogle running just behind it. The wretched thing's head was splashed and engulfed with the cruel false-fire and it fell screeching. As he met the slobberer, fodicar swinging, so Threnody's frission returned and the small gnashers reeled. He swatted at the slobberer with the same thoughtless, clearheaded fluidity, hitting it smartingly on its shoulder. The thing shrieked and flailed its arms, swatting Rossamünd in the chest and throwing him back-first to the road. Threnody's witting caught him and his vision dimmed, threatened blackness; but this was no time for stopping, for lying tamely down just because of a hurt. With a yelping kind of growl, Rossamünd shook himself and rolled on to his side, his vision clearing. What had seemed to him like a dangerous pause had been just an instant. The slobberer bore down on him. Rossamünd whipped his lantern-crook around, smacking the nicker's ankles. Its long legs were tripped out from under it and the thing toppled, a puff of dust erupting from its fall. On his feet in a beat, Rossamünd took his advantage and struck the fallen monster wildly, not caring where, just hitting, hitting, as Threnody's frission lashed out again.

WORMSTOOL BRODCHIN

It was too much now—the bogles had had enough. They were quitting the fight, running back up the Wormway and off into the wilderness. Not satisfied, Threnody trod determinedly toward the cothouse, striving at the monsters inside. Still flailing in fury at the slobberer as it struggled to rise, Rossamünd was vaguely aware that lumpy bogles were fleeing the tower: one even leaped from the roof, landing with a mighty crash in some bushes and, yipping girlishly, disappeared into the scrub. With their escape, the malice of the threwd flared strong for a moment then subsided, leaving only confused watchfulness.

Rossamünd kept hitting, and only when he had smote the utter ruin of the stomping, slobbering nicker did he cease. He stared down at the shattered, mangled creature at his feet: somehow it still lived, glaring up at him, still defiant, still baleful, still hungry. Yet now Rossamünd could not hate the fiendly thing, no matter what it had done to the doughty, friendly lighters of Wormstool. Now he just felt tired and sorry: sorry for the death of his comrades; sorry for the harm he had done the monster before him, to all the monsters; sorry that *he* had become the murderer, the hypocrite.

"I am sorry to have slain thee," he whispered, little knowing from where the words came. "But we were at odds and I could not let you hurt my friends."

The creature's eyes glazed, a sadness—an ancient longing—seeming to dwell in them for a moment, and it ceased.

Gory fodicar still in hand, Rossamünd dropped to his knees and wept.

"Surely you don't weep over the monsters!" he heard Threnody croak as she picked up her doglocks, still lying where she had discarded them. She sat exhausted on the road and thirstily downed a milky blue liquid.

Rossamünd doubled over, keening agony in his very depths. He felt a subtle touch on his lantern-crook. Looking up, he saw that same familiar sparrow perched on the bunting-hook. It gave a single firm chirp as if it were chiding him, and whirred away.

"Oh, go away!" Threnody shied the empty alembant bottle at the departing bird. "A fat lot of good you did for us just now! Go back to your master and tell him the happy news!"

"Threnody!" Rossamünd cried as the flask missed well wide and disappeared into the thistles below.

In her sudden fury the girl turned on him, and for a moment he thought she might throw something at him too. But she did not.

Rossamünd stood, leaning on his fodicar as if it were a geriatric's cane.

Though smoke was billowing from the upper stories and carrion crows were already perching upon the chimney pots, Rossamünd and Threnody still walked to it and climbed to the front door, stepping with heavy grief over the body on the steps. It was Theudas. In the watch room the doors to the cellars had been torn from hinges and cast aside. The collapsible stair, now nothing more than a wreckage of timbers, had worked perfectly; yet this had not been enough to stop the murderous nickers from gaining the higher floors. It was, however, more than adequate in preventing the two survivors from getting above. They called out, screamed and screeched till they were hoarse, hoping to hear the answering plaints of a survivor from the upper levels. But no such answers came, only the hiss and crack of fire unchecked.

Together the two hastily scrounged whatever they could from the litter—food parcels and water skins found in the cellars and with them a flammagon. Among the ruination they discovered the inert white mass of Sequecious, bloodied and cold, collapsed across an equally fat, bilious-looking bogle with great bloodred fangs. It too was dead, the boltarde that slew it still clutched by Sequecious, the aspis-smeared blade thrust full through its ribs, scorch marks showing that it had received the blast of a firelock. Man and monster had died together. Whelpmoon lay faceup by his squat lectern, his glasses missing, his dead eyes staring. By the kennels the dogs had managed to destroy a brace of scaly, big-nosed bogles, perishing themselves as they did.

Men and dogs and monsters, everything was dead. Rossamünd could only imagine the gore and carnage on the floors above. *Too much . . . too much . . .* His extremities began tingling, and just as his anguish became overwhelming it was quickly obscured by a weird, empty flatness.

A terrible smashing report thundered from the floors above and shook the fortalice.

"We must go," Threnody insisted, standing at the top of the cellar steps.

Back down on the road, the two survivors tried to bring Rabbit with them, but the loyal, stupid beast would not leave his friend and master. Flat cart still hitched, it had slowly followed them and now stood forlornly by Splinteazle's remains and would not move. Not even a sprig of swamp oak could induce it to come away. The two young lighters would have had to drag it every single step to get the beast to Bleak Lynche, and they might have done but were desperate to be gone. So they unhitched the cart and left the faithful donkey standing at the base of the tower, ears down, head down, nosing the seltzerman's cooling corpse.

"What a waste," Threnody spat, venting her angry grief as they fled. "It's idiotic. Even out here, with hardly anyone to benefit, they still go on risking lives to light the lamps each evening and douse them each dawning. No one in the cities cares—not even in the towns around about are people mindful or grateful. Whoever uses this part of road? The Bleaksmen stay put. That place is nothing more than a cothouse with a fistful of desperadoes setting up shop about it—what's the point? Imperial waste!" She gagged back a sob.

"But if they did not make a stand here everyone west would suffer!" Rossamünd's contradiction was reflexive, yet in truth he actually agreed with her.

"Do you really think the flimsy string they call the Worm-way, with its few tottering towers so close to the Gluepot and the tired quartos that habit them, is a match for the gathered might of the monsters? Look how easy it was for a small band of brodchin to annihilate one cothouse. It's the work of my sisters that keeps your precious western folk safe!"

Rossamünd had no answer for this—he just wanted to get to somewhere secure. He found himself hoping Mama Lieger might shuffle from the scrub and lend them aid. *How can she have let this happen? Did* she *cause all this? Was the threwd of the land itself the culprit? Is that what I felt?*

An almighty shattering boom roared behind them, scaring them so much they both let out a yelp. They looked back to see the shingle roof of the cothouse collapsing inward with a seething eruption of smoke, sparks jetting from the shell of the tower. Rossamünd spied a hasty little shadow scuttling after them.

Freckle?

Walking on, Rossamünd ached to speak with the glamgorn, to ask question after question, but most of all—why? Why were they attacked? Why did the glamgorn not help? Why was he still following him? However, with Threnody by Rossamünd's side, Freckle would never come near. Strangely, irrationally, the young prentice felt safer with Freckle at their backs.

The day grew darker still and, as poor dead Splinteazle had predicted, it began to rain. Monsterlike shapes seemed to lurk and lunge in the gloom, phantasms made by the rapid fall of water. *At least I have my hat,* Rossamünd thought bitterly.

A far-off cry—a shriek and a gabber—came from somewhere out on the flatland. It was an inhuman call, a monster's voice. Rossamünd cringed at the noise and almost tripped, expecting any moment to be waylaid again. Though they were exhausted, desperation and blank terror set the two lighters running, a weary stumbling lurch, each helping the other if ever one flagged.

When the glimmer of the lights of Bleak Lynche hove in sight, Rossamünd eagerly took up the flammagon and shot its spluttering pink fire into the air. The flare drew a high, lazy arc, the falling damps carrying it northward. It winked out as it fell on the downside of its curve. They had little hope of it attracting attention, yet it did: a ten-strong foray of the Bleakhall day-watch.

The band of lighters that found them could little believe what they were told: a whole cothouse slaughtered? Surely not! Several lampsmen gave shouts of lament. Scrutineers were sent to Wormstool, the sneakiest of the band, while Rossamünd and Threnody were hustled back to Bleakhall. There the astounded Fortunatus the house-major conducted a hasty inquiry. He kept asking the same questions: "What happened? Where are the other lampsmen? How is it just you two survived?"

Rossamünd did not know how to answer except with the truth.

Fortunatus could not accept their shocking tale until the piquet of scrutineers returned, dragging Rabbit, braying mournfully, with them. These doughty fellows confirmed the blackest truth: a whole cothouse slaughtered; friends torn and all dead, the ransacked fortlet open to the elements. They brought with them body parts and several bruicles of cruor as proof, and offered one of these to the two survivors. "So ye might mark yeselfs proudly!" they said.

Rossamünd refused. The handing out of awards at such a time seemed so wrong to him——ill-timed and disrespectful. It did not occur to him that his feats would warrant a marking, maybe even four according to the grisly count that revolved ceaselessly in his mind.

"Not want a mark?" was the general, incredulous reaction. "That ain't natural!" But they did not press him.

Threnody, however, gladly received the blood, and this was a great satisfaction to the other lighters. "My first cruorpunxis," she murmured, scrutinizing the bruicle closely. Either way, all agreed that Grindrod must have improved greatly in his teaching of prentices to raise such doughty young lighters.

27

A LIGHT TO YOUR PATH

obsequy what we would call a funeral, also known as a funery or inurment. These rites typically include a declaration of the person's merit and then some traditional farewell given by the mourners. In the Haacobin Empire it is most commonly thought that when people die they simply stop: a life begins, a life ends. In the cultures about them and in their own past there have been various beliefs about afterlife and some all-creating elemental personage, but such notions are considered oppressive and outmoded. They would rather leave these ideas to the eekers, pistins (believers in a God) and other odd fringe-dwellers.

GIVEN his own room in the Fend & Fodicar and saloop spiked with a healthy dose of bellpomash, Rossamünd slept two days through after the attack, while outside the rain became a fierce storming downpour. He did not know till he had woken again that a dispatch had been sent to Winstermill informing them of the terrible things done at Wormstool and of the two young survivors. Neither was he aware that the loss of that cothouse had occasioned the temporary suspension of lamplighting along the entire twenty-five-mile stretch of highroad between Bleak Lynche and Haltmire. Nor did he know that

Europe had returned from a course while he slept and after a brief inquiry into his health, left again, quick on the trail of the surviving nickers. How the young lighter wished she had been with them at Wormstool; what lives might have been spared with the Branden Rose at the task.

As he slowly awoke, eyes heavy and senses murky, Rossamünd was gradually cognizant of a figure looming at his side. In fright his senses became sharp and he sat up swiftly, pivoting on his hands ready to jump, to run, to shout red-screaming murder. With clarity came truth and with truth came the profoundest delight. It was Aubergene—his old billet-mate—sitting by Rossamünd's recovery-bed on an old high-backed chair, dozing now as if he had been waiting at the bedside a goodly while. Even as Aubergene's presence fully dawned on Rossamünd, the older lighter snorted awake.

"Aubergene!" Rossamünd exclaimed. "Aubergene!"

"Ah, little Haroldus." The older lighter grinned, though sadness lurked at the nervous edges of his gaze. "Dead-happy news to find you and the pretty lass hale! I've heard from the house-major here how you won through. A mighty feat for young lighters."

Rossamünd swallowed a sob of relief. "I thought y-you were killed with the rest!"

Aubergene nodded leadenly in turn. "Aye, I suppose you would—but me and the under-sergeant and Crescens Hugh were sent out with deliveries for the Mama not so long after you went off with Splint." He hesitated. "Poor Splint, poor Rabbit . . ." He put his chin in his hand. "We weren't anywhere nigh the Stool when those wicked unmentionable baskets did their worst there. We were still set on, though. We'd only just begun the return. Mama Lieger warned us not to venture out again, but we figured she was just feeling for some comp'ny. Yet we weren't more than half a mile gone when Hugh put his box on and, certain enough, kenned something odd in the air and had us hurrying back to the Mama's seigh with a whole handful of the blightenedest hob-boggers in chase."

Rossamünd listened with amazed relief, glad to hear that Mama Lieger was not to blame, glad to know that some had won through that day. Yet these three fellows had survived in that small high-house where the might of Wormstool had failed. "How—how did you live through it?"

"We tried our aim from the Mama's windows and hacked at 'em by the door if they tried to shimmy up, Mama Lieger laughing and shrieking like a soul gone mad, poking at the baskets with this great long prod of hers." A strange, troubled thought suddenly haunted Aubergene's brow. He looked to his right and hunched as if he was about to enter into a conspiracy. "Rossamünd," he said low and halting, "we—we was defended by other—by other bogles too."

A chill shivered down Rossamünd's scalp. His hearing whined. "You were defended by monsters?"

Aubergene looked at him hard, almost aggressively, yet there was something pleading in his brittle gaze; he seemed more troubled by what he had just said than by the destruction of his billet-mates. "It's not sedorner talk, Rossamünd!

I'm no bogger-loving basket—it's just what I saw with the same eyes that look on you now . . ."

"You'll never hear me call you a sedorner, Aubergene," Rossamünd answered, an image of Freckle flickering in his mind. "I know there are kindly monsters . . ."

The older lighter's dogged expression loosened. "Poesides warned Hugh and me about speaking on it," he said in a grateful hurry, "but I reckon the Mama might be right about you, Rossamünd, that you do see things more in her way; I reckoned you'd not begrudge me what we witnessed," he finished, almost imploring Rossamünd to say it was so.

The young lighter gave a bemused, shrugging kind of nod. Rossamünd would never cast a stone at the unusual revelations of another.

"I reckon them hob-possums fought for the Mama's sake," Aubergene continued. "Remember that little doll you said winked at you?"

"Aye." Rossamünd barely dared a wheeze.

"Well, you were right! It was a beastie—some weensome bogle-thing made of sticks and bits that's been just there on the mantel all the while, and up it jumped, leaped out the Mama's door without a pause and wrestled baskets dead-near ten times its bulk. Something else joined it—we could scarce catch a sight of the fellow, but something heavy and all bristling beard came, and with great crashings and flashes like some fulgarine. This new nicker set our enemies on a run. I've never seen such a thing, never knew it was

AUBERGENE

really so—just eeker talk, naught but bewilderment and nonsense. When all was quiet, the Mama called out in her old tongue—whether it was to her weeny bogle friend or bristle-beard or the birds themselves I could not reckon. Either way, magpies began to sing as if in answer, getting loud, sounding for all the lands like speaking—dead eerie and unhuman. The Mama became satisfied then and we were left in peace." Aubergene looked out the window.

It was beginning to rain again, a pelting rat-a-tat on the mullions. Rossamünd found he had almost forgotten such a merry sound after two months without.

"If nickers weren't enough"—the troubled man nodded toward the wet—"this storm set itself against us and Poe daren't let us out till Hugh was sure we were clear. The Mama said she'd have her 'friends' watch over us, but Poe refused her. The old dame shrugged at us all contrariness and secrets, but Crescens never caught sight or smell of any escort."

"I am"—Rossamünd could not think of how to put his sad relief—"glad some of us have survived, Aubergene . . . ," he tried, feeling a little daft.

"Aye, though I sorely wish I were at the Stool to defend her, though your deadly feats near won the day." The man looked to him with evident pride. "You earned your name aptly I reckon, Master Harold, smashing every nicker that crossed you—though I'm sure you were dead-glad to have Lampsman Vey with you."

Rossamünd nodded. "She saved us both," he said softly. "But it was not enough to help the—the others."

"No." Aubergene dropped his gaze. "No, I s'pose it - weren't."

Two days later, the remains of their comrades were recovered, brought back to Bleakhall and buried. Even the nonlighter folk of Bleak Lynche attended. Rossamünd had never attended an obsequy before; any foundling who died was buried privately, just for Madam Opera and the masters to see. Here, in the deepest cellars of Bleakhall, with the lighters gathered about, their heads and his own covered over with black mourncloths, he was privy to the whole somber process.

With every burial came the ritual intonation: "A light to your path. A way in the dark."

Rossamünd was surprised, even in his sorrow, by the smallness of the tombs and the thoroughness with which they were sealed with plugs of clay once the corpse was interred. There was something bitterly oppressive about this hurried, repetitive rite, the lives of the passing grieved as a waste, their honor grimly asserted by House-Major Fortunatus and attested to by silent, angry nods from the lighters. "Lampsman 2nd Class Fadus Theudas," the senior officer said, "true of heart and quick of shot, who sought to serve, so young and so well."

"A light to your path. A way in the dark."

Blinking back tears, Rossamünd looked furtively to Threnody, standing across from him at the memorial, and marveled that she and he had survived a theroscade together. The girl looked haunted as they slid the remains into small tombs deep below, glancing reluctantly at him with dark, imploring eyes.

"A light to your path . . ."

She was to be puncted that night. He had no desire to see her marked, for to do that would be to relive the horror and violence—and he simply could not. Providentially—when the time came that evening—he was not made to attend.

After the burial day the young survivors were given light duties about Bleakhall, small tasks to keep them from dangerous brooding.

Any unoccupied time Rossamünd and Threnody had they spent sitting together and talking in the room given to him in the wayhouse.

"Rossamünd"—the girl lighter looked at him with sad earnestness, fingering the bandage that covered her still-forming puncting—"how did you slay those monsters?"

"You were there, Threnody! I just did—I hit them and they died. Isn't that the way it is meant to happen?"

"Yes . . . but Sp-Splinteazle was not able to even bruise one and he is—was thrice your size."

"Sequecious skewered at least one," Rossamünd tried. "Probably more!"

"A huge man using a blade coated in aspis. Did your crook have a venificant on it?"

"No." He had no other answer for this but the one he had already given the house-major.

Threnody squinted at him. "You catch heavy barrels and slay monsters with one blow."

Rossamünd had nothing to say to this.

A welcome silence stretched out.

"Will you go back to Herbroulesse now?" he asked eventually.

"And let Mother win?" Threnody scowled. *"Never.* I am a lighter now, like you, and we shall serve on just as we ought. Once a lighter, always a lighter—isn't that what they say?"

"Aye . . . Maybe." Rossamünd could not conceive of what his future might be now. What little enthusiasm for lighting he had managed to find had been slaughtered out at Worm-stool. Between the violent malice of monsters and the ruth-less ambition of men, where was he to go?

A week after the attack they were talking quietly about unimportant things when Europe entered Rossamünd's room, unannounced and without a knock. She had only now returned, and looked haggard beneath her fine clothes and manners.

There was an uncomfortable hesitation.

With a resigned sigh, Threnody stood, bowed stiffly to the fulgar and left the room.

The lighter and the fulgar peered at each other, Europe's expression impenetrable.

Strange feelings boiled within Rossamünd's bosom, but most of all, with her there he felt truly safe. Without thinking, he leaped from the bed where he had been sitting and flung his arms about the fulgar.

Startled, she relented for a moment, hands placed lightly on his shoulders, but Rossamünd could feel her gathering discomfort and, shamefaced and awkward, he let her go.

"I-I am glad you are safe," he stammered, feeling small and stupid. He sat back on the cot.

Europe nodded. "I know how funny you can get about a monster's dying," she continued circumspectly, "so you may or may not be glad to hear that I have found and slain every hob-thrush, botcher or gnasher I could."

She was right: Rossamünd did not feel any better for the news.

"That old eeker-woman, Mother Lieger, even helped me—if you can credit that." Europe pulled a wry face. "I must give part of my success to her guidance: she knew very well where the baskets might be hiding at—and a girl will never refuse aid however it might come. Here is me all along believing these foolish eeker-folk were in love with the nickers. Indeed, she even asked me to send you her greetings, and tell you that she declares it a 'terrible wicked thing to have happened.'" She sighed a deep, heartfelt sigh. "Now the folk of Bleak Lynche want to fete me, and the house-major wants to cite my deeds for some kind of Imperial commendation . . . I refused them both, of course."

Rossamünd nodded sadly. "They wanted to give me a mark, but I refused them too."

Europe let out a small laugh. "Of course you did." She sat on the edge of the bed. "By-the-by, I saw your glamgorn friend. It was loitering out there near the edges of the town and keeping downwind of the dogs."

"You didn't do anything to him, did you?" Rossamünd sat up sharply.

"I cannot quite believe I am saying this but, no, I let the wretched thing be. I had little choice, actually." She folded her hands in her lap. "Once it knew I was about, it left rather smartly."

Rossamund lay back. "I feel so tired, Miss Europe. I don't know why, but I cannot seem to raise much eagerness for anything."

"I can tell you why, Rossamünd." Europe looked at him appraisingly. "You have stood victorious in a desperate stouche. Dark moods always follow. Your potential as a factotum increases almost every time I see you. Dear Licurius, in all his might, may well have struggled where you have won."

"But all I did was survive!"

"I don't think you comprehend what you have done." Europe leaned toward him. "A wit, even a clumsy, new-cut one, should be able to win through a pack of monsters, else

543

what would be the point of all the pain and inconvenience? But you, an ordinary little man, have not just won through, but—from what I hear—beaten to death three nickers, full-formed and ancient."

Rossamünd hung his head. "I was not counting."

"No," the fulgar said, fixing him with serious eye, "but others are."

The reply from the Marshal-Subrogat arrived two weeks after that horrid Dirgetide day. It declared tersely that the circumstances of the sacking of Wormstool were too unusual for the limited jurisdiction of the ignoble end of the road. It demanded that Rossamünd and Threnody leave immediately on the return post, strangely omitting to summon Under-Sergeant Poesides or Aubergene or Crescens Hugh the lurksman. They had not been witnesses to the fall of the cothouse and were to stay and serve at Bleakhall until further directed from Winstermill. Having stated this in the firmest terms, the dispatch went on to deny any immediate relief to the beleaguered lighters of Bleakhall. The Master-of-Clerks did not see the wisdom in rushing men into the fray when he knew so little of the current situation.

Under the escort of one of the scrutineers who had seen the aftermath, the two young lighters were to be on their way, messengers of the tragedy and bearers of a second urgent request for reinforcement.

Though Rossamünd knew Europe had gone again, hunting somewhere out on the flat with her hired lurksman, he nevertheless looked out for her in hope, even up to the moment of departure. Before boarding the return post, the young lighter left a desperate scrawl for her with Goodwife Inchabald, a plea for the fulgar to follow after him to Winstermill. It was a lot to ask, but he was about to return to the den of that black habilist Swill, and the Branden Rose was the only one who he felt could protect him anymore.

In somber silence, the post-lentum left for the Idlewild proper, farewelled by only Aubergene, sadly waving, and a silent Poesides. Not sparing of the horses, it hurtled west. What little was left of their belongings Rossamünd and Threnody now carried with them in the cabin. All the rest was charred to smithereens in the burning and collapse of his old billet—including, to Rossamünd's great woe, his peregrinat and the remarkable valise given him by Madam Opera.

Out of exhaustion and an unbearable gloominess at his enforced retreat to the manse, Rossamünd slept much of the journey. The return became a bizarre blur of unhappy, cataclysmic dreams; hurrying landscape glimpsed from the thin slot allowed between sash and door frame; strange, anxious faces at whatever stop they made; and tasteless meals he had no appetite to stomach. Threnody too sat in silent grieving, seemingly diminished without her fine furs and traveling bags.

Rossamünd lost the reckoning of time. All seemed dark to him, whether day or night; he could have well done with

House-Major Grystle's hack-watch now. Consequently he was unable to share in the wonder of their escort, who stated that they had achieved Winstermill in a record four days—rather than six—and "that done at the end of the bad traveling season and all!" Four days, six days, ten days, twelve—this was no relief to the young lighter. He had once gloried that he had escaped the oppressive, now-corrupted place, yet here he was, returning to the manse after only two and a half short, violently terminated months.

Now he feared he might never be allowed to leave this den of massacars again.

Their arrival at Winstermill went unheralded, and from the coach yard they were met by Under-Clerk Fleugh and hurried directly through the manse to wait with their escort in the Marshal-Subrogat's anteroom.

"No happy welcomes for us, I see," Threnody muttered as they were let through to the Ad Lineam, the hall-like gallery of tall, many-mullioned windows that took them to the Master-of-Clerks' file, their feet slapping *thump thump thump* as they were hastened along.

As if there was some kind of criminal inconsistency to be found in their accounts, Podious Whympre saw fit to meet with each of them separately. The Bleakhall escort was interviewed first; this was a long meeting that gave the two young lighters time to catch a breath as they sat under the impassive gaze of a foot-guard.

"What do you think will happen?" Threnody wondered quietly.

"I don't know."

"What more can Odious Podious want to know?" she persisted.

"I don't care."

"Hmph." Threnody folded her arms and leaned back as best she might in the high-backed chair.

Their escort reemerged looking harassed and disappointed. Threnody was called for next.

"Do well," Rossamünd offered. The encouragement sounded weak in his own ears.

"And you," she returned with a dazzling smile, and disappeared through the portentous door.

Finally, as the sun westered, shedding gold on the west-facing angles of the mess-hall window frames, Rossamünd was shocked from his doze by a summons. His time with the clerk-master at last. As he was let through to Podious Whympre's file, he could hear the tail of the previous interview.

"In such startling and tragic circumstances," came the Master-of-Clerks' smooth voice, "I have taken the liberty of sending for your mother."

"I do not want *her* here!" Threnody objected.

"But she is here already," Whympre returned evenly. "I shall have my man take you to her immediately. Ah, Master Bookchild, our little teratologist! It would appear you have an unfortunate aptitude for being right in the thick of troubles." The Master-of-Clerks glowered at him almost as soon as Rossamünd entered the narrow, unfriendly room. "Thank you, Lady Threnody. That will be all."

The girl pivoted on her heel, her nose in the air. They exchanged a quick look, Threnody rolling her eyes and exiting without another word.

Rossamünd stepped into the Master-of-Clerks' file and stood at the far end of the great table that ran most of the length of the room. The first thing he noticed was the enormous antler-trophy of the Herdebog Trought, thrusting out into the upper atmosphere of the room. The trophy was hanging from the wall as if it had been Podious Whympre himself who had bagged the beast. Rossamünd gave a brief scowl of disgust. The musk of the horns cloyed the air in here, joining the sweet fragrance of that old wood and the sharp bouquet of the unguents in the Master-of-Clerks' wig. Rossamünd hated this narrow unfriendly room, wallpapered in a fussy pattern of velvet and gold, with its too-high ceilings of dainty white moldings, too-tall windows looking out to the treacherous fens north of the manse. Its morbid silence hummed with distracting, lurking echoes. In the far-end wall, underneath an enormous painting of some ancient Imperial victory, were three doors. Remembrance made his gizzards tight as Rossamünd wondered which it was he had burst through on the night he slew the rever-man.

The Master-of-Clerks sat tall and stiff, aloof in a great gilt chair at the farther end of the ostentatiously carved table. Dressed in the brilliant scarlet of the Empire, he had removed his thick black wig of long complex locks—an inconvenience when shuffling sheaves of paper. It was also a subtle reminder that neither Rossamünd—nor Threnody, nor their escort for that matter—were important enough to warrant the trouble of being fully dressed.

To the left of the clerk-master, seated on a markedly smaller stool of drab wicker, was Witherscrawl, with stylus in hand and giant book on lap. The indexer scowled through his glasses at Rossamünd, who could feel those beady eyes and ignored them. Laudibus Pile was there too, of course, sitting just behind his master, leaning forward, ready to expose false speech. Rossamünd refused to be daunted—he had nothing to hide.

"Please sit, Lampsman 3rd Class Bookchild," the Master-of-Clerks purred.

There was not much new about the interview itself. The same kinds of questions were asked as had been asked by the house-major of Bleakhall: the why, the where, the how—and Rossamünd's answers were the same. Whympre kept pressing for more detail on just how the young, prematurely promoted lighter had fought and beaten his foes. Rossamünd was troubled by the inkling that there was more to the queries than simple, official inquisitiveness. Nevertheless he answered every question truthfully.

"All this loss of life is very alarming and vexing." The Master-of-Clerks stroked his face and looked anything but alarmed or vexed. Indeed, he seemed more troubled by the destruction of property. The most significant thing he had to tell was that there was to be a formal inquiry of the Officers of the Board into the affair, "to be held here, hence the brevity of this evening's fact-finder. A disaster of such magnitude requires proper bureaucratic process." The man smiled coldly. "Also, I wish to investigate some . . . irregularities. The people of the Idlewild, and the Sulk End too, need to see that their Marshal-Subrogat is not a slouch at the important end of the day—*ad captandum vulgus* and all that, you understand."

Actually Rossamünd did not understand. What irregularities? The events were straightforward.

"I shall allow you a day to gather yourselves, after which we will begin, first thing on the first day of the new week. Understood?"

"Aye, sir."

Shortly after, with his attention waning and sleepiness waxing, Rossamünd was dismissed. He was led to a small room on the first floor of the manse, away from Threnody or any other lighter. Missing mains, he lay on the foreign cot in the cold foreign room and slept.

28

BEFORE THE INQUIRY

heldin(s) mighty folk of ancient history who fought with the monsters, employing their infamous therimoirs to keep the eoned realms of humankind safe. Known by many collective titles, including beauts (common), haggedolim (Phlegmish), herragdars (Skyldic), heterai (Attic), orgulars (Tutin), sehgbhans (Turkic) and what we would call "heroes". The time of their supremacy, when they were relied upon to stand in the gap between everymen and iintermen, is known as the Heldinsage. Said to have begun with the Phlegms— those most ancient forebears—and ended with the Attics, their heirs, it was the time of Idaho, the great queen of the Attics, and of Biargë the Beautiful, among many other glorious and infamous folk and their usually tragic stories. Not all of the weapons of the heldins were destroyed in the violent cataclysms that punctuated and finally concluded that time: many are said to remain, and are most highly prized by collectors and combatants.

T HE next morning, gray and misty and eerily still, Rossamünd was already harnessed when the ritual call came—"A lamp! A lamp to light your path!" Without stopping for breakfast, Rossamünd went straight down to the Low Gutter, through the labyrinthine Skillions. Kneeling over the deserted grate that led to Numps' desecrated bloom baths, the young lighter called and called Numps' name till he was hoarse, but no pallid, welcoming, twisted face loomed on the darkened steps below.

Rossamünd pulled on the grate and found it was locked.

He gave one last cry, and ran to the lantern store, looking dusty and seldom used, but the glimner was not in there either. Rubbing his face, Rossamünd tried to marshal his increasingly anxious conjectures.

Doctor Crispus will know! To the infirmary he went, and found the physician working as he always had, tending the few ill or wounded fellows there.

"Have you seen him?" Rossamünd pressed intently. "Is Mister Numps recovered from his grief?"

"Cuts and sutures! No, I have not had sight of Numps, young Master Bookchild," the profoundly startled Crispus replied. "And well betide you, young sir, all questions and no greetings!" he added. "I had no notion you would ever be back with us!"

"Sorry, Doctor Crispus. Hallo, sir. I was just down in the Skillions looking for Mister Numps."

The physician laughed, a tight nervous sound, and directed Rossamünd into his study. "All I can confirm," the man said when the door was shut, "is that the astute fellow has taken to living in the damp cellars under our very feet. I put out food in his lantern store at the start of every week, and each time I have returned to do it again, the previous parcels are gone. It seems a satisfactory arrangement, though it probably cannot last. Nevertheless, I shall keep at it till events dictate otherwise. And for you, my boy, why are you here? I heard of the terrible things done at Wormstool. It does me a great good to see you hale."

"The clerk-master has called Threnody and me back," he said, sitting upright and tense on the seat Crispus offered him. "He says that the things that happened at Wormstool are too terrible to not inquire after properly. He also says he wants to investigate 'irregularities.'"

"I am sure he does," Crispus exclaimed. "Guilty minds are suspicious minds."

"You received my letter, Doctor?"

"I did, my boy, I did." The physician stared at his well-ordered desktop for a moment.

"I sent the same to Mister Sebastipole," Rossamünd added, fishing out the letter from Sebastipole and passing it over. "This was his reply."

Crispus took the missive and "hmmed" a lot as he read. "The gears of bureaucracy turn against us, Master Book-child," he said at last, waving the letter. "The most difficult thing in all of this topsy-turvy hubble-bubble is proof."

"Have you discovered any, Doctor?"

"Regrettably, no," Doctor Crispus said flatly. "Our not-so-temporary Marshal has reversed my position, and against all custom and decency that sawbones Swill is my superior: a surgeon over a physician! I am not certain that it is even legal. But that is the lay of things, and consequently my movements about the manse are severely restricted. So you and Mister Sebastipole and I can wonder and surmise all we like, but like the leer says, it is all useless without tangible proofs, and these none of us is in the position to obtain."

"Miss Europe says the same." Rossamünd's shoulders sagged. Then a bright idea struck. "I could find proof. I got into the cellars before, I can do it again."

"Lah! The boy is a heldin reborn!" Crispus exclaimed. "They cover their activity too well. If Mister Sebastipole could not find evidence or even traces of the same, what hope have you with your less cunning senses? No, no, no, Rossamünd. You are in things deep enough, I think! Having said that, you should destroy this letter—their finding proof against *us* . . . against *you* . . . would be terribly counteractive."

"How is it that we are not able to stop such clear wrongdoing?" Rossamünd said in suppressed indignation.

"I am afraid, my boy, our foes are well ahead of us in the use and experience of cunning and shrewdery," said Crispus resignedly.

"But it can't be that they are allowed to go on making rever-men and ruining lives!"

"No, it cannot," the physician concluded softly. "No, it cannot," he repeated, and lapsed into introspective silence.

Flummoxed, Rossamünd went silent too. Railing about the wretched situation did naught to solve it. "The manse seems empty, Doctor," Rossamünd eventually observed.

"Joints and gristle, my boy," Crispus exclaimed, "this place has gone to blight after that sis edisserum caper. All the best folk are leaving as fast as schemes will let them. Whympre said something about Grindrod being overburdened by the rigors of learning prentices their trade. The poor fellow has been sent on half pay to some other fort—I never did catch where—some remote and difficult place. Benedict has taken his sweet little wife back to High Vesting."

Rossamünd could not believe his ears. Benedict gone? Grindrod disposed? The lamplighter-sergeant had seemed as permanent as the rock of Winstreslewe itself. "But who is drilling prentices, then?"

"There are no more prentices," returned Crispus. "Master Whympre says that the road is in too great a disarray for prenticing to continue. He says that after he has brought things back in order and reformed the whole Wormway, the question of prentices shall be addressed again."

"Who else has gone?" Rossamünd asked, saucer-eyed.

"Let me see . . ." The physician began counting off fingers. "As you know, that Mother Snooks woman evaporated without a glimpse some months ago; I have heard some dreadful rumor that she was declared mentally unsound and exiled to some terrible far-off place. Then there is that amiable young register, Inkwill. He set off last week to some sinecure—a sweet-and-easy station I believe the common roughs call it— in the bureaucracies of Brandenbrass, got for him through a cousin, or so he said. The lurksman-general is seeking a position elsewhere. Most of my epimelains have left; they said they would not work with that butcher at the lead—bless their eyes. I have precious few like-minded fellows to converse with now, and a sore trial it is too, I might say. If it were not for Numps, I might find a way to a new posting myself. Now let me look you over." Crispus reached for a special monocle like Swill had worn when searching out the calendar Pandomë's hurts. "It might be near on a month since you were in your fight, but I do not trust Mister Trippletree"—by which he meant the dispenser at Bleakhall—"to have been thorough enough."

While he was looked over, Rossamünd explained the many events that had crowded his life since last he was in Winstermill, though he omitted any mention of Freckle. ". . . And all I hear," he concluded after a long telling, "is what a remarkable thing it was to have slain those nickers."

"Well, my boy, I cannot say that I blame them. To come out unscathed from one of the worst assaults on a cothouse in recent history would be a most remarkable thing even for a fully formed man. But fret not: the body is capable of remarkable deeds when the soul is under great pressure. Now, Rossamünd, you look fit enough, though I think you need to eat more."

So, with morning transformed to midday, Doctor Crispus invited Rossamünd to share middens.

"Ahh." Crispus waxed cheerful as the food was brought in by silent maids. "Middens is a meal not to be missed! One can go without breakfast, and a missed mains won't do you harm, but to skip middens"—he clucked his tongue rapidly—"that is to risk a sluggish and interminable afternoon."

Rossamünd basked in the physician's dependable unflappability.

There was tench pie, boiled leg o' veal, carrot collique, peas with a great wedge of butter melting on them and sweet wine jelly for puddings—like a Domesday feast, served right in the physician's study. In this prandial refuge they talked a little about lighter things, but mostly they ate in heavy, ruminative silence.

The meal approached its end and Doctor Crispus pushed back his chair and, with a show of sangfroid, said, "Don't fuss about Numps, my boy. Together we just might preserve the poor fellow from further harassments." He sucked down the last of his tepid sillabub with a clear yet dignified snort and said, "Back to the coughs and croaks and running sores for me, my friend. Nights can be as long as days for one in my line of work: several wounded lighters have been sent to me from beyond the Tumblesloes. They did not do as well as you against the bogles, but are not beyond repairing. Good day to you, Master Bookchild, until anon."

Standing to bow, Rossamünd bid the physician good afternoon and left, spirits lifted, pleased to have such an estimable man of physics call him *friend*.

Rossamünd spent confinations alone in his tiny room. In the afternoon he had gone back to the Low Gutter to seek Numps, but still to no avail. After this he made an attempt to meet with Threnody, but she was now closeted with her mother and was refusing all visitors. She had not been hard to find: he simply asked Under-Clerk Fleugh, who, though sneering and supercilious, told him without hesitation. Even as he approached down the dark, aromatic passage, he could hear the rumor of a terrible ruckus. It became a terrible female screech as the door of Threnody's apartment was opened to his knock.

"You shall tell everything as you saw it, child," is what it sounded like, coming from some other room farther within.

Before him at the door stood Dolours. She wore a wimple to cover her bald pate and a dogged expression. "Hello, young lampsman. Threnody will not be taking any callers today."

"Our clave has *no* liars!" the screeching continued behind. "How would we look to others if it were known my daughter—the Right's heiress—was a black-tongued deceiver?"

"Not even me?" Rossamünd had persevered.

"Not even you, young lampsman," Dolours had answered with a sad and not unfriendly smile. "She is being prepared for tomorrow's inquiry. Be on your way, Rossamünd Bookchild. We are grateful for your aid to our senior-sister's daughter, but bigger wheels are turning here."

Lying on his lumpy, lonely bed, he worried over this odd display. *Will she tell of Freckle?* The chilling thought froze his innards. Flicking disconsolately through an old pamphlet to distract him from such inconvenient anxieties, he heard a call come for him. "Lampsman Bookchild, you are required by the Marshal-Subrogat!"

What now! Rossamünd fretted as he was taken to the Master-of-Clerks' file. *Is the inquiry coming early? Is it canceled? Are they letting us go?* All sanguine hopes, he was sure. Arriving, he closed his eyes and took a deep breath and readied himself to face the foe. The doors swung back and he saw Whympre, sitting at his usual place at the far end of the long table, within the light of the only lamp lit in the room. He was apparently on his own for the only time Rossamünd could ever recall, until the young lampsman saw that there were shadowy figures in the gloom, standing about halfway down the clerk-master's long table beneath the Trought's great antlers. Did he know those figures?

With a great, weird, leaping exultation he realized he was staring straight at Fransitart and Craumpalin, his old masters, the former stiff and steady, the latter fidgety and trying not to be. They had come, as they said, all the way from Boschenberg, even though it was the worst time for traveling. It was so utterly strange to see them there, his two worlds—old and new—overlapping. Rossamünd was struck dumb.

On seeing him, Craumpalin made to hurry down to greet him, yet was halted by a subtle hand of Fransitart's.

"Ah-ha, Lampsman Bookchild!" the Master-of-Clerks almost cried in disingenuous eagerness, clearly making a kindly show of it for Rossamünd's old masters. "You have visitors, see: your old wardens come to offer you succor in these darkest of days."

Rossamünd blinked at the man. "Thank you, sir," he managed.

"Hullo there, lad," said Master Fransitart huskily, his hard face made soft by the dampness in his soulful eyes. Rossamünd realized he had near forgotten the once-so-familiar face. "We were about on our ways to Wormstool but heard ye'd returned unexpected. We understand troubles are athwart yer hawse."

Nearly bursting into tears, Rossamünd wrestled with the knot in his throat. "H-Hallo, Master Fransitart. Hallo, Master Craumpalin."

" 'Ello, my boy." The old dispensurist grinned through his white beard.

"I have allowed them to join with you in the prentices' mess hall for a light supper before douse-lanterns." The Master-of-Clerks did a brilliant simulation of the kindly host.

Mercy of mercies, Podious Whympre let them leave promptly, and the promise of a late meal was actually honored. Left alone in his tiny accommodation, the reunited finally gave expression to truer feelings as Rossamünd threw himself into Fransitart's arms. He buried his face in the rough weave and old, unique scent of his dormitory master's cheap proofing. The mildly startled ex-mariner cooed, "There, there, me hearty" several times till the young lighter loosened his hold.

Craumpalin fussed and exclaimed, "Look at thee! All bones like a mouse in a miser's kitchen. What, don't they feed thee, lad?"

"Why are you here so soon?" Rossamünd's voice wobbled. "Your letter said you would not be here till . . . till . . ."

"Till now, lad," Fransitart said gently. "And we're actually

CRAUMPALIN

late. It took some organizin', but finally there was naught else for us to stay for, no marine society, no—no children to look after with 'em all now safe at other places . . ."

"And no Madam to employ us neither," Craumpalin added solemnly.

Rossamünd did not know what to say about Madam Opera. There had been little warmth between them. Still, she had done more than many ever would in the aid of the "undeserving," even if her labors lacked motherly sentiments.

"A fine woman," the dispensurist murmured. "Not the friendliest, but fine an' upstandin'!" He raised a mug in silent salute.

Fransitart did the same, and they bumped mugs together.

"And now we're loose-footed." Craumpalin chuckled stoutly. "Just like afore all this settling down to care for wee babbies. Roll on them old days!" He looked meaningfully to Fransitart, and Rossamünd became aware of a great weight of history between the two. Here, when he thought them so very familiar, they were revealing parts of themselves to which he was a stranger.

"Old days indeed." Fransitart frowned. "And thankee to yer Marshal fellow for our ales!"

"Don't be tricked by that trickster, Master Fransitart," Rossamünd warned. "He is the most cunning basket of them all."

His two old masters blinked at him in surprise.

"I do believe the lad's filling out his baldric nicely, Frans." Craumpalin winked. "Don't be troublin' thyself, Rossamünd, we know hay from straw; caught sight o' his colors right quick, di'n we, Frans?"

"That we did, Pin—a regular lamb-clad wolf is he."

"Aye aye, enough to make thy meat crawl," the old dispensurist agreed. He looked sourly at the food before them. "Blight and blast me, these wittles are uncommon bland!"

Rossamünd did not care how tasteless or unsatisfactory the food was, he was all a-joy to be safe with his masters. Yet while they ate together and the first enthusiasm receded a little, he became aware of an unfamiliar awkwardness.

Determined to enjoy their company, Rossamünd launched into the most full and hearty recounting of his life since leaving Madam Opera's. Describing the fight with the rever-man, he made direct connection with Swill, expressing his suspicions as part of the tale. The sorrow of the ruination of Wormstool flooded out like relief. He even talked a little of Freckle too; of the *Hogshead* and the wood near Wormstool; of the sparrows and Cinnamon, and especially of Europe and of Numps. His masters listened to it all in utter silence, a sign of respect, till he was done. It felt so good to have out with the whole tale, start to end and all the in betweens. When he had finished, a great weight had lifted from his shoulders.

"This Miss Europe lassie sounds like an uncommon remarkable woman," Craumpalin enthused. "I remember her mentioned in thy letters."

"I was alarmed to hear ye conjecturin' about yer surgeon bein' a dastardly, naught-good massacar!" said Fransitart.

"Oh, aye, Master Fransitart! And that Podious Whympre fellow is right in it with him!"

"What's the place comin' to?" Craumpalin growled. "Why ain't he in hand with the authorities then?"

"Doctor Crispus knows, and Mister Sebastipole and I reckon the old Lamplighter-Marshal does too, but there is nothing any of them think they can do about it." Rossamünd spoke quickly in his frustration. "About the only one who could do something is Miss Europe, and she says let them choke on their own rope."

"Always the way with them lahzars." Fransitart shook his head. "Crotchety and crosswards. Still, her notion has wisdom."

"What have we sent the lad into, Frans?" Craumpalin exclaimed. "We've got to get thee away from 'ere, Rossamünd!"

"And I would go with you, Master Pin, but that I made an oath to serve as a lighter and I've been paid the Billion."

"Aye, right ye are, Rossamünd." Fransitart smiled his approbation. "We raised ye 'onorable and that way ye should stay. It's a difficult task to stay faithful beyond endurance. We'll figure a loose for this impossible-seemin' knot yet."

"Aye aye!" Craumpalin added. "Might be possible to get thee an acquittance."

"An acquittance, Master Craumpalin?"

"Aye, an all-encompassing, all-official release from bound service. Prodigious handy."

Fransitart nodded. In a firm hush he said, "And did I hear ye right when ye spoke of that Freckle fellow that 'e's a bogle?"

Rossamünd felt a guilty leap in his belly. "Aye, he's . . . he's a—a glamgorn."

"Thee what?" Craumpalin exclaimed, spitting some ale.

"He helped me—" he added quickly, "more than once."

"Do others know ye 'ave been talkin' with this wee thing?" asked Fransitart. "To be talkin' civil with a bogle is a sedorning offense, Rossamünd. They can gibbet ye for that! I know we taught ye to use yer own intellectuals, but speakin' with a nasty bain't quite where I thought ye'd take me advice."

"Sorry, Master Fransitart," Rossamünd squeaked.

"Once said is done," the master said, sighing deeply. "Whatever happens to ye from here on, lad, Master Pin and I'll be right by ye."

"Too right!" agreed Craumpalin.

They continued their meal, Rossamünd losing his appetite to worry.

"Master Fransitart? Master Craumpalin?"

"Aye, lad," the two said together.

"Freckle has said some prodigious strange things to me."

"What manner o' things?"

"That he could tell what I am by my name."

Fransitart and Craumpalin looked blank at this.

"That people were my friends who would not be my friends if they knew . . . knew something," Rossamünd pushed on. "That I was safer with him. That he wanted to take me to the Duke of Sparrows."

The two old salts became glassy-eyed, the kind of expressionlessness that hid deeper workings.

"Such is one half of the trouble ye get from talkin' to bogles," Fransitart reflected soberly. "They rarely make sense."

"You've spoken to bogles, Master Fransitart?" Rossamünd peered at the man in astonishment.

"Aye, lad. And this is the first time I've said on it."

"Miss Verline once wrote me that you had something to tell me. Something not for letters but for ears alone." Rossamünd tried, thinking this must have been that *something*.

The old dormitory master went a gray color Rossamünd had never seen him go before. The two old salts swapped meaningful glances and the awkwardness, instead of dissolving, got worse.

"Well, that I did," Fransitart said slowly through a mouthful of salt pork, "and . . . and bless 'er for lettin' ye know."

"Are they the same strange and shocking things you wanted to tell me before I left?" Rossamünd pressed.

"Aye, they just might be." Fransitart chose his words carefully. "Be that as it might, though I have yer ears 'ere open and ready, I reckon now is not th' time for them ears to hear." He leaned in. "Ye know we've always sought yer best, aye, lad?"

"Aye, Master Fransitart."

"That Master Pin and I have worked only for what we reckoned as right for ye, aye?"

Craumpalin nodded in emphasis.

"Aye, sir." Rossamünd frowned, baffled.

"Well, trust us that when it's time for telling, then that'll be th' time we'll tell ye. Aye?"

Rossamünd nodded. He could not fathom what manner of despicable revelation his old master knew that made him so reluctant. Either way he knew he would not get any more on this from his old masters tonight.

The three ate and looked at each other uncomfortably for a time, but talk gradually returned to happy things: to tales of the old vinegaroons' long-gone adventures together at sea; to fond memories of marine society days—whatever it required to lift them and bring them close again. Rossamünd could have stayed forever in that cozy, happy womb of cheer and love. Anything to smother the growing dread.

29

A FALSE FALSEMAN

Imperial Secretary highest ranked of all the Haacobin Empire's bureaucrats; men and women of great influence and power, not so much because of their own rank, but because of the status of the ears and minds they have such ready access to—the senior ministers of the Emperor, and even the great man himself. The favor of an Imperial Secretary can be the making of you: disfavor your ruin. Though often of common birth, they are typically courted and feted by peers, especially the lowly ranked, and by gentry and magnates too, eager for some kind of advancement or boon. One does not strive to be an Imperial Secretary for dreams and hopes of reform, but for the sake of pure ambition and ego.

THE morning of the inquiry after a brief wash and short breakfast, Rossamünd was led to the offices of the subrogat-marshal between two foot-guards, like a prisoner. Fransitart and Craumpalin went with him, heads high and dignified, vinegaroons of tested worth in support of a worthy mate. They were recognized as interested parties on Rossamünd's side and as such were allowed to sit with him during the questioning.

Within Whympre's file Rossamünd was surprised to find more people gathered than he had expected. Dismayed, he scrutinized the lofty folk sitting at the far end of the table. It was a tribunal of men, ready and waiting, most ignoring the young lighter before them as inconsequential fluff. This tribunal comprised foremost the Master-of-Clerks, preeminent in the central position. Upon his right was indexer Witherscrawl, a pen ready in each hand and two ledgers open before him, acting as his assistant and glaring at Rossamünd for no good reason at all. Next to him was the General-Master-of-Labors assisted by the Surveyor-of-the-Works—two of Whympre's chief cronies. In the shadows of the far corner Rossamünd was startled to find that black-eyed wit, standing with his head bowed, not bothering to look at Rossamünd but rather peering darkly through brows to the corner behind the young lighter. Most astounding and disconcerting of all, sitting impassively at the Master-of-Clerks' left, was an Imperial Secretary, distinct in shaven head and coattails of clerical black. His role was as an independent eye, yet this was probably the very same esteemed personage under whose support the Master-of-Clerks had blossomed.

To the right of these—as Rossamünd saw it—on a chair to the side of the Board sat Surgeon Grotius Swill, the official adviser for any inquiries on physics, picking at lint on his breeches. Rossamünd knew this was rightly the task of Doctor Crispus, but he was not present. Halfway down the left side of the table sat Laudibus Pile, designated the inquisitor, and assisted by Fleugh, the under-clerk, already scribbling away in a ledger. Rossamünd's innards gave a painful, sick twist. Anyone without an intimate knowledge of the workings and the personalities of Winstermill would think this collection of officers and bureaucrats before them a worthy and impressive bunch. But from Rossamünd's view it was a tribunal stacked against his favor.

As Fransitart and Craumpalin took their seats behind him at the back of the room, Rossamünd caught a flash of deep magenta silk in the corner behind. He turned. There was Europe, legs crossed, an easy expression on her face; she was making a grand entrance into his life again, even while she simply sat, serene.

"Hello, little man," she said smoothly. "We meet in some of the most peculiar circumstances, don't you think?"

"But how—"

"Quiet, please," came the Master-of-Clerks' tight call.

Rossamünd's old masters looked from the fulgar to Rossamünd and back, Craumpalin nodding toward her as if to say, "Is that *her*?"

As Rossamünd took his place at the end of the table, there was a rustling and a hustle as the Lady Vey proceeded into the hall, attended by Dolours, a gloomy-looking Threnody and Charllette in full mottle-and-harness: all four women—even Threnody—wore wings and high hats and bright-patterned bossocks, a startling display of their unity. Threnody was a lighter no longer. With some fussing, the Lady Vey and Charllette took their places on the right side of the table opposite Laudibus Pile. With Dolours joining Fransitart, Craumpalin and Europe at the back, Threnody sat at Rossamünd's right hand. He tried to catch her eye, but she refused to look to him.

Clearing his throat loudly, Witherscrawl stood and called the room to order, introducing each member of the tribunal to the other, calling it collectively a "Board of Officers." He paid particular honors to the Imperial Secretary, naming him Secretary Imperial Scrupulus Sicus. The alert-looking official stood and gave a gracious bow to the Master-of-Clerks, to the Lady Vey, Dolours, and then, almost as an afterthought, to Europe, far down the other end of the room.

To Rossamünd it very much appeared like boys playing at "Lords and Magnates," a child's game of grandiloquence and false civility.

Introductions done, it was now Pile's turn. "Secretary Imperial Sicus. Marshal-Subrogat Whympre," he began, standing and pacing into the broad oblong gap between all the various tables. "We have done our preliminaries regarding the occurrence of the assault on His Serene Highness' Imperial Cothouse of Wormstool not two weeks gone. The purpose of this inquiry is to lay out what we have found, Mister Secretary, and derive conclusions for the satisfaction of all." He took a pause. "First I shall begin with the Lady Threnody of the Columbines of Herbroulesse, who served briefly with us as a lampsman 3rd class, m' lady." Pile bowed to Threnody, all snide and obscure sarcasm, his tone hovering expertly on the divide between deference and offense.

Threnody sat a little stiffer.

Pile began. "You were present at Wormstool Cothouse during the attack on the twenty-third of Herse, correct?"

"Yes." Threnody frowned. "I arrived back there after restocking a stone-harbor with Rossamünd and Splinteazle."

"By which you mean Lampsman 3rd Class Bookchild—present here, and Seltzerman 2nd Class Splinteazle—who sadly died at the attack of which we speak, yes?"

"Yes."

"How did Seltzerman 2nd Class Splinteazle die?" Pile rocked on his heels with deliberate gravity.

Threnody hesitated. "He was torn to death by a pack of brodchin and other nickers."

"And did you and Lampsman 3rd Class Bookchild do all you could to save him?"

Rossamünd shifted in his seat. *Of course we tried to save him!*

"Yes, leer, we did," Threnody returned coldly. "Rossamünd—"

"You mean Lampsman 3rd Class Bookchild," the Master-of-Clarks interrupted.

The girl went quiet for a moment, to prove her displeasure at the man's rudeness. "Yes, who would be Rossamünd." She waited to be corrected again. "He was in a better place to help Splinteazle and fought most vigorously, while I had my own gnashers to confront."

"And why did Lampsman 3rd Class Bookchild fail to save the unfortunate seltzerman?" Pile asked softly.

Are they trying to blame poor Splinteazle's end on me?

"He didn't *fail* at anything." Threnody scowled. "The

LAUDIBUS PILE

beasts were too quick, and overpowered Splinteazle before Rossamünd could help. He threw a blaste at the beasts to hinder them, but it was not enough to stop them all."

"So Lampsman 3rd Class Bookchild did his utmost, but Seltzerman 2nd Class Splinteazle was overwhelmed regardless, correct?"

"Correct."

"So how is it that this undergrown child"—the leer indicated Rossamünd—"was able to best a nicker that a hardened veteran seltzerman could not?"

Threnody shrugged. "He's stronger than he looks, I suppose."

"Stronger . . . ?" Laudibus Pile looked genuinely intrigued. "How do you know this?"

"I've seen him catch a butt of musket balls that should have crushed him flat," the girl returned easily, as if this was nothing.

"And . . ."

Threnody gave a small cough. "Because I watched him kill a monster. But that event is plain enough," she added quickly. "You don't need me to tell you of it."

Pile's shrewd eyes narrowed. "Indeed." Apparently careless, he picked at some spot or mark upon his soutaine. "Yet tell me . . . m'lady, do not these events strike you as unusual, almost impossible?" The leer looked piercingly at her with his all-seeing eyes.

Threnody cast an anxious glance toward her mother.

The Lady Vey was sitting more stiffly than ever, looking

not at her daughter but directing her brittle gaze at the wall between two windows.

"I suppose they do," the girl said in a small voice Rossamünd had never heard her use before.

"You *suppose* they do? Hmm . . . Is what she says true, Lampsman Bookchild?" Pile asked, looking to his palm as if the question were a trifling thing.

The young lighter shied. "Ah . . .Y-yes . . ."

Murmurs from the observers.

Rossamünd did not know what else to say. What was the use in dissembling? With this false-hearted falseman his questioner, who would people believe? Such a fellow in command of a room could do anything with the truth; with no other telltale present, no one could credibly challenge him.

"Of Lady Threnody's part in the battle, her success is clear: a wit, however young, fighting off a beastie is perfectly proper, and this young peer should be commended as the bravest and best of her clave. Maybe it is only me who is bemused by this, but elucidate for me—if you are able, Lampsman 3rd Class—how a mere lad of your slight stature manages to defeat a man's share of nickers! How does one so small win through unharmed, where a cothouse-full of the Emperor's own was bested and slain?"

Rossamünd had no answer. It was a fair question: he wondered it himself.

"I agree with you, Master Leer," interposed the Master-of-Clerks, "that this is highly irregular."

"Thank you, sir." The leer spoke smoothly, in an even, convincing voice. "Give your answer, Lampsman."

Rossamünd obeyed. "I-I don't rightly know, sir."

Pile seemed to be smirking. "M'lady Threnody of Herbroulesse, is there anything else about Lampsman Bookchild's manner you would describe as irregular?"

Despite the firm set of her jaw, Threnody went pale.

"There is nothing to be hidden here, m'lady," Laudibus Pile purred, his disconcerting eyes daring a contradiction to his honeyed voice. "This is but an inquest into the whys and wherefores, for the sake of record."

The calendar looked to her mother again.

The Lady Vey just glowered meaningfully.

Threnody looked at Rossamünd again, her expression confused and intention unclear.

"*And,* m'lady?" Pile persisted, completely undaunted.

With a deep breath she said, "He wears a bandage soaked in a kind of nullodor around himself all the time."

Pile pursed his lips. "Surely an odd and unnecessary habit?"

"He does it only for the sake of his old foundling masters," Threnody insisted.

"I see." The leer set his cunning attention on Fransitart and Craumpalin. "How the count of oddities increases."

The two old salts stared back angrily.

Swill shifted in his seat stroking his mustachios thoughtfully, and regarded Rossamünd and the two retired vinegaroons closely.

"Is it not *also* true—as the report I have declares," Laudibus Pile continued, looking like a hungry dog, "that this young fellow *refused* to be puncted even after such a great feat as done at the Imperial Cothouse of Wormstool? Would you not also call such refusal—so dishonoring the memories of the fallen—odd, my dear?"

Threnody's mouth stayed shut. With a brief glare at the leer, she fixed her attention stubbornly on the wall before her.

"I can see that you know it to be very much the case." Pile tapped his cheek just below one of his red-blue orbits. "So you might as well just speak out those things you cannot hide . . . Or may I take it that by your silence"—Pile scratched his nose daintily to hide his subtle, goading expression—"you think it right for the courageous dead to be dishonored?"

The Lady Vey bridled, her seat moving with a clatter of chair legs on hard, polished floor. "I will not tolerate my daughter's being accused of dishonor, sir!"

Pile turned his cold, unnerving eyes to the august. "Maybe she might be free of such an accusation if she ceased hedging for this *fine fellow*"—he pointed dismissively to Rossamünd—"and told this esteemed panel fully what I can clearly tell she knows!"

"Have a care, sir," the Lady Vey warned, soft and low. "Now speak, my dear," she demanded of her daughter, "and let this ridiculous fiasco come to its end!"

Threnody darted a look to her mother. "There is nothing more to say, Mother," she said, a darkly victorious look growing in her eye. "Rossamünd is no more odd than any other in this *ridiculous* inquiry."

Laudibus Pile puffed his chest and lifted his haughty head. "*I* am a thrice-proven telltale in the Emperor's Service," he declaimed with quiet, frosty arrogance, "under charge of our Serene Highness' most humble minister, the Marshal-Subrogat. My eyes see true, and I say to you, young peerlet, that that is an utter and thorough-going *lie!*"

The Lady Vey rose, crying her disapproval. "How dare you, sir! That is twice now you slander her; there shall not be three! I will not hesitate to use my privileges to make my displeasure felt on you, leer. Blast your eyes to flinders! If my daughter says there is no more, then—by the foul depths—that is the end of the matter!"

"If you wish your daughter free from slander, madam," Pile seethed, his façade failing, "then you should have schooled her better in honesty!"

"Please, Laudibus!" interjected the Master-of-Clerks. There was genuine alarm in his voice, yet that predatory look never left his eye. "I am most positive this fine young peeress would not dream of soiling her clave's honor by obfuscating truths or uttering falsehoods in a properly convened Imperial Inquest. Our good Lady Vey has indeed taught her too well." He smiled winningly at the august. "Is this not correct, Madam August?"

The Lady Vey looked at him proudly, her own chin in

the air. She cleared her throat ever so softly—a subtle, female threat.

"My exulted madam," Pile said with wounded dignity,
bowing most humbly, "I merely seek the truth, and if my
zeal for it has offended your person I apologize."

Imperial Secretary Sicus raised a hand. "Falseman Pile,
I thank you," the vaunted clerk declared regally. "You have
sought your trail as far as it might take you, but I warn you
now to let it go. We cannot have these gracious ladies harried so."

Rossamünd heard Threnody give a scornful sniff.

"Most Honorable Secretary!" The leer faced him and
clasped his hands piously. "One might be tempted to disregard any of these on their own as either minor offenses
or just an idiosyncrasy, sir. Yet when so many irregularities
find themselves embodied in one soul, my intuitions and
insights as a falseman start to tell a darker story." Laudibus
Pile pointed to Rossamünd. "There he sits, Master Secretary,
with his face so po, but is it possible this solemn young toad
hides a wicked treachery? Is it possible that this apparent
servant of the Emperor is in league with the nickers, that
he survived because of this league, and not through some
act of individual prowess? That is why he wears a nullodor
all the time—to mark himself out to his nickerly friends!
He killed them only for a show, and this is why he refused
a mark! I say to you, Master Secretary, surely this one is
a wicked sedorner! Surely it is he who, with his monster

friends, orchestrated the attack on Wormstool! *Surely* that is why he survived!"

Rossamünd gritted his teeth against a sudden fury within. So this was their game—to accuse him a sedorner and shuffle him off to the gallows. He almost sprang to his feet.

"So I must ask you, most honored Master Secretary," the leer said, bowing low and long, "that I forthwith be allowed to examine Lampsman 3rd Class Bookchild, so getting to the root of this tragedy."

Imperial Secretary Sicus stood, hand still lifted in placation. "This is a *most* serious charge. It is most persuasively put, and I thank you, Mister Pile; yet I believe I shall continue the inquiry from here."

The leer bowed, his mien unreadable.

The Master-of-Clerks did not look best pleased, and surreptitiously gave an unhappy look to the leer.

Secretary Sicus turned his powerful attention to Rossamünd. "What is your answer to this charge, Lampsman 3rd Class? You have been accused a sedorner, lad. What say you?"

Before the young lighter could open his mouth, Grotius Swill, calm and calculating, stood, a hand raised. "If I may interject on proceedings, good sirs!" the surgeon inquired politely. "I have been listening now to these most troubling details, and I declare to you esteemed officers of the table that a possibility yet more disturbing has revealed itself to my thoughts. I ask your indulgence to pursue my own inquiries." He bowed low to the collected personages seated at the long table.

The Master-of-Clerks nodded, all pomp and smugness, covering his surprise at the interruption. "Indeed, dear surgeon, you are our eminent physical man here. Let us take a brief recess for breaths to catch and minds to clear."

The room was emptied but for Rossamünd. Even Europe went, leaving him to worry alone on what terrible revelations might follow. Pile had already claimed he was a sedorner—a claim, in truth, he could not deny. What other crimes was Swill to lay upon him?

QUO GRATIA

libermane potive used to prevent the cruor of a monster from clotting too quickly as it is stored in a bruicle. Useful as this is, it also affects the quality of the blood, thinning it and making the cruorpunxis it is used for pale, less distinct. Therefore libermane is used only when teratologists believe they are more than a couple of days' journey from a punctographist. Another function of libermane is its application on swords, knives and other blades of war, to make a wound flow more than it ought, though by the Accord of Menschen this practice is deemed unacceptable in modern conflict.

H ONORIUS Ludius Grotius Swill peered about at the many personages who had reconvened in the clerk-master's file. "It may be that when I first declare the notion that has occurred to me," he began, "you shall think it a mad genius-leap, so I ask you, gracious Officers of the Board, to please bear with me. The full play of my thoughts *will* clarify if I am given the time." He cleared his throat histrionically, giving Rossamünd an odd look from the corner of his eye. "Officers of the Board, paritous inquisitor, peers, ladies, gentlemen, I have listened this whole morning to the witness of these two young Imperial servants—listened long and keen—and what I have heard troubles me greatly. However, one question vexes me over all others. What truly does all this evidence point to, and how is it such a runty . . . *lad* might do such feats as he has done?" He pondered a moment, a fine act to focus people's attention upon him. "In view of an answer, if I may I would like to address the whole room with this question: how many of you have heard of Ingébiargë? Perhaps you know her as Biargë the Beautiful?"

The Master-of-Clerks and Scrupulus Sicus, the Imperial Secretary, nodded.

The Lady Vey made a face as if to say, *What does it matter if I have or have not?*

No one else indicated either way.

Rossamünd knew of Ingébiargë. Craumpalin had told him of her more than once. She was meant to be a cannibalistic woman living in the remotest coasts of the Hagenlands who, by forgotten habilistics, had kept herself alive many thousands of years and made prey of any who passed too near. Such an unnatural length of life had apparently twisted her: she was gray-skinned, with red and yellow eyes more terrible than any leer's.

"Some of you might dismiss this Ingébiargë as a fiction, but any vinegaroon who has sailed east beyond the Mare Periculum through the Beggar Sea, or harbored in the roadstead off the Stander Lates near Dereland's western shores, will tell you she is a very real and very factual danger. If we could ask a mariner of one thousand years gone of her, he too would give the same ghastly report."

The normally indulgent Master-of-Clerks, most likely aware of Secretary Sicus sitting immediately to his right, started to show impatience at this bizarre divagation.

The surgeon lifted his hands appeasingly. "Now please, sirs, attend to me, I do have a point. Ingébiargë, the great abomination, the shame of the Hagenards, known as an ever-living monstrous everyman—or woman." He corrected himself with a peculiar look to the calendars and Europe. "Yet she is not the only one. The obscurest corners of history will reveal the occurrence of other such abominations, though most, when discovered, were destroyed before they could become the terrible canker Ingébiargë is to southern shipping to this day. For this Biargë is not some clever skold, as some might reckon, but rather a manikin—a monster in the shape and form of a person, and as such more assuredly an abomination."

Fransitart had become a wan gray.

Craumpalin had a haunted glimmer in his eye.

"Pray, Surgeon Swill, you must bring us to your point of view, sir—the morning runs long," purred the Master-of-Clerks, a hint of chill in his voice, though he never let slip his patient façade.

"Most certainly, Marshal-Subrogat." The surgeon bowed a third time to the Officers of the Board and went on as if he had not been interrupted. "But how can such a wicked abomination happen? I see the question clear on your corporate faces: how can a monster be found in the form of an everyman? As you are all well familiar, we know so little of the where and the why of the monsters, of how they perpetuate themselves. What we do know is that most teratologica survive so long they can be considered—as the short generations of men reckon it—to live forever. Yet the monsters *do* replace their numbers. We *know* some repeat themselves, budding like so many trees, dropping bits of themselves to grow into replicas of the original. This can be most commonly observed in the kraulschwimmen of the mares or the vicious brodchin of the wildest lands such as the Ichormeer or Loquor."

Here Swill paused, took a breath.

An awful, sick sensation was blossoming in Rossamünd's gut.

Everyone expectant, the surgeon poured himself some wine from a sideboard, drank it all and continued.

"But what we have never seen is the creation work of the ancient gravid slimes, those places said to have been the nurseries of the earliest monsters, the eurinines—the first monster-lords—and used by them in turn to bring forth the lesser types of the theroid races." As he went on, a quaver of fervent enthusiasm entered the surgeon's voice. "Some of you might even know the history that was before history, the rumors of the beginnings; that these eurinines were granted by the clockwork of the universe to be able to put forth their threwd and make the muds fertile. Heated by the sun, worked on by the threwd, the very ground was made womblike and would pop to bring forth from the foul cesspits of the cosmos many of the worst and most notorious of the monsters that still stalk this groaning world today."

Rossamünd did have some small understanding of the things said, but he had never heard the most ancient of histories put so directly. If he had not been in such a great anxiety, he would have eagerly listened to Swill wax learned like this for hours.

Wiping his mouth, Grotius Swill took up the cause once again. "Now these gravid muds continued to be used by the monster-lords, even through the rise and fall of ages, whereby they take the remains of some fallen nicker and bury them in the slimy womb-earth. After a time this spews forth some vital regeneration of those parts, another full-fledged monster to terrorize the homes of men." He looked about shrewdly.

Not one person moved. Swill had intrigued them all.

"But here is the rub, you see. The movements of the races of men and tribes of theroid, all those risings and fallings, have left many threwdishly fecund places untended by their monster-lords, deserted but still oozing with foul potential. Yet unattended and unchecked by a eurinine's will, these most threwdish of places we seldom if ever dare to navigate can still produce life, making strange beasties of whatever creatures might fetch up and die there. This abominable process we learned few call abinition, and this, lords, ladies, gentlemen"—Swill raised a salient finger into the air—"*this* is how Ingébiargë was made: a woman, some woman, nobody knows who, three thousand years ago perhaps, dies in one of these gravid places and falls, her remains swallowed by the hungry ooze. Sometime later out

SURGEON
GROTIUS SWILL

comes—what?" The surgeon shrugged and stared at his audience expectantly.

Expressions were blank, except Fransitart and Craumpalin: both were gray-faced, as ill-looking as Rossamünd felt. Despairing, Rossamünd looked to Europe. The fulgar was not paying him any mind, her astute, raptorial gaze fixed on the surgeon.

"Is it human? Is it monster? This thing sprung from the muds. We do not know for certain," Swill pressed on, unaware of this calculating regard. "What we do know is that what is 'born'—for the need of a better term—is reformed from the debris of human matter, *birthed* from the threwd, a wicked repeat of some lost and departed person. This we call a manikin, and whatever it might be, this reconstituted creature is certainly not human. I commend to you that if it is not human, then rationally it must be monster, and even if it is not, a manikin is not something we want walking free among us." He paused and looked about the room with evident academic pleasure. "In the case we have before us today, things, I fear, go much deeper than simple sedonition. Rather, events must have proceeded upon similar particulars as I have just related. In some blightedly threwdish dell in the hinterlands of Hergoatenbosch, some poor lost fellow dies and falls. His remains are sucked up by the mud and slowly, by action of heat and threwd, maybe over centuries, they are remade, an abominable simulacrum birthed from the loam; another manikin. And what becomes of it? This manikin is somehow found and taken to a wastrel-house in the city to be raised as an everyman. Yet it is, in fact, *not* one of us at all."

There was a baffled pause, people's faces intent or dumbly wondering.

"Now, ladies and gentlemen, we all know the name Rossamünd—a sweet and apt name for some lovely, cherished girl . . . and, as it happens, the unfortunate and completely inapt name of this young lighter here"—Swill looked about keenly—"but who of you has heard of a rossamünderling?"

Vacant faces met him.

"None of you?" The surgeon's satisfaction was evident. "I am not surprised; such a word has never appeared on any of the usual taxonomists' lists. I, with all my reading, had not encountered such a word—until recently, that is, a happy accident of my persistent study. How does that interest us? Just so: Ingébiargë is a rossamünderling. All manikins are. You see, after much esoteric study I discovered in the most obscure of texts a most fascinating word: *rossamünderling*. It means 'little rose-mouth' or, more vulgarly, 'little pink lips.' More astonishingly yet, this word is a name the monsters of the east have for manikins. *Rossamünderling*—an ünterman in the appearance of an everyman. Rossamünd." The man now pivoted on his heel, spitting in his passion, and pointed ferociously at Rossamünd. "For that is my point! That you— *YOU*, young Rossamünd whatever-you-are—you are that mud-born abomination! You are a manikin! You are a rossamünderling! A thrice-blighted wretchling in human guise!"

There was a great shout of disbelief, of horror, from almost every throat in the room. Threnody jerked away from him, staring at him in dismay.

Rossamünd could barely breathe. He did not know whether to laugh or cry or shout down the surgeon's foolishness. Mastering himself, he stood and looked to his old masters, and something in their eyes struck him more than any preposterous accusation of some strutting massacar. For their faces declared more eloquently than explanations that the words of Grotius Swill, secret maker of gudgeons and clandestine traitor to the Empire, might possibly be true.

Europe's gaze was narrow and inscrutable as she peered at Rossamünd.

What does she think?

Laudibus Pile sneered, stroking his chin in wicked satisfaction.

The Master-of-Clerks actually managed to look stunned, and the Imperial Secretary with him.

"Yet if you need proofs of my logic, I simply quote this fine young peeress," Swill pursued, "the daughter of the august of our very own faithfully serving calendars."

The Lady Vey sat erect, her face hard and supercilious with hidden distaste, not giving a hint whose side she was for. She turned this brittle gaze to her daughter, and Threnody dropped her head, either unwilling or unable to look at Rossamünd.

"This fine girl speaks of his great destroying strength," Swill continued, "a bizarre aberration that immediately piqued my curiosity. Then she explains of his habit of always hiding his smell behind a nullodor. *Why would one perpetually wear a nullodor,* I asked myself, *when one spends one's life safe in the world of men?* And the answer came: unless you were trying to hide that you were not a man at all!" The surgeon said this last with a very pointed look at Rossamünd. "And *of course* you did not want to be marked with the blood of your own kind," he cried, "for not only would the idea be repugnant, you *know* that on your flesh a dolatramentis *cannot show, for one monster's blood will surely not make a mark on another!*"

The young lighter's thoughts reeled, and he blinked in dismay at the surgeon's accusations.

"More so," Swill pursued, "if what the august's daughter says is true, then this one's masters have conspired with it to hide its nature—a foul and deplorable act of outramour as has ever been documented!"

Fransitart and Craumpalin looked hard at the surgeon and refused to be cowed.

The Master-of-Clerks stared squarely at Rossamünd, a conquering glimmer in the depths of the man's studied gaze. "What do you have to say for this, Lampsman 3rd Class?"

Rossamünd felt the blood leave his face and sweat prickle on his brow and neck. He could not let these puzzle-headed fallacies pass unchallenged. But what could he say to such outlandish poppycockery?

"Tell me, surgeon," Sicus asked firmly, "how by the remotest here and vere do you propose to substantiate such a bizarre accusation? This young lighter as a sedorner is a charge I am prepared to hear out, but a monster who looks like a person! This is a *very* long line you plumb, sir. How do you intend to substantiate this obscure conjecturing?"

Swill balked, momentarily stumped, but rallied, a solution clearly blossoming in his thoughts. "If you would but indulge me just a little further, we could but take a little of this—this one's blood; someone could be marked, and in a fortnight or so the proof would be there. Only a monster's blood will make a mark on a person if pricked into the skin."

Threnody gasped.

Sicus and Whympre and his staff were thunderstruck, and the Lady Vey too.

"I'll not let ye cut 'im!" Fransitart cried, half standing but held back by Craumpalin.

Europe still did not move or comment, and the black-eyed wit kept his heavy-lidded scrutiny ever fixed on her.

To the universal surprise of the room, it was Rossamünd who spoke in Swill's support. "Take my blood," he said firmly, not quite believing what was coming out of his own mouth. Yet he was resolute. "How else can I show that this . . . that Mister Swill is wrong?"

"How else indeed? Bravely said, young fellow!" Swill enthused. "And to make it a truly impartial test, it would be best for one member each of the interested parties to be marked. In that way none can accuse the other of fabricating a result."

"This is most irregular, surgeon," Secretary Sicus cautioned.

"A serious and far-fetched charge has been laid at this young lighter, sirs," the Lady Vey interrupted. "I say let a little blood be taken from him and the poor boy's innocence and heritage be established."

"As you wish it, m'lady." Sicus nodded and made a dignified bow.

This sealed it.

Swill chose himself to represent the Empire and the lighters. Fransitart quickly offered himself on Rossamünd's behalf.

A small dish, a small bottle, a guillion and an orbis were called for.

Grimacing, Rossamünd held out a finger, profoundly aware of the trust he was suddenly placing in a man he considered the blackest of all black habilists.

From the small bottle, Swill dabbed the young lighter's fingertip with a thin, straw-yellow fluid, then dipped the guillion-tip in the same.

"This is libermane," he explained to the room. "To make the sanguine humours flow easy."

The surgeon deftly punctured Rossamünd's fingertip with the guillion and more blood than Rossamünd expected began to drip out.

Feeling stupidly giddy, the young prentice let many drops of his blood splicker into the dish to form a little puddlet there.

"That will be sufficient," Swill said when a coin-sized

puddle of it had collected in the dish. With professional regard, he automatically passed Rossamünd a pledget to stanch the tiny wound.

"Hark ye, clever-cogs! I shall go first," Fransitart insisted, looking very much as if he wanted to pound the surgeon to stuff. With a look of deep revulsion he removed his wide-collared day-coat and, rolling up the sleeve of his shirt, presented the inside of his wrist. "Right there'll do fine, ye bookish blackguard," he growled malignantly at Swill.

The surgeon swallowed nervously. "As you wish, Jack tar," he answered and, taking up the orbis, dipped the guillion in Rossamünd's blood and began to tap away on the old dormitory master's blotched skin. Gripping the pledget to his finger, Rossamünd could not watch, and he looked up at the great antlers of the Herdebog Trought splayed above them. Even in these strange circumstances he still felt revulsion at the tap-tap-tapping of orbis on needle.

Swill seemed to have barely made a start when Europe stirred. She stood and stepped directly to Rossamünd.

The black-eyed wit straightened, looking ready to fight.

Distracted by Europe's action, the surgeon hesitated then stopped his tapping.

Standing by the young lighter's side, Europe looked with serene confidence at the powerful men gathered before her. "This has all been greatly diverting," she said with a tone of mild amusement, "but I must now say, gentlemen and strigs, that it is time Rossamünd and I were going. His tenure with the lighters has, I think it is safe to say, come to an end." She touched him lightly on the shoulder. "Come along, Rossamünd."

"Stay where you are, Lampsman!" The Master-of-Clerks stood in turn.

Rossamünd hesitated out of martial habit.

"You cannot take him, madam," Whympre contradicted disdainfully. "This is a court-martial of our Most Just Emperor, trying one of the Emperor's own servants, and *we*," he said, turning a haughty glance to the Imperial Secretary sitting officiously by, "we shall deal with him according to our own right rule."

"Don't come at me with that sneer in your nostrils, sir!" Europe warned. "You may have your dour Haacobin friend there"—she nodded to the Imperial Secretary—"but he is still just a clerk—whomever he might know, and you *and he* are together beneath me by more degrees than you have fingers or toes collected."

The Imperial Secretary began to rise, declaiming loudly, "You flagitious shrew! How dare you interrupt an Imperial proceeding while—"

"You, Master Secretary, tread dangerous turfs!" Europe's eyes went wide in indignation. "You are addressing Europa, Duchess-in-waiting of Naimes, Peer of the Haacobin Empire, Marchess of the Vewe, shareward of the Soutland states, descendant of Euodice—speardame of the immortal Idaho, and of Eutychë her granddaughter—spurn to Dido, and the Branden Rose, terror to man and nicker alike, and I *will* dare, sir, and I *do!*"

The Imperial Secretary opened his mouth to remonstrate, but Europe spoke him down. "If *that* will not silence you, impudent wretch, then I say simply QGU and now the matter is done!"

QGU? Rossamünd stared. *Quo gratia!* Europe was using her ancient right as a peer to overrule any court. She was using it for *him* . . .

The Lady Vey glowered at the fulgar scornfully.

The black-eyed wit took a step forward, but was stopped by a brusque wave of Secretary Sicus' hand.

"Good day to you, Master Secretary," she concluded. "*You* are at perfect liberty to go tell of my wielding of this venerable privilege to your cunning masters and all your fellow glaucologs up in Clementine, babbling away and filling the world with words; it will do you little good. For if it is a trading of status and influence you seek, I come ready prepared."

To this not even the Imperial Secretary had a fit or contrary answer.

"Come, Rossamünd, we go." The fulgar took him by the hand.

Rossamünd glanced quickly at the thunderstruck Board and fumbled the chair out from the table, tripping on one of the legs in his haste. Without a word needing to be said, Fransitart took a pledget from the table, rolled down his sleeve, put his day-coat back on, and he and Craumpalin followed after. The rest of the room were too stunned to act. Heading not too briskly down the passages of the manse—far be it for Europe to hurry—Craumpalin handed Fransitart a handkerchief to wrap the puncting-wound upon his wrist.

"We can't thank ye enough, my lady!" the old dormitory master gruffed.

"Don't wax too grateful, old salt," Europe returned tartly, more intent on exit than gratitude. "I had not intended on rescuing the boy's entire staff, but you may come if you wish!"

"We wish it, madam," Fransitart said quickly. "We'll not leave our boy to the world's scarce mercies. Carry on—we shall get Rossamünd's dunnage," the ex-dormitory master insisted. "We shall be returnin' presently!" Before any argument could be made he hurried off, no sign of any limp, Craumpalin close behind, both disappearing up the stairs to their temporary quarters.

Rossamünd hesitated with his old masters' departure, feeling a strange conflict. The fulgar detained him with a touch to his sleeve. "Stay, little man. You are safest with me!"

They were out of the manse and walking the gravel drive to the coach yard when the Master-of-Clerks and the rest of the Board finally followed, gathering on the steps before the manse. Imperial Secretary Scrupulus Sicus gave a great cry, hollering for the day-watch to "descend and prevent these blighted rascals from escaping!"

Some haubardiers from the wall responded and hurried down from the battlements to the Mead to cautiously bar the way. They were clearly uneasy to be confronting a lahzar. Europe stopped before them and turned to face her pursuers.

The black-eyed wit stepped forward, grim satisfaction clear.

"Cease where you are, Madam Fulgar," the Master-of-Clerks decried boldly. "Whatever the surgeon's wild speculations, there is still the question of this lad's alleged sedonition to be answered for!"

"Tilly-fally, sir!" Europe returned with a sneer. "Bestir me not with your lip-laboring. If talking with a nicker makes one a sedorner, then I would be guilty almost every other day! Stand your men aside! Do *not* force me to use more physical arguments!"

The black-eyed wit hesitated.

Laudibus Pile snarled and glared.

Podious Whympre puffed himself up, spluttered and even cursed, but did not continue his intervention.

The day-watch haubardiers happily stepped aside even before the order to do so was on the clerk-master's lips.

Among them Rossamünd could see Swill at the clerk-master's back, wrapping his own arm with a bandage, staring with inordinate, slow-blinking fascination at him.

Fransitart and Craumpalin returned bearing all their baggage. Somehow Doctor Crispus was with them, bearing some part of the load.

"Clear the way, thank you!" the doctor demanded, pushing through to the young lighter and the fulgar.

With some jostling and snarls, Fransitart, Craumpalin and the doctor were allowed to pass and Europe led them and Rossamünd away from the flabbergasted crowd. A lentum rolled up for them—Europe's own hired carriage.

The Lady Vey and her calendars now emerged from the manse and stepped about Whympre's party and out on to the gravel drive. With profound calm Europe and the Lady Vey regarded each other as they passed. Threnody stood alongside her mother, safe among her calendine sisters. She stared at Rossamünd with inscrutable intensity, the tracks of tears on her cheeks.

This difficult, abrasive witting girl had stayed true through it all, and Rossamünd wanted to thank her, to embrace her. Yet dazed, and baffled by the sudden turn of his fortunes, he remained close by Europe.

"Greetings, Branden Rose," said the august.

"And to you, Syntychë," Europe returned icily.

There seemed a self-satisfied gleam in the Lady Vey's steady gaze. "We had heard you lost that foul fellow Licurius in a theroscade. How sad you must have been."

Europe's top lip twitched. Her iciness became a grim freeze. "Yes, I was," she said, ever so quietly—and that was all. She let herself be handed on to their transport by the - side-armsman.

Desperate to leave this miserable fortress, Rossamünd mounted the carriage step. "Good-bye, Rossamünd," he heard Threnody call as she was borne away to the coach yard. He was about to cry a farewell of his own when Doctor Crispus suddenly stepped before him, filling his view.

"Fare-you-well, young Bookchild." The good physician extended his hand for a manly shake. "It has been a pleasure to have one of your quality serve here. May you and your masters," he said, looking about the cabin, "find kinder stops along your road."

Rossamünd swatted away tears. "Good-bye, Doctor Crispus! Good-bye!"

"Come with us, good doctor," Europe offered, standing on the top step as Fransitart and Craumpalin hastily loaded their goods. "Though I do not know you, the boy trusts you and that says much for me. A man of physics standing ready by is always an asset."

The physician nodded a bow. "I thank you, madam—your offer has its merits. But I would remain, for there are others here who need my care yet."

Rossamünd knew Crispus was speaking of Numps. Poor, poor Numps hiding somewhere below them in the dank ancient cellars and pipes. Rossamünd was suddenly sharply aware he would probably never see the glimner again.

"I know you will keep care of him, Doctor," he said low and fast. "Tell him good-bye from me if you see him."

Luggage stowed, Fransitart and Craumpalin clambered aboard with admirable activity in such aged fellows.

"Leave now." Crispus slammed the door of the coach shut. "Each moment makes tensions thicker." He called to the driver, "Drive hard, sir, and safe! Get these good people to better places!"

A crack of whip and shout of starting and the carriage shot forward. Rossamünd held his breath, not quite believing he was actually winning free of this place. He caught one last confusing sight of Threnody staring after the departing carriage before they were through those mighty bronze gates. Only when the lentum clattered off the Serid Approach and on to the Gainway did Rossamünd manage to breathe evenly again. As Craumpalin more properly bandaged Fransitart's puncted arm, Rossamünd looked to his old master. Fransitart turned his gaze to him. Deep conflicts showed there, old sorrows and new, a great agonized confusion. It was the nearest Rossamünd had seen his old dormitory master come to tears, and it terrified him more than any anger could.

"Master Fransitart?" Rossamünd reached out with his hand. *Don't cry . . .* he wanted to say, but did not know how. A thousand thoughts collided. *Who am I? Is what Swill says true?* And as he looked again at his dormitory master, a small frightened voice, right down in his most inward place . . . *Do you still love me?*

"Don't ye fret, lad," the old salt said with a determined smile, taking Rossamünd's hand, "we'll fathom ye out of all this." The dormitory master looked to Europe.

The fulgar sat straight and proud, staring out of the opposite window, taking small notice of the man.

"Listen to thy ol' Master Frans," Craumpalin encouraged

as he finished his mending. "He and I 'ave been in worse dilemmas. We'll see thee right."

Yet as Rossamünd smiled to reassure the old dispensurist, it was only face-deep. The doubts persisted. *Am I truly some kind of half-done monster? Am I a manikin? A rossamünderling? It's like my stupid name . . .* And a worse thought: *Have Fransitart and Craumpalin been lying to me all these years?* His smile failed altogether. *WHO AM I?* his soul cried. In a small voice he dared to ask, "Master Fransitart, who am I?"

The confusion in the old vinegaroon's eyes deepened. His wrinkled lips pressed and squeezed together as, for the first time Rossamünd had ever known, Fransitart was struck speechless.

In the aching muteness Europe turned and looked at Rossamünd with a mild expression. "Why, little man," she said, "you're my factotum."

. . . And with the sun just reaching its meridian, the carriage clattered down the Gainway, bearing him, his one-time foundlingery masters and the mercurial fulgar to Silvernook, then perhaps to High Vesting and unguessable ends.

FINIS DUOLIBRIS
[END BOOK TWO]

EXPLICARIUM

BEING A GLOSSARY OF TERMS
& EXPLANATIONS INCLUDING
APPENDICES

NOTES ON THE EXPLICARIUM

A word set in *italics* indicates that you will find an explanation of that word also in the Explicarium; the only exceptions to this are the names of *rams* and other vessels, and the titles of books, where it is simply a convention to put these names in italics.

"See (entry in) Book One" refers the reader to the Explicarium in *Foundling,* Monster Blood Tattoo, Book One by D.M. Cornish.

PRONUNCIATION

ä is said as the "ar" sound in "**a**sk" or "c**a**r"

æ is said as the "ay" sound in "h**ay**" or "**eigh**t"

ë is said as the "ee" sound in "scr**ea**m" or "b**ee**p"

é is said as the "eh" sound in "sh**e**d" or "**e**veryone"

ö is said as the "er" sound in "l**ear**n" or "b**ur**n"

ü is said as the "oo" sound in "w**oo**d" or "sh**ou**ld"

~ine at the end of pronouns is said as the "een" sound in "b**ean**" or "s**een**"; the exception to this is "Clèmentine," which is said as the "eyn" sound in "f**ine**" or "m**ine**."

Words ending in e, such as "Verline" or "Grintwoode": the e is not sounded.

SOURCES

In researching this document the scholars are indebted to many sources. Of them all the following proved the most consistently sourced:

The Pseudopædia

Master Matthius' Wandering Almanac: A Wordialogue of Matter, Generalisms & Habilistics

The Incomplete Book of Bogles

Weltchronic

The Book of Skolds

& extracts from the *Vadè Chemica*

A

abinition spontaneous generation of life from muds and clays warmed by the sun in powerfully threwdish places. Such soils are called fecund or abinitive muds, or in the uncommon vernacular, life-loams. Some more extreme theories hold that these life-loams, these dipherbiosës (literally "seats of life") can exist even in the heart of an urban park or rural lumber plantation, that where plants flourish (even domesticated varieties) *threwd* can concentrate in boggy dells and the ground become fecund. When known beyond the esoteric provinces of the teratological habilists this concept is generally rejected as being too terrible to contemplate.

Accord of Menschen, the ~ what we would think of as an "international" agreement upon the rules of conduct in warfare, standardizing procedures of victory, surrender, the treatment of the loser and of neutrals; a reratification of a much older document known as the Usages of War, a set of dogma governing behavior to foes, prisoners, noncombatants, and the wounded and infirm during war. Though it was primarily drawn up in reference to land warfare, naval officers will also cite it, though they have their own accord— the Articles of Conduct; however, this is not as comprehensive in its statutes.

"ad captandum vulgus" a *Tutin* political term literally meaning "toward courting the crowd" but used more in the sense of doing things to please the people, to inspire confidence.

alembant(s) broadly speaking, *scripts* that alter the biology of a person, such as the washes that make a *leer's* eyes. Specifically, the term can be used to refer to the *potives* taken by *lahzars* to keep their surgically introduced organs from vaoriating (spasming). The best known of these is Cathar's Treacle. See *lahzar* in Book One.

almonder assistant to a *dispensurist* or a skold, who does much of the fetching and carrying and reordering and other less glamorous work.

alternats, the ~ catch-all name for the secondary or subcapitals of the *Haacobin Empire,* being the *Considine* and the Serenine in the *Soutlands,* and the Campaline on the Verid Litus.

amanuensis *clerk* who takes minutes, makes duplicates and triplicates of documents and writes notes on the details of official conversations.

Approach, the ~ steep "driveway" that leads up to *Winstermill* from the *Harrowmath*. It is actually split in two, one way continuing east down to the *Pettiwiggin* and the other curving south to join the Gainway.

Arabis, Arimis son of a poor *peltryman*, Paddlin Arabis from *Fayelillian* way, who died of exposure on a desperate winter's foray along with his crew of trappers. Raised by his mother in deep squalor, Arabis was first prenticed to another *peltryman;* when things turned foul he escaped, living by his wits and making his gradual and circuitous way to the capital. There he chanced upon a recruitment drive for the *lamplighters* of *Winstermill,* and took the Emperor's Billion there and then.

ash-dabbling(s) working with organs and other parts of corpses. The "hobby" of *massacars* and other *black habilists,* taking this name from "ash" as a synonym for the remains of a person.

Ashenstall last *cothouse* east before the *Wormway* descends out of the highlands of the *Placidine* down onto the *Frugelle* and the start of the *"ignoble end of the road,"* taking its name from the gray land about it, and perhaps from the local stone of which it is mostly built.

ashmonger(s) part of the chain of supply in the *dark trades.* When stocks of body parts are low, the worst of these will stoop to abduction and murder to get the required items. If such items need to be of a certain "ripeness" to be useful, they will achieve this artificially, with chemistry. Stolen bodies are sometimes called anthropelf. See entry in Book One.

aspis as stated, this is a *venificant,* a highly toxic contact poison that allows the often harmless blows of a person against a *monster* to have rapid and deadly effect. The only problem with such *potives* is that they are deadly to people too, one touch being enough to cause some great discomfort in the very least. Aspis is one of the more preferred *venificants* because it is a little slower to act, meaning that accidental touch will not do much harm, although it is deadly once a good dose of it has entered a body's system.

Assimus surly, sandy-haired, pinch-faced lampsman 1st class serving at *Winstermill.* In semiretirement owing to the early onset of arthritis, this *lighter* has been granted the easiest stretch of the *Wormway* on which to work and see out his days. Along with his old mate *Bellicos,* he has seen service on most of the inner stretches of the highroad, even enduring a spell at the *"ignoble end of the road."*

astrapecrith the correct technical term for a *fulgar.* The equivalent for a *wit* is *neuroticrith.*

Atopian Dido reference to the time when Dido, the great ancient queen and founder of the *Empire,* was without a home, wandering the region once known as Opera and the Witherlends, driven to flight through the attempt on her life by jealous ministers wanting power for themselves. For several years she wandered from kingdom to kingdom, staying where she might, till the monarch of Patris took her in and rallied in support of her as the last surviving shoot of Idaho's line.

Attic language of the ancient people of the same name, a mighty race of great learning and sophistication, the direct inheritor of Phlegm's cultural, technological and sociopolitical legacy. Much of what they knew is now lost, the remnants still considered the acme of wisdom and habilistics. Idaho is considered their greatest ruler, and Dido, her great-granddaughter, second only to her. The language itself is based on the real Attic (otherwise known as classical Greek), and with this comes the author's usual apology for any offense his current usages might incur.

Aubergene *Lampsman* 1st class billeted at *Wormstool* and a native of Burgundis, he is renowned for his steady aim even in the most trying situations. Though little is said of it now, early last decade he earned deep respect and not a few *cruorpunxis* when defending a search party in the *Ichormeer.* These foiled rescuers had been attempting to find the lost family of the Warden-General of *Haltmire,* who disappeared in the terrible swamp. Few traces found could be followed, and those that could led only to disaster as the swamp swallowed men whole and its denizens preyed on them like cats in a mouse plague. As part of a rear guard, Aubergene's deadly shots bought space for the retreating party, who found only one child—the middle daughter—to take back to her agonized father. For his deeds the young *lighter* was awarded the Carpa Virtus (the Hand of Valor), the highest honor available to a mere *lighter.*

aufheitermen said "owf'*high*'ter'men"; the Gott word for *lamplighters,* meaning literally "the gloom lighteners" or "those who bring lightness to the gloom."

august ruler of a single *calendar clave;* typically a woman of some social stature, perhaps a *peer,* or noble, with a social conscience. To have any chance of affecting their surrounds, *calendars* need money and political clout, and those with high standing socially possess these attributes natively. A *clave* that does not have ranking gentry or nobility at its head and core, or at least as a sponsor, will most certainly be marginalized. Augusts are seconded by their *laudes,* who are their mouthpieces and their long reach. With a well-organized and talented *clave* with her, an august can be a daunting and influential figure in Imperial politics and society. Within her own *clave* the august is often referred to as the *senior-sister.*

aurang in the Half-Continent's version of a card deck the aurang is the fourth station (card value) in the house of brutes (animals), below the daw (3) and above the crocidole (5). An aurang is what we would call an orangutan, being found on the smaller islands of the northern *Sinus Tintinabuline* and found in the Half-Continent usually only in books, though wide-faring vinegaroons may well have seen one or two. The aurang lends its name to one of the winning hands in the card game *pirouette,* "Kindly Ladies Watch the Happy Aurangs Again."

auto-savant a person who, by the exercise of extremely sensitive and attuned intuition, is supposed to be able to tell a person's thoughts and needs. Most of these are rejected as humorless fakers and *fabulists* by those of the more serious habilistic turn of mind.

auxiliary, auxiliaries in this circumstance the people in support of *Winstermill* and her *lamplighters,* including the house guards of musketeers, *haubardiers* and *troubardiers; leers* and *lurksmen* and other "creepers"; skolds and other *thaumateers;* and the artillerists tending the great-guns on the walls.

ax-carabine also called axe-carbine or fusiscuris, a *combinade* made of a *fusil*-like firelock with an ax-blade attached to the muzzle.

B

bane *teratologist* who is both *wit* and skold, either beginning as a skold then choosing the *neuroticrith's* path to increase his or her power, or beginning as a *wit* and becoming adept at *skolding.* This second path is not uncommon: a *wit* has to take many more concoctions than a *fulgar* to keep healthy—and many of these are more complex to make than Cathar's Treacle. *Wits* may well opt to make these themselves rather than be tied to other suppliers, which is said by some to be a risky business as far as consistency of quality and efficacy are concerned. In the way of learning their own *scripts, wits* may well discover that it is within their abilities to make other potives, and branch out into skolding. A bane is therefore considered more versatile and greater in power than a plain *wit*.

bastion-house strongly fortified house or other such dwelling reinforced to withstand the rigors of conflict. *Cothouses* are often a form of bastion-house.

Baton Imperial of Fayelillian, the 8th Earl of the ~ the *Lamplighter-Marshal's* proper title, the hereditary rank granted to his *Fayelillian* family by Menagës Scepticus Haacobin I, the usurper of the Sceptics and the original Emperor of the current dynasty. Even so the *Lamplighter-Marshal* will not allow others to address him by any other title than "sir," as befits his military rank.

bee's buzz, the buzz gossip and rumor, so called for the buzzing sound of folks engaged in hushed mutterings about another.

Beggar Sea the body of water off the *Stander Lates* and the southern coasts of Hagenland, the Stafkärlsstig or "wandering beggar" in Brandenard. In the Half-Continent it is known as the Pontus Mendicus.

Bellicos one of the three semiretired *lampsmen* who look after the *prentices* as they practice at lighting along the *Pettiwiggin*. A little younger than his two compatriots, Bellicos is probably the surliest of the three, though he is generally forgiven this for the feats of valor he performed during his full service out *Ashenstall* way.

bellpomash mild restorative which, though drunk, is said to help the clotting and healing of wounds by fortifying the body's functions from within.

belugig(s) also belungs; large *monsters,* especially ettins or even the great beasts of the mares.

Benedict, Under-Sergeant-of-Prentices ~ red-haired assistant to

Lamplighter-Sergeant Grindrod. Benedict's carrot-colored hair is remarkable in northern *Soutlands,* showing his Wretcherman heritage. He and his sweet little wife, Daisy, live down in the *Nuptarium* in the Target Row, on Target Street.

benthamyn constituent of *Craumpalin's Exstinker;* a distillation of oils found only in the rock of certain regions of the *Sinus Tintinabuline,* Wretch and the Gottskylds, with the best quality part coming from the Heilgolands.

Berthezene artist sometimes going by the name of Berthezar, once a native of Turkeman, come to the *Sundergird* in flight from the husband of a mistress, and shopping his considerable skills as an imagineer (an illustrator) to any buyer, including pamphlet makers both reputable and disreputable. His talent is lauded by some as the most remarkable of the age, rivaling even the legendary Gouche, though that fellow's admirers disagree.

besomer(s) broom-makers.

Biargë the Beautiful (said "bee-*arr*-gee"—with a strong *g* as in "get"); common, easier to pronounce form of *Ingébiargë* (said "*Ing*'ga'bee'arr'gee"), the name of the cannibalistic monster-woman of Hagenland's southern shores, also known as Biargë the Salt-skold or, in Gott folklore, as Beogerthë the Cruel. Of the few manikins known to history, Biargë is perhaps the best documented, though few ordinary folk know her origin—or even know of her. Her origin is found in times long gone, in the lands of the Skylds, during a period of particular and morbid conflict there between human and *monster* known as the Volkammerung—a time of decay after the Heldinsage when heroes prevailed and civilization flourished. A faithful servant and yrrphethäl ("*earr*'feh'tharl," equivalent to a rhubezhal—see *skold* in Book One) to Ulfe Pytr (said "*Ull*'fer *Pie*'ter"—the great Hagen king who drove the Skylds from their rightful land), Biargë was hailed for her cold beauty and treacherous use of her great skill to aid the *Hagenards* against her own people. As time passed, and well after the Skylds had fled west across the Gramlendenmeer ("The Sea of Heavy Sorrows") Biargë became noted most of all for the longevity of her beauty, and it was soon rumored that she had brewed a potion of powerful virtue to prolong life and youth. Puzzled as to her own juvenescence, Biargë encouraged this rumor, yet it doubled back on her: Uthoedë (said "yoo'*tho*'dee"), Ulfe Pytr's wife, pressed her husband mercilessly to insist that their court's beauteous concocter make this tender brew for the queen as well. Many times he cajoled, remonstrated with and railed against *Ingébiargë*, and each time he was refused, first with kind excuses then with outright obduracy. On each occasion he had to return to a furious wife and a night spent banished from the conjugal bed. Goaded by her imperturbable obstinacy, Uthoedë went herself to Biargë's *test*, taking with her a number of mighty men of the Volkammerung—Skarphethinn (said "*Skar*'feh'thin") and Grettir preeminent among them. They took Biargë into custody, ransacked her home, turned up no vital *potive* and imprisoned the rhubezhal in the darkest depths of Steindurom, the regal stronghold. There, under pain of torture, Biargë confessed that there was no potion of youthfulness, that she did not know why she was still young after so long. Väkr, the royal *signifer* ("watcher of stars") tested her for *threwd*. On finding its subtle but definite presence, he renamed Biargë the Tvymadthrmaen—the twice-false maid—and she was declared a samligr (something akin to a sedorner). Uthoedë screamed for her doom and Ulfe Pytr sentenced Biargë to be executed at next moon's dark. Yet not all were against her. One Freyr, brother and equal of Grettir and nephew to Ulfe Pytr, was besotted with the long-lived beauty, and when time came for her burning, contrived to set her free. In their flight Väkr was slain by the chemistry of the damned maiden and many houseguards with him. The two lovers fled to the Illr and lost themselves in that haunted land; not even Skarphethinn, Biarkamil, Syfyrd, Gudbrand or the wounded and anguished Grettir nor any other of the men of renown would follow after. So Biargë and One Freyr wandered in the wilds, aided by strange and inscrutable folk—the haustayr or hausti, the autumn-folk that men were forbidden to converse with—till they made their home across the Leith Fol, on the Stendrlaeti (see the *Stander Lates*), the shores of the Linden Finné. Here Biargë suffered the deep grief of watching her young love One Freyr age, and decrepitude approach, while she stayed forever young. In bitterness and grief her thoughts blackened, and she cursed the cosmos and plotted useless revenge—for all but Biarkamil, the warrior-poet, had withered and died. She searched and brewed and scoured the lands, trying to find the secret of the vital brew she had once been so mistakenly condemned for making. She terrorized communities and stole their parts and *potives,* slew young men out of spite or abducted them to test and refine her concoctions. Many of these poor subjects did gain a kind of prolonged life, but each one was twisted and broken by the experiments he endured. No matter what the increasingly crazed Biargë tried, she failed utterly to find the perfect elixir to keep her lover and rescuer whole and by her side for always. The common end for Freyr is that he went the way of all people, yet awed stories remain that, among the many walking, shuffling horrors that make the Stendrlaeti an impossibly dangerous place, is the moldering mindless hanuman of One Freyr, aching with longing he no longer understands. As for Biargë, she is said to live still, her skin gone gray with time and her eyes red and yellow from centuries of *skolding*—utterly mad and insatiably ravenous, seeking to devour all men she can find, wanting in twisted love to take them unto herself, where they might continue on and not wither with age. She is said to have devised many ways to lure vessels and their crews onto the risky shores of the *Stander Lates,* whereby she desires to consume each one. The best source of information on Biargë can be found in that ancient *book* of horrors, the *Derereader.*

billet   where *pediteers, lamplighters* or other military personnel sleep and live when not on duty.

Billeting Day   day when *prentice-lighters* are granted status as full *lampsmen,* having completed their training. In a solemn ceremony, *prentices* reswear their vow of service to the Emperor and are assigned to a *cothouse* where they will serve out what days are left to them lighting and dousing the lanterns on the appropriate stretches of road.

biologue(s)   any device or machine that uses actual living organs to provide its functions. See *sthenicon* in Book One.

Bitterbolt   *cothouse* on the *Wormway* situated just beyond the eastern bank of the *Bittermere.*

bitterbright   powerful and rare *potive,* a delicate *fulminant* that, by the cunning artifice of its chemistry, produces light to hurt the gaze of any who look at it. Unless it is actively replenished, bitterbright burns for a limited duration, its effect lessening dramatically as it burns low. Therefore you must be constantly working to keep it "burning" if you want its painful glow to remain.

Bittermere, the ~ small river running from high in the *Owlgrave* that swells greatly in size before joining the Migh on the northern edge of Needle Greening. Said to be threwdish, it derives its name from the sharp, foul taste of its tealike waters, sweetened only slightly by the joining of its flow with the swift-flowing *Mirthlbrook*.

black habilist(s) term most commonly used to refer to *massacars* or *transmogrifers;* those considered to be dabbling in the darker sides of learning; the great patrons of the *dark trades,* which would not exist without them. See *habilists* in Book One.

blaste any fulminating *potive* or *script* that erupts or explodes, *loomblaze* being an excellent example.

Bleakhall *cothouse* at *Bleak Lynche,* upon which its inhabitants are greatly dependent for safety and the dispensing of justice. It is one of the more irregular duties of the *house-major* to preside over the smaller local civil disputes. Built before the town, as a position of retreat for those dwelling at *Haltmire,* Bleakhall is one of the larger *cothouses* on the way and is meant to be *billet* to an overstrength platoon of *lamplighters* and their *auxiliaries.*

Bleak Lynche last civil settlement in the eastern edges of the *Idlewild,* gaining its name from its remoteness and the poor prospects of the land about it, and from the bridges spanning between the high towerlike houses built there—otherwise called "linches." Founded by the state of Doggenbrass, the settlement's best source of corporate income is tending to the needs of the *lamplighters* and postmen posted there, and as a trading post and "stopover" for those few travelers coming up on the Wettin Lowroad from Burgundis and Hurdling Migh. This is still thin pickings, and the lords of Doggenbrass have found themselves paying frequently to prop up the ailing colony, many of whose citizens have moved to the more prosperous mining settlements in the region, the Louthe or Pot. One can find pathsmen here: private wayfarers who contract out their energies as guides and guards to those foolish few who wish to travel the *Wormway* into and through the *Ichormeer,* or take the Wettin Lowroad down to Hurdling Migh and beyond.

blighted of or pertaining to *monsters* or *threwd,* especially the worst kinds of *threwd.* Used as an emphatic curse—with "twice" or "thrice" or some other preceding qualification for extra emphasis—to declare a person or thing bad or unworthy or worthless.

bloom shortened form of "*glimbloom*," also known as frons lumen or collucia, and sometimes referred to as *stuff* (though this is a catch-all term); the aquatic, weedlike plant possessed—in certain circumstances—of bioluminescence used to provide the source of illumination for *bright-limns* and the *great-lamps* of the highroads and cities. It is a wonderful, regenerating source of light, but there are those who hold that having it, and particularly growing it, is an enticement to *monsters,* who are said to like the taste of it. Others disagree, particularly *lampsmen* out on the roads working with bloom each day, who argue that the *monsters* tend to find them much more toothsome. Some *seltzermen,* on the other hand, might complain of a disproportionate incidence of *theroscades* when they are out replacing the worn-out bloom of a *great-lamp.*

blunderer offensive term for a nonmilitary person, used by *pediteers* and their like in the same way a vinegaroon might call a landsman a lubber. Very rude when said to another soldier.

boltarde a *combinade* or weapon made of a combination of two or more other tools of violence. Essentially a boltarde is the bringing together of a helmbarde (what we would call a halberd) with two wheel-lock pistols formed as part of the shaft, one short barrel on either side of the ax-and-spike-head. The wheel locks are fired by means of triggers farther down, just above the rondel that protects the hand. Shallow grooves run down the middle of the blade to allow the ball to fly unhindered. An invention of the Sebastians, it is unwieldy but highly effective in the right circumstances, although boltardes have not gained much popularity in the *Haacobin Empire.*

book(s) in the Half-Continent there is a whole library of catalogs and matters on *monsters,* habilistics, necrology and more; among the more necessary (other than the *Vadé Chemica*—see Book One—and related texts) are *Ex Monsteria* (by Wytwornic) and *Phantasmagoria.* Also there is the *Nomenclator Animantium* (unknown author), *Historica Monstorum* (a modern publication by Pellwick), *De Dinpiscibus* (on sea-*nickers* and kraulschwimmen by Aldrovand), *Labyrinthion* (an ancient text on *teratology* by Stabius and translated by Wünderhuber) and the strange and antiquated *Historie of Fourfeeted Beastes* by Topsell—to name but a few.

Clysmosurgical Primer is a learned and rare book on the actual techniques involved in transmogrification (surgery making a person into a *lahzar*) complete with diagrams. Its sources are the ancient and even rarer writings of the Phlegms and most particularly the Cathars, now extinct races known for their skills and learning in such things. This is not a proscribed book as such in the *Empire,* but owning one is a sign of dabbling in unusual, esoteric things. Because of what is deemed dangerous content or encouraging *outramour,* it is illegal to sell many of these within the *Empire,* though not necessarily to own them. The banning of books is an inconsistent practice, with each state interpreting the laws differently, and it tends to be the paleologues (the "ancient texts") that suffer the most restrictions. People of yore often thought very differently of the race of *monster* than folk of the Half-Continent do now.

Bookday Rossamünd's birthday, as it is for every ward of Madam Opera's Estimable Marine Society for Foundling Boys and Girls. See entry in Book One.

bossetation making gardens (what we would call landscaping). Though the making and planting of gardens might seem a worthy and peaceful pastime, its main purpose is to expunge the *threwd,* to keep the land tame.

bossock also known as a mayotte, the basic well-fitting proofed-silk *(soe)* harness of the *calendars* and one of their most distinctive items of apparel. It is made close to allow free movement and, while it prevents moderate lacerations, thicker items of proofing must be worn over it to give better protection.

Brandenard language of the Brandenards, the race who populate much of the northern *Soutlands* and even beyond and have contributed much to the exploration and expansion of the *Empire's* mercantile and geographical interests; the Half-Continent equivalent of English. In HIR 1311 the Imperial declaration on the languages of its subjects, "The Correct Sounds to Instruct the People," officially recognized Brandenard as the vulga lingua—the common language among peoples of differing states and even countries, the tongue of trade. *Tutin,* however, was declared—and is still regarded—as the language of education and politics.

Brandenbrass major city of the Grume. See entry in Book One.

bravo(es) generally any hired killer, but also used specifically to describe what we would call assassins; also known as pnictors or pnictardos ("stranglers").

Briary, the ~; Briarywood small thorny woodland that stubbornly grows about the eastern end of the *Pettiwiggin*. It has been allowed to remain, as a source of firewood and small timber for the needs of both *Winstermill* and *Wellnigh House*.

bright-limn(s) small portable *seltzer* lights. See Book One.

Brisking Cat, the ~ wayhouse on the highroad of the *Conduit Vermis*, and one of the longest established in the *Idlewild*. Situated near the confluence of the *Mirthlbrook* and the *Bittermere*, it was founded three generations ago by the father of the current enrica d'ama, Madam Oubliette. The family of Parleferte (said "*Par'leh'fert*"), her steward, has served there for as long as the "Cat" has been open. A popular *billet* for many *teratologists*. Ever prone to grumbling, local townsfolk will complain bitterly of the coxcombry and inconvenience of *knaves* when they are bunked in the townships. It's all very tedious. They want the work but not the persons who do it, so most pugnators prefer to stay in knaveries, cot-rents or wayhouses and avoid the nonsense.

brocander(s) sellers of secondhand clothing, particularly proofing.

bruicle tool of *physics* used for holding blood, made usually of glass or porcelain. *Teratologists* and *punctographists* use them too for storing *cruor*. The arrangement of one bowl inside another within a bruicle insulates the stored blood, keeping it viable for longer and making it ideal for carrying *cruor* back to your friendly neighborhood *punctographist*. See *graille(s)*.

bully-dicey what we would call a meat pie.

burge(s) small flags for signaling, made in sets of distinct patterns for the representation of letters, numbers, cardinal points, titles of rank or social elevation, even whole words. The color of a burge is first and foremost for distinction, though the meaning of the colors can be inferred if a small multistripe, multicolored flag—known as the parti-jack—is flown with them. Burges are used for both civil and military purposes on land and the vinegar seas.

C

caladine also aleteins, solitarines or just solitaires; *calendars* who travel long and far from their *clave* spreading the work of good-doing and protection for the undermonied. The most fanatical of their sisters, caladines are typically the most colorfully mottled and strangely clothed of the *calendars,* wearing elaborate *dandicombs* of horns or hevenhulls (inordinately tall thrice-highs) or henins and so on. They too will mark themselves with outlandish spoors, often imitating the patterns of the more unusual creatures that their wide-faring ways may have brought onto their path. *Claves* tend to confine their actions to a defined jurisdiction known as a *diet,* and customarily seek permission to enter another *clave's diet.* However, caladines have a unilaterally agreed right to travel freely from one *diet* to the next, though it is considered polite and proper to visit with the *august* while you are there. Sometimes a caladine is called by the local *laude* to produce credentials before getting an affirming nod.

calanserie, calanserai, calansery headquarters and home of a *calendar clave*, and therefore also called a clariary. Usually situated well away from urban buildup, out in more rural places where there is a greater need for the *calendars'* work, though there are a few notable exceptions: the oldest *clave*-homes are found near cities and there are even calanseries in Catalaine, Millaine, Ives and Chastony. Calanseries are typically fortified against assault from both *monster* and man, especially given that several are home to *sequesturies* as well.

calendar(s) sometimes called *strigaturpis* or just *strig*—a general term for any combative woman; the *Gotts* call them mynchen—after the do-gooding heldin-women of old. Calendars gather themselves into secretive societies called *claves* (its members known as claviards), constituted almost entirely of women, organized about ideals of social justice and philanthropy, particularly providing teratological protection for the needy and the poor. They usually live in somewhat isolated strongholds—manorburghs and basterseighs—known as *calanseries.* Some *claves* hide people—typically women—in trouble, protecting them in secluded fortlets known as *sequesturies.* Other *claves* offer to teach young girls their graces and fitness of limb in places known as mulierbriums. Calendars, however, are probably best known for the odd and eccentric clothing they don to advertise themselves. Over the years a distinct nomenclature has emerged for the various "trades" within a calendar *clave*, for example:

- ♣ *fulgar* = stilbine
- ♣ *wit* = pathotine
- ♣ dexter = cacistin
- ♣ skold = pharmacine
- ♣ *scourge* = cheimin
- ♣ *bane* = sceptine
- ♣ *sagaar* = purrichin
- ♣ *pistoleer* = *spendonette*
- ♣ *leer* = astatine.

All kinds of *teratologists* form secret societies, but calendars are one of the few who generally seek the welfare of others. The calendar ranks in descending order are:

- ♣ carline—rare, revered and retired, sought for wisdom and adjudication
- ♣ *august*—the head of a *clave*
- ♣ *laude*—the second in charge and herald of the *august*
- ♣ cantin—assistant to the *laude*, lifeguard of the *august*
- ♣ *caladine*—equivalent in rank to a tome (but operating alone and errant)
- ♣ tome—leader of a number of chapters and pagins
- ♣ chaptin—fully approved and initiated sister
- ♣ pagin—initiate serving probationary period, entry-level.

See Appendices 2 and 3.

calendine of or pertaining to *calendars*.

Callistia, Damsels of ~ fabled beauties from the Heldinsage, ever-living beauties dwelling in the autumn-lands of the urchin-lords. Many tales of love unrequited and rapacious appetites and much misery surround them. The salient lesson in the histories of not putting too much stock on physical beauty is lost, however, on modern folk. For the idea of these mythic ladies has given rise to parades known as Callistia or callic-shows, beauty galas with awards for the most poised, graceful, well-turned out and rational girl in the show.

cantebank(s) peregrinating songsters and prosodists who also sell their talent for words to pen panegyrics for *teratologists* wishing to boast of their skills either to prospective employers or to be read out in a common room or other public place.

cantus properly called the cantus-and-laude, this is the creed by which a *calendar clave* lives and dies. Often it is rendered in abbreviated verse form so that it stays in the mind. *Calendars* are continually indoctrinated with their cantus till obedience to it is reflexive. The *In Columba Alat* is an excellent example of a cantus, and each clave will have its own variation of such a creed. See *In Columba Alat*.

carum, dust-of-~ pronounced "kar'*room,*" one of the parts that go into the making of *Craumpalin's Exstinker.* It comes as a gray powder made from the dried and ground buds of a type of seaweed commonly found along the entire southern coast of the Half-Continent. The dust is a common base for many powdered *scripts.*

caste small, fragile flasks usually made of glass or delicate porcelains designed to fracture when dashed against a hard surface. These are used to hold liquid *potives* that burst and react violently when released. Castes have to be stored and carried in padded receptacles; a *salumanticum,* for example, will have a reinforced pocket as part of the inner linings, divided into softly cushioned slots in which individual *castes* can be kept. Another method of carrying them is in a digital, a small, sturdy, well-cushioned container, usually of tin or pewter or wood, worn handy on a belt or in a pocket, into which four or five castes can be kept for easy use. There are some different types of digital, and they are common accoutrements of a well-prepared *hucilluctor.*

castigation(s) • (noun) severe punishments starting with time in the stocks and moving on to increasing strokes of the *lash* • (noun) period in the afternoon when defaulters are named and their punishments determined. These will typically be impositions; only very rarely will actual castigations be given, despite the grim name—only for larceny or brawling or some gross dereliction of duties. *Prentices* are often threatened with castigations, but these are empty threats (not that the *prentices* are usually aware of this) to keep them well in line.

cathared to be made into a *lahzar,* to have undergone transmogrification.

Cathar's Treacle also called *plaudamentum*; draught imbibed by *lahzars*—both *wits* and *fulgars*—to keep their introduced organs from rebelling inside their bodies. See entry in Book One.

catillium, catillium-hat round, broad-brimmed, squat-crowned hat, usually made of straw and lined with felt.

catlin also called a catling; a long-bladed, long-handled surgical knife, sharply pointed and double-edged. The preferred tool in amputations and the making of major incisions.

Childebert one of Rossamünd's fellow *prentices;* a fairly quiet but capable lad who paid Rossamünd little mind as they shared their lives in *Winstermill.*

Chill often used as a synonym for winter, but more specifically referring to the coldest months in the year—Pulchrys, Brumis, Pulvis and Heimio, considered usually an ill time for travelers.

chymistarium or *test-barrow;* cupboard or portable barrow where skolds and their ilk can make their *potives.* Very compact, with ingenious drawers and foldable sections, an entire miniature *test* crammed into as small a space as possible. Skolds may port the cupboard variety on a cart or carriage to take about with them or pull the barrow (or hire some sturdy rough to pull it for them) to make what they need when they need it. Not to be confused with a *test* itself, which is a whole room and its tools given to this purpose.

cicuration said "*kick*-u-ray-shun"; determined process of bringing the wilds under control by farming and cultivation, by digging and cutting and landscaping, and by colonization to bring the land fully under *everyman* control. It is a slow form of taming, but its effects are deep and long lasting. Even so, some places refuse to be brought under heel—such as the *Harrowmath,* large parts of the Mold, the *Frugelle* and so on. See also the *Idlewild.*

claustra small booths used in the more fancy alehouses, coffeehouses, wayhouses, tomaculums and any other such public place, made to seat no more than four comfortably. Designed to provide a modicum of privacy to guests, they were originally used in the less salubrious establishments to allow nefarious conversation to happen somewhat publicly without being too public. As is so often the case, the fashions of the wealthy romanticize and ape the daily realities of the less well-heeled, who in turn copy things they like from those of higher station—and so it goes around.

clave(s) group of *calendars,* particular and distinct, set to protect a defined area. A clave has its own unique mottle and spoors that its *phrantry* are expected to wear at all times with pride. *Calendars* in general hold to universal beliefs and rules, but a clave is free to emphasize or add bits as they see fit. The *augusts* of all the claves in a region may meet every so often to coordinate and bond. There is normally no real animosity between claves, and *caladines* tend to be the glue that keeps it all one big happy family.

Clementine capital city of the whole Empire; some may use the name Clementine when referring to the Emperor and his ministers as a collective; a general term for all the powers that govern the *Empire.* See entry in Book One.

clerk(s) at Winstermill these are essentially civilians with a military rank: few states have professional military staff. Given this, the most preferred clerks are concometrists, the combat-clerical graduates of athenaeums such as Inkwill, who are highly trained in both paper shuffling and the *stouche.*

clerk-master another rendering of the title *Master-of-Clerks,* slightly less formal and typically allowable in use only by those of higher rank.

coach-host harbor for *post-lentums* and other public carriages situated at a convergence of routes, where a passenger can while away minutes and hours either eating and drinking in the refectory or sitting and waiting in the *parenthis.* Coach-hosts are not wayhouses: they have no facilities to accommodate travelers, though folk are allowed to sleep in the *parenthis* if they wish, at no charge, sitting on hard benches and locked in at night with limited access to the *jakes* or refreshments and no bedding. Still, for those short of money this is a better option than a night exposed on the streets or in the wilds.

color-party small group bearing the colors before a body of soldiers. A typical color-party holds the colors—the flag that signifies the pride of its soldiers—and the pensills—the personal pendants of the officers in charge of that unit. A marshal's color-party will also carry the spandarion. With the color-party will also go a drummer boy and a fyfesman beating time and encouraging their comrades with martial music.

Columbine(s) *calendars* belonging to the *Right of the Pacific Dove*.

Columbris *calansery* and *sequestury* of the *Right of the Pacific Dove* who otherwise call themselves *Columbines,* from the *Tutin* for "dove."

combinade(s) hand arms that are a clever combination of melee weapon and firelock. The firing mechanism on most combinades is an improved wheel lock, being more sturdy than a flintlock, and able to take the jars that come when the weapon is used to strike at a foe. Added to this, the lock mechanism, trigger and hammer are usually protected by gathered bands of metal, a basket much like those protecting the hilts of many foreign swords. When edges and bullets are treated with *gringollsis,* combinades become very effective *therimoirs* (*monster-killing tools*).

commerce men smugglers and other such illegal traffickers working in concert and with some kind of centralized leadership or organizer, an unduly respectable title for a very unrespectable lot. It is applied, a tad sarcastically, to all such folk whether they belong to an actual commerce society or not.

compeer how one *peer* may refer to another.

compliment what we would call a toast, when glasses are filled and touched together as things are declared and wished for.

Compter-of-Stores chief accountant of *Winstermill,* apparently of equal rank to the *Master-of-Clerks,* though in practice very much under the latter's sway.

Conduit Felix, the ~ reputed to be the longest highroad in the *Empire,* reaching from Clementine, the Imperial Capital far in the north, through the very midst of the Grassmeer and on to Andover in Hergoatenbosch. The Conduit Felix is used to mark the separation of the Grassmeer into the Ager Magnus on the eastern side and the Solum Magnus to the west.

Conduit Vermis, the ~ proper name of the *Wormway*. See entry in Book One.

confectioner any seller of *potives,* whether skold, *hedgeman* or simple shopkeeper; also sometimes called fargitors ("makers of potpourri"), an ancient *Tutin* name for skolds given them when the first rhubezhals arrived from across the eastern mares.

confustication confusion or fight, particularly a wild brawling fight or a fight that has turned out badly.

Considine, the ~ one of the *alternats* or subcapitals situated at strategic places within the *Haacobin Empire. Alternats* were founded to allow the *Empire* to keep greater control over its subject states, most of which lie beyond inveterately threwdish land, well past easy reach. Large armies and navies are kept at each *alternat,* ready to venture forth and chastise any overweening state or peer or defend the lands against the *monsters.* In the *Soutlands,* the Considine is the larger, older and therefore senior of two *alternats,* the other being the Serenine, farther south.

corser(s) grave robbers and traffickers in dead bodies for the service of high-paying *massacars* and all the rest. Probably their best-known tool-of-trade is the corpse-fender, a long pointed pole driven into the mold to test the location of a possible grave. Apart from the dangers of *monsters* and the ever-vigilant *obstaculars* and revenue officers, you might also come into conflict with other corsers over a prize tomb. Edgar Shallow, a somewhat well-known corser, wrote a *book* on the subject; part treatise, part sage advice, part fictional license—*The Ashmongers' Almanac.* Other *books* on the subject include *Codex Necropoli* by Tichanus, an old catalog and guide to all the known cemeteries of the Old World (recent revisions by Tidswell include references to Turkeman grave sites); and *Fossae Magnum* (or "The Book of Graves"), a treatise on the trade of the corser with a cursory guide to the main cemeteries in the larger cities. See *corsers* in Book One.

costermen small-time traders who travel about selling fruits and vegetables and any other foodstuffs they might have.

Cothallow built between *Makepeace* and the Three Stile Junction, this is one of the best *cothouses* on the *Wormway,* with a reputation for smartness and punctuality and for the comforts of its cot-rent. The *lighters* serving there are a happy bunch (as *lighters* go), flourishing under an uninterrupted string of competent, good-natured *house-majors.*

cothouse(s) type of *fortalice,* the small, often houselike fortresses built along highroads to provide *billet* and protection to *lamplighters* and their *auxiliaries.* Cothouses are usually built no more than ten to twelve miles apart, so that the *lamplighters* will not be left lighting *lamps* and exposed in the unfriendly night for too long. Their size goes from a simple high-house with slit windows well off the ground, through the standard structure of a main house with small attendant buildings all surrounded by a wall, to the fortified *bastion-houses* like *Haltmire* on the *Conduit Vermis* or Tungoom on the *Conduit Felix.* Sometimes called a little manse.

coty gaute pronounced "*co'*tee *gort,*" a delicate pastry from the Patricine stuffed with quail cooked so long the bones are edible.

course • (verb) to hunt, particularly to hunt monsters. • (noun) the hunt itself, usually referred to as a coursing-party, or in such phrases as "to go on a course." A course is, obviously, a dangerous affair. One undertaken lightly will always result in the doom of some, if not all, of those involved. A prospective courser is always advised to take at least one skold and one *leer*—or, if they are unavailable, a *quarto* of *lurksmen,* even a navigator or wayfarer, and a hefty weight of *potives* and *skoldshot.* Not to be confused with "corse," meaning (of course) a dead body, a corpse.

court-martial a court or tribunal made up of military or navy officers who try their own for any offense committed by *pediteers* or vinegaroons against military—and even sometimes Imperial—law; a martial court rather than a civil court (court-civil), where everyday folk are tried. To be subject to a court-martial does not necessarily mean being cashiered from one's chosen service; the tribunal of officers in a court-martial have to establish guilt or innocence, just as in a civil court. Therefore you can be tried in a court-martial and be found innocent and so return to service.

crank in habilistics this term is used to mean something that is of dubious or unknown origin and/or effect, something made with little skill and giving little real benefit; it is also used to refer to something that is broken or impaired in some way.

crank-hook(s) another name for *fodicars,* so given for the blunt spike sticking from one side that is used to wind the mechanism of a *seltzer lamp* to draw out the *bloom* into the *seltzer water.*

Craumpalin's Exstinker *nullodor* made by Master Craumpalin for Rossamünd, which Rossamünd is meant to apply frequently; he works hard to do so, keeping a careful eye on how much he has used and how much he has left.

crinickle bonnet of muslin or silk worn by women to bed at night to keep their hair in place during the night's sleep.

Cripplebolt *cothouse* situated on the *Frugelle* built atop the ruins of an ancient Burgundian tollhouse; most famous for the horse-stud kept within the old, still-intact cellars protected by three sets of strong doors and the vigilant maintenance of powerful *nullodors.* The stocky nags bred there are not the sleekest beasts, but they still pull a load as they are meant to.

Critchitichiello, Mister itinerant *ossatomist* hailing originally from Seville who finds life down in the cooler climes of the *Soutlands* more to his liking because people are not so aware of his unusual past, and rumor so far has not managed to follow him across the Grassmeer. A *ledgermain* of natural gifts, he is talented at basic *skolding* too, and has made a comfortable living in the less traveled habitations of the *Empire's* southern conquests.

Crofton Wheede *prentice-lighter.* See *Wheede, Crofton.*

cruor monster's blood once it has been taken from the beast.

cruorpunxis *monster-blood tattoo.* Though *cruor* is used to mark a *monster*-slayer, this is not because of any special properties in the blood of a dead *monster* over the blood from a live *monster* (*ichor*). It is simply that getting a *bruicle* of blood from a still-living *nicker* might seem a difficult task: the author would defy anyone to attempt it and come away whole. See Book One.

curricle light two-wheeled cart or carriage usually pulled by a team of two horses or, in a pinch, a pair of strong mules or donkeys—though at a slower pace.

cursor(s) mathematical *clerks* employed for their ability to count and arithmecate (do all manner of sums) quickly and without the aid of counting devices.

D

dancing calendar(s) more properly *calendine sagaars*.

dandicomb(s) large, gaudily decorated "novelty" hats, designed to attract attention. Worn almost exclusively by *teratologists,* dandicombs declare very much that the wearer is serious about killing *monsters*. They come in a variety of forms with wings (ailettes), horns, multiple crowns, twisted crowns; whatever the imagination of the wearer, the depth of his or her purse and the skill of the milliner might conjure.

dandidawdler(s) rich, affected men who dress expensively in fussy, frilly threads; those of the modern fashionable set known as *fluffs*. See Appendix 4.

dark trades illegal trade of body parts and *monster* bits. See entry in Book One.

day-clerk(s) in *cothouses* much of the clerical work—filing of indents, sorting of work cards, auditing of stores, concatenation of papers—is in the hands of one person, the day-clerk, who may have an assistant, if he or she is fortunate. Day-clerks are also responsible for the transit of mail through their station and the dissemination of the same to and from postmen serving the area.

day-watch *watch* in a *cothouse* responsible for guarding their *billet* and the sleeping *lantern-watch* and the immediate road during the day; for driving off *monsters* from their stretch of the way; for aiding in the chasing and apprehension of *lurchers* and other *commerce men;* for participating in *fatigue parties* either on ditch duty or as laborers themselves; and for whichever other duties might present themselves for the doing. At determined intervals that vary with the needs of each house, the day-watch and *lantern-watch* will swap duties, making it a long day for the previous day-watch and a shortened *vigil-day* for the relieved *lantern-watch*.

Dead Patch, the ~ the common grave of the *lamplighters* and *auxiliaries* in *Winstermill*. Indeed there are many graveyards throughout the Half-Continent and beyond with this name. A noteworthy feature of the one in *Winstermill* is that the dead are buried feetfirst—standing upright, as it were—to conserve room, so that as many as possible might be interred there.

degree another term for the situations of social status and rank. The highest degree is a duke/duchess, then marche/marchess, followed by a count/countess, then viscount (or reive)/viscountess (or revine), after which are baron/baroness, then companion/companine, then armige (or esquire)/armigine and finally gentleman/gentlewoman. Each degree above companion may be referred to as "lord" or "lady," and those below as "sir" or "dame."

Dereland the vast southeastern continent beyond the Liquor and the Mare Periculum (Gramlendenmeer), a region which includes the Hagenlands, the eoned home of the *Gotts* before they were driven out by the *Hagenards*.

diet the defined range of a *calendar clave's*—and therefore its *august's*—influence as stipulated by the *clave's Imperial Prerogative* (a commission from the Emperor). Any *calendar* entering another *clave's* diet must seek permission either from the *laude* or the *august* herself, depending on circumstances.

dispensurist(s) in *Winstermill,* dispensurists occupy a rank between *sergeant* and *under-sergeant,* meaning they are one step down from a *leer* and therefore subordinate to the same. See entry in Book One for more on dispensurists in general.

distinct acid(s) acidic *scripts* made especially for a reactive corrosion upon contact, properly known as *mordants*.

ditchland(s) also known as fossis, ditchlands are the last march of human habitation, being disputed territory where men and *monsters* vie for control of the land. Essentially you could think of a ditchland as the "front line" in the never-ending war between *everymen* and *üntermen*.

doglock heavy firearm, somewhere between a pistol and a carbine in length, and often with a very large bore. Also known as a *hauncets,* they make excellent *salinumbus*.

dolly-mop(s) a fairly recent social innovation, these are the working girls of a city or town, ones living for fun and fashion, using their self-earned income in pursuit of the same.

Dolours, Lady ~ pronounced "doll-loors," a power *calendine bane* and the *laude* of *Syntychë*, the *Lady Vey* and protectress of *Threnody*. Her origins are uncertain; she perhaps comes from the Patricine state of Vauquelin or Haquetaine. Only a handful of years younger than the *Lady Vey,* she arrived at *Herbroulesse* as a teen, already well along the path of *skolding*. There she was so well cared for by *Syntychë's* mother (the existing *Lady Vey*) and by all of the Right that she willingly transmogrified to become the personal protectress of the heiress of the *clave*—a young *Syntychë* herself. Dolours is the oldest serving friend of her mistress, and though she does not agree with all *Syntychë* does or says, she remains fiercely loyal to her, taking on the role of *spurn* to Threnody, the next heiress of *Columbris,* with pride (even though in some ways this is a demotion). There are rumors about, vague hints that Dolours has been spied in conversation with *monsters,* suspected of discerning between *monsters* that must be slain and those that should be spared, of being affected with *outramour.* All of this is conjecture, and the *bane* herself remains taciturn when asked: what business is it of others? It is unknown if the title of "lady" is a courtesy or a declaration of rank, and Dolours has never sought to clarify this either way.

domesticar(s) *pediteers* in the employ of a particular individual, serving as the personal guard and even army of the same.

Dovecote, the ~ also known as *Herbroulesse* or *Columbris;* the home and headquarters of the *Right of the Pacific Dove,* gaining its name from the title of the *calendar clave* living within.

Dovecote Bolt *cothouse* situated nearest to the *Dovecote* and one of the smallest *cothouses* on the *Wormway,* known as the Bolt by its inhabitants; an unremarkable *billet,* and notable only for its proximity to the incidents involving *Numps* and his fellow *seltzermen.*

Drüker derived from the Gott word for "crush," the name of one of *Winstermill's* fourteen *tykehounds,* and their curregitor. See *tykehound(s).*

Duke of Sparrows, the ~ also called the sparrow-king or sparrow-lengis; urchin (see entry in Book One), and one of those known as a nimuine, or monster-lord, who have sway over the behavior of the lesser *monsters* about them. Though most do not believe he exists, the common myth states that the sparrow-king is a friend of the Duke of Crows. He is said to hold court in the woods of the *Sparrow Downs,* resisting the conquering actions of those *monsters* set against the realm of everymen. Even so, reputed autumn-land or not, few dare to venture too far into the Downs. People of the *Haacobin Empire* have dismissed the ancient foolishness that there are two kinds of monster-lord: the nimuines who are kinder, seeking to benefit *everymen*, and the cacophrins or tlephathines, who seek their own ends and the destruction of *everymen*.

dust-of-carum see *carum, dust-of-~*.

dyphr said "*die'*ferr," from the *Attic* for "seat" or "chair"; a light, two-seater, four-wheeled carriage with a high dashboard, open-topped and open-sided before the driver and with the back wheels much greater in diameter than the front wheels. Built for speed and recreation, it is driven by the owner, with no lenterman's seat at the front. For inclement weather, a foldable top can be pulled over the occupants, and higher sides can be folded up to help protect against a *theroscade,* though a hasty retreat is a dyphr's best protection.

E

einsiedlerin the Gott word for an eeker, those people living by choice or imposition on the fringes of society. See *eeker* in Book One.

Emperor's Own Lighters the formal and glorious title of a *lamplighter* in the service of the Haacobin Emperor. Declared boastfully to the listener, it is used particularly by *lighters* when referring to themselves.

Empire, the ~ meaning the *Haacobin Empire* of current rule or the Sceptics whom they overthrew. See entry in Book One.

enkle Gott for "grandson," a name kindly old Gott folk sometimes give to any young person.

epimelain pronounced "eh-*pihm*-eh-layn" or "eh-*pihm*-eh-line" and sometimes shortened just a little to pimelain, also known as an abergaile, a person we would call a nurse, employed in infirmaries and *sequesturies* to tend to the routine cares of the sick and recovering; regarded as a superior class of maid.

Eugus Smellgrove see *Smellgrove, Eugus*.

eurinine(s) said "yoo'rah'neen"; the original *monsters* who were granted the capacity to make life come from the earth. In some texts they are written of as the Primmlings—the first. All the nimuines, tlephathines and cacophrins were once of these kind—or so some antiquated sources say.

everymen people, humankind.

Evolution Green also called Evolution Square; the oblong space south of the Grand Mead in *Winstermill* designated for marching and other drills of movement.

evolution(s) training in the correct movements in marching and the right handling of weapons and other equipment. Evolutions are taken very seriously in military organs, especially in armies, where *pediteers* are drilled over and over and over in all the marches and skills required until they become a habit. Failure to perform evolutions successfully is punished, sometimes severely, and this is usually enough to scare people into excellence. Evolutions form part of a hierarchy of military motion and drill starting with manual exercises (individual drill), evolutions (quarto and platoon movements), great exercises (company and battalion movement), and maneuvers (in concerto movements of regiments or forcces of greater size). To evolve is to be put through drill maneuvers such as marching or handling weapons.

Ex Monsteria also known as the *Liber Beluafaunis* or "Book of Monsters"; an exceedingly rare tome written by the eminent and assassinated scholar and Imperial *teratologist* Hubritas Whittwornicus of Wörms or, more simply, Wittwornick. It is considered the most learned and thorough study of *theroids,* but is unofficially considered a banned book for the dubious conclusions Wittwornick comes to about the nature of the ancient foe. It is so hard to get, however, that few but the most learned know of it, and fewer still have a copy to read. A thoroughly abridged form exists—*The Incomplete Book of Bogles*—but even this is regarded as containing *sedonitious* information despite the truncation of its contents.

expungeant(s) another rendering of expunctants; those *scripts* that slay instantly.

Exstinker the *nullodor* made by Craumpalin for Rossamünd before he left Madam Opera's, given to him to keep our hero ". . . safe from sniffing noses." See *Craumpalin's Exstinker* and *nullodors* in Book One.

F

fabulist(s) one practiced in and gaining income from the arts of sleight of hand, juggling and other feats of prestidigitation. Also used to refer to artists and other image makers.

false-fire *potives* that cause kinds of chemical burning and melting; the glowing, often firelike reactions of these same *potives;* chemical "flames" and burning.

falseman a *leer* whose eyes have been altered so that she or he can detect when another is being truthful or not. See *leers* in Book One.

fascins said "*fass*'skins," coming from infula fascia, the retardant-treated bandages or wrappings and covers worn by *scourges* to protect them from the workings of their own chemistries.

fatigue party group of laborers, *peoneers,* and/or *seltzermen* set to manual labor. If a fatigue party ventures out beyond its protective bounds, it will be accompanied by a *quarto* or more of *pediteers* and maybe a *lurksman* or *leer.* Soldiers so engaged are said to be on ditch duty.

Fayelillian small northern *Soutland* state, north of *Brandenbrass* and directly west over the River Humour from *Sulk End;* one of the states that during the Dissolutia (see *Gates, Battle of the ~* in Book One) did not venture out against the Imperial Capital. As a reward in HIR 1413 the new dynasty expanded Fayelillian's borders (much to the disgust of her neighbors), elevated her existing peers, granted patents to the most eminent nonpeer families and bestowed hereditary responsibilities, such as the peerage-marshalsy given to the forebears of the *Lamplighter-Marshal.* To common folk the people of Faylillian have a reputation for gentle simplicity and hospitality greatly at odds with their conquered ancestors, the fierce and indomitable Piltdownmen, who well over a thousand years ago vied with the Brandenards, Burgundians and Wretchermen of aulde for control of lands about the Grume.

fenceland also called sokes or scutis, fencelands are a marche or region of human habitation, where people have a firm hold of the land but still come into frequent contact with *monsters.* See entry on *marches* in Book One.

fend any long pike or spear-like weapon with long barbettes or other crossing-pieces protruding perpendicularly at the base of its head or along the shaft, manufactured so to prevent a *nicker* from pushing itself down the shaft.

Fend & Fodicar wayhouse in *Bleak Lynche* lovingly known by the locals as "the Pointy Sticks" and run by a kindly widow, Goodwife Inchabald—a large, socially fearless and universally genial woman, as all good enrica d'amas should be. As the only wayhouse in the whole *Frugelle,* it actually does a stiff trade despite its remoteness.

fetchman also fetcher, bag-and-bones man, ashcarter or thew-thief ("strength-stealer"); someone who carries the bodies of the fallen from the field of battle, taking them to the manoeuvra—or field hospital. Despite their necessary and extremely helpful labors, fetchmen are often resented by *pediteers* as somehow responsible for the deaths of the wounded comrades they take who often later die of their injuries. Indeed, they are regarded as harbingers of death, sapping their own side of strength, and as such are kept out of sight till they are needed. Such a thankless task. What we might call a stretcher bearer or orderly.

fettle mental fitness and stability, general soundness of attitude and emotion.

feuterer(s) the hundfassers, hound-hands or hundsmen who look after dogs in their kennels, feeding said animals and mucking out their dwellings. Feuterers are usually required only in the care of *tykehounds,* which need special care and calming, raised as they are to be nervous (and so give quick alarm to the presence of a *monster*) and cruel (so that they may not shy from attacking a *monster*). Nevertheless, even a half-decent feuterer and his fellow hundsmen will train their charges to react only to *monsters* and not *everymen.*

file what we would think of as an office, where *clerks* labor and leaders complete all the necessary and burdensome paperwork their positions require.

firing by quarto a platoon giving fire by division of *quartos,* each *quarto* firing separately while the other two reload.

fish, fishing common, vulgar term for the sending of a *wit;* a corruption of *frission.*

fitch attachable collar of feathers, themselves proofed or fixed into a gaulded cloth or buff lining and consequently a kind of armor.

flammagon stubby, large-bore firelock used to fire flares high into the air. In a pinch it can double as a weapon, but it is best suited as a launcher of bright signals.

flam-toothed saw medical tool used by *surgeons* to saw bones.

flanchardt similar to *shabraques* but used on oxen, bullocks and other beasts of burden. It is made of lower quality proofing but uses more layers to achieve comparable protection.

flash swell(s) idle rich young men who carouse and duel and woo the wrong women and are more trouble to the city folk than all the *monsters* combined. See *dandidawdlers*.

fleermare meaning "the weeping of the sea," an extraordinarily thick and drenching fog that comes in off the seas, most commonly in more arid places, acting as the "waterer" of the land in the place of highly infrequent rains. A fleermare can be so thick that it leaves everything dripping as if sodden by a good downpour.

Fleugh, Mister *clerk* of *Winstermill*, subordinate to *Witherscrawl* and very much in that man's sway.

Flint founded by a collective of *Soutland* states: a small but very wealthy non-Imperial state belonging unwillingly to the Sigismündian hegemony of the *Gotts* and its allies. The first stop on the way inland to *Sinster*, it has grown wealthy on gold and silver mining and on the trade of *gretchens*, which are most commonly found in waters off their coasts, and has recently begun to expand its navy—each vessel having as its aft-lantern a beautiful *gretchen* pearl. This militarism has people alarmed on all sides of the Pontus Canis, for a belligerent state could easily upset the fine balance of power that currently exists in the south of the Half-Continent.

fluff(s) wealthy people, peers, especially those who dress showily. No one really knows for certain where the term comes from; some suggest it is because of the continuing fashion for the well-to-do to wear all kinds of expensive furs and trim their hats and boots and even parasols with the same. See Appendix 4.

fodicar(s) (noun) also *lantern-crook,* lamp- or lantern-switch, poke-pole or just poke; the instrument of the lamplighters, a long iron pole with a perpendicular *crank-hook* protruding from one end used to activate the *seltzer lamps* that illuminate many of the *Empire's* important roads. The pike-head allows the fodicar to be employed as a weapon—a kind of halberd—to fend off man and *monster* alike. The bunting-hook on the reverse side to the lantern-hook can also be employed as a sleeve-catcher, making the fodicar a useful tool to parry and tangle fellow people should the need arise.

fortalice any small, usually freestanding building built or reinforced for use as a fortification, seldom used to garrison more than a platoon.

frank to be an accurate or "true" shot with a firelock; to shoot accurately.

Frazzard's powder one of a powerful set of repellents known as urticants, Frazzard's powder affects the mucous membranes and eyes most, reacting sharply with the moisture to sting painfully and even burn, scalding the eyes and rendering a foe permanently blind. Harsh stuff, by convention it is used only on *monsters*.

Friscan's wead one of the more common *alembant* treacles required to be taken by a *wit*. Its main purpose is to stop those specific organs inserted into the cranium from driving a *wit* mad and vaoriating (See *spasm, spasming* in Book One), witting anyone unfortunate enough to be near.

frission the collective and general term for the invisible energetic "pulse" of a *wit;* see *wit* in Book One.

fronstectum what we would call an eye-shade or visor, made of solid felt with a three-quarter-circle band of cloth-covered bone that fixes about the head.

Frugal, the ~ starting in the hills about the lead mines of the Louthe, this small river is noteworthy as the largest water source running through the *Frugelle.* Many tiny tributaries flow into it as it in turn flows into the *Ichormeer,* running right by the wall of *Haltmire* and serving as that fortress's source of water before bending away to the northeast and on into a great swamp.

Frugelle, the ~ great plain upon the western shores of the *Ichormeer* and the source of many small runnels and creeks that feed the wet of that notorious bog. It gains its name from the lack of arable soil and little rain there, moisture coming to the hardy plants and beasts by way of thick fleermares (fogs) off the *Swash,* the great bay to the south.

fugous cankers terrible and contagious disease spread by sneezing and showing worst as excruciating, rupturing, suppurating ulcers all over the body. Can be fatal if left unchecked, with the worst sufferers having to be shipped to a pestilentarium or pestifery, isolated houses for the separation of the sick from the living. The best run pestiferies will even treat and heal the sick held there; the worst are no better than prisons.

fulgar(s) *lahzars* that make powerful electrical charges in their body and use them to fight *monsters*. See entry in Book One.

fulminant(s) *potives* that cause explosions and flashes and bursts of fire.

furtigrade secret staircase hidden in the cavities of a wall. Such things were once built into almost every structure of more decent size, though now they are included only by request of the architect and builder.

fusil also known as a fusee or carabine or harquebus; a lighter musket with a shortened barrel that makes for simpler loading, is less cumbersome to swing about in thickets and woodland and saves considerable weight. Its shorter length also makes it handy as a club when the fight comes to hand strokes. This makes the fusil a preferred weapon of ambuscadiers and other skirmishing foot soldiers, and also comes a-handy for the drilling of smaller folk in the handling and employment of arms.

G

g the symbol for guise, the lowest monetary denomination in common currency of the *Soutlands*. See *money* in Book One.

Gall, Foistin near relation to the *Lictor* of *Winstermill*, Foistin was not proving to have either much aptitude or inclination for the lictoring trades (in which the Gall family has been a proud participant for thirteen generations) and, after a little "*playing of strings*" by his relation, was afforded a place in the *lamplighters* of *Winstermill*.

Gall, Grizzelard *Lictor* of *Winstermill*, the continuer of a greatly esteemed family trade, who delights in terrorizing the *prentices* with the power of his threat.

gallant *monster*-hunter, a more vulgar term than *teratologist*. Sometimes used to refer to venators (non-surgically improved hunters of *monsters*) but is a general appellation too.

gargant any large *nicker*.

gaudery odd and colorful garb that many *teratologists* wear: actually a stage term for the overdone costumes worn in plays and other performances.

geese vulgar term for the smallest denomination of Imperial coin, the guise piece, often used as a general reference to money of all kinds and amounts.

Gethsemenë blue glowing planet and one of the brighter heavenly bodies in the night. Not nearly as large as *Maudlin* or Faustus, it gains it prominence for being, after Phoebë (the moon), the closest object in the cosmic sky.

Giddian Pillow see *Pillow, Giddian*.

glaucolog sweet-talker; the less-than-polite name given to politicians, ministers, bureaucrats, lobbyists, factors and clerks—anyone in an official position who needs to persuade or coerce with words.

glimbloom see *bloom*.

Gomroon porcelain one of the finest kinds of porcelain, coming from the tiny kingdom of Gomroon far away on the shores of the *Sinus Tintinabuline*. This place has grown rich and powerful almost solely from the export of its much sought after tableware.

good-day gala-girls women of ill repute.

Gotts the proud race of people living in the southeast of the Half-Continent, their ancestors—the Skylds—coming once from far over the western waters, from the Hagenlands, driven out by crueler men and settling first in Wörms (see entry in Book One). From there they spread, mingled and merged with the local wildmen and eventually forged a small empire of their own to resist the rise of the Haacobins and the Sceptics before them. Gott, their language—sometimes still referred to as Skyldic—is somewhat akin to German in our own world.

gourmand's cork also known as a throttle or a gorge; the projecting "knuckle" of cartilage in a person's throat, in which is situated the vocal cords; what we would call the Adam's apple. It is called the gourmand's cork (a gourmand being one who is a gluttonous or greedy eater) because of the tight sensation you can get there when feeling nauseated, which vulgar folk hold is your throat trying to prevent or "cork" any further eating.

graille(s) tools of a *punctographist*. A marker needs four particular utensils to make a *cruorpunxis* upon the skin. These are the:

♣ guillion—also called an acuse or zechnennadel—the needle dipped in *cruor* and then pricked into the skin;

♣ orbis—in full, orbis malleus, a disc-headed mallet with which the guillion is tapped to puncture the skin and leave a mark.

♣ *sprither*—the device used to extract the blood from a *monster* in the first place.

♣ *bruicle*—the container in which *cruor* is kept till needed and into which the guillion is dipped every twenty taps or so to refresh the blood.

Other tools necessary to a *punctographist* are a notebook and stylus to take an observation of the fallen *monster's* face (either by description or by the presence of a corpse—or the head at least). From this is then figured the design of the *mark,* usually in consultation with the "markee."

great-lamp(s) also called a *vialimn,* the roadside *seltzer lamps* that illuminate the conduits and conductors of the world. They are larger, brighter and more robust than the street-lamps of the cities. In safer places, they are placed about 400 yards apart, and in more wild lands from 200 to 300 yards apart, though this is not a hard rule. The action of winding out the lamp is sometimes known as a hoist or lift-and-drop, each lamp requiring a different number of hoists to wind out fully. A lamp that has not been fully wound does not really pose any problems, but simply cuts down the amount of light thrown and is not good practice.

Greater Derehund(s) one of the larger breeds of *tykehound* with brindled hindquarters, a blunt, squarish snout and small, sharply pointed ears; originally from *Dereland* (hence their name), where they have served for centuries as defenders of *everymen*. Among the biggest of the *tykehounds,* the largest specimens can attain the size of a donkey and are a genuine terror to the lesser kinds of *monster.*

gretchen(s), gretchen-globe(s) also called *liaphobes* or Phoebë's Daughters (after a most famous collection of them); giant, beautiful "pearls" gagged up by kraulschwimmen. Formed in the bellies of the mighty sea-beasts in much the same way as the small nacreous globes are made inside an oyster, their most remarkable trait is that, from no cause the habilists can currently fathom, they glow naturally. The best, those considered flawless, are perfectly round and glow with such intensity that they are hard to look at. By action of currents and the occult movements of the sea-*nickers,* gretchens are found in greatest number along the Enne. Consequently the near-independent duchy of *Flint* and its lesser neighbors have a monopoly on the "harvesting" and trade of the beautiful globes. The smallest *liaphobes* can be no bigger than a typical oyster-made pearl, but the largest known—the Great Gretchen, from which all others take their name, which was found washed up on the shore of the Flintmeer after a mighty storm—was the size of a cottage. The cause of much envy and, in the end, a terrible war, it was lost along with the Phoebë's Daughters and a vast collection of the biggest *liaphobes* ever discovered. All those since found by the foolishly brave divers—encouraged by the great wealth to be had from their labors—have never come close in size.

Griffstutzig the name given to the best canignavor of *Winstermill's tykehounds.* Derived from the Gott for "dim-witted."

Grindrod, Lamplighter-Sergeant ~ said "*Grind*'rod"; senior non-commissioned officer in charge of the training of *prentices* at *Winstermill.* Covered with scars, he has, as he would put it, "survived more *theroscades* than ye've had puddings on Domesdays." He is a rough man but is genuinely concerned that the young souls he trains are prepared well for the labors of a *lamplighter,* that they well understand the terrors they face and are ready to cope with them.

gringollsis *potives* made to paste on to blades or coat the lead bullets of firelocks, making these better able to harm a *monster.* See *skold-shot.*

gromwell inexpensive and barely effective restorative having the equivalent impact on the imbiber of a shot of brandy, a warming jolt that does not last terribly long. Some who take it might also suffer the "runs" and bouts of austeration (meaning farting, taken from auster = "the south wind").

Grystle, House-Major ~ once a highly successful captain of a ram. An indiscretion in money and being outspoken about a clear tactical error of his commanding admiral on a blockade led to Grystle being broke (dismissed of service). Finding himself a bachelor without hearth or immediate prospects, he chose the next best military service (where folk are not fussy of your origins) and took the Emperor's Billion to become a *lamplighter*. Long years of habit mean he quite naturally runs the small stone world of *Wormstool* like the wooden ones he was used to on the vinegar seas. Indeed, he would tell you that there is little difference, both ram and *cothouse* being isolated in hostile regions and beyond immediate recourse to outside assistance, where survival depends upon the smarts and skills of its watches. Grystle is tight-lipped about his origins and the navy in which he served, though certainly by his accent and turn of phrase he is a native of the Grumid states (those states whose shores lie on the Grume).

gudgeon(s) sometimes rendered "gudjins"; also called nandins (meaning "simpleton," "idiot"); man-made *monsters* built by *massacars* (*black habilists*) from bits of people, animals, vat-grown organs, bits of machines and *monsters*. The most common are the corpselike *rever-men* or *revenants*. The major objection to the manufacture of gudgeons is that many body parts used once belonged to people, usually exhumed corpses. *Massacars* argue that this must be, especially with the brain, for without this the gudgeon will not be in any way controllable or useful. Yet with the rise of demand, kidnapping and murder have been employed to furnish the ever-needy *black habilists*, to the great sorrow of many. Publicly the Emperor is set against *black habilistics*, though his "backroom" opinion remains unknown. The more common uses people find for gudgeons are:

♣ for scouring—also known as bog- or bogle-toiling or hob-baiting: the hunting and driving out of *monsters* where the gudgeons are used both as the bait and the main tool of killing. There have been reports of *teratologists* known as reveners who cart around packs of *rever-men,* keeping them obedient with special *potives* and using them in this way.

♣ *hob-rousing.* See that entry.

♣ as guards for vaults and other sensitive, confined places.

♣ for intellectual pursuits, where *black habilists* tinker with the possibility of making a half-living thing. The ultimate goal of this is to make a tractable superhuman *teratologist,* a kind of logical progression from a *lahzar,* that will fight on no matter how injured. The goal is to send such as these into the wilds to seek out the *monsters* where they dwell and turn back the tide.

♣ in the search for longer life, perpetual youth; gudgeons and particularly *rever-men* are made by some for this purpose.

gyrovague one who wanders; a *hucilluctor,* a wayfarer.

H

Haacobin Empire, the ~ see *Empire,* the ~ and the entry in Book One.

hackle(s) • (noun) also called a *fitch,* a broad collar or shoulder-cape made of proofed fur; • (noun) any fur or unshaven animal hide that has been proofed. The gaulding process also affects the hairs themselves, adding to the protective qualities of the material. To gauld furs and keep the hairs, however, requires care and low apseric gaulds, of high quality, which of course increases the cost of the hackle, making it accessible only to the wealthy.

hack-watch pocket watch used by vinegaroons on a marine vessel as an aid to navigation and to determining noon by the sun.

Hagenards, Haganards, the ~ people of the Hagenland and much of the *Derelands* who, long, long ago, drove the Skylds out of their homelands and across the western seas. The Hagenards took possession of Ald Skyld and the Skylds took possession of what is now known as the Gottlands.

half-pay poker(s) older or worn-out *lampsmen* serving lighter duties either within a *cothouse* or on quieter stretches of road. The name *"poker"* is a somewhat derogatory reference to putting a *lantern-crook*—otherwise known as a poke—into the ratchet workings of a *great-lamp.*

Hall of Pageants large meeting hall built in the southwestern corner of *Winstermill's* vast grounds. It is used for all ceremonies, from the *puncting* of its victorious *monster*-slayers to the bestowing of commissions and other noteworthy promotions and awards, and usually the *Billeting Day* parade, held amid much pomp and splendor for each "batch" of fully trained *prentices*. Situated by the *Dead Patch,* the hall has in its cellars and foundations the tombs and sepulchres of its seniormost officers, who served with distinction over the century of its existence. Indeed, the hall is said to be actually erected over the old grave site of the original fortification of Winstreslewe.

Hallow Sill commonly known as the Hagwood, the forest surrounding *Herbroulesse,* which takes its less than friendly name from the very presence of the *calendars,* or hags, in that wood.

Haltmire very last fortress before the eastern borders of the *Soutlands* give over to the *Ichormeer;* built originally as a bastion, dormitory and storehouse for the engineers and laborers attempting the enormous work of building a road through the dread swamp. Not as large as *Winstermill* or the *Wight,* yet it is mighty enough to provide a permanent foothold in the isolated and threatened lands—with a reputation similar to the manse's for impregnability. Stationed there is the Warden-General, who has secondary command of the *"ignoble end of the road,"* and is the highest-ranking officer of the *lamplighters* on the road itself, topped only by the *Lamplighter-Marshal.* Like every other *cothouse* on the *Wormway,* Haltmire is undermanned, its company of *pediteer auxiliaries* reduced to one full platoon and one at half-strength, its *lighters* down to a *quarto,* its *thaumateers* limited to two skolds. There was once a *fulgar* employed there who was lost in the *Ichormeer* protecting the wife of the Warden-General as she desperately searched for their young children gone missing in that wretched place. The *lighters* of *Wormstool* and *Bleakhall* joined a greater and near futile search for the wife and daughters in which Haltmire's *scourge* was also lost and many *lighters* and *auxiliaries* barely returned with their lives. Managing to at least save the Warden-General's middle child, men of courage and a *frank* aim such as *Aubergene* proved their worth that day, and many were awarded by the grief-struck father. Situated so near to the southeastern city of Hurdling Migh, Haltmire gets most of its supplies from there and is a stockpile of resources for the *cothouses* to the west.

hand strokes close combat where blows with hand arms such as swords or cudgels are exchanged. The opposite is to "stand a pull," that is, to trade shots ("pulls") over a distance.

harlock means, quite simply, "white hair." See *Hermogenes, Cot-Warden~*.

Harrowmath, the ~ wide, boggy plain upon which *Winstermill* is situated, gaining its name from an ancient intention to drain the area and replant it with crops. However, all attempts to run off water from it and mow it failed: the water just kept seeping back and the grass resprouted stubbornly no matter what was done. Now it is left alone, home to frogs and salamanders and small water snakes, egrets, herons and screaming curlews, coties (small quail) and tiny hopping mice, and mown only occasionally to prevent it from becoming a perfect matted hiding place for *monsters*.

Harrowmath Pike, the ~ another name for the *Pettiwiggin*. It gained the name "pike" from the time when people were taxed a toll for its use, levied at *Wellnigh House* when travelers went to pass through in either direction.

haubardier(s) essentially a heavily armored musketeer. See entry in Book One.

hauncet(s) very heavy barreled pistol that takes great skill and strong wrists to fire and delivers a heavy, crushing blow of a shot. Loaded with *skold-shot* they become deadly tools against the *monsters*.

hedge, hedgeman "part skold, *dispensurist* and *ossatomist*"; often not especially well versed in any of the three trades, or particularly talented at one while offering the others out of need or sheer mercenary intent; one of the many types of *gyrovague* wandering the Half-Continent and indeed the entire world offering services to any paying person.

Heil glassware high-quality glassware coming predominantly from the city of Tüngasil in the fabled southern marches of Tüngusia in Heilgoland, the huge continent and empire south of the Gurgis Magna—the great southern ocean. The glass is made from the extra-fine sands mined from beneath the permafrost of the steplands on the borders of Magog.

heldin(s) mighty folk of ancient history who fought with the *monsters*, employing their infamous *therimoirs* to keep the eoned realms of human-kind safe; known by many collective titles, including beauts (common), haggedolim (Phlegmish), herragdars (*Skyldic*), heterai (*Attic*), orgulars (*Tutin*), sehgbhans (Turkic): what we would call "heroes." The time of their supremacy, when they were relied upon to stand in the gap between *everymen* and *üntermen,* is known as the Heldinsage. Said to have begun with the Phlegms—those most ancient of forebears—and ended with the *Attics,* their heirs, it was the time of Idaho, the great queen of the *Attics,* and of *Biargë the Beautiful,* among many other glorious and infamous folk and their usually tragic stories. Not all of the weapons of the heldins were destroyed in the violent cataclysms that punctuated and finally concluded that time: many are said to remain, and are most highly prized by collectors and combatants.

Herbroulesse also known as the *Dovecote* or *Columbris;* the home of the *calendars* of the *Right of the Pacific Dove.* The original name of the old, moldering fortress that the *Right* occupied when they first moved into the region at the *Idlewild's* beginnings.

hereward westward. In the Half-Continent, although the usual north, south, east and west are common terms, directions of the compass are often given more classical names:

♣ north = nere, said "near"; also nout, said "nowt"

♣ south = sere, said "seer"; also scut, said "scoot," or sout, said "sowt"

♣ east = vere, said "veer"; also est

♣ west = here, said "heer."

See *"by the precious here and vere"* in Book One.

Hermogënes, Cot-Warden ~ said "Her-*moj*-anees"; once a native of Seville, far to the north, he has carried with him for a long time the name *harlock,* which means simply "white hair," having been born with those unusually pallid locks. Cot-Wardens are the senior-most sergeants (sergeant-master) of a cothouse.

Hinkerseigh said "*Hink*-ker-see"; a small city/large town in the *Idlewild* whose founding state is the Sangmaund state of Maubergonne. It gets its name from its most prominent founding family, the Hinkers, and their grand fortified high-house (a *seigh*). Hinkerseigh is most noted for its many water-driven mills and heavier industry, a small copy of the original city of its founders—one of the more industrialized of the *Soutland* states.

hirsuite partially cured animal leather with the hair left on, the hair usually being shaved or trimmed short but not removed. See *rimple.*

hob-rousing also known as sheboggery, or pit-fights; a recent invention of the affluent bored and a major customer of the *dark trades*. Hob-rousing is the practice of pitting a *gudgeon* and *nicker* against one another and betting on the outcome. Under the charge of a *rouse-master*, gents known as pit-bobs (or *tractors*) wrangle these beasts together into a pit (10-plus-foot deep x 12-plus-foot wide), initially separated by bars. This barrier is removed and the two allowed to *stouche* it out until one is left alive (with *gudgeons* usually proving the more aggressive but the less robust). *Gudgeons* that survive for many bouts can gain a kind of fame among the hob-rousing regulars (the gamers or cubes, who come to watch and wager, and the nullards or pigeons, who come only to watch), gaining names like "the Matschig Mauler," "Old Feisty" and such like, "Mary's Long-Dead Mother" being one of the more gruesome and ironic appellations. Indeed, even some *monsters* who have survived for many fights have gained grudging admiration. The *rousing-pits* are typically maintained by either a peer or magnate or by a cartel of mercators (*dark trade* bosses)—someone with the will and money to establish and maintain such a place. They will be found deep in the foundations of a manor house (with tunnels and their entrances leading well away from the host) or some abandoned hall or cave out in the country. Hob-rousing is a big money-spinner for the organizers, with fights sometimes rigged in the *rever-man's* favor to give the spectator some much-needed satisfaction against the monstrous foe. Of course, if a *rousing-pit* is secreted out in the wilds, any *gudgeon* kept there will eventually attract *nickers;* this, although highly risky, usually suits the organizer/owners, who will try to trap any *monsters* lurking near and use them in the next fight.

Hognells, the ~ broad gray escarpment regarded as the natural division between the *Idlewild* proper and the poor lands of the *Paucitine.* They form part of the range of hills rich in mostly as yet untapped ores: lead, copper and, some say, even silver. Fossickers can often be seen ranging about the surrounding lands, sent by the big states to find sources of these precious metals.

horrors, the ~ • (noun) common term for *threwd.* • (noun) lingering and malingering effects of *pernicious threwd,* the sufferers remaining in a fragile, frightened and broken state. Some folks hold that those touched by the horrors have a greater sensitivity to threwdish things and are more aware of the monstrous in the world around them. More sensible people dismiss this as arrant rustic nonsense. The horrors are related to the blue ghasts, which is a more darkly depressive state.

house-major more properly titled *Major-of-House,* this is the most senior officer of a *cothouse* with charge over all the doings therein and along the span of road put under his responsibility. If something happens to or along that span, then it is his duty—and the duty of those he commands—to initiate a solution, whether it is road repairs, clearing the verge, rescuing stranded travelers, hunting *lurchers* or brigands or *monsters.*

house-watch permanent staff of a *cothouse* who do not go out on the *lantern-watch.* These can include the *house-major,* the *day-clerk, uhrsprechman,* the kitchen staff (if present) and the various trades and laborers required for daily tasks such as *tinkers, proofeners, seltzermen* and the like. Some *cothouses* were once manned well enough to possess a large house-watch of *pediteers* as well to relieve the *day-watch* at intervals and provide them with extended rest.

hucilluctor(s) said "hyoo-sil-luck-tor"; a wayfarer. The word comes from the *Tutin* term meaning "hither and thither."

hugger-mugger one of the many synonyms for *monster,* referring to a common manner of attack among the *üntermenschen,* which is to leap from an ambush—to "hug"—and grapple closely with their prey—to "mug."

huque said "hyook"; a long cloak with split sides to allow the wearer's arms free movement.

I

ichor when talking of *cruorpunxis,* a *monster's* blood when still inside it is known as ichor, and when extracted by a *sprither* into a *bruicle* it is called *cruor.*

Ichormeer, the ~ great threwdish swamp to the east of Sulk and west of Wörms said to be the origin of *monsters,* the place where they are "born" from to terrorize the *Soutlands.* See entry in Book One.

Idesloe *calendar* purrichin of the *Right of the Pacific Dove,* originally coming from *Flint,* and once speardame to Sophia Idaho II, its ruling Duchess. The eldest purrichin, she is the mentor of the other *sagaars* of the *Right,* going into a *stouche* bearing her ancient *therimoir,* a sword-of-wire called Glausopë—or "Asp's Tongue," a relic of the Heldinsage.

Idlewild, the ~ officially known as the Placidia Solitus, a gathering of client-cities (colonies) along the Imperial Highroad of the *Conduit Vermis.* Each town, village or fortress is sponsored by a different state of the *Empire*—*Brandenbrass,* Hergoatenbosch, Quimperpund, Maubergonne, Termagaunt, even Catalain. Established in the late fifteenth century HIR, it is the latest great project of what is grandly termed *cicuration*—taming by farming; *purgation*—taming by force; and *bossetation*—taming by landscaping, originally proposed by *Clementine* itself. The Inner Idlewild or *Placidine,* from *Tumblesloe Cot* to the *Wight,* was declared "regio scutis"—a *fenceland*—over a decade ago. This heralded a brilliant success of the great labor of pushing back the *monsters* and the *threwd.* The marches from the *Wight* to *Haltmire*—otherwise known as the *Paucitine* (also the *Frugelle*)—are still considered *ditchland.* These two divisions of *Placidine* and *Paucitine* are known as *themes,* or military districts, the western governed by *Winstermill,* the eastern by *Haltmire,* with the *Wight* situated at their meeting and concerned only with the taxation of trade from Sulk.

"ignoble end of the road" title given to the remote and dangerous stretch of road that runs along the flat of the *Frugelle,* beginning at the *Hognells* and ceasing at *Haltmire,* and to the *cothouses* found thereon.

IMIR In Ministerium Imperia Regnum (or Rex), meaning either "In Service to the *Empire*" or "In Service to the Emperor"; the motto of any ministry or body working for the *Haacobin Empire.*

Imperial fumomath *scourge,* skold or *dispensurist* in the direct employment of the *Empire;* the term can be used to refer to such skolds and *scourges* that are employed at *Winstermill* and elsewhere, but more properly means those who serve in the Emperor's courts in *Clementine,* especially those tending to the Emperor himself.

Imperial Prerogative a mandate from the Most Serene Emperor granting limited yet often far-reaching rights to certain individuals or groups (such as many *calendar claves*) allowing them to operate outside the governances or interference of state or other local authorities. It can even be pushed (some might say abused) to allow things contrary to the Imperial interest to proceed unhindered, such as the breaking of an Oath of Service.

Imperial Secretary highest ranked of all the *Haacobin Empire's* bureaucrats; men and women of great influence and power, not so much because of their own rank, but because of the status of the ears and minds they have such ready access to—the senior ministers of the Emperor, and even the great man himself. The favor of an Imperial Secretary can be the making of you, their disfavor your ruin. Though often of common birth, they are typically courted and feted by peers, especially the lowly ranked, and by gentry and magnates too, eager for some kind of advancement or boon. One does not strive to be an Imperial Secretary for dreams and hopes of reform, but for the sake of pure ambition and ego.

In Columba Alat meaning "a dove's wing" or "the wings of a dove," and also known as the Columbinale; the *cantus* (or creed) of the *calendar clave* known as the *Right of the Pacific Dove* to which each adherent must ascribe and swear:

> *Defend the oppressed where e'er thee can,*
> *Defend the woman e'er 'gainst man;*
> *From thy own chattels another soul aid,*
> *Clear the writs that cannot be paid;*
> *Shelter the shelterless through heat or snow;*
> *Set wings of Dove 'gainst cunning crow.*
>
> *Live thee rightly, ready to die,*
> *Uphold the true, expose the lie;*
> *Gentle yet strong, humble yet bold,*
> *Guidance for young and succor for old;*
> *And where e'er thee walk and whither thy go,*
> *Set wings of the Dove 'gainst monstrous foe.*

Another version replaces "chattels" in the third line for "labors"—though the idea is held to be the same. Other *claves* will have similar creeds, for *calendars* of any stripe live by such things.

Ingébiargë pronounced "*Ihng*'geh'bee'arr'gee;" or *Biargë the Beautiful,* as she is commonly known, a powerful creature who relishes the taste of vinegaroon and has lived as long as modern matter can tell. See *Biargë the Beautiful.*

invidist(s) commonly thought of as loathards, those who utterly hate *monsters,* who feel *theiromisia* (deliberate and pointed malice against teratoids), as opposed to those who feel a general dislike or habitual, mindless fear (the average citizen of the *Empire*). Also known as aspex (typically used in reference to a *teratologist*), theirmisers, execrats, these are the inveterate enemy of sedorners.

ipse adversus as the Marshal says, this roughly means "standing alone" and comes from "(ipse) solus adverso malus," literally, "(oneself) alone against the evil."

"I will wait for thee / If thou wouldst come with me" a quote from "The Wide-faring Merchant," also called "The Plaint of the Merchant's Wife," a popular tune heard the *Soutlands* over.

> *Off go thou to a fabled land,*
> *To mystic Fiel and Samaarkhand,*
> *For prospect's grasp at money's hand*
> *and that fortune's making;*
> *I wouldst go with thee,*
> *If thou wouldst wait for me.*

> *We'll sit on plushest gala seats,*
> *Eat mani-plattered sweetest meats,*
> *A plethora of toothsome treats,*
> *till our stomachs' aching;*
> *I will wait for thee*
> *If thou wouldst come with me.*

> *We'd charter ram to Hagen'Sere,*
> *Ply the mares to farthest vere,*
> *From Tintinabuline to Quimpermeer*
> *and see the world a'passing;*

Thou shouldst wait for me,
For I would come with thee.

And if I catch a morbid ill,
From Heilgoland's most wretched chill,
And spend my days on Death's doorsill
till morning turns to mourning;
Wouldst thou stay with me,
As I wouldst stay with thee?

J

jakes, the ~ toilets, also called *heads* (navy), or garderobe, water closet, the gong and the rest.

Josclin said "joss'lyn"; *scourge* of *Winstermill*. Hailing from *Brandenbrass* yet said to be descended from Cloudeslee stock, that quasi-mystic land beyond the southern bounds of the *Haacobin Empire*, reputed to be populated with sedorners and most famous for its deadly accurate archers— or toxothetes. Josclin does not elaborate on his heritage and, as a *scourge*, has chosen a profession quite at odds with the principles of his reputed forebears. He trained at the Madrigoll, the much-vaunted rhombus in Maubergone, rather than at the Saumagora—or "Soup Pot"—in *Brandenbrass*, won by the former's well-earned reputation for producing first-rate *scourges*. He so rarely ventures forth without his *fascins* that though he has served with the *lighters* at *Winstermill* for nigh on a decade, only a few of his fellows know what he actually looks like.

K

knave(s) • (noun) the opposite of a *spurn*; broadly any *teratologist* who hires services out to the highest bidder or any other paying customer, but used in reference to *lahzars* particularly—a nonlahzarine *monster*-slayer is sometimes called a hack, because these nonsectified *gallants* have to "hack" at a *monster* to battle it (as with a sword or cudgel or the like). How this includes skolds (which it does) is unknown and also unquestioned. • (verb) to hire oneself out, especially as a *teratologist;* to sell one's services.

knavery offices where a person can go to hire a *teratologist* or three or as many as are needed. Such establishments gain their name from the term "*knave*," that is, any person who sells services to any paying client, as opposed to a *spurn,* who serves a retaining lord or master. When entering a region for the first time, a *teratologist* may register at the local knavery to make it known that he or she is about and going on the roll offering services. In doing this *monster*-hunters are agreeing not to shop their skills through other neighboring knaveries or their own advertisement, thus denying the knavery its commission. The knaving-*clerk* will take a request from a customer and offer a selection of *monster*-hunters they believe will solve the dilemma. Once the *teratologist* has been selected, he or she is approached with an Offer of Work, which may be accepted or rejected. Work is more steady for *teratologists* who use the knaving system, though they usually make less money for service rendered.

L

lackbrained empty-headed, slow-witted, not very bright or clever.

Lady Dry-stick vulgar term for an uptight, unfriendly, upper-class woman.

Lady Vey, The ~ see *Vey, the Lady ~*.

laggard(s) *leers* specializing in the detection of hard to see things and things far off, getting greater use out of a *sthenicon*, which is made in part to enhance such senses, than a *falseman*.

lahzar(s) said "luh'*zahr*"; the premium *monster*-hunter, gaining peculiar and deadly abilities through surgery. See entry in Book One.

lale short afternoon break usually held at 4 P.M., where the *lantern-watch* ready themselves to depart, taking a small meal to help them on the road. The word is an antiquated rendering of "lull," a time of quietude.

lambrequin simple proofed cover-all armor, worn over the top of normal clothing, like a kind of heavy gaulded poncho.

"Lamp East Winst(ermill) *x* **West Well(nigh House)** *y*** system for designating the placement of a *great-lamp* on a highroad, *x* and *y* being the number of *lamps* away from a *cothouse* or other fortification.

lamplighter(s) *pediteer* responsible for the lighting and dousing of *lamps* along highroads, low-roads and any other roads in between. One of the benefits of experience is knowing just how many winds it takes for each lamp to be fully wound out, for not every *great-lamp* requires the same number of lift-and-drops to bring out the *bloom*. Upon joining as a *prentice,* a *lighter* is issued with the following items:

- ♣ 1 *quabard,* Imperial mottle
- ♣ 1 sash, twin-pattern, rouge blank and rouge and cadmia checks
- ♣ 1 *fodicar,* Scutid pattern
- ♣ 1 thrice-high, felt, black, with gaulded band
- ♣ 3 shirts, linen, white
- ♣ 3 longshanks, proofed, black
- ♣ 3 pair undergarments, white
- ♣ 3 pair trews or stockings
- ♣ 1 trencher, wooden
- ♣ 1 cup, tin
- ♣ 1 set turnery or cutlery
- ♣ 2 blankets, woolen
- ♣ 1 pillow, hay-stuffed
- ♣ 1 clasp-knife (for paring toe- and fingernails, cleaning fouled equipment)
- ♣ lug-pipe, pewter (used in the cleaning of firelocks)
- ♣ 1 ox trunk

Of course, if fellows possess equivalent items of their own, then these are employed instead, and they may expand their equipment as they wish. At some *cothouses* each *lighter* is also issued with charges of repellents or *blastes* (such as bothersalts, *Frazzard's powder,* salt-of-asper and the like) and given a little training in how to use them, thus acting as his own skold. Every second *lighter* is also issued a record: a small book in which the disrepair of a lamp can be recorded and left for the *seltzermen* to read and act upon. See entry in Book One and Appendix 7.

Lamplighter-Marshal, the ~ his correct title is the *Eighth Earl of the Baton Imperial of Fayelillian.* Though he comes from a well-to-do family, an entire life spent in military service in close association with the common *pediteer* has meant the Marshal has picked up their less-than-couth manners. He is the kind of leader who shows by example and has fought several *stouches* in the front with his men, gaining himself their deep respect, several gruesome scars and no small number of *cruorpunxis*. The rank itself is the highest possible for a *lamplighter*, an Imperial commission that is usually only granted to peers—with the heroic Protogenës being a notable exception. In order for the Lamplighter-Marshal to succeed at his tasks he is heavily reliant on the cooperation and skill of the Comptroller-Master-General and with him the *Master-of-Clerks* to keep the more bureaucratical gears of the lighters' world turning efficiently.

Lamplighter-Sergeant Grindrod see *Grindrod, Lamplighter-Sergeant.*

lamps collective noun for all lights, and particularly those that give light to streets and roads.

"A lamp's worth is proved by its color" also "a lamp's weal (health) is proved by its color," an old *lamplighter* truism meaning that someone's moral value is proved by his or her actions, or "actions speak louder than words." It comes from the idea that you can tell a *seltzer lamp's* condition by the color of the light coming through the *seltzer.*

lampsman 3rd class the lowest rank of a properly qualified *lighter*, being the rank *prentices* are promoted to once *prenticing* is done. See Appendix 6.

lampsmen another name for *lamplighters,* meaning generally the non-officer ranks.

lamp-watch also called the *lantern-watch;* the nightly duty of moving along a stretch of road to light the *lamps* and then spend many hours on watch in your *bastion-house* till early morn when you go out once more and put all the *lamps* out again. After this it's a well-earned sleep during daylight hours. The term also refers to the folk involved in the performing of the lamp-watch.

landgrave a rank of peer in the Lauslands, equivalent to somewhere between a duke and an earl of the *Haacobin Empire;* essentially the now hereditary rulers of their lands, the ranks formerly granted by a long-gone dynasty of kings when the Lauslands were once a part of Ing. Now they elect for themselves a valastin (chief elector) from among their own, who rules for a set period and is responsible for those troubles of state that require centralized governing. The Haacobins and the Sceptics before them have long coveted these fertile western lands of the landgraves and have long waged war to get them. Yet they have never been able to prevail over their western neighbors. The soldiers on those failed campaigns have claimed that the *monsters* of those lands are actually working in the favor of the landgraves and their peoples; the ministers back in *Clementine* dismiss this as an excuse.

landsaire also spelled landtseir, an organized group of *lesquins* of battalion strength or greater. Sometimes they include "legio" or "legion" in the names, after the *Tutin* armies of old.

lantern-crook another name for a *fodicar.*

lantern-span distance between *great-lamps* on a highroad, the agreed standard being 400 yards, though the lamps themselves can be anything from 200 to 600 yards apart, depending on where in the road they are situated.

lantern-stick(s) mildly deprecating name for *prentices* given them by full-ranked *lampsmen*. It comes from the name for the lighter wooden practice-crooks that are sometimes employed to help young would-be *lighters* in winding a *great-lamp's* mechanism. It is also an insulting nickname infrequently given to *fodicars* by nonlighters.

lantern-watch another rendering of *lamp-watch,* used especially to refer to the period of duty itself rather than the group of *lamplighters.*

lark-lamp also called a swadlimn, a 1:6 to 1:10 scale model of a *great-lamp,* used to instruct *lamplighters* on the workings of the lights used along the Emperor's highroads. They are lights in their own right, fully functioning, with the *bloom* capable of being wound in and out of the *seltzer.* Unlike *bright-limns,* however, they do not suffer being tipped about, such action generally causing them to spill *seltzer water* and foul up the fine gears of their workings.

laude assistant, voice and rod of the *august* of a *calendar clave* who knows all the comings and goings of the local area. It is to her and her assistants that all appeals, requests and visitors must come before being referred to the *august* for final arbitration. Highly capable and dangerous in her own right, a laude is the deliverer of all the censures and commendations of her *august* and *clave.*

leakvane kind of tarbinaire, a *potive* composed of two parts that combine to make the required reaction. Leakvanes themselves are small elongated boxes of thin light wood, designed to break apart, divided into two wax-sealed halves between which is a heavy film of treated velvet that protrudes from the top of the box. When this tab is pulled the two *potives* kept separate in either half mix together, and after anywhere from a few seconds to a minute they will react with the desired effect. The best tarbinaires will have the expected time for reaction stamped on them, and it is recommended never to shake one, as this can cause an almost instantaneous effect while the device is still in your hand.

ledgermain(s) person who has learned *skolding* from books and not from another skold. Ledgermains are considered grossly inferior to the genuine, once-prenticed article.

ledgerstone stone carved with pretty words commemorating the life of some noteworthy individual. They are usually used as part of a floor or path, and sometimes are actually placed over the remains of the great personage. What is remarkable about this is that the body is typically laid right out rather than placed vertically or crouched in the fetal position. The latter is the common practice in cities not wanting to dispose of the beloved dead outside the city walls where *monsters* can dig the corpses up and *corsers* too, and where they need to conserve space in the tight confines of the city itself.

leer(s) people who soak their eyes in remarkable concoctions to achieve extraordinary feats of sight. See entry in Book One.

lentum shorthand for a *post-lentum* or any other covered and enclosed carriage of four wheels.

lesquin(s) • (noun) honored mercenary regiments and brigades of the obdacar or freebooter (mercenary) class, wandering the lands or stationed in home cities waiting for the highest-paying master. They are special societies of soldiers with elaborate initiation ceremonies that emphasize loyalty to the particular *landsaire* (a lesquin legion). Much used in the squabbles between cities because they are a way—a loophole—around the stringent recruiting restrictions of the *Accord of Menschen* (where numbers within a state's standing army are limited). The use of lesquins also allows a certain amount of immunity from accountability should it ever be required by the Emperor—"So sorry, your

Imperial Highness, the lesquins got out of control and we were not able to stop them," or that kind of thing. Lesquins dress as gaily as *lahzars* and *calendars,* though with differences that make them immediately recognizable, wearing such things as sammosh (big baggy hats) with guirlandes (enormous dyed feathers worn on the head), plunderhose (baggy pants tied off at the knee), exotic hide proofing such as crocidole (reptile skin), and favoring exotic weapons, especially *combinades.* Lesquin legions, or *landsaires,* originating from nonsignatory countries (Gottingenin, Wörms, the Lausid States and anywhere north of the Marrow and the Foullands) are preferred, though their numbers may still be stocked from Old World (meaning "Imperial") populations. They will often charge their fee in accordance with their reputation. Still, less expensive *landsaires* have their uses—most notably affordability. The elite regiments are marked out with fancy mottle accoutrements: ospreys and other *hackles,* ailettes, and bonnets to rival a *calendar's dandicomb.* Champions, known as machismards, are awarded harness and gear of exceptional manufacture, beyond regular issue, to recognize their prowess and encourage such ambition among brother fighters. Lesquins make excellent soldiers, rivaled only by a few standing armies or, more particularly, units within the same. Contests with such as these are fought bitterly to prove, of course, who is best. Ragtag bands of ill-trained, ill-equipped, ill-led and very cheap mercenary regiments are called foedermen, and are not considered worthy of the lesquin name. • (noun) card game commonly played by serious gamblers between a dealer (known as the colonel) and any number of wagerers. It is based on matching cards, and who holds what card determines whether the colonel or wagerers get the pot or ante. It takes its name from the soldiering lesquins, for some mistakenly believe it was invented by these sell-swords, but it is more likely that the lesquins are responsible not for its invention but for spreading it about the known world. They are certainly among its most frequent players. The *prentices* of *Winstermill* would be playing it to feel all manly and brave; the *lighters* on the *Wormway* would be playing it because all soldiers the lands over do.

letter-fall that is the apt sequence, or "fall," of the letters as they are in what we would call the alphabet; alphabetical order.

liaphobe(s) see *gretchen(s), gretchen-globe(s).*

libermane *potive* used to prevent the *cruor* of a *monster* from clotting too quickly as it is stored in a *bruicle*. Useful as this is, it also affects the quality of the blood, thinning it and making the *cruorpunxis* it is used for pale, less distinct. Therefore libermane is used only when a *teratologist* is more than a couple of days' journey from a *punctographist*. Another function of libermane is its application on swords, knives and other blades of war to make a wound flow more than it ought, though by the *Accord of Menschen* this practice is deemed unacceptable in modern conflict.

Lictor person in charge of punishment and discipline, the deliverer of the lash, the clapper of irons, the locker of stocks, pillories and durance doors; the tightener of the noose or the cords of a Catherine wheel. In more extreme regimes, the Lictor is also the chief torturer.

lighter(s) shortened name for a *lamplighter*.

limes short, universal morning interval designed purely to make certain *pediteers* get some citrus juice into them. After the discovery by Callio Catio (reputed—along with Asclipides and others—to be the founder of modern *physics*) of the prevention of scurvy and other nutrition-related diseases, military organizations the lands over have fastidiously ensured their men take their lime or lemon juice (Juice-of-Orange is a more recent advent, reserved for those who can afford it and not your ordinary foot slogger).

limulight(s) small box-light whose source of effulgence is living bio-luminescent mosses and lichens. See *moss-light*.

linen package wrapped parcel containing one's underclothes.

liripipium hat with a peak that hangs down at the back in a "tail."

locum usually a physician in training or someone working as assistant to a physic with a view toward attending a physactery and gaining a full qualification.

long-rifle smooth-bore musket with an extraordinarily long barrel to provide greater accuracy. The name is a misnomer, for the bore is not in fact "rifled," but left smooth, though the great length of the barrel does make for very true shots.

loomblaze powerful repellent that is also part *fulminant*. Because it both poisons and burns with *false-fire*, it is regarded as a very versatile agrise (violent *potives;* as opposed to palliates—helpful, healthful *po-*

tives; or obstrutes—most other *potives*), useful against both human and *monster.* The nature of its violence means its use is recommended only when deadly force is required.

lordia mild restorative that is meant to balance the humours (see *Four Humours, the ~* in Book One). Balancing the humours restores equilibrium to intellect and soul, pith and thew, calming the imbiber and setting agitations to ease. Its mild efficacy is matched only by its small expense; a cheap pick-me-up that has been said to be the cause of addiction in some.

lorica also known as a corslet, a *proof-steel* back-and-breastplate, worn most by *troubardiers* and the few heavy equiteer regiments in the Half-Continent. Its front is fairly steeply peaked to allow shots from a firelock to more easily ricochet. It is a common practice to adhere *lour* or *soe* or villeny to the metal or to black it in order to eliminate or reduce shine.

Lornstone, the ~ also known as the Heptafornix or "seven arches," a bridge and causeway built as part of the great project to run a road through the *Ichormeer.* The causeway that runs east from it was built on the pattern of the *Pettiwiggin* and had been intended to carry the road all the way through the *Frugelle.* The attrition of economies and a lack of desire meant this ambition was soon abandoned after only a few miles of raised-road were completed. The first of many small failures that dogged the great work of the laying of the *Conduit Vermis.*

Lot's Books popular diagrammatic readers written on a whole host of topics—navies, *monsters,* famous people, animals, weapons, etc.—and filled with helpful diagrams. Expensive, they are a favorite educational tool for children among the well-to-do.

lour • (noun) velvet that has been treated with gauld; other gaulded cloths include linteum (lint) = cotton; duram = hemp; buff = leather; ombyx = gauze or other filmy materials; *soe* = silk; pellis = fur; fustian = hessian; villeny or lawn = felt. • (verb) to frown.

Low Gutter, the ~ in the distant past of *Winstermill's* history, the southern end of the huge mound upon which it was erected collapsed with loss of life, the historied rubble on which it was founded failing at last. Rather than abandon the fortress, as some advised, cooler minds

657

prevailed to have that ruined section of what was once an enormous open ground shored up and leveled, a stable shelf several score feet lower than the main Mead. Upon this shelf it became practicable to construct servants' quarters and mills for laboring work as the staff of *Winstermill* expanded beyond the simple barracks it once had been. It was during the early repairs that the name the Low Gutter was coined, for the ruined foundation would fill with the rains and spout water from many cracks and corners like a roof gutter.

lurcher(s) • (noun) also called finegars, the vernacular for those who especially trap *monsters,* doing their level best to keep them alive. They are considered worse than poachers and other such slyboots, and often trap on lands otherwise declared out of their bounds, such as the private lands of a peer. • (noun) derogatory name used to refer to someone who killed a *monster* for which another had the Writ of the Course to slay, thus robbing that second *gallant* of his head-money.

lurksman, lurksmen sometimes called pathprys, these are trackers and spies, and are often nonleers practiced in the use of a *sthenicon.* Given that a *sthenicon* is made to be used and understood by a *leer,* it takes a lot for nonleers to achieve such skill, and once they have mastered it they are never as good as a box-faced *laggard.* Still, a lurksman is far better than no sensurist at all.

lurksman-general informal name for the General-Master-of-Palliateers and the commanding officer of the *Palliateer-Major.* Palliateers are those soldiers and *auxiliaries* concerned with sneaking and spying and tracking, including *leers, lurksmen,* ambuscadiers, sneaksmen and other clandestine agents.

M

mabrigond one of the constituents of *Craumpalin's Exstinker* made from the dried and ground buds of the flower of the same name; a typical inclusion in *nullodors,* where its own flat smell helps obscure other scents.

maiden-fraught any woman given to a life of combat, including *calendars.* In a typically patriarchal society, *skolding* and more recently becoming a *lahzar* has been an oft-used path for young women seeking relief and independence from their fathers, uncles, brothers and the usual social mores. *Lahzars,* particularly, occupy an unusual place in society, outside of it in an ill-defined way: respected, feared, despised and needed. And a woman as one is regarded as the acme of all things "modern"—and modernity is generally regarded as a bad thing by those of breeding. "You look very modern," one might say with a sneer.

Maids of Malady, the ~ *clave* of *calendars* from Burgundia. Little is known of them in the *Empire,* for they direct their activities more to the eastern lands, though any who have had dealings with the *Soratchë* will have likely heard of their allies the Maids as well. Indeed the Maids are said to be aspex (see *invidists*), treating sedorners most severely, going out of their way to chase down a proven *outramorine.* They are even more zealous than their allies in their pursuit of *black habilists.*

mains last official meal of the day, usually begun at 6 P.M. Much to Rossamünd's early discomfort, mains is later in the day than he was used to at the old marine society, and he was terribly sharp-set in the first week as a *prentice lighter* at *Winstermill,* as his tummy emptied on habit two whole hours earlier than it would be filled again.

Major-of-House the correct title of a *house-major.*

Makepeace one of the smaller settlements in the *Idlewild* sponsored by *Brandenbrass.* The sister colony of the mining village Gathercoal, this hopefully named township is the main source of supply and support to the *peltrymen* of the Ullwold to the north, and pastoralists of the Swiddenlands or Swide—the narrow hilly stretch of farms to the south along the northern fells of the *Sparrow Downs.* It is also home to the *cothouse* of Makepeace Stile.

manchin(s) thick sleeves of proofed materials, usually voluminous enough to be pulled over other sleeves, then tied to the body with straps or ribbons. They serve as extra protection for the arms, and are often lined with fleece for added warmth.

maraude(s) *theroscades* on a large scale, with an abnormally large collection of *monsters* in one attack or many attacks across a range or, most frightening of all, both at once. For reasons not properly understood, winter has proved to be the more usual time for such things, but they are mercifully less common than might be expected. Unless they are beasts who naturally pack together, it takes a mighty showing of will to get *monsters* to behave in concert. Even so, history both popular and obscure is filled with the hushed tellings of these terrible days and the *Empire* is still recovering from the aftermath of the greatest maraudes—those civilization-ruining massings of *nickers* great and small.

Maria Diem old *Tutin* word meaning "Meerday"—the Day of the Sea. For the other days of the week there are Newwich = Prima Diem, Loonday = Luna Diem, Midwich = Media Diem, Domesday = Festus Deis, Calumnday = Caelum Dies, and Solemnday = Gravis Deim.

mark • (noun) *monster-blood tattoo;* • (verb) to apply a *monster-blood tattoo.*

marshal-lighter alternative rendering of *Lamplighter-Marshal.*

massacar(s) common name for a *black habilist,* especially those loathsome dabblers who make *rever-men* and other *gudgeons.* See *habilists* in Book One.

Master Come-lately a mildly derogatory name for Rossamünd, given to him first by *Lamplighter-Sergeant Grindrod* and quickly adopted by the other *prentices.*

Master-of-Clerks, the ~ also known as the *clerk-master,* the rank of *Podious Whympre,* the youngest son of a youngest son of a line of glossagraphs (foreign *clerks*) from *Brandenbrass.* There is money in the family, but Podious is not likely to inherit. The parsimonious fellow is an ambitious and shrewd administrator who loves a complete and thorough system of paperwork. His substantive (actual) rank is the highest non-commissioned *clerk* in a military establishment; his brevet (temporary) rank as Comptroller-Master-General puts him equal with the second highest ranks in *Winstermill,* though its position as the leader of all bureaucracy makes him the second-in-command. His appointment to this powerful position, after the original Comptroller-Master-General took sudden leave of his senses and the manse, was due to the influence of the *Imperial Secretary* stationed in High Vesting. An old friend of the family's scrupulus sicus has taken to patronizing Whympre, exerting influence at the political end in the *clerk-master's* favor. Ultimately taking his orders from Imperial bureaucrats, the *Lamplighter-Marshal*, whatever his personal take, has had to promote as directed. It is very frustrating for a military leader to have his affairs meddled with from afar.

mathematician(s) bitter rivals of the concometrists (see entry in Book One), trained at an institution known as an abacus, and more interested in the beauty and function of pure numbers and systems than the functions of society. Trainees of an abacus are prized for their sharp minds, rapid calculations and other skills of genius and mental aptitude. Indexers, for example, are those who can organize figures and information in their heads without writing anything down, then remember it all and retrieve some point of fact for you at will, like thumbing through a file. Probably the most famous kinds of mathematician are the Imperial Computers, striving up in *Clementine,* figuring probabilities and sums that might affect the *Empire.*

Maudlin said "*Moord-lin*"; a planet, and one of the brightest lights in the night sky, having a distinct greenish tinge. See entry in Book One.

mercer public messengers and parcel deliverers with a distinctive red-and-yellow-checked mottle. Usually employed within the confines of Imperial bureaucracies, they are sometimes sent to roam the lands taking notes, letters, invitations, packages and advertisements from someone to another and back.

middens meal between breakfast and mains, around the middle of the day; lunch.

milt the depth of one's self; the core of one's soul and convictions, deeper even than the heart.

Mirthlbrook, the ~ sometimes spelled Myrthlbrook; also known as the Mirthbyr or Mirthlstream or just the Mirthle, the fast-running stream that runs the length of the main valley that is the western *Idlewild* (otherwise known as the *Placidine*). The origin of its name is unclear; some say it is because of the many kinds of myrtle crowding along great lengths of its bank; yet others hold that it is because of the merry sound of its waters bubbling along its stony bed.

monster(s) the nonhuman denizens of the Half-Continent. See entry in Book One.

monster-blood tattoo *cruorpunxis;* see entry in Book One.

monster-making province of the *massacars*—or monster-makers—its practitioners are either called cadaverists (working in fabercadavery—making monsters from parts) or theropeusists or theropusists (working in theropeusia—making *monsters* by growing them). See *habilists* in Book One.

mordant(s) *scripts* that work by corrosion, otherwise known as *distinct acids.*

moss-light also known as a limnulin or *limulight,* this is a small, pocketable device, a simple *biologue* consisting of a small, lidded box holding a clump of naturally phosphorescent mosslike lichens (either funkelmoos or micareen), set on a thick bed of nutrient to keep it alive. This nutrient bed can be reinvigorated with drops of liquid similar to *seltzer.* The light provided by a limnulin is not bright, but can give you enough to see your way right on a dark, dark night, and is diffuse enough to not attract immediate attention. The color of the light varies widely: white, yellowish, green, blue and reddish illumination. The light produced has a distinctive natural glow and discrete focus that keeps it from being seen by unwanted eyes at oblique angles.

munkler(s) also known as holzkreggers or nimsmen, being the fellows whose dangerous task it is to go into the deep wild woodlands, seek out, cut down and carry away as much almugwood, black elder and other are growths (see *sectithere*) as they can find. These woods are found mostly in the dark forests of Wörms and the central Gottskylds (as well as the uninhabitable spaces between Wencleslaus and Ing), and the name comes from the Gott word for "whisper." It is given to them because of the silence and care with which they must proceed into the remote places and the relative quiet they must employ when taking down a tree. This is done using a great array of tackle and ropes strung from surrounding trees, which prevent the felled logs from crashing noisily. Munklers are therefore skilled climbers and knot-tiers. Animals are never taken on these expeditions, and the munklers carry out only what they themselves can bear. This is not much as woodcutting might go, but such a high price can be got for their precious cargo that four or five back-loads is enough to set a man up for more than a year's living. Consequently, munklers make their dangerous forays only once or twice a year. One of the characteristic practices of munklers is to always cover themselves in *nullodors* so as to attract as little monstrous attention as possible as they extract the rare timber.

muttony-greasy rich stew of lamb-gristle and goat meat, cooked all day to make it digestible, its sauce rich and salty, the best aromatic with a myriad of herbs.

N

Naught Swathe also known as the Blank Swathe or the Dodderbanks, a region of the eastern bank of the Humour, near its mouth, and the lands farther east, inland to the Tumblesloe Heap. Home to several villages, the most prominent being *Red Scarfe* and Sodbury Wicket. Rossamünd actually made his way through the southern end of the Dodder Swathe during his flight from the Spindle to High Vesting.

neuroticrith technical or proper name for a *wit*.

new-carved used to describe a *lahzar* who has only recently been operated upon to become one.

nicker(s) generally any *monster*. See entry in Book One.

night-clerk an *uhrsprechman*.

nihillis one of the parts that make up *Craumpalin's Exstinker,* being a distillation of the odor-absorbing chalks dug from the mines of the Orpramine and Euclasia on the Verid Litus. The best chalks come from the pits at Caulk Sinter, Ferdigundis Rex and Calcedonys. It is a common ingredient in *nullodors.*

nullodor(s) any *potive* that changes or hides an existing smell. See entry in Book One.

Numps, Numption Orphias highly talented, semiretired *seltzerman* kept in service at *Winstermill* by the goodwill of the current *Lamplighter-Marshal.* Disowned by his family after the terrible incident of three years ago.

Nuptarium, the ~ also known as the Collocation; lines down in the *Low Gutter* where married *pediteers* and *lampsmen* live with their wives and even children—though fortress life is not considered best for little' uns. Married men with rank are still expected to spend two or more nights sleeping in the bachelors' lines each week.

nutrified wine usually claret that, along with pear or apple pulp, is mixed with concentrates of oranges, lemons and limes and other decoctions of healthful herbs to provide a method of keeping folks healthy by duping them with alcohol.

O

obsequy what we would call a funeral, also known as a funery or inurment. These rites typically include a declaration of the person's merit and then some traditional farewell given by the mourners. In the *Haacobin Empire* it is most commonly thought that when people die they simply stop: a life begins, a life ends. In the cultures about them and their own past there have been various beliefs about afterlife and some all-creating elemental personage, but such notions are considered oppressive and outmoded. They would rather leave these ideas to the eekers, pistins (believers in a god) and other odd fringe-dwellers.

obstacular(s) often billeted alongside the *lighters* might be a small garrison of suicidally zealous obstaculars: thief takers and excise-men who make oaths with their own blood to ferret out all *lurching,* smuggling, banditry and *dark trades* in their range.

Ol' Barny the Old Barn Owl, the affectionate epithet given to the Parracallid, also known as Sagax Glauxës or Saxo Glauxës, the Sagacious Owl of the Haacobins, the sigil of the *Empire,* which common *pediteers* of old held to look like a barn owl.

Old Gate pensioner, stiff as an ~ Old Gate in *Brandenbrass* is a hospital for aged pensioned *pediteers* to spend what years are left to them in a quasi-military environment, still performing *evolutions,* though not as easily as they once did—hence the expression.

Old Lacey the name the *lighters* of the *Paucitine* have given to the *fleermare*—more properly called the Lacrimaria—that comes in from the *Swash.* They use this name both as a corruption of its proper designation and because commonly as it is falling or lifting it looks like a web or "lace" of foggy tendrils.

ossatomist sometimes also called a bone-setter; the proper name for a person whose job is indeed to reset broken bones, a practice known as ossatomy. Because proofing is so effective in stopping lacerations, the more common wounds are bruises and breaks, as the body beneath the gaulding absorbs blows. There are no colleges or insitutions that train ossatomists; they rather pass their trade on through *prenticing,* and yet are still considered higher in value than *surgeons.* Ossatomists also perform dentury, that is, many of the functions we might recognize as the work of a dentist.

outramorine one accused or taken by *outramour,* a monster-lover.

outramour high regard for or love of *monsters;* the crime of which sedorners are guilty. Technically this is known as theiragapia (and its perpetrators as theragapins), and is also called sedonition (of course), and sometimes bewilderment (the state of being dazzled by—and therefore sympathetic to—the wilds).

Owlgrave, the ~ a thick wood at the eastern end of the Ullwold, in which can be found many boneyards—threwdish places where *monsters* of the region will take their prey and where they go to die when the weight of the everlasting war with the *everymen* weighs too heavy or wounds too deeply. Most animals eschew such places and they are characterized by the absence of birdsong—but for the hoots of owls and other scavenging birds who dare to go there at night for the promise of a feast of moldering *monster*-meat.

ox dray large, long, heavy, flat wagon with 4, 6 or even 8 wheels for the carting of big loads and pulled by teams of 6, 8 or even 10 oxen. When there is a paucity of these beasts, great trains of 20 or more mules are used instead to achieve the same hauling strength. In tamer places, dobbins—great draft horses as strong as any ox—are employed.

P

pagrinine also known as a filzhüt, the soft squarish cap of proofed felt (lawn) worn by *troubardiers.*

palisade cloth and wire cap favored by women of the southern Patricine and Frestonia.

Palliateer-Major in charge of small groups of *leers, lurksmen,* sneaksmen and other erapteteers (those who creep), with captains to aid in their command. Palliateers tend to be divided into ambuscadiers (sneaking, ambushing soldiers) and erapteteers (sniffing, ferreting spies and trackers).

palliatrix one who is trained to lie and deceive without giving any hint of mendacity, gaining mastery over reflexive gestures and nuances of expression—any small tic or twitch or stutter of the eye or voice that could give away a falsehood. Not a very common class of person and typically used only by less-than-savory employers.

pallmain(s) heavy, oiled coat used to keep the wearer dry rather than for warmth. Typically they are proofed, which adds to their water-resistant qualities as well as their protective ones; among the few items of proofing vinegaroons will wear in service.

Pandomë one of the *calendars* of the *Right of the Pacific Dove,* a *pistoleer* (or *spendonette* as she would be called by her "sisters") of great skill and fiercely devoted to *Dolours,* even over her loyalty to the *Lady Vey.* Her name, given her when she joined the *Right,* means "of the people, of the house," essentially "woman of the people."

Pannette a purrichinn—or *calendine sagaar* of the *Right of the Pacific Dove,* young and fairly newly joined to the *Right,* being with them not even a year. It is said she was banished from her *clave* back in Grawthewse for undisclosed "irregularities" of conduct, though word has filtered through from visiting *caladines* of other *claves* that it involved a series of assignations with a married peer. The *august* of the *Right* has not pressed her for clarity, but rather has welcomed the increase to their numbers regardless of any reservations.

parenthis waiting room in a *coach-host* or any other establishment requiring such a place. They are so called because of the Parenthine in *Clementine,* the great waiting hall where honored and lofty folk tarry before a meeting with the Emperor.

park-drag very large carriage that can carry up to eight passengers, needing at least a team of six to pull it; it is more common in cities than the country.

parti-hued multi-colored; mottled with bright hues.

Paucitine, the ~ eastern half or *theme* of the *Idlewild,* from the *Wight* to *Haltmire,* gaining its name from the poorness of farming and the harshness of life in general in that region, so much of which is taken up by the *Frugelle*.

pediteer any kind of foot soldier. See entry in Book One.

peltrymen trappers and fur traders living rough lives; tough and resourceful, these fellows know well how to avoid monstrous encounters and some even dare to trap the same and sell them to agents in the *dark trades,* doing so to supplement their meager earnings.

pen(s) also imagineer or (derogatory) fabulist; what we might think of as an illustrator or commercial artist. Somewhat confusingly, the term is also used for freelance writers.

peoneer(s) military laborers with particular skills in constructing fortifications from surrounding materials and sapping, that is, digging trenches near enemy positions and undermining walls.

pernicious threwd the worst kind of *threwd,* said to drive people mad with fear. It is the kind of *threwd* that is said to grip the inland places of the Half-Continent: the Grassmeer and the Witherlends. Some of the more crafty *monsters* are actually able to amplify the effect of the *threwd* to terrify an individual. The most mighty of the *monsters* are said to be able to awe whole armies with such amplification.

Pettiwiggin, the ~ meaning "little worm," the more common name for the *Harrowmath Pike.* Part of the *Wormway,* running from *Winstermill* in the west to *Wellnigh House* in the east.

phrantry specifically the collective membership or sisterhood of a *clave* of *calendars.*

physician(s) highly respected, these are the main practitioners of *physics* in the Half-Continent. See entry in Book One.

physics what we would call medicine. See Book One.

Pile, Laudibus a native of *Brandenbrass* and *telltale* to the *Master-of-Clerks.* From a middle-class family brought to near ruin by the cheating and falsehood of a viciously unscrupulous peer, Laudibus decided by his tenth birthday that when he was old enough he would become a *false-man* and bring that same peer undone. This he did, rescuing his family though corrupting himself in the process and earning a short stint in gaol. Thinking his prospects ruined, Pile yet managed to work his way into a minor Imperial clerical position—such is the demand for *falsemen*. There he was "discovered" by one *Podious Whympre*—then a senior tally-clerk in the Imperial Usury Bureau—who took him under his wing, anticipating a general upward movement in his own propects and knowing full well how handy your own *falseman* can be. When the promotion and shift to *Winstermill* arrived for his new master, Pile happily followed in Whympre's wake.

Pill eminent illustrator of broadsheets and other periodicals known for the firm, confident quality of his lines and the precise detail he can achieve in a relatively short time.

Pillow, Giddian native of Doggenbrass, Pillow is a younger son of small-time middle-class merchants who was taken out of school and sent to the *lighters* when his parents inherited an old family debt. This had them put in the sponging house and all the children set to work until the debt was paid. Though Pillow does go on *vigil-day* trips to *Silvernook*, he does not spend much there but sends most of his pay back home. He would much rather continue in his father's line of work than live a life of danger on the road.

piquet a small collection of ambuscadiers, *lurksmen, leers* and other sharp-eyed individuals sent to scout or spy and return with their report unnoticed.

pirouette card game where the highest hand makes the lowest hand dance a particular dance as dictated by the cards of the winner. It is a complex game where knowledge of all the many ranks and meanings of cards is essential if you do not want to find yourself hopping and bopping embarrassingly all night. Each combination of cards or "route" has a name: "the Kindly Ladies" are any combination of queens and duchesses; the four of brutes is "the dancing (or hopping) *aurang*" and so on. Knowing *all* these names and their combinations is held as proof of your skill with the game.

pistoleer *teratologist* who performs services with pistols and other handheld firelocks loaded with various kinds of *skold-shot*. They are often skolds who make their own *potives* to be discharged from the barrel of a pistol, though many would be considered *ledgermains* with just enough habilistics to achieve the chemistry they need to make *skold-shot* or any other *potive* that can be discharged. Pistoleers prefer to use *hauncets* and *salinumbus* rather than just a simple *pistola*, though they might possess one to deal with more mundane threats.

Placidine, the ~ western half of the *Idlewild,* so named because it is considered safer (and thus more peaceful) than the eastern half. The Placidine is regarded by most (especially those who dwell therein) as the true *Idlewild,* the only part that really counts or has value. See *Idlewild, the.*

plaudamentum the proper name for *Cathar's Treacle*, which is taken by *lahzars*. See *Cathar's Treacle* and entry in Book One.

"playing of strings" also known as "pulling the cords," both meaning using influence, favors, nepotism and whatever other means at your disposal to achieve an ambition within or through a bureaucracy, political body or anywhere else really.

pledget(s) absorbent bandages, often made from lint or pullings of cloth and used mostly to staunch flows of blood, such as might occur in a surgery.

Plod, Punthill *prentice* in the same course with Rossamünd. A native of *Brandenbrass* and the youngest of fifteen children, Plod has joined the Imperial Lighters of the *Conduit Vermis* to escape his poverty. He will not be missed by his overtaxed and half-soused mother.

plush elegant finery, clothes of expensive make often finished with flourishes of lace and fur and metallic cloths and the like. Especially used of uniforms so made; what we might call livery.

po solemn, serious or innocent-looking; also sometimes used to mean unconcerned or indifferent.

poker unflattering name for *lamplighters,* so given because of the pole-pokes (see *fodicar*) they carry to light the *lamps* with.

poleax(es) not actually an ax, but rather a nasty-looking war hammer upon a long pole. At the end of such a length of handle the head can achieve a terrible blow and as such they are the preferred tool of *troubardiers* wanting to hammer people to stuff inside their gaulded covers.

po'lent shortened form of *post-lentum,* "po(st)-lent(um)," and a common vernacular term for carriages of that kind.

poll person's head, or the top or "head" of anything.

669

pollcarry "on-seller" of a skold's *potives,* unable to make them, but buying them from one zaumabalist (or skold) or more and reselling them for whatever price the local market will bear. They have a variable reputation, and are often the only source of *potives* in some remoter places.

post-and-six or lentum-and-six, simply the name of the carriage and the number of horses in the team pulling it: in this case, a *post-lentum* and a six-horse team.

post-lentum(s) among the carriages more commonly used to traverse the highroads and byroads of the Half-Continent, post-lentums deliver mail and taxi people (for a fare) from one post to another. They are manned by a lenterman or driver, an escort (usually armed and armored) known as a side-armsman or cock robin (if wearing a red weskit of Imperial Service) or prussian (if wearing a deep blue weskit of private employment) and one or two backsteppers—either *splasher boys* or post runners or amblers—sitting upon the seats at the back of the roof. When travelling dangerous stretches, another backstepper may join—a quarter-topman possessing a firelock and a keen gaze—for extra protection. This crew is collectively (and confusingly) referred to as lentermen. The delivery of post in remoter areas is irregular, the lentermen waiting for there to be enough missives and parcels to warrant the dangerous journey (usually a post-bag over half-full). If possible they also prefer to take passengers along with them, the extra income making the risk of travel worthy. *Po'lent* is the common term for these vehicles, an abbreviated derivation of po(st)-lent(um).

potive(s) any combination of parts (chemicals) for a particular and definable effect. See entry in Book One.

prentice(s), prentice-lighter(s) "prentice" is the name given to any (typically young) person taken on to learn a skill-set, in the case of this book, those training to be *lamplighters.* A prentice-lighter's duties will include workings (hands-on learning), targets (shooting practice), *evolutions* (marching and drill), readings (very basic reading, writing and rimitry [arithmetic] lessons from books), refections (meals), impositions (minor punishments), *castigations* (the period after mains when punishments are read out to remind the prentices of who needs to be where for doing what. This is also the term for major punishments, including time in the pillory and flogging—very *very* rare) and confinations (when prentices are kept in their cells). The life of prentices is governed by strict routine, and every moment of their day is taken up with military and practical lessons in fighting and lighting the *lamps*. Four months (roughly thirteen weeks) is deemed long enough to turn a *blunderer* into a *lighter*, though once the prentices have been promoted to *lampsman 3rd class* they are typically billeted to the safer western end of the road till they have achieved the rank of lampsman 2nd class. Because there are far fewer of them, prentices are treated better than other military recruits, husbanded as a precious resource and fed well and trained intensively (though briefly) in their tasks. Given this and that they are better paid (slightly) than your usual *pediteer*, it is surprising more lads do not sign up for a life tending the *lamps* on the highroads.

prentice-watch(es) *lantern-watch* conducted for *prentices*, where the platoon of *prentices* is divided into *quartos* and each one is sent out onto the road on set nights to learn the job in the field. The *quartos* are named after noteworthy military persons from history or the current regime. When Rossamünd was *prenticing* he and his fellows were sectioned into three *quartos*, or *prentice* quarters, named as follows: 1st Quarto = Q Protogenës (1st PQP), 2nd = Q Io Harpsicarus (2nd PQIH), 3rd = Q Hesiod Gæta (3rd PQHG—which is Rossamünd's *quarto*). Each one was sent out on this roster:

Quarto	1st	2nd	3rd	1st	Vigil	2nd	3rd
Day	Newwich	Loonday	Meerday	Midwich	Domesday	Calumnday	Solemnday

Each *quarto* sets out to light the *lamps* in the late afternoon of the day named for that *quarto*, staying overnight at *Wellnigh House* when they are done. The next morning they wake before dawn, ready themselves and set out at sunup to "douse" the lanterns, arriving back in *Winstermill* to rest and ablute before rejoining their comrades for the usual day of training. These two days either side of a prentice-watch are long for those involved, hence the two or three days' break in between for each *quarto*. See Appendix 8.

prenticing training and initiating people into a trade.

"present and level" to present your arm is to hold it out in front of you; to level is bring it up and point it in the general direction of the enemy.

private room *Winstermill* has a few small chambers it dedicates to the accommodation and intimate meetings of distinguished guests, found on the second floor of the manse. These are somewhat self-contained, possessing their own *jakes,* small conference rooms and a wet area for ablutions. Even so, these rooms are still quite spare as city standards go—more on par with a provincial wayhouse.

privers long sturdy tongs used to grip toxic articles, especially such things as *skold-shot.*

proofener one who supplies proofing but does not manufacture it.

proof-steel metal (usually forged iron and the like) that has been backed with buff or some other sturdy proofed material. This allows the metal to be thinner and therefore lighter while still offering superior protection. The wearing of metal proofing of any sort is regarded as flashy or *showing away* or old-fashioned or all of these in one, though regardless *troubardiers* and *lesquins* typically reserve the right to don-proof-steel.

pudding(s) what we would call dessert.

punct, puncting to *mark* someone with a *cruorpunxis.*

punctographist(s) also called a nadeller (Gott) or marker. A person who is skilled in marking or *puncting* a person with a *monster-blood tattoo.* A punctographist's tools are known as *grailles,* used for either extracting the *cruor* of a *monster* or for tattooing (*puncting*) a *mark* on a person. A punctographist typically views the head and face of the slain *monster* in advance of the actual *puncting,* and makes a design for the tattoo in a book or on some other paper from what they see or are told.

punt-royale card game where the highest ranked cards are the least desirable. The game revolves around passing these cards off on each other till all the cards are played or a predecided number of passes (turns) have occurred. The loser, or knave, is the one with the most high cards; the winner, or free-man, is the one with none. More of a recreational game rather than one for gambling, though inveterate wagerers have found ways to win and lose money with it.

purgation taming the land and quelling the *threwd* through force and violence, especially against the *monsters* themselves. It is the more immediate way to begin conquest of the wilds, but its effects are only short term, for *monsters* will always return to places they consider their home, their original/proper range of wandering. See *Idlewild, the*.

Puttinger said "*Putt*'ing'ger"; lampsman 1st class of *Winstermill,* once a native of Gottland, being born in Wittzingerod; how he came to be in the Emperor's Service is a tale he isn't telling. He is the eldest of the three *lampsmen* set over the young *prentices* and probably the friendliest—though only just barely. Struggles to make himself understood to the lads through his thick Gott accent.

Q

q the symbol for sequins, the middle-value denomination in the common currency of the *Soutlands.* The average weekly wage for your common working fellows is 8 q, which in turn is about the average hourly rate of hire for your high-class *teratologist*—such as Europe, the Branden Rose. See *money* in Book One.

QGU abbreviated reference to *quo gratia.*

Q Hesiod Gæta the *quarto* of *prentice-lighters* to which Rossamünd belongs. The *Q* stands for quarto, and Hesiod Gæta was once lamplighter-marshal in charge of the *lighters* at the time that the *Idlewild* was founded. The names of the other *prentice quartos* are also taken from other noteworthy *lighters* of old. Io Harpsicarius was the founding marshal of *Winstermill,* while Protogenës is probably the most renowned, performing great feats in defense of the fledgling colonies of the Placidia Solitus.

quabard vestlike proofing for the chest, sometimes referred to in full as "quarter-bard," usually reaching down over the abdomen. See entry in Book One.

quacksalver doctor or *dispensurist,* but particularly a bad one or one who passes himself off as a person of *physics* without possessing the actual qualifications or skills.

quarto(s) the smallest designation of a group of soldiers. It goes:

quarto = 10 men

platoon = 30 men = 3 *quartos*

company = 100 or more men = 3–4 platoons

battalion = 300–500 men = 3–6 companies

regiment (million) = 1,000–3,000 men = 3–6 battalions

tercion (brigade) = 3,000–12,000 men = 3–4 regiments (millions)

legion = 10,000–40,000 men = 3–4 tercions (brigades)

division = 30,000–40,000 men = 2 or more legions

army (marshalsy) = 60,000 or more men = 2 or more divisions

quiet-shoes also called pattens; soft, heelless, pliable shoes with stoutly proofed soles, usually tied on to the foot with ribands wound way up the leg. Very useful for walking quietly and for activities that require nimbleness, grip and a near-silent step. Easily the most preferred shoe of *calendars* and *sagaars* and even some *fulgars.*

Quinault northernmost town of the *Idlewild,* founded by the Sovereign State of Quimperpund with backing from the peoples of the Maund. Situated on the borders of Sulk, it is a major supplier and trafficker of foodstuffs from the Sulk to the other colonies immediately to the south.

quo gratia shortened form of the *Tutin* term "quo gratia ex unicum," "the favor of the peerless," and often invoked in its abbreviation—*QGU;* it is the right of a peer to circumvent certain laws—civil or military, though the latter is a little harder—or the due process of the judicial system, or even nullify a court's ruling, all for personal ends. Based on an ancient code known as the Wittenrood that existed before even the occupation of the *Empire, QGU* is preserved most in the *Soutlands,* where the Emperor tolerates it to keep the peers there on his side. It is not common to use this right too frequently, though a peer with enough swagger might carry off even the most outrageous affront under the cover of *QGU.* Most, however, are careful and sparing in its use, for its invocation can get you unwelcome attention from *Clementine.* Generally if you are to use it, you want to be pretty sure you can get away with it, either through corrupt practices, the justice of your cause or the power of your lobby in the Imperial Capital.

R

Red Scarfe rural center considered a part of *Sulk End,* though many of its inhabitants have family and associates in the *Idlewild* and so consider themselves as being part of the westernmost end of the *Idlewild*. It gets its name from the red bricks that were originally used to make its encircling, sloping walls (a scarfe or scarp).

revenant simply a more formal, educated rendering of *rever-man*.

rever-man "zombielike" *gudgeon,* and the most human-looking of the same. See entry in Book One.

Right of the Pacific Dove, the ~ *calendar clave* found in the historied fastness of *Herbroulesse,* led by *Syntychë, the Lady Vey.* The *clave*-members are usually called *columbines,* from the *Tutin* word "columbarium," meaning "dovecote." Originally dwelling in *Brandenbrass,* the Right—as it is called by its own—was founded over three hundred years earlier in the time of the Sceptic Dynasty. After too many rivalries with local lords, as well as with another, better connected *clave,* they had their charter to exist in that city revoked. Acquiescing meekly, the Right moved to remoter lands, finding *Herbroulesse,* where it has endured ever since. Their motto is "Semper Fidelis"—"always faithful."

rimple a curious-looking hairy-leather purse made from the entire skin of a small rodent, shaved, with a drawstring at the neck hole, and the skin of one limb sewn back on itself as a loop to fix on to a belt. Actually looking like some bloated rat, a rimple is all the fashion as a coin-bag among the wayfaring classes.

Roughmarch, the ~ the combination of two deep gorges cutting through the southern tip of the Tumblesloe Heap, worn down into the rock and earth by the action of two ancient, now-dry waterways: one running roughly west, the other east.

Roughmarch Road, the ~ road that runs through the *Roughmarch* gorge, running along the serpentine wendings of the dry streambeds. The middle part of the road is straightest where Imperial *peoneers* and road-builders blasted and cut the small spur of rock that separated the two original gorges to allow the road to continue through. The *threwd* is never far gone from this place, and the thorny plants that grow along its edges are in need of constant pruning and lopping. *Fatigue parties* are sent out at least every two months to do this, thus preventing a *monster* from having a place whence to ambush passing traffic.

rouse-master one in change of a *rousing pit*. See *hob-rousing.*

rousing-pit(s) holes in the ground with stalls or stands or make-shift seats about and in which *gudgeons* and bogles are set to fight to the death while the spectators above wager on the outcome. Such pits are usually situated well away from prying authorities and common paths, kept hidden and secret to all but to those initiated into the local rousing brotherhood.

ruttle to clear the throat; the sound of mucus in the windpipes.

S

sabine expensive weave of soft wools from the small kingdom of the same name, found beyond the northern shores of the *Sinus Tintinabuline*. It would be held as mythic by southern folk but for the existence of its exquisite wools, and there are many imitators of their product, some so good only a connoisseur can tell the difference.

sagaar(s) the combatant *teratologist* dancers who use their nimbleness, the prescribed movements of their chosen "dance," and *therimoirs* to defeat the *nickers* and the bogles. See entry in Book One.

salinumbus meaning "salt-shaker" and also called a salt-gun; a straight-handled pistol made to fire special *potives* designed for the purpose. The inside of its barrel is treated with coatings to reduce the corrosive damage done by the chemistry of its shots.

Sallowstall a *cothouse* on the *Wormway* situated in a small dell, by a ford-crossing on the *Mirthlbrook*. Sallowstall is thickly surrounded by a small wood of maples and ancient willows, and gains its name from the thicket of willows—sallows being the local name for willows—that grow about it and along the banks of the *Mirthlbrook* on which it is built. It is actually a cot-rent, with a few extra, cramped rooms where non-lampsmen can stay for modest board.

salpert(s) small, fragile sacks of cloth that hold *potives,* especially those that need to burst when they are thrown and hit something. A fair amount of care must be taken when handling them, and the recommended method for carting them is inside some kind of padded box such as a *stoup* or digital.

salt-bag(s) simple name for a *salumanticum,* and so called because it is designed to hold the parts or "salts" of a skold or other habilist or - parts-dealer.

salt-horse a useless person, taken from the idea of a horse that is so old it is no longer good for anything but being turned into dried, heavily salted meat.

salumanticum (*Tutin,* meaning "salt-bag") also known as a *salt-bag,* usually a satchel with various pockets, flaps and slots for holding *potives* in all their varied forms. The arrangement of a salumanticum should facilitate easy access to the right chemical at the right time, and skolds will know and recall the inside of their *salt-bags* better than their own birthdays.

Scale of Might, the ~ originally an anecdotal reckoning of the number of *everymen* it takes to best an *ünterman,* it has since been extensively codified by Imperial Statisticians, but simply put it is deemed possible for three ordinary men armed in the ordinary manner to see off one garden-variety bogle, and for about five to handle your more common *nicker.* Add *potives* or *teratologists* to the group and this number fluctuates significantly—depending on the quality of *potive* or skill and type of *monster*-slayer.

scarlet-powder what we would think of as washing detergent, bright red flakes of crystalline surfactant that lose their color as they form suds in water. Seeing them for the first time you might expect the water in which they are placed to turn red too, but it remains clear.

scourge(s) skold who specializes in the use of the most potent *scripts* known. See entry in Book One.

scratch-bob short, powdered wig with dainty curls at the sides and a short tail of hair hanging at the back. Usually referring to those of cheap manufacture, but a common term for all such items of apparel.

script(s) *potives* or the "recipes" for their making. See entry in Book One.

scrubber(s) very large tubs made from the halves of old brewing butts and used as washing basins to clean dishes or clothes or any other thing that needs a lot of room for a good scrubbing.

Sebastipole, Mister *Lamplighter's* Agent of *Winstermill* and *telltale* to the *Lamplighter-Marshal.* See entry in Book One.

sectifactor(s) transmogrifying *surgeons*; that is, those people who conduct the surgeries that make a person into a *lahzar.*

sectithere said *"sek'*tih'theer," kind of *therimoir;* knives made by a profoundly ancient method, used for the effective cutting of *monsters,* who are otherwise hard to harm with more mundane blades. They were once the standard weapon of the *heldins*—the mighty folk of renown from obscure history—and the weapons of these near-mythical folk are prized relics today, as the quality of manufacture cannot even be approached currently. In more recent times sectitheres are the tools of *sagaars* and *therlanes* ("*monster*-butchers" from the *Tutin* "therilanius") and some *punctographists.* They are very hard to make, which means they are prohibitively expensive, and as such, very uncommon. The best kind, of course, are the relics. Some sectitheres come in the form of scissors. The blades are made of spiegeleisen (also vitrine or festverglas): a highly refined, almost glasslike ceramic containing powerful *mordants, expungeants* and pestilents such as *gringollsis.* This is applied over metal, or allowed to soak into wood which is then fired many times till it is tempered-steel hard. Different woods give different results: the best woods for the strongest, most potent blades are made from now near-mythical almugwood or exceptionally rare black elder. Wood so treated is known as glanzend (Gott for "gift-glass") or giftwood.

Secunda Loca the "bottom half" of the *Haacobin Empire,* encompassing the lands south-southwest of Tuscanin and Catalain, down to and including the Lent, reaching west as far as the Patter Moil and east to the shores of the *Ichormeer.* The "top half" is the Prester Regnum, and includes the Seat and the Verid Litus.

seigh the local Sulk and *Idlewild* name for the more fortified highhouses built in wilder places.

Sellry, wine-of ~ constituent of *Craumpalin's Exstinker,* a fairly common decoction made from the juices of several common plants that, when put together, have the qualities required by a wide variety of fluid *potives.* Mildly poisonous, it is most frequently used as a base for repellents, though it is seldom seen in *nullodors.*

seltzer, seltzer water salts-infused "waters" used to cause *bloom* to give off light. Depending on the origin of the very first *bloom* from which your stock was raised, the constituency of your seltzer will need to vary to allow for the different marine environments from which each kind of *bloom* was once retrieved. This knowledge tends to be possessed only by *seltzermen*, the suppliers of *bright-limns*, and some skolds, who can tell what breed of *bloom* they might have before them and what mix of seltzer to nourish it in. Generally the composition of seltzer water is:

22 parts brine

5 parts chordic vinegar

3 parts wine-dilute penthil salts

2 parts spirit-of-cadmia

1 1/2 parts bluesalts

Some *seltzermen* might also include varying parts of ethulate, of which there are different varieties for the particular breeds of *bloom*.

seltzer lamp larger version of a *seltzer lantern*, though the terms are interchangeable.

seltzer lantern any *lamp* that uses *bloom*-and-*seltzer* to give light, but most particularly a portable light of larger size than a *bright-limn*.

seltzerman, seltzermen tradesman responsible for the maintenance of all types of *limulights*. Their main role is to make and change the *seltzer water* used in the same. Among *lamplighters*, seltzermen have the duty of going out in the day to any lamp reported by the *lantern-watch* (in ledgers set aside for the purpose) as needing attention and performing the necessary repair. This can be anything from adding new *seltzer*, to adding new *bloom*, to replacing a broken pane or replacing the whole lantern-bell. See *seltzer, seltzer water*.

Senior Service the navy—a name it gives itself; see entry in Book One.

senior-sister the name *clave* members use among themselves to refer to their *august*, being the highest active "rank" among them. Carlins are the revered "retirees" who often no longer actively serve but live lives of

679

quiet contemplation or—if they are peeresses—return to the glamour of their former lives as wise old dames.

Sequecious pronounced "seh'*kwee*'shuss"; enormous, easygoing and almost unquenchably jovial, he is a native of the independent realm of Sebastian, a direct western neighbor of the Seat, the heartland of the *Empire.* A war over the fertile lands of the downs of the Agrigentum and the plateau of the Stipula has been waxing and .waning between Sebastian and the Haacobins (and the Sceptics before them) for centuries. Sequecious was a camp cook for an eminent Sebastian officer and was captured when the baggage train of that officer's regiment was ambushed and ransacked by Imperial ambuscadiers. Spending time first in a war prison, he was processed and sent out to serve as a soldier-slave—as with so many of the Haacobins' prisoners of war—on the *Empire's* more southerly borders, despite his size. This found him as the cook for the *lighters* of *Wormstool,* as remote a post as you could want for. The good dealings he has in the hands of the *lighters* give him hope for a better life as a citizen of the *Empire,* as does the promise of actual pay he is due should he become a native of the Haacobin domains.

sequestury, sequesturies places of quiet and contemplation well within the protecting walls of a *calanserie,* originally established to provide well-to-do women with a refuge to which to retreat from undue attention or unpeaceful lives. Accommodated in their own apartments, these anchoresses (hermit women) are granted the rights of their degree and live in familiar worldly comfort. They are the great benefactresses of the *calendars* the world over and with their support sequesturies are able to take in battered wives, destitute widows, *good-day gala-girls* and other ladies of poor repute fleeing their handlers and seeking a better life. They also seek social justice for women as a sex in general.

sergeant(s) second highest rank of non-commissioned officer, below master but above *under-sergeant,* involved in the training, *evolving* and supervision of the lives of their charges. A good sergeant will play "mother" to a lieutenant's or captain's "father", tending to the welfare of his subordinates.

sergeant-lighter alternative to *Lamplighter-Sergeant,* a slightly less formal way of addressing one of that rank and normally allowed only to those of equal or higher rank.

shabraque(s) proofed coverings for horses, commonly made of panels of buff (gauld-leather), fixed together by rivets or points (reinforced ties) or both, flexible yet solid. Every time a horse goes out with its shabraque, the proofing is smeared or splashed with a *nullodor,* either deadening the horsy odor or transmuting it to smell like some other less tasty creature. Over all this may be hung a couvrette, a colorful, sturdy blanket in your chosen mottle and even marked with sigils, a purely decorative feature and the kind of excess insisted upon only by the conspicuously wealthy.

♣ chaffe or equiperson: a mask covering *poll,* forelock and forehead, down to the nostril and over the cheeks with holes for the eyes. Not often used, as it limits a horse's vision.

♣ crinarde: covers mane, neck and often hangs over the points of the shoulders as well.

♣ petraille: covers withers, shoulder, chest and foreparts of ribs down to the knee.

♣ crouppere: covers back, loin, flank, croup, thigh and buttock, down to the hock, and typically leaving the tail free.

sheer crane or winch used to lift loads up and lower them down.

showing away boasting or showing off.

siccustrumn any *script* used to staunch a flow of blood from a wound. This is achieved by pastes, fast-setting liquids and powders. The better siccustrumn will not only stop a flow quickly, but will act like sutures and keep the wound from opening and bleeding again. Best results are achieved by a siccustrumn combined with bandages.

signifer(s) the distinct parts of a scent or other trail that aid *leers* or *lurksmen* in their work. One of the more remarkable applications of a signifer is a group of *potives* known as anavoids, which *leers* use to *mark* someone or something they want to trail, following the distinct scent wherever it may lead. The best anavoids will last for weeks even in water and are hard to detect by fellow *leers* and other "box-wearers," seeming more like a natural smell to all but the person who used it. It has been known for talented and well set-up *leers* to follow an anavoided trail even over waters from one harbor to another.

sillabub honey-sweetened milk mixed with either strong wine or, in a *Skyldic* twist, with vinegar—a taste for the dead of mouth and strong of stomach.

Silvernook miners' town on the northern edge of the Brindleshaws. See entry in Book One.

Sinster the best place to go to be made into a *lahzar*. See entry in Book One.

Sinus Tintinabuline called the Sin Tin for short, and meaning the Bay of Bells, it is the great body of water to the northeast of the Half-Continent, its western shores home to the ports of the Turkemen, its east coast hiding the pirate-kings of the Brigandine States. The Sin Tin gets its name from the many, many buoys and markers with their warning-bells that have been moored by the myriad of submerged hazards for as long as history records. These buoys are freely maintained by all who use the waters of the Bay; even the pirate-kings play ruses with them only very occasionally, otherwise doing their part to tend the ancient warning system.

sis edisserum *Tutin* term, loosely meaning "please explain," this is an order from a superior (usually the Emperor) to appear before him and a panel of peers forthwith, to offer reasons, excuses, evidence, testimony and whatever else might be required to elucidate upon whatever demands clarity. A sis edisserum is normally seen as a portent of Imperial ire, a sign that the person or people so summoned are in it deep and must work hard to restore the Emperor's confidence. A sis edisserum is a "black mark" against your name, and very troublesome to remove.

Skillions, the ~ south-eastern corner of the *Low Gutter* in the fortress of *Winstermill*. It gains its somewhat derogatory name from the many small, wood-built single-story sheds, warehouses and work-stalls found there. These are a recent addition to this part of the Gutter, previously being the site of a stately old building designated for multiple uses, including the growing of *bloom* and the making and storing of all lanterns. This reputedly burned down in mysterious circumstances two generations ago, outside of any current occupant's memory.

skilly gruel or broth made from scrap meat and leftovers from the previous evening's mains.

skittle-alley what we would think of as a "fun-parlor," where folks pay to play at skittles (obviously), hoop-a-ring, bowlers (essentially carpet bowls) and pegstops (a game that involves using batons known as pegs to knock your opponent's pegs down and get a ball into their "goal"). The best skittle-alleys also possess billiard tables.

skolding practices and arts of a skold; to work as a skold or to go out hunting *monsters* with *potives*. See *skold(s)* in Book One.

skold-shot leaden balls fired from either musket or pistol, and treated with various concoctions of powerful *venificants* known as *gringollsis*, particularly devised for the destruction of *monsters*. These *potives* are corrosive, damaging the barrels of the firelocks from which they are fired and eating gradually, yet steadily, away at the metal of the ball itself. Left long enough, a skold-shot ball will dissolve completely away. Very effective against most *nickers* and bogles, some of the best *gringollsis* actually poison a *monster* to the degree that it becomes vulnerable to more mundane weapons.

Skyldic coming from or of the Skylds. In modern parlance it is used in reference to the people of Wörms or Frissia.

slot and drag a slot is a trail of smells and a drag is a trail of prints and other visible *signifers* of passing. These two trails are much more acute to a *leer's* augmented senses.

slug(s) truly insulting invective against profound dim-wittedness and tardiness.

Smellgrove, Eugus wastrel from *Brandenbrass* and fellow *prentice* with Rossamünd who loves his sleep. Smellgrove started out promisingly as a journeyman rat-catcher before being enticed by the romance of Imperial Service and the immediate glory of a whole Imperial billion.

Snooks, the culinaire of the *Winstermill* kitchens, who rules her boiling, bubbling, savory domain from the head of a long scarred bench—a scale and weights always handy—attended on either side by a row of hanging carcasses glistening in the heat—mutton, bully beef, coney, pullet, venison for the officers. She reads from recipes and writes lists of comestibles required while kitchen hands chop and carve before her and the harried bustle spins about her. She rarely moves; certainly she never lifts a limb to help her henpecked staff, tyrannizing all with her wheezing, penetrating voice. A near-mythic fear of her makes pots-and-pans an excellent punishment for defaulting *prentices*.

snuftkin what we might call a muff, a "tube" of fur worn over the hands, wrists and lower arms, for the warming of the same.

sobersides one who does not drink or get drunk.

soe gaulded silk; already a strong material, silk made into soe is an expensive but highly sought material for proofing. See *lour*.

Soratchë said "Saw'*rat*'kee"; a small but widely spread and well-known *calendar clave* consisting almost entirely of *caladines*, those wandering loner *calendars*. The Soratchë's stated mission is not so much to fend for the poor and helpless, but to eradicate the *dark trades*, especially the abominable practices of the *massacars*. Strangely, they have not been granted an *Imperial Prerogative* (an official commission from the Emperor). Notwithstanding, they are infamous for the vigor and violence with which they pursue their self-appointed mandate.

sot-headed drunk or acting as if you are drunk; to be slow-witted and stupid.

soutaine long coat with dead straight hems reaching to the knees or even ankles. A foreign style imported from Heilgoland and worn by those seeking to look serious and unaffected by fashion.

Soutland(s), the ~ the large southern part of the *Haacobin Empire,* requiring two secondary capitals—the *alternats*—to govern properly and keep under the Imperial thumb. See entry in Book One.

sovereign lime thickened lime juice mixed with lemon juice and other fortifying traces. Often mixed with cheaper alcohols to add flavor and encourage people to ingest some kind of antiscorbutic.

spangled whelp-hound(s) smaller kind of *tykehound* but still big as dogs go, white with black spots on the rump and flanks and black points. Probably one of the more people-friendly of the *tykehound* family, and very similar to our own Dalmatians, yet a little larger and bulkier.

Sparrow Downs, the ~ range of hills between Small and the *Idlewild* that acts as a boundary between the two. It is the reputed home of the *Duke of Sparrows,* an urchin-lord said to lurk and hide within. There are no official reports of a sighting of this mythical monster, and many doubt the truth of the tale. The deeps of the forest (the Nigflutenwald—"the Wood of Little Wings") are held to be a tykewood—a woodland haunted by *monsters,* impenetrably threwdish and thickly grown. Those few *peltrymen* who dare to venture there report skulking threats and an inordinate number of sparrows and other small fowl.

Sparrows, the Duke of ~ see *Duke of Sparrows.*

spatterdash(es) also known as spats—which are usually a shorter version of the same—these are leather-and-buckle coverings for the shins and reaching over the top of the foot. Often proofed, they provide excellent protection for the lower leg.

spendonette the term used among *calendars* for a *pistoleer.*

spittende(s) a kind of *fend,* spittendes are very long pikes used especially to fend away *monsters* and sometimes large game, with barbed points and strong flukes to prevent a skewered beastie from pushing down the pole and harming the wielder. Also known as a durckshlägen.

splasher, splasher boy most junior member of the *lentermen* crew, sitting at the back of the carriage ready to open doors, haul luggage, run messages, carry the post when necessary and otherwise serve the needs of the passengers, the driver and his side-armsman. It is a dangerous job, but a good one for a lad of between twelve and eighteen, paying pretty well, near as much as the *prentices* of *Winstermill* earn in a year, and without quite the same constrictions on their lives. When a carriage is in port and the splasher's chores are done his time is his own.

Splinteazle, Seltzerman 2nd Class ~ bosun to *House-Major Grystle* when he was a ram captain, following him from vessel to vessel and so loyal he went with the man when he was ejected from the navy. As the best fit for his previous skills he has taken up the role of *seltzerman,* and though in the ranks of *Winstermill* he no longer has quite the same authority, he is known as the old servant of the *house-major's* and is respected accordingly.

sprither said "sprih-ther," with a short *i;* the common name for the tubelike needle used to extract *ichor* (*monster* blood) from a slain *monster;* also known as a bludspritz, its technical name being a cruorclyst. It comprises a long, thick, needle-pointed, steel tube known as a clystron; a round pewter or tin receptacle known as a curbit is fixed to the clystron's blunt end. Usually, a preserved gut tube—the intestin—is attached to the other side of the curbit, upon which the user draws with the mouth, sucking the *ichor* out of the *monster* and into the curbit. The more advanced cruorclysts will have a small preserved bladder instead of the intestin, which is squeezed rapidly to achieve the same outcome. *Ichor,* once taken out of the *monster,* is known as *cruor*—"spilled blood." If the curbit becomes full, the *cruor* is siphoned into a *bruicle*. See *graille(s).*

spurn(s) *lahzar* or other *teratologist* who faithfully serves one master or organization. The word is used more generally to mean someone acting as personal bodyguard to an individual, the non-teratologist kind sometimes known as harnessgarde.

Squarmis a *costerman* who dares the long stretch of the *Frugal* Way (see entry on the *Wormway*) to make occasional deliveries to *Haltmire* with an old boneshaker of a cart harnessed to a crotchety she-mule, Assanina, hiring out his services as a kind of wayfaring porter; a native of *Brandenbrass,* come to the *Idlewild* to escape some unpleasant business back home.

"Stand While You Can" rousing military tune with an up-tempo beat despite the grim turn of its content, showing typical bravado in the face of a violent end. Sung by soldiers throughout the *Haacobin Empire,* it goes something like this:

> *Though foemen press hard, lads*
> *Though foemen press hard;*
> *Fight for* Ol' Barny *and*
> *Stand while you can.*
>
> *Stand while you can, lads,*
> *Stand while you can:*
> *With a shout of* "Ol' Barny!"
> *Stand while you can.*
>
> *Don't tarry o'er death, lads*
> *Don't tarry o'er death;*
> *Just put your thew forward, and*
> *Stand while you can.*

Stand while you can, lads,
Stand while you can:
For the Glory of Ol' Barny,
Stand while you can.

And so on like this for a whole twenty verses. Its history is obscure, though the tune is of some antiquity and was around in other songs well before these words were put to it.

Stander Lates, the ~ *Brandenard* rendering of Stendrlaeti ("shores of fiendish howling"), the *Hagenard* name for the southwestern coast of the Hagenlands, where *Ingébiargë* is said to dwell, devising her wicked brews and waiting for sailors to eat.

sthenicon these sensory-enhancing *biologues* are worn by nonleers as well; such folk are called *lurksmen*. For both *lurksmen* and *leers* the sensation of removing a sthenicon is, for a very brief moment, powerfully disorienting as the wearer's senses adjust back to normal input: the world seems dull and colorless, sounds oddly muted, the air too still and bland. This confusion is properly known as accosmia or more commonly as the dulldrins or dimmings. In a few this can continue on for several days, characterized by the squints—or strabismic droop—with squinting eyes and disorientation. The squints is almost guaranteed if you wear a sthenicon for more than a week without respite.

stingo(s) a common term for pints of beer.

storm-bird(s) cuckoo-shrikes, whose appearance is said to precede and therefore announce the arrival of rain, especially heavy, storming rains.

stouche • (noun) a fight, a battle. • (verb) to fight.

stoup also called a fistulum, a cylindrical case of (usually) leather-covered wood or just layers of stiffened leathers, in which *scripts* are carried for easy access. The interior of a stoup is well padded and so arranged with removable platelike layers that allow the most needful *potives* to be got to first, with others arranged by priority beneath. Most stoups have about 4 or 5 layers, but some are double-ended and can be up to 12 layers long. See Appendix 7.

stovepipe hat vernacular for a copstain or capstin, a tall cylindrical hat with a flat crown and a somewhat narrow brim. Some varieties are a little more conical.

strig(s) shortened form of *strigaturpis;* not considered a very polite word.

strigaturpis originally the wild *heldin* fighting women of the Phlegms and then the *Attics* during the Heldinsage. The term is used now to refer to any combative female, especially a *teratologist.* Such women are also known as beldames. See *calendar(s).*

stuff • (noun) clumps of thread or frayings from rope or cloth. • (noun) synonym for *bloom.* • (noun) flesh—though this is not a common use except in the phrase "*stuff and bits.*"

"stuff and bits" flesh and bones.

sturdy rough(s) hired muscle, as they say; your "heavies" used to do dirty work and intimidate opponents.

Sulk End south-westernmost part of Sulk of which the *Harrowmath* is considered a part. See entry in Book One.

Sundergird the Half-Continent, including all the lands outside the *Haacobin Empire:* Escatoris, the Gottskylds, the Herelands, the Netherlands and beyond, and the southern reaches of the Witherlends.

surgeon(s) considered the lesser counterpart of *physicians.* See entry in Book One.

swab • (noun) small child. • (verb) the action of washing a floor with a mop, which is also called a swab.

swaggerer *knave* or hack or other hired tough; those who put themselves forward as monster-hunters or *spurns;* a mercenary.

Swash, the ~ the great bay east of Needle Greening, south of the *Frugelle* and northwest of *Flint,* the source of thick *fleermares* that are blown inland by strong southerlies to saturate and water the parched *Frugelle.*

Swill, Honorius Ludius Grotius named after an empress-dowager of old, Honoria Ludia Grotinia—said to be a revered distant relative of Swill's line—Grotius is the young and gifted *surgeon* and *physician's* ward at *Winstermill,* gaining the position through the influence of the *Master-of-Clerks.* A true Imperial subject, being born and raised in the *Considine,* his original poverty did not prevent him setting up shop as a talented carver. He soon got the attention of the *surgeons* of *Sinster* and became an articled man there under the tutelage of Flaccus Fusander, a sectifactor of great and irregular vision. There is a strange, suspicious cloud over Swill's departure from *Sinster,* a departure he says was due to the near-violent jealousies of his rivals. A voracious reader with a large personal library, Swill is ambitious for knowledge—the more obscure the better—and with this the power it might bring.

Syntychë see *Vey, the Lady;* forename of the *august* of the *Right of the Pacific Dove,* and *Threnody's* mother. A peer of middling rank, she possesses the hereditary title of marchess and, like most peers, claims a blood-link to Dido's race. It is said she was transmogrified when in her twenties, though none beyond the intimacy of the *Dovecote* have ever seen her perform a lahzarine act, and her true nature remains a mystery.

T

tally-clerk person responsible for counting and recording the comings and goings through whichever door, gate or other portal he or she is assigned to watch. The use of such a function in a place like *Winstermill* is to regulate trade, traffic and even emigration, and for awareness of who and what is within the manse. They are assisted greatly in their duties by *cursors.*

tandem, tandem chair finely carved, two- or three-seater cushioned seat; what we might call a chaise lounge.

telltale(s) *falsemen* retained by one of office or status to inform their employers of the veracity of others' statements or actions, to signal if fellow interlocutors are lying or dissembling or masking the truth in any other way. If they could afford to, most people of any significance would employ telltales, but there simply are not enough *falsemen* to fill so many vacancies. This means that a *leer* can earn a truly handsome living as a telltale, many commonly charging a premium for their service at fees usually beyond all but the very well off, or serving with promises for advancement and personal advantage. Then there are those honorable few who do it simply because it is their job and responsibility. Despite this rarity, many of the prominent work hard to nullify the advantage a telltale will give, either by employing their own *falseman,* or having a *palliatrix* (a highly trained liar—even rarer than a *falseman*) attend in their stead.

tempestine military term for a *wit*, gained from the notion that they cause a tempest within the minds of the enemies.

teratologist(s) *monster*-hunter. In truth there are not a great number of teratologists in the Half-Continent, and those who are there are stretched thin and typically prefer the higher financial recompense of *knaving* themselves to the poor pay received in direct Imperial Service. This is especially true of *lahzars*, who may well have a large debt to service, incurred to pay for their original transmogrification. Consequently it is only a few teratologists ever feel community-hearted enough to work permanently in the government's pay at fortresses, manses and other outposts on the edges of civilization—and when one dies he or she is very hard to replace. See entry in Book One.

test place where skolds, *dispensurists* or other habilists do their makings, their brewings and combinations of parts. What we might term a "laboratory." Consequently, to brew or otherwise make a *potive* is to testtelate.

test-barrow or *chymistarium* or testtle; a wheelbarrow-like device, a sizable oblong box striated with hinges and doors, drawers and locks, that folds open to reveal many compartments and a small yet fully functioning and very portable *test*. This includes a small but remarkably well-appointed portable *chymistarium* (what we might think of as a chemistry set) that can include a little stone-lined stove-plate, kept hot even when on the move, providing the clean puffs of smoke from its chimney. Test-barrows are ancient tools, more basic versions used first by the rhubezhals of old and refined over the centuries. Expensive items, their possession proves the affluence and (assumedly) the successful skill of its possessor.

thaumateer(s) term for a *teratologist* in military service; taken from the *Attic* word for "a wonder" or "a marvel." As may be expected, the various kinds of *teratologist* are given their own military designation, such as tempestines for *fulgars*, torsadines for *wits*, bombastines for *scourges*, avertines for skolds and so on.

theiromisia also known as theiraspexthis, apexthia or, most commonly, invidition: the implacable hatred of *monsters*. The opposite of *outramour*, which is the love of *monsters*, as an *invidist* or execrat is the opposite of a sedorner (see *sedorner* in Book One). See *individist(s)*.

theme(s) military districts that are given into the charge of a general or even a marshal—who may even be in charge of a multiplicity of them. All matters military or to do with the defense of the people are under the control of the marshal or general. There are two kinds: Static themes—under the control of a state, and Imperial themes, established by *Clementine* and not necessarily conforming to sociopolitical boundaries established by the states. Where Static themes and Imperial themes overlap there can be a great deal of wrangling and collision of jurisdictions.

therimoir(s) pronounced *"there'*ih'moyr" (*Attic*, literally, "*monster*-fate"), also tierschlächt (*Gott*); weapon designed or fitted to slay *monsters*. The most famous and useful of these are ancient devices, many of which have been lost in the many rises and falls of civilization.

therlane(s) literally, "*monster*-butchers," typically members of the *dark trades* who, by experience, are usually able to make a common sense of the varying anatomies of dead *monsters* and cut them up with *sectitheres* for the various uses for which each part will be employed. Those who use such parts are utterly reliant on these *monster*-carvers, and skilled therlanes can command high prices for their expertly dissected bogle-bits.

theroid(s) a more technical term for a *monster*.

theroscade(s) quite simply, an attack by *monsters*, particularly an ambush, but the term is used to mean any assault by *üntermen*.

Theudas, Fadus young *lamplighter* serving at *Wormstool*, born and raised in the *Considine*. His father is a midlevel bureaucrat in the Imperial Service. Theudas could not bear the idea of the desk life and fled his home; after many adventures he found the active simple life he desired with the *lamplighters* of the *Wormway*. An eager fellow who, through persistence and the excellence of his brief service record, gained a *billet* out on the "*ignoble end of the road*."

691

thill(s) shafts on a cart or carriage onto which a horse or other such animal for pulling the vehicle is harnessed.

Threnody of Herbroulesse, Marchess-in-waiting, the Lady ~ only child and daughter to the *Lady Vey,* conceived outside of the banns of any intended marriage, simply for the purpose of producing an heir. She is a self-determined girl, stubborn and quick-witted, and even quicker tempered, sent to *Sinster* by her mother on the advent of her thirteenth birthday to be transmogrified into a lahzarine *wit*. Consequently, when Rossamünd was still at Madam Opera's despairing of his chance at getting work, Threnody was under the knives of Spedillo and Sculapias, said to be among the best *surgeons* to have ever held a *catlin*. *Dolours* and others of the *clave* advised the *Lady Vey* to wait, but she would not, determined to have her daughter as a powerful *wit,* well learned in antics by the time she was old enough to begin to share the lead. Threnody has ideas of her own which (of course) do not always correlate to her mother's ambitions for her. The tension between them is continual, often emotionally violent, to the point that Threnody's request to become a *lamplighter* was granted her, if only to give *Syntychë* and the *columbines* of *Columbris* a rest from all the agonies of mother-daughter angst. One of the "joys" of Threnody's new state is the endless imbibing of the necessary chemistry to keep her new organs in check.

Threnody's Alembant Schedule

	Morning	Noon	Night
Newwich	*plaudamentum,* Iambic Ichor, nephushe	nil	*plaudamentum, Friscan's wead*
Loonday	*plaudamentum,* Iambic Ichor	Cordial of Sammany	*plaudamentum*
Meerday	*plaudamentum,* Iambic Ichor	Friscan's wead	*plaudamentum*
Midwich	*plaudamentum,* Iambic Ichor, Cordial of Sammany	nil	*plaudamentum*
Domesday	*plaudamentum,* Iambic Ichor	Friscan's wead	*plaudamentum*
Calumnday	*plaudamentum,* Iambic Ichor	nil	*plaudamentum,* Cordial of Sammany
Solemnday	*plaudamentum,* Iambic Ichor, Friscan's wead	Friscan's wead	*plandamentum*

threwd at its mildest, the haunted feeling of watchfulness that can be felt in wilder, less populated places. See entry in Book One. See also *pernicious threwd*.

thrice-blighted emphatic curse meaning that someone is truly wicked, useless and unwelcome.

thrombis healing *script* of the *siccustrumn* group related to the restorative realm, and one of the better kinds of powders used to quickly clot a wound and staunch blood flow.

thrumcop also called a bog-button and related to a larger, tasty and oddly threwdish fungus known as austerpill, thrumcops are a mushroom with a deep brown pileus spotted with swollen off-white circular patches. The essence of thrumcops can be used in rudimentary repellents, giving rise to the idea that eating them on their own will cause this essence to seep through your pores and make you less appetizing to a *monster*.

tinker sometimes mistakenly called a trifler (seller of cheap cutlery and other pewter and tinware), a tinker is a mender of metal items not requiring a forge to fix. One of the wayfarers that go "huc illuc" about the lands to find work, though *Winstermill* employs a whole bunch of the fellows to look after their myriad of small metal-working needs.

toscanelle any lovely rich red wine coming from the Tuscanin region; actually named after the stream that runs through that country.

tow rough fabric made from hemp fibers or from jute—a somewhat finer kind of hessian or burlap.

tractor(s) also called feralados or feraloderoes; handlers of animals and beasts of war whose task is to feed and clean their charges and make intractable creatures eager to do their master's bidding.

transmogrifer(s) *surgeon* who specializes in the making of *lahzars*. See *lahzar(s)* in Book One.

troubardier(s) heavily armored *pediteers* trained to fight at *hand strokes* with a variety of hand arms, including *poleaxes, fends,* huge swords known as claughs and spadroons, and other exotic tools. See entry in Book One.

trunk-road(s) roads made by the need for trade and the easy passage of goods.

Tumblesloe Cot one of the primary duties of the *lighters* here is to take part in the *fatigue parties* that venture regularly into the *Roughmarch* and clear it of *monster*-harboring vegetation.

Tumblesloes, the ~, Tumblesloe Heap, the ~ Known by the Plutarch *Tutins* of old as the Arides, for they were ancient and withered even then; the north–south running range of hills to the east of *Winstermill* and the *Harrowmath*. Their tops, constantly buffeted by strong winds and covered with only a thin soil, support no vegetation other than mean, stunted stubble. Their low places, however, are choked with dense knots of brambly plants, sloe, briar and blackberry. Among the oldest hills in the *Soutlands,* they are known as the "heap" for their tumbledown appearance and the great cracklike gorges that cross them, the evidence of some tectonic violence eons before.

Tutin language spoken by the inhabitants of *Clementine* and the lands about. (It is based loosely—or not so, at times—on Latin, and to those troubled or offended by this, the author might dare to say: *excusationes offero propter licentiam quam cum hac pulchra lingua in libello meo cepi. Habete eam artificiosam libertatem et, obsecro, mihi ignoscite*).

Tutins the ruling race of the *Haacobin Empire,* descendants of Dido and her people, speakers of the language of the same name; also called the Plutarchs (actually their ancient forebears); a refined people of great capacity who once, under Dido's rule, conquered the regions now known as the *Soutlands* before their decline. For a time they seemed to vanish entirely from the southern parts of the Half-Continent, abandoning their allies and dependants to the ravages of their foes. It was only several hundred years later that they reappeared to rewin lands lost, a lesser people—a shadow of their mighty forebears—but still strong enough to conquer.

twelve of the best twelve lashes of the straight-whip, or worse yet the three-o'-tail bob.

twin keep(s) bastions or other small forts built side by side, one to support the other. Some are joined by bridges and covered galleries, others by tunnels, and still others are separate from each other. The most common use of twin keeps is to straddle a roadway, with a tollgate hung between them for duties to be collected from travelers.

Twörp, Tremendus said "twerp"; a rather fat young man whose now-dead parents were exiles from Gothia. Found wandering and starving by a cruel *cantebank* man, he was fed and set to work by this fellow as a pan-

694

handler and mute beggar (for he could not speak a word of *Brandenard* beyond "yes" and "thank you"). Providence stepped in when, while passing through *Winstermill,* the *Lamplighter-Marshal* saw the small abused wastrel and bought him from the suspicious *cantebank.* The Marshal then installed the startled child in Hand Row, the small foundlingery down in the *Low Gutter,* and taught him the common tongue until Twörp was old enough to begin *prenticing.*

tykehound(s) • (noun) collective noun for a set of dog breeds raised to hunt and slay *monsters.* The collection of tykehounds includes tykehounds themselves (sometimes also called selthounds—see next point), *spangled whelp-hounds, Greater Derehunds,* garmirvithars and stafirhunds. Their counterparts are the slothounds, who are trained to track *monsters* from even the faintest trail and corner them, rather than come to grapple with them. A curregitor is the leading dog in a pack of tykehounds, what in our world might be termed an "alpha male"; it runs at the front and is first into the fight. A canignavor, from the *Tutin* word meaning "lazy dog" (also langsbain, a Gott word meaning "slow-leg"), is the second dog of a tykehound pack; it periodically runs back or lags behind the main chasers waiting for its *everyman* masters to tell it the path of the rest of the hunt. These animals are anything but lazy, as their title misnomically suggests, usually running twice or three times the distance any of its fellows covers in a *course.* • (noun) also selthounds, specific breed of hound, the largest of all the *monster*-hunting dogs: with long, heavy snouts; wide mouths and overlarge teeth for an irresistibly gripping bite; thickly gathered hide about the neck to prevent a *monster* throttling it; covered in thick, short, wiry black hair and with powerful hips and shoulders, large paws and great cunning. Some of the most famous dogs of matter—such as Garngagarr—are of this breed.

U

uhrsprechman (Gott, literally "clock-speaking-man") also called a *night-clerk,* found only in *cothouses* and other military outposts. Their main task is to complete any paperwork not finished by the *day-clerks,* sort mail as required and read the clock and tell the time for the unlettered soldiers about them—of which there are many.

umbergog ettin-like *nicker*, but possessing an oversized head in deformed simulacrum of an animal's *poll*. If it were possible, umbergogs are even more dim-witted than their more manikinlike (personlike) cousins, the ettins, more bestial—as their heads might imply. Typically they are a little smaller than ettins, but this does not mean that there are not examples of umbergogs of numbingly enormous size; rivaled only by the singular, portentous appearances of the mighty, mindless false-gods lumbering across the doomed land.

under-clerk assistant to a *clerk,* a kind of corporal-clerk, put upon to do the most menial of clerical tasks, the dullest and most repetitive duties, the ones sent to the less friendly places to act as bureaucrat and - paper-shuffler.

under-sergeant military rank used by landed armies but not navies, and the next in rank under a *sergeant* and above a *pediteer* or other 1st class of any type. The equivalent of corporal.

Under-Sergeant-of-Prentices Benedict see *Benedict, Under-Sergeant-of-Prentices.*

ungerhaur one of many Gott names for monsters.

üntermen Gott word for *monsters,* roughly translating to "undermen," meaning that *monsters* are less than men. As a name for *monsters* it has gained some currency all over the Half-Continent.

V

venificant(s) poison-*scripts,* also sometimes known as pestilents—these are particularly the more corrupting and wasting *potives.* Either way they are all very nasty.

Vey, the Lady ~ official title of *Syntychë,* the *august* of the *columbines* of *Herbroulesse.* Born to the role and following her mother through five generations of *augusts,* five generations of the Lady Vey. Her title comes from a local corruption of the word "fey," thought to mean that she "convenes with *monsters,*" yet it actually comes from Feye, a tiny *Soutland* state that was absorbed by another larger state almost two centuries ago. Fleeing the subtle conquest, the Lady Vey's ancestors made their way up to the *Idlewild* to seclude themselves in a small *sequestury* there, and, by ambition, rose to rule it and expand its work. *Syntychë* is profoundly aware of her proud heritage, of the aggressive nature of her family's historied grasp on the control of the *Right of the Pacific Dove* and the dubious honor it is to be a *calendar*. Her zeal for her *calendars* and her heritage is almost consuming.

Vey, Threnody See *Threnody of Herbroulesse*.

vialimn meaning "path-light," the "correct" name for a *great-lamp*.

vigil-day what we would call a holiday.

Volitus *dispensurist* of *Winstermill,* originally simply a *confectioner* from High Vesting, he has managed to gain status as a true dispenser, though the quality of his work is not always guaranteed. It is fortunate for the others of the manse that his assistant has a better grasp of habilistics.

W

wandlimb type of ash tree with a narrow trunk whose gracefully long, straight branches are a favorite for withies, cudgels and the basis for fulgaris.

watch(es) among the *lamplighters* there are three main watches that do not revolve so much about four-hour intervals as in the navy, but rather on duties and whether it is day or night. During the day there is the *house-watch,* whose task it is to maintain the day-to-day running of their posting; the *day-watch,* who keep lookout during the sunny hours and rove out beyond their posting to accomplish the various tasks the day requires. At night while these two watches sleep it is time for the *lantern-* or *lamp-watch* to shine (ha! Get it?). Their duty starts with traveling from their place of day-rest, lighting *lamps* along the way to the next *cothouse* or other fortress, where they stay up all night to keep guard.

wayfood(s) other favorites among *hucilluctors* are twice-pickled gherkins and evercap, a dainty mushroom that preserves well when dried and can last for many years still edible, though these too are preferred pickled—either with pepper or honey. See entry in Book One.

Wayward Chair, the ~ a hostelry of barely a dozen rooms found in the more down-at-heel suburb of Marlabone in the city of Compostor; run by a Mr. and Mrs. Phile, and not particularly well known for its appointments or refinements. Why Europe chooses to stay there is a bit of a mystery, for she usually prefers the finer establishments if she can have them, and there is certainly more than one of those in that city.

Wellnigh House the small *twin-keep cothouse* most immediately east of *Winstermill,* gaining its name because it is well-nigh to both *Winstermill* and the *Tumblesloe Heap.* It was once the tollhouse for those coming through or entering the *Roughmarch,* the toll helping to pay to keep the marche clear of the thick briars and thorns that ever seek to choke the path.

Wheede, Crofton a somewhat clumsy and ineffectual boy of average build and average intelligence, and one of the other *prentices* at *Winstermill.* He is actually a native of the *Idlewild* itself, from a line of cobblers in *Hinkerseigh.* His mother was slain in a *theroscade* during a summertime Domesday stroll, his father killed by grief and the viscid humours (a terrible contagious disease said to be spread by *nickers*). Young Wheede has been shipped off by surviving uncles and aunts to serve with the *lighters.*

"When falsemen disagree . . ." comes from an aphorism, "When *falsemen* disagree, to whom then can the truth be known?"

Whympre, Podious pronounced *"Po'dee'us Wim'per";* see *Master-of-Clerks.*

Wight, the ~ also known as Wightbury: Imperial designation of the Imperial fortress-city of *Wightfastseigh,* built to collect tolls on goods coming down from Sulk and eastern Catalain and the Undermeer states. It is a center of military might in the midst of the *Idlewild* and the pivot between two *themes* of the *Placidine* and the *Paucitine,* with each settlement of the *Idlewild* providing contingents of *pediteers* and even *swaggerers* to its guard. Yet despite its size and impressive fortifications, it has no direct jurisdiction over the *Wormway* or in political affairs in the *Idlewild* (though citizens of influence might have their say). Indeed the *cothouses* in the Wight are no larger than those along the lonely road; this city is all about taxation revenue and the protection of its collection and the trade route that most supplies it. The citizens of the Wight themselves are generally very concerned with the latest fashions, importing all the new fads and baubles they can from down south—where all the best people dwell.

Wightfastseigh see *the Wight*.

wine-of-Sellry see *Sellry, wine-of-~*.

Winstermill great Imperial fortress of *Sulk End* and home to the *lamplighters* of the *Wormway*. Winstreslewe, the ancient, abandoned *Tutin* fortress upon whose foundations it was built, was itself constructed about and upon an even more ancient great hall and motte. This great hall was once a seat of power for the Burgundian kings before they were pushed aside by the greater might of the *Tutins* of old. Winstermill is the first port of call for anyone wishing to enter the *Idlewild*. It is the administrative center, whence are issued all Imperial writs and certificates that allow easier passage through the varied bureaucracies of the colonies along the *Wormway*. See Appendix 5 and entry in Book One.

Winstermill, serving staff of ~ an astounding collection of people somehow find their home in the fortress: metalsmiths, wheelwrights, coopers, gaulders, cobblers, tailors, house-tinkers, glaziers, armorers, ostlers, farriers, *feuterers*, storemen, stewards, cooks, menservants, parlor maids, bower maids, scullery maids, fullers, porters, lighter's boys, pageboys and general hands.

wit(s) *lahzars* who are able to send out pulses of invisible "static" to afflict people's minds. It is well known that wits lose their hair as they continue to use their potency, and a calvine or calvous wit is a wit completely without hair. There are those wits known as mesmerists, who are skilled in and prefer subtle and gentle techniques of *frission,* coercing and quietly manipulating their targets without giving themselves away, rather than blasting them with great feats of striving. To be a mesmerist takes great skill, but overspecializing makes one less able to put forth powerful yet well-controlled *frission* in singularly destructive striving. The opposite of mesmerists are striveners, who practice mighty yet tightly controlled assaults of *frission,* the perfecters of the nex aspectus—the killing look or "eye of death." In a similar way coruscists are *fulgars* who do not thermistor, who do not wish to take the risk of blasting themselves apart if they botch the summoning of lightning. See entry in Book One.

Witherscrawl trained as a *mathematician,* he is the indexer and stooge of the *Master-of-Clerks.* See *Witherscrawl, Mister* in Book One.

withy-wall(s) usually naturally occurring barriers of sapling stems (withies).

works-general properly called the General-Master-of-Labors, the highest ranked *peoneer* in *Winstermill*. His charge includes all of the maintenance and works about the fortress and on the road too; he also has charge over the *seltzermen* as well as the more common laborers. This is part of the reason why *lighters* do not truly consider *seltzermen* to be their equals—they belong to another corps.

Wormstool very last *cothouse* on the eastern end of the *Conduit Vermis* (from which it gets its name) with only the fortress of *Haltmire* between it and the untamed wilds. Built simultaneously with *Haltmire,* at the time when the Wormway was being forged through the *Ichormeer,* Wormstool is an octagonal tower rather than the usual fortress-house. It shares this trait with *Dovecote Bolt* and is reached by narrow steps wrapping about three of the structure's sides. On every level, the windows are shuttered loopholes through which defenders can fire down upon attackers. There is provision for cannon on the third level and on the roof, yet pieces have never been supplied and Wormstool remains without great-guns, despite the presence of *umbergogs* and other *belugigs* on the *Frugelle.*

Wormway, the ~ vernacular name for the *Conduit Vermis* (see both entries in Book One); also called the *Harrowmath Pike.* The Wormway is divided into named lengths:

♣ *Pettiwiggin*—from *Winstermill* to *Wellnigh House*

♣ *Roughmarch Road*—from *Wellnigh House* to *Dovecote Bolt*

♣ Mirthway or Mirthle Road—from *Dovecote Bolt* to *Makepeace*

♣ Half-wiggin Pike—from *Makepeace* to the *Wight*

♣ Pendant Wig—from the *Wight* to *Bleak Lynche*

♣ The *Frugal* Way—from *Bleak Lynche* to *Haltmire* and through to the *Ichormeer.*

Wrangle poor boy of obscure origins who goes by this name and this name alone—of too destitute a beginning, it seems, to have more than a first name. A fairly slow-witted but physically adept lad, he is the perfect candidate for a soldier—or *lighter.*

wrench-of-arms what we would call arm wrestling.

X

Blood and sutures! No entry for *x!*

Y

yesternight last night, the counterpart of yesterday.

Z

Pullets and cockerels! Still no entry for *z!* How is this possible?

THE 16-MONTH CALENDAR OF THE HALF-CONTINENT

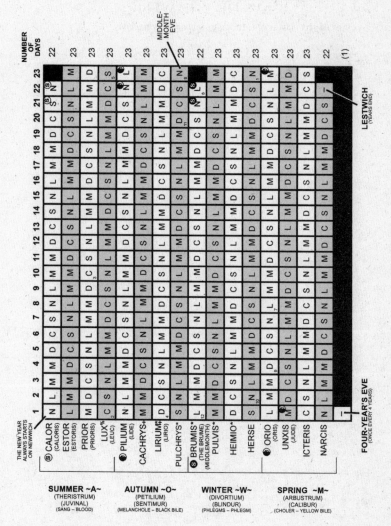

SUMMER ~A~
(THERISTRUM)
(JUVINAL)
(SANG – BLOOD)

AUTUMN ~O~
(PETILIUM)
(SENTIMUR)
(MELANCHOLE – BLACK BILE)

WINTER ~W~
(DIVORTIUM)
(BLINDUR)
(PHLEGMS – PHLEGM)

SPRING ~M~
(ARBUSTRUM)
(CALIBUR)
(CHOLER – YELLOW BILE)

DAYS OF THE WEEK (7)

N - NEWWICH first day of the week
L - LOONDAY
M - MEERDAY
M - MIDWICH
D - DOMESDAY a day of rest
C - CALUMNDAY
S - SOLEMNDAY

VIGILS - DAYS OF OBSERVANCE
(THESE NUMBERS CAN BE FOUND IN THE CALENDAR)

1 - DIRGETIDE		7 - PLOUGHMONDAY	
2 - HALFMERRY DAY		8 - EIGHT-MONTH'S EVE (CLERK'S VIGIL)	
3 - MALBELLTIDE		9 - THISGIVINGDAY	
4 - MANNER		10 - GALLOWSNIGHT	
5 - MELLOWTIDE		11 - VERTUMNUS	
6 - NYCHTHOLD		12 - MIDTIDE	

(S) = SOLSTICE

(☯) = EQUINOX

THE DATE UPON WHICH
THE SOLSTICE & EQUINOX
OCCUR IS VARIABLE, HENCE
THE TWO POSSIBLE TIMES
SHOWN FOR EACH EVENT.

* SAID TO BE THE COLDEST MONTHS,
UNFRIENDLY TO TRAVELERS.

% IN THE OLD CALENDARS THIS WAS
ONCE THE FIRST MONTH OF THE YEAR.

+ THESE TWO MONTHS WERE ONCE IN
THE REVERSE ORDER. THEY CAME TO
BE SWAPPED WHEN THE EXCEEDINGLY
TALL AND EXCESSIVELY SPOILED
DAUGHTER OF MORIBUND SCEPTIC III
COMPLAINED SO BITTERLY THAT SHE
SHOULD HAVE BEEN BORN IN THE
BEAUTIFUL-SOUNDING MONTH OF
LIRIUM RATHER THAN THE UGLY-
SOUNDING (AS SHE THOUGHT IT)
MONTH OF CACHRYS. SHE MADE
COURT LIFE IMPOSSIBLE UNTIL HER
MUCH-HARASSED FATHER DECREED
THE SWAP BY IMPERIAL EDICT. THE
CHANGE HAS REMAINED EVER SINCE,
EVEN AFTER A WAR WAS FOUGHT
OVER IT.

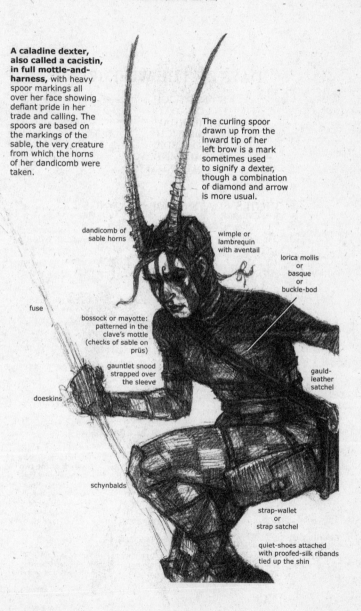

A caladine dexter, also called a cacistin, in full mottle-and-harness, with heavy spoor markings all over her face showing defiant pride in her trade and calling. The spoors are based on the markings of the sable, the very creature from which the horns of her dandicomb were taken.

The curling spoor drawn up from the inward tip of her left brow is a mark sometimes used to signify a dexter, though a combination of diamond and arrow is more usual.

dandicomb of sable horns

wimple or lambrequin with aventail

lorica mollis or basque or buckle-bod

fuse

bossock or mayotte: patterned in the clave's mottle (checks of sable on prüs)

gauntlet snood strapped over the sleeve

doeskins

gauld-leather satchel

schynbalds

strap-wallet or strap satchel

quiet-shoes attached with proofed-silk ribands tied up the shin

APPENDIX 3

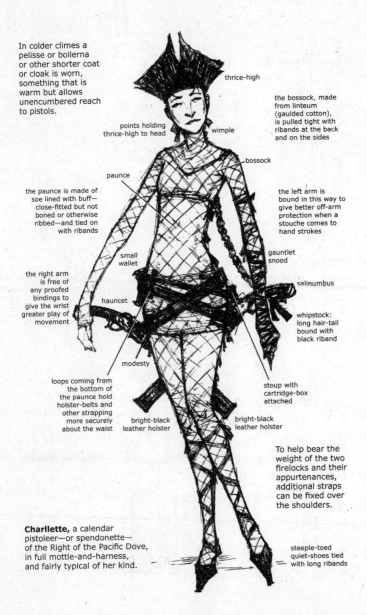

In colder climes a pelisse or bollerna or other shorter coat or cloak is worn, something that is warm but allows unencumbered reach to pistols.

thrice-high

points holding thrice-high to head

wimple

the bossock, made from linteum (gaulded cotton), is pulled tight with ribands at the back and on the sides

bossock

paunce

the paunce is made of soe lined with buff—close-fitted but not boned or otherwise ribbed—and tied on with ribands

the left arm is bound in this way to give better off-arm protection when a stouche comes to hand strokes

small wallet

gauntlet snood

the right arm is free of any proofed bindings to give the wrist greater play of movement

hauncet

salinumbus

whipstock: long hair-tail bound with black riband

modesty

loops coming from the bottom of the paunce hold holster-belts and other strapping more securely about the waist

bright-black leather holster

stoup with cartridge-box attached

bright-black leather holster

To help bear the weight of the two firelocks and their appurtenances, additional straps can be fixed over the shoulders.

Charllette, a calendar pistoleer—or spendonette—of the Right of the Pacific Dove, in full mottle-and-harness, and fairly typical of her kind.

steeple-toed quiet-shoes tied with long ribands

705

APPENDIX 4

A GENERAL MANNING-TABLE OF LAMPLIGHTERS & AUXILIARIES OF WINSTERMILL MANSE

and the cothouses beyond, in order of rank & authority from highest to least

~ COMMISSIONED OFFICERS ~

LIGHTERS	PEONEERS (LABORERS)	PEDITEERS (SOLDIERS)	CLERKS & STORES	PHYSICS	THAUMATEERS
Lamplighter-Marshal (marshal-lighter)					
	General-Master-of-Labors (works-general) **[Warden-General]**	**General-Master-of-Palliateers** (lurksman-general)	**Comptroller-Master-General**		
Lamplighter-Major [Major-of-House] (house-major)	**Surveyor-of-the-Works** (master-surveyor)	**Palliateer-Major Major-of-Foot**			
	[Road-Warden]	**Adjutant**		**Physician***	
Lamplighter-Captain (captain-lighter)		**Captain-of-Pediteers** (pediteer-captain)			**Captain-of-Thaumateers** (skold-captain)
		Captain-of-Palliateers (ambuscadier-captain or captain-lurksman) **Captain-of-Ordnance** (artillerist)			
		Lieutenant			
Altern-Lighter		**Subaltern**			
		Ensign			

Master-of-Lighters (sergeant-master) **[Cot-Warden]**	**Master-of-Works**	**Master-of-Pediteers** (sergeant-major) **Master-of-Ordnance** (gun-sergeant-major) **Master-Lurksman**	**Master-of-Clerks*** (clerk-master) **Compter-of-Stores*** **Quartermaster**	**Skold** **Scourge** **Wit** **Fulgar**
	Master Proofener (gaulding-master) **Master Armorer**	**Color-Sergeant**	**Librarian*** **Lamplighter's Agent**	
Lamplighter-Sergeant (sergeant-lighter)	**Peoneer-Sergeant** (sergeant-labourer) **Carpenter** (houseman) **Housemason** **Armorer**	**Pediteer-Sergeant** (sergeant of ~ musketeers haubardiers troubardiers) **Sergeant-Armorer** (gun-sergeant) **Leer**	**Provenderer*** **Secretary** (~ to the "rank")	
	Ostler **Proofer** (gauldsman)	**Lurksman**	**Indexer***	**Ossatomist*** **Dispensurist***
Lampsman-Corporal (lantern under-sergeant)		**Corporal 1st Class** (pediteer-corporal) (gun-corporal)	**Register** (registry clerk)	
		Corporal 2nd Class (under-corporal)	**Almonder***	

~ * means a civilian position with substantive rank in the manse

~ [ ] means ranks used at cothouses only

707

~ OTHER RANKS ~

LIGHTERS	PEONEERS (LABORERS)	PEDITEERS (SOLDIERS)	CLERKS & STORES	PHYSICS	THAUMATEERS
		Troubardier (foot-guard) Franklock (marksman)	Culinaire*	Surgeon*	
	Seltzerman 1st Class Farrier, Groom	Ambuscadier 1st Class	Clerk 1st Class* (amanuensis)		Factotum*
Lampsman 1st Class	Seltzerman 2nd Class House-Tinker	Ambuscadier 2nd Class Pediteer 1st Class (musketeer, haubardier) Artilleryman 1st Class	Steward* [Uhrsprechman]		
Lampsman 2nd Class		Pediteer 2nd Class (musketeer, haubardier) Artilleryman 2nd Class Turnkey	Clerk 2nd Class*		
Lampsman 3rd Class	Driver	Pediteer 3rd Class (musketeer, haubardier) Under-Turnkey (gaol-watch) Lictor	Under-Clerk* Night-Clerk Storemen Cooks, Baxters, etc.* Chief Servants*		
		Drummer Boy Fyfesman			

Maid*
Mansservant*

Mercer

Porter

Page*

Laborer 1st Class
Stable Hand

Laborer 2nd Class

Laborer 3rd Class
Box-Boy
(splasher)

Prentice-lighter
(lantern-stick)

Lighter's Boy 1st Class   Hand 1st Class

Lighter's Boy 2nd Class   Hand 2nd Class

Lighter's Boy 3rd Class   Hand 3rd Class

~ * means a civilian position with substantive rank in the manse
~ [ ] means ranks used at cothouses only

APPENDIX 5

THE EQUIPMENT AND ACCOUTREMENTS OF A LAMPLIGHTER

A lamplighter dressed ready for the lantern-watch.
Individual lampsmen will vary what bits they do or do not wear, and those of different cothouses on different stretches of a highroad will often don coats of distinct color underneath their quabards. Along with this, lampsmen are allowed to wear the baldric of their native state, though if they are from another realm entirely they must don the baldric of the Empire. The lamplighters recruit from all paths of life; many are from other parts of the world, with pasts they would rather forget. The Emperor does not care—the more grist for his "mill," the better.

pike-head
or
pike-end

bunting-hook
or
sleeve-catcher

bright-limn
(detachable),
not usually
attached to the
fodicar. Some
lighters prefer
to fix these to
the shaft with
iron clasp-rings
rather than let
them swing
freely and
make noise.

crank-hook

fodicar

tricorn

black aventail
or stine pulled
over mouth and
nose to protect
from potive
fumes

quabard
bearing
the sigil
and mottle
of the
Empire

feathered
baton

high, proofed
undercollar to
protect back
of neck

baldric

710

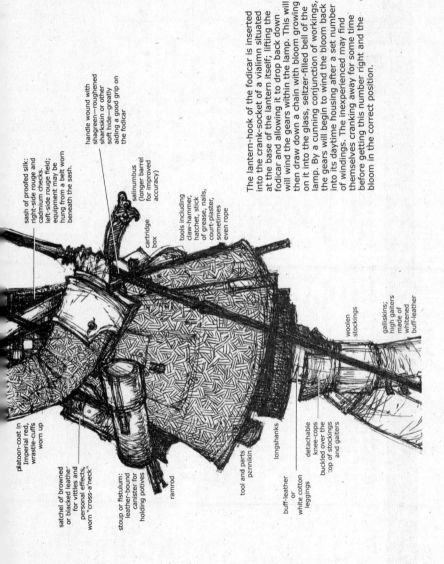

sash of proofed silk: right-side rouge and cadmium checks, left-side rouge field; equipment may be hung from a belt worn beneath the sash.

handle wound with shagreen—roughened sharkskin or other soft hide—greatly aiding a good grip on the fodicar

salinumbus (longer barrel for improved accuracy)

cartridge box

tools including claw-hammer, hatchet, stick of grease, nails, court-plaster, sometimes even rope

platoon-coat in Imperial red, wrastle-cuffs worn up

satchel of browned or blacked leather for vittles and personal effects, worn "cross-a'neck"

stoup or fistulum: leather-bound canister for holding potives

ramrod

tool and parts pennikin

longshanks

buff-leather or white cotton leggings

detachable knee-cops buckled over the top of stockings and galters

woolen stockings

galliskins; high galters made of whitened buff-leather

The lantern-hook of the fodicar is inserted into the crank-socket of a vialimn situated at the base of the lantern itself; lifting the fodicar and allowing it to drop back down will wind the gears within the lamp. This will then draw down a chain with bloom growing on it into the glass, seltzer-filled bell of the lamp. By a cunning conjunction of workings, the gears will begin to wind the bloom back into its daytime housing after a set number of windings. The inexperienced may find themselves cranking away for some time before getting this number right and the bloom in the correct position.

711

APPENDIX 6 PRENTICE SCHEDULE

	NEWWICH	MEERDAY	LOONDAY	MIDWICH	DOMESDAY	CALUMNDAY	SOLEMNNDAY
5 A.M.	3rd Lantern-watch (Q Hesiod Gæta) wakes (Wellnigh)	1st Lantern-watch (Q Protogenēs) wakes (Wellnigh)	2nd Lantern-watch (Q Io Harpsicarus) wakes (Wellnigh)	3rd Lantern-watch (Q Hesiod Gæta) wakes (Wellnigh)	1st Lantern-watch (Q Protogenēs) wakes (Wellnigh)	SLEEP	2nd Lantern-watch (Q Io Harpsicarus) wakes (Wellnigh)
5 A.M.–5:30 A.M.	L-W ablutions & **Breakfast**	L-W ablutions & **Breakfast**	L-W ablutions & **Breakfast**	L-W ablutions & **Breakfast**	L-W ablutions & **Breakfast**	SLEEP	L-W ablutions & **Breakfast**
5:30 A.M.–6 A.M.	L-W leaves for dousing	L-W leaves for dousing	L-W leaves for dousing	L-W leaves for dousing	L-W leaves for dousing	SLEEP	L-W leaves for dousing
6 A.M.	Rest of prentices wake	Rest of prentices wake	Rest of prentices wake	Rest of prentices wake	Rest of prentices wake	All prentices wake	Rest of prentices wake
6 A.M.–7 A.M.	*Morning Forming*	*Morning Forming*	*Morning Forming*	*Morning Forming*	Preparations & **Breakfast**	*Morning Forming*	*Morning Forming*
7 A.M.–7:30 A.M.	Ablutions (bath day) & **Breakfast**	Ablutions & **Breakfast**	Ablutions & **Breakfast**	Ablutions (bath day) & **Breakfast**	*Pageant-of-Arms*	Ablutions & **Breakfast**	Ablutions & **Breakfast**
7:30 A.M.–9 A.M. 1st Morning Instructions	Evolutions	Evolutions	Evolutions	Evolutions	*Pageant-of-Arms*	Evolutions	Evolutions
9 A.M.–9:30 A.M.	**Limes** 3rd PQHG returns	**Limes** 1st PQP returns	**Limes** 2nd PQIH returns	**Limes** 3rd PQHG returns	*Pageant-of-Arms* 1st PQP returns	**Limes**	**Limes** 2nd PQIH returns
9:30 A.M.–11 A.M. 2nd Morning Instructions	Readings	Evolutions	Workings	Readings	Vigil-day outing departs	Workings	Readings
11:30 A.M.–1 P.M. Middle Instructions	Workings	Evolutions	Workings	Readings	Private-stalls	Evolutions	Evolutions

712

Time	Middens	Middens	Middens	Middens	Middens	Middens	Middens
1 P.M.–2 P.M.	Middens	Middens	Middens	Middens	Middens	Middens	Middens
2 P.M.–3 P.M. 1st After Instructions	Targets	Evolutions	Evolutions	Targets	Private-stalls	Workings	Labors
3 P.M.–4 P.M. 2nd After Instructions	Targets	Evolutions	Evolutions	Targets	Private-stalls	Evolutions	Labors
4 P.M.–4:15 P.M.	Lantern Forming **Lale** 1st Q Protogenês leaves for lighting	Lantern Forming **Lale** 2nd Q Io Harpsicarus leaves for lighting	Lantern Forming **Lale** 3rd Q Hesiod Gæta leaves for lighting	Lantern Forming **Lale** 1st Q Protogenês leaves for lighting	Private-stalls	Lantern Forming **Lale** 2nd Q Io Harpsicarus leaves for lighting	Lantern Forming **Lale** 3rd Q Hesiod Gæta leaves for lighting
4:15 P.M.–5:30 P.M. Evening Instructions	Targets	Private-stalls	Evolutions	Targets	Private-stalls	Evolutions	Labors
5:30 P.M.–6 P.M.	Evening Forming	Evening Forming	Evening Forming	Evening Forming	Vigil-day outing returns	Evening Forming	Evening Forming
6 P.M.–7 P.M.	Mains	Mains	Mains	Mains	Mains	Mains	Mains
7 P.M.–7:15 P.M.	Castigations	Castigations	Castigations	Castigations	Mains	Castigations	Castigations
7:15 P.M.–8 P.M.	Evenstalls/ Impositions/ 1st L-W arrives at Wellnigh & Mains	Evenstalls/ Impositions/ 2nd L-W arrives at Wellnigh & Mains	Evenstalls/ Impositions/ 3rd L-W arrives at Wellnigh & Mains	Evenstalls/ Impositions/ 1st L-W arrives at Wellnigh & Mains	Evenstalls/ Impositions/	Evenstalls/ Impositions/ 2nd L-W arrives at Wellnigh & Mains	Evenstalls/ Impositions/ 3rd L-W arrives at Wellnigh & Mains
8 P.M.–9 P.M.	Confinations/ Impositions	Confinations/ Impositions	Confinations/ Impositions	Confinations/ Impositions	Confinations/ Impositions	Confinations/ Impositions	Confinations/ Impositions
9 P.M.	Douse-lanterns	Douse-lanterns	Douse-lanterns	Douse-lanterns	Douse-lanterns	Douse-lanterns	Douse-lanterns

SLEEP

713

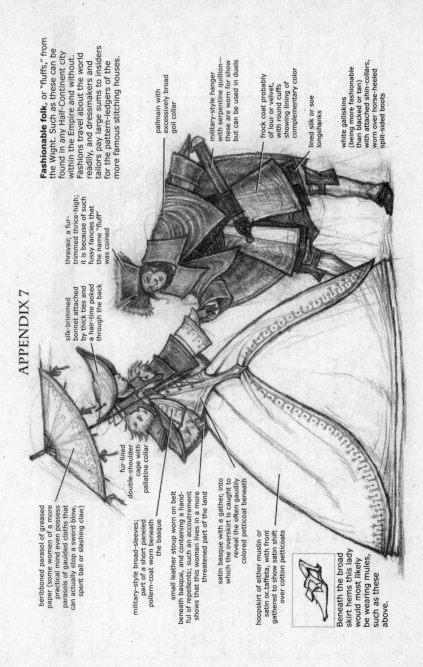

Fashionable folk, or "fluffs," from the Wight. Such as these can be found in any Half-Continent city within the Empire and without. Fashions travel about the world readily, and dressmakers and tailors pay large sums to insiders for the pattern-ledgers of the more famous stitching houses.

silk-brimmed bonnet attached by thick ties and a hair-tine poked through the back

threvair, a fur-trimmed thrice-high; it is because of such fussy fancies that the name "fluff" was coined

pallmain with excessively broad goil collar

military-style hanger with serpentine quillon—these are worn for show but can be used in duels

frock coat probably of lour or velvet, with round cuffs showing lining of complementary color

lined silk or soe longshanks

white galliskins (being more fashionable than blacked or tan) with attached shin-collars, worn over horse-heeled split-sided boots

beribboned parasol of greased paper (some women of a more practical mind even possess parasols of gaulded cloths that can actually stop a sword blow, spent ball or slashing claw)

military-style broad-sleeves; part of a short paneled pollern-coat worn beneath the basque

fur-lined double-shoulder cape with pallatine collar

small leather stoup worn on belt beneath basque, and containing a hand-ful of repellents; such an accoutrement shows that this woman lives in a more threatened part of the land

satin basque with a gather, into which the overskirt is caught to reveal the often gaudily colored petticoat beneath

hoopskirt of either muslin or satin or taffeta, with front gathered to show satin shift over cotton petticoats

Beneath the broad skirt hems this lady would most likely be wearing mules, such as these above.

WINSTERMILL

**HIS MOST SERENE IMPERIAL HIGHNESS' STRONGHOLD
& THE MANSE OF THE EMPEROR'S OWN LAMPLIGHTERS
OF THE CONDUIT VERMIS**

Ⓐ   ANGLE TOWER

Ⓑ   BLOCK-HOUSE

Ⓢ   STRONG POINT

    WELL

    GREAT-LAMP

    BED/TABLE & OTHER FURNITURE

    STAIRWAY UP
    ARROW SHOWS DIRECTION OF ASCENT

    STAIRWAY DOWN
    GRADIENT SHOWS STAIR GOING DOWN

    FURTIGRADE

    DOOR

    HIDDEN DOOR

    PORTCULLIS

    TREE

    EARTHEN BANK

GRATE

◯   VAT OR TUB – OR OTHER WORKINGS

    CANNON

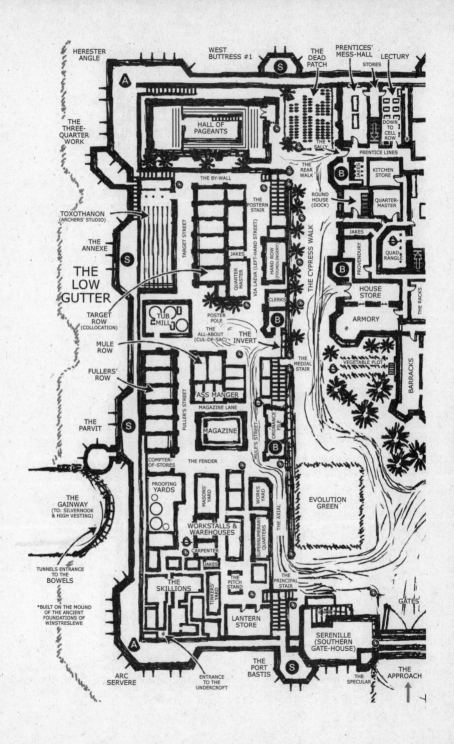

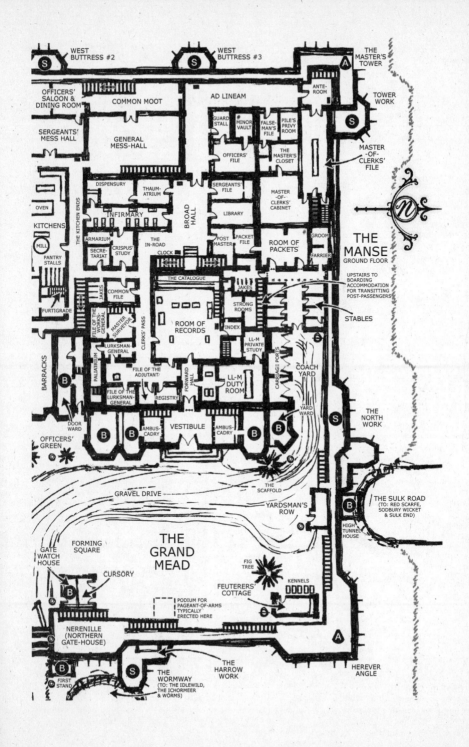